LINDA BYLER

Lizzie Searches
for Love

TRILOGY

Three Bestselling Novels in One

Based on true experiences from an Amish author!

Good Books

Intercourse, PA 17534
800/762-7171
www.GoodBooks.com

Running Around (and Such), by Linda Byler © 2010
When Strawberries Bloom, by Linda Byler © 2010
Big Decisions, by Linda Byler © 2011

Cover design by Koechel Peterson & Associates, Inc.,
Minneapolis, Minnesota

Design by Cliff Snyder

LIZZIE SEARCHES FOR LOVE TRILOGY
Copyright © 2013 by Good Books, Intercourse, PA 17534
International Standard Book Number: 978-1-56148-794-3
Library of Congress Catalog Card Number: 2012954498

Publisher's Cataloging-in-Publication Data
Byler, Linda.
 Lizzie searches for love trilogy : three bestselling novels in one / Linda Byler.
 p.m.
 ISBN 978-1-56148-794-3
 Contents : Running around (and such) –When strawberries bloom –Big decisions.
 1. Amish --Fiction. 2. Teachers --Fiction. 3. Love –Fiction. 4. Courtship –Fiction.
I. Title.

PS3602.Y53 L59 2013
813.6 --dc23 2012954498

Table of Contents

LINDA BYLER

Running Around

(*and Such*)

LIZZIE SEARCHES *for* LOVE
• *Book 1* •

Chapter 1

LIZZIE GLICK NOTICED THE CHANGE IN DAT one evening when he came in from checking things over at the pallet shop one last time before bed. He stood at the sink, washing his hands much longer than usual. Lizzie watched her father from the corner of her eyes, knowing something was about to give.

Things had been tense between Dat and Mam for more than a week, ever since Dat had announced he wanted to move to the new settlement and try his hand at farming. Mam most decidedly did not want to go. Her despair and total dislike of the whole idea had turned the usual peaceful, happy atmosphere of the Glick home tense.

Lizzie and her sisters had done the best they could to keep the peace, trying to understand Dat's ambition to become a farmer like his father and brother-in-law, even as they knew Mam didn't want to move again.

Lizzie thought she knew how Dat felt. There wasn't much of a challenge in Jefferson County anymore. The house was almost paid for, there were few financial concerns, and the pallet shop made an easy living. Dat was bored.

"Annie," Dat said.

"Hmm?"

Lizzie's heart leaped to her throat at his tone of voice. Dat meant business. Here it comes, she thought wildly. We're moving.

Dat dried his hands on the dark green towel, then turned to face his wife and daughters before he sat down opposite Mam at the kitchen table. He took a deep breath.

"Annie," he said a second time. "Doddy Glick and Daniel were here at the pallet shop this afternoon again."

Mam stiffened, her fingers working the straight pin in and out of her dress, which she often did when she was nervous.

"And?"

Lizzie bit down hard on her lower lip, drying a plate over and over again.

"They want me to go along over to Cameron County to look at a farm. It's only about two miles from Daniel's place and four or five from Doddy's place."

"I'm not going, Melvin."

"Ach, Annie, I thought you said the decision was up to me. If I make a choice, can't you find it in yourself to honor it?"

"I didn't say I wouldn't move. I said I'm not going along to look at the farm. You know I don't want to move, Melvin, but I have no choice if you decide to go."

"Annie, why don't you want to?"

"Melvin, think a little!" Mam's voice rose, desperation almost making her choke.

Lizzie felt like running out of the kitchen, her hands over her ears, far away where she'd never have to hear this painful conversation. Her older sister, Emma, sat quietly at the table, playing with their little twin sisters, KatieAnn and Susan.

Mam continued, "Emma will soon be 16 years old. She has all her friends and interests here. As far as I know, there are no other youth in that...that settlement, Cameron County, whatever you want to call it."

She clenched her hands.

"Another thing, Melvin," she continued. "We've talked of this before. How do you know we can make a living farming? You've never farmed. You don't know the first thing about it. Even if Uncle Eli gives you a good price for the pallet shop, the cost of starting up, with cows and equipment plus the farm itself, is completely frightening."

Dat sighed. He pleated the tablecloth with his fingers, then he sighed again, watching Mam's face as she stared at the floor.

"Where's your faith, Annie?"

Mam made a sound much like a snort. "I guess I don't have any where Cameron County is concerned.

I'm so afraid we're making a big mistake. The *Ord-nung* here is plainer; our young people are well behaved —"

Lizzie thought of high heels and ice cubes in the refrigerator and gas stoves with a broiler to make toast. "Do they wear high heels in Cameron County?" she blurted out.

Dat glared at her, clearly perturbed that she should even think of anything like that at a time like this. Mam tried to hide her smile, but Lizzie could tell she had to laugh.

Lizzie had loved heels forever. Ever since Mrs. Bixler had stopped in for a visit with Mam when Lizzie was five years old, Lizzie had wanted to grow up to wear shoes like Mrs. Bixler had—shiny and white with high heels. Maybe Cameron County was her chance to wear fancy things.

Watching the brief smile on Mam's face, Lizzie said, "Because if they do, I'm going to wear them."

Mandy, Lizzie's younger sister, yelled out from the living room, "Me, too!"

There was silence for a while, and not altogether a comfortable one. No one was smiling about wearing high heels anymore. Mam and Dat both looked desperately unhappy again. Mam broke the silence with a sigh.

"Well, Melvin, you know I am supposed to submit like every good Amish wife should. And I will go along if that's your decision." That was said in a much softer tone of voice, but there was a line of steel running through it, too.

Dat looked at Mam, then looked away. Lizzie knew that her mother thought Doddy Glick was responsible for all this. Dat always wanted to have his father's approval and praise. It was just how Dat was, Lizzie realized.

"I need a challenge again," he said. "Besides, I farmed growing up. I know how to milk cows, load hay, plow, and till the soil. I know plenty."

Suddenly enthused, excitement lighting up his blue eyes, he said, "Well, I'll tell you what, Annie. I'll go look at the farm, and if it's alright, I'll come back, and you and the girls can look at it before I buy it, okay?"

Mam didn't answer.

"I want to," Lizzie said. Emma and Mandy nodded.

"It's 120 acres. Can you girls imagine how much you would have to do? There's a large creek bordering the property and hills to sled-ride! Doddy said it would be perfect for you girls."

"It sounds exciting," Emma said politely, but her heart clearly wasn't in it.

Dat's smile folded up like an unplayed accordion. The light went out of his eyes just as quickly, leaving his face a picture of disappointment mixed with false bravado. His shoulders sagged, and he turned to go into the living room, first looking searchingly at Mam, who would not return his gaze.

Lizzie felt sorry for Dat, she really did. She knew how much it meant to him to be able to buy a farm and live in a new community. She wished Mam

wouldn't act so stubborn and would be nicer to Dat about moving.

Later that evening, lying in the bed that they shared in the little room at the top of the stairs, Mandy told Lizzie, in her wiser-than-her-years kind of way, that a husband should honor his wife's wishes.

"But, Mandy…" Lizzie said lamely.

"I don't care, Lizzie. I don't care what you say. If Dat loved Mam with all his heart he would not make her move to a place she does not want to go. I pity her so much I can hardly stand to even look at her poor face. Her hair is so gray, Lizzie. She coughs all the time."

Mam's hair was turning completely gray so rapidly it almost scared Lizzie, especially since she so often looked pale and tired, too.

Lizzie rolled over to face Mandy. "Mam is not pitiful. She's stubborn."

"Lizzie!" Mandy was furious. She seized her pillow and flung it at Lizzie.

"You don't know one tiny bit, Lizzie Glick!" she yelled. "You were always Dat's pet. You can read German better, drive ponies better, and you even stole nails out of the nailer and he never blinked. So why wouldn't you pity Dat? Huh? *Huh?*"

Lizzie muffled her giggles in her pillow, but her shaking shoulders gave her away.

Mandy made a fist and got a few good raps on Lizzie's shoulders. "So there. You don't have to have such a righteous attitude about Mam. I pity her. You

can just see how hard she's struggling to let Dat have his own way."

She plopped down on her side of the bed, turned her back to Lizzie, and mumbled a "Good-night." It didn't sound like a real "Good-night"; she just kind of swallowed the word till it sounded like "Gnat."

"Gnat!" Lizzie said loudly.

There was a sputter and Mandy burst out laughing. She snorted and laughed, rolling off the bed, hitting the floor with a whump, all the while whooping and laughing. It was so infectious, Lizzie stuck her head in her pillow and laughed along with her.

"Be quiet!" Emma called from her room.

"What is going on?" came Mam's anxious voice from the bottom of the stairs.

"M-M-Mandy fell out of bed," Lizzie gasped.

"Gnat, Mam!" Mandy called, which reduced them both to helpless waves of mirth.

Mam had flown up the steps to see what was going on. She shook her head and then leaned down and blew out the kerosene lamp that sat on the table next to the girls' bed.

"Sleep tight," she said as she closed the bedroom door.

Soon Mandy's breathing became regular and even, accompanied by soft little snores. But Lizzie lay awake, a thousand thoughts and fears swirling through her mind.

She wondered what God thought about all this. She also wondered if he cared. Surely Dat had prayed for direction. She wondered if Dat and Mam

had asked God for exactly opposite things. How could he answer each of them fairly?

Lizzie rolled over and rearranged the blankets. Mam had said there were hardly any young people in Cameron County. What would that mean for Emma and her, so close to 16 but with no one to date? Besides, she had heard that the bishop in Cameron County was strict, so she would probably never have high heels or anything fancy at all, so what did boys matter anyway?

And of course there was the farm, too. What if Mam was right and Dat wasn't a farmer? Then they'd live in Cameron County with no money. She had absolutely no clue what the farm looked like. Dat didn't even know. Why wouldn't Mam go with him to say if she thought it was alright to live there? What if it was so old and tumbledown, it wasn't even fit to live in? What if they had no money to fix it up? Mam would stay angry and grouchy for the rest of her life. It was all too troubling to think about.

Money had been an off-and-on touchy subject for the Glick family ever since Lizzie was a little girl. Even now, Lizzie got sad whenever she thought about Teeny and Tiny, their beautiful miniature ponies. She had been only eight when Dat had sat down at the breakfast table one morning. She knew something was wrong.

"I guess I may as well tell you now, girls," he said.

"What?" Emma asked. She had looked up and smiled.

But Lizzie's heart had sunk way down with a sickening thud. She knew. She knew exactly what Dat was going to say, because she had overheard Mam trying to persuade him to part with Teeny and Tiny, along with the glossy black spring wagon with the golden pinstripes along the side.

"We are going to have to sell Teeny and Tiny," he said.

"Why?" Emma asked, stopping halfway with a bite of potato soup.

"Because we really need the money, and because it costs too much to feed three ponies. Mam thinks it would be best. I do, too, of course, but I wish we could keep them, I really do," he finished.

Lizzie was heartbroken. It was just unthinkable, selling their miniature ponies. They were pint-sized little animals, a perfectly matched team of copper-colored ponies with blond manes and tails that Dat had made a little wagon for. The girls just loved when Dat hitched them to this wagon, and they went clipping down the road with their heads held high.

"When do we have to sell Teeny and Tiny?" Lizzie had asked so she wouldn't cry.

"I've decided we'll sell them soon at Harrison's Horse Auction in Taylorsburg."

Dat had spent several nights teaching Lizzie and Emma to drive the ponies. Lizzie loved the way the

two creatures stepped together as if they were one animal instead of two. Their coats had glistened in the evening sun, and their blond manes and tails streamed behind them as their little black hooves pattered.

Lizzie was thrilled to sit on that seat in the little black spring wagon, up so much higher than the ponies, and feel the power of their sturdy little bodies. Driving ponies made Lizzie so happy that she smiled to herself without even realizing it. Dat said he loved it, too, which made her even happier.

The neighbors stopped their work and waved at Dat, calling out to him or shaking their heads in wonder at the size of those miniature ponies, Lizzie remembered. She had tilted her head back to see Dat's face, and he was smiling and waving. He was so proud of this matched pair of ponies and the little spring wagon he had made all by himself.

As they pulled into the gravel driveway, Lizzie said to Dat, "We should get lots and lots of money for these ponies and never be poor again, ever— right?"

"Yes, Lizzie, you're right," Dat agreed.

But Lizzie wondered how Dat could have been laughing so much one minute and sound quite so sad the next. She thought he was probably as sad as she was to be back home so soon after that ride.

❧

Lizzie jerked awake and rolled over. Her throat was dry and her tongue was parched. She needed a drink of water. Shivering, she slid out of bed. She still did not like to go roaming about the house at night after hearing of that creature in Alaska they called Bigfoot. He was as tall as a second-story window, with shaggy hair, and no one had proved yet that he did not exist.

Mam told Lizzie over and over that this was all untrue. God did not make big horrible creatures like that. Lizzie had put Bigfoot to the back of her mind, but she still pulled her blinds the entire way to the windowsill every evening before she went to sleep. She told herself it wasn't because she was afraid or anything; she just felt safer that way.

Lizzie stepped out of her room, half asleep, feeling tired and groggy. Suddenly she stopped and her eyes flew open. Directly in front of her was a huge, shaggy shadow. Its hair stuck out wildly, and the shape of its grotesque head advanced slowly on the wall ahead of her.

Lizzie grasped the door frame, her eyes opening wide with pure terror. Her breath came in ragged gasps as she watched the shadowy creature on the wall. Just when Lizzie could take no more without screaming, cold with fear and her hands pressed tightly to her mouth, a very small voice said, "What are you doing?"

It was her little brother, Jason, stumbling out of his room, his riot of brown curls sticking up every which way. As he passed the kerosene lamp on the

hall dresser, his woolly head had been illuminated on the opposite wall, blowing it way out of proportion until his headful of curls had taken on the appearance of a huge creature.

"Jason!" Lizzie gasped. Her knees were shaking so badly, she dropped down to the floor.

"What's wrong with you?" he asked innocently.

"You just scared me, that's all." She couldn't tell him that his woolly head resembled an imaginary Bigfoot. He was self-conscious enough about his thick head of hair without her telling him what it had appeared to be.

"I'm thirsty," he said.

"Me, too. Come with me."

After they each had a cold drink from the gas-powered refrigerator, they made their way carefully back up the stairs. At the top, Lizzie turned to watch Jason walk down the hall to his room, grimacing again when the same shaggy head appeared on the wall as he passed the kerosene lamp.

Still, weak with relief, she turned into her room and quietly got into bed, not wanting to wake Mandy. Maybe that's how it was with her worrying. Everything looked so big and so terribly frightening, but if you refused to let it grow in your mind, it wasn't half as scary as it seemed. A dog barked in the distance, and a chill crept up her spine. She flopped onto her back, seeing again the expression on Dat's face years earlier when she had begged him not to sell Teeny and Tiny.

❧

"Do we…I mean…do we have to, really have to sell Teeny and Tiny?" she had asked, raising her eyes in misery.

"Ach, Lizzie." Dat's face softened, and for a minute Lizzie knew Dat felt exactly the same way she did. Emma stopped brushing Tiny, resting her hand on his back to listen. Dat didn't say more, and Lizzie waited expectantly, brushing back Teeny's forelock. His hair was so soft and blond, and…

"We have to, Lizzie. We need the money, and that's all there is to it," Dat said gruffly.

"Oh," said Lizzie, knowing deep down that Dat was only saying what she knew all along.

When Lizzie drove Teeny and Tiny into the ring, with Emma riding beside her, the crowd had gone wild. People stood up in their seats, clapping and cheering, smiling and waving their hats. The auctioneer could barely be heard above the thunderous applause. He laughed, put his microphone down, and waved his white cowboy hat. Emma and Lizzie had looked at each other and laughed.

Around they went, back to where Dat was standing, shaking his head and laughing, although Lizzie thought he looked as if he could cry at the same time.

"Keep going, Lizzie!" he yelled.

The auctioneer had opened the sale of the ponies at $500. He had to lower it to $300, and Lizzie dared hope that maybe, after all, Dat could not get

a good price for them and they would be taken back home. Then the bidding escalated so fast and at such a confusing rate, with the auctioneer talking so fast that his words were a blur. Lizzie just kept driving the ponies steadily, eventually stopping them in front of the auctioneer's stand.

Lizzie remembered hearing the amount of the bid. "Emma!" she whispered. "One thousand dollars!"

"That's a lot, isn't it?" Emma smiled at Lizzie, wringing her hands nervously in her lap.

Dat ran over to hold the ponies' heads, patting their necks as he spoke to them.

"Eleven hundred dollars!" yelled the auctioneer. "Do I hear $1125?" A pause and a resounding, "Sold!" with a whack of his gavel, and the ponies were officially sold to buyer number 520.

Dat looked at the girls, a broad smile on his face and tears in his eyes. Lizzie and Emma smiled back, but Lizzie's smile felt funny, as if it could slide downhill and pull tears along with it, like ice cream melting off a cone.

"Come, girls," Dat said firmly, and they walked away, Dat in the middle with Emma and Lizzie on either side looking straight ahead. None of them had looked back at their ponies — not once. There was simply no use.

❧

Lizzie pulled the covers up and sighed. She had done what she could to help their family have enough money then. And things weren't as tough now as they were once. She would do what she could now to make the move to Cameron County as smooth as possible.

Chapter 2

LIZZIE HURRIED INTO THE KITCHEN, CLUTCH-ING two pieces of wood that she had collected from the back porch. She lifted the metal handle from its hook on the wall behind the kitchen range and opened the round black lid so she could feed the wood into the fire. But the fire was hot and she couldn't quite arrange the wood so that it would fall in the way it was supposed to. She pulled back as smoke burned her eyes.

"Shut that lid!" Mam said loudly.

"I can't get the wood in right," Lizzie answered.

"Here." Emma came quickly to her rescue. Lizzie stepped back as Emma removed another section of the cast-iron top, and the wood fell to the grate. She quickly replaced the top and turned to wipe her hands on her apron.

Lizzie rubbed the smoke from her eyes. What is ever going to become of us? Lizzie wondered. She dreaded the future, so afraid Mam and Dat would

never be the same. Mam had never gotten this upset when they had moved in the past.

Suddenly, Emma squared her shoulders and turned to face Mam, looking directly into her eyes. "Mam, there's not one thing that is going to keep us from moving. I wish you wouldn't be so dead set against it. You're just making it hard for all of us."

Lizzie was shocked to see Mam burst into tears. She lowered her head, bringing her hands to her face and turning away. Emma watched without expression before looking at Lizzie and raising her eyebrows. Lizzie could hardly bear what was happening. She let her eyes drift out the window at the dreary landscape, the dry grass, the pallet shop, and the overcast skies.

After a moment, Mam took off her glasses and wiped her eyes with the corner of her apron. She breathed a trembling sigh, replaced her glasses, and said, "I'm sorry, Emma. I really am. I know I'm acting like an absolute baby. I have to get a hold of myself and stop this bitterness. But we have it so nice here…" Her voice trailed off.

"Mam, I know. I don't want to move either. But we have no choice. We have to be strong and look forward now," Emma said.

Mam sighed. "I've always been able to give up before this and never minded moving so much. But this time, I don't know why, but it's different. My whole being resists this move. I have never *not* wanted to do anything so badly."

Lizzie sat down on the bench opposite Mam.

She put her hands on her knees, leaned forward, her eyebrows raised hopefully. "But think, Mam, it might not be so bad. Didn't you say we can wear a different kind of apron? A bib apron? Do you know how to make them? We could see if we have material, and you could make some for us."

Mam looked at Lizzie, a blank expression in her eyes. "Not today."

That was all she said, but Lizzie knew it would take Mam a while to accept this move. The weight of Mam's struggle would fall mostly on Emma's responsible shoulders since she was older and closer to Mam. Lizzie and Mandy would try to make everything seem normal by acting as if nothing had happened.

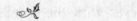

The next day, Lizzie and her family piled into the van Dat hired to take them to Cameron County and the farm that Dat and Doddy Glick were buying. The road into Cameron County didn't seem very big, at least not like the four-lane highways Lizzie was used to. She leaned against the cold window of the van Dat had hired to take them to the new farm as they crossed the bridge at Port James. The road wound through the countryside, past mountains, through wooded areas, and along tumbling streams. They passed through a few small towns, but there were no cities or shopping centers—nothing big or exciting.

"Look, girls, there it is," Dat said.

He leaned forward and pointed out the window as the driver slowed the van. Lizzie moved up in her seat so she could see where Dat was pointing. All of a sudden, there it was. The farm. Lizzie's heart sank. She did not dare look at Mam's face, or Dat's, or anyone's. It was so awful.

The barn appeared first on the left, towering over them like a dark, scary thing. There was not a drop of paint on its black weatherbeaten boards. A row of cracked, dirty windows stood along its front.

"That's the cow stable," Dat said.

Lizzie couldn't understand his excitement. A rickety barbed-wire fence made a barnyard of sorts, with sagging locust posts and rusty, broken wire. The barnyard was a quagmire of trampled black mud, with broken concrete blocks, pieces of brick, and old boards scattered through the oozing sludge.

The drive turned up a small slope, and the house was on the right behind a large oak tree. The house itself was brick, with a smaller mismatched brick addition that someone had tacked on as an after-thought. A wide porch ran along the small brick addition, with three or four steps going up to it.

The thing that shocked Lizzie most was the length of the grass in the yard. It looked like a hayfield, but there was no way you could have cut it, there was so much junk in the yard. The porch was filled with old stoves, chairs, boxes, barrels, chicken crates— just about anything you could imagine.

There were a few outbuildings, with broken

weeds left over from the summer alongside them, hanging their heads like tired, sleepy sentries.

Despair washed over Lizzie, enveloping her in a thick cloud. Emma's face was white, and Mandy whispered, "Wow!"

"Here we are!" Dat sang out.

"Melvin," Mam said weakly.

"Now, Annie, I told you it looks bad. It's just their junk, that's all. By the time we get everything cleaned up and painted, this can be a lovely home. I tried to tell you," he pleaded.

"But...but...Melvin, nothing could prepare me for *this*!" Mam gasped.

"Mam, now..." Emma said quietly.

Mam's mouth was pressed into a thin, hard line, and Dat's gaze never left her face as she climbed down from her seat in the van. It was heartbreaking to see how much he wanted Mam to like this farm. But it was so hopeless-looking that Lizzie pitied Mam with all her heart.

Mam stood uncertainly beside the van, her fingers working the straight pin in the front of her dress. She looked as if she could burst into tears any minute but was trying hard to put on a brave front. Dat talked to a small man in at the house for a while before motioning them all to come up on the porch.

The first thing that struck Lizzie was the bare light bulb hanging from the ceiling. It looked so stark and so ugly it reminded her of a prison. The interior of the house looked no better than the porch

or the yard with dishes, clothes, boxes, shoes, and toys strewn everywhere.

The living room was an unbelievable mess. Once, when Dat had started the harness shop and things were slow, Mam had spent as much time helping him as she had working in the house. Emma had done her best to keep things clean, but sometimes things got away from her. But things at their house had never been as dirty and disheveled as this. The only thing Lizzie could really see was the television set in the corner. The sofas were sagging with pillows and afghans and two cats, a gray one and a yellow one that was so big he reminded Lizzie of a bobcat. Books teetered on the wide arm of an old brown sofa, with tablets and pencils scattered beside them. Lizzie guessed it must be someone's homework.

Two long, narrow windows looked out over the fields to the south. The walls were papered, or had been at one time. The paper was peeling off in layers but was still intact on some of the walls. Curtains sagged at the windows, which were so dirty Lizzie could barely see the fields beyond.

Lizzie glanced at Mam to see if there was a spark of interest in her eyes. She was talking with the heavyset woman, who still had not introduced herself. Lizzie couldn't tell how Mam felt, so she soon forgot about watching her as they finished their tour of the house.

When they had seen all the rooms, Lizzie and Mandy headed outside and toward the road, looking for bright sun and fresh air. They spotted Dat

and Edwin, the small man, coming out of the cow stable. Dat looked happy, talking animatedly and pointing to the distant slopes. The two men walked along the fields to survey the property lines. Mandy and Lizzie turned back toward Mam in the house, hoping that they would soon leave.

Mam was talking to Edwin's wife, trying to keep the twins out of mischief and looking very tired and impatient.

"Where's Dat?" she asked as the girls entered.

Mam sighed when the girls told her he was walking along the property line with Edwin.

"Should we tell him you're ready to go?" Lizzie asked helpfully.

"No."

The girls sat on the porch, mostly because they didn't know what else to do. They both felt awkward because Mam was so impatient and Dat wouldn't be back for a while, Lizzie knew. So they sat side by side on the steps, their chins in their hands, looking out over the muddy pasture that went down to the creek.

Mandy sighed. So did Lizzie. They said nothing for a very long time.

"Mam said we're allowed to wear sweaters here."

"So?"

"Which would be better? Living in a nice house with our cousins and friends in Jefferson County, or living in this...this...ugly place and wearing sweaters?"

"I don't know. Be quiet. That's dumb."

"You're grouchy now."

"Well, you don't have to say things like that."

They sat in silence as the birds twittered high in the old oak tree.

"We have to slap water on our hair and roll it if we live here," Lizzie offered.

"I'm not going to."

"You have to."

"I don't know how."

"You'll learn."

"From who?"

"Mam."

Lizzie felt mixed up. A part of her wanted to live here, to try new and strange things, but another part of her clung to Jefferson County. She felt as if everything secure was being taken away from her, and there was nothing to do but let it go.

Chapter 3

A FEW WEEKS LATER, DAT SOLD THEIR HOUSE and the pallet business to Uncle Eli. Dat couldn't wait to move to Cameron County. He loved change, and this was a brand new challenge, probably one of the greatest ones he ever faced.

Mam did her best to hide her misgivings. She spent lots of time at the sewing machine, making dresses and bib aprons, so different from what they wore now, for the girls. Emma giggled as Lizzie tried to put one on but got stuck. She held the strange apron in front of her, trying to figure out how she could ever get it over her shoulders.

"Here," Mam said, throwing it over Lizzie's head and settling it around her neck.

"Now, stick your arms through here," she instructed.

Lizzie held her arms up, and suddenly the whole apron slid into place. She reached back to tie the strings as she hurried into the bedroom, excited to

see herself in the dresser mirror.

"Lizzie's hardly fat at all anymore," Emma whispered to Mam.

Lizzie heard her and smiled as she turned this way and that, swiveling her head to see the back, and adjusting the front, smoothing it down over her stomach. Lizzie hated dieting. Every morning she would get up and vow silently to herself that today was the day she would start her diet.

Mam had even bought diet soda for her to drink, mostly to be encouraging without being rude. But the diet soda wasn't very tasty all by itself. The only way Lizzie could really appreciate her diet soda was with a big, thick sandwich made of ham, cheese, lettuce, tomato, and lots of mayonnaise. And a handful of potato chips, too.

Maybe Cameron County wasn't so bad after all, if the new aprons made her look slimmer. She studied herself in the mirror and sighed. Emma had dark hair and green eyes, with a round cherubic face which made her look a lot like Mam. Lizzie didn't resemble Mam and Emma at all, so she guessed she must look like Dat's side of the family. Her hair was straight and mousy brown, and her eyes were gray.

Since she had slimmed down some after becoming a teenager, her nostrils didn't seem quite as long and slanted anymore. She supposed that when you lost weight, the size of your nostrils diminished as well, which was a very interesting thing. She never read that in a magazine though, or heard of anyone else discovering this fact, but that's how it was for her.

And now, of all the nightmarish fears of Lizzie's 15 years, she was getting blemishes on her forehead. Ugly red pimples that popped if you squeezed them. When the pimples had first appeared, Mam was concerned, peering closely at Lizzie's forehead through her glasses, clucking worriedly as she did so.

"You shouldn't squeeze them," she would say.

Eventually Mam bought her a tube of Clearasil lotion the same color as her skin, and that helped the pimples dry up quickly. It was the single best thing anyone ever invented, Lizzie always thought, because it certainly did make a difference and it was almost like makeup.

Emma and Mandy hardly ever had one pimple, and if they did, it soon disappeared. But they were always careful of Lizzie's feelings, because they knew that Lizzie's skin troubles really weren't fair.

"Do you like it?" Mam asked from the doorway.

Lizzie smiled and glanced one more time into the mirror at her new apron. Now all Lizzie really needed to feel attractive was a nice pair of shoes with heels on them. She was not allowed to wear heels till she turned 16, but that was the one single goal of her life—to wear high-heeled shoes. She often told Emma she wanted some that would make a clacking noise when she walked. Emma said that was *grosfeelich*, or vain, and if that's why she wanted high-heeled shoes, she had better forget about it.

"I love the apron," she said. "It feels so comfortable."

"This style will be ideal for milking cows and carrying hay bales," Mam said.

That was closer to genuine happiness than Mam had come in a long time, Lizzie thought. She knew Mam was trying very hard to accept the move. Lizzie found that it made the future much less frightening if Mam at least tried to be a good sport about moving to the tumbledown old farm.

She turned to smile at Mam as she wriggled out of the apron, handing it back to her. "Now, when are you going to teach us how to roll our hair?" she asked since Mam was almost happy.

Mam narrowed her eyes, looking at Lizzie's profusion of loose waves. "Go wet your hair. The whole top of your head," she said.

"Sopping wet?" Lizzie asked.

"Well, wet."

Lizzie giggled and ran into the bathroom. It wasn't the wet hair that made her laugh as much as the fact that Mam was finally warming up a little bit. Kind of like an ice cube just beginning to melt. But she *was* melting, which made Lizzie's heart feel light.

She pulled the pins out of her covering and laid it on the counter. She took down her bob, or hair bun, running her fingers through her waves as they tumbled down her back. Her hair was getting to be so long and thick she could hardly make a decent bob on the back of her head. She used 10 straight hairpins and still she could hardly keep her hair up till the end of the day.

Quickly she held her hands under the water faucet, ducked her head, and patted the water onto it. The water felt cold as she wet her hair twice before going out to Mam.

"I need a fine-toothed comb," Mam said.

Lizzie returned to the bathroom, found a comb, and came back to sit on a chair. Mam combed through her wet hair, then stopped, and taking both hands, pulled back dreadfully hard.

"Ouch!" Lizzie winced.

Mam laughed, stepped back, and said, "You had better get used to this."

"But it hurts! Look at me. I have tears in my eyes."

"Alright. I'll be careful." Mam started rolling in the wet hair along the side of Lizzie's brow, smoothing it back with her hand as she rolled. She completed the other side before stepping back to see the finished result. Before she had a chance to say anything, Emma and Mandy started laughing hysterically.

"Li-i-i-zzie! You look so—!" Emma tried to say, but she was laughing too hard.

"Homely!" Mandy sputtered between giggles.

Lizzie got up and hurried to the bathroom to look in the mirror. She did look so ugly! Her forehead was twice as wide as it should be, making her eyes appear way too low on her face.

"I look...I look like a drowned rat!" she wailed.

Mam was hanging onto the back of the kitchen chair, she was laughing so hard. Emma and Mandy

were sitting on the couch, their heads thrown back as they laughed with Mam.

Mam took a deep breath to answer but was overtaken with a fit of coughing. She leaned over the kitchen table, her hand covering her mouth as spasms racked her body. She clutched the table for several minutes until she could breathe normally again. Finally, she lifted her apron to retrieve the handkerchief in her dress pocket, gasped, and shook her head.

"My goodness, what a cough," she said.

"Mam, you should see a doctor," Emma said, gazing worriedly at her mother.

"I know, Emma," Mam said. "I'll see if the cough gets better this week. If it doesn't, I promise I'll go."

Lizzie shivered. She hoped Mam wouldn't wait too long.

Chapter 4

MAM AND DAT HAD STOPPED ARGUING IN front of Lizzie and her sisters.

Lizzie knew why.

One of the last evenings the family was in Jefferson County, Lizzie couldn't relax and fall asleep. She lay in bed, thinking once again about all they were leaving behind for Cameron County, when she heard Dat and Mam talking in the kitchen.

Mandy must have left the stairway door open because Lizzie could hear her parents more clearly than usual.

"I still don't want to move," Mam said. "But I won't argue with you anymore."

"Thank you, Annie," Dat said. "I know this has been hard."

"Not just for me," Mam said. "It's hard on Emma, too, knowing that she's moving some place new where there aren't many young people her age to run around with. But there's no point in making

it harder for her by arguing, so I'm going to just let it go."

"What about Lizzie and Mandy?" Dat asked.

Lizzie lay very still, waiting to hear what Mam would say.

"They aren't turning 16 yet," Mam said. "Besides, they're like two colts full of life. They don't mind moving. It's exciting to them."

Lizzie rolled over so she couldn't hear anymore of their conversation. Mam had done it again. Emma, Emma, Emma. Poor Emma. Well, what about me? Lizzie thought resentfully. Maybe I mind it more than anyone else. I'm just scared to bring up the subject for fear it will make it harder for Mam.

Lizzie always wanted to be like Emma, but she couldn't seem to be, no matter how hard she tried to be good and sweet like Emma was. Emma loved to cook and bake and try new recipes, even copying a whole boxful of them before she had a boyfriend, which Lizzie couldn't imagine doing. Emma loved to sweep and dust, wash clothes, and sew. She had even started sewing their white organdy coverings, which was a skill in itself.

She had copied every song from the many hymn-books they had, writing them all down neatly in a composition book, so that when they felt like singing they used Emma's handwritten songbook. Emma had first started copying songs in a thick composition book in sixth grade, so now she had a collection of over 100 songs—hymns, school songs, and little funny songs—actually, anything she could

learn or that Mam and Dat taught her.

Lizzie often started copying songs, but she never finished any of them. The thing was, it took too long. Her hand got awfully tired of writing, and she became so horribly bored that she felt numb all over, so she never had a songbook of her own.

It had always been like this, Lizzie thought. Even when they were little girls and Dat was under a lot of pressure to have their very first house "under roof," as he said, "before the snow flew."

Emma, Lizzie, and Mandy went off to school every morning, while Mam cared for the twins, who were babies then, and cooked meals for the men who helped Dat build the house. Emma was clearly under plenty of stress, too, coming home from school every day to a sink filled with dirty dishes, and the house strewn with toys, baby bottles, diapers, and loads of unfolded laundry on the kitchen table.

One evening, after Mam had spent the whole day cooking for a tableful of men, the house was such a mess that Emma burst into tears of frustration when she stepped in the door. She tossed her lunchbox on the table, ran into her bedroom, threw herself on her bed, and cried.

Lizzie had looked up from her after-school snack of cold leftover meat loaf with ketchup, chewing methodically.

"What's wrong with Emma?" she asked.

"Close your mouth when it's full of meat loaf, Lizzie. She's just upset because everything is such a big mess. It's no wonder. If you and Mandy would help more around the house, she wouldn't feel quite so responsible. All you do when you come home from school is eat and read the comics in the paper. You're lazy, Lizzie. You're actually getting quite overweight and you are *lazy*." Mam's face had been red with frustration and anger as her voice became louder.

The meat loaf that had been so delicious a moment earlier turned to sawdust and stuck in her throat. Lizzie was shocked. She felt hot all over, her face burning with humiliation.

"I don't mean to be rude, Lizzie. I know I'm losing my temper. But you need to shape up and help Emma and me more over this time. We're building a house and this house is for you, too, so your duty is to help along with everyone else."

Lizzie hadn't said one word. She couldn't. She supposed what Mam had told her was true. She was fat and lazy. The truth hurt so badly, Lizzie felt like crawling under her bed and never coming out again. She would stay under her bed until she died and turned into one big dust ball. They would never know what had happened to her.

That evening, when Emma set the alarm clock properly as she always did, climbed into bed, plumped her pillow, rolled over, and said, "G'night," Lizzie didn't answer. After a while, she said, "Emma."

"What?"

"Do you think I'm fat?"

"Ach, Lizzie, it's mean to say someone is fat. I'm not thin, either."

There was silence as Lizzie stared wide-eyed into the darkness. It was not a nice thought, but Mam wasn't very kind. How could she be so mean?

"Emma?"

"Hmm?"

"Mam likes you a lot better than me, doesn't she? I mean, she likes me as good as you can like a fat, lazy person, but she likes you a lot better. Not just because you're thin and you work harder, but she really, really, really likes you a whole pile more than me."

"Lizzie, now stop it. You know that's not true."

Lizzie sat straight up. "Emma, I know what's true and what isn't. Don't you try and tell me. Mam said I am overweight and lazy, so that's exactly what she thinks of me. And I don't care."

Lizzie plopped back down on her pillow, snorted, and then twisted and arranged herself in a comfortable position before she said, "G'night."

"Lizzie."

"What?"

"You can't go to sleep thinking that. Mam would never love one of her daughters more than another. It's just that you *could* help more since we have the twins. There is about three times as much work now as there was before they were born."

"See?"

"See what?"

"I tried to tell you. What do we want another baby for? And then she goes and has two."

"You think it's her fault? God gave us those babies."

At least Mam had decided to stop being upset about their move to Cameron County. Lizzie wished now that Mam could bring herself to care as much about her as she did about Emma. Dat did, but Mam still seemed to think first of Emma and her needs. Lizzie shifted in her bed, listening to the sound of Mandy sleeping. Maybe when they were little, Emma had been right about Mam loving all her girls the same. But that didn't mean she did now. Lizzie was going to have to do something about this whole dilemma in the morning.

Chapter 5

L IZZIE POUTED ALL THROUGH BREAKFAST, barely touching her food. When someone asked her a question, she shrugged her shoulders and looked at the cold, congealed egg on her plate.

"Alright, what's wrong?" Mam asked finally.

Lizzie blinked her eyes rapidly to hold back hot, angry tears of shame and resentment. She got up from the table. At the sink, she started throwing dirty dishes out of the way and slamming plates on the countertop as hard as she could. She would show Mam and Emma who could get work done around here. She held the bottle of dish detergent upside down and squeezed, producing mountains of white, frothy bubbles. The rinse water was foamy with soap when Mam came back to the kitchen to heat water for formula.

"Lizzie, how many times do I have to tell you? Don't use so much dish detergent!" she said.

Lizzie didn't answer. She turned away from Mam,

blindly looking for more utensils. Just go away, she thought. Go away and leave me alone.

"Lizzie?"

"Nothing." Lizzie kept her mouth clamped shut tightly. She refused to turn around and look at Mam.

Mam sighed and started to clear the food from the table.

CRASH!

Lizzie jumped as the milk bottle she was holding slipped through her soapy hands and landed on the floor. The whole glass gallon jar lay in a hundred pieces on the linoleum as milk streamed in every direction.

"Lizzie! You did that on purpose!" Mam shouted.

"I did not!" Lizzie yelled back. She grabbed a roll of paper towels and dropped to her knees, swabbing at the flow of milk.

"Ouch!" she yelped, as a large chunk of glass embedded itself in the palm of her hand. She sat back on her heels as blood spurted from the wound.

Emma knelt down beside her and calmly wiped up the milk with an oversized towel from the bathroom, absorbing most of it. Mandy gingerly picked up pieces of the glass jar with her thumb and forefinger. Mam bent over Lizzie, her face red, scolding and fussing anxiously. Jason sat on the bench at the table, his curly hair sticking out every which way and said calmly, "This is about a mess."

Lizzie sat with her back against the cabinets, holding her bleeding hand while Emma filled a bucket

with warm, soapy water and finished mopping up the milk. Mam stood up and turned to Lizzie.

"Whatever in the world were you doing? Banging the pots and pans around because you were mad about something again, Lizzie? Well, you just let me tell you something."

She paused and took a deep breath.

"Emma, go get the gauze and tape. Union salve, too."

While Emma hurried to the bathroom, Mam pressed the paper towel down hard until Lizzie winced.

"Ow. Watch it!" she said.

"Oh, sorry. As I was saying, you can just straighten yourself up right this minute, Lizzie Glick."

"I heard you and Dat talking about Emma last evening," Lizzie snapped, pulling her hand away.

Mam grabbed her hand again.

"Well, you're going to have to learn to stop being so selfish. All you ever think about is yourself, and whether or not I like you as much as I like Emma. Now listen to me."

Mam took off the paper towel, releasing the pressure on the wound, and only a small swell of blood seeped out of the cut. She cut off a piece of white sterile gauze and laid it aside.

"As long as you are planning to go through life thinking only of yourself, you're going to have an awfully hard time. I've often told you girls, Jesus first, others next, and yourself last spells J-O-Y," she said.

Lizzie shrugged. Emma and Mandy stood in the doorway listening.

"You know, too, Lizzie, that I've had an awful time giving myself up to moving to Cameron County. It's a struggle to think of Jesus first. But if it's his will that we move—which I hope it is—and if I don't want to give in to that, then I most definitely am not putting God's will first. And Dat…" Her voice trailed off.

Lizzie watched the emotion on Mam's face. She wanted to be truly submissive, Lizzie knew, but it was very hard.

"You think it's stupid, don't you," Lizzie asked.

"What?"

"Farming."

Mam held Lizzie's hand tightly as she applied the dark brown pungent salve before laying the gauze carefully on top of the wound.

"I shouldn't say this, Lizzie. Especially not to you. But, yes, it's stupid. Financially, for sure. I don't know about spiritually. Maybe it will be good for all of us to do without money again." She tore off a few lengths of adhesive tape, wrapped them around Lizzie's hand, and stood up.

"There. No more washing dishes for you." She bent down, her face level with Lizzie's. "And quit your pouting."

Lizzie looked squarely into Mam's face before she said, "I will, if you quit treating Mandy and me like we're two years old. Mam, I am 15, not four. And I have feelings, too, you know."

Mam laid a hand on Lizzie's shoulder, softly rubbing it back and forth. "Ach, yes, Lizzie, I know. You're just so very, very different from Emma that it seems as if you're younger than you are."

Lizzie swallowed the lump in her throat. She could never understand why she felt like crying when Mam was kind.

But that was often how it was. Maybe when anger dissolved, it brought a lump to her throat and tears to her eyes. Probably.

Chapter 6

When moving day arrived, Lizzie was glad to see the moving truck pull in. She just wanted to put the worst part behind her, get to the new farm, and begin living her new life in Cameron County.

The sun shone with a golden light on the new spring leaves as they wound their way along the twisting mountain road, following closely behind the loaded moving truck in a van Dat had rented for the day. It was a lovely time of year to move, with a fresh spring breeze making everything seem soft and new. Lizzie supposed the four seasons would be the same in their new home, which was somewhat comforting.

When the van turned down the farm's steep drive, the front door of the house opened and Lizzie's Glick aunts and uncles filled the yard, ready to help unload their belongings and carry them into the house. The yard looked so much better without all the pieces of junk strewn about, Lizzie thought.

Inside the house, the girls ran excitedly from room to room. The place didn't seem nearly as hopeless as it had on their previous visit. Mammy Glick and two of Lizzie's aunts, all of whom lived right there in Cameron County, had emptied the house as soon as the English family had moved out. The tall, old kitchen windows shone, the glass sparkling in the spring sunshine. Even the grayish white tile of the kitchen floor was waxed to a glossy shine.

While most of the family helped unload the van, Dat and his two brothers worked in the kitchen, connecting the gas stove and refrigerator to the propane tank that sat outside the kitchen wall. When they were finished, Lizzie turned the burner handles, one by one, and watched as an even blue flame burst forth. Next she opened the refrigerator door and stuck her head in, enjoying the cold air that brushed her cheeks. Now they could have ice cubes again and ice cream whenever they wanted.

Mam came into the kitchen, carrying a box.

"There is so much to be done," Lizzie said.

Mam nodded. "We could paint for a year and still find something to paint. But that will have to wait till we're settled and everything is put in order," she said.

Lizzie knew that Mam was right. The walls looked dirty, even after Mammy Glick had scrubbed them clean. But at least they had nice things in this new house.

That hadn't always been the case, especially when Mam and Dat had first started the pallet shop. Then, it seemed, they were so poor that all they had to eat was lumpy potato soup.

"What's wrong with Mam and Dat?" Emma had asked one evening back then as she scraped Lizzie's uneaten soup into her own bowl and added the crusts of leftover bread.

"I think we're very, very poor," Lizzie had said as she gathered a handful of silverware from the table and carried it to the sink.

"Why are we so poor?" Emma asked. "I mean, Dat and Mam are always busy in the shop. Dat makes lots of pallets, and the little bell above the door rings an awful lot lately."

"I know," Lizzie said. "But they argue all the time."

"No, they don't, Lizzie. Mam and Dat really like each other, and they don't argue all the time," Emma said.

"I don't care what you say, Emma. I heard them."

"When?"

"One time."

"Lizzie, you stretch stuff. Everything isn't nearly as bad as you make it sound."

"Well," Lizzie sighed, grabbing a washcloth and wiping the plastic tablecloth furiously. There were little rips and holes in the cheap fabric, and Lizzie caught her washcloth in one. "See, if we weren't so poor, we wouldn't have this pitiful-looking, old, torn tablecloth on our table."

"Lizzie, you should be ashamed of yourself. Lots of Amish families have torn plastic tablecloths on their tables. When I get married, I'm not going to go buy a new tablecloth just because it has a hole in it. Everybody has holes in their tablecloths," Emma said.

Lizzie drew herself up to her full height.

"Emma, I don't care what you say. Anyone that has a torn plastic tablecloth on their table is poor. If they weren't, they'd buy a new one. When I'm married, I am not going to keep mine that long. It looks sloppy and makes you look like you're poor, anyhow," she said.

Emma added dish detergent to the hot water in the sink. "Well, I pity Mam."

"Why?"

"I don't know. I just do."

"I pity Dat," responded Lizzie.

"I pity Mam most, because she's always working in the shop and it's just a fright how sloppy this house looks," Emma had said.

❧

Lizzie shook her head, remembering Emma's words and the terror in her own heart. Well, at least they weren't poor anymore. Not yet, at least. She turned to help Mam finish putting the pans away.

"Do you like it here now, Mam? I mean, better than you did that first time we saw the place?"

Mam turned and gazed across the kitchen. "Yes,

Lizzie, I do," she said quietly. But Lizzie heard a sigh in her voice, a kind of hollow undertone that wouldn't quite go away.

"But you're worried about Emma, right?"

"Well...yes, I am. I mean, turning 16 years old is hard enough in a settled community like Jefferson County. But here...I don't know."

"She'll be 16 in six days."

"I know."

"Are we having a birthday party?"

"Who would we invite? There are no young people here." There was an edge of bitterness to Mam's voice.

Lizzie pushed the last pot into the cupboard and then quickly closed the door so it wouldn't fall out.

"Who will Emma marry if there aren't other Amish youth in this area," she asked.

"I don't know. Two new families are moving into the area from a neighboring community, but they have only a girl about Emma's age," Mam said.

"That's nice!" Lizzie said, even though she knew Mam didn't think that was enough to be happy about.

"Yes." Mam opened a new box and started to unpack silverware, placing it into a drawer next to the sink.

"Mam, how does God's will work if there are no boys to marry, anyway? How will poor Emma ever get married? I mean, this is getting serious. She's soon 16, and in a year I'll be, too. What are we going to do?"

Mam put down a handful of forks so she could look at Lizzie. She was clearly trying to muster her own conviction about this subject.

"Lizzie, if you would only read your Bible more and try to be more mature about your faith, you would not be so troubled. If you pray honestly, God will direct you to the right husband. Even if right now you can't figure out how that's possible."

Lizzie nodded, but she couldn't help but wonder how God would direct her if there weren't any boys nearby. Before she could ask Mam more about God's will and future husbands, Mommy Glick called them to dinner. Lizzie followed Mam into the dining room where the table was covered with food.

Mommy Glick had made chicken potpie with large chunks of potatoes swimming in thick chicken gravy. Chunks of white chicken meat were mixed with the potpie squares and sprinkled with bright green parsley. Mommy Glick made her own noodles, too. She mixed egg yolks with flour, and the potpie turned out thick and yellow and chewy. It was the best thing ever to eat with creamy chicken gravy.

Lizzie also admired the baked beans that had been baking most of the forenoon and now were rich with tomato sauce and bacon. Bits of onion floated among the beans, and steam wafted from the granite roaster. Applesauce, dark green sweet pickles, and red beet eggs completed the meal.

Lizzie was so hungry she forgot all about her diet for the day. When they finished eating the main part

of the meal, Lizzie and Mandy helped themselves to pieces of shoofly pie and sat on the steps of the porch together. They each bit off the very tips of their pieces.

"No one else in the whole world can make shoofly pies like Mommy Glick," Lizzie said.

Mandy nodded, her mouth full as she ate her way through the whole delicious piece.

"Do you think we'll ever feel at home here?" Mandy asked, finally.

"Probably."

"It's going to take a while."

"I know."

"We can't hear any traffic or see any lights. We don't even have neighbors."

Lizzie pointed toward a white house in the woods down by the creek. "There are people," she said.

"Who are they?"

"Old people, Dat said."

"How does he know?"

"I have no idea."

They sat in silence, the breeze stirring the leaves of the walnut tree beside the sidewalk.

"We can make a nice farm out of this junky place," Lizzie said, even though she wasn't sure that was true.

Mandy nodded.

Chapter 7

MAM CAME OUT TO THE ENCLOSED BACK porch, her back bent as she coughed deeply, her handkerchief to her mouth. Mommy Glick and Emma followed close behind her.

"Emma, how long has she been coughing like that?" Mommy Glick asked, her brows drawn with concern.

"Most of the winter, it seems like," Emma said, her eyes filling with unexpected tears.

Mommy Glick turned to Dat. "Melvin, I think Annie needs to see a good doctor, and soon," she said.

"I've begged her to go," Dat replied.

"I don't like the sound of that cough," Mommy continued as she helped Mam into a chair.

Mam sat down slowly. One of the twins ran over and buried her face in her apron. Mam stroked her head absentmindedly as she cleared her throat repeatedly. Mommy Glick watched Mam, while

Emma hurried back into the house to get Mam a drink of water.

Lizzie and Mandy huddled together. "I wish Mam would stop coughing."

"She's going to end up in the hospital."

"She can't. We need Mam more than ever now."

Lizzie gazed across the field and the trees beyond that, where the creek ran wide and cold. She shivered. She hoped fervently that God would watch over them way back here on this winding country road in the middle of nowhere. She had never felt quite so alone, or quite as old as she did right this minute, sitting on the concrete porch steps.

About a week after they had settled in, Mam's cough became an alarming rasp. She held a Kleenex to her mouth as she bent over, painfully hacking from the persistent ache in her chest.

She had gone on as best she could, even as her strength sometimes failed her, Lizzie knew. But she worked more slowly every day.

One afternoon, Lizzie was outside pulling weeds around the little log cabin. She was tugging with all her strength on a very stubborn weed almost as tall as herself. She didn't notice Emma running down the sidewalk until she called for Dat in a tone of voice that made Lizzie stop yanking on the weed.

She watched as Dat emerged from the barn and listened to what Emma was saying. When he walked

toward the house with her, Lizzie knew there must be something wrong. She wiped off her grimy hands on her apron and hurried up the slope to the house.

As she entered the kitchen, Dat pulled up a chair and sat close to Mam, a concerned look making his tired face seem soft and vulnerable. Mam was struggling to breathe and her complexion was almost blue in color.

"Annie, you should have done something a long time ago," Dat said. "You just go on and on and on, even if you feel so bad."

"Well, Melvin, I can't go on. I need to go to the hospital now. Every breath I take burns in my lungs, so I suppose I have a bad dose of pneumonia. I guess we'll see a doctor first, but who? Everything is so strange and new here."

Dat sat up resolutely.

"No, Annie, you won't go to the doctor. You're going straight to the emergency room in Falling Springs. There are no two ways about it."

"I'm just so sorry. It will cost thousands of dollars if I'm admitted," Mam said anxiously, searching Dat's eyes.

Dat smiled at her tenderly, covering her hand with his own. "What are thousands of dollars compared to losing you, Annie?"

Mam tried to smile at Dat, but her nostrils flared as they always did when she had to cry. Her face turned a darker shade as her tears came uncontrollably.

"Ach, now you made me cry," she said.

"I'll go call a doctor. You get yourself ready and we'll leave for Falling Springs."

Dat glanced anxiously at Emma. Lizzie knew she was the one who would keep everything else going. She would take full responsibility for the laundry, the cooking, and the cleaning. She was naturally a very capable girl for her 15 years, as she had always been, even as a child.

Lizzie met Dat's concerned look and smiled bravely, consoling him with her cheerful appearance.

"We'll be all right, Dat. Please don't worry about us," she said, although Lizzie could see that Emma's smile was a very good cover-up, hiding her own worries. Lizzie vowed to do all she could to be a good helper, working along with Emma, even taking on jobs she didn't want to do.

Chapter 8

Dat left to call a driver, and Mam went to take a bath, even if it was mid-afternoon. Mam was very particular about being clean when you went to see a doctor. Even when she took the twins for a checkup, she gave them a bath in the middle of the day.

Emma hurried anxiously after Mam. "Are you sure you should be taking a bath, Mam?" she asked.

"Why, Emma?"

"Suppose you pass out?"

"I won't. I'll be fine."

Mam always said that. Lizzie twisted her fingers nervously around the small hem of her bib apron. She could not bear to hear Mam coughing from the bathroom, so she hurried outside to the porch. Jason was sitting on the porch swing.

"Is she going to die in the hospital?" he asked, his voice quavering.

"No, Jason. She is just really, really sick. I'm sure the doctors can make her well."

"Are you sure?"

"Oh, yes." Lizzie said this with a lot more bravado than she felt inside. People died of pneumonia every day. That's how Mommy Miller had died. But she didn't say that to Jason. She just pushed the porch swing back and forth with her one foot.

The porch swing comforted Lizzie. It was the one thing that made her feel at home these first days of living on the farm. There was something very soothing about swinging back and forth on it in the clean spring air. Even if Lizzie was troubled, the porch swing always calmed her spirit.

Dat hurried up the sidewalk and into the house without even glancing at Lizzie. Emma called him, and Lizzie heard their low tones as they discussed something in the kitchen behind the screen door. Soon Dat reappeared, looking sternly at Lizzie.

"Where's Mandy?"

"I don't know."

"Well, Emma said she doesn't want to tattle or make you and Mandy angry at her, but you don't always listen to her when Mam and I are away, that you just run off to the creek or go drive Billy, or do anything you can to get away from doing jobs she asks you to do."

Lizzie watched her foot on the concrete floor of the porch, not sure what to say. She knew it was true. There was just something about Emma asking her to do a job that ruffled Lizzie's feathers. She

wasn't as bossy as she used to be, but whenever Emma asked, Lizzie always felt like not doing the job Emma wanted done.

"Do you hear me?"

"Yes."

Lizzie wished her toes weren't so crooked. She had the ugliest feet she had ever seen on anyone. She decided then and there that she would never go barefoot except at home. Her toes were hideous.

A dull thump from the direction of the living room and a piercing scream made Lizzie leap to her feet, almost upsetting the porch swing. Dat sprang to the door of the kitchen as Emma screamed again. They yanked open the bathroom door to find Mam in a heap on the floor beside the counter. She had been pinning her apron when she fell. Pins were scattered all over the floor.

Dat cried out as he stooped to lift her, but he wasn't able to pick her up because she was so limp. Her face was so pale, Lizzie couldn't bear to look.

"Emma open the windows," Dat said.

He rolled Mam over.

"Lizzie, go get a pillow. Hurry up!"

Lizzie dashed to the bedroom, her heart racing. Poor Mam! Poor, sick Mam who just went on and on, feeling horrible all week. She grabbed a pillow off of her bed and ran back downstairs.

Dat lifted Mam's head and gently placed the pillow underneath it. Lizzie was terribly alarmed to see how Mam's head rolled around on her shoulders, just like a rag doll's. Dat stood up and held a

clean washcloth under the cold water faucet. After he wrung it out, he knelt to bathe Mam's face.

Mam's head rolled to the side, and she moaned as her eyes fluttered open.

"Annie!" Dat touched her face. "Annie!"

Mam's eyes blinked, and she struggled to focus.

"Ach, my," she whispered weakly.

"Annie, you'll be all right. You fainted," Dat said tenderly, as he kept stroking her forehead with the cool washcloth.

"Ach, my," Mam said again.

Dat was just helping her to a sitting position when the kitchen door banged shut.

"Hey," Mandy yelled.

Lizzie hurried out. "Shh!"

"What?"

"Mam passed out on the bathroom floor!"

Mandy clapped a hand to her mouth, her big green eyes opening wide. Hay was stuck in her hair, her face was grimy with dust, and she had torn a big hole in the sleeve of her dark purple dress.

"What happened?"

"Mandy, she's terribly sick. She has to go to the hospital. Where were you?"

"In the haymow. Hey, I found a bunch of kittens. You know all those wild cats around here that have no tails? There's a whole nest full of kittens and *not one* has a tail!" Mandy was so excited, the veins in her neck stuck out like cords.

"Shh! Mandy, calm down! Mam's sick."

"I know. Are they...is she...how are they going

to the hospital?" Mandy asked as she made her way to the bathroom door.

Dat was helping Mam to her feet as Emma hovered nearby, picking up the pillow and comforting the twins who were crying.

Mam sank wearily onto the sofa, just as they heard the crunch of tires in the driveway.

"Your driver's here," Lizzie announced.

Dat helped Mam back to her feet while Emma hurried over with her black Sunday apron.

"Your apron, Mam."

Mam could not answer. Her mouth was pressed into a straight, thin line as she used all of her concentration to stay on her feet. Dat shook his head at Emma as they slowly made their way across the kitchen, through the door, and into the waiting car. This was the first time Lizzie ever saw Mam go away without her black apron, but she supposed it was all right to do since Mam was so sick.

As Mam and Dat got into the car, the twins started crying uncontrollably. Susan wailed steadily, and no one was able to console her. KatieAnn finally sat in her little chair with great sad eyes and sniffled, her teddy bear clutched to her chest.

Emma reached down and scooped up Susan, holding her close until her wails at last subsided.

"Poor little things, Emma," Lizzie said over the top of KatieAnn's dark head.

"I know," Emma agreed. "We just moved from the only home they've ever known, and now Mam leaves them like this."

"Let's rock them on the porch swing," Lizzie suggested.

They took both little girls and held them, gently rocking the old wooden porch swing in the warm spring sunshine. Jason sat on the steps, his curls lifting and falling as the breeze played with his hair. Mandy found a flashlight and ran across the yard to the barn, returning to her newly found nest of baby kittens.

Chapter 9

EMMA STARTED HUMMING AS SHE ROCKED BACK and forth on the swing. Here they were, way back in the sticks, or so it seemed to Lizzie, the twins crying, Mam sick, Dat on the way to hospital with her, everything frightening and unsure.

Lizzie felt as if her life was a jigsaw puzzle, all finished, each piece fitting perfectly into the next, until now when it seemed someone had suddenly come along and scattered the whole thing. Now nothing made any sense.

She thought of praying, but she didn't really know how to word her scattered thoughts and fears. Would Mam die? Could God be so mean? The thought was so unbearable that she got up from the porch swing and went into the kitchen, balancing KatieAnn on her hip.

Just as she was opening the refrigerator door, she heard the dull, muffled sound of a car engine. Quickly she closed the door of the refrigerator and

watched as an old green pickup truck ground its gears to a stop beside the sidewalk. Her heart leaped in her chest as she saw a young man leaning out from the window, his thick, hairy arm bent in a V shape. Huge red, black, and blue tattoos covered most of his arm.

His hair hung straight down over his face. His eyes were half closed. Lizzie clutched KatieAnn so tightly that she began to squirm and push at Lizzie's arms.

"Sorry," Lizzie muttered, without thinking.

Another passenger turned the handle of the old truck and climbed down to stand beside it. Looking more closely, Lizzie saw that this second person was a woman, dressed in ragged jeans and an old, torn T-shirt. Her hair was swept up in a tight ponytail that bounced as she moved.

Finally, the driver opened his door and ambled around the front of the truck. He was very heavy, with holes in the stomach of his shirt, white skin showing through. His hair was just as long and dirty as his companions'.

Lizzie shivered with raw fear. She swallowed, thinking wildly of where she could run. The attic. That would be the best. They would never find her in the attic back under the eaves behind some cardboard boxes.

But what about Emma? Or Jason? She had to stay here. She couldn't leave Emma alone. She wished Emma was not out there on the porch swing. If only she was in the house, they could hide somewhere

and those awful people would think there was no one home.

What should they do? Lizzie glanced wildly around the kitchen, still looking for a place to hide. But she couldn't leave Emma alone to talk to them. Who were they? What did they want?

Mustering all of her courage, she made herself walk to the screen door. Her legs felt like wooden stilts, she was so afraid. She was fairly gasping for breath because of the unnatural rhythm of her racing heart.

Without thinking, she prayed in silent little screams. Please, please. Help us, dear God. Help Emma to know what to do.

The dark-haired man stepped up on the sidewalk in front of Emma. Emma stopped the porch swing with both feet. She clutched Susan tightly on her lap, her face very white and as still as a stone. Jason sat beside her, not even a curl ruffling his stillness, his eyes big, round, and absolutely terrified.

"How you?"

Lizzie jumped as the man spoke to Emma in a raspy, deep-throated voice.

Emma's mouth opened, but no sound came from it. She cleared her throat and tried again to speak.

Lizzie pushed open the screen door and stepped out. She did not know if these people were dangerous; she just knew she could not trust them. First of all, they must never know their parents were not at home. The man's eyes were on her. The woman stepped up on the sidewalk beside the man and

glanced at the twins that Emma and Lizzie were holding. For a moment, Lizzie thought she would smile, but she didn't. She only lowered her eyelids farther.

"How y' doing?" the man asked.

"I'm fine," Lizzie said, louder than she had wanted to.

"Y' Mom and Dad home?" he asked.

"Y-yes," Lizzie lied.

"Can I talk to 'em?" he asked, eyeing Lizzie suspiciously.

"No. My mom is too sick and my dad is with her. He can't come to the door right now," Lizzie said.

The dark-haired man glared at her, and Lizzie glared back.

"Y' think your dad would let us look for arrowheads along your bottom field, here close to the creek?" he asked, jerking his thumb in the direction of the line of trees bordering the creek.

"What do you mean?" Lizzie asked bluntly.

"These." He came forward, reaching into the pocket of his jeans for a few arrowheads. He held out his hand, showing her pieces of grayish brown stones in the shape of an honest-to-goodness arrowhead.

Lizzie bit down on her lip as she surveyed the stones from her spot on the porch.

She looked at the arrowheads, and then looked up at the man's face. His eyes were chocolate brown and not unfriendly now. She looked at the arrowheads again, and then up at him. What should she

do? She glanced at Emma.

"Could...could you come back later this evening?" Emma asked.

The man smiled widely and Lizzie took a step forward.

"Your dad ain't home, huh? Your mom ain't, either," he stated.

Lizzie stepped back. She felt extremely foolish.

"That's okay. We're not going to hurt you. We live a couple miles from here. I own a machine shop in the nearest little town. Everybody knows me, Evan Harper, my wife, and brother-in-law.

"So you bought this farm from ol' Edwin. Don't look the same with his junk gone. We'll be back later when your dad's home. See ya."

He headed down the sidewalk toward his truck with the woman close behind him. The truck starting with an awful-sounding roar.

Lizzie sank onto the porch swing, letting out her breath in a long, slow whoosh. Emma looked over at Lizzie and said, "Oh, I mean it, I was never so scared in all my life!"

"It was awful," Lizzie agreed.

"You lied, Lizzie," Emma said.

"Not really a bad lie, Emma. I was only trying to protect both of us, Jason, and the twins. They looked so...so, well...just like you would imagine kidnappers or thieves might look."

"It was still a lie."

"Emma, now don't scold me. What if they were dangerous, and I would have let them know our

parents weren't at home? I couldn't do that."

"He knew you lied."

"So? If he knows, he could wash his hair and cut it and stop acting so big and tough. Then I wouldn't have to lie, because I would trust him in the first place. It's his own fault, not mine."

"You better ask God to forgive you."

"I will."

Dat came home toward evening, leaving Mam at the hospital. As the girls crowded around him, he told them how sick Mam was, how they took X-rays of her chest and admitted her as soon as they could.

Dat said she was resting well, and they had already started medication and it would help her fight the pneumonia.

"The doctors said that Mam is very, very sick and it will take a few days to tell which medication works best," he said with tears in his eyes.

"Is...is she in pain?" Emma asked.

"No, not really. Only when she coughs. She seems relaxed, and all she wants to do is sleep. She told me to come home to you children. You know how she says, 'I'll be fine.'" Dat shook his head ruefully.

Then the girls told him about the old green pickup and its occupants, their fear, Lizzie's lie, and the arrowheads.

"Never let rough-looking men like that know you are alone," he said.

"But Lizzie lied."

"I know it isn't right to lie, but what else could

she have done? In a way, it was the right thing to have done, and yet..." Dat just didn't know.

Later that evening Dat sat all alone on the porch for a very long time. Lizzie wondered what he was thinking. The tree frogs' chorus from the creek was deafening as a half-moon appeared in the sky. Lizzie hoped Dat was a strong enough person to make it through the next few weeks without Mam. She hoped she was, too.

Chapter 10

Lizzie was very nervous, sick to her stomach with apprehension. Today was the first day of school in Cameron County. She didn't know what to expect. She wished Mam was here, but she was still recovering in the hospital.

Lizzie had completed eighth grade before they left Jefferson County, and so now she would attend vocational school just one morning a week until May. She needed to hand in her diary where she kept account of the homemaking jobs and farming chores she had done that week. And along with the other vocational "scholars," as the Amish called them, she would study arithmetic, spelling, and German, a few hours each week.

Earlier in the week, Dat had made arrangements for them to travel with an English van driver who also hauled two other Amish families' children to school. Because there weren't enough families in Cameron County to build an Amish school, the few

Amish children that lived in the area attended an Old Order Mennonite school. Lizzie didn't know one thing about these Mennonites. Dat said they drove horses and buggies, but they had some practices that were different from the Amish.

Lizzie tried to remain calm and serene as she wet down her hair and worked at combing it in the new Cameron-County way. After four or five attempts, she decided it was good enough, especially since there wasn't much time to try again. She smoothed her new dark purple dress, pinning her black apron and her covering into place. After one last glance in the mirror, she was ready to go.

"How do I look?" she asked as she stepped into the kitchen.

Emma was at the counter, kneading bread.

"You look fine," she said. "You're hair doesn't even look too bad."

Lizzie tried to smile, but she felt as nervous as Mandy looked. It was also Mandy and Jason's first day at school, and both of them were near tears over breakfast. Outside, Jason made up songs as he ran little circles in the driveway.

"I wish you were coming with us, Emma," Lizzie said.

Emma added some more flour to the bread and began to shape the dough into a loaf. She had finished her vocational class before they left Jefferson County and now worked at home full-time, like other Amish girls her age.

"You'll do fine," she said.

Lizzie nodded. She took a deep breath as a black pickup truck with a flat camper on the back popped over the hill and rolled to a stop at the end of their drive.

A white-haired, balding gentleman jumped out and helped them into the truck. Inside were two boys and two girls. The boys looked so much alike with their very blond hair and blue eyes that Lizzie thought she must be seeing double. They didn't say anything as they watched Lizzie climb into the back of the pickup as gracefully as she could.

"Hi," said the girl with the same blond hair and blue eyes as the twins. "My name is Sara Ruth. These are my brothers, Joe and John."

"I'm Lizzie," she said. "This is my sister, Mandy, and my brother, Jason."

Jason squirmed in his seat, while Mandy smiled.

"And this is my cousin, Sharon," Sara Ruth said.

"Hi," Sharon said quietly.

Sharon wore a navy dress that had little lines in it and lovely sleeves with pleats in the shoulders. Lizzie could hardly wait to ask Mam to make a similar dress for her. Sharon's hair was dark brown and very straight, rolled up neatly along the side of her face. Did her hair look that nice? Lizzie wondered.

The truck rolled to a stop outside of the brick schoolhouse and they all clambered out. Lizzie slipped her hand in Mandy's.

"I hope the Mennonites are half as nice as the Amish are," she whispered.

"Me, too," Mandy said quietly as they followed

Sara Ruth into the cloakroom. Pretty floral sunbonnets hung from hooks around the room, next to narrow-brimmed boys' hats made of black straw.

A large group of girls followed them into the classroom.

"Lizzie, this is Viola, her sister Irma, and Marlene," Sara Ruth said, pulling or pushing each girl forward. Some of the girls giggled and others shrugged as they tried to free themselves from Sara Ruth's grasp, but they all managed to say, "Hello."

Lizzie knew she met Lucy, Etta, and Jean, but she could not keep their names or their faces straight. She thought there were three sisters in the Zimmerman family and two in the Hoover family. One—no, two—with the last name of Martin had eyes as brown as she had ever seen. They had straight brown hair and skin tanned almost the same shade from their long days in the summer sun.

"So! These are the *new* girls!" the Mennonite teacher said, welcoming them in a rush of color and warmth as she came into the room.

"We heard for a while already that you were moving in," she said. "You're not from Lamont, where the rest of the Amish are from, right?"

"N-no, we're from Jefferson County," Lizzie said.

"Same kind of Amish? I mean, is there a difference?" the teacher inquired.

"Yes, there is," Lizzie said, uncertain about how to explain the distinctions between the two Amish groups.

"Really? That's interesting. Did you like it in... did you say Jefferson County?"

"Oh, yes. We loved it. Well, I did. I...I...we had lots of cousins and friends there."

"Well, hopefully, you'll find lots more friends here. We're happy to have you in our school!"

Lizzie didn't know what to say. Mandy smiled and said, "We're glad to be here."

Lizzie wasn't sure that was quite true. She didn't know how she'd feel until she had spent the morning in vocational class.

"Time for the bell!" and the new teacher was off in a whirl of tiny little flowers. "Oh, I didn't even tell you my name! Esther!" she called over her shoulder as she disappeared behind the tall white doors.

Esther reappeared promptly, clanging and banging an old hand-held bell. At the sound, boys of all shapes and sizes charged past her into the school, dust flying and gravel spitting as they ran. They milled around the entry, hanging up straw hats, clomping their feet, and talking loudly. But as soon as they stepped into the classroom, they quieted down until every noise faded away and there was complete silence.

As Teacher Esther read the Bible, Lizzie chewed her fingernails in her seat at the back of the room. The Mennonites did dress differently. The boys wore jeans and plaid shirts, or striped ones, and their hair was cut short like English boys'. The only thing that made them look like Mennonites was their suspenders.

The Mennonite girls were so pretty. They combed their thick, wavy hair back and secured it with clasps, and then wove it into a heavy braid on each side of their heads. What really caught Lizzie's eye was that they were allowed to wear rubber hair bands with brightly colored baubles on the ends, and that they had barrettes in their hair. She would love to look so fancy.

Joe and John sat one row in front of her. The twins were decidedly good-looking. They were a bit small for their age, but they'd probably grow taller soon. Lizzie thought she would probably marry one of them and Mandy would marry the other. Of course, that left Emma out, but these boys were too young for her anyway.

Lizzie was relieved to know there were boys here in Cameron County whom she could marry. Of course, Mam said it was not up to them. They needed to pray every evening and ask God for his will, not their own. That was all very good and right, Lizzie was sure, but it was hard to know exactly what that meant. You couldn't help it if you thought some boys were nice-looking and others weren't.

The way Mam sometimes made it sound, all the handsome boys weren't good husbands—just the homely ones. It caused Lizzie to fall into a great state of sadness most times when Mam gave them that lecture.

"You don't go by looks," she would say, shaking her forefinger at them. "God has a special person for each one of you, so it's very important you don't

go by his looks."

Well, Lizzie was too young to take this husband matter very seriously, but she certainly hoped one of these twins would be God's will, as Mam put it. She couldn't wait to talk to Mandy after school to ask her which twin she wanted.

Lizzie leaned back in her chair. Were lovely girls bad wives, too? she wondered as she studied the girl next to her. Viola was strikingly beautiful. She was beautifully tanned and had deep-brown, wavy hair with gold overtones, almost as if sunlight had reached in and dyed some of her hair, just not all of it. Her eyes were slanted and very dark, and she had white teeth that flashed when she laughed.

Marlene sat on the other side of Lizzie. She looked a lot like Viola, suntanned with such dark eyes, except her hair was straight and soft and pulled back into heavy braids that fell below her waist. Lizzie had never seen such pretty girls before. She shifted in her seat, suddenly aware of her skin and how much she weighed and how her dress was made. Why couldn't she be prettier? Each miserable thought settled on her like a huge, wet blanket until she could barely breathe.

Then Lizzie remembered what Aunt Vera had told her when she visited just after they moved to Cameron County. Aunt Vera walked like a duck. She was short and round, with solid little legs on solid little feet that rocked her from side to side when she moved. Her face was round, with big blue eyes and a small nose, and Lizzie had discovered,

much to her joy, that Aunt Vera's nostrils looked exactly like her own.

"Aunt Vera!" she said gleefully.

"Now what?"

"Your nostrils look like mine!"

Vera had thrown back her head and laughed her raucous laugh. "Now, mind you, Mousie! You think my nostrils are ugly and you think I'm short and fat and I walk like a duck. You wait! When you're as old as me, you'll be shaped like me. Yessir, you will. Now mind, won't be long!"

How did she know what Lizzie had been thinking?

"No, no, Vera. I think you're just right. You wouldn't be Vera if you didn't walk like you do," Lizzie assured her.

Lizzie sat up straighter. She wouldn't be Lizzie if she didn't look like she did. She would have to "brace up" as Mam said. She tried to think of all her attributes. Brown hair rolled flat in this Cameron-County, slicked-down fashion that she would never get used to. Ordinary eyes, slanted nostrils, flat nose, and teeth that looked like a rabbit's. Her covering didn't fit right; her dress that had seemed so pretty this morning was just downright drab-looking now. She could not think of one good thing about herself.

Fortunately, the bell rang. The classroom quickly emptied outside into the school yard. Lizzie followed the others slowly, blinking as she stepped into the sun.

"Over here, Lizzie," Sara Ruth called. "We're picking teams for baseball."

Lizzie hurried over to the group. Joe and John were leaders of the two teams. They took turns choosing from the group of pupils, picking the big boys first. The first girl picked was Viola, who giggled and batted her eyelashes while John grinned at Joe, or Joe grinned at John. Lizzie had absolutely no idea which boy was which.

So...Viola must be a top ballplayer. Lizzie's heart beat faster as she thought about when she'd be chosen. She knew she could play ball every bit as well as some boys and better than most girls. That was one of the reasons why she got into so much trouble in Jefferson County. She was hot-headed and fiercely aggressive when it came to winning in baseball.

The twins were looking at her and Mandy, trying to decide if they should choose them before some of the smaller children, Lizzie realized. She felt her face heat up and quickly scuffed the toe of her shoe in the dust.

"Lizzie!" one of the twins said.

"Mandy!" the other one echoed.

Viola walked over to John or Joe and asked for his glove, holding her pretty head to one side. A tug of raw jealousy pulled at Lizzie. Oh, so Viola even shared gloves with them.

Her eyes narrowed as she set her chin resolutely. I may not be as pretty as she is, but I'll show her a thing or two about playing baseball, Lizzie thought.

When Lizzie's turn came to bat, she was so

nervous, she felt like fainting. She hoped no one could see her heart beating through the fabric of her dress. The blood pounded in her ears and her mouth was dry as sand. She licked her lips nervously, biting down hard on the lower one to steady herself.

The first pitch was too high, but she swung anyway, misguided by nervous energy, sending a foul ball just shy of third base. No one said anything. There were no groans or calls. A strange silence hovered over the ball field. Lizzie was one of the new girls, so everyone had to be nice.

Lizzie had never wanted anything quite as badly as a good solid hit to show all of them what a good ballplayer she was. But she was far too nervous. She knew she had to calm down and relax.

The second pitch she let pass on purpose, taking a few deep breaths to get her bearings. The third pitch came in fast and low. She swung with every bit of strength she could muster.

A solid THUMP! and Lizzie was off. The girls screamed and the boys yelled as loud as they could as she ran for first base. Somewhere out beside the road the boys scrambled in the tall grass, still looking for the ball as she rounded first base and streaked for second.

"Go! Go! Go to third!" Everyone sounded hoarse from yelling. Just as she reached third base, one of the twins caught the ball at the pitcher's mound, and she knew she had to stay. She was panting and her heart was swelling as the third baseman said, "Good hit for a girl!"

Lizzie tried to think of some witty answer, but nothing came. So she just smiled at the boy whose name she didn't even know.

Sharon was up to bat next and made a good solid hit, sending Lizzie to home plate. Her teammates crowded around, asking her if that was how she always hit. Lizzie told them demurely, no, not always. But she knew there was a good chance she probably would quite often.

By the end of the game, Mandy and Lizzie had both established themselves as good baseball players. Mandy was very quick, dashing fearlessly to catch grounders and tagging people out quite easily, amazing even the boys.

It was so exciting and so much fun to be a part of a serious baseball game that Lizzie felt like hopping and skipping the whole way home.

And when Viola told Lizzie that she and Mandy were good for the team, Lizzie forgot all about her jealousy. Touching Viola's sleeve she said, "You are, too. You were picked first."

After school, Lizzie and Mandy walked slowly up the lane towards their house. Lizzie swung her arms and smiled.

"I think I'm going to marry Joe or John," she said.

"Lizzie!" Mandy shrieked.

"I'm serious. They're so cute," Lizzie said happily.

"They would never want us. We're way too...I don't know how to say it, plain, or *fadutsed*, or whatever. We don't near know how to dress and do our hair like Sara Ruth and Sharon."

"We can learn!"

"Don't you know it's just common knowledge among the upper graders that Joe likes Viola and she likes him?" Mandy said, eyeing Lizzie skeptically.

She stopped and looked at Mandy, her mouth open in surprise. "Who said?"

"Sara Ruth."

"They can't like each other—he couldn't date a Mennonite!"

"Lizzie, you're so bold, even *thinking* they would even *notice* us. We're just like…country mice going to the city!"

Lizzie's heart sank along with her happy plans. Well, she would not always be a country mouse. It was a horrible feeling to be left out and way behind everybody else, just because she wasn't as pretty and her dresses were plain. How would she ever marry? There were lots and lots of Violas in the world.

"Don't worry, Lizzie. We're too young. Mam would have a fit if she knew how you talked," Mandy said. "We don't have to worry about such things now!"

Lizzie knew Mandy was right, as she usually was. But no wonder she doesn't worry, Lizzie thought. She's thin and pretty and her complexion is as smooth as silk.

Chapter 11

Later that week the girls were allowed to go with Dat to the hospital in Falling Springs.

Jason and the twins weren't old enough to go, so they stayed with Uncle James and Aunt Becca who lived about five miles away. Aunt Becca drove her horse and buggy over to pick up the younger children and take them home with her. Dat said the way Becca drove her horse, she'd be over in a hurry and be back home just as fast.

Lizzie laughed because she loved the way Aunt Becca drove a horse. Becca's horse was little, with deep lines running down his haunches. Lizzie thought this made it look as if he had lots of loose skin on his behind and his haunches flapped up and down along with the breeching on his harness.

Sometimes when they turned a corner, Lizzie had to bite down on her lower lip and clutch the seat, because it seemed as if they were only on two wheels. When Aunt Becca clucked to her horse after

picking up Jason and the twins, she started off so fast that the children's heads flew backward. Gravel scattered beneath the buggy as it rounded the corner past the barnyard. Dat laughed and shook his head.

"There she goes."

Emma laughed with Dat. "How can she stop that horse?" she asked.

"Oh, she'll get him stopped."

Sure enough, Becca tugged the reins just in time and the little horse stopped at the very end of the lane.

After Becca left, the girls only had an hour to get ready to go to the hospital. Emma picked up the twins' toys and straightened the house while Lizzie and Mandy went upstairs.

"Which dress are you wearing?" Lizzie asked.

"Oh, I don't know. I guess it doesn't matter too much."

"I know. But most of our dresses are still all from Jefferson County."

"Guess I'll wear that new lavender one."

"Are you nervous about going to church, Mandy?" Lizzie asked, taking the hairpins out of her hair.

Lizzie could hardly believe that only a few days had passed since they had first arrived in Cameron County and so they hadn't attended church yet.

"Sort of, I guess."

"We probably don't have to go because Mam's sick and can't go with us."

"I hope not."

"We don't know one single person except our Glick relatives."

"I dread it."

"Me, too."

Lizzie yanked at a tangle in her hair. She pulled out the hairbrush and gazed at it. "Look at all this hair! I'll be bald!"

Mandy giggled. "You can lose a bu-unch of hair before you'll be bald."

"Can you roll your hair?" Lizzie asked.

"Not really."

"Do we have to, just to go to the hospital?"

"I don't know."

"I hate to wet my hair down and roll it."

"Ask Emma."

So Lizzie yelled down the stairs, asking Emma if they had to roll their hair.

"Of course you do," came Emma's exasperated reply.

"Why?"

"Because we live here now. That's how we have to do."

"I can't get it right!" Lizzie wailed.

There was no answer, so Lizzie knew Emma wasn't going to extend any mercy to her. She went back to her dresser, peered closely into the mirror, and yanked her hair back as hard as she could. Lifting both arms, she grasped some of the hair growing along her forehead and twisted it back.

A big mound of hair above what she was already twisting poofed up and away from her head. She

tried to smooth it back, but lost the whole part she had been holding, so she had to start all over.

She snorted, stamping her foot impatiently.

This was going to be impossible, that was all there was to it. She dashed to the bathroom and wet her hair until water ran off the tip of her nose. Using the palms of her hands to flatten her hair, she ran back to the bedroom, picked up the fine-toothed comb, and raked it along each side of her head.

"Are you done?" Emma asked, popping her head in the door.

"No!"

"Here." Mandy came over and stood in front of Lizzie. She took the comb and used it to push some of Lizzie's wet hair up and away from her forehead. "Now try rolling it."

Lizzie leaned over the dresser, her face inches from the mirror, and gently twisted her hair back. Mandy stood back and watched, her arms crossed.

"Go ahead, laugh. You're going to anyway!" Lizzie snapped.

Mandy turned and hurried out of the room, her shoulders shaking.

Good, she's gone, Lizzie thought as she tilted her head to one side, trying to roll the other side the same way. The sides looked all right, but in the front, at her part, one roll went straight up and the other roll hung down. When she pushed the bobby pin in place, both rolls stood up and away from her head, making her look like a frog.

She sighed, tears close to the surface. The driver

was coming any minute. She pulled her hair back securely and started twisting it into a bob again. She was not, absolutely *not*, going to call for Mandy. Mandy, her younger sister, could roll hair perfectly. Well, not perfectly, but much better than Lizzie could.

She pulled her hair back as tightly as she was able, only to discover that her rolls of hair now lay flat along the side of her head. So that was how it was done! She finished twisting her hair on the back of her head and stuck in hairpins as fast as she could. She grabbed her good covering and flopped it on top of her head, turning to look for a black belt apron.

"Driver's here!" Mandy yelled from the bottom of the stairs.

Lizzie pinned her apron as fast as she could, adjusted her dress, and ran down the steps. Emma stood in the kitchen, carrying a bag with extra clothes for Mam.

"Come, Lizzie," she said. And she sounded so like Mam that it made Lizzie miss Mam unbearably much. She couldn't wait to get to the hospital.

Chapter 12

DAT HELD THE DOOR FOR THE GIRLS AS THEY entered the cool interior of the hospital. The glass doors were huge. Lizzie gazed at the tall ceilings as she followed Emma into the lobby. The vast windows looking out at the pink trees and the warm sunlight brightened the soft carpet.

Dat went to a desk that said "Information," where a small, white-haired woman was adjusting the glasses on her nose.

"Hello," Dat said. "Could you tell me which floor Room 377 is on?"

"The numbers go by the floors; the 300s are on the third," she said.

Dat thanked her and herded the girls toward the elevator past a gift shop with pretty plants, balloons, cards, and flowers making a bright display along the windows. Dat stopped to look at the price of a bouquet of yellow carnations and white daisies.

"Dat, you should get it," Emma said.

"Twelve dollars!"

"So? Mam probably doesn't have any flowers because we don't know our English neighbors like we used to in Jefferson County. Please?"

Dat reached into his pocket for his wallet, one Mam had made for him years ago. He held it sideways, checking to see how much cash he had, then he smiled and lifted the pretty cut-glass vase.

"I'll have to write a check for the driver," he said gruffly, but Lizzie could tell he didn't mind. Dat was like that, she thought.

They found Mam's room on the third floor. Tears sprang suddenly to Lizzie's eyes when she saw Mam. Her face was ashen—even her lips were pale. She looked so thin and so sick, it made Lizzie feel awful.

"How are you feeling?" Dat asked, going to the side of her bed.

"Oh, I had a rough night, but I can tell the antibiotic is working."

She smiled at Dat and then looked at the bouquet in Emma's hand. "Ach my, Emma. Aren't they pretty? You shouldn't have," she said, turning to Dat.

Lizzie and Mandy stood back, almost shyly. Mam didn't seem like their ordinary, everyday Mam, lying in that hospital bed wearing a green hospital gown. That gown was about the ugliest thing Lizzie had ever seen.

"Mandy, come here. Come, Lizzie," Mam said, patting the bed. So they sat sideways on Mam's hospital bed, while Lizzie tried not to cry.

"What were you doing last evening when I was here?" Mam asked, tucking a stray hair behind Mandy's ear.

Mandy told Mam all about the pickup truck and the strange man with tattoos and long hair. Mam shook her head at Dat.

"Ach my, Melvin."

"There wasn't a thing wrong with him. Not a thing," Dat assured her.

"I guess," Mam said. "And I've often told the girls we can't judge a person by his looks, can we? But...I would feel better if you stayed at home as much as you can, Melvin."

"I will," Dat said.

Mam told them the doctor's diagnosis of her condition. She had acute pneumonia, the worst kind. The doctor wanted to keep her in the hospital for another three to four days to see if her cough stabilized. He warned Mam that it would take months to gain back her usual strength and that she should take it easy as much as she could.

Emma plucked at the crisp white sheet covering Mam's legs. Lizzie knew she worried about the farm. The herd of cows Dat was buying would not arrive for a few weeks, so that would give them time to finish cleaning up. There was so much painting to be done, but Dat assured Mam that would have to wait until she felt better.

Mam sighed and turned her head.

"We're making you too tired, talking about all this work, aren't we?" Emma said.

"No, I just wish I wouldn't have to be here in the hospital."

There was silence while Dat gazed out the window. She would help Emma, Lizzie decided, and try not to complain about anything. She wished their house was not so ugly. She knew they had the sloppiest house of anyone in Cameron County, and now they couldn't paint or fix it up for months.

Suppose someone came to visit? She wouldn't even go to the door. It just wasn't right, having Mam in the hospital and they couldn't do a thing to improve their awful house.

"Why can't me and Mandy paint?" she asked.

"Oh, I don't know," Mam said. "You're hardly old enough to do the woodwork. I don't know if you could use a roller on the walls or not. Maybe if Emma did the trimming."

Lizzie's face lit up with enthusiasm. "We can! Me and Mandy can use rollers and Emma can use a brush along the edges!"

"We watched you when you painted the new house!" Mandy chimed in.

That seemed to cheer Mam immensely. She told the girls how to set the roller pans on newspaper, and how much paint was the right amount when they put the rollers in them. She decided they were allowed to do their rooms upstairs, but the woodwork would have to wait. She didn't want the girls working with that high gloss enamel. Besides, they would not be able to do it without making a mess on the walls.

When a nurse came in to take Mam's temperature, Dat said it was time to leave. Visiting hours would soon be over. Mam smiled, even if her eyes were bright with unshed tears. Lizzie thought she must be the bravest person in the whole world right at that moment.

Chapter 13

THAT FIRST SPRING IN CAMERON COUNTY, Lizzie's life seemed to take on new meaning. Mam was home from the hospital. And Lizzie loved every minute of that one day a week when she went to school. She would get up in the morning, fret and worry about her looks, her hair, how her dress was made, how her covering fit, and whether her complexion was normal or if she was breaking out with those dreaded pimples.

The warm sun and frequent rains meant that their new garden was full of produce. Lizzie ate crisp, red radishes and long, thin spring onions that crunched like a pretzel but tasted even better.

At lunchtime, Dat would spread butter on a thick slice of homemade bread, sprinkle salt beside his plate until he had made a little pile, then select a spring onion. He would dip the onion in the salt, bite it off and quickly take a bite of the buttered bread, and then chew the two together.

Lizzie piled four or five spring onions on a piece of bread and folded it over to make a thick onion sandwich. Sometimes she put mayonnaise on both sides of the bread, which was absolutely delicious, but so fattening. Lizzie couldn't always be careful. As hard as she worked here on the farm, she had to eat enough or she'd feel weak and her head would start to hurt. She wasn't exactly thin, but she enjoyed good food so much, she didn't always care if she was as thin as Mandy and Emma.

The morning before Emma's sixteenth birthday, Lizzie was out hanging laundry on the wash line while Mam worked in the garden. Mam was still recovering from her time in the hospital, but she liked to spend sometime outside each day in the garden. The sunshine made her feel better, she said.

"Lizzie, come look at all these peas!" she called.

Lizzie dropped the towel she was holding and headed to the garden. She stopped in one row and reached down, separating a few pea stalks to have a closer look. Sure enough, thousands of pea pods were hanging in thick clusters, all ready for picking.

"There's a bunch of them!" Lizzie said.

Mam rushed into the house and came back with Mandy, Emma, and even Jason, each carrying a bucket or basket.

At first it was fun picking peas. The buckets filled up fast, and they ate many tender green peas

straight from the pod. They chattered and laughed and threw peas at each other as they watched little toads and snails crawl through the dirt.

But as the sun rose in the sky, the rows seemed longer and longer. Lizzie stretched and rubbed the small of her back. In the next row, Mandy was sitting on the ground between pea stalks, shelling one pea after another and gobbling them down. She wasn't putting any in her basket.

"Mandy!" Lizzie yelled.

Mandy had a mouthful of peas and didn't answer.

"Stop eating peas and help pick!" Lizzie shouted.

Mandy chewed, swallowed, and turned to glare at Lizzie. "Stop hollering!"

"Well, pick!"

"Pick, pick, pick. Pick, pick, pick. You sound like a chicken."

"That's enough, girls," Mam called. "Finish your rows and then come inside to help me get ready for Emma's birthday party."

The girls nudged Emma and laughed as they rushed to finish their rows. Emma kept her head down as she worked, but Lizzie could tell she was excited, too. It must be just absolutely wonderful to turn 16, Lizzie thought, especially if you looked as slender and pretty as Emma.

When Lizzie and Emma were little girls, they were chubby, actually more than chubby as they

got bigger and older. But when Emma turned 13, she stopped eating calorie-laden foods, becoming steadily thinner until she didn't look one bit like Lizzie anymore.

Lizzie had continued to take three sandwiches in her lunch to school, more than the eighth-grade boys took for their lunches, and Emma was terribly embarrassed by this. Lizzie tried to watch what she ate, especially when Mam was around. But it was hard. Often, when Mam was upstairs working and Lizzie had to watch the twins, she ate two whoopie pies.

Once, after Mam had made creamsticks, Lizzie ate four. Creamsticks were homemade doughnuts, but instead of being round with a hole in the middle, they were cut in an oblong shape. After they were deep-fried, Mam cut a long slit in each of their tops, filled them with creamy vanilla icing, and then put golden caramel frosting on the tops. They were the very best thing in the world of desserts, but Mam didn't make them very often because they were so much work, with two different kinds of icing and all.

Lizzie learned quickly that it paid to be careful what she ate around Mam and Emma, but it didn't matter if they were busy and couldn't see her. When things were stressful, nothing made Lizzie feel better about her upside-down world than a good whoopie pie or doughnut. They were so comforting.

The girls rushed to clean the house and prepare Emma's favorite foods for her birthday meal. When the table was set, Emma and Lizzie went out to the woodshed to gather more fuel for the fire.

Emma went straight to the woodpile. Lizzie trailed behind her, admiring Emma's blue dress and neat hair. It wouldn't be long until Emma had a boyfriend, she thought.

✁

The sight of the stacked wood sent Lizzie right back to a long-ago afternoon, when she had played Mrs. Bixler with Emma. "I'm going to see if I can find some wood to make me some high-heeled shoes," Lizzie had told Emma. But Emma ignored her and continued to pick up wood.

"Hello!" Lizzie yelled in what she imagined to be a stylish, grown-up voice. "How are you, Emma?"

Emma turned to look at Lizzie's feet. Sure enough, she had securely tied a block of wood with baler twine to the bottom of each foot.

Emma extended her hand to shake Lizzie's. "Why, come in, Mrs. Bixler! I'm just fine. And where did you get your new high-heeled shoes?"

Lizzie held her head up high, and in a genuine, English-lady imitation said, "Oh, I just bought them at the store!"

Both girls collapsed on the floor in a fit of giggles. When Lizzie hit the floor and her high heels fell apart, they laughed even harder.

Emma sputtered, "L-L-Lizzie—your shoes!"

Lizzie gasped, "Well, they did feel like high heels a little bit." She picked up the blocks of wood and twine, trying to reattach them to her shoes.

She looked at Emma. "There's hardly any use, is there? These aren't really high heels, and I'm not really English." Lizzie squeezed Emma's hand and loved her so much she thought her heart would burst.

Dear, bossy, big sister Emma. And now Emma had turned 16. Tonight the family gathered around the dining room table to celebrate Emma's big birthday. Each person had a lovely glass dish filled with chocolate cake and vanilla ice cream while Emma opened her gifts. The birthday cake had two layers covered with vanilla frosting—everyone's favorite— and they enjoyed every last morsel of it with spoonfuls of creamy vanilla ice cream.

Emma opened the largest package and found a pair of candleholders with blue candles for her bedroom. Another package contained fabric for two new dresses, a robin's-egg blue and a light dusty green material. Emma was quite overwhelmed, and her cheeks flushed a beautiful pink color as she gasped, exclaiming over the pretty fabric.

After they finished celebrating, the girls washed the dishes while Mam bathed the twins. Jason went out with Dat to finish up the chores, making sure

the barn doors were closed properly against the approaching chill of the night.

Suddenly Mam appeared at the kitchen door, looking at the girls and listening for a sound she thought she heard.

"Did someone knock?" she asked.

"No," the girls answered.

But now there was a decided knocking on the kitchen door.

"I thought I heard someone," Mam said, hurrying to open it.

"Come on in," she said, stepping back to let a young Amish man into the kitchen.

"Hello. Sorry to bother you so late in the evening," he said, smiling apologetically.

"That's quite all right. It isn't late yet," Mam answered.

"Looks like you have plenty of help," he said, nodding toward the girls who were clustered around the kitchen sink.

"Oh, yes. My girls are growing up so fast I can hardly keep up with them," Mam laughed.

"That's good. We need *mauda* here in Cameron County." Lizzie's heart sank way down, leaving her stomach feeling all hollow and helpless.

Mauda! Oh, no! I'm not going. Emma can. Mam and Dat can't make me be a *maud*. I'm not going to do it. I'll run away, she thought. She had a wild impulse to run upstairs and hide under her bed where no one would be able to find her and make her go be a *maud*, or maid. Sometimes being a

maud meant staying for weeks at a time in a family's home, which really, Lizzie thought, was much like being a slave.

She had told Emma that one evening when they were discussing the fact that eventually they would probably need to be *mauda*, with so many young families moving into the community who would need help with housecleaning, canning, or assisting when a new baby arrived.

Emma said, no, that a *maud* was not nearly the same. Lizzie argued vehemently, saying it was the exact same thing, except there was no cruel overseer who cracked his whip above your head when you didn't pick cotton fast enough. Emma told her she should be ashamed of herself, that slaves lived in little hovels or cabins with only bare necessities.

"Well, the reason I'm here is...," the Amish man cleared his throat. "My wife needs some help house-cleaning, and I think she wants to paint the kitchen, too."

"Let's see, you're John King, aren't you?" Mam asked.

He nodded.

"Well, I don't see why not. Emma, would you like to go? When is it? Next week?"

"Monday till at least Wednesday. Maybe two of the girls could help with the painting on Wednesday," John offered.

"Why, yes! Lizzie could go Wednesday, and Emma will go the rest of the time. Will you send a driver on Monday morning?"

Lizzie glared at Mam but said nothing. She hadn't even waited till Emma said yes or no. But, really, what difference would it make whether she did say yes or no? It was all the same. Either they could go willingly or rebelliously. Either way, they had to go.

As soon as John King left, closing the kitchen door behind him, Lizzie put her hands behind her back and said staunchly, "I'm not going."

"Lizzie!"

"I'm scared to paint other people's houses. I'm afraid I'll make streaks."

Mam turned to look at Lizzie.

"Oh yes, Lizzie, you're going," she said. "The Kings will show you what to do."

"Why must I go?" Lizzie wailed, flopping on a kitchen chair, her arms flung across the back in a gesture of rebellion.

Mam took a deep breath.

"Because. When you girls reach a certain age, you need to learn about working outside of our home. You need to earn some money and learn how to obey and do jobs you would ordinarily not experience at home. Besides, it won't hurt you to give up your own will. That's what a lot of your life consists of." Mam paused, seating herself at the kitchen table, gathering Susan in a big hug on her lap. Not Mam's favorite line again, thought Lizzie. It had been hard enough for Lizzie to learn to do her part at home.

"When I was your age, I was almost never at home," Mam was saying. "Either I was cleaning

houses or I was caring for elderly people. These are all good experiences for young girls to have before they get married."

"Good for *you*," Lizzie muttered.

Mam chose to ignore that comment, and Mandy blinked her large green eyes in Lizzie's direction. Lizzie caught her gaze, and Mandy blinked again. Lizzie knew she meant she had better watch it.

"I'm kind of excited to go. John's wife, Hannah, always talks to me at church. She's so full of fun, sometimes it seems as if she's my age instead of being a mother with children," Emma said, wiping the counter clean.

"Well, good! Then if you feel that way, we'll just forget about me going. You can paint the kitchen, and I'll stay here and do the work for Mam. Right?" Lizzie looked hopefully in Mam's direction.

Mam shook her head. "You'll go," she said, and she was not smiling.

Chapter 14

So that's how Lizzie found herself at the Kings' new house at the bottom of the mountain, six miles away from her family's farm. Because John had come to get her in his horse and buggy, the drive there was long enough to give her a good chance to think about painting for a very long time.

Emma and Hannah had already spread newspapers on the floor. They had set up a stepladder in the middle of the kitchen and had gallons of paint and fresh new rollers and brushes scattered across the plastic-covered kitchen table.

Hannah greeted Lizzie warmly and explained that she needed to help John in the fields that forenoon so the girls would start painting the kitchen on their own. After Hannah left, Lizzie went upstairs to change into her old dress and tie a bandanna around her head. She clattered back downstairs to find Emma covering the stovetop with an old sheet and then carefully moving everything away that

could accidentally be spattered with paint.

"Where's the paint?" Lizzie demanded.

"Lizzie, this isn't our house. You need to be careful," Emma said.

"I know what I'm doing," Lizzie said.

Lizzie picked up a paint can and set it on the table without bothering to put any newspaper underneath it. She pried off the top and started stirring the light green paint so vigorously it sloshed over the side of the can.

"Watch it!" Emma yelled.

She dashed over to grab the wooden paddle from Lizzie's hand.

"What?" Lizzie asked.

"The paint! It's spilling down over the side. I mean it, Lizzie, if you don't slow down and listen to me, I'm not going to help."

"Good, then I'll do it!"

Emma gasped as Lizzie tilted the bucket of paint into the roller pan.

"Not so much! Not so fast!" Emma wailed.

"Oh, calm down," Lizzie said.

Emma sighed. She picked up a tray and brush and put them carefully on a sheet of newspaper that covered the floor. Lizzie slid her roller deeply into her own tray before heading straight for the wall in front of her, a trail of sticky paint dripping behind her.

The kitchen walls and ceiling were old plaster with deep cracks, some broken spots, and peeling paint. Covering them well would be hard work,

she knew. She smacked on the paint as if her life depended on it, furiously rolling straight up and down in long, uneven rows.

Emma grabbed an old rag and wiped up the paint Lizzie had dripped on the floor.

"Lizzie, see what you did? Don't fill your roller quite as full next time," she said.

"Okay," Lizzie said cheerfully, continuing her mad rolling.

The two girls worked side by side, covering the walls with new paint.

"How do we do the ceiling?" Emma asked.

"That's easy—with a broom handle stuck in here," Lizzie said airily, pointing to the end of her roller.

Lizzie used the rollers as if she was brandishing a serious weapon and the ugly old plaster was a great enemy she needed to conquer. She dashed back and forth from her paint tray to the wall, spattering paint on the floor, on the table, on anything that was not sufficiently covered. Emma tried in vain to keep all the paint spills under control. She continued to clean up drops of paint while brush-painting the trim.

"I love this color!" Lizzie said.

"It is a nice shade," Emma agreed.

The forenoon passed quickly with Emma chattering happily, going from one subject to another. Lizzie could tell that Emma enjoyed painting. Lizzie hoped that someday soon she would be as confident as Emma was in new situations. It hadn't always

been that way. Lizzie remembered when Emma would get scared and would even admit it—like when they were eight and nine and going sledding with the big kids at school.

❧

"Lizzie, don't tell anyone, okay? But..." Emma had lowered her voice, "I am so terribly afraid of going sledding that I...well, Lizzie, don't tell anyone—promise?"

"I promise," Lizzie answered solemnly.

"Cross your heart?" Emma asked worriedly.

"Cross my heart."

"Okay. I was so scared at lunch that when I tried to eat my bologna sandwich, I almost threw up. Really, I had to take a drink and put my sandwich away."

Emma stopped and looked squarely at Lizzie. "And Lizzie, I don't want to go sledding. Don't tell anyone, but I'd almost rather sit at my desk and do my lessons."

Lizzie's eyes squinted as she looked out over the sparkling white hill. She watched as the boys tried to push each other off their sleds while they were flying down at quite an alarming rate. Then she turned to look at Emma, who looked back quite solemnly at Lizzie.

"Emma, that doesn't matter one bit," Lizzie had said staunchly. "I will not tell one single person ever that sled-riding scares you if you don't tell one single

person that I put five whoopie pies in my lunch this morning."

"Five?" Emma was horrified. "Why five?"

Lizzie looked carefully over her shoulder and whispered to Emma, "Because. And I'm not even giving one to the teacher!"

Emma had laughed, throwing back her head, and Lizzie had smiled, glad that her sister was feeling better. And now here they were together today, but with Emma stepping out ahead.

❧

The Kings' house was new, built only a few months earlier. It offered a lovely view of the mountain, which really was only a big hill, but quite a beautiful one, nevertheless. Lizzie thought she could have stood at the kitchen window for a very long time and watched the trees swaying like natural dancers with the mountain providing the stage.

John King's brother, Elam, lived on the same farm, with only the large white barn separating the two houses. His wife, Priscilla, was a small, dark-haired woman, and she was good friends with Hannah.

Lizzie wondered if she and Emma might marry brothers and live together on the same farm. That would be all right as long as Emma and her husband did the milking. They might share a farm, but her husband would most definitely *not* be a farmer. Even to imagine a whole cow stable full of huge

black and white Holsteins was so depressing, she could not think about it too long. Smelly creatures!

Mam always told the girls they must learn to pray for God's will for their lives. Lizzie didn't know if it was alright to ask him to please not make her milk cows, though. There were lots of other ways to make a living that were just fine. Would Joe and John ask her and Emma for dates? She doubted it, but then, you never knew.

"I'm hungry!" Lizzie said.

"It's not even 11 o'clock!" Emma said.

Lizzie glanced out the window and across the front yard toward the team of horses and the wagon moving slowly across the hay field. Hannah was driving the horses while John stood on the back of the wagon, stacking bales of hay.

"Oh, that almost scares me, Emma. I cannot imagine Dat plowing a field with those huge, fear-some-looking workhorses. They're five times as big as Bess and Billy."

"Not that big!" Emma laughed.

But Lizzie found the idea of Dat working as a serious farmer both exciting and scary. How could he handle those large, heavy horses? He was not a big man. It was all too much to think about, Lizzie realized. The only way she could have any peace was to think Dat and Mam must know what they were doing. Everything would turn out alright, especially with Doddy Glick helping Dat to get started.

Lizzie kept rolling paint onto the ceiling. She grimaced as she put one hand up to rub the back of

her neck. The ceiling was a lot bigger than it looked. Her arms ached and her lower back hurt, but she wasn't going to complain.

She thought about what kind of horses Dat would buy and if she would ever be allowed to drive them. If Hannah could, then so could she, Lizzie thought. That would be much more of a challenge than anything she had ever experienced before in her whole life.

She was thinking about driving the new workhorses and walking backwards as she painted the ceiling.

THUMP!

Lizzie's foot hit the edge of the roller pan. Warm, sticky paint flowed over her foot, across the newspaper, and onto the tile floor. She dropped her roller and held up her foot. Paint dripped steadily onto the floor.

"Oh, my word!"

"Don't move!" Emma shouted, as she dashed to the back porch for rags.

"I didn't do it on purpose. Maybe you should have offered to do some of the ceiling!" Lizzie wailed.

"Be quiet. Stop your yelling. You weren't watching what you were doing," Emma ground out between clenched teeth as she knelt on the floor and grabbed Lizzie's foot. "Hold still."

Emma muttered and grumbled to herself as she swabbed Lizzie's foot viciously.

"Now go to the bathroom and stick that foot in the bathtub," she instructed.

"Go to the bathroom?" Lizzie shrieked. "How?"

"Hop on one foot, of course," Emma said.

So Lizzie hopped through the living room, tears rolling down her cheeks.

Emma followed her, trying to clean up any paint that fell on the floor.

"Stop your crying, Lizzie, you big baby," she said. "Maybe if you'd grow up once and stop being so... so much in a hurry when you do something, things would go better for you. I didn't say anything on purpose, so we could get along, and look what happened. Nobody can ever tell you one thing, Lizzie Glick, so you're only getting what you deserve."

With that Emma closed the bathroom door. Lizzie sat on the side of the bathtub, letting water run over her foot and crying her heart out. She just wished she could go dig a nice big hole and crawl in it, never to show her face until everyone liked her again.

Emma thought she was goofy and dumb, Lizzie was sure. She had it easy, being so thin and without one blemish anywhere on her face, while Lizzie struggled with awful-looking skin. And she was fat. Well, not really fat anymore, but not as thin as Emma.

The water sloshed over her foot, and tears ran down her cheeks as she squeezed her eyes shut. She pitied herself so much she wondered if this is how you felt right before you died. She hoped God still liked her at least.

Sometimes she was still afraid of God, especially

at times like this. She had just wanted to hurry up and get the kitchen painted so Hannah would think she was a hard worker. She hadn't stuck her foot in that pan on purpose. It was probably just God punishing her for some other things she had done wrong. That's always how it was.

After her foot was clean, she wiped her eyes and her nose, smoothed back her hair, and went back out to the kitchen. Emma was on her knees, mopping up paint, her cheeks flushed to a rosy color. Hannah, who must have just come in from the fields, sat beside her rubbing furiously at some other paint spots.

Lizzie just stood there, both hands to her mouth, still not quite able to comprehend what she had done. It was so embarrassing and so awful, watching that green stain spreading across the Kings' linoleum.

"I...I'm really sorry," she managed in a hoarse croak.

"Oh, don't be sorry. It wasn't your fault. It could have happened to anyone," Hannah said.

Lizzie didn't know if she wanted to laugh or cry. She could hardly believe that Hannah wasn't angry at all. Lizzie felt like crying partly because of her kindness. Hannah surely couldn't be as nice as she sounded.

But she was. Hannah laughed as they scraped up the last of the paint, pointing at the nice shade of mint green that her linoleum became. Emma laughed with her, while Lizzie went to the washhouse for

some clear naphtha gas. After they applied the naphtha, rubbing at the massive green spot, Lizzie was so terribly relieved to see that the floor wasn't ruined at all that she felt like crying again.

They finished painting the kitchen without any further incidents. Then Hannah made a special meal of delicious cheeseburgers much later than the usual lunch hour. She served tall glasses of Coke with tinkling ice cubes, and lots of ketchup, mayonnaise, tomatoes, onions, and lettuce to put on their sandwiches.

She tried so hard to make Lizzie feel better, to help her forget about spilling the paint, and certainly not to blame herself, that Lizzie decided if she ever got married and had to have a *maud*, she would treat her exactly like Hannah treated her. Of course, she was not going to hire a *maud* unless it was *absolutely* necessary.

Chapter 15

The alarm clock on Lizzie's nightstand jangled loudly. She groaned and rolled over to turn it off. The hands showed five o'clock. She could hear Dat moving around downstairs in the kitchen.

She swung her legs over the side of the bed and sat there, her elbows on her knees. This just isn't right, she thought. I never in my life had to get up this early. I hate it. She could tell it was going to be a warm, sultry day, as humid as it was already. She yawned and reached for a dress in the closet.

She never brushed her teeth or combed her hair at five o'clock. What was the use? Dat didn't care what she looked like as long as she helped milk.

And another thing—those cows. Cows were the dumbest animals on earth. They smelled bad and she was still afraid of their hooves, those big, dirty, split feet caked with a load of manure that squooshed up between the cracks in the hooves whenever they walked.

The cows had arrived almost two months earlier, but these ignorant, slow learners still did not come in from the pasture early in the morning when it was time to be milked. Usually they were at the farthest end of the pasture, lying down and chewing their cuds.

All they did was chew. You could watch a cow for hours, and she did nothing except chew, her lower lip making half circles all day long. When she did stop the constant movement, a sort of rumble came up from her throat, and she began chewing again in earnest. It was so disgusting.

Down in the kitchen, Dat was heading for the door.

"The grass is soaking wet this morning," he called to her. "You better put on some boots so your legs and feet stay dry."

Lizzie snorted. The hem of her dress always seemed to get soaked, and if she held it up, the dew-soaked grass slapped against her legs and water dripped down into her boots creating bigger problems. Then her bare feet slipped and slid around inside those filthy rubber boots.

This morning she headed to the meadow without any boots. Her skirt trailed behind her in the wet grass as she yelled, "Coom, Sook! Coom, Sook!" her voice scratchy with sleep.

Lizzie wondered why Dat had taught them to yell that when they gathered the cows, especially the "Sook" part. She guessed it was probably a tradition of sorts. Doddy Glick had probably called to

his cows the exact same way, and his father before him.

Lizzie's right foot slid into a warm, soft pile of cow manure. She grimaced as she stopped to wipe her foot on the wet grass. It always happened sooner or later as she stomped around in the dark yelling. She had almost gotten used to stepping in cow manure, which meant she had become a full-fledged farm girl. When her foot was clean, she lifted her head, pushed back her tousled hair, and kept on yelling.

No sign of the cows. Lizzie plodded on. Her skirt was wet and snapped against her legs. She winced as a thistle pricked the side of her leg and she stepped into another pile of cow manure.

They had to be around here somewhere, she thought. She had almost reached the edge of the field. Dat would be done with the feeding, wondering where his cows were.

"Coom, Sook!"

Then, quite suddenly, in the half-light of dawn, all sorts of shapes emerged as cows slowly rose from their comfortable positions in the grass. Cows were the most ungraceful animals, Lizzie thought as she watched. When they got up, their hindquarters stuck pointedly into the air for quite a long time until they finally got their front legs unbent and into a standing position. Then they arched their backs, while holding their tails straight out behind in the most ridiculous manner, before starting their slow shuffle to the barn.

"Get! Get! Come on, get going!" Lizzie said,

starting the herd moving toward the barn. A few of the cows glared at her in the most rebellious manner, but she felt a bit of kinship with them. So...get up, cows. I had my alarm clock, and you have me to wake you up, she thought.

Dat met them at the gate, swinging it wide to let the cows through. Typical cows, they began to hurry the minute they smelled their feed.

"Where were you so long?" Dat asked. "It's almost five-thirty."

"The cows were at the other end of the pasture," Lizzie said.

"You're soaked," Dat observed, holding up the gas lantern. "Why don't you wear the barn boots?"

"They don't help anything," Lizzie said.

"They would if you'd wear them."

Lizzie didn't answer. She sloshed into the milk-house to fill a black rubber bucket with warm, soapy water, yawning as she dropped in a clean cloth.

Dat was whistling, rattling chains as he tied the cows in their stalls. Lizzie wished he wasn't so cheerful in the morning because it only made her tired and grumpy. Absentmindedly, she reached under a cow's udder to wash it clean before a milker was attached. Dat was still whistling, but Lizzie wasn't listening. She was thinking about her last day of vocational class only a week before.

She had been feeling a bit blue as she thought about Joe. He still hardly ever noticed her. He talked to her sometimes about baseball and school subjects, but never for very long. If he didn't notice

her more than that, this business of finding a husband was going to be a lot more difficult than she had anticipated.

The last day of school, she was leaning against the old porcelain sink—she could still remember exactly where she was—when Viola and Mandy came charging through the door, arm in arm, giggling and laughing, their eyes shining. Viola was absolutely stunning that day in a dark burgundy-colored dress that set off her long dark braids and tanned skin. Mandy was equally beautiful with her large, expressive eyes and creamy, flawless complexion.

Lizzie had tried to smile at them, but her heart sank steadily as she compared herself to them. She could still feel the panic about being unattractive and, worst of all, absolutely unpopular. She had wanted to go home and talk to Mam or Emma, whoever wasn't busy at the time, and get them to explain this thing about God's will for a husband again. She was never going to get a husband without some help, that was certain.

She stepped into the next stall, bent her head, and was just about to start washing the cow's udders when the cow shifted away from her. This movement was followed by a sharp tugging on her hair. It felt as if every hair on her head was being pulled individually out of her scalp. Was the milking machine sucking up her hair?

"Ouch!" she yelled.

She backed away and turned in time to see the

cow, her neck extended into a long turn, reaching out her tongue towards the top of Lizzie's head. Lizzie jerked back.

That cow thinks my hair is hay! she realized. She brought her fist down on the cow's bony hip, hollering, "Stop that!"

The minute her fist contacted the hip bone, pain exploded through her hand and along her arm, all the way to her elbow. She stepped over the gutter, holding the side of her injured hand, and groaned with pain.

"What in the world is wrong with you, Lizzie?" Dat called.

"Nothing!" Lizzie shot back. She knew her face was red and contorted with the effort to keep from crying.

Lizzie marched into the milkhouse without looking right or left. She went straight to the stainless steel rinse tubs and held her bruised hand under the faucet so the warm, soothing water could wash down over it. She had never disliked anything or anybody as much as she disliked cows.

Any other animal would have been intelligent enough to know her unkempt hair was not hay. Couldn't she smell the difference? Animals were supposed to have a keen sense of smell, weren't they? According to the size of their nostrils, they should be able to smell a bale of hay from a great distance. They had no business slurping at someone's head.

Lizzie hurried back to the cow stable, wiping her

hand on a paper towel. She finished washing udders, carried milk into the milkhouse, and swept the aisle. Dat untied the cows, and, one by one, they backed across the gutter and made their slow, clumsy way out the door.

"Your hand feel better?" Dat asked, as she was sweeping.

"Mm-hmm."

"What happened?"

Lizzie narrowed her eyes. Should she tell him? She shrugged.

"I just hit the cow in the wrong place and hurt my hand."

Dat raised an eyebrow but said nothing as he started sweeping the feed aisle.

"I'm going for breakfast," Lizzie called back as she headed out the door.

"Be right in," Dat answered.

Lizzie slammed the back door a bit harder than necessary. Her future seemed very long and dark if herding cows was her future.

In the house, Mam was frying eggs on the big griddle, her hair combed and her covering positioned neatly on her head. Emma's hair wasn't combed, but she had covered it with a man's handkerchief, which she wore to do barn chores or outside work so her coverings wouldn't get dirty. Emma always wore her dichly or some sort of head scarf if she wasn't wearing her covering, because she was conscientious and a good girl who wanted to do what was right. The girls were taught to cover their heads

when they prayed, which included the silent prayer before and after meals.

"All done?" Mam asked, smiling at Lizzie.

"Mm-hmm." Lizzie bent to wash her hands and face at the small sink in the kitchen.

Emma poured orange juice as Mandy came clattering down the stairs, with Jason a few steps behind her.

"Good morning!" Mam sang out.

"Good morning, Mam!" Mandy answered.

"Morning, Mam," Jason echoed, going to stand beside her so she could reach out and put an arm around his shoulders.

"Mandy, would you please make the toast for me?"

"Sure." Mandy hurried to do her bidding, while Lizzie stood at the sink glaring at herself in the mirror. Oh, great, another angry-looking pimple, she thought, dragging a fingernail through it. She winced as the pain moved across her forehead.

"Don't pick your face, Lizzie," Mandy said from her vigil at the oven door.

"I'm not!"

Mandy raised her eyebrows. But Lizzie just smoothed back her hair and sat down at the table. Lizzie couldn't stop a huge, gaping yawn. Tears formed in her eyes, and she blinked back her tiredness.

"Boy, Lizzie, you look as if you're about at the end of your string," Mandy said.

"The word is *rope*, not *string*," Lizzie growled.

"Grouch," Mandy muttered.

"I had to milk, remember?" Lizzie hissed, stifling another yawn as she expertly flipped two fried eggs onto her plate. Mandy was always happy in the morning. She bounced out of bed, humming under her breath as she raced down the stairs to chirp a warm greeting to anyone who was happy enough to answer.

Dat looked closely at Lizzie. He wished she had a better attitude about her new job, but it seemed no matter how hard he tried to make the cow stable a pleasant place, she was always impatient, wanting to be finished with her chores before they had even started. Mandy was exactly the opposite, cheerfully helping and asking questions, learning all she could about the cows, the butterfat content of the milk, or whatever.

"Lizzie, you surprise me," Dat said as he ate a forkful of egg and toast.

"Why?"

"I guess because you were always the tomboy with the ponies and the ridge. But you really resent milking cows."

"Is it any wonder?" Lizzie asked sarcastically.

"Why do you say that?"

"Cows are stupid."

Mam laughed.

"Lizzie, that's not one bit respectful of my profession," Dat said.

Lizzie looked up sharply, almost choking on her bite of egg. "Profession? You mean milking cows is

a profession, like teaching or making furniture...or ...or...stuff like that?"

"It's a part of farming, a very important part. If it wouldn't be for the milk we're shipping, I don't know how else we'd make a living."

Lizzie had put a spoonful of fried eggs and toast in her mouth so she couldn't answer.

She was so hungry after her morning's work that she ate and ate without even thinking of calories or her weight. She couldn't wait to cut a fresh piece of shoofly pie and pour a mug of steaming hot chocolate over it. Shoofly pie was one of her favorite foods. Mam's shoofly pies were almost as good as Mommy Glick's, with a thick brown sugar and molasses goo on the bottom and a soft crumb cake on top.

When she was finally finished eating, Lizzie pushed back her plate.

"But, Dat, you have to admit it. A cow is not nearly as pleasant as a horse. They swat you in the face with their smelly tails every chance they have. They step on your toes without even thinking about it. They...they take a *huge* slurp of your hair if they think it's hay!" She started laughing.

"What?" Mandy squealed.

Dat started choking and sputtering, pointing a finger at Lizzie.

"So that...," he coughed, before he resumed speaking, "so that is what happened to your head and your hand this morning, Lizzie!" He laughed so hard Mam raised her eyebrows.

"Oh, my!" Dat sighed. He was still chuckling as he told the others about how Lizzie had hopped around the aisle with a sore hand.

"When I asked her what had happened, she said 'Nothing!' so loudly and so angrily, I *knew* something had happened," he said.

"So…the cow reached back and tugged at your *shtrubbles* with her tongue, thinking it was hay, right?" he asked.

Mandy squealed, holding her hands over her mouth, her eyes wide. Jason guffawed loudly. Mam threw back her head and laughed with Dat.

"Ewww!" Emma said. But she started laughing with everyone else.

The whole table was in such an uproar, Lizzie started laughing as well, because there was nothing to do if everyone else thought it was so funny.

"That will teach you to comb your hair before you go out in the morning!" Dat sputtered, wiping his eyes.

"Oh, my, Lizzie!" Mam gasped.

"Your hair does look a lot like hay!" Jason said. "It always does."

The morning sun shone through the kitchen windows, casting a soft, yellow glow into the kitchen. Lizzie smiled. Everyone thought she was hilarious, and she felt the glow from Dat's eyes. She was so thankful for Mam's health, for Dat's laughter, for this old house which they were continuing to clean up, for Mandy, for dear, proper Emma, and for Jason's curls.

She smiled straight into Jason's eyes and said, "Just be glad my hair doesn't look like yours. Then the cow would probably have eaten my whole head!"

Jason punched Lizzie's arm as Mandy slapped the table and laughed again.

"Alright," Dat said. "Enough now."

Dat was like that, Lizzie thought happily. He was so full of fun and jokes, and then he would remember that he shouldn't be too silly and he would say something serious. But family was such a grand thing, Lizzie thought. Cows and old farmhouse or not, having family around her was one thing that was utterly safe and dependable. Together, she believed they could conquer any troubles they would meet.

Even if life handed them disappointments, like Mam's pneumonia and moving here to the old farm, their loyalty to each other would see them through. Mam would correct her if she said that, insisting that God would stand beside them, which Lizzie knew was true. But the thing was, God seemed so undependable to her. Family you could see and actually touch. God was so far away. He just seemed a bit harder to figure out.

Chapter 16

Emma was the first one to go away to work as a *maud* and stay all week. The man who came to the door looked a bit weary and very anxious to have one of the girls come to help his wife with a new baby and all that goes with it. The family had also just started milking cows, so the man would need help with the milking in the morning and evening, too.

Lizzie held her breath, desperately hoping that Emma would offer to go, and, of course, she did. Emma sat at the table crocheting a blue and white afghan, the crochet hook flashing in the gas lamplight. She looked perfectly calm and poised, her cheeks flushed to a delicate shade of pink.

She looked up and smiled. "Yes, I can come. Monday morning will be fine."

Lizzie actually felt her chest deflating as she let out a whoosh of air. Bless Emma's heart. Lizzie felt like jumping up and down with relief, but she stood

quietly beside the refrigerator, chewing her thumb-nail to the quick.

How did Emma do it? How did she manage to always do what Mam wanted? It had been that way forever, it seemed to Lizzie. It happened even on days when they were little and some celebrating seemed in order—like the first day of summer after school was out for the year. Early one spring morning, Emma had come running down the stairs, shouting for Lizzie. Sure enough, she had something bossy to say. Emma told Lizzie loudly that as soon as Mam was done washing, they had to help mow the yard, trim around the existing flower beds, and make new ones.

Lizzie hadn't felt like working in the yard that day any more then than she did now. Emma just upset her, always spoiling a perfect day, telling her what she had to do. So she didn't turn around. She acted as if she hadn't heard Emma and kept her back turned.

"Lizzie!" Emma voice rose. Lizzie could tell she was angry at her. Good for her. Emma could go mow the yard with Mam and she'd stay in the barn with Dat and the horses.

"Lizzie!" Emma yelled louder.

Dat stopped combing Dolly's mane. He did not look very happy as he spun Lizzie around. "Lizzie, answer your sister when she calls you," he said.

Lizzie looked at the floor, pushing a piece of black leather with one toe as Emma stomped into the barn.

"Dat, you have to make Lizzie listen to me. She's just mad because she has to work. I already swept the floor for Mam and she didn't do a thing," Emma said.

"Lizzie, now go on, and don't be so stubborn," Dat said, giving her a shove. He looked frustrated as he turned back to brush Dolly.

"I don't want to, and I'm not..." Lizzie retorted.

Dat turned very suddenly and loomed over Lizzie. "Don't say it, Lizzie, or I'm going to have to find my paddle. You go right now and be nice. I'm busy here, and Mam needs you to help her. Now go."

Lizzie had burst into howls of rage and disappointment. First of all, Emma was bossy, and now Dat was on Emma's side and was being so unkind. She wailed her way out the door and plopped down hard on the porch step, refusing to budge while she cried loud howls of self-pity.

"Lizzie, if you don't shut up right this minute— oh!" Emma stood by helplessly. When she simply couldn't take Lizzie's crying one more second, she stomped off to the little shed and found the push mower.

Lizzie stopped crying as she watched Emma mow. It looked like fun, and it made the lawn look nice and even in size and color. She sniffed and wiped her eyes and watched Emma some more.

Lizzie wished she were back in school. School was much more fun than this. Emma would boss

her around all summer. Mandy was too little to be much fun, but Lizzie guessed if Emma was going to be so grown-up all the time, sweeping floors and mowing yard, Mandy would have to be her playmate. Even Dat was unkind to her today.

Tears welled up in her eyes, because it all hurt dreadfully. She turned away so Emma couldn't see and ran to the tool shed. She found Mam's trimming shears and hurried over to the flower bed farthest away from Emma.

She clipped halfheartedly at the edge of the flower bed. A fat brown earthworm wriggled in the grass, and Lizzie clipped him in two pieces. It served the slimy old worm right—he had no business crawling over the grass where she was supposed to trim.

Mam came over and sat down beside Lizzie. The two parts of the earthworm were wriggling furiously, and Mam could see Lizzie's swollen eyes and tear-stained face.

"What's wrong with the worm, Lizzie?" she asked.

"I cut him in half."

"On purpose?" Mam asked.

"I don't know."

"Lizzie, why were you crying?" she asked.

"Mam, I–I—" and Lizzie burst into a fresh wave of weeping. "It's always the same. Emma is so good and I am so bad. She always makes me do things I don't want to do, because she likes to sweep and do things like that. And she makes me so mad I could… I could kick her. And you like her a lot better than you like me. Dat does, too."

Years later, Lizzie sometimes still fought back those feelings of being second best. That evening after the man came looking for a *maud*, Lizzie slipped over to Emma's room and sat down beside her on her bed. She cleared her throat nervously before she said, "Emma?"

Emma looked up from the Bible she was reading and asked serenely, "Hmm?"

"Emma, don't you...? I mean, don't you mind going so far away to those strange people and staying for an entire week?" Lizzie's voice rose to a hysterical yelp.

"I don't know. I'm not exactly looking forward to it, but I feel like it's my duty to go if Mam and Dat think I should."

She closed her Bible and put it carefully in her nightstand drawer, taking out her diary and pen.

Lizzie couldn't believe it. How could she? How could she be so deep-down and honest-to-goodness obedient to Mam's wishes?

"Emma, aren't you one bit angry?" Lizzie asked, watching as Emma opened her diary.

Emma thought, chewing on the tip of her pen.

"No, I guess not. I mean, what good would it do? I have to go and, like Mam said, it will be a good experience, learning to work for other people."

Lizzie took a deep breath, leaned back, and gazed at the ceiling.

"Well, I'm not ever going to do it."

Emma glanced at her sharply. "You shouldn't say that."

"Well, I just did say it. I'm not going to stay for a week, ever. I couldn't take it. Emma, ewww! Are you actually going to get up in the morning and milk? I guarantee you have to get up at 4:30, if not earlier."

Emma didn't answer. She was writing in her neat, slanted handwriting. "Can I read your diary?" Lizzie asked, leaning over to see what she had written.

"No."

"Why not?"

"Because."

Lizzie yawned sleepily, got up, stretched, and said, "Okay. G'night, Emma."

"G'night. Don't worry too much about being a *maud*. You'll be all right when the time comes for you to go."

That was nice of Emma to place so much trust in me, Lizzie thought as she walked down the darkened hall to her room. But she need not worry, because I'm not going. Mam and Dat can't make me.

She guessed she would have to start saying an extra prayer in the evening. Maybe that was why so many scary things happened to Lizzie, because Emma knelt beside her bed faithfully to say her little German prayer, and Lizzie hopped into bed and said it under the warm quilts. And often Lizzie didn't really say her prayers right. She felt silly, or sometimes she felt like God didn't hear her say them. How could he hear it if she just thought her prayer?

And yet she felt silly to say it out loud.

When they were small and Mam helped them say their prayers, she didn't feel silly. Praying had felt just right, because God heard Mam—Lizzie was positive of that. He heard Emma, too, because Emma was a good girl. She was always straightening up the living room or sweeping the kitchen floor, and she loved to wash dishes. Lizzie just didn't feel comfortable with God yet.

The next day, an ordinary-looking postcard arrived in the mail. Mam read the card out loud from her place at the kitchen table. The card came from a Mrs. Mary Beiler whose town Lizzie didn't even recognize. Lizzie sat on the bench along the wall, eating a piece of apple crumb pie with milk before she went to feed the horses and help with the milking. She was perfectly relaxed since she had resolved not to go work as a *maud*.

"So... Mrs. Beiler needs you to help with the fall housecleaning. They just moved, and the house is small, but in need of a good cleaning," Mam said, smiling at Lizzie.

Lizzie blinked, chewing methodically. "Mmm. Mam, this apple pie is the best thing you ever made."

"Didn't you hear me?" Mam asked.

"What?"

"It's your turn to be a real *maud* now."

"That's no problem, Mam. I'm not going."

Mam's mouth dropped open in surprise. What blatant form of rebellion was this? Her cheeks flushed, but she spoke quietly and patiently.

"Why aren't you going?"

"I just decided when Emma went for a week that I could never do that. She's so good, Mam. You know how it is with her. Same as it always was. So I made up my mind that she can be a *maud*, and I'll stay here with you."

Lizzie set down her glass of milk, wiped her mouth with a napkin, and got up to go do chores.

Mam cleared her throat.

"But, Lizzie, both you and Emma can be *mauds*. Mandy can help me here at home. It would certainly not be fair to make Emma work away while you do as you please."

"I don't do as I please. I work at home." Lizzie pulled on her old sweater, preparing to go to the barn. She lifted her nose a few inches as if to remind Mam how pitiful she was, thinking that she would ever work away from home for an entire week.

The screen door was as far as she got.

"Lizzie Glick!" Mam said in a tone of voice that stopped Lizzie in her tracks. Just as luck would have it, Dat stepped up onto the porch at the exact same moment.

"Now what?" he asked, glancing at Lizzie and noticing Mam's heightened color as well.

Lizzie stood stone-still, her shoulders erect, staring out across the brown fields that led to the creek. Mam explained about the postcard from Mrs. Beiler,

and Lizzie's arrogant assumption that Emma was the only one who would ever be a *maud*.

Dat sat down.

"Lizzie," he said in a terrible voice.

She tasted defeat, a sickeningly sour, green-apple flavor that would not go away. They were actually going to make her go. Not just Mam, but Dat, too. Dat! Now he was on Mam's side, and those two sticking together meant she had no more of a chance than a chicken feather in a hurricane.

"Let me tell you something, young lady. If you think you're going to tell us what to do, you have another guess coming."

Lizzie whirled around, the sour-tasting defeat bringing tears in its wake.

"I don't want to go!" she cried.

"But you're going," Dat said softening his tone.

"Listen, Lizzie," Mam broke in. "I know it seems cruel to you now, but you have to learn to have a job anyway, from now until you get married. That's what Amish girls do. You may as well give in now, because you're just making it hard on yourself and on us."

"Emma's different than me!" Lizzie wailed, sinking onto the wooden bench, putting her head in her hands.

"That's just an excuse, Lizzie. You can try and grow up and become a bit more like her. I know there's a difference in your natures, but you can't use that as a stepping-stone to just skip out of any situation you don't want to be in," Dat said.

"I don't want to wash other people's dirty laundry and wipe their walls and eat with them and sleep in their beds!"

Mam hid her smile but winked at Dat.

"It's not as bad as you think, Lizzie," she said.

Dat's eyes shone, and he smiled at Mam. "Oh yes, I remember you hanging out wash at Aaron Kanagys. I thought you were the prettiest *maud* I ever saw!"

"Ach, Melvin!" Mam smacked his arm playfully.

That made Lizzie so mad, she literally saw red. How could they be so happy and tease each other when they should pity her? She got up, hurrying around the table in a desperate dash to the stairs, but her sweater button caught on a kitchen chair. She stopped to loosen it, and Dat caught her eye.

"So Mam will write Mrs. Beiler and tell her you'll be ready Monday morning?"

"Well, *I'm* not going to write," Lizzie snapped, turning on her heel and stomping up the steps as loudly as possible.

"Let her go," she heard Dat say, followed by a soft murmur from Mam. She paused at the top of the stairs as Dat said, "She'll get over it."

Lizzie flung herself on her bed. Dat and Mam were cruel. They were mean. She wasn't going to go.

Chapter 17

EMMA CAME HOME ON SATURDAY, TELLING all kinds of stories about her week, happier than Lizzie had ever seen her. She hugged the twins and fussed over Jason, telling Mam and Dat how good it was to come home. Lizzie began to suspect that working away couldn't be that bad, or Emma would not be so happy.

So when the driver stopped at the end of the sidewalk on Monday morning, Lizzie grabbed her suitcase and said good-bye to everyone without a trace of anger.

Still, when the driver pulled up to a small white house on the left side of the road, with a huge red barn on the right side and maple trees in the front lawn, Lizzie nearly fainted with nervousness. One of the upstairs windows was flung open, and a slender young housewife looked down at her.

"Well, good morning! You aren't looking for work, are you?" Mary Beiler laughed.

Lizzie looked up and smiled back. She's pretty and neat and so much younger than I thought she'd be, Lizzie thought.

After Mary paid the driver, Lizzie followed her into the kitchen where they sat at the table and talked awhile. She introduced her two young children, a dark-haired, brown-eyed boy named Abner and a sweet little girl named Rhoda.

Lizzie could hardly keep from staring at Rhoda's tiny pink dress. It was the cutest thing she had ever seen. She would make a dress exactly like that for her own little girl one day, she decided.

That afternoon, Lizzie was introduced to the world of Mrs. Mary Beiler's housecleaning expectations. Mary was extremely thorough, much more so than Mam or even Emma. Together they washed walls that were already clean, scrubbed drawers that were already spotless, and washed windows and screens that may have been only a bit dusty. Lizzie learned to use one kind of soap for the furniture and the woodwork, another kind for the walls, and yet another mixture for the linoleum on the floor.

Every quilt, sheet, doily, and rug was whisked off to the kettle house and washed in the wringer washer. Lizzie didn't mind doing the wash if it just meant running it from the wash tub, through the wringer, into the rinse tub, and through the wringer again. But more than that was plainly unnecessary, she thought, though Mam didn't agree. Earlier that week, Mam had frowned when she saw how Lizzie had washed Dat's socks.

❧

"Lizzie, you didn't soak those socks in Clorox water, did you?" she asked.

For one wild moment, Lizzie had a notion to lie and to just say, "Yes." She knew she was supposed to, but she detested the smell of Clorox, and besides, Mam would never know. How could she tell?

"No," Lizzie said.

"You know I don't like yellow socks on the line, Lizzie. Next time you wash, remember to use Clorox."

Lizzie didn't answer. She was too angry. What was the difference? A man's socks were hidden the whole way under his shoes, which came clear up to above his ankles anyway. And his pant legs covered his shoes. Lizzie never saw one peep of Dat's white socks, unless he was ready to take his bath or had just gotten up in the morning. Lizzie never, or hardly ever, saw Dat's socks, so she was positive no one else did. What did it matter if they were soaked in Clorox or not? It was just a bad habit, soaking socks in that awful-smelling stuff.

"Once I'm married, no one is going to tell me to soak my husband's socks. If they aren't white, he will just have to wear them that way."

She had thrown the socks in the washer.

"And another thing, our farm is so old and ugly and sloppy, brown socks on the line would match it just fine," she said, her head held high.

Mam sighed.

"Lizzie, you're going to have to learn," she said.
Your attitude is not good, especially about the farm.
We'll get this place looking just fine in a few years,
you watch."

"And in the meantime, we'll be ashamed every
time someone comes to visit," Lizzie burst out.

"Lizzie!" Mrs. Beiler called.

Lizzie jumped.

"What?"

"Do they always call you Lizzie? Doesn't anyone
call you 'Liz' or 'Elizabeth?'"

"No."

"Well, you should be called Elizabeth. It's pret-
tier.

"Come on down now. Dinner's ready."

Lizzie was sincerely thankful that it was 12 o'clock
and time for lunch. She was almost weak with hun-
ger, since she had been too nervous to eat much
breakfast that morning. As she went down the
stairs, the delicious smells from the kitchen made her
mouth water. Mary Beiler must be a good cook, she
thought happily.

"You can wash the children's hands in the bath-
room," Mary said. "Abner, go with Liz. She'll wash
your 'patties!'"

Liz! Didn't that sound classy! Imagine how nice
it would be if everyone called her Liz! That would
make it seem as if she was already 16 years old.

She turned to Abner, smiling into his dark brown eyes.

"Do you want me to wash your hands?"

Abner placed his hand in hers, melting her heart with his liquid dark eyes.

"Are you our *maud*?" he asked in his slow, proper speech.

"Yes, I am this week."

"Are you going to sleep here?"

"Mm-hmm."

"Good," he drawled, which warmed Lizzie all over again. She hoped with all her heart she could have a little boy that looked and talked like Abner some day.

Lizzie had just sat down at the table when Mary's husband, Jacob, walked into the kitchen. He was big and broad-shouldered with dark curly hair and a slow smile. A tall young man followed him into the kitchen, wearing a short-sleeved white shirt, his face tanned from the sun. Lizzie had never seen anyone whose hair was cut like this young man's. Maybe it was a style she hadn't seen yet because she wasn't running around with the young people.

When he took his place at the end of the table, Lizzie tried not to stare. Yet she had to look sometimes because he was the most handsome person she had ever seen.

"Jacob, this is Lizzie Glick, our new *maud*. Daniel, Lizzie will be here this week," Mary said.

"Hello. So you come from way up at the other end of the county?" Jacob asked.

"I guess," Lizzie managed to croak.

She glanced furtively at Daniel, but he was looking at his plate. He didn't say anything at all, which Lizzie couldn't understand, because surely he would not be embarrassed in front of her. She was only plain Lizzie, with brown hair and clothes that didn't look half as neat as other people's.

"Daniel is my brother," Mary smiled. "He's not quiet usually."

"The cat got his tongue," Jacob teased, and Daniel smiled back.

After they had bowed their heads in silent prayer, they passed dishes of hot, steaming food—fluffy mashed potatoes, thick beef gravy, and succulent young peas in a cream sauce. Applesauce and small red peppers stuffed with cabbage, crisp green pickles, and lots of bread, butter, and jelly completed the meal.

Lizzie tried desperately not to eat too much. She loved Mam's food, but there was also something deliriously wonderful about eating in other people's homes. But today Lizzie didn't eat as much as she would have liked to, mostly because Daniel was sitting so close to her. He was very good-looking, Lizzie decided. She would never, ever have a chance of having him as a boyfriend, and for sure not as a husband. If neither Joe nor John was interested in her, than Daniel wouldn't be either.

She wondered if he had a girlfriend at home. Probably. She would ask Mary if she had enough nerve.

"Does your dad milk cows on your farm?" Jacob asked. Startled, Lizzie dropped her spoon.

"He does now, yes, but I don't know how long yet. They just die."

The men laughed loudly. Oh, dear. Her cheeks felt hot and she blinked self-consciously. Why did she say that? They didn't have to know about their old run-down farm and the fact that so far Dat was not very successful with the cows.

"Why are they dying?" Jacob asked, chuckling.

"I don't know. The vet comes out quite often."

Mary clucked sympathetically. "That can be hard on a pocketbook," she said.

❧

Lizzie had long wondered if Dat knew enough to be a good farmer. When Mandy was little, Dat was a harness-maker. When that business didn't grow fast enough, he started building pallets. So what did he really know about how to run a dairy—with all its expensive equipment, plus animals. What if the crops didn't grow? What if the cows didn't make it?

Lizzie had always been a worrier, all the way back to when she was five and got Snowball the cat and was afraid she'd wander out onto the road and get killed. Lizzie would get up during the night to check that the kitten was still breathing. Now that Lizzie was bigger, she was worrying about bigger things.

Dat had bought their whole herd of 30 Holstein dairy cows from a dealer in Ohio, and they

were trying to make a living by milking cows. It still seemed like a risky enterprise, one that often bothered Lizzie as she went about her work. Cows were living creatures who died or got sick, so it all seemed quite unpredictable. She had a hunch that Dat was not thinking carefully enough. He seemed quite positive that the milk would just keep flowing freely and the big stainless steel bulk tank in the milk house would be filled to capacity every time the milk truck rolled in the driveway.

It was the same way with planting corn and making hay. What if it didn't rain? Sometimes it didn't. Or what if it rained when they needed dry weather to cure the hay?

Lizzie took another bite of bread. It was Dat's responsibility, not hers. Everything would be just fine. If only Dat had more experience.

Emma had often told Lizzie that if she prayed more, God could help her not worry so much. Lizzie wasn't too sure he cared enough to quiet her fears. God wasn't as real to her as he was to Emma.

Mary was slicing a chocolate cake and topping each piece with home-canned peaches. Lizzie desperately wanted a large piece of cake soaked with sweet peach juice like she ate at home, but she was too embarrassed to eat that much in front of Daniel. She wasn't exactly thin, but she was trying. She certainly didn't want it to look as if she overate.

Lizzie was relieved when the meal was finally over.

The rest of the day she housecleaned, ironed curtains, and did any job Mary assigned to her. By the end of the day, she was bone-tired and wished she could go home. She missed Mandy and Mam and Dat, their supper table in the old kitchen, and Jason talking with his mouth full. Everything about home seemed so dear and precious. A wave of homesickness enveloped her in a gray mist.

Finally, it was time for Lizzie to take a warm bath and get ready for bed. The bed in the guest room felt strange, so different from her own lumpy mattress with skinny Mandy beside her, reading as Lizzie fell asleep. The sheets were smooth and luxurious, the pillow twice as thick as her old pillow at home. She lay in the dark, thanking God for a room of her own, this nice soft pillow, and the cool sheets. Even if she had to be a *maud*, there were little things along the way to give thanks for.

Mary proved to be a good, kind person to work for. She was very fussy about the way things were to be done. But Lizzie didn't mind. She just remembered to ask when she wasn't sure how to do something. Mary always explained in detail how she wanted jobs to be handled.

The best day was when Mary sent her outside to rake leaves and mow the lawn for the last time before winter set in. Lizzie loved to work outside. She clipped dead plants, hoed flower beds, raked leaves, and pushed the Beilers' new reel mower.

Abner ran alongside the lawn mower, asking

a dozen questions whenever Lizzie stopped. She always took time to answer, loving the way he drawled out his words and rolled his brown eyes for emphasis as he talked.

Toddlers certainly beat babies in Lizzie's estimation. She didn't really like babies that much, especially if they yelled and screamed and drooled on your hand when you held them. In church, each little girl wanted to get someone's baby after services, so they could pretend they were its mother. Lizzie never liked that. Babies were such a mess, and they made Lizzie nervous. She was never sure how to hold a baby. They were too soft and slippery, and Mam said you had to hold their heads carefully. Lizzie was always afraid she had the wrong end up. But a two-year-old was plain-down entertaining. Most of the time.

When Mary came out to bring in the laundry from the line, she threw her hands up in the air and made quite a fuss about everything Lizzie had accomplished.

"It looks like a different yard!" she said.

Amazing how it worked, Lizzie thought. If you made someone else's day brighter, just like magic your own was bright, too. Maybe that was why Emma had been so happy when she came home from being a *maud* for a whole week. She had made other people's lives happier by lifting their workloads.

When the driver came on Saturday afternoon, Lizzie couldn't wait to go home to her family, but

she felt almost sorry to leave the Beilers, too. Mary thanked her profusely, handed her a check, and gave her some lavender-scented stationery with matching envelopes.

When Lizzie reached the farm, she flew in the sidewalk, burst through the door, threw her suitcase on the floor, and yelled, "I'm home!"

Everyone made a good and proper fuss, so much, in fact, that Lizzie wondered why she had acted like such a baby to begin with. Being a *maud* had a goodness all its own. The best part, probably, was learning to be a less selfish person.

Chapter 18

Now that Emma was 16, she spent Saturday evenings and Sundays with a group of young people in the neighboring county where there was a larger Amish community. Her new girlfriends invited her to stay at their houses. She was also learning to know many young men. Together they ice-skated, took buggy rides, and gathered for supper crowds and hymn-singings. Emma always came home late Sunday evenings with a driver. Her eyes shone Monday mornings as she told Mam, Lizzie, and Mandy all about her weekend.

Lizzie was thrilled as she listened to Emma. How unbelievably exciting it would be when she turned 16 and went to the neighboring county. She still had to stay at home most of the time, although sometimes she and Mandy were allowed to have fun with their friends from vocational class.

One morning when Emma came down the stairs, her cheeks were flushed with excitement. She looked

as if she could absolutely walk on air. In fact, her
feet hardly seemed to touch the floor.

"Good morning, Emma!" Mam said, turning to
add another egg to the pancake mixture.

"Morning!"

She said it louder than usual, and Mandy turned
toward her as she placed the last of the forks beside
the plates. Lizzie looked at her, narrowing her eyes.

"Boy, you're happy!" she said.

Morning was not Lizzie's favorite time of day,
although for some strange reason, she was *never*
very happy it seemed. She was usually fine until
Emma or Mandy became too chirpy, too enthused
about their day, or just too plain-down good for
mornings. Then Lizzie felt grouchier than ever.

Why couldn't they eat breakfast a few hours
later? Lizzie wondered. But no, Dat and Mam got
everyone up and to the breakfast table before the
sun came up. No one was allowed to stay in bed.

"Yes, I guess I am," Emma said, ducking her
head shyly, her cheeks absolutely flaming.

"You have a date!" Lizzie burst out.

"Yes, I do!"

Mam dropped her spoon into the pancake bat-
ter and gripped the edge of the countertop with one
hand. Slowly she turned toward Emma, her mouth
open, but no sound came out. She put one hand to
her chest and took a deep breath.

"Who?" Lizzie squealed. "Who? Who?"

"Let me guess!" Mandy said, jumping up and
down. "David?"

"No."

"Sam?"

"No. Of course not."

"I know. Joshua," Lizzie said.

Emma said nothing, turning away as she tied her bib-apron string.

"It is him, right? Right, Emma? Joshua asked you for a date. This weekend? Is he coming here? Here to our house?" Lizzie asked.

Emma covered her face with her hands and laughed.

"Stop it, Lizzie. One question at a time. Yes, Joshua asked me for a real honest-to-goodness date for next weekend, and yes, he's coming here to pick me up!"

Mam found her voice. "But...but, Emma! You're so young! You just turned 16. Are you sure this is what you want?" she said, rather quietly and a bit weakly for Mam, Lizzie thought.

"I've been 16 for awhile, Mam," Emma replied. And then she said something that Lizzie often thought about afterward, and it never ceased to amaze her.

"Mam, I've known for quite some time exactly who I want. The first time I met him, I knew he was the one I wanted for my husband. It's just so real."

Mam sat down almost as if her knees could no longer support the weight of her body.

"But...but...did you pray about this, Emma?"

"Of course, Mam, many times. Now I feel as if God answered," she said softly.

"Did you ask God for Joshua, Emma? I thought we weren't allowed to do that? Aren't we supposed to ask only for God's will when it comes to finding a husband?" Lizzie asked.

"Now don't start that whole thing," Mandy said as she placed plates on the table.

Lizzie thought about the last day of vocational class, about Mandy and Viola giggling together in the cloakroom.

"Mandy," Lizzie said quietly, standing almost against her.

"Hmm?"

"You know the last day of school?"

"Mm-hmm."

"When I was in the cloakroom, you and Viola came barging in there, your cheeks all red, and giggling together in a corner. What was that all about?" Lizzie felt a thud in the pit of her stomach, already knowing what Mandy would say. She didn't even know why she asked her this question now, but she had to know the answer for sure. She had to know before she could handle another morning in the cow stable.

"What?" Mandy shrugged. "Oh, that!" She turned away to pick up the milk bottle and put it on the table.

"You know what I mean, Mandy. You know, too, why I'm asking. Just tell me the whole truth."

When Mandy finally raised her eyes to Lizzie's, she seemed almost apologetic. "Ach, Lizzie, I can't help it that Joe likes Viola and not you," she burst

forth, quite miserably.

"Then he still does," Lizzie said, just as miserably.

"Well, Lizzie!" Mandy said. "What does it matter anyway? We're only schoolgirls who are not nearly old enough to even think about a husband."

"But you know we do! And you know that John likes you, and the only reason you talk like that is to make me feel better. Good, if Joe likes Viola. That's just great! I don't care one bit! I'm never getting married, anyway." Her voice rose to a hysterical screech. "And besides, I'm fat and homely-looking with pimples all over my face, and you're thin and pretty with no pimples!"

There was an awful silence, with Lizzie's outburst hanging in the air like a choking cloud of dust.

"O-oh, Lizzie! You make me so angry! Your favorite cry for attention is telling me how ugly you are. You *know* that's not true. You know, too, that you are not absolutely unattractive. You just...you just wallow around in self-pity like a pig who is *addicted* to its mud hole."

"Mandy, stop it. Now you listen to me. I *would* stop saying those things if you would understand how it feels to be me. Every time I kind of, sort of, you know, not *real* love, but I like someone, they don't like me. The only person who ever liked me was Ivan, and he's my first cousin. So, how, Mandy, tell me how, am I ever going to be able to get a husband? See, you have no idea, because John likes you, for real, and I guarantee he'll end up marrying you. So what do you have to worry about? Nothing!"

Mandy just looked at Lizzie with her big green eyes; then she wiped her face with the hem of her apron.

Dat hurried into the kitchen with Jason right behind him, the cold air whipping past them.

"No girls to help milk this morning?" Dad asked good-naturedly.

"Mandy's turn," Lizzie informed him.

"That's all right. Jase is about as good as you girls. Thirty degrees out there this morning," he said as he hung his coat and hat in the closet.

"More snow?" Mam asked, trying to ease the tension in the room.

"Emma has a date with Joshua King!" Lizzie blurted out.

"What?"

Dat's face broke into a warm smile. "Really?"

"I guess," Emma said, turning toward the stove.

"Well," Dat said, sitting down at his place at the head of the table. "I suppose you are 16 years old, after all, and that's what keeps the world turning," he said, grinning broadly.

"Not exactly," Mam smiled.

"Is he nice?" Dat asked.

"You'll see, Dat. Of course, he's a nice young man. He's...he's the one I thought about for a while."

"Good, Emma! I'm glad you take this seriously," Dat said.

Mam returned to the stove saying happily, "Oh, Emma, we'll have to see what good things we can think of!"

"You mean to bake and cook?" Emma asked, hurrying to help her finish breakfast.

"Why, of course!"

Later, when Lizzie and Mandy were on their way to the barn, Mandy said, "Maybe we need to talk to Mam about all of this."

"No!" Lizzie barked.

"Why not?"

"Well, you know how Mam is. She'll give us this whole row about God's will and I don't understand what she means."

"Lizzie, surely you know there's a higher purpose than just our own selfish wills?"

"Stop acting like a little preacher!"

"Lizzie!"

"Well, you know I don't understand God when he seems so far away."

"I don't always, either."

"Okay, then."

"But we shouldn't feel that way. Mam says God should be more real in our lives."

"Jesus is more real. He's not as big and scary as God is to me."

"That's nice, Lizzie. I suppose it's different for everyone. But I never think too much about a husband, not in a serious kind of way."

Chapter 19

Saturday evening Lizzie sat in Emma's room, watching every move she made. She couldn't believe Emma was going on a real date with a young man Lizzie had never met. Emma combed her hair for the third time, leaning in over her dresser to get a better view of the right side of her head.

"Aren't you nervous?" Lizzie asked for the fifth time.

"Of course, Lizzie. Stop asking me that question or I'm going to scream as loud as I can!" she said.

"Do! I want to hear you," Lizzie laughed.

"It's not funny. Go on out of my room. You're making me nervous for sure. Go on."

"No. I want to watch you get ready."

"All right. But you have to be quiet."

So Lizzie sat silently, her arms wrapped around her knees, watching as Emma finally got her hair combed to her satisfaction. Lizzie sighed with relief. She wasn't too sure about having a date if it made

you so nervous. Suppose Emma would just pass out flat on the floor from nerves? Then she'd have to go tell Joshua he couldn't see Emma that evening because she had passed out, and he'd have to turn around and go home again. Wouldn't that be the most embarrassing thing ever? She giggled to herself until Emma frowned.

"What's so funny?" she asked.

Lizzie told her, and Emma laughed and seemed to relax.

"Lizzie, I'm not that nervous."

Lizzie wandered off to find Mandy, and together they sat at the upstairs bathroom window and watched for Joshua and his driver to pull in the lane. They turned out the kerosene light so he couldn't see their silhouettes against the sheer white curtains. Settling themselves comfortably against the wide windowsill, they giggled together in the thick darkness.

Lizzie and Mandy had become good friends as Emma spent more time helping Mam. Mandy was even getting close enough to being Lizzie's size, so that that winter when she started school, she got Lizzie's hand-me-down coat. Mam did have to open some seams and make the coat smaller, because Mandy was really thin compared to Lizzie.

The linings made the girls' coats slippery on the inside. Lizzie loved the feeling of wearing a new coat with a slippery lining inside, because if she held out her arms and turned first one way, then quickly in the opposite direction, her coat swished around her, making her feel like she was being twirled. Emma

always told her to stop that, because it looked as if she was dancing. Lizzie couldn't see anything wrong with holding out her arms and twirling around, so she kept going. Mandy just giggled.

Now together they watched headlights coming down the creek road, holding their breaths as each car swerved around the bend in the road but kept on going past the barn.

"Nope, not him," Mandy whispered.

Suddenly the bathroom door was yanked open, and Emma said, "Where is the bathroom light?"

"It's out," Mandy said.

"We blew it out," Lizzie said.

"What are you doing?" Emma asked.

"Watching for Joshua."

"Why in the dark?"

"He'll see us if we let the light on."

"Here come lights!" Mandy yelled.

"In the drive?" Emma asked.

"Yep!"

Emma whirled away with a nervous little yelp and ran into her room while Lizzie and Mandy stayed at the window with its bird's-eye view of the front drive. Headlights turned up the drive, stopping at the sidewalk.

"He's here," Lizzie yelled to Emma. "Go down the stairs!"

"Shhh!" Mandy said, smacking Lizzie's arm hard.

It took forever for the door to open. The interior light went on in the car, but they couldn't see very much of Joshua as he paid his driver. He climbed

out of the car, closed the door, and turned toward the house, pausing at the end of the sidewalk as his driver backed the car down the slope.

"Why doesn't Emma go out to him?" Lizzie hissed.

"Oh, goody, there she goes."

Lizzie was silent, her heart thumping in the quiet as she imagined how nervous Emma must be.

"He's not very tall," Mandy whispered loudly.

"Taller than Emma," Lizzie whispered back.

"Emma's short."

"I pity him. Now he has to meet Mam and Dat. I bet he wishes he didn't have a date. Now I bet he feels like running out the driveway and never coming back."

"Not if he likes Emma enough."

"He's supposed to love her."

"Not yet."

"Oh, yes, he is."

"You don't know."

They held their breaths as they heard low voices in the living room.

"Should we go down?" Mandy whispered.

"Let's just sit on the stairs for a while and listen. I feel kind of sorry for Joshua, having to meet the whole family all in one Saturday evening."

They settled themselves on the lower step, pushing the door open wide enough to allow a bit of light and noise to enter their hiding place.

With Emma slipping away into her new life, Lizzie was glad that Mandy was still nearby. She shivered as she remembered how close they had come to losing Mandy during the auction when Dat bought their Jefferson County house.

"Where's Mandy?" Mam had suddenly asked in the middle of all of the excitement over their new house.

"Mandy?" Lizzie looked up from the doughnut she was eating. "I don't know, Mam. Emma and I were walking around looking at everything. I thought she was with you or Dat."

"Go look for her," Mam said. "I need to sit down."

Mam sat down weakly on a porch chair, holding Jason. She looked drained and tired after all the suspense of the sale, Lizzie remembered. Emma and Lizzie had pushed through the crowd of men standing in the big open doorway of the barn. She had followed Emma back to the house, and they had looked in every room, calling Mandy's name, more frantic by the minute.

"Mand-dee! Mand-dee!"

They burst back out through the screen door.

"We looked everywhere," Emma told Mam. Lizzie was trying hard not to panic because kidnappers were one of her worst fears. In a crowd this size, and with Mandy being so little and skinny, Lizzie could not bear to think about what might have happened.

Mam got up from her chair.

"Lizzie, we have to find her! Please go get Dat!"

They looked for what felt like hours, but Mandy was nowhere around. Lizzie and Emma were walking slowly back to the house when suddenly Emma stopped.

"I think I see her," Emma said, still looking across the lawn. Lizzie looked, and, sure enough, a small brown head was barely visible out at the end of the lawn. It might be Mandy! They both hurried out across the flat yard, and there she was, her thin little arms wrapped around her knees.

"Mandy!" Lizzie said breathlessly.

"She's here!" Emma called to Mam who started to run towards them.

"What?" Mandy had asked.

"Where were you, Mandy? We couldn't find you," Lizzie said.

"Lizzie, look!" she said, pointing to the yard across the road. Two pure white cats emerged from beneath a flowering bush. They were long-haired, and even their tails were long, thick, and glossy, every strand combed and flowing with the delicate movement of the cats' dainty feet.

"What kind of cat are they?" asked Mandy.

"I don't know. All I ever saw were ordinary barn cats and Snowball. But Snowball looked common compared to those cats," Lizzie said.

On the way home, Mandy would talk of nothing else but the Persian cats which had so dazzled her.

Lizzie reached over and squeezed Mandy's hand. Mandy slapped Lizzie's arm and hissed, "Here they come!" But it was only Emma on her way up the stairs for her coat.

"Wha... Wha... Watch it!" she stammered as she hurriedly yanked open the stair door to find her two sisters huddled directly inside. "What are you two up to?" she asked.

"N...nothing," Lizzie said, trying hard to appear nonchalant.

Emma bent low and said menacingly, "Get up. You act like you're three years old. Go out there and say hello to Joshua and talk to him while I get my coat. Go!"

So Mandy and Lizzie went.

Joshua was standing at the sink, leaning back, his arms crossed, and looking at ease in his strange surroundings. He was of medium height with wavy brown hair and deep-set, blue-green eyes. He was quite good-looking, and when he smiled, he had a wide grin which made Lizzie feel a bit less self-conscious.

"You must be Lizzie and Mandy," he said in a deep voice.

"Mmm-hmm," Lizzie said, lowering her eyes as she bit her lip.

"You must be Joshua," Mandy said, smiling.

Tonight Emma was planning to take Bess the horse and Dat's buggy. She and Joshua would spend the evening with Emma's best friend, Sara, who was dating a young man who had recently moved

to Cameron County. He had purchased his own farm and lived there all by himself, so Dat said he must have lots of money for such a young person, as prosperous and well kept as that farm was. Sara was a tall, light-haired girl with large blue eyes, whom Emma was grateful to have as a best friend.

Then there was nothing else to say. The water faucet dripped steadily. Joshua cleared his throat and looked out the kitchen window. Mandy slipped behind the table and sat on the bench. They listened to Emma opening and closing her closet doors upstairs.

Lizzie searched frantically for something to say. Should she ask him how many brothers and sisters he had? Definitely not. That would be too personal. The weather! That was it. If Dat needed something to talk about, it was always the weather. Oh, why didn't that Emma hurry back down from her room? She was probably just checking her covering and her hair again.

"Is it still as cold outside as it was today?" Lizzie blurted out.

"It probably is. It usually turns colder at night," Joshua answered with just a hint of a twinkle in his eye.

"Uh, yeah, I guess so," Lizzie said.

Much to Lizzie's great relief, she heard Emma close her room door and then her light steps raced down the stairs.

She came through the door, her coat slung across her arm, her green eyes sparkling as she crossed the room. Joshua watched Emma, never taking his

eyes from her face with such a soft expression in his deep-set eyes that Lizzie felt like an intruder. Emma smiled at him as she stopped to put on her coat, and Joshua stepped forward to hold it for her.

Lizzie was mesmerized. Her very own sister seemed like a sparkling Cinderella and Joshua was her prince. So this was how it was to have your very first date.

"Ready?" Joshua asked.

"Yes. Oh, we need a flashlight to get Bess hitched up," Emma said as she opened the cupboard door.

And then they were gone. Lizzie and Mandy looked at each other for a very long time, saying nothing at all. Mandy pleated the tablecloth with her fingers, and Lizzie sighed as she looked at the kitchen door.

"I'm surprised they didn't leave a solid trail of stardust as they walked out the door," she said.

"They like each other so much it isn't even funny," Mandy said.

❧

But Lizzie couldn't put another thought out of her mind. Sometimes being married seemed like a lot of trouble. Take Mam, for instance, and the fact that she had to move far away from her family when she and Dat got married. Lizzie decided that she was going to be very careful about whom she married, and then they were going to talk a lot before they moved from one settlement to another.

Maybe Mam should have stayed in Ohio to begin with, Lizzie thought. Then she wouldn't have to be so homesick for her relatives. How had Mam and Dat met, and why had they never lived in Ohio where Mam's people were from? How could you love someone enough to move 300 miles away from your parents? Lizzie snorted, thinking that a man would have to be either extremely good-looking or wonderfully kindhearted to get her to move that far away from Mam and Dat. It was just safer not to get married at all.

Suppose you did get married and your husband decided he wanted to move? If you were Amish, you had to go with him wherever he went; it didn't matter if you wanted to or not. If you were English, and you really, really did *not* want to go, you could get a divorce.

Amish people didn't believe in divorce, Mam said. Lizzie wondered why not. Once she had asked Emma what she thought about all of this while they were in the pea patch.

"Emma, would you move to Alaska if your husband wanted you to?" Lizzie asked, opening a pea pod and scraping out the tender green peas.

"I'm not thinking about Alaska!"

"But, Emma, how did Mam and Dat get married?"

"By a *preacher*! Now come on and pick *peas*!"

Emma wanted to be finished as soon as possible.

Lizzie picked another pea and ate it. "No, I mean, how did they meet?"

"Didn't Mam ever tell you? Of course you know, Lizzie," Emma said.

"How?"

"Mam's brother Eli and his wife lived in Jefferson County and needed a *maud*. So Mam came to work for them, and Doddy Glicks lived there, too, so Dat used to go to the singings and Mam did, too, so they started dating."

"That sounds boring," Lizzie said indignantly.

Whack! A pea hit the back of Lizzie's head.

"Stop your talking and pick peas, or I'm telling Mam," Mandy said.

So Lizzie bent her back and picked, her thoughts wandering back to Mam and Dat and moving so far away from your family to live with your husband. It's not like Dat was astonishingly tall or handsome. He was short, actually, although he had very blue eyes and nice, wavy brown hair with a neat beard. He could sing any song you could possibly think of and was very talkative, always entertaining company when they came to visit. Lizzie bet he was fun to have a date with.

She wondered if Mam had been very pretty and slender. Hardly. She had told the girls she was never thin. That was comforting.

Suddenly Mam came bustling out to the kitchen, her cheeks flushed, excitement making her eyes snap. Dat followed her, a big silly grin on his face as he sat at the table. Jason slid in beside Mandy, looking at Lizzie and back again to Mandy.

"Bet you wish you had a boyfriend," he teased.

Dat laughed, slapping the table with his open palm. "Now, Jase!" he said.

Mam opened the refrigerator door, checking to see if her seven-minute frosting had cooled properly. She tasted it, nodded her head, and got the bowl out of the refrigerator so she could ice the big round chocolate cupcakes.

"They might be hungry when they come home," Mam said softly.

"What did you think of Joshua, girls?" Dat asked, as he poured coffee from the pot on the stove.

"He's nice," Mandy answered.

The wind whistled softly around the eaves of the farmhouse as Mam frosted cupcakes and Dat sipped his coffee. It was a cozy, secure feeling, being there in the kitchen with Dat and Mam, both of them smiling contentedly.

Somewhere out in that dark night, Emma and Joshua were traveling steadily down the road, away from them, to spend the evening with Sara and her boyfriend. It was a good feeling to know Emma and Mam and Dat were so happy, but it also stirred up Lizzie's old worries.

Why did changes have to happen? Couldn't Emma just wait awhile before she started dating

and stay home with her family on weekends? Lizzie already missed her, mostly because she seemed too grown-up now, too preoccupied whenever Lizzie tried to talk to her. It seemed as if Emma's thoughts were a million miles away, and half the time she didn't even hear Lizzie when she said something.

Lizzie sighed, suddenly feeling very tired and a bit old. "Guess I'll go to bed," she said, getting up and stretching. As she went up the stairs, she heard Dat ask Mam what was wrong with Lizzie, and Jason said that Lizzie wished she had a boyfriend herself.

Not really, Jase, not really, Lizzie thought. Too many changes too fast made Lizzie feel as if she needed Mam for a very long time.

Chapter 20

LIZZIE'S HEART SKIPPED A BEAT WHEN SHE read the postcard from Sara Ruth inviting Mandy and her to attend a skating party.

"Oh, my!" Lizzie breathed as she leaned against the mailbox, reading the postcard. "Oh, my," she repeated, her eyes narrowing as she contemplated the message on the postcard. Mandy would be thrilled to see Joe's brother, John, again. Some of Sara Ruth's cousins from Lamton, a huge Amish settlement 50 miles away, would be there. Joe would be there, and Viola, who was not Amish, would be nowhere around. Sorry, Viola, Lizzie thought.

A grin spread across her face as she tucked a strand of hair nervously behind her ear. She yanked her scarf tightly under her chin, then she burst into a run, racing up the driveway, her breath coming in short hard puffs. The frigid air hurt her lungs, but she didn't care one bit. She was going skating!

"Guess what!" she yelled as she clattered through

the kitchen door.

"Shut the door!" Mam said, as she bent to open the oven door. "I declare it hasn't gone one degree over zero today!"

"Guess what, Mam! Sara Ruth wrote a card saying she's having a skating party! Can we go? Huh? Can we?"

Lizzie bent down beside her mother, peering into her face as Mam squinted, testing a shoofly pie with a toothpick.

"Better not," she muttered to herself as she closed the oven door, straightening her back to look at Lizzie.

"Better not what?" Lizzie asked. What if Mam wouldn't let them go? She wouldn't be so cruel, would she?

Mam threw her pot holders on the countertop and sat down at the kitchen table. She sighed as she gave Lizzie her full attention. "I meant better not take those shooflies out quite yet," she said. "Now what are you so excited about?"

"Sara Ruth wrote and said she's having a skating party," Lizzie said patiently.

"Where?" Mam frowned.

"I guess at her house," Lizzie answered.

"Is the ice thick enough? And how would you go?"

"I bet the ice is a foot thick!"

"I wonder."

Mandy came clattering down the stairs. Lizzie jumped up and grabbed Mandy's shoulders. "Sara Ruth is having a skating party!"

They squealed and hopped and danced across the kitchen until Mam said they had to calm down because the whole house was shaking.

And so, the following Friday evening, Lizzie and Mandy took their baths earlier than usual. Lizzie carefully combed her hair and chose a pale blue dress to wear. She couldn't wait to see her friends from vocational school again.

Dat hitched up Bess and made sure the battery in the buggy was charged so their lights would stay bright on the way home. He also double-checked that the turning signals and the orange blinking rear lights worked as well. He complained a bit about letting the girls drive so far by themselves in the dark, but he was smiling as he told them to be careful.

It was almost six miles to their destination, but it didn't seem far. Bess clopped steadily through the star-strewn evening. The heavy, warm buggy blanket covered their knees, and the steel wheels rattled gently on the macadam. Lizzie and Mandy chattered on about lots of subjects as Bess pulled the buggy up hills and around bends, through little tree-filled hollows and across different roads.

"They have a beautiful farm," Mandy said as they approached the well-lit house.

"I know," Lizzie said. "That's because their house is bigger and better than ours, and it has classy white shutters on it."

"They have more money than we do, don't they?"

"Probably. Yeah, I'm sure they do."

The Kings' red brick house stood like a sturdy

sentinel in the night with warm yellow light radiating from the windows. Isaac King, Sara Ruth's Dat, finished up his evening milking in the glowing barn. He helped Lizzie unhitch Bess beside the big new cow stable with a rounded roof and the two new silos which towered over the other buildings.

Through the darkness, Lizzie could see a bonfire burning down by the pond next to a line of willow trees. On the pond, dark figures dashed across the ice, while others huddled around the bonfire. Lizzie shivered with cold and something almost like fear. For one wild instant, she felt like hitching Bess back up again and heading home as fast as she could.

"M...Mandy!"

"What?"

"Aren't you...I mean...don't you feel afraid, or... shy or anything?"

"Kind of, yes. But we won't for long."

Sara Ruth and Sharon came running towards them, calling their names.

"It's so good to see you again," Sara Ruth gushed as she linked her arms in theirs. "You'll have to meet our cousins. And, oh yes!" She let go of their arms as she skipped forward, then turned to face them as she walked backward. "Do you know that new Beiler family who moved in from Allen County?"

"Who are they?"

"I don't know. Their oldest boy is 16 already. They have a girl about exactly our age named Anna."

"Are they coming tonight?"

"Probably."

They reached the pond where they met Sara Ruth's cousins from Lamton. These girls were perfectly thin and so pretty, Lizzie could only stare at them. They wore pretty colors in the latest style, and their hair was combed so beautifully, Lizzie could only hope to be able to comb herself half as neatly someday.

They look like little dolls, Lizzie thought miserably, feeling very much like the fat little country mouse being shown the trim city mouse. But the cousins, Linda and Louise, smiled so honestly, welcoming them so sincerely, that Lizzie soon forgot about being self-conscious.

Joe and John skated up to the bank, their grins welcoming the girls to the pond.

"Did someone help you put your horse away?" John asked.

"Your dad did."

"Good!"

And they were off, racing across the pond with a few of their smaller cousins.

The girls sat down on the straw bales and pulled on their white socks.

"Do you always wear white socks?" Sharon asked.

"Yes, to go skating."

"That looks nice."

Sara Ruth started giggling, saying she never even thought about wearing white socks to skate. She was going to bring a bunch of the twins' socks down to the pond. Then the girls were off, leaving Lizzie and

Mandy to put on their skates.

They were still struggling to lace up their skates when a dark shadow hovered over them. Lizzie looked up from tying her skates at a tall, thin guy standing beside the fire, holding a pair of black skates.

"Hi," Lizzie offered.

"Hello. Are John and Joe here?"

"They're skating. Oh, there they are."

A grin spread across the boy's face as the twins swooped up on the bank, almost colliding with the youth.

"Stephen!"

"Hey!"

So that was his name—Stephen. Lizzie glanced at him sideways. His hair was way too long in the back, and his bangs almost fell over his eyes. His eyes were big, huge, actually for a boy, and a light baby blue. Long, dark lashes surrounded them, unlike any Lizzie had ever seen. She wondered why he didn't get his hair cut.

Girls swooped down on Lizzie and Mandy like a bunch of blackbirds in the fall. Lizzie couldn't help giggling. Sharon pushed Lizzie over on her hay bale and started pulling on a pair of socks. Stephen stood watching in his eerily quiet way.

"You sound like a bunch of wild geese," he said.

"Where's your sister, Stephen?" Sara Ruth asked.

"Too cold for her."

"You should have brought her. Lizzie and Mandy don't know her yet."

"They'll see her in church."

And with that, Stephen moved off as quietly as he had come. Lizzie burst out, "He's different! He's so quiet, he gives me the creeps."

Lizzie jumped up and skated onto the pond. She threw back her head and laughed. She loved skating with all of her heart, and this was the first ice-skating of the season. She didn't think about boys or fancy girls as she glided across the ice with wings on her skates. She twirled and turned, skated sideways and backward, warming to the thrill of being alive.

Suddenly she heard girls clapping and cheering from the bank. She slid to a stop.

"What?"

"Can you ever skate!" Sara Ruth called.

"Show-off!" Sharon teased.

Lizzie laughed happily as Mandy, who was even more graceful because of her slight form, joined her. They skated together until the boys hooked arms with them, and they all met in the middle of the pond and decided to play Freeze Tag.

This was one of the best nights of Lizzie's whole life. The stars were so close she could almost reach out and grasp one. The air was sparkling cold, burning her nose the way it did when she drank Pepsi and then burped.

Stephen was an extremely fast skater. No one could escape once he decided to pursue them without mercy. Joe chased her a lot during the evening. Maybe he might someday like her without Viola around. Who knew?

Lizzie's heart was light. She was chased and held captive, dipping and swaying, breaking free, being caught again, all under the light of the too-close stars. Before Lizzie had even begun to tire, Sara Ruth announced that her mother would serve an evening snack just as soon as they went to the house. Lizzie wanted this evening to go on forever, this perfectly crisp, thrilling, heartfelt, starry, wonderful evening on the ice.

Inside the house, Mrs. King had all kinds of delicious food for the skaters, which helped ease Lizzie's sense of disappointment about leaving the pond. The dining room table was filled with big thick slices of homemade pizza piled high with cheese and browned ground beef, root beer in glass mugs, crackers, pretzels and potato chips, and warm chocolate chip cookies for dessert.

Sara Ruth beamed, Linda and Louise flitted about like rose-colored parakeets, and Sharon giggled in a corner with Mandy. Stephen was quite shy, staying well away from the bright gas lamp in the kitchen. Lizzie wished her family could have a skating party at their house. They had the creek that was perfect for swimming in the summer, but no pond on the old farm for ice-skating.

When the evening finally ended, they all walked to the barn to hitch up their horses.

"Does the creek ever freeze solid?" Lizzie asked Joe.

"I don't know," he said.

"I doubt it," John echoed.

"Is the water pretty swift? How deep is it?" Stephen asked.

"It depends. Some places it's way deep and quiet, and other places it runs real fast over rocks."

"If it stays this cold, it'll freeze over."

Lizzie and Mandy talked the whole way home. Bess plodded faithfully, her breath coming in hard, round little puffs of steam as she pulled the buggy safely back to their farm.

In their kitchen, a kerosene lamp shone bright. The girls hurried to the warmth of the coal stove, quickly shedding their snow boots, pushing their stocking feet against its glowing warmth.

"Mmmm!" Mandy closed her eyes, enjoying the stove's wonderful heat.

"You home?" Mam tiptoed out from her bedroom, her housecoat clutched in her hands. She smelled of talcum powder just as she had when Lizzie was a little girl.

"Yes, Mam. We're almost frozen."

"I'm glad you're here. I haven't slept yet." She turned to go back to bed, relaxed now that her girls were safely in the house.

"She looks like an angel."

"She smells like one."

Lizzie could hardly bear the feeling of love she felt for Mam. Wasn't it just wonderful that God made soft, warm Mams who smelled so good? Her soft housecoat felt like Lizzie imagined heaven must feel.

Lizzie decided there was no place sweeter than

home, and she wanted to stay there for a very, very long time.

She only blinked at the moonlight once before she fell into a deep, lovely sleep.

Chapter 21

ONE DAY MAM FROWNED WHEN EMMA handed over her paycheck. She had been away for five days, but the money she brought home wasn't much for an entire work week.

"Emma, I don't mean to criticize or complain. I know you work hard, but if I need to think about buying your hope chest and starting to fill it for when you get married, we're going to have to earn more money somewhere. I know these young dairy farmers who you're helping are struggling, and they have to spend a lot on your transportation, too, so it isn't their fault that you aren't earning more. I just wish we could find a better paying job for one of you, at least," she said.

"Mam, I could work in town at a restaurant," Lizzie volunteered.

"I guess not. We're not that desperate," Mam said, shaking her head.

Lizzie knew that was what Mam would say. But

ever since she was a little girl she had wanted to be a real waitress in a real restaurant.

Her first restaurant meal was etched forever in her mind. On the second morning of their once-in-a-lifetime family vacation to Luray Caverns, they had eaten breakfast in a real restaurant! Lizzie had never eaten in a restaurant, so she didn't know what the inside would look like.

There were lots of electric lights, and a shiny green floor with dark blue lines and streaks running through it. The place was filled with so many tables and chairs, Lizzie could not imagine how the waitresses could remember who sat where and what they wanted to eat. It was all a bit frightening and confusing, until a smiling lady with a small white apron came to seat them.

She was so friendly, Lizzie felt much more at ease, especially when she made a big fuss about the twins as she helped Mam put them each in a high chair. Some of the other waitresses had watched Lizzie and her family as they sat down around the table. That was one thing about being Amish that Lizzie did not like—when people unfamiliar with their plain clothes stared at them. Most people were just curious about their long dresses and coverings, but some people were not very polite.

When the kind waitress handed them a large plastic-covered paper, Mam told them it was the menu,

and they should look for food listed under "Breakfast." That breakfast was plain-down unforgettable. Lizzie didn't think of her weight once, as they all enjoyed bacon, eggs, and pancakes topped with huge globs of butter and all the syrup they wanted. Tall glasses of ice-cold orange juice and crispy toast that was also saturated with butter made their meal extra special.

Mam was smiling and saying they had the best coffee she ever tasted. Dat was smiling at Mam as they all enjoyed the delicious food. Emma was fascinated by how fast the waitress poured coffee. She had never seen anything like it, she told Lizzie.

"You could pour coffee every bit as fast as she does if that's what you did all day. That doesn't look as hard as balancing all those trays of food. Did you see how many plates were on that one tray?" Lizzie asked.

"Yes. That would be fun," Emma answered.

"I wonder if Amish girls are allowed to be waitresses," Lizzie said.

"No. Certainly not," Emma said.

"We could go English and all work in the same place," quipped Mandy.

They had giggled together until Mam said they had to be quiet since they were not being respectful.

Lizzie spun around on her kitchen chair. She had eaten in restaurants only a few times since that first meal, but each time she thought it would be so fancy to wear a small white apron, writing down orders and putting her pen in the pocket of her little white apron.

"But Mam, I would love to work in a restaurant," she said.

"Absolutely not," she said. "No daughter of mine will be prancing around a whole roomful of English men. No good could come of it."

That's how Mam was. She wouldn't think of letting her daughters work at questionable establishments. She was very careful about everything, even the van drivers she chose.

"Lizzie, you shouldn't complain," Emma said. "Mam is only being careful because she cares about us."

Lizzie stuck her nose in the air and made a snorting sound as she left the kitchen. Mam was a bit over-protective.

❧

Lizzie continued to pester Mam about working in a restaurant. But Mam wouldn't agree. Instead, Mam was overjoyed when Darwin Myers, a local Mennonite man, came to the kitchen door a week later.

Mam was washing dishes at the kitchen sink when Darwin stepped up onto the porch. "Oh, I

know who that is! I bet he wants some help," she said to Lizzie.

Quickly, Mam dried her hands on her gray work apron and went to open the door. She greeted him warmly, and he asked how they were. They talked about the weather, as people always did, Lizzie mused.

Finally, Darwin got down to business.

"I need someone to help with the egg-grading," he said. My wife does too much of it for her age, and she's not as well as she once was, so would you consider letting one or two of your daughters come work for me? I would need them on Mondays, Wednesdays, and Fridays."

"Oh, yes!" Mam responded eagerly.

So that was that. Lizzie would go, and if he needed more help on summer days, Mandy would also help at the hatchery, whatever that was.

After he left, Lizzie picked up a dish towel and absentmindedly wiped at a dry plate. She always dreaded starting a new job, but she knew she was getting older and everyone had to have a job after they were out of school.

"How many hours do I have to grade eggs in a day?" she asked, turning to look at Mam with what she hoped was a sweet, martyred expression. She thought that if she lifted her eyebrows at just the right angle and made her eyes look as sad as possible, there was a slight chance that Mam would take pity on her and make Emma go.

Mam was busily reading a recipe card, but she

stopped and looked at Lizzie. A smile tugged at the corners of her mouth.

"Didn't he say he'd pick you up at eight o'clock? Then probably until four or five in the evening. Around eight hours."

Lizzie grabbed another plate and wiped it ferociously. Well, that hadn't helped.

"Well, Mam, I think if we need money to fill Emma's hope chest, shouldn't Emma be the one to make the most money?" Lizzie ventured again. She was trying to complain in a very polite way.

Emma sat at the table cutting sheer white fabric that she would make into coverings, whistling under her breath as she worked.

"Lizzie, I do work away most of the time, but someone has to sew our clothes, too. Do you want to stay home and make coverings?" Emma asked.

Lizzie turned her back and didn't answer. She was too old to cry, and she knew it was plain childish to complain.

"Lizzie, you know you're very fast with your hands. You can do anything you try, and rapidly too," Mam said. "That's why grading eggs will be a good job for you. You do your work just like Mommy Glick, so be glad you inherited her talent. I think you will make a very good egg-grader, and a competent one. Emma is much better at doing fine, careful work like sewing our coverings, so I think this is the best arrangement."

Emma started whistling under her breath again as she watched Lizzie. She didn't say anything. She

just looked at her.

Lizzie swallowed all the rest of her complaints, because what Mam had said made her feel good. Maybe that was true. She probably would be a good egg-grader. She just wished the first day was over.

Chapter 22

THE NEXT MONDAY MORNING, WHEN DARWIN
stopped his car in front of a long, low, silver build-
ing, Lizzie's heart sank. The chicken house was a
corrugated steel box with huge round fans on each
side. An unruly jumble of weeds and briars grew
along the building's base, and old chicken coops
leaned in an odd pile-up beside the door.

The door itself was wooden with layers of paint
peeling off the front. The window was so splattered
with fly dirt you could barely see it was a window at
all. Cardboard cartons lay strewn beside the chicken
coops, and eggshells littered the gravel drive.

When Lizzie opened the car door, a stench filed
her nostrils and turned her stomach. Her first
thought was to make a wild dash for freedom, but
instead she followed Darwin into the hatchery.
Inside, a lone yellow light bulb hung from the ceil-
ing, reminding her of a jail cell. The bright green
walls were barely visible between the stacks of

cardboard boxes and dull metal carts piled high with square gray cardboard trays used to hold eggs. A huge machine stood along one wall, which Lizzie assumed was the grader.

Through a door at the far end of the room Lizzie heard a rustling, cackling sound. Apparently that was where the chickens were housed. A green door burst open, and an older gentleman pushed out a darker green cart, piled high with cardboard trays of white eggs. He wore an old denim coat and denim overalls, and a navy blue hat covered his white hair. His face was still quite handsome, Lizzie thought as his light blue eyes shone and he smiled.

Lizzie smiled back and said, "Hello."

"This is Enos Martin. He gathers the eggs every day and pushes them into the cooler room," Darwin said.

He pointed at another large green door. When Enos opened it, Lizzie saw that it was insulated, like a refrigerator door. The dim interior of the cooler room gave her the creeps. A wet, rattling sound from up high on the wall came from a cooling unit. Water dripped down the walls into a round granite tub. Would it be her job to empty that tub of cold, dirty water? Lizzie wondered. She shivered and wished with all her heart that Emma was here in this new, scary place and that she was still in school with Sara Ruth and Joe and John.

Darwin showed her where to stack the boxes of jumbo eggs, the extra-large, large, medium, and pullet-sized. That's a lot of eggs, Lizzie thought. Oh, I

hope I can do it without breaking them. She chewed her lower lip nervously and took a deep breath to steady herself.

Darwin flipped a switch on the wall and the long lights attached to the ceiling flickered on, filling the room with bright, white light so that the area was no longer haunted and shadowy.

Pulling a cart of eggs over to the machine, Darwin flipped switches, opened boxes, and adjusted dials. The whole machine purred, rattled, and hummed into action. He stepped to the right of the machine, motioning to Lizzie to come and watch.

"Come closer so you can see," he said.

Using both hands, he lifted six eggs and quickly laid them on the moving belt. He did it so rapidly and with so much ease, Lizzie almost forgot that he was holding fragile eggs. The eggs rolled across a light so bright that the eggshells appeared transparent. A dark round object appeared inside each one.

"That's the yolk," Darwin said.

"Now watch," he said. "The reason for this bright light is to find any blood inside the egg. If there is any, you'll be able to see it quite easily, and you put that egg on this flat."

Lizzie nodded. So that was what the cardboard containers were called—flats.

Darwin led her down to the left side of the machine where the eggs were already rolling out, washed and dried to a glistening finish. Stepping up to the machine, Darwin showed her how to pack the eggs.

"Now, if you can't keep up, just holler and I'll stop the machine. You probably won't be able to go very quickly at first," he said.

So the egg-grading began in earnest. Lizzie felt as if someone had pushed her off a cliff and she was hanging in midair. It was absolutely terrifying, all those eggs coming down the moving belt and rolling across the shining stainless steel trays. What if she couldn't keep up and all the eggs got stuck in the moving belt, breaking apart with yellow egg yolks dripping all over the floor?

Darwin was calmly dropping eggs on the light, whistling under his breath. Just like Emma, Lizzie thought. At that moment she resented Mam, Emma, the hope chest, Joshua, growing up, and everything else in her life. This was awful. Mam may as well give up, because she would not spend one more day in this stinking, creepy place.

But Lizzie set her jaw and lifted eggs off the belt, trying to put them into the flat with the pointed side down. It was impossible. There was no way she could lift six eggs at a time and then get them into the right position. Her hands moved quickly, but she needed to stop and turn eggs over so often that the trays were soon overflowing. Meanwhile, the flats were filling up. She was supposed to reach over and lift another one on top of the already filled ones. Once there was a stack of six flats, she had to place them into the big brown cardboard box marked "EGGS."

Lizzie struggled to keep her tears from showing

when she finally asked Darwin to stop the machine. He smiled as he came over to help her, but the lump in Lizzie's throat was so big she couldn't respond. What a dreadful job, she thought, pushing a strand of hair away from her face with trembling hands.

After Darwin helped her catch up, he returned to his station, and Lizzie started picking up eggs again. She wondered how she could ever run back to the cooler room, get the cart, push it under a stack of eggs and take them back, all while the eggs kept steadily rolling into the trays. But as the forenoon wore on, she calmed down enough to holler to Darwin whenever the trays got full. He took care of moving the stacks back to the cooler room since it was her first day.

By lunchtime, she was becoming much more accurate at directing six eggs into each cardboard flat, but her back felt as if there was a knife between her shoulder blades. She swung her shoulders, trying to ease the pain. But there was no time to stop and really do anything about it, so she kept going.

At noon, Darwin turned off the egg-grading machine.

"I'm going to the house for lunch," he said. "I'll be back at one."

Oh good, Lizzie thought, I get a whole hour for lunch. Her mouth watered, thinking of the good food she had packed in her insulated lunchbox that morning.

Lizzie washed her hands in the bathroom and went outside to eat her lunch. She found a

freshly-mowed strip of grass that stretched beneath a towering oak tree. If only the smell wasn't so bad, my lunch would taste a lot better, she thought as she sat down on the grass.

She opened the lid of her lunchbox and pulled out her plastic container of juice. She took long gulps of the ice-cold drink. She felt so much better as she unwrapped her sandwich made with Mam's homemade bread, sliced turkey, white American cheese, and lettuce. It was so good, she thought, as she munched it down with a handful of crunchy potato chips. She was so hungry that she didn't worry about counting calories at all. After all, you couldn't work if you didn't eat.

Her spirits lifting, Lizzie watched the leaves swaying in the breeze. Trucks and cars sped past on the road below her. She wondered where they were all going. She sat up straight when a truck pulled into the drive leading to the chicken house. She was all alone and quite a distance away from the house and hatchery, she realized.

The truck ground to a stop, and a middle-aged man leaned out the window, looking at her. Lizzie drew her knees up, pulling her skirt and apron down over her shoes, wrapping her hands around her legs. She gazed up at the driver, hoping he was only asking for directions and would soon be on his way.

"Hello," he said, looking down at her while a slow smile spread across his face. His hairline had receded to such a point that his forehead looked huge. When he took off his dark sunglasses, his

brown eyes twinkled at her.

Lizzie smiled up at him. He looked quite harmless, she decided, so she took another bite of her chocolate chip cookie.

"Hello," she said.

"So, why is a young thing like you eating her lunch in a place like this?" he asked, all his white teeth showing as his smile widened.

For some reason, Lizzie thought of the wolf in *Little Red Riding Hood*.

"This is my first day grading eggs for Mr. Martin," Lizzie said.

He opened his door and climbed down from the truck. Lizzie blinked, holding her breath as he adjusted his belt and walked over to her. He was very tall, his shoulders bulging beneath his flannel shirt. He put his hands on his hips and stood quietly in front of her. Lizzie took a deep breath.

"You don't suppose he'd give me a job, do you?" he asked, laughing now.

Lizzie didn't know what to say or think about this man. He was not unattractive. Actually, he was rather good-looking in a masculine way, and he certainly was friendly enough. She felt guilty smiling too much, remembering all Mam's warnings about strange men and that you could never tell what their intentions really were.

Lizzie lowered her eyes and said, "I don't know."

Suddenly he sat down on the grass beside her.

"Do you mind if I wait until Darwin is finished with his lunch?" he asked. "I'm here for an order of

eggs to take to Harrisburg."

Lizzie snapped the lid on her lunchbox.

"N...no, that's all right," she said, edging away from him.

He turned to look directly at her.

"You don't need to be afraid of me. I'm quite harmless. I have no bad intentions. Darwin knows me really well. I've been buying eggs from him for years."

"Oh," was all Lizzie could think of to say.

"What's your name?" he asked, still watching her.

"L...Lizzie. Or Elizabeth," she added.

"Elizabeth. That's a beautiful name."

Lizzie turned to thank him, but his brown eyes were too disconcerting so she looked down at the grass, a slow blush creeping across her cheeks. Now she was absolutely at a loss. She didn't understand her rapidly beating heart. Was it fear, or just the unusual way he spoke to her? She couldn't remain sitting here beside this man. What would Mam say?

So she tucked back her hair and got to her feet, bending to pick up her lunch.

"I...I have a bit of cleaning to do," she stammered, without meeting his eyes.

"Really? I bet your lunch hour isn't up yet. Why don't you stay here and talk awhile?"

"I really should...shouldn't."

"Are you Mennonite?" he asked suddenly.

"No. I'm...I'm Amish."

"Really?"

There was nothing to say to that, so she stayed

quiet, holding her lunch with both hands, her eyes downcast.

"Let me guess how old you are. Seventeen? Eighteen?"

Lizzie shook her head, a small smile playing around the corners of her mouth.

"I'm 15."

"I don't believe it."

"Yes, I am. I'll be 16 in a few months."

He said nothing, and Lizzie was puzzled, so she looked at him again. His brown eyes were still as unsettling as ever, and she knew that she needed to get away, anywhere, do anything, because something, she didn't know what, made her think of Mam's warnings. A whisper of guilt was beginning to shadow her.

That afternoon, Lizzie's thoughts were completely jumbled as she continued to grade eggs. She couldn't understand them. Her lunch hour had turned into a jigsaw puzzle of questions, but without a design and without many of the pieces.

Lizzie had not really been afraid of the man. Yet, why had she walked away from him? He was very friendly, actually. She felt like she should go home and tell Mam and Emma all about her lunch hour, but she knew she couldn't. How often did he pick up eggs?

She let go of the eggs and raised her cold hands to cool her face. It was just the way he said "Elizabeth." That was all. She needed to go home and tell Mam. She also knew she wouldn't.

Chapter 23

OVER THE NEXT WEEK, LIZZIE LEARNED TO love her job at the egg-grading machine. A week after she started working, a young woman named Dora joined her. They split the work, with Lizzie putting all the eggs on cardboard flats, while Dora placed the eggs on the belt.

Dora was older and had never married, perhaps because of her health problems. She was an epileptic and her seizures could occur at any moment. She was soft-spoken and shy when she first met Lizzie, but as the weeks passed and the two of them worked side-by-side at the grading machine, she became friendlier.

Every day at lunch, they sat beneath the oak tree in the soft fragrant grass and shared the food they had packed. Dora's mother made soft, light-as-a-feather dinner rolls, which melted in Lizzie's mouth. Sometimes she also sent chicken salad made with great succulent chunks of white chicken and crispy

pieces of celery and onion, mixed with creamy white mayonnaise. Lizzie shared Mam's homemade cupcakes filled with lovely white frosting or her big, round molasses cookies sprinkled with sugar.

They covered many subjects as they ate. Dora even talked about getting married, although shyly and a bit wistfully. Lizzie felt so sorry for her, it actually hurt. Lizzie admitted that she couldn't wait to turn 16 and start dating. But who would ask her?

One afternoon, when the leaves were turning colors and the breeze was a bit chilly, Lizzie and Dora sat by the oak tree with their sweaters wrapped around them as they finished their lunches. Lizzie leaned back against the rough bark of the oak tree and closed her eyes, sighing. Dora turned toward her.

"Lizzie, you better be careful with that Don Albert," she said.

Lizzie's eyes flew open and she sat straight up, staring at Dora, her cheeks flaming. "Dora! I'm not...I'm not...," she stammered.

The eggman's name was Don Albert, and he wasn't married, he had told her. He always stopped to talk to her when he came to pick up the eggs. His attention made her heart flutter each time and the color rise in her cheeks. Lizzie wondered if that was how it felt to have a real boyfriend. Dora always watched him when he talked to Lizzie, her eyebrows drawn down and her mouth unsmiling.

There was no doubt about it, Lizzie was flattered by this handsome stranger's attention. It brought

a thread of excitement to her otherwise mundane job. But she kept her feelings to herself, never telling Mam or Emma. She almost confided in Mandy one evening when she was feeling especially guilty. But she convinced herself that there was no harm done as long as she only talked to him and stayed polite and respectful.

"I know. I know exactly what you mean, but I can also tell how glad you are to see him come for eggs on Tuesdays. He's a nice-looking man, and no matter what you think, you are an innocent young girl. If I were you, I would be extremely careful."

"I wasn't even thinking about him. I would never go out with him or try and ...flirt with him," Lizzie said.

Dora looked at her steadily, as if she knew more than Lizzie was willing to admit. Finding it hard to meet her gaze, Lizzie lowered her eyes and felt a little cheap and guilty.

"Lizzie, I know you want to be a good Christian, and you haven't met many temptations in the world, as young as you are. But be careful, because you could be playing with fire. Does your mother know about this man who talks to you every week?"

"Of course not!"

"Why not?"

"I...I don't know."

Lizzie twisted her gray apron around and around on her finger. There was no harm in talking to Don. It was only natural to be attracted to a good-looking man who called you Elizabeth and made you feel

like a princess. Besides, there was no chance of them getting to know each other better. He was English and she was Amish. Talking with him was just a harmless thrill to lighten up an otherwise ordinary week. She was sure.

The following Friday, Dora felt weak and ill with a headache, and she left work early. Lizzie finished cleaning up the egg-grader by herself. When she was finished, she threw out her bucket of soapy water just as a cool wind blew, tugging at her skirt. She glanced up and saw that the sky was thick with clouds.

She stood for a moment, her blue dress billowing around her legs, searching the rolling gray clouds for the first raindrops. Most of the leaves from the oak tree were already lying in brown heaps at its base, reminding Lizzie that winter was fast approaching. The fresh, autumn breeze felt wonderful after grading eggs all afternoon. She lifted her arms and stretched, glad her work week was over.

Suddenly two large, heavy hands encircled her waist. She yelped with surprise. She tore loose of the hands, whirling around to face her assailant as she stifled a scream. Her eyes were large with fear and apprehension, and she clenched her hands at her throat.

"You!" she burst out.

"Me!" Don Albert said, laughing. "Scared you, didn't I?"

"W...what are you doing here? It's Friday."

"Where's Dora?" he asked, not bothering to answer her question.

"She went home early with a headache."

"Good."

He took a step toward her, and Lizzie backed away. His eyes held hers, but with a strange new light, terrifying her so that she pressed both hands to her mouth. Her breath came in rapid gasps.

"Now, don't act all scared of me. I just came down here to ask you to go to the movies with me. It's Friday night, and I want to be alone with you. Let's go into town and have a good time."

Lizzie shook her head, her hands still pressed to her mouth, her eyes wide, watching him.

"Come on. I will be the perfect gentleman. I just want to get to know you better. Please?"

He spread his hands, and for one moment Lizzie thought how exciting it would be to throw all her fear to the wind and go to town with him. But the next moment, Mam's face and all her admonitions brought her back to her senses.

"No."

"Why?"

"I...I can't. I'm Amish. My parents would never allow it."

"They wouldn't need to know."

Lizzie shook her head, refusing to look at him.

Suddenly, he gripped her shoulders, shaking her gently. "You shouldn't have talked to me for so long and been so happy to see me. I know you were glad. I could tell."

"I'm sorry," Lizzie whispered.

Rain started falling in large splattering drops and

he relaxed his grip diverting his attention. Lizzie wanted to run back into the hatchery, but she was afraid he would follow her. She wouldn't feel safe once they were in the building and out of sight. She had to leave, and she had to leave now.

"It's raining. I have to go get my paycheck down at the house. I...I have to leave now."

She backed away as she spoke, her skirts blowing in the wind and her hair coming loose beneath her navy blue kerchief.

"Wait!" he called, as she turned and started running down the drive. "Come back!"

But Lizzie ran blindly down the lane, rain pelting her face. She never looked back, knowing she couldn't risk that. A sob tore at her throat and the raindrops on her face mixed with her tears, cooling her warm cheeks.

She heard his truck bumping down the lane before he pulled up beside her.

"Elizabeth!" he called, leaning out of the truck window.

Lizzie's pace slowed, and she lifted her face to him.

"Leave me alone," she said.

"Get in. It's raining."

"I can walk."

"No. Get in."

Lizzie stood in the rain.

"Elizabeth, trust me. I'll take you to the house. I promise."

Slowly, Mam's face burning her conscience, Lizzie walked around the truck, opened the door, and slid

onto the passenger's seat. He didn't look at her. He sat gripping the steering wheel with both hands, the knuckles of his hands showing white. Finally, he put the truck in gear and drove slowly down the lane and out onto the road. He turned left and then pulled to a stop in front of the Martins' house.

The wipers whispered across the windshield as the rain increased. It pelted the top of the truck and coursed down the windows.

Don Albert did not say one word as he stared straight ahead at the rain. Lizzie gripped the door handle as she opened her mouth to say something, anything to break this awful silence. She cleared her throat.

"I...I have to go."

He turned slowly and reached for her hand.

"Elizabeth, yes, you do have to go, but wait until the rain slows down."

He held her hand until Lizzie pulled it slowly away from his grip.

"So. That's how it is. Amish girls don't go out with ordinary men."

"No."

Suddenly, Lizzie felt horribly ashamed of herself. She had no business harboring flirtatious thoughts, of being glad to see him. It was not right. Oh God, please, please forgive me, she prayed, as tears pricked the corners of her eyes. Just please, God, let me get home safely and talk to Mam and Emma and Mandy.

She had never felt as if she had done something

so horribly wrong as she did at this moment. Little things in her life had never bothered her much, as they had Emma. But sitting here in this stranger's pick-up truck, the rain rushing down its sides, she begged God to forgive her. She felt as low as she could ever remember.

"Good-bye," Don whispered.

Lizzie didn't say anything. She couldn't. There were no words to convey the depth of her shame and misery. She opened the door and slipped out, standing in the rain as he drove away without looking back. Rain fell on her head, running in little rivulets down her cheeks. Guilt mixed with longing, obedience fought with yearning, all in one churning moment of time like the pinwheels Mam used to buy for them at the Ben Franklin store. When she blew on them as hard as she could, the two different colors became one constant whir of blended color. But as soon as she stopped, the colors separated and became distinct again.

"Lizzie! Get in out of the rain!" Darwin called from the house. Lizzie snapped to attention.

"Oh, yes, I will," she said running up onto the porch.

"You look like you've seen a ghost. Either that, or been scared out of your wits. How did you get to the house?" Darwin asked, peering into her pale, wet face.

"I...I walked," Lizzie said, unable to meet his eyes. "I...I mean, partways."

Luckily, Darwin left it at that as he helped her

into the house. He picked up her paycheck from the kitchen table and handed it to her.

"You will need a ride home, won't you?"

"I suppose."

"I'll see if Carol can take you."

Lizzie sat down at the kitchen table. The warmth of the room suddenly made her very, very tired. She crossed her arms tightly, pulling her sweater closely around her shoulders as she waited for Carol.

In the car, Carol kept up a running conversation, talking on and on about the flock of ducks she raised by the creek. She loved to see the white Muscovy ducks paddling along the water's edge, she told Lizzie, as they hungrily fed on the abundant watercress that lined its banks.

Lizzie answered in monosyllables, never quite sure what the conversation was about, her mind repeatedly drifting back to the events of this long, rainy, mixed-up day. She felt worse than she had ever felt in her whole life. As Carol talked about church and their need for a stronger youth group, Lizzie planned her way out of this miserable, alone feeling.

She would tell Mandy what happened as soon as she had a chance. She would help Mam as much as she possibly could. She would set the table, play with the twins, Susan and KatieAnn, and agree to help with whatever task Mam assigned her.

Then when supper was over, she would start at the very beginning and tell Mandy every detail of her ... what would she call it? It certainly was not a

friendship, and "flirtation" sounded too plain bad and disobedient. Well, she wouldn't call it anything at all. She would just tell Mandy. Mandy was so wise and attentive to all Lizzie's fuss about everything, always taking Lizzie quite seriously.

Lizzie was so deep in thought that when Carol pulled up to the sidewalk in front of Lizzie's house, Lizzie actually had to shake her head a bit to clear it.

"I'll see you on Wednesday," Carol said.

"Oh... oh, yes, of course," she stammered.

"Good-bye," Carol said.

"Bye," Lizzie answered, turning to walk up to the porch, certain of her plan that would not fail.

Chapter 24

After dinner, Lizzie went up to her room. She found her Bible in her nightstand drawer and carried it with her as she climbed into bed. She propped up both pillows and leaned back against the headboard. She bent her head over her Bible in her lap.

Very little about the Bible made sense to Lizzie. Plus reading it was usually inconvenient. Even on gorgeous Sundays when their church district wasn't meeting, Dat insisted on taking time to study the Bible.

Once when Lizzie was little and the leaves were orange and red, Dat said to Mam, "Let's hitch up Bess and go to the mountain today."

"We could," Mam agreed and smiled at Dat.

"Good. After dishes and a Bible story, I'll hitch up the buggy and you can pack a lunch."

"We don't have to have a Bible story," Lizzie said.

"Oh, yes," Dat told her. "Every Sunday."

While Mam gathered the dirty breakfast dishes and put away the leftovers, Dat sat on the couch and read the story of the lost sheep. Emma sat beside Dat and listened attentively, but Lizzie wasn't interested in that little sheep story.

So what if he didn't make it into the pen with the others? He could stay out on the mountain till the next morning, when the shepherd drove his sheep back down that way. Lizzie thought the shepherd wouldn't have had to light his lantern and go look for the sheep in the dark. That was a lot scarier than waiting till morning. The shepherd was lucky he didn't get eaten by a bear, walking around the mountain yelling for one sheep.

Lizzie remembered Dat telling Emma to always remember to be a good little girl and do as Mam said. Lizzie had picked at a scab on her knee and wished he'd be quiet now. She just wanted to go for a ride in the mountains.

❧

But now Lizzie was reading her Bible intently because she wanted to be good again.

Mandy opened the bedroom door. Lizzie didn't look up so Mandy cleared her throat, but that failed to get Lizzie's attention. Finally, it was too much for Mandy, and she plopped down on the bed beside

Lizzie. "Why are you reading your Bible?"

"What's wrong with that?"

"Nothing, Lizzie, of course not. If it was Emma, I'd think it was good and natural, but to see you reading it so seriously is kind of a surprise. Did you have a bad dream?"

Lizzie put down the Bible and turned to swing her feet off the side of the bed. She lowered her head and whispered, "I wish it would all have been a bad dream."

Mandy gasped audibly. "Lizzie, what in the world?"

Lizzie sighed and ran her hand through her already tousled hair. "Mandy, you have to promise, cross-your-heart-promise, not to tell Mam or Emma, or I won't tell you."

"I promise," Mandy said. She placed her hand on her heart as she leaned forward.

"Okay," Lizzie began. "You know how dreadfully dull that egg-grading job is? I hate it so much. I would never, ever go near that smelly place if it wasn't for Dat and Mam."

"Ye-e-ss," Mandy said slowly, kind of as if she was carefully walking on thin ice, knowing it could break at any moment.

"Well, it's all right, I guess. The job itself, I mean. It's just that this very…well, kind of very handsome, but not very, *very* good-looking man started coming to the chicken house to pick up an order of eggs to take to Harrisburg every week."

"Go on," Mandy said, her fingers plucking nervously at the tufted chenille bedspread.

So Lizzie launched into the whole exciting, miserably tormenting story, trying to make it appear innocent, but also trying to honestly relate the parts that pricked her conscience.

Mandy listened attentively. She nodded her head wisely, her green eyes a portrait of her inner feelings—fear, suspicion, surprise, and, as Lizzie's story spun to an end, disbelief.

"Lizzie, I cannot believe how dumb you are," Mandy said when Lizzie finished.

"Why did you say that, Mandy? Why?" Lizzie wailed.

"Because!" Mandy shrieked.

"Not so loud!" Lizzie hissed.

Mandy lowered her voice and bent her head so close to Lizzie that she cringed.

"You are old enough to know better. How could you? How could you even dare to get in his pickup truck? Lizzie, can't you see? He could have driven off with you, and none of us would ever have seen you again. It happens all the time."

"Not Don Albert. Mandy, you don't understand. He's nice. He was serious. He liked me."

Mandy snorted.

"He did!" Lizzie cried.

"As long as you're going to stick to that part of your story and refuse to admit that you did anything dumb, I'm going to tell Mam."

And before Lizzie had a chance, Mandy was up and running down the stairway.

"No-no, no!" Lizzie called.

There was no use. Mandy was already clattering down the stairs. Lizzie flung herself on the bed and stuck her fingers in her ears. She was in a barrel of trouble now. Even the Bible did not give her too much hope. She felt like a real sinner. She would have to pray for a very long time, which she planned to do, as soon as she survived Mam's wrath. Probably, with Mandy telling everyone her secrets, Dat would get involved, too. Maybe even Doddy and Mommy Glick and all the preachers in Cameron County.

Chapter 25

Sure enough, Mandy stood at the bottom of the steps calling her name. Lizzie went downstairs without answering. She felt like a prisoner being led to her fate, alone and condemned because of what had occurred.

Mam, Emma, and Mandy sat around the kitchen table. Dat was in the blue platform rocker reading a farm magazine. Surely Dat didn't have to hear this, she thought fiercely. He was acting more and more suspicious of her ever since she started combing her hair a little more fancy. Lizzie sat down without lifting her eyes.

"So, Lizzie, what happened? I could tell the minute you walked in the door that you were not your usual happy self," Mam said, not unkindly.

Lizzie glanced nervously in Dat's direction. She swallowed the lump in her throat and knotted her hands in her lap. Slowly, resolutely, she retold the events of the past few months. She did not leave out

any details or skip over anything that had led to that afternoon.

She felt as if she was hacking her way through dense underbrush, and that the further she came through it, the closer the soft, yellow light of a relieved conscience warmed her. She couldn't believe how good it felt to be free of her hidden feelings in just in a few moments' time. For so long she had tried in vain to decide what was wrong and what was right. Sitting here at the kitchen table with her family, Lizzie knew. She knew so suddenly and with such clarity that the huge backpack of guilt, which had tugged her strength away, was suddenly lifted off her shoulders. She felt as light and airy as a feather floating on a breeze.

Mam was silent as Lizzie finished her story. She shook her head slowly. "Lizzie, it just makes me weak in the knees, the danger you could have been in," she said quietly.

"That's what Mandy claimed, same as you. But the part you don't understand, Mam, is that Don is very nice. He never would do anything dishonorable. I mean, the thing that actually scares me most is how much I wanted to go with him."

Mam stared at Lizzie. Dat put down his paper and looked at her as if he were seeing her for the first time. Emma's jaw dropped, and her mouth formed a perfect O. Mandy gawked at her as if she had gone completely crazy.

"Lizzie!" she gasped.

"Oh, my!" Mam said.

Dat stared sternly at her, his eyebrows drawn down over his blue eyes. "What did you just say?" he asked.

Then Mam found her voice. "Lizzie, let me tell you something. I believe that the real danger in this situation is not the kind all of us are thinking about. It is a far more exciting danger, isn't it?"

Lizzie nodded, her eyes lighting up with the knowledge that Mam really did understand. She knew!

"Yes, I mean... Mam, I want you to know that if it hadn't been for your face and my remembering you, I probably would not have realized that something was wrong. My feelings of *wanting* to go with him were very strong."

Mam bit her lip as quick tears sprang to her eyes. "Oh, Lizzie," was all she could say.

Suddenly, Dat sat up straight, put away his magazine, and, directing his voice to Lizzie, said quite harshly, "You're just a flirt, Lizzie."

Lizzie looked away, biting her lip.

"I don't ever want to hear anything of this sort again. You're only 15 years old. How do you plan to behave when you're 16, if you're already acting like this with an English man?"

Dat's words hurt as badly as if he had spanked her. Lizzie's face reddened, and she slid down in her chair, trying to become as small as possible. Every word was true, but Dat's harsh, biting tone produced a rebellion in her which reared its ugly head, blotting out the light of Lizzie's clear conscience.

"I wasn't doing *anything* wrong!"

"No, Lizzie, probably it didn't appear as if you were," Mam cut in. "That's the scariest part of raising all my daughters. You girls are not unattractive, and there are many pitfalls out there for innocent young girls. You knew there was something wrong going on, Lizzie, or you would have come home in the evening and told us all about this man coming for eggs. Why didn't you?"

Lizzie blinked, her face reddened again, and she stammered, "I...I guess I knew you wouldn't like me to...to...look forward to seeing him."

"So you knew then already that it wasn't 100 percent harmless?"

"Yes, I suppose so."

Mam sighed again. "Let me tell you something. When I was a young girl, I worked as a *maud* and became a bit too familiar with some of the family's hired hands. To make a long story short, I got involved in a frightening situation. You girls must learn that there is a line, sometimes a very thin line, separating friendliness from flirtation. There is nothing wrong with friendliness. But if you become too familiar, even nervous or thrilled about seeing a young man — or an older one, for that matter—you've already crossed over that line of safety." Mam laughed a bit, before she said, "Actually, it would really be nice if there was a piece of plastic tape surrounding you all the time, so you could clearly see that line."

Dat was nodding his head, agreeing with everything Mam said. "So, you see, Lizzie, it would

probably be best if you wouldn't work there any-more," Dat finished for Mam.

Lizzie was incredulous. Not grade eggs! That seemed like a dream come true until she thought of the fact that she needed to be working somewhere, and then grading eggs didn't seem quite that awful.

"We'll see," Mam said.

"Does this...this man still come for a load of eggs every week?" Dat asked.

"I guess. I mean, I don't know why he wouldn't," Lizzie said.

Dat gazed at her with a serious look in his blue eyes. "No, I think you had better find another job, Lizzie. The way it sounds to me, I see no wisdom or common sense in having you continue at that place."

Mam nodded her head in agreement.

Emma and Mandy watched Lizzie, their eyes large and staring and each of their faces set in a serious expression. Lizzie wondered if this was what it felt like when a criminal appeared before a judge to be handed her sentence. Everyone looked like unblinking owls, watching every emotion and inner feeling portrayed on Lizzie's face.

Quite suddenly, she knew she didn't detest her job. It wasn't nearly as bad as working away from home as a *maud* when you got so homesick that you had to try not to burst into tears at a strange, new supper table.

"But, Mam!" Lizzie protested.

"No, Lizzie, don't even try. There's just no sense

in letting you go back. I'll call Darwin this evening yet."

When Dat picked up his magazine and resumed reading, Lizzie knew without a doubt that her sentence had been handed down. A mixture of rebellion and resentment coursed through her, and she picked at the tablecloth with her thumb and forefinger, her eyes downcast. There was nothing more to say.

She sighed, stood up, and headed toward the stairs and her room. She needed time to think about the whole situation alone, away from all of them, even Mandy. As she went up the steps, low voices resumed in the kitchen, and she knew that they were talking about her again. Let them, she thought angrily. I'm always the one to get into trouble, and even Mandy is always on Mam's good side. They just don't like me.

Within her, self-pity fought with the warm brightness of a cleared conscience. Lizzie closed the door to her room quite firmly. She knew one thing. She wanted to go back and grade eggs again, not so that she could see Don Albert again. Well, not totally anyway. Instead, she was afraid of the unknown, of the new job which she knew could be a whole lot worse.

❧

Sure enough, that evening Mam walked over to the neighbors and made the phone call to Darwin and Carol. They were very kind and understanding

about the situation. In their conversation, Mam learned about a very good, new opportunity for Lizzie. Darwin and Carol's son, Lawrence, and his wife had just had a new baby. They lived almost 20 miles away on a farm close to Dunnville and needed someone to help with their other small children, the laundry, and the housework.

Mam thought it was perfect, a job for Lizzie that would take her away from the egg-grading plant.

The following morning Mam watched Lizzie a bit warily as she came down the stairs, unkempt and the last one to appear, as always. Mam hardly knew how to approach her about this new job offer, knowing she was still smarting from the previous evening's conversation.

Through breakfast, Mam said nothing while Dat cheerfully described the milkman's account of the weather prediction. They were going to have record snowfalls this year.

"It's going to snow in a few weeks, I bet," he finished, as he buttered his toast generously.

Lizzie watched with narrowed eyes, irritated this morning because he used so much butter. How could they all be chatting away happily as if nothing in the whole world had happened the evening before? Didn't they know she was extremely apprehensive about her future and fighting back some rebellion about having to quit grading eggs?

"Lizzie, pass the jelly."

Lizzie didn't hear Emma, so she asked again.

"Lizzie!"

"What? You don't need to yell at me," Lizzie retorted sourly.

So Mam kept the news of the upcoming job to herself until the dishes were washed and Dat had gone to the barn. She was wise enough to know she could not successfully approach Lizzie at the breakfast table when she was in such a stormy mood.

After the girls were chattering among themselves, Mam told Lizzie about Darwin's proposal that she work for their son in Dunnville.

Lizzie dropped her mouth open in disbelief. She stared at Mam without saying a word.

"Well?" Mam finished.

"Darwin's son? They're Mennonites and use electricity, don't they? Well, you know that I don't know the first *thing* about sweepers and automatic washers and dryers and…and…*toasters*!" she wailed.

Mandy burst out laughing and Emma promptly joined in. Mam hid her smile as she assured Lizzie that she was able to learn how to use electric appliances and that she was sure Darwin's daughter-in-law would willingly teach her.

Lizzie sagged on the bench and leaned against the kitchen wall, her arms crossed defiantly in front of herself.

"Emma can go!" she burst out.

"No, Lizzie, Emma cannot go. You can," Mam said.

"I'd rather grade eggs!"

"No, you're not going back there, Lizzie. We can't trust you after the things you told us last evening."

Lizzie was so angry she could not speak. The lump in her throat threatened to choke her as she bit her lip, glaring at Mam.

"You know that this new job can't be any worse than staying an entire week in Amish homes," Emma volunteered, trying to cheer Lizzie.

"You like to work away!" Lizzie spat out vehemently.

"Now girls, that's enough. I worked in English homes at your age, Lizzie, and it's not going to hurt you a bit. And yes, you'll be staying for a week at a time, sleeping there overnight, so you'll need a suitcase," Mam said firmly.

"But... but... it's my birthday, Mam! I'll be 16! Surely when your daughters turn 16, they should be treated at least a bit special, shouldn't they?"

"We'll have a birthday cake when you come back on the weekend," Mam assured her. "Plus we'll have all your presents, just like we did for Emma."

Lizzie clamped her mouth shut and said nothing. Maybe if everyone was so mean to her, she'd just become English.

"I think I'll leave the Amish," Lizzie ventured out loud.

Emma and Mandy stared at her. Mam frowned.

"Lizzie, now grow up and act your age," Mam said. "That kind of talk is exactly why we can't trust you to grade eggs for Darwin anymore."

"I'll be so old and tired when I get back, I'll never get a boyfriend," Lizzie said, trying not to laugh.

"Well, then, I guess you'll be an old maid," Mam said.

For a moment, Lizzie indulged herself, imagining how it would feel to be English. She had taken these mind excursions every since she was a little girl. They had started when she had sneaked a moment by the magazine racks at the grocery store while Mam shopped.

She loved to look at all the fashionable girls on those glossy pages. They were so fascinating, with long, shining blond hair and wearing all kinds of beautiful clothes. How would it be to look like that? She had always longed for high-heeled shoes after all. But she knew there was no way she could be like the women in the magazine.

She was Amish, and Amish people dressed plain. She had been content most of the time to dress in the clothes Mam made, pin her covering on, and go. She was starting to understand that there was a lot more to life than trying to get Mam to buy her a pair of high heels or even seeing Don Albert.

Being Amish kind of settled things. The English world was beyond her reach. That was just how life was if you were Amish, and Lizzie was pretty sure that she really didn't want to be anything else. She loved her secure circle of family and friends. And how could she ever hurt Mam and Dat by telling them she was going to leave the church? She wouldn't know how to be English now even if she tried.

Chapter 26

THE WEATHER TURNED PREDICTABLY COLDER
with gray skies and a biting wind as Lizzie carried
her suitcase to Darwin's car a few days later.

She had used up all her protests, including the one
about a snowstorm keeping her stranded in Dun-
nville. There was absolutely no use. Mam smiled at
her lovingly, telling her to keep her chin up when
she left, which did very little to help her depressing
thoughts.

The farther they traveled, the more Lizzie fought
her anxiety. It seemed to take forever, through the
large town where Mam had lain in the hospital
with pneumonia, onto a big three-lane highway,
past industrial sites and places of business, until the
countryside turned into an agricultural area with
large red barns, neat white houses, and tall blue
silos. Seeing that hospital only heightened Lizzie's
anxiety on this harsh morning—and she couldn't
shake the uncertainty that suddenly filled her. The

last time she had been in this town, Mam was very sick.

But soon they were winding their way through the countryside again. At a crossroads, Darwin slowed the car and turned onto a winding gravel road. They snaked between hills and woods, twisting and turning until it seemed as if they had entered another world. The fields were brown and bare with only the stubbles of the corn crop showing, along with dead grasses flattened by the icy rains of autumn.

As they turned right and started the steep ascent up a winding dirt driveway, Lizzie clutched the door handle until her knuckles turned white. A large, rambling old farmhouse stood at the top of a hill with a huge barn and outbuildings opposite it. The whole farm looked as if was run by a very busy person trying to do all the work by himself.

"You are about to meet young parents who need some help right now," Darwin remarked. He turned to look at Lizzie whose eyes were wide with consternation.

"I hope you can feel at home here," he added.

Lizzie took a deep breath, mostly to summon all the courage she could. "I...I'm sure I'll be fine," she said without much conviction.

Darwin led her down the sidewalk to the front door, streaked with mud from the farmer's boots. The entry was cluttered with children's clothes, boots and shoes, boxes, and newspapers, with a smell which belonged to all farmers' clothes. Darwin opened the kitchen door, and Lizzie walked into

a large white room with bright lights illuminating every object. She saw dishes waiting to be done, a table holding the remains of the evening meal, and clutter everywhere.

Darwin heard the delightful squeals of his grand-children in the living room. He headed for that side of the house. Lizzie didn't know what she should do, so she stood rooted to the kitchen linoleum, blinking in the strange, brilliant lights, and wishing with all her heart that she could go home to Mam and Dat.

"Lizzie, come meet Amanda," Darwin called, already seated on the recliner with a toddler on each knee.

Lizzie set down her suitcase and walked across the carpeted area. Amanda smiled up at Lizzie from her comfortable position on the sofa and extended her hand. "So you're Lizzie! My, I'm so glad to have someone come to help out. You'll have to excuse everything, because it's just a grand mess."

Her tinkling laughter captivated Lizzie, and she smiled back, immediately feeling relaxed. Amanda was small and round. She had beautifully thick, wavy, dark hair combed loosely over her head, with a small Mennonite covering pinned on the back. Her complexion was flawless. Her small upturned nose made her look like she was 16.

Lizzie told her that things really didn't look that bad, explaining how much work was involved when the twins were born.

"You have twin sisters? Oh, I would so love to

have a pair of twins someday."

Lizzie stiffened slightly, going a little queasy in her stomach as she thought about any babies, but especially two at once. Lizzie still didn't like babies. But that would appall Amanda. Emma didn't understand Lizzie's feelings about babies either. She loved to sew, whistling under her breath, which indicated that she loved what she was doing. And anywhere there were babies, Emma was watching the mothers, hoping for a chance to hold one.

Lizzie figured that she didn't like babies because she had been around them too much when she was younger. After all, Jason was still a baby when the twins, KatieAnn and Susan, were born. Emma and Mandy had been much more excited about the new babies than she was, Lizzie remembered.

"Are we really going to have another one? Jason is still a baby, sort of. And besides, he's finally cute, and now we don't have to have more, do we?" Lizzie had asked.

"Lizzie, you just aren't normal! Why don't you like babies more? You should be ashamed of yourself," Emma said.

"I guess," Lizzie said slowly.

"You could grow up and be glad. It's a blessing to have children," Emma told her.

Lizzie sighed as Amanda showed her around the kitchen. Maybe she wasn't normal, like Emma said. Oh, she knew she was normal as far as her brain working well because schoolwork was not hard for her. But maybe she wasn't normal where babies

were concerned. That was something new to worry about, seeing that Emma seriously thought so.

But sometimes babies screamed for a very long time, their faces looking awfully contorted. Some babies opened their mouths so wide you could easily see their tonsils, all bright red and looking like kidney beans. Babies were just not something Lizzie was very happy to think about.

But she had learned to hold a baby and figure out which end was up. Emma was a much better helper, because Lizzie got tired of babies quickly. But Mam told her she did well and that she would be a good mother someday, which made Lizzie feel considerably better about babies in general. Well, now Amanda needed her. Maybe she'd discover that babies and toddlers weren't nearly as annoying as she used to think they were.

Chapter 27

Amanda's children looked just as charming as their mother. Two boys with reddish brown hair and large brown eyes full of mischief bounced around on Darwin's lap. And littlest of all was a wee child of about two with a riot of reddish curls all over her head, a face peppered with tiny little freckles, and huge blue eyes. She was so tiny and looked so fragile that she reminded Lizzie of a porcelain doll. She hid behind the recliner, and when she thought she wasn't being noticed, peeped out at Lizzie. She resembled a rabbit, blinking her eyes without moving otherwise.

Amanda watched and smiled at Lizzie. "They'll be a handful for you. The oldest one is Timmy, then Martin, and the little girl is Bethany."

What an adorable name for an adorable child, Lizzie thought. Her ruffled dress had lavender daisies strewn into the fabric, which now, Lizzie thought, made her seem like a fairy.

Suddenly, Lawrence appeared. A husky farmer, he wore a red bill cap with a seed corn logo on it, muddy jeans, and a green work jacket. He smiled appreciatively at Lizzie and invited her to make herself at home, just as Amanda had done.

After peeping at Rosanne, the tiny newborn, Lizzie followed Amanda upstairs. Amanda showed Lizzie where she would sleep and apologized for the fact that she had to go through the children's room to get to her own.

The upstairs was freezing cold, but Lizzie was quite accustomed to a drafty old farmhouse, so it didn't bother her much at all.

She was just grateful to have a room of her own, even if it was cold. The tall, dark four-poster bed had a clean white quilt on it, and plenty of thick pillows made it look very comfortable. She hung her dresses in the closet and unpacked her suitcase as Amanda returned to the children.

Lizzie took only a moment to part the white curtains and gaze out at the barren, lonely-looking fields. Her longing to be at home with her family only deepened, but she resolutely turned and, with a deep breath, made her way downstairs and to her duties.

She rolled up her sleeves, washed dishes, emptied garbage, burned trash, swept, dusted, scrubbed floors, and prepared meals. The hardest part was making meals, because Mam did almost all of the cooking at home. Amanda helped her get each meal started, but then Lizzie was on her own to figure

out how to fix everything and get all the food on the table at once and on time.

The kitchen had never been Lizzie's favorite place, except for eating, of course. Lizzie would need every ounce of resolve today. At home, they mashed potatoes by hand, plunging a sturdy hand-held masher into a steaming stainless-steel kettle filled with soft-boiled potatoes. But Amanda brought out a strange contraption that she plugged into an electrical outlet. She pressed a button and the beaters began to spin at an alarming speed.

"Here, use the mixer to mash the potatoes. It's so much easier," she said, heading into the living room as the baby's shrill cry sounded through the house.

Carefully, Lizzie held the mixer in what she hoped was the right position and pressed the button. Instantly her hand vibrated and chunks of soft, hot potato flew out of the bowl, landing with soft, sodden plops at her feet. Lizzie quickly bent to pick them up, hurriedly rinsing the globs of potatoes under running water before returning them to the bowl. Grimly, she repositioned the mixer, pressed the button, and tried again. This time the potatoes hit the back of the countertop and slid behind the glass canister set.

Her face turning red, and her mouth tight, Lizzie returned the steaming potatoes to the bowl, held the mixer as straight as possible, and pressed the button only halfway. She was rewarded by the beater starting more slowly. The potatoes began to mash, and then all at once, the thing stopped.

Oh, dear, Lizzie thought wildly. Now I've clogged everything up. She pressed the button as hard as she could and was horrified to hear a high, thin whine. The potatoes flew first around the bowl, and then out onto the countertop, onto Lizzie's shoes, and onto her apron. Some even landed in the sink.

She was almost in tears when she heard Amanda's giggle directly behind her.

"The mixer giving you a hard time?" she asked as she patted her baby's little bottom, a diaper draped across her shoulder.

Lizzie turned sheepishly, her face red with embarrassment. "I just can't seem to get the right speed," she said nervously.

"It takes some getting used to," Amanda said easily and handed the baby to Lizzie. With a skill born of practice, she pressed the button lightly, finding the proper speed. The potatoes whirred into a fluffy mass. She added salt and butter and a small amount of milk at regular intervals until the mashed potatoes were finished.

With Amanda's easygoing, good-natured attitude, Lizzie learned to relax, ask questions, and take her time discovering the whole world of electricity. Toasters, blenders, automatic washers, dryers, and even the steam iron, which she used to iron Bethany's small ruffled dresses, were all new and strange to her.

Every evening she was bone-weary, grateful for a good hot bath and her warm bed with the heavy quilts which kept her snug and warm through the long winter nights. The children's chatter kept her

awake a few nights, but not for long, she was so tired.

Lizzie's sixteenth birthday fell on Thursday of her week at Lawrence and Amanda's. She woke up feeling much the same as always, although she knew she was crossing a big threshold into a new chapter of her life. Turning 16 was a long-awaited moment. Now she could be with the youth every Sunday. She could even start dating. How thrilling to wake up on a Thursday morning and realize that she had become a young woman.

Lizzie sat up in bed and stretched, wondering if Mam and Emma were remembering her birthday, and if they had gifts ready to wrap for her. She missed Mandy terribly, and the thought of being with her whole family made her giddy with anticipation.

Only two more days and I'll be going home, she smiled. Home had never seemed more dear to her than at this moment. She had often been away from home, but never over a birthday, and certainly never for her sixteenth.

Lizzie dutifully went about each task, whistling lightly under her breath as she hurried along. Two more days, two more days, she hummed in rhythm to her movements. The children could sense her lively mood and teased her playfully. They kept getting in her way and being generally annoying with little mishaps that wore on her patience.

Later that afternoon the door burst open and Lawrence stepped into the kitchen, shaking his hands and blowing on them to warm up. His cap

was pulled low over his forehead, his collar was turned up, and his ears were red from the cold.

"We better get ready!" he announced in his usual enthused manner. "Feed man says there's about two feet of snow on the way with high winds."

Lizzie dropped the towel she was folding and opened her eyes wide in absolute disbelief. How could he come in like that, as if this was the most exciting event of the year? Didn't he know how desperately she wanted to go home?

Lizzie's mouth turned dry with fear and anxiety. She walked quickly to the kitchen window, parting the ruffled white curtains to survey the sky anxiously. Oh, mercy! The sky was a flat, leaden gray with not a glimmer of sunshine or any puffy clouds to dispel her fears.

Amanda talked animatedly with Lawrence as the children skipped and sang about the coming snow.

Lizzie fought back her fear, trying to hide her feelings from the family. No one even noticed her, so she went on folding towels, trying to conjure up enough courage to mention the fact that she would like to go home sometime before the storm hit.

She opened her mouth a few times, glancing edgily in the direction of the living room where Lawrence and Amanda stood talking, only to lose her nerve and resume her towel-folding. Her confidence melted like an ice cube in hot water. They talked so long that she panicked, certain that they had forgotten she existed, let alone even thought about taking her home.

Lizzie set her mouth determinedly, waiting for a lull in the conversation. "Do...do you suppose you could take me home before the storm arrives?" she asked loudly. *I said it too loudly,* she thought. *Now they won't take me home for sure.*

Lawrence looked at her, considering her request before shaking his head. He raised his eyebrows at Amanda and said, "We really need you until Saturday afternoon. No use worrying about getting home before the storm gets here."

So that was that. Lizzie spent a long evening trying not to think dismal thoughts. She wished with all her heart Lawrence would change his mind after the snow began to fall in earnest, but she knew there wasn't much hope. She wondered if it was all right to ask God to wait to let it snow until she got home.

That evening she knelt beside her bed, her knees on the braided rug and her bare feet on the cold wooden bedroom floor. Lizzie prayed as urgently as she had ever prayed in her young life. She felt like Emma, but she was so desperate to be with her family, that this time she wasn't self-conscious about being on her knees. She begged God to get her home safely, and please, please not to make her stay for another week without seeing Dat, Mam, Emma, and Mandy.

But who knew if praying really made a difference? Emma believed it did. She always had, even when they were still poor and Dat wanted to move to the worst ramshackle farm ever. Back then, Lizzie had tried to pray for help even though she was barely 10. How could God resist a 10-year-old's prayers?

She remembered lying awake, listening to Mam and Dat talk way into the night. Dat's voice would rise, followed by a soft murmur from Mam, until her voice would yank Lizzie to reality again as she talked fast and loud, almost as if she could cry at any moment. It had been quite an ordeal, listening to their conversation. Dat had bought an expensive piece of equipment from a salesman, which Mam felt they could not afford. Lizzie knew they were poor, but she didn't know it was as bad as Mam said.

The thing that struck terror in Lizzie's heart, that caused her to lie awake deep into the warm night, was when Mam said she just didn't see how they could hang on any longer. Dat had answered Mam in the most awful, loud voice, stomped across the living room, and went out on the porch, the door slamming behind him. Lizzie thought she would surely die when she heard Mam crying softly, sighing, and blowing her nose. She thought of crawling out of bed to get on her knees to ask God to please come help them all. Dat and Mam didn't know what to do because they had so many bills and no money.

But that would have made her feel too dumb, so she didn't. She did turn on her back and clasp her hands over her chest and think a loud thought to God, asking him to help Dat and Mam. Later she thought maybe Jesus would have heard her better, because he was much smaller and not nearly as fierce-looking. He didn't look one bit scary, except

he wore a long, white dress, which was very strange. So Lizzie thought the same thought, except this time she directed it to Jesus.

She felt strangely quiet and not so scared after that. Maybe it was because the light went out in the living room, and Dat and Mam went to bed. Or maybe it was really that God had heard her, or Jesus. She was pretty sure that one of them had because she felt so much better.

The next morning when they were getting dressed, Lizzie had turned to Emma.

"Emma, did you go to sleep early last night? I mean, as soon as we went to bed?" Lizzie asked hesitantly.

"Why?"

"Did you hear Mam and Dat argue last night?"

"Were they arguing?"

"Well, yes, Emma. Really bad. Mam was crying. Emma, we're so poor that we can barely hang on here, whatever that means."

Emma sighed.

"Emma, who hears prayers the best, God or Jesus?" Lizzie asked, very suddenly.

"They both do the same," Emma said firmly.

"How do you know?"

"Oh, I just know."

"Does God hear it better if you go on your knees or not?"

"You have to ask Mam that. You should pray on your knees, though. I mean, everyone does in church," Emma had said.

Now here she was, on her knees with Lawrence and Amanda's children giggling and jumping on the bed in the adjoining room. But Lizzie barely heard them, she was so engrossed in wondering if God was hearing her prayer and would answer somehow. She certainly knew from experience that you couldn't just pray for a million dollars, or to be really thin, and have God promptly answer your prayer, even if you got on your knees in the middle of a freezing cold, upstairs bedroom.

But she had a faint glimmer of hope that maybe, just maybe, this request was not too selfish or ridiculous. She hadn't really stated specifically or exactly how she wanted to get home, or how much she wanted it not to snow. She didn't understand very well how God thought, but then, she wasn't sure she was supposed to. Mam said God was her Master, so she guessed that explained a lot.

The following morning the cold tingled Lizzie's nose until she snapped awake, alert in an instant, the knowledge of her predicament crowding out the warm fuzzy comfort of sleep.

She leaped to her feet, throwing back the heavy covers, and tiptoed to the window. Sure enough, exactly as she had feared, tiny pellets of wind-driven snow whirled past the old farmhouse, covering the fields, roads, and everything in their path.

Her heart sank as she put both hands to her mouth and thought another silent prayer. Please,

God, just get me home. I don't want to stay here on Sunday. She wondered how many days it would take to dig out from two feet of snow. Why did God allow this snowstorm? Didn't he know she was stuck in Dunnville? Did he even care?

Biting her lip, she grimly resolved to take the day with whatever it brought and to do the best she could. She could not be a big 16-year-old baby, crying because she had to stay a few extra days.

It was a long day. The children were more noisy and active than usual, making Lizzie extremely tense and nervous. There was not one single lull in the storm all day. Every time Lizzie looked out the window, the same swirling whiteness beneath a grayish sky loomed overhead.

Lawrence and Amanda loved the snow, teasing Lizzie relentlessly about staying over on Sunday. They thought the snow was fun and exciting, so Lizzie tried to hide her feelings of desperation. Oh, how she longed to go home!

Chapter 28

THE FOLLOWING MORNING THE SNOW MEA-
sured almost 20 inches deep. Snowplows inched
their way along the township roads. Lawrence
announced at breakfast that he couldn't risk taking
Lizzie home that day since it was still snowing.

Without thinking or even caring, but desperately
longing to be at home, Lizzie blurted out, "Well, I
want to go home very badly. I miss my family, so
maybe if you won't take me, you could think of
someone who will."

Lawrence looked startled at her unexpected out-
burst. Amanda was immediately sympathetic when
she saw how upset and close to tears Lizzie was.
"Why, of course, Lawrence, your brother Philip
would enjoy the challenge of driving in this snow,
wouldn't he?"

Lizzie blinked back tears of genuine relief and
gratitude. She felt like jumping up and hugging
Amanda, wanting to shout and leap high enough to

touch the ceiling in her pure, unrestrained joy. When Lawrence went to the telephone, then turned to tell her that Philip would be there at one o'clock that afternoon, she thanked him with her whole heart.

Lawrence pushed the snow off the steep driveway with his tractor and at a few minutes past one, sure enough—oh, unbelievable sight—a four-wheel-drive pickup came bouncing up to the house. There were wings on Lizzie's feet as she sprang to the truck, waving good-bye to Amanda and the children. Then she was on her way through a white, white world as pure and crystal-clear as her joy. She was going home! Philip was a good driver, so Lizzie wasn't afraid. But she did keep pushing her feet against the carpeted floor, trying in spite of herself to make the truck go faster.

When he turned onto their road, Philip looked over and said, "You won't get there any faster leaning forward like that."

Lizzie laughed, sat back, and tried to relax. Then— oh, happy day—she was running up the sidewalk, up the porch steps, and through the kitchen door, dropping her suitcase and greeting everyone at once.

The house smelled wonderful. Mam's Saturday baking was cooling on the countertop—apple and blueberry pies with crumb toppings, a fresh batch of cupcakes with caramel frosting, and, her favorite, molasses cookies.

Emma was cleaning the upstairs, but she came running to meet Lizzie. Everyone talked at once, and no one listened to what anyone else was saying.

The evening wrapped around Lizzie's heart like a soft warm blanket, etching itself forever in golden letters in her memory. Welcoming love enveloped her, soft and secure, topped off with all kinds of pretty things wrapped in beautiful birthday paper and finished with bows on top.

Emma gave her soft, rippled, robin's-egg blue dress material and a small chest to keep her little treasures safe. Mam and Dat gave her a piece of navy blue fabric and two beautiful pillar candles with artificial flower rings to arrange around their bases. Mandy's present was a new scarf and gloves with a white bandanna to wear when she went skating. Jason even gave her a small package containing two pairs of warm, woolly knee socks. The twins helped Lizzie open her packages while Dat looked on, his blue eyes beaming at her.

When Mam served the birthday cake and ice cream and everyone sang, "Happy Birthday," Lizzie's eyes shone with happiness and some other emotion that seemed to make her eyes produce tears. She wondered if it was possible to be so genuinely happy that you cried for no reason at all.

Chapter 29

Aᴏᴛᴇʀ ʜᴇʀ ʙɪʀᴛʜᴅᴀʏ, Lɪᴢᴢɪᴇ ᴡᴇɴᴛ ʙᴀᴄᴋ ᴛᴏ spend one more week with the family in Dunnville. And then she stayed home for a week so she could have intensive lessons in learning to make her own dresses, capes, and aprons. It was time, now that was 16.

Emma was already sewing most everything, including coverings for the whole family, which at 17 years of age was no easy feat. She was naturally an accomplished seamstress, taking her time and measuring carefully, while constantly whistling under her breath. She was never happier than when she sat at the sewing machine after she had finished all the cleaning. It was her reward. That was just how Emma was.

Lizzie used to envy Emma's ability to sew, embroider, and crochet, but she never had the patience to sit still with hand-sewing like Emma did. It wasn't that she hadn't tried, especially embroidering. Mam

loved to buy cute iron-on transfers of little houses or animals for the girls to cross-stitch. Even Mandy sat patiently still as she learned how to tie a knot at the end of thread, how to thread a needle, and how to separate the strands of embroidery floss. But Lizzie got tired very quickly.

Lizzie knew that this time Mam wouldn't let her escape sewing lessons, even though she had so long dreaded and detested every part of it. Lizzie had tried many times to use their treadle sewing machine, halfheartedly teaching herself until the fabric got all bunched up on the wrong side of the presser foot. Lizzie's left-handedness was a real hurdle. The seam she was trying to sew should have been to the right, while the large piece of fabric she was sewing should have been to the left on the sewing machine's flat surface.

But for Lizzie, everything was exactly opposite. She needed to stuff all the fabric under the machine itself, which meant she couldn't see well. Inevitably, she sewed the seam crooked. Of course she disliked any sewing project. And until she was 16, she refused to trouble herself with the thought that someday she would need to learn how to sew. Unfortunately, Lizzie often thought, you couldn't just walk into a store and buy Amish women's clothes.

The happiness she felt from having completed two weeks in Dunnville spread its warm glow through her heart for quite a while. She was so glad to be at home and so happy to sleep with Mandy in their bed. They giggled and read books by the light

of the kerosene lamp, which they perched precariously over their mattress. Sometimes they tiptoed to the kitchen for bologna and cheese sandwiches, along with some lemonade, taking the goodies back to their room for a late-night picnic on the floor.

These days Lizzie was happy to hang out the family's laundry, even whistling under her breath sometimes, which actually alarmed her. Had she picked up Emma's annoying habit without even trying? She worked as fast as she possibly could because the frigid air soon numbed her fingers. She rapidly picked up the clothes and clipped them onto the wash line with wooden clothespins.

Then she scuttled back to the protection of the old washhouse, which wasn't much, but the hot water felt good to her hands as she lifted the clothing out of the washer tub and put the soaking laundry through the wringer piece by piece. The air motor hummed at her feet. As steam rose to envelop her face, her soft whistle turned full-fledged and shrill. It was wonderful to be home and using Mam's wringer washer in the tumbledown old washhouse. She must be growing up, she realized. She used to despise Monday mornings.

❧

She had first learned to do the family wash when she was 10 and Emma was 11. First they had sorted mountains of laundry from a big plastic hamper packed full of dirty clothes. A hose hung in the

white Maytag wringer washer with steaming hot water pouring out of it. They had pushed the granite rinse tub up against the washer, ready to fill it with rinse water.

The washing machine was powered by a small gas engine, which Dat would start for them when they were ready. They were too small either to fill the engine with gasoline or to try to start it. Lizzie always made sure she was close when Dat poured gasoline into the engine because she loved the smell of it.

Everything seemed to be going fine the first time Lizzie and Emma did the washing on their own, until Emma suddenly howled in despair. She had reached into the fast-moving water, only to grab a big blob of tightly knotted diapers. Water sloshed over the side of the washing machine as she dropped the knotted clump back in.

"Lizzie!" Emma yelled at the top of her voice so her sister could hear her over the "putta-putta-putt" of the gas engine. "Go get Mam!"

Lizzie cast one wild-eyed look at the water slopping out of the washer and dashed madly out the door and up the steps to the kitchen. She burst into the house, shouting, "Mam!"

Mam looked up from cleaning the stovetop, an alarmed expression on her face. "Lizzie, whatever is wrong with you?" she asked, turning pale.

"Come quick! Water is slopping out over the sides of the washing machine and the diapers are so wrapped up in each other that they're as hard as a stick," Lizzie panted.

Mam followed her down the stairs, scolding as she went. "Lizzie, you have to stop leaving the diapers in so long. I have often told Emma that. What were you doing?"

They came to the washhouse where Emma stood wringing her hands, despair on her face. She looked relieved to see Mam and burst out, "Mam, the diapers are knotted so tight it isn't even funny!"

Mam pinched her mouth, pulled up her sleeve with one hand, and plunged the other into the washer. She came up with a mass of very white, very knotted diapers, which she proceeded to pull apart with strong hands, objecting loudly as she did so.

"Emma, where were you and Lizzie? You know you can't let these diapers wash for so long! Ach, I should just wash by myself, I guess. You girls mustn't be old enough yet." Mam twisted and pulled on the hard knot of diapers, dropping them back into the swirling, sudsy water as she loosened each one. Emma stood beside her, watching with a bewildered expression.

"Well, Mam, I can't understand why they knotted like that. Me and Lizzie were just sitting on the steps talking for a little while."

"Just be careful. You have to mind your business when you wash." Mam wiped her hands on her apron, watching as Emma put the diapers through the wringer, which pressed out the water from the diapers and then deposited them into the blue rinse water.

Mam turned to go but paused again to watch

Emma rinsing them. "Be sure and rinse them thoroughly. The last time you washed, the diapers were as stiff as a board."

That did it. Lizzie decided she didn't like Mam that morning. Who felt like washing now? Maybe the last time the diapers were stiff and not rinsed very well, but they weren't as stiff as a board. Mam stretched stuff. Lizzie supposed that's where she got it. At least Emma claimed Lizzie did, too—stretch the truth that is, not rinse the diapers.

These days, Lizzie didn't mind doing the laundry as much, even when it was bitterly cold. She lugged the wicker clothes basket filled with wet clothes out to the wash line and then used wooden clothes pins to hang the snowy white, sweet-smelling shirts. They blew straight out and away from her on the sharp winter breeze, flapping quietly as Emma hung each one up.

Things were better at home since Lizzie returned from Dunnville. No one mentioned Don Albert anymore. Lizzie thought about him less, too, now that she was 16 and would soon be running around with Emma on the weekends.

After she had hung the final load of laundry on the line, she swept the last of the water across the old wooden floor, washing out the wringer washer and rinse tubs well. Banging the wooden washhouse door, she ran down the steps and dashed into the

kitchen, drawn by the rich aroma of freshly baked molasses cookies.

Ever since Lizzie was a small child, Mam's molasses cookies were her favorite. Mam made them large and perfectly round, not too high but not flat, with little ditches across the top that she sprinkled with sugar. The cookies were perfect for dunking in hot chocolate. You could soak them real well without having them crumble and fall apart. And these didn't sink to the bottom like some did while you raced to the kitchen cabinet drawer for a spoon to save your drowning cookie. When that happened, the worst part was having ruined a perfectly good cup of hot chocolate. It never tasted quite the same when drowned cookie crumbs floated across its surface.

Mam smiled at Lizzie as she came into the kitchen. "All done?" she asked. "Did the wash freeze as fast as you hung it out?"

"Not really," Lizzie answered. "Mmm, these look good. May I make hot chocolate?"

"Go ahead," Mam said, turning to flip more freshly baked cookies expertly.

Emma joined them for a cup of cocoa, and the conversation turned to Lizzie's sewing.

"Oh, I dread it," Lizzie groaned. "Why can't Emma just sew my dresses like she does my coverings? I hate to sew and I can't do it."

"You have to learn, Lizzie," Emma said. "Who will sew for you after you get married?" she asked, her eyes wide and incredulous.

"You can!" Lizzie laughed.

"Oh, no. I won't have time on my old farm with all my children," Emma said, chuckling.

"Oh, Emma! You'll never change. I hope you do marry Joshua and spend all the rest of your days on his old pig and cow farm. You will live there until you're old and fat and wrinkly."

Emma threw back her head and roared. "And you'll probably be my next-door neighbor on another old pig and cow farm!"

"Oh, no, I won't! I will not marry anyone who milks cows, it doesn't matter how nice-looking, kind, or wonderful a person he is," Lizzie shot back.

"Now, now," Mam laughed. "Exactly what you vow and declare you will never do is usually what you end up doing."

"Not me," Lizzie stated firmly.

"Lizzie, you better start thinking about a husband. Four more days and it's your very first weekend to go with me to Allen County. Ephraim Yoders are having the supper for all the youth. Imagine that! Everything is planned already! I'm so excited to be able to take my younger sister along."

Lizzie smiled at Emma appreciatively. "Do you really feel that way?"

"Why, of course, Lizzie."

In that moment, Lizzie realized how good a sister Emma had become to her. Emma helped her style her dresses, she was teaching her how to sew and how to make her coverings fit well, and now she was actually looking forward to taking her along

on Sunday evening. Emma was a dear a lot of the time, no doubt about it. She seemed less bossy and more generous and unselfish than ever, devoting her time and energy to helping Lizzie successfully join the young people's social events.

"Lizzie..." Mam began a bit hesitantly.

"Hmmm?"

"I worry about you starting to run around."

"Why?" Lizzie turned to Mam, her anticipation still brightly evident.

"I just do. I suppose that incident with that... that English man, whatever his name was, just put a fear in me. You're not very...how can I say it? You need to be very careful, Lizzie. Remember how we talked about the thin line between friendliness and flirtation?"

Lizzie sighed and rolled her eyes to the ceiling. "Mam, here we go again. Aren't we allowed to flirt a little after we're 16? I bet you did."

Mam pursed her lips as she told Lizzie in no uncertain terms that finding a husband was not about flirting with handsome boys or thinking the decision was entirely up to her or depended on her appearance. Neither, she said, did fanciness and style have anything to do with it. Lizzie should learn to pray sincerely for God's will in her life with a humble spirit, Mam said emphatically, so that God could lead her to the right man.

Lizzie wasn't against praying. She had just never been sure how to do it right. Ever. She had always put her patties down, as Amish children were taught

to do. At mealtime, Amish people never prayed out loud like English people did, so Lizzie always felt especially ill at ease when she heard someone praying aloud.

Concentrating seemed to be Lizzie's problem. Dat told them to thank the Lord for their food and to look down at their plates as they prayed. Lizzie often forgot to pray because she was peeping at someone or thinking other thoughts. She didn't know why, but it seemed she could never stop her mind and pray a long prayer during patties down. She tried hard though. Emma dropped her head far and moved her lips as she said her silent prayer. Lizzie often watched her sideways, fascinated by her goodness.

Chapter 30

As Mam talked earnestly, Lizzie's spirits fell into a downward spiral. She wished it would all make more sense. "Well, Mam, you know I don't understand what you mean. If I comb my hair flat as a pancake and make my dresses as long as yours and sit on a chair with my hands folded my first weekend, no boy is ever going to look at me, you know that. That's what you mean by being humble, isn't it?"

Emma burst out laughing and Mam joined her helplessly. As Emma showed Lizzie a dress pattern that she recommended and Lizzie picked the fabric for her first "running-around" dress, Mam resumed the conversation. She first tried to explain to Lizzie how important it was to obey God's will, which basically, for a young person, meant letting her conscience guide her and trying to do what was right in all matters.

Every so often, Mam and Dat got all worked up about the girls' spiritual lives.

That whole year after Emma turned 16 and Lizzie's 16th birthday approached, the girls were learning how to live a new life, trying to live the way that Jesus taught. They learned the rules of the church, and they promised to obey and help build the church.

Mam even had tears, talking to them about all of this. Lizzie could tell that Emma took it very, very seriously. But the whole business depressed Lizzie to the point of tears. This would not be fun. They had to be so careful. What if they said or did one thing wrong ever again in their lives? And if they grew into old people, imagine the hopelessness of their situation, unless they all stayed at home and read their Bibles almost continuously.

Mam read her Bible a lot, urging the girls to as well. Emma read her Bible every evening before she blew out her kerosene lamp, but half the time Lizzie wasn't sure where her Bible was. Mam would have a fit if she knew.

Lizzie never told anyone, but the Bible scared her a lot. It just seemed too holy, too righteous, and too impossible to follow. She often wished she wouldn't feel that way, wondering if she was normal. Emma said the Bible comforted her, which went beyond Lizzie's understanding. That made her feel so guilty that she could never, ever tell Emma how she felt about all the talk about spiritual things.

As Mam launched into one of her speeches that just gave Lizzie the blues, Lizzie quietly slipped out of the room and went up to her bedroom.

She heard steps coming up the stairway, so she quickly closed her door. Nobody had to know where she was.

"Lizzie, are you in there?" Mandy called.

No answer.

"Lizzie?"

She still didn't answer.

The steps turned, the sound ebbing away before starting down the stairs. Good, Lizzie thought. Mandy can go play with Jason.

Lizzie rolled over, searching for a book to read. She had read them all so many times she hardly knew what to read anymore. If only Mam could spot more mystery books, but they were getting harder to find. Lizzie just loved those books about teenagers not much older than she and Emma solving exciting mysteries, some of them even a bit dangerous. They were all interesting, good, clean books that Mam approved of. They weren't allowed to read just anything.

The last book she read was about a huge colony of bats living in a cave—vampire bats. If one of them bit a horse or a human being, the bats gave them a disease called rabies, which caused you to lose your mind and die a slow, painful death.

After Lizzie finished that book, she wouldn't go outside after dark. There was an electric pole light at the corner of their yard, which was actually the

neighbors'. Every night in the summertime, a cloud of insects whirled around the light. Bats often swooped in among them. Dat told Lizzie they didn't have rabies; well, only rarely. Bats also have radar that warns them of an approaching object, which makes them steer clear of people.

Lizzie told Dat that vampire bats are thirsty for blood; in fact, they'll sit on horses and drink their blood. Mam said she should quit reading those mysteries if she was going to be afraid of bats. Besides, very likely none of what they had in them was true.

Lizzie's Uncle Marvin had often told her about the time a bat flew into Aunt Rachel's room and sat in her hair. Rachel screamed and screamed, picking up the horrible creature and throwing it against the wall with all her strength, where it slid to the floor, quite dead. The bat was probably rabid, or why would it have become tangled in Rachel's hair? Evidently its radar wasn't working, which meant it had already lost its mind. So Lizzie remained unconvinced of Dat's reassurances, refusing to go out at night for a very long time.

She found her *Tom Sawyer* book, but she had read it so many times that it was boring now. She kept looking. *My Friend Flicka.* Oh, that was a different one. She had only skipped through it before. So happy to have something to read, Lizzie rearranged the pillows, flipped on her back, opened the

book, and started in. She was soon transported to a horse ranch in the West, where she worked alongside a family who owned a great herd of horses and cattle.

All at once she became aware of her name being called quite anxiously. It sounded as if it came from outside in the yard. She listened a while but didn't answer. Then she heard someone at the foot of the stairs.

"I *did* look up there!"

"Well, where could she be? Lizzie!"

It was Mam, and her voice sounded as if she was close to tears. For an instant, Lizzie felt like remaining quiet, but her conscience made her do what was right. Putting her book aside, she yelled, "What?"

"Where *were* you?" Mam asked weakly. Lizzie could hear the great relief in her voice. "We looked all over the place for you."

"I was up here."

"Then you didn't answer when I called you the first time," Mandy said.

Lizzie didn't say anything.

"Come on down now, Lizzie. We're having a snack," Mam said.

Lizzie sat up, fixed her hair and covering a bit, and checked her face in the mirror before starting downstairs. She was so pleased that Mam was worried. That was so good for her, because now she would be more careful about what she said and would like her every bit as much as Emma.

Dat and Jason were making popcorn. Lizzie was

instantly hungry. Mam had made a pitcher of ice-cold chocolate milk and put out pumpkin whoopie pies and blueberry pie. Lizzie sat in a chair, smiling at Emma, feeling quite pleased because everyone had been worried.

"Where were you, Lizzie?" Mam asked.

"In my room."

"What were you doing?"

"Reading."

"Didn't you hear us looking for you?"

"Hm-mm."

"I bet you did," Emma said.

"No, not until someone was calling for me in the yard." She unwrapped a pumpkin whoopie pie and took a huge, soft bite. The icing stuck to her cheek, and she wiped it away with her hand. Mmmm. Mam made the best whoopie pies.

The popcorn was ready, and Dat poured it into a huge, stainless-steel bowl, adding salt and melted butter. Everyone took a colorful plastic dish and dug into the bowl, shaking them down, piling more on top to make their dishes heaping full.

This was one of Lizzie's favorite snacks. Buttery, salty popcorn, washed down with cold chocolate milk. Amazing how you could have a whole mouthful of popcorn and the minute the chocolate milk hit it, the popcorn all dissolved and went to nothing. Kool-Aid, iced tea, or water did the exact same thing. She supposed that if they were English and drank Pepsi, it would dissolve popcorn, too. That was because popcorn was mostly air.

"Where's church next time?" Emma asked around a mouthful of popcorn.

"At Levi Kanagy's," Mam said.

See? There Emma talked with her mouth heaping full and Mam did not say one word about it, Lizzie observed to herself.

"I wonder," Emma said, clearly thinking about the main subjects of conversation for the last few weeks, "if everybody's sins are all forgiven when they're baptized, what happens when they sin again?"

"That's a good question, Emma," Dat said. "Actually, that's when the power of Jesus' blood goes into effect. After you profess to believe in Jesus, you become one of God's children, and your sins are forgiven when you repent and pray to be forgiven. That happens over and over again as we go through life."

Okay, Lizzie thought. Well, that makes everything seem much more possible. It didn't seem quite as dangerous to join church if you had a chance of making some mistakes afterward.

Lizzie wished they'd simply stop talking about all this serious stuff. Everything had been strict enough around the house lately. It just gave her the blues. She didn't know why things had to change so much when you got older.

"You girls probably think Mam and I have become a bit hard on you recently. We don't mean to be, but watching the youth join church this summer, and seeing how fast you're growing up, kind of

puts fear into us. We want to do all we can to help you girls be the mature young women you should be as you join the youth and go to singings on Sunday evenings." Dat said this so soberly, it sounded as if there were tears in his voice.

That was nice, what Dat said, Lizzie decided. She believed him, and she felt like trying hard to please Dat and Mam in everything. But that was enough now.

Chapter 31

Lizzie's intensive sewing lessons continued during the week after her birthday. One morning, after the breakfast dishes were done, Lizzie and Emma spread out dress fabric on the kitchen table while Mam baked cookies

"It's not straight," Lizzie wailed, as she started to cut into the fabric.

"Hold your scissors upside down, Lizzie. You're left-handed."

"Ow! Ouch. That doesn't work either. It cuts right into the soft part of my thumb."

"Well, it's one way or another, Lizzie," Emma said measuredly.

"Mam!" Lizzie screeched.

"What?"

"Didn't anyone ever invent scissors for left-handed people?"

Mam dried her hands on a dish towel and went to see what Lizzie was yelling about. After watching

her attempts, which were more like chewing the fabric than making a clean, slicing cut, she nodded.

"I see what you mean. Yes, I'm sure we can find a left-handed scissors for you at a fabric shop somewhere. Next time we go shopping we'll look for one."

So with a black cloud of impatience and frustration already forming over Lizzie's head, sewing at the machine went quickly from struggle to disaster.

"Not so fast, Lizzie!"

"Yes, you have to zigzag the seams. If you don't, they'll ravel apart, leaving long strands of thread dangling. Lizzie, you have to!"

Mam winced when she heard the chair thump on the floor, and Lizzie came charging toward the counter. Her hair stood out wildly every which way, her covering was crooked, and bits of fabric stuck to her bib apron.

"Mam, why do I have to zigzag? That's the dumbest thing I ever heard of. The fabric is already sewed tight with a straight stitch twice, so why do I still have to zigzag? I'm not going to." And with that, she flounced back to the sewing machine, leaving a trail of loose threads floating behind her.

Emma's patience was already stretched to the limit, so when Lizzie came huffing back, she put her hands on her hips and announced quite firmly, "If you don't do it right, I'm not going to help you anymore."

"But that's so stupid!"

"Do you want to have sloppy-looking pieces of thread sticking out of your neckline or from under

your cape on your very first weekend?" Emma shouted.

Lizzie narrowed her eyes, considering. "No-o-o."

"Okay, then settle down and watch me turn this knob. You have to stay on the *edge* of the fabric. You can't just zigzag anywhere you feel like."

Lizzie's sigh of resignation assured Mam that she was well on the way to learning how to sew, so she relaxed as she started a batch of homemade bread. Susan and KatieAnn pushed their chairs up to the kitchen cabinets. Mam let them stir the yeast into the water, her heart melting as it always did when they wanted to be her helpers.

The treadle on the sewing machine thumped fairly rhythmically without too much noise between the two girls until Emma showed up at Mam's elbow, looking peeved.

"Mam," she whispered, "Lizzie's dress is going to be way too fancy. She cut her sleeves so wide, she can hardly gather all the fabric neatly at the bottom of the sleeve."

Mam's heart sank as she looked at Emma. Dat was already asking Mam why she allowed Lizzie to comb her hair so stylishly. She was increasingly in that difficult position between Lizzie's strong will and Dat's fear of what other people would say about his stylish daughter.

Mam strode purposefully over to the sewing machine. "Lizzie," she said quietly, peering over her shoulder at the alarming length of fancy ruffles which Lizzie was arranging along the bottom of the sleeve.

Lizzie jumped nervously. She had thought it was Emma coming to watch her make the sleeves. "What?"

"You can't have so many ruffles, Lizzie. That's just not allowed. Emma's dresses aren't cut or gathered like that. You're going to have to take some fabric out. Dat will have a fit. It simply looks too fancy."

"Emma's dresses have exactly this many gathers," Lizzie snorted defiantly.

"No, Lizzie, they don't. And if that's how you're going to be, you may as well close the sewing machine right now and wear a dress that you already have for your first weekend in Allen County."

Lizzie set her jaw in a firm line and held her shoulders stiffly as she sat gazing out the window without moving a muscle.

"It's up to you," Mam said, turning to go back to her bread.

Tears welled in Lizzie's eyes as the battle between giving in and having her own way raged. Why did Mam have to have all these plain ideals for her daughters? And Dat was worse yet.

Well, they would soon find out that she was not nearly as good and well behaved as Emma. Why would she be? She never was when they were little girls. And besides, Mam didn't understand how important it was that she was right up there, dressed like all the other girls, especially since she always felt a bit different, coming from Jefferson County and living on this ugly old farm. Why, the barn wasn't

even painted, and they weren't nearly as classy as almost everyone else in their church district.

She knew, too, that her fight to look good would be a long battle. She didn't necessarily want to outdo the other girls. She just wanted to look pretty and be noticed as someone who was tastefully fancy. Was that so terribly wrong?

It made Lizzie sad, though, to think of hurting Mam and Dat. For a moment, she looked at Mam and thought about all she had to overcome, living on this terrible run-down farm. She had recently asked Mam, "Do you like it here now? I mean, better than you did that first year?"

Mam had gazed across the living room, seeing nothing as she struggled for the right answer. "Yes, Lizzie, I do," she said quietly, but there was a sigh in her voice, a kind of hollow undertone that wouldn't quite go away when she tried to use words to cover it.

Lizzie couldn't help wondering if Mam believed it was God's will for them to move here. Not only were they trying to make a livable farm and home on this heap of a place, but Dat's and Mam's daughters had to travel to another county for friends, both girls and boys.

She wanted to ask Mam how God's will could work if there were no Amish boys to marry in Cameron County and very few in Allen County. How will Mandy and I manage to get married if there aren't boys?

"Mam," she said when she got her nerve back.

"Hmm?"

"What does 'God's will' mean?"

"It just means he will be able to guide our lives."

"Oh."

"He has a perfect plan for each of you, and if we pray and seek that will, everything will work out."

"How do you know what it is?"

Mam paused. "You don't always. Although, I suppose if we made more of a sacrifice, instead of seeking our own selfish desires, we could tell so much better."

Lizzie's mind conjured up Abraham sacrificing a lamb in the Old Testament. Now that was confusing.

"What do you mean, 'sacrifice'?"

"It's hard to explain, Lizzie. I guess the more we learn to give up our own selfish desires, the easier it is to discern and be content with God's will."

"What do you mean, we have to listen for God's will for a husband? I mean, this is getting serious. I'm 16, and I still don't understand."

Mam put down her sewing and searched Lizzie's face. "Lizzie, if you read your Bible more, and tried to be more mature about your faith, you wouldn't be so confused."

Lizzie's face felt warm and she said quietly, "Right now, I don't know where my Bible is."

"Lizzie, I do not believe it!" Mam was shocked, as Lizzie knew she would be.

So Mam talked, explaining to her how she would understand more fully as the years went by. She had nothing to worry about because God knew her heart

and would help her through every situation as life went on. It was all very comforting that day, sitting in the gaslit living room, with the rain and the dark, scudding clouds.

Lizzie's heart felt lighter and quite unafraid as Mam talked. She still did not understand everything, although she was comforted when Mam said that finding the right husband was not a hit-or-miss kind of thing. Apparently it wasn't like Lizzie thought. Mam said that if you prayed honestly, God would direct you to the right husband, although somehow it was still your own choice. *Of course* you could marry someone that you wanted to! she said.

Lizzie walked slowly into the living room, trying to make sense of that slim ray of light that had pierced her soul as Mam talked about finding a husband. She picked up the sleeve with all the gathers, then looked out the window and down across the fields that led to the creek. Her shoulders slumped as she slowly, slowly let out some of the gathers, the battle within far from resolved.

She threw down the sleeve when the thread snapped and yelled at the top of her voice, a sound mostly driven by frustration at her sewing and her own personal battle. "Emma!"

"Coming," Emma said, dashing to her rescue.

As the afternoon wore on, Lizzie finally realized that it was perfectly possible for her to make a dress. It wouldn't have happened without plenty of help from Emma, but she began to see how the pieces fit together. Everything made more sense than

ever before.

When she pulled the new dress over her head, letting the soft blue folds of the skirt hang almost to the floor before Emma pinned the hem, she was so happy she felt like a princess. Whirling her way from the kitchen to the living room, she lifted her arms and told Emma she was Cinderella.

Emma grinned wryly. "Well, you're not exactly Cinderella, scrubbing floors as your sisters while away the hours in luxury."

Emma's own patience had nearly run out. Now here was Lizzie, the cause of a whole afternoon of stress, suddenly happy as a lark, showing off, in Emma's opinion, her still too-fancy sleeves. But Emma said nothing as Lizzie climbed up on a chair so Emma could pin up the hem.

"Shorter, Emma," Lizzie commanded.

"Lizzie, your dresses are short enough. No."

"I'm 16 now!"

"So?"

"Mam!"

Mam walked over, assessing the new outfit as Lizzie stood on top of the chair. In Mam's view, the sleeves still looked a bit too fancy. She narrowed her eyes as Lizzie asked if she could have her dresses a bit shorter now because she was 16.

"Why would you want to, Lizzie? Your dresses are too short as it is."

"They are not, Mam. They hang almost to my ankles."

"Stop it. No."

Mam turned to go back to her baking, and Emma pinned the hem securely. Lizzie hopped off the chair and glared at her.

"So, if I don't get a boyfriend by the time I'm 25, it's all your fault, Emma. Yours and Mam's."

"Stop being so childish. Joshua says that's about the last thing he notices about me."

"What?"

"The style of my clothes. Boys don't always think about such things. They think more about a pleasing personality."

"Joshua isn't the only boy in the world. Some boys notice how you look. I'll never be asked out on a date, as long as that dress is."

Mandy abruptly changed the atmosphere when she walked into the house from her day's work at the hatchery. She took one look at Lizzie's lovely new blue dress and shrieked her admiration.

"Li-izzie, you look so nice! You are so lucky to be 16! Mam, I want a dress exactly like that when I turn 16!"

Emma exhaled in relief as a big smile appeared on Lizzie's face and she said, "You think so, Mandy? Isn't it too long?"

"No-o. Not a bit. It makes your gray eyes look blue, Lizzie!"

"I made this dress all by myself, Mandy!"

"Did you really?"

"Yep!"

Mam and Emma exchanged knowing glances. Emma wondered later if Cinderella would be back.

Chapter 32

Uncle Marvin was Dat's youngest brother and only a year older than Emma. He had started accompanying Emma on the drive to the young people's gatherings in Allen County a few weeks earlier. Marvin paid half the amount the driver charged them, which helped cut down on expenses for Dat and Mam.

Dat's youngest sister, Elsie, was 16, too, but she had already joined another group of young people in a larger community about 90 miles away. She had found friends there who were more conservative like she was. She was still a dear aunt whom Lizzie and Emma were very fond of, but during their years of being with the youth, Elsie went her separate way on the weekends.

Not Marvin. He joined Emma most weekends and she loved his companionship, each of them sharing their own thoughts and opinions on many subjects as they traveled to and from Allen County,

where there was a larger settlement of Amish. Marvin had always said what he thought to Emma and Lizzie without inhibition. In fact, he had recently told Lizzie in no uncertain terms what he thought about her looks, her behavior, her attitude. In a way, Marvin was like her older brother. He cared deeply about her and wanted her to mature and find good friends.

One afternoon, he stopped at their farm to make plans with Emma for the coming weekend.

"Are you excited to come with us to Allen County?" he asked Lizzie as he sat at the table eating a whoopie pie.

Lizzie nodded as she watched Marvin eat. She had already had a whoopie pie that forenoon, but she wanted another one.

Marvin brushed the crumbs off his hands as he leaned back in his chair.

"Lizzie, I know you hope to meet some boys during these weekends in Allen County," he said. "But I have to be honest. Boys will think you're a lot prettier if you lost more weight. You're still a bit on the heavy side."

Lizzie was appalled. She didn't think she was one bit fat anymore. Well, she knew she wasn't skinny and rail-thin like some girls, but she didn't feel heavy at all. Marvin's comments stung, but Lizzie liked that he was honest. She believed he wanted the best for her.

That night at dinner, Mam was busy filling everyone's plate with steaming chicken stew. Large chunks of chicken, white cubes of soft potatoes, orange carrots, peas, and slivers of onion and celery floated in a thick, creamy sauce. Specks of black pepper and little pieces of dark green parsley dotted the broth. Best of all, Lizzie thought, were the mounds of fluffy white dumplings on top. Mam plopped half of one on each plate, and then spooned gravy over it. Cold macaroni salad and thick slices of homemade bread with butter and peach jam completed their meal.

Everything tasted wonderful, even the macaroni salad. Emma didn't eat very much anymore, picking daintily at her dumpling with her fork. She didn't eat any macaroni salad at all, saying it was too fattening with all that mayonnaise. Lizzie took a huge bite of dumpling and gravy, chewed thoroughly, and looked at Emma with narrowed eyes.

"Mayonnaise isn't fattening."

"It is."

"No, I know it isn't."

"Lizzie!"

"It isn't." Lizzie scooped a large spoonful of macaroni salad onto her plate, her second helping, before taking a large bite.

"Lizzie, mayonnaise is one of the most fattening things you can eat," Dat said.

"Who said?"

"I don't know. I guess everybody just knows—it's quite a common fact."

Mandy jumped up, opened the pantry door, and

came back with a jar of mayonnaise. "One hundred calories for one tablespoon!" she announced. "See?"

"If you're on a strict diet, you are allowed 1,000 calories. So imagine! One-tenth of those are used up by putting mayonnaise on your sandwich," Dat said.

"I'm not on a diet!" Lizzie said loudly.

"No doubt," Emma muttered.

"Mam, Emma is being mean," Lizzie said.

"Emma," Mam said.

So Lizzie ate a large piece of pumpkin pie for dessert, free of guilt, because it seemed as if Mam was on her side. That one piece was not quite enough for her, so when they were clearing the table, Lizzie ate another piece, only smaller, when Emma wasn't looking. That left kind of a yucky sweet taste in her mouth, so when she took the pie back to the pantry, she got a handful of stick pretzels from the jar. Emma came into the kitchen just as Lizzie grabbed another handful of pretzels.

"Lizzie," she said. "Are you still eating?"

Lizzie turned and ran out of the room. She felt miserably full. It just wasn't fair. Look at Mandy. She naturally didn't like to eat a lot. She certainly did not like creme-filled doughnuts. The filling made her gag, she said. Lizzie loved those doughnuts, easily wolfing down two of them at a time, the last bite tasting every bit as wonderful as the first. Lizzie threw herself on the couch, crying, sniffing loudly, snorting, and blowing her nose in a crumpled paper towel she had found on the floor.

"You just like Mandy better. You're both so much thinner and prettier than me," she sobbed when Emma followed her into the room.

"Eww! Lizzie, don't use that dirty paper towel!"

"I will if I want to."

Emma shrugged her shoulders, watching Lizzie crying on the sofa. Suddenly, Emma could stand it no longer. She sat down beside Lizzie, touched her knee and said, "Lizzie, listen to me."

"What?"

"Why do you have this thing about nobody liking you? That gets really old. You claim Mam likes me better than you, and now you're saying Mandy and I stick together. You know that's not true. It's always you and Mandy doing things together, not me. Now you even sleep with her in the same bedroom, and I'm always by myself. You know I like you just the same as I always have. Mam gets impatient with you sometimes, but Lizzie, she has reason to. All you do is..." Emma hesitated, because she couldn't say what needed to be said.

"Eat! Just say it, Emma. I'm fat and lazy. Go ahead, say it!" Lizzie burst out.

"No, seriously, Lizzie, I honestly don't think you like yourself right now—that's why you feel as if no one else likes you. Your weight does bother you, only you won't admit it."

"I'm not that fat, Emma."

"But you are."

Lizzie looked steadily at Emma. Emma looked steadily back.

"See, Lizzie, Mam doesn't mean to be unkind. She's so busy with the twins right now and wrapped up in her own little world. So why don't you and I write each other a diet every day? You write what I can eat, and I'll write what you can eat! That would be fun! Do you want to?"

There was a long pause. "Hm-mm."

"You know what, Lizzie? You're just not yourself anymore. You're not even *happy*!"

"Are you allowed to have *any* mayonnaise on a diet? Emma, I mean this—seriously—I can't eat sandwiches without it."

"No, Lizzie, you can have mayonnaise. But instead of eating three sandwiches at lunch, try taking one. You can have all the mayonnaise you want on one sandwich."

Lizzie thought about this long and hard. Emma watched anxiously as Lizzie blinked, chewed her lower lip, and stuck a straight pin in and out of her dress.

"Lizzie, don't."

"What?"

"Don't jag yourself with that pin."

"I have a rash from doing it."

"Let me see."

Lizzie showed her.

"Lizzie!"

"I guess it's a nervous habit."

"Why are you nervous?"

"I dunno."

They sat in silence before Lizzie said. "Okay,

Emma, you may write me a diet for tomorrow, and I'll write you one. Only don't make it too strict, or I won't stay on it anyway."

"I won't, Lizzie. This is going to be fun!" Emma beamed.

Lizzie didn't say anything. After a while she said, "I'm only 16, Emma."

"Sixteen is old."

"Is it?"

"Yes, it is. You're getting older." Emma nodded her head wisely.

Lizzie sighed. But secretly, she was pleased. How nice of Emma to worry about her. She really did care. Suddenly she leaned over, put her arm around Emma's shoulder, and squeezed. "Thanks, Emma."

"Now you can never say I don't like you, Lizzie. I do."

⚜

The first morning of Lizzie's diet, she stepped on the scales for the first time without hanging onto the bathroom sink. She had learned long ago that if you crept onto the scales a bit slowly while you held onto the bathroom sink, you didn't weigh quite as much.

She knew she weighed a lot. Way too much for a girl in her mid-teens. She stepped off the scales. Why? How in the world could she weigh so much? She needed to lose at least 25 pounds. No one had noticed anything different that morning. Lizzie ate a bowl of Cheerios and a piece of toast with butter.

But she drank only a small glass of orange juice instead of a large one. Later, when Lizzie packed her lunch, she took only half a sandwich.

"Lizzie, are you sick?" Mam asked.

"Why?"

"Half a sandwich? You?"

"I'm going to lose weight."

"You are?"

"Good for you!" Mandy had said.

"You can do it," Emma encouraged her.

All those words helped so much, Lizzie could hardly believe it.

That evening at supper, Dat had asked Lizzie why she was eating less.

"I'm not hungry," she said.

"You must be sick then," Dat said, taking a big spoonful of macaroni and cheese.

Lizzie swallowed, watching him lift a steaming forkful to his mouth, shaking his head because it burned his tongue. She could eat the whole dish of macaroni all by herself, she was so hungry. For a moment, she felt like crying, but the thought of her weight and the size of her waistline filled her with determination. She would go through with it.

And she did. The first few days were the hardest, but slowly the weight came off, until one Saturday morning she stood on the scales and weighed exactly 25 pounds less.

She was so thrilled she put her hands to her face and shrieked. Emma and Mandy came running into the bathroom.

"Look! Oh, Emma, look at the scales!" Lizzie had gasped.

"One hundred thirty!" Emma said. "You did it!"

Mandy clapped Lizzie's shoulder. "You really did!"

Mam smiled broadly.

"Well done, Lizzie," she said. "But you know, Lizzie, you'll need to be careful from now on. They say it's harder to keep it off than it is to take it off."

"I know," Lizzie said. "I realize I can't eat everything I want to, probably never in my whole life."

Chapter 33

THEY HAD A FULL CARLOAD THAT FIRST
Sunday afternoon Lizzie went to Allen County—
Emma's friend Sara and her boyfriend, Uncle Mar-
vin, Emma, and Lizzie. Lizzie had never been to
Allen County, so she got caught up in looking at
the homes and roads and scenery around this Amish
community. There were fewer hills than in Cameron
County, and so the roads were wider and straighter,
with only gradual slopes instead of long, steep hills.

When they passed a little white schoolhouse,
Lizzie knew they had reached the heart of the com-
munity. They went by a few Amish farms and then
turned into a straight driveway that led to a white
two-story house, a red barn, and a bunch of scat-
tered outbuildings.

The youth were already gathering for supper. The
hymn-singing which followed would be at a differ-
ent home, the same place where church services had
been held earlier that day.

Marvin talked to the driver about where and when to pick all of them up that night. And then they all headed for the house. Lizzie had one moment of wild panic as she tried to walk gracefully in her long-awaited high heels. They actually weren't that high, just high enough for her to feel very much like a young woman and maybe even just a bit fancy. She panicked briefly as she tried to walk smoothly and assuredly on the crooked cement-slab sidewalk. It was certainly much more difficult than when she practiced with the shoes in her bedroom.

Lizzie was plain-down proud of her shoes. Mam had been a real dear and agreed that she could have them when Lizzie found them at the shoe store in town. The heels were not as high as English women wore, and they tied over the top of her feet with black shoelaces, which made Mam feel comfortable about Lizzie having them. Dat frowned when she showed them to him, but he frowned a lot since the girls were running around.

He was just on edge about his daughters joining the youth at suppers and singings and doing things with their friends on weekends. Dat had been raised quite conservatively as far as clothes and certain social events were concerned. In fact, his dad, Doddy Glick, didn't like to see the young people wear anything fancy. Emma and Lizzie thought that Dat was too much like his father.

Dat objected to the way Lizzie combed her hair, he sighed if her dress was too short, and he made her change stockings if he thought they were too

transparent. She felt rebellious sometimes, but when Mam agreed with Dat, there was nothing to do but surrender to Dat's wishes, go back upstairs and redo her hair, change stockings, or try to fix whatever his gripe was at the moment.

A lot of their girlfriends' parents had the same concerns, so they soon decided that Mam and Dat were as fair as most other Amish parents. Emma said they were concerned that if their children didn't keep the *Ordnung* and rules, who would continue to build the church? Lizzie understood that, she really did, but she battled constantly for her own way. She didn't dwell on these tensions all the time; she just liked to look nice. She imagined copying all kinds of fancy things she saw other people doing, even when she was a little girl.

One summer, Mam and the children decided to take the train to Ohio to visit Doddy and Mommy Miller, Mam's parents. Lizzie was all excited because, as she explained to Emma, "When you ride on a train, you can see all the English people and their fancy shoes, and the big tall buildings in the cities that the train passes through."

"Lizzie," Emma said, quite seriously.

"What?"

"You shouldn't be quite so wild in your mind. Why do you have to look at all the fancy shoes, anyway?" Emma asked her.

"Oh, they just look pretty. Especially the white ones with high heels. If I'd be English, that is exactly what I would wear. They make a nice clicking noise, too," Lizzie said.

Emma said nothing, so Lizzie folded her hands in her lap and thought Emma agreed with her. She looked down at her own navy-colored sneakers that had a white sole on them, and thought she had nice shoes for an Amish girl. She was happy with her new lavender-colored dress with a black apron. She liked being Amish—she just liked to watch fancy ladies with high heels. Emma didn't seem to understand that.

⁊

All these years later, her high heels helped tremendously to make her feel more accepted by the young people. They bolstered her self-esteem. Still, this is not going to be easy, she thought, as Emma began introducing Lizzie to the girls her age.

There was a thin, dark-haired girl named Barbara, almost exactly Lizzie's age, who was dating a young man from Lamton County. She also met Mary, who had a round face, narrow, almond-shaped eyes, and very black hair. She was quite talkative and accentuated her sentences with lots of eyebrow-lifting and hand motions. She and Barbara were quite warm, so Lizzie soon felt a bit more at ease, although she still depended on her high heels for self-assurance.

When it was time to eat supper, Lizzie's heart did

an absolute flip-flop. She was almost overwhelmed with a sickening sensation in her stomach as she thought about filing into that kitchen full of boys and parents. Barbara and Mary didn't seem to mind at all. Lizzie sincerely hoped they didn't notice the color draining from her face.

When she passed the little kitchen mirror, she made a desperate attempt to check herself, hoping she didn't appear nearly as agitated as she felt.

Her covering was straight—a nice covering and it fit well, thanks to Emma. Her hair was still combed neatly, although not as fancy as she would have liked, thanks to Dat. She had successfully hidden her pimples with Clearasil. She was biting her lips. Have to stop that; looks too nervous, she reminded herself.

She stepped off to the side and lifted the top of her blue cape, checking the pin in front to make sure it was straight. She couldn't see her black apron or shoes in the mirror, but she felt quite confident that her shoes looked snappy. She wondered if boys noticed shoes.

Now there was nothing to do but face the whole kitchen full of people. Lizzie was aware of a line of young men heaping their plates with mounds of food. A few of them cast cautious glances her way. Emma and her friend Sara had already filled their plates and were talking and laughing with the long line of boys.

Surprisingly, Lizzie wasn't hungry or even very interested in what was in the large roasters and

stainless steel pots and pans on the long table. She just knew that she made it through the line, filled her plate without spilling it, and ate as if she was in a trance.

Running around and going to a strange community, meeting new girls and feeling so afraid was not one bit fun, she decided. Next to her, Barbara and Mary started laughing and giggling together, then suddenly, without asking Lizzie to join them, got up and dashed into the kettle house.

She sat alone, her empty plate in her lap, not knowing which would be the least conspicuous—to remain there saying nothing or to get up and hurry out to the washhouse after Barbara and Mary. Just when she felt like a true misfit, a young man tripped over her foot.

"Whoa there! Sorry!" he said, turning to look at Lizzie as she quickly pulled both feet back under her chair where they probably should have been in the first place.

"That's okay," Lizzie mumbled.

He took his plate to the table, then turned and came back to sit beside her. Lizzie didn't know if she should be pleased or embarrassed, but his friendly smile put her at ease.

"So...you're Emma's little sister?"

"Mmm-hmm."

"Sixteen years old already?"

"My first weekend."

She dared to look at him. His eyes were as dark as Mary's, his skin even darker than hers. A shock

of jet-black hair made him look mysterious, Lizzie thought.

"What's your name?" he asked.

"Lizzie. But I wish I was called Elizabeth, because that's my real name," Lizzie said hurriedly.

"Nothing wrong with 'Lizzie.'"

"It's not very classy."

He laughed unexpectedly, showing a row of very straight white teeth. "What would be classier?"

"Liz. Or Elizabeth."

"Well, Liz, Elizabeth, Lizzie, whatever. Do you play Ping-Pong?"

"Ping-Pong? I used to, but since we moved, we have no place to put the table, so I'm sure I'm quite rusty."

"Come on. There's a bunch playing in the basement."

❧

Lizzie loved Ping-Pong. She was still amazed that years earlier Mam had actually gotten them a Ping-Pong table for their basement. This was not at all like Mam.

One day when Mam was reading the newspaper, she suddenly said, "Girls, listen to this: 'Ping-Pong table. In very good condition. One hundred dollars or best offer.'"

Lizzie had looked up. "What's a Ping-Pong table?"

"Surely you know, Lizzie."

"No."

"Well, it's high time you girls learned. I'll call this number and offer them $75."

"Aren't you going to ask Dat?" asked Emma, looking up from her crocheting.

"Oh, he won't mind. He loves to play Ping-Pong." And with that, Mam was off, hurrying down the driveway and across the street to the neighbors' phone.

"Boy!" Emma said, dryly.

"I'll say," Lizzie agreed.

"She really must want that Ping-Pong table." Emma resumed her crocheting, her needle flashing in the glow of the gas lamp.

In no time at all, Mam hurried back up the steps and into the kitchen, waving the paper with the telephone number on it. "We got it! They'll deliver it this evening! Net, paddles, and all! This will be a big surprise for Dat!"

When Dat came home for supper, Mam was flushed and beaming. She could never keep a secret very long, so before the girls had a chance to say anything, Mam blurted out, "Melvin, guess what?"

Dat was washing up in the bathroom, but he peeped above the blue towel he was using to dry his face and said, "Now what?"

"We're getting a Ping-Pong table tonight!"

"Hah-ah!" Dat said, in disbelief.

"Oh, yes! They're delivering it from close to Marion for $75. It was advertised in the local paper for a hundred!"

Mam turned to the table with a steaming bowl of

chicken stew and dumplings, while Emma poured water into the plastic drinking glasses.

"Wonder if it's any good?" Dat asked.

"We'll see. I'll beat you good and proper, Melvin!" Mam said, her eyes twinkling.

"If I remember right, Annie, I skunked you last time we played!" Dat told her, laughing.

'Skunked?' Lizzie thought. This had to be some childish game they were all worked up about. Dat and Mam sure were acting dumb about it. 'Skunked'?

"What do you mean, 'skunked'?" she burst out.

"Oh, that's a term you use when one person has 11 points and the other has only one or two," Mam said.

"So...Dat was a lot better than you, right?" Lizzie asked.

"Oh, that just happened once or so. He didn't beat me like that all the time," Mam assured her.

Here in the middle of the youth in this basement, Lizzie was transported to that earlier evening. They had all sat down for supper then, and put patties down or folded their hands on their laps as they bowed their heads in silent prayer. Lizzie was so busy thinking about Ping-Pong, she didn't remember to give thanks. When Dat lifted his head she said quickly, "Is it hard to learn?"

"I'm afraid you forgot to say your prayer, Lizzie," Dat said soberly.

"She always forgets. She told me once," Emma sniffed.

"Emma, I do not!"

After dinner, they hadn't yet finished with the dishes when a pickup truck drove up the driveway and stopped. A dark green table with white lines around its edges and another white line straight up the middle stood propped on the back of the truck.

"It's here!" Lizzie yelled.

Dat and Mam bustled out the door, down the steps, and helped unload the huge table. After Dat wrote a check and thanked the English man who brought the table, he showed the girls how to hold the paddle properly. It was not at all as Lizzie had imagined. You had to hold the round, rubbery part in, and the wooden handle out.

Lizzie and Mandy tried to bat the little white plastic ball back and forth, but they hardly ever got it right. Usually the ball didn't go close to where they wanted it to be, and they bent over laughing again and again. They thought they would never learn.

But when Dat and Mam started to play, Lizzie couldn't believe it. They hit the ball back and forth, almost faster than her eyes could follow. It flew low over the net, always hitting the table before Dat or Mam slammed it straight back. Lizzie wasn't surprised that Dat could do this. He was a man and good at lots of physical things. But Mam! Lizzie was astounded. Mam's eyes sparkled, her arms flew fast, and her hand gripped the Ping-Pong paddle until her knuckles turned white. She pinched her mouth with determination, sort of like when she was upset. She moved faster than Lizzie had ever seen her, with

her feet almost dancing to keep up with Dat's furious pace.

Just when Lizzie was positive she could no longer take the suspense, Mam yelled, "Melvin!"

Dat yelled, too, and slapped his knee in triumph. He had hit the ball to the very corner of Mam's side of the table. The ball had gone down over, but first it touched the table lightly, meaning it was Dat's point. If the ball had cleared the table, it would have been Mam's point.

Dat certainly did not skunk Mam that game, because Mam won, 21 points to Dat's 18. Mam's cheeks were red, and she was laughing as she ran over to open a window, saying it was much too warm in the basement. Jason clapped his hands and squealed with excitement as he grabbed Mam's paddle and ran off with it. She caught him, pretending to smack his little pants' seat with it.

They played three games before Mam gasped and said that was it, she was too tired for one more game. Dat had laughed, begging her to play one more, but she said it was high time to put Jason to bed.

Lizzie hadn't played Ping-Pong regularly, so her confidence was a little shaky as she followed the guy down the steps. She smiled, remembering how happy Dat and Mam had looked that evening when they played together. Maybe someday someone would look at her that way.

In the basement, gas lanterns glowed bright and a woodstove in the corner warmed the room. At card tables groups of boys and girls played games, and a lively game of Ping-Pong was underway in one corner. Instead of only two players, there were four, which caused a lot more excitement, frustration, and yelling. When one young man became agitated, he stomped his foot and threw his paddle across the table.

Lizzie turned to look at her newfound friend and found him looking at her, laughing. His smile was so infectious, Lizzie laughed back quite unashamedly until she realized she didn't even know his name.

"You didn't tell me your name or who you are," she said, wondering if that was too bold.

"Didn't I? Guess I forgot or just took for granted you'd know. I'm Mary's brother, Amos."

Instantly, Lizzie saw that he and Mary both had striking dark skin and eyes. When the Ping-Pong game was over, Amos asked her to be his partner and play against Marvin and a girl Lizzie didn't know.

Lizzie hung back, her heart banging against her ribs, not sure she could play well enough to be in a game with four people. She glanced at Amos who gave her a reassuring smile.

"I...I'm not very good," she said.

"Sure you are," Marvin said loudly. "You used to be when you lived in Jefferson County."

Lizzie's face colored and she shot him a "Be quiet" look. He didn't have to say that so loudly in front of everyone in the whole basement.

Marvin's eyebrows spiked, and he said, "What?"

"Oh nothing. Come on, let's play!"

The game started in earnest. Amos proved to be a capable player. He was quick, so Lizzie came to depend on him when an opposing shot was too fast or hard for her to reach. When the opposing players scored nine points to their 10, Lizzie was breathlessly laughing, no longer paralyzed by shyness. She was having so much fun she quite forgot her misery of only an hour ago.

They played two sets, and Lizzie did not want the game to end.

But Amos threw his Ping-Pong paddle down, ran his fingers through his hair, and said, "It's too hot in here! Let's go for a walk!"

Lizzie didn't know what to do. Was he talking to her or Marvin? She couldn't go on a walk with him alone on her very first weekend. That would not be proper at all, she knew that, and she could just hear Mam and Emma on Monday morning if that happened.

But she wanted to go for a walk with Amos. He was fun to be around and quite nice- looking, but… she shouldn't, not her first weekend of running around.

Marvin found his coat and asked Lizzie why she didn't go get hers. "You and Ruthie can go with us."

Lizzie smiled shyly at the strange girl who evidently was named Ruthie. "You want to go?"

"Do you?"

Lizzie cast a sideways glance at Amos who was

looking at her, waiting to see what she'd say. "Yes. If you do."

"All right. My coat's upstairs."

Lizzie ran up the stairs with Ruthie, and they looked straight into each other's eyes, smiling happily. No matter if they didn't know each other before this, they were going for a walk with the boys! Ruthie's eyes sparkled as she tied her covering strings more tightly, checking her face in the mirror. "I'm Ruthie Stoltzfus, and I heard that Emma had a sister who would soon be 16. So you're the one!" she said, smiling at Lizzie.

"I am, yes!"

They laughed together as they dashed down the stairs.

Outside, the air was brisk and cold, although most of the snow had already melted. Lizzie pulled her scarf closer and shivered as they set a brisk pace out through the driveway.

They talked about all kinds of things with Marvin leading the conversation, as he usually did. Lizzie saw a few more Amish houses and learned about the community. She also heard about Amos' home, where he lived, and how many were in his family. Ruthie lived only a few miles away and had four sisters.

Lizzie looked at Marvin and smiled. He smiled back as if to say, Isn't this just the most fun ever? Her heart swelled with genuine fondness and admiration for her uncle. Dear Marvin. Even now, at this absolutely important time in her life, good old

Marvin was enjoying it along with her, just as had happened many times in their childhoods.

The hymn-singing was taking place a few miles away. Ruthie told Lizzie that when a boy took you to the singing, or when he asked you to go along with him, it was because he liked your company. It wasn't like a real date, not even the start of one, but it was exciting to see who asked you to ride along in his buggy. Sometimes a group of girls asked a guy to take them along to the singing in his buggy, which was all right, too. Ruthie giggled a little when she told Lizzie that it was a really great thing if someone asked you to go along.

Lizzie chewed on her lower lip, nervously eyeing the boys getting ready to go out and hitch up their horses. She saw Joshua ask Emma if she was ready to go, and Emma nodded her head, smiling at him. It would be so safe and secure to have a boyfriend, Lizzie thought.

"Ruthie, what about our walk? That didn't mean anything, did it?" Lizzie asked a bit hesitantly.

"No. We were just cooling off after playing Ping-Pong."

Lizzie nodded. But she couldn't help but be disappointed that Marvin and Amos didn't ask them to ride with them to the singing.

Barbara and Mary caught up with the two girls, inviting Lizzie and Ruthie to ride along with them

and Barbara's brother.

The ride to the singing was the wildest buggy ride Lizzie had ever experienced. She was so glad she was in the back seat and that it was dark. Barbara's brother drove so fast that she was immensely relieved she couldn't see the landscape flying past from where she sat.

More teams of horses tore along, both in front of and behind them. One by one, they overtook the buggy Lizzie was in, streaking past them as if they were hardly moving. Lizzie hid her face, hung on, and hoped there was no vehicle approaching from the opposite direction.

She was sure that they turned into the driveway on two wheels, the horse leaning at a 45-degree angle, but she didn't say anything because she was too new to squeal or state her opinions.

Chapter 34

THE YOUTH ALL FILED INTO THE LIVING ROOM of the large house where a long narrow table had been put together. It was made of church benches set on small wooden extenders to form a table top. Other wooden church benches were set on either side, and hymnbooks were piled in the center of the table. The boys sat on one side; the girls on the other.

Emma and Sara started the first song, an old German hymn Lizzie had often sung in school. She knew the words well and loved to sing, especially with a whole group of people. On this very first weekend she discovered the utter beauty of joining the young people's hymn-singings on Sunday evenings.

She was singing heartily when she looked up and saw Marvin and Amos come in and sit down on the boys' side of the table, followed immediately by two girls whom Lizzie did not know.

She blinked her eyes nervously, hastily looking at the words in the hymnbook. So that was how it

was, huh? You could go for a walk with a good-looking young man, and it amounted to nothing.

. Already, only a few hours later, he had asked another girl to go along to the singing with him. Lizzie felt absolutely dejected, her future of running around as insurmountable as Mt. Everest. She would have to have a serious talk with Emma.

She noticed Ruthie watching her anxiously, so she knew she had to paste a smile on her face and start to sing again. But all she could think about was Uncle Marvin having the nerve to do this to Ruthie and her.

She was not only planning a serious talk with Emma about how she managed to go for a walk with Joshua *and* ride to the singing with him. She had also decided to give Marvin a good scolding on the way home.

Lizzie felt almost as confused as she did one morning a few years earlier. As they got ready for school, Emma gave her another lecture about how she should look and behave at school. She wasn't even a teenager yet, but if she listened to Emma, it sounded like she was now too old to horse around with the boys. Let Emma be sedate and domestic, Lizzie decided. But she wasn't going to stop having fun.

Lizzie finished combing her hair in silence that day. Emma pinned on her apron, asking Lizzie to

straighten it in the back. There was a small piece of cloth sewn to the waist of their dresses, called a lebbley, and their black aprons had to be spaced evenly on each side, according to Amish custom.

"Yesterday your apron was so crooked I couldn't even see your lebbley, Lizzie," Emma informed her.

"So?"

"Well, you could let me straighten it for you."

"I can do it myself. Besides, I don't even care much what I look like. Around here, nobody really cares much about clothes. It's relaxed," Lizzie said, sniffing.

"I agree," Emma assured her. "But you looked so sloppy yesterday in school, I was almost embarrassed. Your hair looked a fright. I mean, I don't want to be unkind, Lizzie, but you should hold still and be a bit more quiet. We're not exactly little girls anymore!"

Lizzie narrowed her eyes at Emma. She had a straight pin in her mouth, because she was pinning her black school apron, so she didn't say anything immediately.

"Emma, we're not old yet. I don't want to have to grow up right now and start worrying about what I look like. There's too much to do yet, like playing baseball and going sledding and skating," Lizzie said, holding a straight pin to the lamp to see why it wouldn't pierce the fabric of her black belt apron.

Emma sighed, turning to hang up her flannel nightgown. She shook her head. There was no use trying to persuade Lizzie to act a bit more grown

up. Lizzie assumed she was fine exactly the way she was, although Emma thought she was too noisy in school, often speaking her mind quite loudly and at the wrong time.

As they splashed through the slush on their way to school, Emma hung back a bit because Lizzie was stomping her boots in the shallow ditch beside the road. Bits of slush and water flew in every direction, splattering anyone close to her.

"Stop it, Lizzie," Sadie Mae said. "You got my socks wet."

Lizzie laughed and skipped ahead, trying to catch up with Ivan and Ray. They were talking, never noticing Lizzie's approach. Emma watched as Lizzie sneaked up behind them and then stomped her boot in the slush, splattering their pant legs with cold, wet snow.

"Hey!" Ivan yelled.

"Cut it out!" Ray growled.

Lizzie stomped again, splattering more cold, wet snow across their legs. Ray put down his lunchbox, picked up a handful of wet snow, grabbed Lizzie by the shoulders, and rubbed the snow in her face. Lizzie shrieked and tore out of his grasp, stopping to shake the water off her face. It ran down her chin and soaked her coat. She rubbed a coat sleeve across her face in an effort to dry it. Her face was red as a beet, her bonnet pushed to the back of her head, her hair a disheveled mess, and the day hadn't even begun.

"Lizzie!" Emma scolded.

"What?"

"Behave yourself."

Sadie Mae was scowling at her and Emma looked embarrassed. Mandy walked quietly behind them, but her eyes were at least twinkling.

"That makes Ivan and Ray mad if you splash slush on them," Sadie Mae told her sourly.

Lizzie felt terrible. No one smiled—not even Mandy—so she figured that wasn't a good thing to have done this morning. She pinched her mouth shut and fell behind everyone else. That was just the trouble with getting older, she thought bitterly. There were always these unspoken guidelines about what was nice behavior and what wasn't. Who was to say what was grown up and what was childish? Emma? Emma couldn't always be there with Lizzie to remind her to behave herself her whole life long. And that Sadie Mae had nerve, telling her that Ivan and Ray didn't like slush splashed on them. How did she know? Everybody was mean this morning. Even Mandy was sober and serious.

Now, Lizzie sat at her first singing, wondering again if she had missed some important rule of behavior. She guessed she'd have to ask Emma.

Chapter 35

SPRING ARRIVED, ALONG WITH WARM, MELLOW sunshine and buds bursting from the maple trees in the yard. Even the old walnut tree beside the sidewalk began to shine with a look of light green mist. Thousands of tiny green buds were erupting from its dark branches.

The swollen creek churned on its relentless way to the river, muddy brown from all the April showers. Little green shoots emerged from the moist brown earth under its blanket of wet, decaying leaves which had mulched the baby sprouts to new growth.

Dat was working the horses hard, preparing the soil for another crop. Clyde was back in the harness, still bouncing around as if he had springs in his legs. But the spirited horse was learning to buckle down and behave long enough to pull his share of the plow.

Mam's energy level was almost back to normal a year after her bout of pneumonia, which comforted

and relieved Lizzie and Emma. She asked Dat to bring a few wheelbarrow loads of manure into the yard so she could start a new flower garden. And she asked the girls to help her in the evening with laying out a huge new rock garden on an unhandy slope between the house and barn where no grass could grow decently.

New Amish families were moving into the community this spring. When the Glick family went to church, they often met new girls and parents with small children whom they had never seen before.

Each weekend Lizzie went with Emma and Marvin to Allen County, which she looked forward to each and every other day of the week. Running around was even more fun now that warmer weather had arrived, because there was so much more to do. Lizzie thought that baseball games, volleyball, croquet, and just going for drives to different picnic areas or lakes with a group of young people were the funnest things in the entire world.

She became good friends with Barbara and Mary and often spent Saturday nights with them. One weekend blended into the next until Lizzie's world was filled with warm golden sunshine and so much to do and think about that time flew by like the spring breezes.

She still liked Amos, and she was never quite as thrilled as when he asked her to go for a buggy ride with him. Those times felt like romance to Lizzie, if not true love, although she didn't know what the difference was between the two, or how you could

know whether your feelings were right or not.

She liked everyone, and all the boys were her friends. But somehow, it seemed a little different whenever Amos was around. It was almost as if the group of youth was not quite complete until he arrived. And as soon as Lizzie knew he was there, she was not completely happy until he had noticed her and said hello.

There seemed to be lots of talk about Emma getting married in the fall. Actually, it was only teasing among Mam and the girls because Emma was still too young. She would be only 18 by November. Lizzie knew how Emma felt, though. She had secretly told Lizzie that she would love to get married in the fall and move to Joshua's parents' farm in Allen County.

The old place had a huge brick house with an L-shaped porch, a barn, and lots of sheds and outbuildings. It was the home Emma had always dreamed of, and there were stars in her eyes as she folded towels and sheets and placed them in the cedar hope chest that had her initials on the front.

Lizzie did not want to get married so young. She discovered that soon after she turned 16. Running around was much too exciting to think of settling down on an old farm with a husband and nothing to look forward to except cooking and cleaning for the rest of your life.

Mandy heartily agreed with Lizzie when they talked about the possibility of Emma getting married so young. Mandy nodded soberly though, when

Lizzie said that Emma had always been different as far as working in the house with Mam, and that she really enjoyed all kinds of domestic duties at a very young age.

"Hey, look at Clyde!" Mandy yelled.

Lizzie was in the garden pulling weeds with Mandy. She looked up, shading her eyes with one hand in the morning sunlight. Mandy pointed toward the big brown horse pulling the plow in the old hayfield.

"What's wrong?"

"See how he can barely settle himself down long enough to stay in line and pull his share with the others? He's always prancing or stepping sideways or shaking his head up and down. I guess he's just too full of himself to act decent when he's hitched up!"

Lizzie continued to watch as Dat plowed the hay stubble. He had already plowed enough so that the girls could see a thin line of dark brown, overturned earth following the curve of their gently rolling land. When Dat and the team of horses returned from the far end of the field, they came close enough for the girls to hear the clank of the plow and the squeaking of the leather harnesses.

Mandy shook her head in her wise way, clicking her tongue. "Clyde's never going to last in this heat!" she said.

Lizzie stood, watching anxiously as Dat turned the team of horses at the end of the furrow. What at first seemed to be an impossible turn became a picture of perfect motion, as Dat called and each horse

stepped tightly to the right. It seemed to Lizzie as if they all knew exactly what was expected of them, and they executed the short turn with no effort at all.

Except Clyde. He hopped about three times too often, tossing his head before Dat yelled at him. Lizzie looked at Mandy and they both smiled, knowing how impatient Dat was with Clyde.

As the team pulled the plow up over the slope, making the brown strip wider, the girls bent down and resumed their tedious job of weeding. The sun was very warm, reminding them of the hot summer days ahead.

"Wish we could go down to the creek and cool off," Lizzie said.

She plopped down between the rows of corn.

"Watch out! Lizzie, you sat on some cornstalks," Mandy said.

Lizzie didn't move. Who cared about a few measly little cornstalks? Nine chances out of 10, they wouldn't make it anyway, so what was wrong with sitting on a few?

"Wish we could go down to the creek," she said again.

"Wishing won't get you anywhere. Come on, Lizzie. Help with these weeds."

Lizzie turned and pulled absentmindedly at a few weeds.

This garden is way too big," she said.

"We need a big garden now. We're poor farmers," Mandy said, tossing a handful of weeds into her white plastic bucket.

Lizzie selected a wide piece of grass, stretched it expertly between her forefinger and the base of her thumb, and, lifting it to her mouth, she blew as hard as she could. A shrill explosion of sound followed. Mandy ignored her.

"That was a good one," Lizzie said.

She got no response so Lizzie watched Mandy pulling weeds. She was mad now, Lizzie could tell by the way Mandy jerked on the weeds and hurled them into her bucket. Mandy was so thin, Lizzie thought. These kinds of clothes made her look good, she decided, because the black bib aprons fit her perfectly. She was wearing a dark blue dress with its sleeves made in a looser fashion, which only accentuated her slimness and made her face even prettier.

Lizzie scrambled to her feet, pulled her bucket over, and began pulling weeds in earnest.

"Mandy, did you really, really mind going to church here the first Sunday we went?" Lizzie asked.

"I don't know. Not really, I guess. I mean, Elsie and Aunt Becca and Mommy Glick were there. But it wasn't exactly *fun*, if that's what you mean, with all those strange people staring at us."

"They probably didn't really mean to stare, Mandy."

"I know, but…it felt as if they were all looking at us."

Lizzie walked down the row of corn, lifting her bucket of weeds and tossing them across the fence into the pasture. On her way back, she said to Mandy, "It's because our clothes don't look right."

"What do you mean?" Mandy asked.

"I'll tell you the truth, Mandy. I feel so self-conscious and ugly since we live here. Our coverings haven't been made nearly as neat as everybody else's."

"I know. But you know why? Emma said it's because Mam comes from Ohio, and she doesn't really know how to make neat coverings for young girls. She never did. So Emma told me that's why she's learned to make them. Otherwise, we'd never look any better. She didn't want to insult Mam by saying hers aren't neat enough. They are alright for mothers and little girls."

"Emma can sew anything she tries," Lizzie said.

"I know. Did you see her make bib aprons? They're just as neat as a pin."

"I'm so relieved she's making our coverings now. I was so tired of being embarrassed. I just want to look nice."

Lizzie and Mandy took turns using the hoe to unearth the small weeds as they talked on. Birds circled overhead, calling while they flew into the old walnut tree at the end of the sidewalk. The diesel was droning in the distance as Mam filled the clothesline with load after load of clean laundry.

A desperate cry sliced through their conversation. Mandy dropped the hoe, and she and Lizzie turned to see Dat standing at the corner of the partially plowed field, waving his straw hat frantically.

"Something's wrong!" Lizzie gasped.

"C'mon!" Mandy called, already running across

the garden. Together they raced over the tilled plot and out the lane to reach the hayfield. Breathless, they arrived and discovered immediately what was wrong. Clyde was down.

It seemed as if time stood still, immobile as a huge concrete slab. Lizzie stood looking at the beautiful horse who tried desperately to get up from the ground, who wanted just to keep going. She didn't want to look at this fallen creature. It was so awful and so pitiful all at the same time that she could not take her eyes away.

Dat was panting, his eyes wild with fear and worry.

"You need to help me a minute. Lizzie, I'll hold up his head. You try and loosen some of the snaps that keep him attached to the team. I don't know if we can. Mandy, you might have to run to the barn for my leather shears. If nothing else works, we may have to cut the harness. Let's try and get him up one more time."

Lizzie worked to free Clyde, but she couldn't. Finally, Dat turned toward Clyde, lifting at the bit of his bridle. "Come on, boy, come on. Get up! Get up, now!"

Clyde tried valiantly. His eyes opened until the whites of his eyes showed the whole way around, and he struggled repeatedly to get his forelegs underneath himself for better balance.

Dat urged him on continuously, while Lizzie clutched her hands to her chest, bit her lips, and choked back agonizing sobs. What caused him to go

down? She was afraid she knew why, but she wasn't sure she could face the answer.

Dat kept talking to Clyde, trying to get him to stand up. The rest of the horses stood by patiently, tossing their manes as if they knew something was wrong. Clouds floated overhead as the sun beat mercilessly down on poor, struggling Clyde.

Finally, Clyde heaved once more with tremendous strength and managed to stand on all four legs. He was shaking violently, sweat dripping from his stomach and running down his legs in rivulets, pooling underneath him.

"Quick, Lizzie, help me unhitch him!"

Lizzie hurried to unsnap the traces that attached him, while Dat loosened reins and chains and took off Clyde's cumbersome collar.

"He's loose," Lizzie said, her voice shaking.

"Come, boy," Dat said gently, as he led him beneath the shade of a small locust tree. Clyde took a few faltering steps to the spot where Dat wanted him, away from the sun's relentless heat.

There Clyde stood, his head hanging down as far as it would go as he heaved great, unbelievable breaths. His chest and sides rose and fell, rose and fell, in an almost hypnotic rhythm. Lizzie clenched her hands in despair. She could not believe the amount of perspiration draining from this massive animal.

"Dat!" Lizzie cried. "Isn't there something we can do?"

Dat shook his head as the trembling of Clyde's limbs increased. He shook like an aspen leaf in a

summer thunderstorm, almost as if his legs had a power all their own. His nostrils flared in and out as he breathed in small, gasping, sucking sounds.

"Lizzie, I don't think so. I don't know. I should have been more careful. It's not even noon yet, and he just became overheated, I guess."

"Can you call a veterinarian?"

"I suppose I should. If you'll stay here, I can go, but honestly, Lizzie, I'm afraid he won't make it."

"Why does he tremble like that?"

Dat lowered his head as he turned to walk down the field lane to use the neighbor's phone. Lizzie called after him.

"Dat, could we try and cool him down with water?"

"Let me talk to the vet first," Dat said.

Meanwhile, Mandy had run to the house, looking for Mam, but she couldn't find her. Now Mandy came flying along the field lane, her skirts billowing around her knees, her face pale with fright. She slid to a stop when she saw Clyde standing under the locust tree.

"He's up!" she cried.

"Yes, but Dat doesn't think he's going to live much longer," Lizzie said.

They stood side by side, their nearness giving strength to each other. Lizzie was grateful she did not have to stand out there all alone with this suffering, broken horse. Tears pricked her eyes as she watched Clyde struggling to breathe. Poor, poor boy, she thought.

Then he folded, his limbs buckling, until he slowly sank to the ground. Lizzie cried and reached toward him, helpless, unable to do anything. Mandy stepped back, wrapping her arms around her own waist.

Clyde rolled over once, his legs stretched out, and, for one heart-stopping moment, Lizzie thought he had died. But his side rose and fell, his breathing accompanied by a deep grunting sound.

"He's never going to make it!" Mandy whispered.

And then Lizzie decided to pray. Whether God heard her or not, and even if he seemed far away, she needed to call on him right now and ask him to do something. They could not afford to lose this good, strong workhorse—God would surely know that. So she prayed, turning away from Mandy and toward the remaining team of horses who still waited quietly at the field's edge.

God, you are going to have to look down here and help us. Please let Clyde live because we really need him. Whatever your will is, I guess, but please, please, please let Clyde make it, she prayed.

"Lizzie!"

Lizzie turned to see what Mandy wanted.

"Look, I think he died!"

She turned and saw that his sides were no longer heaving quite as heavily, but he was definitely still breathing on his own. "No, Mandy, he's just quieting down."

It seemed like hours until they heard Dat return. He was half-running, half-walking, his hair and

beard blowing back in the breeze. He was panting as he reached them.

"Is he dead?"

"No, he's still breathing," Mandy said.

"He is, isn't he?" Dat said, bending down to peer into Clyde's frightened eyes. "Well that's something."

He straightened up.

"The vet will be here soon," he said.

"What can they do for him?" Lizzie asked.

"I don't know. I really don't. I just feel awful about this. I'm so ashamed to even have the vet look at him. He'll think I'm some horseman, working my horses until they die of exhaustion."

"Dat, you didn't. You *didn't,*" Lizzie said. She felt like hugging Dat, she pitied him so much, but she didn't, because that was just how their family was. They never hugged, because it would be too embarrassing for a grown girl to hug her father. But she wanted to anyway.

A white pickup truck came bouncing in the lane, a cloud of dust rolling behind it. The driver slammed on the brakes and hopped out. He ran to the side of the truck, quickly stepped into a pair of clean, white coveralls, and then ran to kneel beside Clyde.

"Beautiful animal," he said quietly, touching, kneading, taking the horse's temperature, shaking his head, and muttering to himself. He ran back to the truck, asking Dat to come help him. Lizzie and Mandy watched wide-eyed as they prepared a huge plastic bag of solution. There was a small plastic

line attached, which looked very much like the I-V line Mam had around her wrist when she had pneumonia.

"Mandy! Mandy!" Lizzie breathed excitedly. "I guarantee he's going to make it now. They're going to put all that stuff in him."

They watched breathlessly as the vet attached the plastic line to a long, sterile needle which glinted in the sun. The vet jammed the needle into Clyde's shoulder muscle as Dat held onto the huge plastic bag. Clyde never moved or winced, so for a heart-stopping moment, Lizzie thought again that he had died.

There was silence then, everyone barely daring to breathe, as the life-giving solution trickled directly into the horse's veins. The locust tree's leaves swirled in the hot breeze as a horse snorted behind them, the chain on his collar clanking against the jockey stick.

Dat turned toward the waiting team as the vet watched the I-V fluid dripping into the horse. A grasshopper leaped past Clyde, and Lizzie wondered if God cared about the little grasshopper as much as he did about Clyde. Probably not.

Lizzie jumped when the vet lifted his arm and whooped. Dat grinned.

"Looks like he's gonna make it!" the vet said. Sure enough, Clyde's gasping, grunting breaths were slowing down now to an almost normal rhythm. The perspiration still ran down the sides of his stomach, but his trembling was visibly subsiding as Clyde relaxed.

Dat explained to the vet what had happened. The vet nodded as Dat described in detail how Clyde worried himself, prancing and tossing his head while the other horses conserved their energy for their work.

"He won't be worth too much for the rest of the summer, at least for a couple of months," the vet said when Dat finished.

Lizzie and Mandy heard Mam calling for them in the garden, so they told Dat they had to go. The girls walked slowly down the lane, troubled about Clyde. And Dat. When they reached the garden they told Mam and Jason and Emma what had happened.

"Surely God was with them when Clyde didn't die," Mam said.

Lizzie said nothing then, but later that evening she asked Emma if it was possible that Clyde lived because she had begged God that he would.

"Why, of course, Lizzie," Emma said.

"You think so?"

"I'm sure God heard you."

Every time Lizzie watched Clyde contentedly grazing in the pasture, his beautiful copper-brown color glinting in the sun, tossing his magnificent head until his black mane rippled, Lizzie thought about God. He was probably kinder than she had thought, she realized.

Chapter 36

THAT WEEKEND, DAT BUILT A NICE CHICKEN coop for Mam. It was a tiny wooden building with a tin roof and plenty of windows to let the sun in on winter days. Along one wall was a row of tin nests, or boxes, with wooden perches along the front where the chickens sat to lay their eggs.

A long trough on the floor contained the chicken feed, or laying mash, as Mam called it. A round container that was upended into a tin tray held their water. Lizzie never could figure out how you could set that large container full of water upside down in the tray and have only a small amount trickle out at a time. Just enough came out to allow the chickens to have a satisfying drink of water but not so much that they could slop around in it.

Lizzie disliked milking, but she loved horses. For her, chickens fell somewhere between love and disgust. She liked to gather the eggs, as long as the chickens didn't have a crazy notion in their heads

about hatching the eggs they sat on. Mam said that a "cluck" or a mother hen, had a natural maternal instinct to remain seated on the egg she had laid so it could hatch into a baby chick.

Thinking about the yolk turning into a baby chick was disgusting for Lizzie. But she loved to eat eggs—fried, scrambled, soft-boiled, just any which way, with salt, pepper, or ketchup. They were delicious. Mam often made an egg in a nest for Jason. She began with a slice of bread, cut the center out of it with a small drinking glass, buttered the "frame" of bread on both sides, and then laid it on the griddle. She broke an egg into the hole in the center, then fried it until the bread was browned and the egg set.

So Mam's chickens were a good thing, providing their family with fresh eggs every day, until egg production dropped drastically. When Lizzie brought in only five eggs from the flock of 21 chickens, Mam said it was time to butcher them. They would need to do the entire cleaning, laundry, and baking on Friday so that on Saturday, when all the girls were home, they could help butcher chickens in the morning.

Lizzie sat at the table, trying to get herself in gear for a job she dreaded. She was tired and discouraged as she thought ahead to Sunday. Her last weekend in Allen County had left her extremely irritable and insecure. She hadn't yet had the nerve or the energy to talk to Emma about things. Marvin was grouchy and slept, or pretended to sleep, the whole

way home from the singing. So far, Lizzie was getting no real help in this whole business of how you went about finding a husband, especially one who didn't milk cows or wouldn't suddenly decide to move to another county. Her questions were totally unresolved.

Lizzie stuck the tines of her fork straight into a whole chocolate cake cooling on the kitchen counter and pulled on a small piece. She went back for another before Emma told her that if she wanted cake, she could cut a piece for herself, put it on a plate, and eat it.

Lizzie ignored her. When she heard Mam say that she was ready to start butchering chickens, she tried to ignore that, too.

"It's time you girls learned how to butcher chickens," she said, doing her best to get them all motivated. "You can't be a good wife until you learn," she said, smiling at Emma.

Emma beamed. "Of course, I want to learn," she said happily. "I would love to be able to butcher and can my own chickens."

"I'll have to teach you to make homemade potpie, too," Mam said.

Lizzie snorted but not loud enough for them to hear. Wasn't that just so Emma-ish? Planning all her cozy housewife duties a year or so in advance. She still loved old houses with homemade quilts and rag rugs, and baking bread and jelly rolls, and all sorts of other impossible things.

"I'm not going to help," Lizzie announced loudly,

Mam kept washing dishes and without turning her head, said, "Oh yes, you are."

The emphasis was very strongly on the "Oh," so Lizzie knew there was no use arguing. She had often watched Mam butcher chickens, which was, in Lizzie's opinion, the most horribly unnecessary thing to do when you could go to town and buy chicken already butchered, quartered, cleaned, and sealed in a package.

Mandy didn't mind butchering. She had helped Mam take the insides out of a chicken once, and she said she found it quite interesting. Not Lizzie. So far, she hadn't been able to stay in the kitchen long enough to watch. The warm, wet chickeny smell sent her into the living room, swallowing desperately to keep from gagging.

But that Saturday morning Mam carried a kettle of boiling water out the door, and Emma carried another as Lizzie and Mandy pulled on shoes. Dat had already chopped the chickens' heads off neatly with a hatchet, and so the chickens were ready to be dunked into the boiling water. That step was to make the feathers easier to pluck. Lizzie started swallowing as she approached the chicken house, trying with all her being to help along with this gruesome task. Mam was already bent over the steaming water, holding waxy yellow feet as she swirled a dead, headless chicken in the hot water. Emma grabbed a chicken, held it by its feet, and followed suit.

"Here!"

Mam handed the gray, sodden, headless chicken to Lizzie, the water running off the ghastly-looking feathers as a sickening, steamy smell wafted toward her flinching nostrils.

She swallowed gamely and reached out for the scaly, yellow feet. Gingerly holding both feet with one hand, she started plucking the feathers a bit tentatively from one side of the bird. Blood dripped onto the snow from the severed neck. Lizzie held the gruesome thing as far away from her snow boots as she possibly could until her back started hurting.

"Why are you leaning over like that?" Mandy asked, plucking feathers with nimble fingers, blood splattering all over her shoes.

"Look at your boots!" Lizzie shrieked.

"It's only chicken blood. It's not going to hurt me," Mandy said sensibly.

So Lizzie knew for sure that she was all alone in hating this task. Mandy and Emma laughed and talked, Mam hurried into the house for more hot water, and no one seemed to be sharing her disgust for the dead chickens.

After the chickens were plucked, Lizzie offered to clean up the feathers, anything she could desperately think of to avoid going into the kitchen. She knew Mam wanted to teach her how to "dress" a chicken. In Pennsylvania Dutch, the process was called "taking it out." As Lizzie raked the feathers, she wondered why English people said "dressing" the chicken. Probably because they were more fancy

than Amish people, they wanted to make it sound as if they were dressing the chicken up in a fine suit of clothes. Besides, if they would say "taking it out," someone might think they were going out to a fine restaurant with a chicken. But how did the term "dressing" ever get started? What they were doing was more like *un*dressing the chickens' feathers. The English language was strange, she decided, just like Pennsylvania Dutch was.

When she opened the kitchen door, her cheeks red from the cold, a small pile of raw, dismembered chicken pieces stood on the counter. Emma was holding a plucked chicken while Mam stood beside her, patiently instructing Emma in how to dress it. Mandy was looking over Emma's shoulder, her eyes wide, interested, and wanting to learn, Lizzie could tell.

"Lizzie, this slop bucket needs to be taken down to the fencerow," Mam said, swiping at a stray hair with the back of her hand. No wonder she uses the back of her hand, Lizzie thought, swallowing hard. She bent to pick up the stainless steel bucket of unimaginable objects with waxy feet floating around in it and carried it across the yard, down the field lane, and over another grassy area before heaving the contents of the bucket into the fencerow.

Dat had opened the garage door and was sweeping the forebay of the horse barn, pushing the wide broom in short little bursts.

He stopped, looked at Lizzie, and laughed when he saw her expression. Pushing back his hat, he

called, "Are you happy butchering chickens?"

Lizzie gave him a withering look, and he laughed again, bending his back to resume his sweeping.

"Oh, Dat!" was all she said, hoping he knew she didn't find him or her job funny.

"I 'took out' a whole chicken," Mandy announced triumphantly when Lizzie returned.

"Good for you," Lizzie said dryly.

Mam was cutting the cleaned chicken into pieces and packing the pieces onto trays, which she then set out on the back porch to cool thoroughly before she started canning the meat. Lizzie carried the trays out to the porch, thinking about how the chickens had died with goose bumps all over their skin. They were probably so horrified at the massacre in the chicken yard as Dat started brandishing the hatchet, that they all broke out in goose bumps of pure terror. She had noticed that the eyes of the dead chickens were open extremely wide, which only underlined the fact that these chickens died a most awful death.

She pitied chickens anyway for having to sit in tin boxes and lay one painful egg after another. Then people came along and took away what the hens wanted to keep and what they hoped would hatch into children. She wondered if the clucks forgot about their eggs a few minutes after laying them. Were their brains developed well enough to wish they could have a whole family of baby chicks?

They couldn't be too smart, Lizzie thought, or they wouldn't eat bugs and worms or any insect they

could catch. Chickens ate almost anything you tried to give them, even chewing gum that had already been chewed, so they couldn't be too bright.

"Someone has to guard that meat," Mam said. "I don't want the cats taking all this good chicken."

"I'll watch out for them," Lizzie offered.

That, plus having no enthusiasm for the job, was why she never took out a chicken, she guessed later. Between guarding the trays of chicken, taking the slop bucket to the fencerow, and caring for Susan and KatieAnn, Lizzie escaped touching the insides of the chickens that day. When there were only a few more to take out, Emma alerted Mam to the fact that Lizzie had not cleaned one bird.

Mam sighed and then looked at Lizzie and the remaining chickens.

"Mam, I'll learn next time, all right?" she said quickly.

"Lizzie, you should do at least one now."

"You're getting tired of it, and I don't know the first thing about it," Lizzie reminded her.

So Lizzie ended up not dressing chickens that day. Emma told her she didn't pity her if she couldn't make good chicken potpie or chicken corn soup after she was married.

"I'm not going to get married, so don't worry about me," Lizzie shot back.

Emma looked at her teasingly. "Didn't look like it Sunday evening!"

"What do you mean?" Lizzie asked, her face coloring to a deep pink.

"Oh, nothing," Emma said, turning to wipe down the counter.

"What? What?" Mandy asked, fairly hopping up and down.

Mam stopped dressing chickens long enough to raise her eyebrows at Lizzie. "You didn't say anything to us," she said, smiling.

And so, while they finished the job and cleaned the kitchen afterward, Lizzie let the whole story of her first weekend with the young people tumble out. All her feelings of insecurity and her real fears. She wondered aloud how she could play Ping-Pong with such a nice-looking boy one moment, and even go for a walk with him, and then be left set, "like...like chicken innards in the fencerow," she said as she finished her miserable outburst.

Mam looked genuinely surprised, shocking to Lizzie, and Mandy squealed, clapping her hands excitedly.

Emma looked at Lizzie with disbelief written all over her face. "Lizzie," she breathed. "I can't believe you're saying these things. You always seem so self-assured. You didn't even seem shy on Sunday evening. I wished I could have been so talkative on my first weekend. To tell you the truth, I was even envying your ability to make friends. Just like you were with Amos. I would never have talked to a boy that much my very first weekend. You just have a way of making up to people."

"E...Emma!" Lizzie burst out, incredulous.

"I really have a hard time believing what you're

saying, Lizzie! You certainly didn't act like you felt that way."

Mam smiled. "Lizzie, I hope you realize that the first time you're with the youth is only a very small step on a much longer journey. You know that I believe that God already has a husband picked for you. We just don't know who it will be yet. So certainly, one game of Ping-Pong..."

"Two!" Lizzie broke in.

Mandy giggled and Emma rolled her eyes as Mam continued. "Well, two games. That is certainly not going to have a big effect one way or another in your seeking for your life partner."

"See, Mam?" Lizzie said miserably. "Right there's the trouble."

"What?"

"'Seeking your life partner.' That's not the girl's job. We can't do one thing about it. We just have to sit around and act like we don't even care if we get a husband or not. The boys are the ones who can do something about it. If we'd ask a young man for a date, they'd all have a fit. I bet the whole church, or anyone who found out anyway, would have a fit. It's so one-sided it isn't even right."

Mam sat down, lifted her hands, and laughed, taking off her glasses and wiping them clean with the corner of her apron as she always did. "No, Lizzie, you certainly don't want to go ask Amos for a date," she said, still chuckling.

"Who said I would even want to ask him?" Lizzie retorted.

"Well, it sounds to me as if you'd like to. But you're going way too fast and haphazardly as usual. Just because a young man is handsome, and you feel attracted to him, doesn't mean that you need to know immediately, right this second, whether he feels the same, or if you're even suited for each other, or if it's God's will. You need to let feelings develop over time and learn to pray about it. Ask God to show you the way, Lizzie. You have to slow down. You're far too immature at this stage in your life to be choosing your husband," Mam said wisely, as usual.

"What does he look like, Lizzie? Is he cute?" Mandy asked, leaning toward Lizzie, her green eyes shining. "Does he like you?"

Emma looked at Mam and shook her head in disbelief as Lizzie punched Mandy's arm. "Stop it."

The really good thing about growing older, Lizzie decided that evening as she got ready for bed, was that Mam's talk about God's will made a lot more sense than it had a year ago. She had come to really believe that her future was not based on nerve-wracking life or death, right or wrong, decisions. She was beginning to understand that God had plenty of time to let you grow up in knowledge and understanding. You couldn't run ahead of him, trying to figure things out on your own, because that gave you the blues.

So she would try and calm down, enjoy her weekends in Allen County, and not insist on knowing right away who her husband would be. Mandy

told her that she thought too much and tried to figure things out that were none of her business, which was true. But how could you stop thinking? It just happened.

And another thing. How in the world was God going to show her the way? Mam was just so much further advanced in knowing God than she was, that it wasn't even funny. How did God talk to a 16-year-old girl when that girl's thoughts of him were still not very clear at all?

God was supposed to be way up in heaven, and who even knew if he was there for certain? Nobody did. They just *hoped* he was or *believed* he was. They didn't know for sure.

Lizzie closed her eyes tiredly. She found the turmoil of a budding faith to be a bit too overwhelming. It was much easier just to have fun and be young and enjoy life than to become too serious too soon.

Mam, on the other hand, believed that Lizzie's thoughts were probably very much like the egg under the cluck. Her faith was being well cared for and nurtured into growth by a very loving heavenly father whom she did not yet feel very close to.

Chapter 37

Sunshine and warm breezes found their way into the house and barn. Clyde and Bess ran back and forth across the pasture. Milking cows wasn't even quite as distasteful on these lovely spring mornings.

When Sunday evening rolled around, Lizzie wore a new lavender dress, almost the color of the delicate crocuses bordering the porch. Emma looked very pretty in a shade of green which matched her eyes and made her hair appear darker still.

When the driver came to pick them up, Lizzie was surprised to see Stephen sitting in the back seat. His skin was already tanned to a dark shade of brown, and his hair was bleached lighter by the spring sunshine. He is certainly not unattractive, she thought.

After climbing into the van, Lizzie smiled back at Stephen and said, "Why are you going along to Allen County?" she asked.

"To run around," he told her abruptly.

Marvin laughed loudly at this, and Stephen looked at Marvin, his eyes twinkling. They made Lizzie feel as if she was an annoying little 12-year-old. She turned around and resolved not to talk to Marvin the whole way to Allen County. That Stephen. He may be nice-looking, but when he and Marvin were in one of their moods, they irritated Lizzie to distraction.

Well, she liked Amos anyway, so there was no real problem. As she looked out the window at the light green beginning to appear on the mountain, she was filled with the joy of springtime. No use being grouchy, she thought, as she observed the beautiful tulips, daffodils, and hyacinths growing in neat rows along the bases of the well-kept houses they passed. She loved looking at new homes, at their landscaping and green lawns cut so evenly that they looked like indoor synthetic green carpet. That's what my yard will look like when I get married, she thought happily. No old farm for me.

That Sunday, the day itself was as light and joyous as a feather. Not a heavy, white, waxy chicken feather, but a downy, light blue feather that floated to the ground from a bluebird's wing. The whole earth was full of color and joy, the warm breezes blowing the girls' hair loose from beneath their coverings.

They all decided to go for a long drive to a nearby lake before going to the regular Sunday supper. Marvin, Stephen, and Amos, with Mary, Barbara, Lizzie, and Ruthie, traveling in two different teams,

headed out Barbara's driveway and onto the highway. Amos had his hands full with his feisty little horse who was clipping along at an alarming rate. He didn't say much as he held onto the reins with both hands, his arms outstretched in an effort to hold him back.

Ruthie and Lizzie rode with Amos, while Stephen and Marvin took the other girls with their team and followed them. Lizzie was secretly a tiny bit disappointed because she didn't want Ruthie to go along with her and Amos. She wasn't convinced that Amos didn't like Ruthie. That was the annoying part of liking someone too much; there was always the chance that he wouldn't like you back. What if she wanted Amos to ask her out on a real honest-to-goodness date, the serious kind, and then maybe in a year or so he would ask her to get married? Of course, this would have to involve living in Cameron County, not Allen, and in a new house, not on an old farm. But there was no use thinking too far ahead, not on a day like today, Lizzie reminded herself.

Ruthie was sitting between Amos and Lizzie. The only way three people could sit comfortably on a buggy seat was for the person in the middle to sit on the edge of the seat while the two others sat as far back as they could. Lizzie had been a bit miffed when Ruthie plopped herself beside Amos, where Lizzie had already been seated. But if she leaned over far enough, it seemed as if it was just she and Amos driving together without Ruthie being there. That was a mean thought, Lizzie knew, but she thought

it nevertheless.

"My arms are getting really tired hanging onto this crazy horse!" Amos said, laughing.

"I'll drive!" Lizzie blurted out.

"You!" Ruthie gasped.

"I love to drive! He can't be worse than our old horse Billy was when he was younger," Lizzie said, glancing at Amos.

"You want to try?" Amos asked, a bit incredulously.

"Sure."

They exchanged seats, which was no easy feat with Ruthie in the middle, squeaking and exclaiming about her apron getting wrinkled if they didn't settle themselves soon. Amos apologized profusely, which irritated Lizzie so much that she had a notion to loosen the reins entirely so the horse would run away and throw them all out into a field.

No doubt about it, this horse had a mouth of iron, as Dat described a horse that wanted to run too fast. Lizzie bit her lip and clamped her hands down hard on the reins. It felt so much like driving Billy in Jefferson County that she burst out laughing. This was an absolutely exhilarating feeling, with the powerful little horse lunging into his collar and the breeching across his rump flapping up and down with every frenzied step he took.

The warm breeze swooshed through the window of the buggy until Lizzie's hair flew across her eyes and her covering slid helter-skelter. She remembered the first time Dat had let her drive Teeny and Tiny,

the miniature ponies. She had started to giggle when the ponies went too fast, just like now. There was something about a horse going this fast that made Lizzie laugh.

"What's so funny?" Ruthie asked.

"I always have to laugh when a horse runs too fast. It just gives me the giggles," Lizzie answered.

"It isn't funny, Lizzie. Let Amos drive."

"She can handle him," Amos said, glancing at Lizzie behind Ruthie's back. The twinkle in his eyes caught hers, and they looked at each other rather long, Lizzie thought. She could tell he admired her for driving his horse, or she hoped that's what he meant when his eyes smiled at hers.

Springtime was unbelievably wonderful. Lizzie's heart sang as the little horse kept up his rapid trotting for the next mile. Was it true that a young man's thoughts turn to love in the springtime? At least she was sure that she had impressed Amos by driving his horse, and that felt like butterflies flitting across her heart. She bet it wouldn't be long until he asked to come see her at her home like when Joshua came to see Emma.

When they stopped at the lake, Lizzie was awestruck by the weeping willows and their branches drooping at the water's edge. The softly moving limbs rustled gently while the water lapped at the new shoots of grass. Lizzie thought of Cinderella's long skirts that swayed whenever she danced with her Prince. She supposed God designed willow trees to be graceful and able to talk with the gently

rippling water in the spring. God actually had lots of good spring-time ideas—butterflies, crocuses, baby birds, tulips.

Suddenly she realized that she had wandered alone to the far side of the lake. She turned around and hiked quickly in the direction of the hollering and laughing.

When Lizzie reached the group, Ruthie was clutching a tiny bouquet of purple violets and smiling up at Amos who was smiling back at her. Jealousy, unlike anything Lizzie had ever felt before, clamped its iron jaws around her heart until she thought she would suffocate like a mouse in a trap. She knew instinctively that her feelings were wrong. Mam had always taught the girls that jealousy came directly from the devil.

She turned away, detouring around Amos and Ruthie to find Barbara and Mary unhitching their horse, with Marvin still sitting in the buggy. They were laughing and teasing him, and Lizzie had to laugh in spite of trying desperately to fight off her jealousy of Ruthie. Marvin held a bag of potato chips and calmly munched on them, his feet on the dashboard as if he hadn't a care in the world.

"Marvin!" Lizzie called, laughing.

"What? Oh, Lizzie! How's my niecely?" Lizzie's heart grew warm with fondness for Marvin, for the pet name and for the genuine sense of safety he gave her, as well as the admiration and love she felt for him.

"Come join me, Niecely!"

Gratefully, Lizzie climbed into the buggy beside him, grabbing his bag of potato chips. "Share your chips, Marvin!"

"You want a Pepsi?"

"Do you have extra?"

"Sure!"

Lizzie took a long drink of the refreshing soda until her eyes watered, her nose burned, and she burped.

"You mean you still can't drink soda like a lady?" Marvin teased.

Lizzie hiccuped, smiled, and ruefully shook her head. "Nope, Marvin. You know I'm not used to drinking soda."

They sat in companionable silence, watching the little wavelets slapping themselves to nothing on the pebbly shoreline. The weeping willows danced gracefully above them, the sky full of puffy clouds as white as cottonballs against the blue sky. Out on the lake, two people pulled on oars, pushing their streamlined orange canoe against the little waves. It was all so peaceful that the perfect spring scene here by the lake brought a lump to Lizzie's throat. If she hadn't had these troubling thoughts about Amos, Stephen, and Ruthie, the day would have been wonderfully perfect.

"Marvin, do you think Amos likes Ruthie?" she asked, nervously toying with her Pepsi can.

Marvin looked at Lizzie, noticing the anxiety in her eyes. "Why should you care?" he asked bluntly.

"I don't," Lizzie said forcefully.

"You do!"

"I *don't*."

"Then why do you ask?"

That was as far as the conversation went before Amos came walking over to the buggy. There was a light in his eye and a real spring in his step as he approached them.

"Hey, this guy told me we can take his canoe out. Wanna go, Marvin?"

"Why don't you ask Lizzie?" Marvin asked. "I'm busy eating chips."

Lizzie looked at Marvin and then at Amos, becoming flustered immediately. "Well, I..."

"I can ask Ruthie," Amos said.

"No! I'll go. I just didn't want to go unless you wanted me to. I mean, you didn't ask me. Marvin just said I could go. If you'd rather ask Ruthie, please do. It's not like you have to ask me to go along." Lizzie stopped, noticing the strange look Marvin was giving her. His eyebrows were drawn down, and his eyes seemed to plead with her to be quiet. Why couldn't I just be quiet? Lizzie thought miserably.

The canoe looked awfully long and narrow. But after she was seated, she wasn't frightened because there was much more room than she first thought. Amos clambered in. He held onto the oars and tried not to rock too much before he found his seat, facing Lizzie.

"Ready?" he asked.

"Mm-hmm," Lizzie said, clamping her teeth

down hard to keep her voice from shaking. She certainly hoped he had rowed a canoe before.

He lifted the smooth wooden oars into the oarlocks, set them evenly on each side, and pulled. The muscles in his strong, brown arms bulged as he heaved on both oars.

Lizzie's nervousness evaporated easily, and she laughed out loud at the thrill of gliding so swiftly through the clear blue water. Amos was adept at handling the oars, which propelled them along at a surprising rate. Lizzie put her hand over the side and found the water to be alarmingly cold. She quickly put her hand in her lap.

"Is it cold?"

"It's icy cold!"

"Can you swim?" Amos asked.

"Oh, yes!" Lizzie answered, hoping with all her heart that she had impressed him even more than when she drove his horse.

"Really? Come on! You can't!"

"Of course, I can swim."

Amos stopped rowing and they sat quietly, the canoe rocking gently from side to side. It was the single most blissful moment Lizzie had ever experienced. Here she was in the middle of a beautiful lake on this extraordinary day. With Amos. She had to admit to herself, too, that it was especially sweet because he was with her and not Ruthie. The only thing that bothered her was the fact that Marvin told Amos to take her canoeing. Amos had not actually asked her on his own.

When they got back to the lake's edge, Amos hopped out and held the canoe so Lizzie could step safely onto the grass. She felt warm and a little confused. And almost rapturous. She drifted off to catch her breath under a long-armed willow tree.

A moment later, she heard a step behind her and turned to find Stephen approaching her. How could he have crept up on her like that? He must be part Indian.

"What are you doing here by yourself?" he asked.

"I didn't realize I was by myself. I guess I just walked over here to look at the weeping willow branches hanging in the water. Aren't they the prettiest things you've ever seen?"

"No."

Lizzie looked at him, puzzled at his curt answer. She found Stephen's blue eyes looking intently into hers without a trace of laughter.

"You are," he said.

Lizzie was shocked. She was so surprised that she could say absolutely nothing. In fact, she couldn't look at him so she looked at her shoes, which felt much safer. And her shoes were really quite interesting. She tried desperately to think of a fitting comeback, even a joking one, but she was absolutely tongue-tied. When she looked up, he was gone.

She turned to walk back to the others, putting her hands up to her warm cheeks to cool them. Oh, mercy! Now Stephen had said that, and she liked Amos. How complicated was this whole husband thing going to become? She didn't know Stephen

liked her. Well, maybe he didn't. Maybe he just thought she was pretty, and it was very nice of him to say that. He did intrigue her, but...there was Amos.

Amos had taken her to the middle of the lake alone. Was that, she worried, so indescribably special mostly because Ruthie had to watch?

She would ask Emma to give her honest opinion about whether, when you sit in a canoe with a boy and feel absolutely joyful, you are in real love. And did Emma think she should learn to know the mysterious Stephen better? Who was he really and how could she find out?

Lizzie would have to relate this whole wonderful day, bit by bit, to Emma and Mandy. Thank God for sisters. And for interesting boys. Including Uncle Marvin, who may or may not be helpful.

Linda Byler

When Strawberries Bloom

Lizzie Searches *for* Love
• *Book 2* •

Chapter 1

"AND SO..." LIZZIE FINISHED HER STORY, "that's how it was!"

"Oh, I wonder how this will all turn out?" Mandy sighed.

Lizzie loved Monday evenings when she could tell stories about her weekend, interesting bit by interesting bit, to her younger sister Mandy who always listened with wide-eyed admiration. With dinner over and the dishes done, the sisters worked outside with Mam, planting flowers in the new rock garden that Dat had built beside the house. Lizzie mixed peat moss into the topsoil while Mandy set up the rubber garden hose from the water hydrant by the barn.

Spring had arrived, filling the days with warm, mellow sunshine. Buds burst forth from the maple tree in the front yard, and even the old walnut tree beside the sidewalk shone with a light green mist which, if Lizzie looked closely, was actually

thousands of tiny green buds erupting from the dark branches. The swollen creek churned on its relentless way to the river, already muddy brown from all of the April showers. Little green shoots emerged from moist brown earth, stretching through the blanket of wet, decaying leaves.

During the warm days, Dat worked the horse hard, preparing the soil for another crop. Clyde, the big workhorse, was back in the harness, still bouncing around as if he had springs in his legs, but now he was settled down enough to pull his share of the plow.

In the evenings, barn swallows dipped and whirled through the air like little acrobats, chirping their evening song as they caught mosquitoes for their baby birds in the mud nests inside the horse barn.

"Ach, Lizzie, you're still so young. I wouldn't get too serious about either Amos or Stephen or too worried about Ruthie. You have plenty of time to run around yet. Besides, more importantly, you need to pray about this," her older sister Emma said, as she gently pushed the porch swing back and forth with her foot.

Lizzie flicked some dust off her black bib apron, adjusted the navy blue sleeve of her dress, and shivered. The cool evening breeze reminded her of the evening before when she had paddled across the pond with Amos, handsome Amos, who had always paid more attention to her friend Ruthie than to her until last night. Everything had been perfect until

Stephen appeared as they were pulling the boat to shore.

One moment she had felt warm and a little confused as she watched Amos tie up the canoe. The next moment, Stephen had stepped beside her and told her she was the prettiest thing he had ever seen.

Lizzie shook her head and snorted impatiently. Something about Stephen bothered her. They had become friends, real friends, in the year since his family moved to Lamont County. But even though Lizzie saw him every weekend, she never quite felt like she knew what he thought about her. He was too quiet, not as outgoing and funny as Amos or her Uncle Marvin, and sometimes she caught him watching her as if he knew something more than even she knew about herself. He bugged her!

Besides, how could she know that Stephen liked her in that way? Maybe he didn't really. He was just teasing her, or he thought she was pretty but nothing more. Or what if he wished he hadn't said anything to her now? She certainly wished he hadn't because she felt all mixed up inside.

"Emma, I do pray. You know I'm not as scared of God as I used to be. And you have nothing to say. How old were you when you started dating Joshua? Huh? How old?" Lizzie turned her head and squinted teasingly at Emma.

Emma reached down and playfully pulled at Lizzie's *dichly*, the little kerchief on her head. Lizzie grabbed the top of her head to stop her, but Emma

was too fast, and she snatched it and flung it over the porch railing.

"Emma!"

"You should have a real worthwhile project in your life like drawing, crocheting, embroidering..."

Lizzie pretended to gag, and Mandy threw her head back, whooping and laughing. Emma may enjoy crocheting and embroidering, Lizzie knew, but not she or Mandy.

"I know what I would like to do more than anything in the whole world!" Lizzie said.

Mandy and Emma looked at each other, rolled their eyes, and said simultaneously, "Teach school!"

"Yup. That's right. Teach school," Lizzie said.

They had often listened to Lizzie's vivid accounts of what her classroom would look like, her methods of discipline, her way of teaching, the songs the children would sing, and on and on until both of her sisters became quite weary of listening and started to tease her. It wasn't that they scoffed at the idea of Lizzie teaching. It just seemed a bit improbable to them that the very proper school board would even think of asking 17-year-old Lizzie to teach school.

"But Lizzie," Mandy protested, "you're too young."

"And too fancy," Emma finished soberly.

"What do you mean?" Lizzie wailed. "I'm not fancy!"

"You're way too fancy with your hair, your clothes, your covering. The school board will not

ask a girl like you to teach," Emma said quite mat-
ter-of-factly.

"I'm not fancier than any other girl in our entire
church," Lizzie argued.

"Well, you could wet your hair down and roll the
sides more sleekly. You often look so ... well, I hate
to say 'sloppy,' Lizzie. Maybe you'd like it better if I
used the word 'fancy,'" Emma said.

"The school board shouldn't judge me by my
hair," Lizzie said, her hands on her hips.

"They don't really, Lizzie. But ... well, I don't
know quite how to describe it."

Lizzie plopped down beside Emma on the swing.
The chain of the porch swing creaked against the
hooks in the ceiling as they swung silently together.
Across the lawn, the girls' twin sisters, KatieAnn
and Susan, were playing in the freshly mowed grass
by the clothesline, while Dat whistled as he swept
the horse barn floor with his wide broom. The sun
was sinking behind the hills in a grand show of
yellow, orange, and red. Streaks of dark blue and
lavender made the colors seem almost like heaven,
Lizzie thought.

Mam clapped her hands, brushing off the dirt
as she straightened her back. Lizzie eyed her newly
planted petunias. The old farm had been vastly
improved in many different ways since they had
moved in. It was their home now, and a cozy, homey
one which Lizzie had learned to love with all her
heart. Her heart always sang when she returned
home to Mam's comfy kitchen, whether she had

been at work or coming home from running around during a weekend in neighboring Allen County.

Lizzie truly yearned for only one thing now, and that was to become a real teacher. So if the school board thought she needed to change some things about her dress, she would. She knew there was nothing else in all the world she wanted to do more than be a teacher, so she would show them she could be a plain, old-maidy kind of person, quiet, sober, and very, very mature for a 17-year-old. She made a mental note of who was on the school board, wondering how she could persuade them that she was capable of doing the job.

Lizzie could still remember her first day of school. Emma was six years old then, and Lizzie was only five. Actually, Lizzie was almost too young to go to school, but Mam wanted the two girls to start together. They were only a little over a year apart in age, so she thought it was good for them to start first grade the same year.

On that first day, when the little white one-room schoolhouse came into view, Lizzie's heart had done a complete flip-flop. There was a porch and a fence with a gate that was pulled open. A horse shed and two outdoor bathrooms stood in a corner of the schoolyard. There were already lots of children at school, and Lizzie felt very afraid.

Emma said, "Good morning," to the teacher, but

not very loud. Lizzie didn't say anything. She had just stared at the teacher. She was very thin with a long black dress. Her forehead was wide, and she wore glasses, and her white covering was bigger than Mam's. She looked friendly enough, but she also looked scary. Lizzie wondered if she spanked little first-graders. She looked like she could really spank.

"Come, girls, we'll find your seats," the teacher said. "You'll find your name written on a piece of tape. Let's see if you can find your seats. Can you write your own name?"

Emma nodded her head. Lizzie was too shy to do anything except walk along under that hand on her shoulder. It had seemed so far across the classroom, and she felt like many pairs of eyes were staring at her. She hoped her dress was buttoned properly and that her bob was not falling down.

Lizzie squirmed a little to make herself more comfortable on the slippery varnished seat. She tucked her legs underneath, and her new shoes crinkled at the toes. Teacher Sylvia handed out blue songbooks to some of the children.

"Now we're going to take turns picking songs," she said. The singing started and welled in the room, growing louder and louder. Lizzie bit her lip, trying hard not to feel lonely.

"*My Lord, what a morning,*
My Lord, what a morning,
My Lord, what a morning,
When the stars begin to fall."

On and on the children sang, and lonelier and lonelier Lizzie became. She tried to think of happy things, of good things to eat, and of silly things, but the huge lump in her throat only grew bigger. She looked down and bit her lip, shuffling her feet, but the lump in her throat would not go away. She glanced at Emma, and Emma smiled a weak smile, trying to cheer her up.

In that moment, huge, wet tears coursed down Lizzie's cheeks, and a harsh sob escaped her bitten lips. She was soon crying uncontrollably, wishing she could go home to Mam before the stars fell and the end of the world came. Wouldn't it be awful if the stars fell from the sky and she was in school and Dat and Mam were at home?

Emma took Lizzie's hand and tugged gently. Lizzie followed Emma across that big expanse of schoolroom to the door while the singing went on. Emma led her across the porch and down to the little outdoor bathroom. They huddled together while Emma tried to console Lizzie in earnest tones.

"Lizzie, it's okay. What's wrong?"

Lizzie cried horribly. She couldn't tell Emma about the deep black loneliness she felt when they sang that song. So she just shrugged her shoulders, and Emma wiped her eyes and told her to be quiet. She said Lizzie would have to be a good girl and grow up now and not cry in school. Lizzie gulped and choked and nodded her head. She would be all right, she assured Emma. And much to Lizzie's surprise, she really was.

And soon she learned to love school, in spite of sad songs.

The next morning when Lizzie combed her hair, she made sure it was all put up neatly in an orderly fashion. Dat looked at Lizzie once, then followed up with closer scrutiny before he gave Mam a bewildered look.

Mam checked Lizzie's neat attire, her covering pulled forward to cover her carefully combed hair. Lizzie's eyebrows were raised in a quite pious expression, her eyes downcast in her Herculean effort at humility.

Mam's eyes met Dat's and she shrugged her shoulders. Dat cleared his throat.

"Well, Lizzie, to what do we owe this change of heart you're displaying?"

Lizzie looked up at Dat, her eyes as meek and docile as a sheep's.

"Oh, the girls told me if I want to be a schoolteacher, I need to mend my ways. I mean, comb my hair more severely and act more responsible. How do I look?" she asked, batting her eyelashes demurely.

Mam sputtered. She made a brave attempt to keep from laughing, but in the end her shoulders shook until she gave up helplessly. Dat looked a bit stern, then seeing Mam wiping her eyes, he laughed with her.

When Emma came down the stairs, she was startled to hear everyone laughing so early in the morning until she saw Lizzie's hair and covering.

"Oh, my goodness!" she gasped.

Lizzie was a bit insulted to see everyone laughing at her real effort to appear grown up and responsible.

"Well, go ahead and laugh then," she said.

"We weren't laughing at you, Lizzie. But you are laying it on a bit thick," Dat said. "After all, Lizzie, you have to be yourself. You can't purposefully turn yourself into a whole other sort of person. I do admire you for dressing more respectfully, but I have a good feeling about the school board. If they know you truly want to teach school, they'll be kind enough to give you a try. I'm pretty sure they will."

"Of course, they will," Mam agreed.

Lizzie sighed. It was almost unbelievable that Dat actually thought the school board would ask her to teach! In this community there was only one school for Amish and Mennonite students, and as far as Lizzie knew, its teacher was getting married in the fall. That meant they would need a new teacher, and she knew of no one else who wanted the job. So maybe … just maybe …

Chapter 2

THE NEXT SUNDAY, LIZZIE DRESSED QUITE soberly. During church, she sang along with the congregation, singing quite purposefully, listening to the preacher with no fidgeting or whispering. She wanted the men on the school board to think she was a mature young woman, capable of teaching in the fall. She knew that the responsibility and seriousness of teaching could be completely overwhelming, which, really, sometimes if she thought about it, was about as frightening as ... well, as lots of things about the unknown.

Emma was very supportive, always being positive when they talked about it. She even told Lizzie that she thought she would be a teacher herself someday, but the way things were turning out, she just didn't know if that would happen. Lizzie knew exactly why Emma didn't seriously pursue teaching. It was because she still held the dream of being married soon. She probably thought that if she didn't

commit herself to teaching, Joshua would ask her to marry him.

After services were over, Lizzie helped the other single girls carry trays of bread and pies, ham, soft cheese spread, pickles, and red beets to the long tables where the traditional Sunday dinner was served. She caught sight of Stephen standing on the other side of the room, laughing at something Uncle Marvin had said. Stephen smiled at her and Lizzie's heart sped up. But when Uncle Marvin turned to see who had caught Stephen's attention, Lizzie ducked her head and walked away.

Dat was talking with an unfamiliar man who looked to be about his age. Lizzie wondered if he was part of the Beiler family who had recently moved to the area. She remembered that Dat mentioned one evening at the supper table that this Jonas Beiler was pushing for the development of an Amish school board to help the Mennonites run the local school.

"Who's that?" she asked Emma.

Emma smiled and shrugged.

"I don't know," she said.

Lizzie sighed and went on with her duties, hoping with all her heart that she was making a good impression.

❧

By the next week, Lizzie had almost forgotten about impressing the school board with her good

behavior. She was so busy working as a *maud* for a local family, and her days and evenings were full of spring cleaning and planting. She didn't have time to worry about teaching school. Mandy said they probably wouldn't ask her anyway, because she was only 17 years old. Lizzie quickly reminded her that she would be almost 18 in the fall, and that was plenty old enough to teach school.

She was upstairs cleaning her closet one warm evening, just as the birds were twittering their goodnight songs, when the door of her room burst open.

"Lizzie, get down to the kitchen! The school board is here!" Mandy hissed.

Lizzie dropped the dress she was holding, her mouth open in disbelief. "The real school board?"

"Of course!"

Lizzie felt her heartbeat accelerate, and the color drained from her face. Quickly she dashed to the mirror, checking her hair and covering before she nervously wiped a few fuzzies from her apron. She could think of nothing, absolutely nothing to say. For some reason it felt as if they were there to spank her, like she was still a little girl who had done something mischievous in school, and the stern-faced school board had come to tell her what her punishment was going to be.

Her knees hardly supported her as she went slowly down the stairs, clutching the sides of her covering, checking that it covered part of her ears. Who knew? They might change their minds if she didn't look too fancy.

In the kitchen, Dat and Mam sat at the kitchen table with three men. Lizzie recognized Jonas Beiler from his conversation with Dat at church. The other two men, Elam Glick and Elmer Esh, had lived in the community much longer, and Lizzie knew them well. In one glance, Lizzie could see that Mam was nervous because her hands were closed with her thumbs tucked under her fingers. That's what Mam always did when she was worried about something.

"H... Hello!" Lizzie said in what she hoped was a sweet and humble way.

"Good evening, Lizzie," they all said, looking at her closely.

"How are you?" Jonas Beiler asked.

"Good," was all Lizzie could think of before she swallowed fitfully.

He looked at Dat before he asked how old she was. For all the world I feel like I'm a young cow or horse being taken to an auction, Lizzie thought.

They all talked about the weather, the price of milk, the price of the farm that had been sold recently, until Lizzie felt like screaming. Why didn't they say what they wanted? She began chewing on the inside of her thumbnail until Mam looked at her with lowered eyebrows. Lizzie quickly put her hands under the table and pressed them together as tightly as she could.

Finally, Jonas Beiler looked at Lizzie and cleared his throat.

"So your father says you'd like to try teaching school?"

Lizzie's heart jumped to her throat. But she looked steadily at him, meeting his clear gaze.

"I'd like to," she said.

"Well, that's good. We are going to need a teacher this fall because the Mennonite girl, I forget her name, is getting married. So..."

He left that sentence hanging in the air, and Lizzie felt as if she had been holding a balloon which the wind had suddenly whipped away, completely out of her grasp. He had only mentioned the fact that they needed a teacher; he hadn't really asked her to teach the school.

Just as suddenly, the departing balloon drifted back firmly into Lizzie's hands when Jonas said, "Would you consider being the new teacher in the fall then?"

"Yes!" Lizzie breathed, her eyes shining.

"That's good," Elam Glick said, smiling.

"Yes, we're glad you want to," Elmer Esh added.

"You'll need these," Jonas said, handing her a small orange booklet and a few other papers.

Lizzie flipped through the pages as the men talked about the date school would be opening, the book order, the rules of conduct for a teacher, and many other things that Lizzie hadn't considered before. But nothing deterred her. Not one thing they talked about gave her the blues. She was so thrilled about sitting right there in the kitchen, reveling in the delightful knowledge that the school board had really honest-to-goodness asked her to be a teacher.

Before the men left they each wished *der saya* for her, or God's blessing, which brought tears to Lizzie's eyes. Wasn't that the nicest thing in the whole world for a school board to say? She didn't feel worthy, but their words made her feel as if she could conquer anything. She would do her very, very, absolute best to become the teacher they expected her to be.

After saying good-night to them, Lizzie turned to Mam and clasped her hands to her chest. "Ma-am!"

"Looks like you're a teacher, Lizzie!"

Emma and Mandy clattered down the stairs, congratulating her as she twirled joyously around the kitchen. Jason thought she was making an awful fuss about it, and the twins danced funny little steps of their own.

"Jason, you may as well not look so sour! I'm going to be your teacher, too, you know!"

"I know!" he said, but Lizzie could tell he was pleased. She loved Jason, grown boy that he was now. He was turning out to be a good-looking young man and his curly hair was his most adorable feature, she thought.

❧

Lizzie could still remember the day Jason was born.

"Emma, look at your brother. His name is Jason, and he looks a lot like Lizzie," Dat had said.

Emma whispered, "Jason? Aww, he's cute! Can I hold him, Dat?"

Dat had smiled and lowered the blue bundle into
Emma's lap while Emma stroked the little cheeks
and touched his downy hair.

Lizzie peered under the flap of the soft, woolly
blanket. She was suddenly overcome with horror.
He was so ugly and so bright red she couldn't imag-
ine ever letting Mam take him to church. His eyes
were closed, but he had lots of deep wrinkles around
them. Lizzie could not imagine how he could ever
see around all that skin. His nose was big and puffy,
and his mouth was much too big for his face.

She felt Mam come up behind her and put her
arm around her shoulders. Lizzie leaned against
Mam and tried hard to smile—at least to smile
enough to be nice. But she wished so much her new
baby brother wasn't so ugly.

"Isn't he sweet, Lizzie? You may hold him, too.
Emma, may Lizzie hold Baby Jason now?" Mam
asked.

"I–I don't want to hold him. Emma may." And
much to her shame, Lizzie started to cry.

"What's wrong? Come, Lizzie." Mam sat down
on a soft chair and just held Lizzie till she finished
crying. "Now tell me what's wrong."

But Lizzie never did tell Mam the real reason she
cried. She just told her that her head hurt, because
it wasn't nice to say Jason was ugly. But he really
was.

Now Jason had grown into a strong young man with even features and wild curls that caught the eye of more than one girl Lizzie knew. He was a good brother, and Lizzie hoped he was well-behaved at school because he was about to become her student.

Dat smiled, pleased that Lizzie would be a teacher. That afforded him some status in the community, one of his girls being the first Amish teacher in this school. That fact made him smile, Lizzie knew. Mam was beaming as well, although when everyone quieted down she said she hoped Lizzie was aware of the responsibility that was involved.

"I know, Mam!" Lizzie assured her. "I can handle 20 children. I know I can. I just wish it was the end of August and I could get started. I can already begin on some artwork, can't I?"

"Probably when you come home from work in the evening," Mam agreed.

That evening Lizzie did not sleep for a very long, long time. Thoughts and projects she would try the next year whirled through her head like a child's pinwheel on a stick, turning in the wind until she couldn't make sense of anything.

She did remember to thank God from the bottom of her heart for the chance to be a real schoolteacher before she drifted off to a happy slumber.

Chapter 3

The summer flew by, like a train going so fast you had to turn your head to be sure and see the engine at all. Lizzie continued working part-time as a *maud*, but only part-time because she also needed to prepare for the upcoming school year.

Weekends in Allen County with her friends were still the highlight of her life, marred only by her growing obsession with Amos. He had become the center of her weekends—his attention, or lack of it, was now her main reason for going to Allen County. Of course, she didn't want to miss being with her Uncle Marvin, who was Dat's brother but almost the same age as Lizzie, and the mysterious Stephen, who was her friend, but who had also told her once that she was pretty but never mentioned it again.

Sometimes Lizzie thought it was easier to think about Amos and Ruthie than it was to figure out what Stephen really thought about her. In fact, Lizzie had begun to think that if it wasn't for Amos,

she would have genuine fun with lots of other guys every weekend. But because she was never quite certain whether Amos liked her or Ruthie, she could think of nothing else.

On the surface, Lizzie remained good friends with Ruthie. No one but Mandy knew about the cold, hard jealousy that so often consumed Lizzie. She wondered how long God would have patience with her awful feelings of jealousy. Every Sunday night when she came home, she asked Jesus to forgive her and wipe away her sins and make her as clean and brand new as tablet paper with no marks on it.

Sometimes the whole sinning and forgiving thing was hard to figure out. How could Jesus keep forgiving her if he knew she'd just get jealous again the next weekend? Maybe he recognized that she was still young. She was pretty sure about one thing, though. After she became a member of the Amish church and gave her life to God really seriously, she either had to be dating Amos or quit going to Allen County on the weekend if she wanted to have any peace at all.

On Sunday night she was so positive that Amos would ask her for a date that her heart beat so rapidly and loudly she was sure he could hear it. After the singing and while she waited on her driver, he sat in the yard beside her, just sat there, talking about lots of different subjects. His teeth shone white in the dark, his head outlined against the starlight, and Lizzie was so nervous, just waiting to hear him ask

her for a real date the following weekend. But he didn't. Lizzie was mad all week just thinking about it.

Finally, Mam had had quite enough of Lizzie's crabbiness, her pouting and short answers, her eyebrows raised in anxiety, her obviously being in the center of a great personal crisis of some sort.

"Lizzie, I do wish you wouldn't be so grouchy all the time. The twins are almost afraid of you," she said after Lizzie had shouted at the two girls to leave her alone. The twins stood against the sofa, tears in their eyes.

Lizzie didn't say anything. She just gazed miserably out the kitchen window. Mam sighed and went to the kitchen to make some lunch.

"Oh, dear," she said.

"What?" Lizzie asked.

"I'm out of butter."

"Do you want Mandy and me to drive Billy to Bittle's?"

"It's late!"

"Not that late. We can."

So Lizzie found Mandy, and together they led Billy from his stall and hitched him to the cart. It felt good to brush his coat and his oatmeal-colored mane and tail and to throw the harness across his round, sturdy little back.

As they rounded the corner and headed out the lane in the buggy, Lizzie held tight to the reins so the buggy wheels wouldn't slide. Billy always wanted to run, and to run fast, every time they hitched him

to the cart, although he was much easier to control now than when he was a very young pony.

Mandy sat beside Lizzie, happy and talkative, content to let Lizzie drive as she talked about one subject after another, without too much comment from Lizzie. But as they turned onto the main road, Mandy glanced over at Lizzie.

"What a crab you are this week!" she suddenly said.

"Oh, be quiet. Can't I be a crab all by myself without you noticing every little thing about me?"

"It's Amos, isn't it?"

"No!"

"Mm-hmm. Oh, yes, it is, Lizzie. You know it is. What happened now?"

"Nothing!"

Mandy just shook her head. Billy trotted rapidly down the road, and the sisters waved at a lady mowing her lawn. It was one of those perfect summer evenings, not too hot or humid, not too windy, just perfect to be driving down the road with Billy. Lizzie wished she could tell Mandy the whole miserable story, but so far, she was too proud to admit even to herself that Amos was her problem. So they silently drove on through the little village situated on the side of a long, winding hill, with Billy lunging into his collar steadily until they reached the top.

Lizzie had to hold him back as they started down the opposite side. Billy loved running downhill at what was clearly an unsafe speed. Even as Lizzie firmly held Billy back, the buggy slid to the left as

they pulled into the gravel parking lot of Bittle's Store.

Bittle's was a tiny store situated on the edge of a dairy farm. They sold milk, butter, cheese, and ice cream, among other things. It was a fairly new building, clean and shining on the inside, and the girls always loved driving Billy there because they could each buy a huge ice cream cone after they had made their purchases.

Lizzie tied Billy to the adjacent hitching rack. She quickly grabbed a pound of butter before she met Mandy at the ice cream counter where she was already deliberating over the ice cream flavors. Finally, Mandy chose mint chocolate chip while Lizzie decided on butter pecan.

"Let's sit here at the picnic table," Lizzie said as they left the store. "I always have a problem driving and eating my ice cream at the same time."

"I'll hold your ice cream for you," Mandy offered.

"No, let's stay here and eat it," Lizzie said. She threw down the bag containing the butter on the picnic table before sitting down on one of the benches. A young man drove up to the store, got out of his car, and nodded at them before disappearing through the doors.

"He looks like Amos," Lizzie said.

"Everybody looks like Amos to you," Mandy said, taking her napkin and wiping her mouth.

Lizzie didn't answer. She just gazed across the rolling farmland, watching the black and white

Holsteins grazing as she steadily ate her ice cream.

After awhile, Lizzie said dully, "I wish I was still 15 like you!"

"I'm 15, almost 16."

"So? You're still not 17 like I am."

Mandy bit off a huge chunk of mint chocolate chip ice cream. Lizzie watched her with narrowed eyes.

"Doesn't that hurt your teeth?"

"Nah. So what's wrong with being 16?"

"Oh, I don't know. Nothing, I guess. I mean, I have fun most times but... Mandy, why do you think a guy acts like he likes you and you're really, really, really good friends, but he never asks you for a real date? You know, a date where I can go tell all my friends that I have a date?"

"I don't know, Lizzie. How can you expect me to know if I'm only 15. Almost 16."

Lizzie nodded. She wished that she could ask Mandy about Stephen, too. But what could she say? Amos' interest in Ruthie really upset her, but Stephen bothered her almost as much. He told her he was pretty, but then went back to acting like they were just friends.

Lizzie wasn't sure what she'd do if Stephen asked her on a date. Amos was one thing. He was handsome and fun and interesting, but was he really her friend, she couldn't help but wonder. Stephen was, even if he was too quiet and a little mysterious. What if he decided he didn't like her as much as she was starting to like him? Or what if he wanted to

get married? That had happened to Emma. Lizzie wanted to get married sometime. Probably. But not yet.

Lizzie sighed. Customers drove up to the porch or drove away, some of them with ice cream cones and others with dishes piled high with the cold, creamy confection. Some carried gallons of milk or chocolate milk or bags containing ice cream or cheese and butter.

Lizzie thought that milking cows wouldn't be nearly so bad if you could operate a farm on this level. She could have fun milking a hundred cows a day in a fancy milking parlor and running a beautiful new store like this one with electricity and huge coolers with shiny new tile on the floor. Then Dat could hire men to do the milking, and all Lizzie would have to do would be to comb her hair nicely and look neat and pretty, smiling at customers all day while she rang up sales on the up-to-date electronic cash register.

When they had finished their ice cream, Lizzie and Mandy climbed back into the buggy and headed towards home. Lizzie was glad she had eaten her ice cream on the porch of the store. Billy was in one of his running frenzies, as they called it, and it took all of Lizzie's strength to hold him to a trot.

He bent his head so he could hold the bit better, his ears turned forward, his mane thick and heavy, bouncing solidly along the nape of his neck. His muscular little haunches flapped rhythmically with every clacking step. He had never been shod, which

meant he ran on the hard, unrelenting macadam with no iron shoes tacked to his hard little hooves. He never slipped or fell, being as surefooted a pony as Dat had ever seen.

Once, when Lizzie's family was attending a church service 13 miles away from their home, Dat had allowed Lizzie and Mandy to drive Billy. Little Billy moved in line with a row of other horses and buggies, running steadily up hill and down, his legs taking two steps to the larger horses' one. Dat would tell this story to anyone who would listen, how his little feet went "Blip-blip-blip," and how he kept up perfectly, arriving at church services without being winded.

"He wasn't even blowing. He could have run 10 more miles," Dat would say, waving his hands for emphasis.

Lizzie always felt like crying when Dat told that story, her love of this plucky little pony stirring up an emotion that choked her and melted into tears. He was the best, the strongest, the sweetest pony they had ever owned, and Lizzie hoped with all her heart he would live forever.

They moved down the hill through the village at an alarming pace, Lizzie hanging on to the reins with all her strength. They hit the concrete bridge, bouncing off the seat as they flew across the creek.

Mandy burst out laughing, and Lizzie joined in.

"Don't make me laugh, Mandy!" she gasped. "I can't hold him!" But the harder they tried to hold back their laughter, the more helpless they became,

until Lizzie actually was struck by a panicky feeling that Billy was running away.

"Stop it, Mandy!" she shouted.

"Wheeee!" was Mandy's response, which caused Lizzie to fall into helpless giggles again.

As Billy broke into a gallop going up the opposite hill, the sisters became serious as Lizzie wrapped the reins around her hands and pulled with all her strength. He slowed, but none too obediently, Lizzie thought, sensing through the reins that he would break into another gallop the second she let up on them.

Mandy reached over and slapped her hand down on Lizzie's arm. "Good driver!" she said, grinning.

Lizzie grinned back. She was overcome with a feeling of love for Mandy. Dear skinny, green-eyed Mandy. The love of her life, besides Mam, Dat, Emma, and Jason. She loved Susan and KatieAnn too, of course, but not like Mandy. There was just something about having a sister close to your own age that was unlike any other blessing in life.

When Lizzie said something funny, she knew instinctively that Mandy would find it hilarious. She always did. And when Mandy was joking or in a silly mood, no one caught on faster than Lizzie.

The evening sun shed its warm golden light all around them and around the surrounding woods, fields, and houses. Even the telephone poles etched against the evening sky looked pretty as they wound their way home.

Lizzie momentarily forgot her troubled feelings about weekends, Amos and Ruthie, and running

around in general as she laughed happily with Mandy, skidding the pony cart wheels as they turned in on the country road that took them home.

᠕᠊

The following Sunday evening, not very long after Lizzie arrived at the supper crowd, Rebecca, Stephen's sister, came running toward her.

"Come here, Lizzie!"

"You'll never guess what?"

"What? What? Don't keep me guessing!"

Lizzie's eyes shone in anticipation, her heart beating, her thoughts going instantly to Amos. Maybe... just maybe...

"Amos asked Ruthie for a date this weekend!" Rebecca said. "It's her first one!"

Lizzie felt as if Rebecca had hit her in the stomach with a boxing glove. All the air surrounding her lungs pushed up against her throat, constricting it in an awful choking sensation. She leaned back, reaching for the support of the chair behind her, feeling as if the whole floor was somehow going completely crooked. She hadn't expected this kind of news to hurt this much.

"Lizzie, aren't you happy for them? You look as if you'd seen a ghost!" Rebecca burst out.

"Oh! Oh, no... No, of course I'm happy for Ruthie! It's just such a total shock! I mean... I mean... I didn't know Amos liked her," she ended lamely.

"They liked each other since they went to vocational class together," Rebecca said, absolutely beaming. "It's so-o cute!"

"Oh, yes! Of course, I think so, too," Lizzie said. She felt as dishonest and untruthful as she had ever been in her whole life. Only her pride kept her standing there, knuckles white against the dark wood of the chair, a false smile pasted on her face.

The rest of the evening at the supper passed as if in a haze for Lizzie as she kept trying desperately to control her emotions. When Amos appeared in the kitchen door looking more handsome than ever in a sky-blue shirt, his black vest and pants setting off his very dark hair and skin, Lizzie almost burst into tears of frustration.

She slowly put down her plate and calmly walked to the bathroom where she sat down on the side of the bathtub, held her head in her hands, and cried great tears of annoyance and bitter disappointment. Why? How could he act as if he liked her one weekend and the very next Sunday have a date with Ruthie? She sat up and sniffed, grabbing a tissue from the box on the sink and honking into it loudly. She dabbed viciously at her eyes, going to the mirror to see the damage her tears had done.

Taking a deep breath, she braced her shoulders, pulled up her cape, and adjusted her covering. I don't want him anyway. I hope he marries Ruthie and she gains 50 pounds the first year. I hope he dates her awhile, and then they break up because he

wants me. I'm not going to congratulate her. I'm not even going to talk to her.

No one will ever like me, she thought. First Joe and John, the handsome twins who were in her class at vocational school, who had paid much more attention to their pretty Mennonite classmates. Now Amos had picked Ruthie instead of her. I'm just fat and ugly. I have pimples.

But really, what does Ruthie have that I don't? She can't drive a fast horse or swim. Lizzie's thoughts collided against each other like bumper cars at an amusement park as she struggled with jealousy, self-pity, a low sense of self-worth, and, most of all, her first real disappointment in love.

"Who's in here?"

A resounding knock on the bathroom door propelled Lizzie into action. Dabbing desperately at her eyes with a cold wash rag and answering in a muffled voice, she sprang to the door to unlock it.

"You heard," Emma said.

She stepped into the bathroom and closed the door behind her.

That was Lizzie's undoing. All the pent-up frustration and bitter defeat emerged in one low sob which caught in her throat, bringing a real, little-girl hiccup with it.

Emma put her arms around her, stroking her back, talking in soothing tones, for all the world as she had done so many years before in the privy at school when Lizzie had the blues because of a mournful song the pupils were singing. The thought

hit Lizzie, and in the middle of her tears, her shoulders started shaking uncontrollably as she began to laugh hysterically.

Emma stepped back, her eyes wide with concern. "You're laughing and crying at the same time!"

Lizzie blew her nose, sniffing, and smiling ruefully as she said, "Emma, this reminds me of us in first grade! Remember?"

Emma laughed with Lizzie, saying, "I guess we're still in first grade, as far as lessons in life go."

They sat side by side on the bathtub before Lizzie lifted her head and said, "Oh, well, I guess he wasn't meant for me."

"I guess not."

"Why do you suppose I don't have any luck with finding a husband? I don't really, really think I'm so awful looking. I mean, there are girls homelier than me who have boyfriends, aren't there?"

"Of course, Lizzie. You know you're even better looking than me."

"No, I'm not, Emma."

"Lizzie, please don't think you're ugly and worth nothing at all now. I knew you were going to do this. Listen. You know how Mam always says God knows best, and he already knows that somewhere there is a special young man for you. You just haven't found him yet. Sometimes he takes a long winding road around to teach us valuable lessons on the way."

"Evidently *you* didn't need any."

"Well..."

"Emma, it's always been like this. You don't seem to need lessons in your life, hard ones like this, and I get one right after the other."

"Not everyone's life is the same, Lizzie," Emma said, smiling at her reassuringly.

Lizzie sighed as she intently pleated her black apron across her knee. "Yeah, I guess, but I'll tell you one thing. I'm glad getting to heaven doesn't depend on luck, or I'd never make it. I hardly ever won in Chutes and Ladders even, because most times I landed on the square where you go down the longest chute."

Emma laughed. "You'll land on the square that takes you right back up the longest ladder soon, Lizzie, just you watch!" Emma said, squeezing Lizzie's hand affectionately. "Come on, you can go with Joshua and me to the singing."

Lizzie brightened noticeably. "All right, I will. Then no one will know where I am when I'm not around. Amos will think I walked home, and he'll feel so guilty it isn't e-e-even funny!"

They muffled their giggles in their handkerchiefs as they heard another knock on the bathroom door.

Chapter 4

AFter Amos began dating Ruthie, Lizzie threw herself into her much anticipated year of teaching school. She helped the parents clean the old red-brick schoolhouse, washing down the freshly painted plaster walls and rubbing the old window-panes with a solution of soap and vinegar until they shone. The men dabbed fresh putty outside the win-dowpanes and put a new stovepipe in the well-worn wood furnace. They varnished the old school desks for the 20 pupils who would attend school that year. After the cleaning was done, the men poured fresh oil on the wooden floor, which the boards partly absorbed, making it an easier task to sweep the dust and dirt from it.

There was just something about a freshly oiled floor, Lizzie thought, as she breathed in deeply after everyone else had gone home. It reminded her of her own Teacher Katie and her yellow apple, of a piece of fresh chalk in the blackboard tray, of clapping

erasers in the sunshine while holding her head to the side as she squinted through the white dust at her friends who were doing the same thing. School was just a wonderful place to be, especially now since she was the teacher with so many new plans and ideas floating about in her head. She had a list of all her pupils. Some were Mennonite and some were Amish children, but to Lizzie there was no difference. She looked forward to having each one as her pupil.

Sitting at her desk, she clasped her hands in front of her and took a deep breath of absolute delight. Imagine! This was her very own teacher's desk with a wooden chair that had arms at the side and swiveled just like Teacher Katie's chair. Lizzie reached down and lifted up a plastic bag from the floor which contained new bookends, a pretty apple mug for her pens, and a basket to hold papers that had been corrected. She arranged each item, stacking her teacher's answer keys in sequence, starting with eighth grade on the left through third grade on the far right. First and second grades had workbooks with different answer books, so they went into her deep drawer on the left.

She hung name charts on the wall, each one a covered wagon designed with each pupil's name stenciled on it in black marker. Then she adjusted the A-B-C and 1-2-3 charts that the first-graders used and began taping name tags on each pupil's desk. Eighth-graders in the big seats along the back wall, followed by seats for the seventh-graders, and

on down to the little first-graders at the front of the room whose desks seemed to be only knee-high.

Lizzie smiled to herself as she pictured the incoming first-grade class. Those little Mennonite girls were so sweet in their flowered dresses, with pigtails and barrettes in their hair. She could hardly wait to be their teacher. She frowned a bit, thinking about the upper-grade boys. Only a few years ago she had been a pupil here, playing baseball with some of the boys who would now be her pupils this year. She hoped with all her heart that they would respect her enough to behave most of the time. They weren't openly disobedient boys, just mischievous like all boys.

After everything was in order she stepped back and looked at the classroom, smiling with satisfaction. It was old, no doubt about it, with mismatched desks and chairs, cracked plaster ceilings, and an old wood furnace, but it was sparkling clean with a freshly washed blackboard and long pieces of white chalk lying in the wooden tray waiting to be used. Carefully she took a piece of chalk and wrote, "Monday, August 25," across the top of the board.

Oh, my, she thought. That is the grandest thing, writing on a blackboard like a real honest-to-goodness teacher. She stepped back and admired the teacherly slant to her handwriting, which bolstered her courage to begin teaching. She may not be very good at finding a husband, but she sure could write like a teacher.

❧

Lizzie woke up early on the first day of school. She put on a forest-green dress, pinning the cape carefully into place, wetting her hair so she could roll it back neatly on either side of her head. When she finished combing her hair, she adjusted her black belt apron before turning around at least half a dozen times in front of the mirror to make sure everything was tucked, pinned, and pleated perfectly. Twenty pairs of eyes would be checking her out very closely, and she wanted to appear as neat and teacherly as possible.

Lizzie choked on her pancake before giving up on eating breakfast. She just wasn't hungry with all those butterflies in her stomach. Every time she thought of standing behind her desk to read the Bible story book, her stomach did a perfect flip-flop.

Emma glanced at Lizzie's uneaten food and raised her eyebrows.

"Butterflies?" she asked.

"Sort of," Lizzie admitted, laughing.

Mam put down her coffee cup.

"You'll do fine, Lizzie. You have more gumption when it comes to something like this than any of the other girls," she said.

That was all it took to calm Lizzie's nerves. If Mam placed so much faith in Lizzie's ability to face a classroom filled with eight grades, then Lizzie knew she could do her job well. She sighed, beaming at Mam, and then pulled up on the shoulders of her cape and went to the front window to watch for her driver.

The driver was an older gentleman who made a good living as a driver for Amish people in the community. Lizzie knew him well so she didn't mind sitting up front and chatting with him on the way to school. Jason sat in the back seat with a group of his friends as the van stopped at different Amish homes, picking up more of Lizzie's students en route to the brick schoolhouse.

There was a small group of Mennonite children on the playground when Lizzie arrived. As she unlocked the door she smiled at a few small children who stood in the background. Lizzie's worries faded as the students entered the classroom. The children just took over, crowding around her desk, introducing themselves, oohing and aahing about the name charts on the walls, admiring the cup where her pens and pencils were kept, and finding the desks with their names written on the tags.

Lizzie discovered to her delight that she could move quite unself-consciously about her classroom, the children's unabashed happiness making her forget all about her shyness. It's just like being at home, she thought happily. Oh, this will be so much fun. I'm going to teach school and never, ever get married.

When she rang the hand bell, everyone went quickly to their seats—so quickly, in fact, that Lizzie almost burst out laughing. They were so eager to please her. Surely this wouldn't last for long. Lizzie cleared her throat.

"Good morning, boys and girls!"

The whole classroom, except a few scared first-graders, answered, "Good morning, Teacher!"

Lizzie bent her head and read the very first story in the Bible story book about creation and the Garden of Eden. After she finished, the children stood beside their desks, and they all said the Lord's Prayer. Lizzie was desperately afraid she would forget a line, but she closed her eyes and concentrated, finding it harder to get through the prayer than she had thought.

Next, the children all filed up to the blackboard behind her desk and stood hesitantly while Lizzie sorted them by height for singing class. Jason and the other upper-graders stood in a row along the blackboard, followed by a second row of fifth- and sixth-graders who were a bit smaller, and so on until the first-graders stood beside the second grade in the front row.

"There, that looks pretty good," Lizzie said. "Maybe... Jason, would you trade places with Robert?"

She switched a few more children until the biggest children stood in the middle and the shortest stood on each side. Lizzie handed out the songbooks and picked the first song, an easy hymn that most children knew well, "Life's Railway to Heaven." After she started the song, they joined her, singing along as well as you could expect a group who wasn't accustomed to singing together.

Lizzie smiled at them reassuringly, noticing the one little first-grade girl looking a bit sad. If that little girl

cries, I'm not going to sing one more song. I mean it, Lizzie thought, remembering the time she had been in first grade, so absolutely terrified about the stars falling that she could not wait to go home to Mam. But the little girl soldiered bravely on, trying her best to remain upbeat and positive, although the display of emotions on her small upturned face was heartbreaking. Lizzie couldn't stand another minute of seeing that poor, brave, little girl putting forth so much effort to keep from crying, so she said, "All right, we'll just sing two songs this morning because we only have a half-day today. It's our very first day, of course."

As the pupils filed to their seats, she smiled at the frightened little girl who dipped her head shyly and scuttled to her seat.

Lizzie asked the children to introduce themselves, saying their full names so she could begin to memorize who sat in which desk. The first-graders were Rosa, David, and Arlene, who whispered their names so quietly Lizzie could barely hear them.

The remainder of the day flew by on wings. She barely had time to look at the clock. She helped the pupils with their books and workbooks, passing out clean new tablets, pencils, and erasers. She showed the first and second grade where the scissors was kept on a hook low on the wall. She told them they'd have lots of cutting and pasting to do, which brought a shy smile to Rosa's face.

What an adorable child, Lizzie thought. But I'm not allowed to have teacher's pets. That doesn't work at all.

There were so many things to do, assigning the next day's work, finding the proper pages for the lower grades, answering raised hands in between her other duties, that the clock showed eleven-thirty before she was finished.

They had only half-days that first week, an old custom that allowed the children to go home and help their parents with the end of the summer's harvest. So at noon Lizzie quickly told everyone to put their books away just as the school van driver pulled into the schoolyard. Oh, dear, we haven't even swept or cleaned up a thing, she thought. Oh, well, it's my first day. I'll keep getting better, I hope.

She told everyone they would learn their good-bye song the following day and tapped the bell to dismiss them. She was shocked to hear everyone shout, "Good-bye, Teacher! Good-bye. Good-bye!" as they scrambled for the front door. Lizzie tried to answer, but there was no use. They would never have heard her over the din, even if she had yelled at the top of her lungs. She would have to try and quiet down this enthusiastic parting. But then, maybe the children would be insulted and think she was some doddering old maid who lived a joyless existence. Quickly, she packed a few things in her book bag, locked the door, and climbed into the front seat of the school van.

She sighed as the van pulled away from the school, and the driver smiled at her.

"Big day?" he asked.

Lizzie nodded.

They talked most of the way home, and, as usual, Lizzie could hardly wait to get there because she was bursting with lots of things to tell Mam. Emma and Mandy were away working, she knew, but it was lunch-time, so Dat would be in the house.

"How did it go, Lizzie?" he asked, as she hurried in the door.

"Oh, good! Really good. Except a little, first-grade girl almost cried, and Dat, I mean it, they're so loud after I dismiss them, it isn't even normal. They yell good-bye with all their might."

Dat chuckled as he took a bite of homemade vegetable soup.

"I guess they're glad to be out of there," he said.

As he crumbled a handful of saltines into the soup, he started to blink his eyes rapidly. He bent his head to take off his glasses and rub his hands across both eyes as he continued to blink.

"Can't figure out what's wrong with my eyes this morning. Everything seems a bit fuzzy, especially my one eye," he said, as he put his glasses back on while blinking over and over.

"Didn't you sleep well?" Mam asked.

"Just as good as usual," Dat answered.

"Which must be pretty good by the sounds of your snoring. I can hear you from my upstairs bedroom sometimes," Lizzie said, laughing.

"That's Mam you hear!" Dat said.

"Oh, I wouldn't say that, Melvin. Who knows? We both snore."

Jason slid onto the bench beside Lizzie.

"I'm starved!" he said.

"Here. Take some vegetable soup," Mam said, hovering over him, seeing that he had bread, cheese, and sweet bologna. Jason slapped bologna on a slice of bread, threw a piece of cheese on top, smashed the second piece of bread down on the cheese, and stuffed half of the dry sandwich into his mouth.

Jason's eating never failed to amaze Lizzie. He took bites twice the size of an ordinary person and swallowed promptly. You could hardly ever see him chewing; well, not very much, anyway. He ate so fast, Lizzie could never understand how he didn't upset his stomach when he swallowed his food without chewing properly.

"Pickles!" Jason said loudly.

"Your sandwich is too dry, isn't it?" Lizzie grinned at him.

"No, 'course not. I'm just hungry for a pickle."

"How did it feel to have Lizzie for a teacher?" Mam asked.

Jason's mouth was stuffed with pickles, so he nodded his head before bending it to eat the other half of his sandwich in one bite.

Dat shook his head, watching Jason eat.

"As soon as you have time, you can answer Mam," he said, his eyes twinkling.

Jason swallowed and nodded his head again. "Good. I think she's going to be all right. She's a good teacher!"

He started slurping soup, so Lizzie knew that was as much as he would say. She looked at Mam,

beaming, and Mam smiled back.

"Good for you, Lizzie. I knew you could do it. Do you think you'll like it? This is only the first day, you know."

"I love it, Mam. I really do. I can't imagine getting the blues from teaching school. It's so much more challenging than standing at that egg-grading machine or working as a *maud*."

"There'll be times when you wish life was as simple as grading eggs, though. You can't teach school without occasional troubles along the way," Dat said wisely.

"How do you know?" Lizzie asked.

"Because I taught school one year," Dat said.

"Did you really? I never knew that."

So Dat launched into an account of his one year of teaching school when he and Mam were first married and living in Ohio. It was fascinating to listen to him tell the story of serious discipline problems, among other troubles he had encountered. But Dat's stories didn't worry Lizzie. She was quite sure that teaching school was the single most wonderful thing in the entire world, and there wasn't too much that could happen to change her mind. It was a whole lot easier than finding a husband.

Chapter 5

Lizzie narrowed her eyes as she looked over her shoulder, pinning her white cape neatly into place.

"That's crooked," Mandy said, around a pin in her mouth. Lizzie sighed with exasperation before saying loudly, "Take that pin out of your mouth this second. I hate when you put a straight pin in there. Mam used to do that when we were little girls."

"I won't swallow it."

"Take it out!"

"Grouch."

Lizzie looked over her opposite shoulder, trying to get the pleats in her white organdy cape straight. Of all the clothes they wore, white organdy for church was the hardest to handle.

"Mandy, fix this!" Lizzie said, unable to get the whole thing straight. Mandy helped, adjusting a few pins, before saying, "Lizzie, aren't you thrilled about our new friends we'll get to meet today?"

More new families were moving to Cameron County that fall, including the Marks family with four girls near in age to Lizzie and her sisters. A young man had also recently moved there to help his brother, a bachelor, with the farming.

"Of course! Maybe if we have a few more teenagers we'll start to run around here in Cameron County and not bother going to Allen County at all anymore. Marvin was talking about it last weekend."

"Really?"

"Mmm-hmm."

"Goody, Lizzie! I'll soon be 16, and I don't really want to go to Allen County. It's too far away."

"Hurry up, girls. Time to leave," Mam called up the stairway.

Hurriedly, they pinned their black coverings to their heads, grabbed their black woolen shawls and bonnets and skipped down the steps. Emma ran lightly down the stairs behind them, a bottle of lotion clasped in one hand. In the kitchen, KatieAnn and Susan put on their coats and shawls, followed by their navy blue bonnets, while Mam hurried to get everyone out the door to the waiting carriage.

Lizzie scooped up Susan and planted a kiss on her little cheek. "You look so cute in your shawl and bonnet," she said.

"Let me down!" Susan said, wiping her cheek as she glared at Lizzie. Everyone laughed as they hurried out the door, while Dat stood wiping the mirror on the buggy with his clean, white, Sunday handkerchief.

༺ঔ༻

At church, Lizzie sat next to Mandy on the long, backless bench on the women's side of the room. As the boys filed into the room, they bent slightly to shake hands with the ministers before going to the men's side of the room to sit. A tall boy whom Lizzie didn't recognize joined the group. That must be the new boy who's moving in with his bachelor brother, Lizzie thought. She dug her elbow into Mandy's side.

"Is that him?" she whispered.

"Probably," Mandy whispered back.

He was taller than Uncle Marvin, with long, jet-black hair which hung in loose waves. His eyes were almost as dark as his hair, and he had an almost perfect nose and mouth. His face was expressionless and polite, but Lizzie was fascinated by his dark, good looks. Mandy must be, too, she thought, watching her. Oh, well, no use planning about this one as a husband. He'd probably go the way of Amos and of Joe and John, the twins who had caught Lizzie's eye in vocational school. Or he'd act like Stephen. He'd tell her that he thought she was pretty once and then never mention it again.

Stephen, Joe, and John filed into the room. The twins, once small for their age when they were in Lizzie's vocational class, had grown to almost normal size. They were still as blond and blue-eyed as ever. Stephen stood tall and dark beside them, his blue eyes flashing around the room until they landed

on her. He smiled. Irritated, Lizzie turned away.

During services, Lizzie considered the possibility of staying here in Cameron County on weekends. Allen County had lost much of its charm since Amos and Ruthie were dating, she had to admit. Now there were enough young people in church to have their own supper crowd somewhere nearby and have a singing in the evening each weekend. That would be exciting, something new, and she bet they would have lots of fun once everyone became acquainted.

Doddy Glick stood up to give the main sermon, and, as usual, he preached with fervor. He always became quite loud, waving his arms for emphasis as he exhorted the congregation, adding Old Testament stories as examples for their everyday lives. Lizzie never tired of listening to Doddy preach, enjoying his stories of Gideon, David, and other Old Testament heroes.

After services, Lizzie asked Uncle Marvin if he was planning to stay here for the rest of the weekend. He raised his eyebrows and nodded toward the Marks sisters and said he guessed he'd have to since they had more young people now. Lizzie laughed and hit his arm playfully.

"Oh, you! I know exactly why you aren't going to Allen County!"

"Should we try and have a singing here? Do you want me to ask if Aaron Fishers want to hold one? Or what? What could we do this afternoon?" he asked.

Stephen and the new young man, John, walked up to Marvin.

"Hello," they said, nodding to Lizzie.

"Hi!"

"So ... do we want to go boating?" Marvin asked.

"The water's too low," Stephen said. "We need more rain."

"Volleyball?" Marvin asked.

"We can go down to my brother's place," John offered.

Lizzie watched him speak, quite impressed with this tall guy. Of course, she wanted to go to his brother's place, and now she had several girlfriends and Mandy to go with her, all of whom had recently turned 16.

"I have to do evening chores because Leroy is in Allen County," John said.

"Good! We'll help you!" Marvin volunteered. "Do we want the girls to go along? There are only three of them."

"They can make supper," John said, smiling shyly.

Lizzie was ecstatic! She walked as calmly as she possibly could to the washhouse and almost shrieked as she grabbed Rebecca's hand.

"Rebecca, I'm so glad you're 16. And Mandy and Mary Ann just turned 16! We're going to have so much fun together. First of all, the boys are doing chores at Leroy Zook's place. You know, that old guy that's dating Emma's friend. They want us to go along and make supper!"

"Does that mean we're going to start having suppers and singings here now?" Rebecca asked.

"I guess that's up to the parents, but I think everyone would be glad to have singings, even if the group is small. Should we ask Aaron's wife if they want a hymn-singing this evening after the boys have finished the chores at Leroy's farm?"

And so plans were made, with the small group of youth being "officially" started in Cameron County. The girls had great fun cooking supper through trial and error at Leroy Zook's house as the boys did the evening chores. Mary Ann was easy to talk to and, after a few hours together, Lizzie felt as if they had known each other for a long time. Rebecca was also talkative and good-natured with an easy laugh, and her antics never failed to send Lizzie into rounds of helpless laughter.

The boys came in for supper, filling their plates before sitting in the living room to eat. The girls ate around the kitchen table, laughing about the lumpy gravy on the mashed potatoes.

"This is a nice farm," Mary Ann said.

Lizzie agreed. The house wasn't new, but it had four good-sized rooms with a porch running along the front of the house. The view was nice, overlooking rolling pastures and neighboring farms. Leroy had recently built a new cow stable, and a new silo jutted up against the looming mountain, giving the whole farm a prosperous look.

What would it be like to marry John and live

here in this farmhouse, milking cows every morning? Lizzie thought she could marry a farmer if he looked like John. It wouldn't be so bad to stumble out to a cow stable at five o'clock in the morning if a husband that good-looking was beside you, helping you milk cows.

Was John a farmer, or was he only helping out his brother for a little bit before returning to Lamton with its big community of Amish folks? Did he have a girlfriend? She wondered how he was going to the singing that evening, and if she might be riding in the same buggy.

But when it was time to go to the singing, Marvin, of course, offered to take all three girls in his buggy. So Lizzie knew there would be no riding to the singing with John because it wasn't fair to make the other girls go alone with the boys. Mary Ann was still new, and she couldn't do that to her. So she told Marvin, all right, they would all go with him.

How unexciting, she thought, as she sat in the back seat of Marvin's buggy, slouched down and pouting just a tiny bit. Maybe if Marvin wouldn't have been quite so eager to ask us, John would have gone with me and Mary Ann. Oh well, she decided, that made no sense either, so there was no use being upset.

When they arrived at the singing, the kitchen table was already spread out long enough so everyone could sit around it, boys on one side and girls

on the other. Some parents had come to help sing as well. Aaron Fisher's wife set pitchers of water and some paper cups on the table so no one would get thirsty. Since Lizzie was a schoolteacher, the girls said she could start the first song, an old German hymn she knew well from school and from singing it in Allen County with the youth there.

Glancing nervously at John, she cleared her throat and started the song. Marvin was a good singer, and he joined in heartily. The parents helped along immediately, realizing that there were only a few youth to keep the singing going smoothly. They sang one hymn after another, old German songs that had been sung by Amish youth for years and years. Lizzie especially enjoyed these old hymns, and she loved to sing. The evening sped by.

Mrs. Fisher served a snack of pretzels and cheese, leftover snitz pie, and grape juice after the singing was over. Lizzie and her friends laughed and talked with the parents easily. In this small budding community, the two generations had a close relationship. Some of the parents asked Lizzie how teaching was going and if the children were causing any trouble.

Marvin said he could take Lizzie home after the singing, which puzzled her. Stephen and Rebecca lived closer to her than Marvin, and she was sure they wouldn't mind dropping her off. She told Marvin so, but he insisted, telling her he really wanted to. It was time they had a good old chat to catch up again, he said.

That warmed Lizzie's heart, and she was glad

he wanted to take her home, even if it meant many extra miles for Marvin. They hadn't gone very far before Marvin blurted out, "Lizzie, it's no wonder you don't have a boyfriend."

Lizzie's heart thudded and sank to her shoes. A heart couldn't sink to your shoes, she always thought, but sometimes when something shocked her, she had that kind of sensation, a sinking, downward feeling.

"Whatever makes you say that?" she breathed.

"Well, you know you are my dear 'niecely,' but you need to sit up and take notice. I don't want to hurt your feelings, Lizzie, but I can hardly stand to see something that you are so blind about."

"What on earth are you talking about, Marvin?"

"Well, hey, fix that rearview mirror. When a car comes up behind me, the headlights are blinding."

Typical proper Marvin, Lizzie thought as she opened the door of the buggy and adjusted the mirror.

"Right. Turn it a little to the right. There."

Lizzie closed the door, and Marvin continued.

"Just like now. This John guy coming out from Lamton, I can just see how he thrills you, and you bat your eyelashes, and you're all nervous and giggly when he's around."

"Every one of us girls was!" Lizzie burst out.

"I know. I know. I can see why. I mean, it's only normal, but that really bugs me, and since John is here, I have to say something. Lizzie, don't you even notice Stephen?"

Lizzie was dumbfounded.

"What do you mean, notice him?"

"Well, it's as plain as day, Lizzie. He adores the ground you walk on, he would do anything for you, and you notice him as much as...as an insect!" Marvin said.

"Marvin! I don't!"

"You do!"

"I don't. I mean it. I like Stephen. We talk a lot. All the time, actually. He's one of my friends. I mean...I do not treat him like an insect."

"See, Lizzie. Maybe that's why Amos started dating Ruthie—because he wasn't meant for you. It seems as if you always want someone else, and it's so plain what's happening right under your nose, but you're too busy always chasing after someone else."

"I don't chase after boys!" Lizzie shouted.

"Not so loud. You know what I mean."

Lizzie said nothing, just leaned back against the seat and crossed her arms tightly. Of all the nerve! This was the worst! How was she supposed to know how Stephen felt? All he ever said was that she was pretty once. But what did that really mean?

"I'm sorry, niecely."

Lizzie didn't answer. She was too angry.

"But please, Lizzie. Stephen is a great guy, a really nice, genuine kind of person. He doesn't think highly of himself, and maybe that's why he acts kind of different sometimes. But, ach well, I guess I can hardly stand to see him like you as much as he does,

and you're off on Cloud Nine somewhere."

"I like Stephen, Marvin."

"But not in that way, right?"

"Well… not really. I mean, I guess if I knew he liked me, but…" Lizzie was at a loss for words.

"All right. I won't push some big burden on you, Lizzie. But, seriously, try and pray about it and regard him in a different light. You know, maybe he has all the feelings for you because it's meant to be, and you're just not listening to God's voice."

There was silence in the buggy except for the wheels rattling over the gravel and the horses' hooves spitting it against the bottom of the buggy. When they rolled to a stop by the sidewalk, Lizzie couldn't believe they were at home.

"There you go, Lizzie. Sorry if I offended you." Marvin slid his arm around her shoulders and squeezed affectionately. "Just think about it. Okay?"

There was already a dangerous lump forming in Lizzie's throat, the kind that quickly dissolves into embarrassing tears. She hopped out of the buggy, choking on her "Thanks, Marvin!" as she ran up the sidewalk.

Dear, caring Marvin. Who can stay angry at him? He's so genuinely honest.

When she hurried through the kitchen without speaking to Joshua and Emma, who were having a snack at the kitchen table, they looked at each other and shrugged. It was hard to tell what had happened now.

Chapter 6

Ever since Mandy had turned 16 years old, Lizzie was very happy. She was enjoying running around even more now that Mandy was allowed to go away with her on weekends. To celebrate, they had a great time painting and redecorating a room for Mandy and moving Lizzie's old bedroom suite into her room.

One snowy afternoon, shortly after Mandy's birthday, Lizzie sat at the sewing machine, a frown creasing her brow as she used the seam ripper to open the seam of a sleeve she had accidentally sewed on with the inside out. Finally, she stuck a few stray hairs under her covering, pushed back her chair in exasperation, threw down the offending garment, and marched out to the kitchen.

"I hate that fabric!" she said, much louder than necessary.

Mam looked up from watering the geraniums in the window. "Now what?" she asked.

"Why don't they produce fabric that looks the same on both sides?" Lizzie said, reaching for a warm chocolate chip cookie.

"I don't know," Mam said absentmindedly, her attention on a vine that needed inspection. "Hmm. This thing has mealybugs, that's what," she muttered.

Lizzie watched her mother with narrowed eyes. "You're not listening to me," Lizzie whined.

"Hmm?"

The door opened and Dat came into the kitchen, closing the door firmly behind him as he shivered, pulling off his coat and hat.

"Brrr! That air goes right through to the bones. It's a good thing I fixed those cow stable windows this week. I'm going to warm up and take a bit of a break. I'm just plain cold the whole way through."

Lizzie munched her cookie, saying nothing while Dat rubbed his hands together.

"Oh, yes, the phone was ringing out in the shanty when I went to call the vet. It was Henry's Sharon. She's having a sledding party at their farm this evening."

Lizzie sat up, brightening noticeably. Saturday evening! Maybe they could stay at Sharon's house for the night!

"Oh, goody!" Lizzie shouted.

"You sound like a five-year-old," Mandy said, grinning.

"You're just as excited as I am!" Lizzie said. She stuck out her tongue at Mandy.

❧

The snow continued to fall all day, turning the outdoors into a winter wonderland as Lizzie and Mandy traveled to Sharon's house. When they arrived, they were surprised to see a few other buggies parked by the horse barn.

They knocked lightly on the kitchen door. It burst open, and Sara Ruth and Rebecca pulled them into the house.

"You're late!" they said in unison, enveloping both girls with mittened hands.

"Bess had a shoe missing, so we had to get a driver," Mandy explained.

"It's okay. Sharon's mom made pizza!"

The kitchen had a warm, spicy, tomatoey smell, which mixed well with the aroma of homemade yeast dough. Lizzie's stomach rumbled unexpectedly, reminding her of how hungry she really was. Always watching her weight, she hadn't eaten any lunch or supper, only breakfast and one chocolate chip cookie that afternoon. She always wanted to feel thin, especially on running around weekends, so often on Saturdays she ate very little.

Sharon's mother, Cathy, was bustling between the table and the oven, setting two huge, round pizzas on the table. She grinned at Lizzie and Mandy.

"Where were you?" she asked.

"Late, evidently," Lizzie said, smiling.

"No, you're just in time," Cathy said. She was a small, gray-haired woman, formerly from an Amish

community in Indiana. She had a quiet smile and manner of speaking. Lizzie loved to go to Sharon's house, feeling very welcome to spend the night or just be with Sharon. Her father, Henry, was a farmer who was just as friendly and welcoming as his wife.

"Help yourselves. Pizza's done," Henry boomed to the group of young men who were seated in the living room. They wasted no time in heaping their plates with pizza, potato chips, cheese, bologna, and other snacks.

Lizzie said hello to everyone before helping herself to a slice of the thick homemade pizza. It was one of the most delicious things she had ever eaten. The crust was thick and springy, with hot tomato sauce and cheese melting off the sides. Sausage and pepperoni sat on top of the melting cheese.

Oh, well, we're going sledding, Lizzie thought as she took a big bite, so I'll work off all the calories in this wonderful pizza.

After they finished eating and had helped Cathy with the dishes, Lizzie and her friends zipped up their snow boots, buttoned their coats, and tied their white scarves securely. Talking and laughing, they wound their way across the road and up a long twisting path to the top of a hill. Since visibility was limited with the snow whirling past them, the boys set gas lanterns in the snow at different points to mark the trail they would sled down. The group pulled wooden sleds with runners, a toboggan, plastic sleds, round sleds—anything that would whisk them down the hill.

The girls mostly used the runner sleds and the boys piled on the long wooden toboggan, determined to see how many could fit on at one time and how fast they would go.

Lizzie wasn't normally afraid of sledding, but watching the toboggan streak past her at such an alarming speed terrified her. The boys whizzed by so fast in one long dark blur, often losing one or two riders before they slowed at the bottom of the hill.

Later in the evening, the boys started a roaring bonfire in a small patch of trees, protected from the steady east wind and blowing snowflakes. One by one, the girls tired of sledding and sat by the fire to warm themselves.

Lizzie hadn't realized that she and Mandy were the only remaining girls sledding until John Zook and Paul Esh asked them to try a toboggan ride.

Mandy quickly accepted, which really irked Lizzie. *She's probably as scared as I am, but if John asks her to go, she'll go,* Lizzie thought. *She'd try to fly off a house roof if he asked her to jump.*

"Come on, Lizzie!" Mandy shouted.

"I'm not going."

"Come on!"

"No!"

"We won't go as fast if you girls go," Paul assured them. He was new to Cameron County, but he was easy to get along with and really funny. He had quickly become one of Lizzie's good friends, and she often confided in him.

Lizzie looked at Paul skeptically. "I don't know

about you."

"We'll be careful. Come on, pile on. Ladies before gentlemen!" Paul laughed.

"How many are going?"

"Just you and Mandy, me and John."

"I'll push you," Stephen offered, as he walked up to join them.

Her heart hammering in her chest, Lizzie seated herself behind Mandy. The boys piled on the back, telling the sisters to keep their feet on the sled. When the boys yelled "right" or "left," the girls should lean in that direction in order to steer the toboggan. Stephen showed Lizzie how to hang on to the rope attached along each side of the sled. She bit her lip, sniffed, blinked the snowflakes from her eyes, and tried to stay calm.

Mandy was eagerly leaning forward. "What are we waiting on? Let's go!"

There were a few thudding sounds as Stephen pushed on Paul's shoulders before he leaped on the back. Then the only sensation was black, whirling, blinding speed. It was the most helplessly, horrifying feeling Lizzie had ever experienced. She could see nothing at all, except sometimes Mandy's white-clad head bobbing up in front of her. The wind whistled so fast it was almost like a huge, sucking void that took her breath away.

When she could no longer bear the feeling of falling into a dark, bottomless hole, she screamed. She continued to yell at the top of her lungs, afraid to keep going and afraid to roll off.

She sincerely hoped they would each remain in one piece when they came to the bottom of this gigantic, seemingly endless hill. When her mouth became too dry from screaming, she just clamped it shut and hated Mandy with all her might. It was all her fault. She was just showing off for John. Just when Lizzie thought she would faint from pure terror, the swishing sound slowed to a whisper and they swooshed to a stop.

Mandy was laughing helplessly. "Hooo-boy!" she said, scrambling to her feet and wiping furiously at her snow-encrusted hair and scarf. "Let's do it again!"

John walked over to her side, put a hand on her shoulder, and wiped snow off her scarf. Even in the faint lantern light, Lizzie could see the sincere admiration in his eyes as he bent his head and said, "You really liked that, didn't you?"

"Of course!" Mandy said gleefully, looking up at him, her green eyes shining. So John just kept his hand on her shoulder as they began walking back up the hill. Oh, great! Lizzie thought, seething. How cute. She just turns 16, and already they're this charming little couple who have eyes only for each other.

She was angry. Mostly angry at Mandy for making her go along, but also angry at herself for feeling so horribly jealous of her own sister. She loved Mandy, so why did she struggle with this anger toward her now? John Zook. No, she knew she had no chance with him, but... the truth confronted her

nevertheless, raising its big taunting head, blotting out any happy thoughts of the future.

She tried hard to accept the fact that John had no interest in her, even praying earnestly that God would not let these ugly feelings take control of her. But when Lizzie was with John and Mandy and confronted with their evident admiration of each other, it was more than she could handle. Especially when Mandy acted so sporty. Lizzie guaranteed that Mandy had been just as scared as she, but, oh, no, she would never admit it.

Lizzie yanked off her head scarf, shaking the snow from it, wiping her face with her mittens as she watched the retreating figures. She dusted off the front of her coat, stomped her feet to shake off the snow, and started trudging up the long, winding trail.

Suddenly, there was someone beside her. She turned, alarmed, to find Stephen in step with her.

Lizzie laughed ruefully. "I declare, you have the most annoying habit of sneaking up on someone!"

"I didn't sneak up on you."

"Yes, you did."

He didn't answer and they walked side by side up the slippery slope. Lizzie's breath came in short, panting gasps until she gave up and stopped.

"Whew! This really tires a person, doesn't it?"

"Not like the mountain."

Lizzie peered through the darkness at Stephen's face. He was very nice-looking, she realized again.

He stepped closer to Lizzie and said, "Lizzie, you

should go hiking with me sometime. I love to go tramping around in the mountain. You can always see deer or grouse, squirrels, or just whatever."

Lizzie was quite taken aback. She looked up at Stephen and blinked rapidly. Was he serious? Did he mean that they, just the two of them, should go hiking together, like a real date sort of thing? Or did he mean just in the way he would ask Paul or John to go with him, as a good buddy type of thing? Stephen was just mysteriously different. That's all there was to it.

"You mean in the wintertime?" Lizzie asked, laughing.

"No, some time when it gets warmer."

He paused before continuing, "'Course, I guess we can't go this year anymore. I'm going to another county in northern Pennsylvania to work for my uncle who just moved there a few months ago."

"You mean to live there? You'll stay there on the weekends, too?" Lizzie asked, incredulous. She couldn't imagine weekends without Stephen.

"Yeah."

There was silence as Lizzie scuffed the toe of her boot into the snow, as the soft snowflakes fell around them in the velvety night. Suddenly she raised her head and asked, "Why?"

"Why do you care if I stay there or not?" Stephen asked shortly.

"I...I don't. I mean...I do...I mean, I'm going to miss you. It won't be the same without you. But..." Lizzie shrugged helplessly.

Suddenly, Stephen moved close to her, and she felt the weight of both of his hands on her shoulders. Her breathing stopped, fading away to nothing, her heart hammering even as she felt as if all the oxygen was knocked out of her. She could not look up so she stood quietly, her breath coming in small jagged whispers.

"Lizzie, I'm going away because of you."

She lifted her head in one quick fluid movement. His eyes shone with a light of love or of pain... She wasn't sure which, but she quickly bent her head against his gaze, wanting to defend herself against... against what? She didn't know. She just knew she couldn't go on looking into his blue eyes.

"You know how it is," Stephen continued. "I've always, well, admired you, or in plain words, wanted you for my serious girlfriend. Surely you can tell a little bit how I feel. And there's just never any sign of you returning that feeling. It's always someone else. You care more about every other young man than you do about me. So... I figure the best thing for me to do is leave for awhile and try to sort out my feelings."

Lizzie was speechless. How was she supposed to know how he felt? Okay, so Uncle Marvin had told her. But what did Uncle Marvin really know? Why hadn't Stephen told her, really told her, before now? Lizzie glanced around, wishing that Mandy was nearby. What was she supposed to do?

"I suppose I'm hoping you'll miss me, I guess, which is kind of dumb. But maybe you'll be able

to … well, maybe someday you'll feel differently about me."

"But … but …" Lizzie was searching for the appropriate words. All in one rush she knew she didn't want him to go, but she also knew if he stayed she was not ready to commit herself to him before … Before what? She wasn't sure. Taking a deep breath to steady herself, she said, "Stephen, I do like you. You are a good friend, and I don't want you to go away if you don't want to."

"I do. I want to go," Stephen said.

That left her more confused than ever. He wanted to go. What if he found a nice girl in northern Pennsylvania and stayed there forever?

"Because you'll find another girl and marry her?" Lizzie asked.

Stephen made a derisive sound, stepped back, and started on up the hill. "As if you'd care," he flung back over his shoulder.

"Stephen!" Lizzie called. "Wait."

He stopped. She could talk better if she wasn't so close, especially if she could talk to the back of his head.

"Stephen, listen. Just give me some time. I need a few months to think and to sort out my feelings. Sometimes I feel confused, and I don't always understand myself. My … my mom says I run away from God's will, whatever that means."

Stephen turned, and taking both her mittened hands in his, he said, "Did she? Did your mom really say that?"

"Yes," Lizzie said, puzzled that it should mean so much to him.

"Well, I'll go now, Lizzie. I'm leaving in a few days. Be good, and don't forget about me."

And he was gone. Just as if the night and the swirling snow had swallowed him whole, he was suddenly no longer there. Lizzie searched the area where he had stood a moment before, but he had vanished into the blowing snow, leaving her standing by herself on the side of the hill, as alone and dejected as she could ever remember feeling. She lifted her face to the sky as her heart cried out to God for guidance. Just show me the way, she prayed. You have to make it very clear, because I don't understand very much about how you make your will known.

But she knew, more plainly than ever, that her heart yearned for God to direct her often shaking footsteps.

Chapter 7

A TOUCH OF SPRING SUNSHINE FLOODED THE Glick family's kitchen in a soft yellow glow. The stainless steel teakettle on the stove top sparkled and shone as the light bounced off the shining windowpane.

It was Saturday morning, when breakfast was always later and much more relaxed than on weekdays, because no one had to hurry off to their jobs or to school. Dat and Mam were contentedly sipping their steaming mugs of morning coffee as they laughed at the twins. KatieAnn and Susan were dark-haired and very pretty. Dat said Jason was turning into a tall young man, his blue-gray eyes usually crinkling into an expression of humor. His curly hair was his most attractive feature as he grew older, something which never ceased to amaze Lizzie, having endured all that worrying about his looks as a little girl. She had been so certain that Jason would never know what to do with his head

full of curls springing in every direction.

Lizzie sighed happily as she spread strawberry jam on a crisp piece of toast. Mandy and Emma were already doing the dishes, and when Lizzie finished eating, they started deciding whose job it was to do the Saturday cleaning, who would do laundry, and who would tackle the lawn-mowing.

"Mow grass!" Lizzie yelled.

"Do laundry!" Emma shouted, imitating Lizzie.

"I'm not doing all the Saturday cleaning by myself," Mandy complained.

Lizzie looped one arm around Mandy's shoulders.

"I'll help you do the cleaning, and then maybe we can find some grass that's long enough to mow," she said.

Lizzie was returning from the back porch with the dust mop when the kitchen door opened and Dat came in, sitting down at the table, his eyes open wider than usual.

"Annie, I can't figure this out," he said, his voice rising. "It seems as if there is a fog over my eyes that just won't lift."

"What could it be?" Mam asked, turning to look at Dat with an expression of concern. "Do you have a headache? Are you sure you didn't get some sawdust or something in one of your eyes?"

Dat shook his head.

"Why don't you take off your shoes and go lie down for awhile? Maybe you overworked yesterday," Mam suggested.

Dat turned to go into the living room to rest on the sofa. Lizzie raised her eyebrows at Mam, who raised her shoulders in a gesture of "I don't know."

Turning, Lizzie went upstairs to join Mandy and Emma in cleaning the bedrooms. It was highly unusual for Dat to be in the house midmorning like this. Fear swirled around in her mind like an ugly gray vacuum, threatening to force her into its grip. What if there was something seriously wrong with Dat? What if he was going blind? Some people did. How would Mam manage the farm if Dat was no longer able to work? The vacuum of fear whirred noisily in her head until she found Emma plumping the pillows of her bed.

"What?" Emma turned, straightening her back, seeing the expression on Lizzie's face.

"Emma, Dat came in and said he has a fog in front of his eyes. He hasn't been able to see normally all morning. Suppose he's going blind?" Lizzie said, her voice squeaking with fear.

"Lizzie, now stop it. There you go again. Thinking the absolute worst. He probably just has a headache."

Emma returned to her bed-making, telling Lizzie to hurry up and get started. It was already late enough, and after all, this was Saturday, and Saturday evening came right after that, and Joshua was coming to pick her up at seven o'clock.

Lizzie turned on her heel, biting her tongue to keep the hot, angry words inside. No use letting it show, she thought. I do it often enough.

Her pride arranged properly, she hurried into her own room and started taking up rugs, yanking open the window to shake them outside. Her hand slipped and she tore a fingernail on the sharp, wooden window frame. The window crashed down on the rug as Lizzie hopped around her room, pinching the injured finger with the opposite hand.

"What in the world is going on?" Mandy asked as she stood in the doorway, her eyes wide.

"Oh, don't worry about it!" Lizzie yelled hysterically. "What do you care? I always make everything worse than it is. So who cares if Dat has a brain tumor or he's going blind? As long as the cleaning gets done and the yard looks nice!"

Great big tears of pain and frustration rolled down Lizzie's face as she continued hurling senseless accusations at her sister. Mandy stood in the doorway, her wide green eyes filled with alarm as she stared open-mouthed at Lizzie.

"Wha … what?" she finally managed. "Lizzie, what has gotten into you? You act like … like you're not even normal."

Lizzie sat down hard on the floor, still holding the injured finger. Sighing, she grabbed a few Kleenexes from the nightstand, honked loudly into them, and dried her tears. She pushed back a few strands of her brown hair, adjusted her covering, and straightened her black bib apron. Mandy sat down quietly, watching as Lizzie regained her composure. She knew it was better to remain quiet for awhile once Lizzie was in one of these moods.

"All right," Lizzie said finally. "Sorry."

Mandy still said nothing.

"I said, sorry," Lizzie repeated, glancing at Mandy quickly before her eyes fell at Mandy's pitying gaze.

"I know."

"Well, say something."

"What?"

"I don't know."

Lizzie took a deep breath before the words began tumbling out miserably. She was very, very worried about Dat. She had a feeling deep down inside that it was something more than just a fog in front of his eyes. And she couldn't stop thinking about what Marvin had said about Stephen and his feelings for her.

"Lizzie, I could just shake you," Mandy said sharply. "Don't cross the bridge before you get to it about Dat. Nobody knows, and it might not even be serious. What crawled over you?"

That was their favorite question to ask when they wanted to know what was wrong, or what had suddenly made the other person act in a strange way.

Lizzie jumped up and started sweeping furiously. "Come on, Mandy. We'll never get done at the rate we're going."

So Mandy closed her mouth, turned and left, and resumed cleaning her own room. Lizzie swept and dusted her room, carefully arranging her pretty things a bit differently. She stood back to survey a basket of dried flowers she had placed in another

area and smiled with satisfaction. That was better. Turning, she placed a candle on the opposite end of her dresser, only to frown at the emptiness beside it. She started whistling under her breath as she found a small wooden dish to place beside the candle, which really evened things out.

Catching sight of herself in the mirror, she leaned forward to check her complexion. The dreaded blemishes were no longer as evident as she became older, so that was comforting. Same brown hair, plain, mousy, homely old brown, same as 75 percent of the population, she thought. Blue-gray eyes that sometimes turned green when she wore a dark, forest-green dress, which still made no sense. Same old rabbit teeth, but very white and not too bad when she smiled, she thought. She tried smiling deeply to watch for dimples, but even if she had some, they weren't natural, quirky, cute dimples, instead more like an extra line in her cheeks.

She smoothed her bib apron over her hips, wishing she was as thin as Mandy. Oh, well, too bad, so sad, she thought wryly. I'm not thin, never will be, but I'm not fat either.

I wonder ... I really wonder ... She hardly let herself think. How did she feel? Why should she care? Why was she nervous? Why would she even think about all this? Stephen was just ... well, he was just a good friend, that was all.

She finished cleaning the bathroom, her thoughts in a constant whirl. Maybe that was why she was so upset about Dat's eyesight. It was her yet

unexplained, unaccepted nervousness about this evening.

She had almost nothing to say as they finished the kitchen downstairs. Mam had cleaned the refrigerator, stove, and cabinets, wiping down the countertops as she always did. Lizzie and Mandy got down on their hands and knees, a bucket of soapy, clean-smelling water between them, and scrubbed the kitchen floor.

"Good job, girls," Mam said. "That's a great feeling, having the cleaning done."

"Where's Dat?" Lizzie asked.

"He got up and went back to work. He said he'll just have to ignore it awhile, and maybe it'll go away. Oh, I certainly hope so," Mam said as she watched Dat through the kitchen window.

After lunch, the girls went down to the lawn shed for the mowers. Dat had eaten a hearty meal, saying his eyesight seemed a bit better and hopefully that would be the end of it. So Lizzie's heart felt lighter as she found her favorite red mower beside the one Mandy always used.

Before they pushed them out the door, Lizzie blurted out, "I'm not going away tonight."

"Why?" Mandy asked in disbelief.

"Oh, I just don't feel like it. I'm tired and... and I... well, I just don't think I will."

"Lizzie, that is so absolutely not *you*," Emma said. "You always love to go away and be with your group of friends."

"Mandy and Emma, do we have time to talk?"

"Of course."

Lizzie bent down and picked a piece of grass. She looked at her sisters, then looked down at the piece of grass in her hand. She opened her mouth, made a sound, then closed it again.

"What?" Mandy urged. "You are one strange person today."

"No, I'm not. Okay, promise me you will not laugh."

Mandy's serious green eyes looked directly into Lizzie's, and neither one wavered as Emma said, "I promise I will not laugh."

They all lifted their faces and howled with laughter. They laughed until tears squeezed from Lizzie's eyes. Then they looked seriously at each other once more.

"I trust you both. You're always so wise; you really are. Now let's not laugh. Okay?"

"All right."

"Marvin told me that Stephen really likes me. Then Stephen told me he likes me so much he needs to leave the County for a while to get away from me. He's going to help his uncle farm. How am I supposed to feel? I mean, you know how it always was with us. He … he …"

"Likes you," Mandy finished matter-of-factly.

"Yes."

"Go on."

"But the thing that really bothers me most is that I feel so nervous and worried. I don't really want to see him ever again. And yet I do. I'm afraid that

when he comes back, he won't seem like plain old Stephen anymore. Not at all. How am I supposed to feel? How does it feel, Emma, when you're in love like you and Joshua? So how am I going to know if he's the right one for me? Suppose this nervousness is all wrong, and Marvin's wrong, and Stephen doesn't like me one tiny bit anymore when he returns, and I'll like him as much as I used to like Amos?"

All Emma said was, "You'll know." That was all.

Then she was gone, off with her lawn mower, whistling in the nearly spring-time air. Lizzie looked over at Mandy who shrugged. Lizzie got up and hurried after Emma.

"Stop, Emma! You can't just go walking off like that. How will I know?"

"Lizzie, you'll know. You already do. God probably knew for a long time. You were just too thickheaded to hear him."

"Now stop acting like a prophet of some sort, Miss Know-It-All!"

Lizzie grabbed Emma's apron strings and pulled the bow loose, then ran to her mower and started pushing it as fast as she could. Oh, my! Oh, my! I'm going to go out tonight after all, Lizzie thought. That Emma. She thinks she knows everything. But really, she does.

Lizzie's heart sang as the mower cut the light green grass in an even swath. She loved to mow lawn, and today's taste of spring was certainly no exception. She felt some heat rise in her face, but

she was used to the exertion of lawn-mowing. She kept steadily at her task. Her concerns about Dat's eyes were pushed to the background of her mind as she watched him clean the cow stable. Surely there was nothing too seriously wrong with him or he wouldn't have the strength to lift those huge fork-fuls of cow manure.

Jason whistled at her as she stopped to rest, and she waved at him, smiling to herself. What would Dat do without Jason's help? He certainly was a hard worker for his age, and Dat appreciated him every day.

She shook her head ruefully as if to clear it, then stood up straight, took a deep breath, and put her mower away. It was time to clean the flower beds, too, and trim around them, so that would be a good place to be for awhile. On her knees.

Chapter 8

As spring began to warm toward summer, Lizzie's concerns about Stephen were overshadowed by her interest in Emma's future. Mam had begun fussing to Emma, wondering when Joshua would ask her to marry him, or if he had any plans of marrying her this year.

"You're young, Emma, but you've been dating well over two years, and sometimes it's better not to be dating for too long," she said, hurrying between the stove and refrigerator, preparing a quick supper for Dat.

Some Amish youth weren't ready to settle down right away, but not Emma. She had always been conscientious, aware of right from wrong. She had become a member of the church the previous year, taking instruction classes during the summer until she had been baptized in the fall.

It was all very serious for Emma, and she did not have a hard time giving in to the instruction of the ministers. She seemed to understand about the new

birth, and that the water poured on her head was the outward sign of an inward change of heart, of giving her life to God.

Lizzie and Mandy both knew very surely, like the button on the flap of a pocket being buttoned securely, that they wanted to do exactly the same thing as Emma did. It never occurred to them that they wouldn't be Amish their whole lives. They each had a deeply ingrained knowledge that when the time was right, they would become baptized members, the same as Emma. God was very real to Emma, and she calmly listened to Bible stories at a very young age without getting the blues like Lizzie did.

Sometimes church made Lizzie sad. The feeling had started when Lizzie was a little girl. Some daughters sat with their fathers on the men's side during church. Lizzie and Mandy often sat with Dat because they were both better behaved with Dat. When Dat walked into church, Lizzie would take Mandy's hand, and the three of them would find a seat on a bench along the wall.

Once an unfamiliar man sat down beside Lizzie, along with his two strange-looking boys. He looked a bit scary to Lizzie. His boys were wriggling around on the bench, trying to take their coats off. He didn't help them, and Lizzie guessed he was mean to them. Lizzie moved as close to Dat as she could and put one hand under Dat's arm. He looked down at her and smiled. Lizzie felt a bit better.

Someone picked a song, saying the number in German. Dat found the page, and soon the room

was filled with the sound of the slow German singing. Usually Lizzie enjoyed that, but for some reason, she felt like crying today. She blinked and tried to think happy thoughts, or at least something funny.

Suddenly, the strange man reached over and pinched one of his little boys. Then he twisted the boy's arm as he talked to him quite sternly. The little boy opened his mouth and let out a crying howl of pain and surprise.

Dat looked over at the howling little boy, but then politely looked away. Lizzie sat and looked straight ahead, too. The boy's father did not try to comfort him or make him feel better. He just sang loudly as his little boy wailed beside him. Lizzie had the blues. She was so afraid of that strange man, and Dat was singing as if nothing was wrong at all. She felt more and more dejected, even though she knew she was much too old to cry in church.

Her nose started to run, so she got out her little flowered handkerchief and carefully wiped it. Even before tears formed, a sob tore at her throat. Dat looked down at Lizzie. He put his arm around her, bent low, and whispered, "What's wrong, Lizzie?"

With Dat's kindness, her blues dissolved into tears, and she sobbed quietly. She hid her face in Dat's *mutsa*, or suit coat, and cried. He patted her shoulder and asked her again why she was crying. Lizzie couldn't tell him, because maybe she was acting like a baby. But she really did not like that man and his little boy. So Dat just kept his arm around her and let her cry quietly.

Lizzie felt a bit better after she was finished crying. When Dat patted her shoulder, she relaxed. She thought of snitz pie and cheese bread and wished it was time for church to be over. She drifted off to sleep, dreaming that she was eating peanut butter bread and bologna, and that the black-haired man took it from her and dipped it in his coffee.

Emma had never had any hesitation about church, just as she seemed so certain about Joshua.

"Mam, don't you know that old tradition of being asked to marry when the strawberries bloom?" Emma asked, her eyes twinkling.

"Pshaw!" Mam snorted. "Never heard of such a thing."

Lizzie giggled. That was Mam, all right. Because she came from Ohio where the culture was a bit different, she didn't like "these eastern old wives' tales." If it was an old Ohio tradition, it was all right, which always made Dat smile and shake his head. Mam was born and raised in Ohio, and that's just how she was.

"Joshua's parents come from the real old traditional state of Maryland," Emma said.

"His mother doesn't," Mam argued.

"Wherever. She knows all those sayings and even abides by them. Her favorite saying is, 'We didn't use to do that in the old days.'"

"Well, if Joshua waits to ask you to marry him until June…"

"Not June, Mam," Emma broke in. "Strawberries bloom in May!"

And sure enough, the next Monday morning, the first in May, Emma fairly danced down the steps, her cheeks flushed as she whistled nervously under her breath.

Uh-oh, here it comes, Lizzie thought from her seat on the bench where she sagged wearily after a late evening at a singing.

Mam had her back turned, flipping pancakes on the griddle.

"Is that you, Emma? Come put the toast in the broiler," she said.

Emma obeyed, saying nothing as she pulled out the broiler drawer from the gas stove, arranging the sliced white bread in neat rows. Lizzie yawned, her eyes watering, and she dabbed at them with the back of her hand. It was nearing the end of school, and she was happily looking forward to sleeping in during the summer.

"Boy, I'm tired! Wish school was over this week," she mumbled.

"Why?" Emma asked, straightening her back.

"I could sleep later in the morning."

"You won't be sleeping late too many mornings if we have a wedding at our house," Emma said, blushing.

"Who's having a wedding?" Mam asked without turning around.

"We are, Mam. Joshua asked me to marry him this fall," Emma said.

"What?"

Mam's spatula clattered to the floor as she whirled around, her eyes wide. Emma was laughing with tears in her eyes.

"Really, Emma? For real?" Mam quavered.

"Yes, for real, Mam."

Mam returned to her pancake turning, but Lizzie knew she only went back to her duty to hide her emotions. After awhile, when the pancakes were arranged on a plate, she turned.

"So, Emma, this is what you always wanted, isn't it?" But there was a catch in her voice, and her eyes glistened.

"Yes. You know it is," Emma said, almost shyly.

The breakfast table that morning was absolute bedlam. Everyone congratulating Emma, everyone asking about the wedding plans, everyone talking at once while no one listened.

Dat was very excited. His eyes weren't bothering him as much these days, and Lizzie hoped that whatever had ailed a few weeks ago was gone. Dat could hardly wait to tear down the dilapidated old washhouse, add a new basement for the laundry, and build a large, new living room. He loved to remodel, fix things, and make them look nice. Mam always said Dat was never happier than the times he was building something.

They planned, laughed, and talked until Lizzie had only 20 minutes to put on her cape and apron. She flew up the stairs, threw on her clothes, and hurried down just in time to grab her coat as the school van pulled up.

That evening as Lizzie and Emma swung on the newly painted porch swing, Lizzie suddenly became a bit wistful. She could not imagine life without Emma, and that thought suddenly took away some of the excitement of preparing for her sister's wedding.

"Emma, doesn't it make you one teeny bit sad about moving away from here?" Lizzie asked.

Emma looked over at Lizzie.

"You sound sad, Lizzie. You're such a strange duck!" She pinched her arm affectionately.

"Emma, it isn't funny. Don't you kind of ... well, just sort of wish you weren't getting married and could live here with me and Mam and Mandy for always?"

"Li-i-zzie!" Emma shrieked.

"Well, don't you? Not a teeny weeny bit, even?"

"Of course not!"

There was a quiet calm as the porch swing creaked and Emma slid one foot along the concrete floor in a rasping noise.

Well, Lizzie thought, either I'm not ready to get married or else I'm just different. If I knew I had to move to Allen County, 50 miles away, into an old farmhouse with some strange person I hardly knew, I would most certainly have the blues.

She looked out over the pasture that led to the creek near Charlie Zimmerman's house, then back at the new living room and the freshly painted wash-line poles. She loved her home so much, there was no one going to get her to move away.

Mandy came through the door with a cereal dish held in one hand and a spoon in the other. She backed up to the porch swing and looked down at Lizzie.

"Slide over."

"If you give me a bite of whatever's in your dish."

"Okay."

Lizzie sat tightly against Emma, and Mandy wiggled in on the other side. Lizzie peered into her dish. Chocolate cake and vanilla pudding. Mmmm!

"One bite!" Mandy said, knowing Lizzie's appetite.

"A big one."

Mandy cut off a huge piece of cake, loaded it with vanilla pudding, held it in front of Lizzie's face.

"Open wide!"

Lizzie did, and her mouth was promptly filled with a huge bite of cake, the whole spoon, and vanilla pudding squishing everywhere. Lizzie made funny noises, and Mandy threw back her head, howling with glee, as Lizzie struggled to keep everything in her mouth. After she had swallowed, Mandy jumped up, knowing from experience she would catch it from Lizzie.

Sure enough, Mandy tore down the steps and across the yard with Lizzie in hot pursuit. After racing circles in the yard, Lizzie plunked down on the porch swing beside Emma, panting.

Emma grinned.

"I don't know why you don't give up. You can never catch Mandy anyway."

"She's so skinny," Lizzie panted.

Mandy ran up to the porch swing, backed up, and said, "Slide over."

The peaceful swinging resumed as Mandy finished her cake and pudding.

"Emma, you're going to miss us when you move!" Mandy said.

"You'll come visit me, I hope."

"Yes."

"But you know very well how I always was, Mandy. This is what I wanted since I was a little girl, not much older than eight years old. To be alone in my old farmhouse, cooking and cleaning, baking good things and washing my very own dishes—it's just too good to be true."

"What if you get homesick? What if Joshua is mean to you?" Lizzie asked.

"He won't be. You don't understand, Lizzie. You were never in love."

"Oh, yes, I was!"

"With who?"

"You know. Remember?"

"Well, yes. But I mean, you've never dated anyone seriously for years like I have. I feel actually closer to Joshua than I do to you and Mandy. Or Mam, for that matter. I just look forward to spending the rest of my life with him. Growing old together and having a whole pile of children."

Suddenly, Mandy sat up very straight, blinking her large green eyes seriously. "I think I'm falling in love."

"Mandy!" Lizzie shrieked.

Lizzie looked closely at Mandy. She could tell Mandy was dead serious. She had that certain set to her upper lip when she was not joking at all. Lizzie called it her "professor" look, all smart and wise and knowing.

"John Zook comes to church every two weeks," she said, as matter-of-factly and rock-solid as a mountain.

Lizzie's heart sank. Don't tell me that Mandy will be exactly like Emma, she thought. Oh, please.

"I think he's very handsome, and I think he likes me," she said.

"How do you know? You never said a word to him, and he never talked to you either," Lizzie said.

"Oh, I just know," Mandy said. She started to hum in the most grating manner.

Emma got up, saying it was time for her to give KatieAnn and Susan their baths. Mandy and Lizzie continued to swing, watching the pasture as if their life depended on it. The tension between them was as thick as Mam's potato soup. Lizzie was still secretly hoping John would ask her for a date, and that's all she thought about Monday evenings. Well, she just had a feeling she knew why he didn't ask her out. It was because he was very likely Mandy's "meant to be."

"Lizzie," Mandy sighed, "I don't want to hurt your feelings, but you may as well not like John Zook. From the first moment I saw him, I had a little feeling that someday, if it was the Lord's will,

John Zook would be my husband, just like Emma and Joshua."

"I don't like him anymore," Lizzie said, surprisingly quiet and reserved.

Mandy looked at her sharply. "You used to."

"Let's not talk about it, okay?"

"If you don't want to, all right."

The thing was, Lizzie had some thinking of her own to do. For the last few weeks she had been busy thinking of Emma's wedding and pushing all thoughts of boys and dating aside. Uncle Marvin's words about Stephen were stuck somewhere out of reach, failing to wake her conscience or reason. She wanted John to ask her, just as she had wanted Amos to. And now Mandy said she liked John, and it was almost scary with that Mandy, once she said something in that wise way of hers.

She sighed. Oh, well... if John liked skinny, big-eyed Mandy, then so be it. I'll just never get married. They are building the new Amish school, the school board has already asked me to be the teacher, and I can hardly wait to get started at the end of the summer. So if that's what God has for me, fine. At least if I'm an old maid, I can pack two whole sandwiches in my lunch with all the mayonnaise I want, and who is to care if I weigh 200 pounds?

She sniffed, and she shook her head.

"What's wrong with you?" Mandy asked.

"A fly flew up my nose."

They giggled and continued to swing.

Chapter 9

THE SUMMER BEFORE EMMA'S WEDDING WAS full of one busy day following another. Lizzie and Mandy often did the milking alone, since Dat was working on the new addition. Mam's garden was full of vegetables for Emma as well as for the wedding. Earlier that summer, Dat had plowed a large area behind the house, past the apple trees, and planted potatoes and sweet corn. Mam called it her "patch." Lizzie said it was more like an acre than a patch. It was huge, and often she and Mandy spent hours hoeing and weeding on hot summer days.

They also had a frolic on a Saturday in June, when they invited all of their relatives and friends to work on the addition to the house. Mam cooked and baked the week before, preparing huge amounts of food to feed the hungry workers. She made two roasters of fried chicken and filling. Emma was always proud of Mam's culinary skills and worked diligently to learn all of Mam's cooking and baking

secrets. Lizzie didn't care. She just ate the food.

Of course, Mam made cream sticks for coffee break in the morning. They were homemade doughnuts, with the dough cut in rectangles, fried in deep fat, a slit cut along each top, and filled with creamy vanilla frosting. Golden caramel icing was spread on top, resulting in achingly sweet, oblong, filled doughnuts, which in Emma's words were so good it wasn't even right.

When the men finished eating, they paid Mam warm compliments. She dipped her head, her cheeks flushed, basking in the words of praise. Dat acted so conceited when someone praised Mam's cooking that the girls hid their smiles behind their hands. He wasn't very tall, but he grew a few inches whenever that happened, Emma would say.

After the frolic was over, the addition was well on its way. Just like a miracle, a new basement and the skeleton frame of the living room with a new roof and windows were put in place. All through the summer, Dat and Jason kept steadily on, building and finishing the new living room until the day came when Mam went to town for a few gallons of primer and semi-gloss paint for the walls. Mam was thrilled with the light shade of blue she chose, saying this old farm was looking pretty good of late.

It was a happy summer, an exciting one, with Mam being more energetic and enthused than she had ever been since moving to the farm, Lizzie thought. And when Dat put down the hardwood flooring, rented a sander to smooth it, and then put

on three applications of polyurethane varnish, she was almost in tears of gratitude.

"What a lovely, lovely, big living room!" she exclaimed, as she finished the final coat of varnish. "I'm almost afraid to have a wedding in this beautiful new room!"

There were five new windows, all freshly stained and varnished, letting in the fresh air and sunshine. Mam hung blinds in the windows. In Ohio they hang white cloth curtains and tie them back, but here in the East that was considered too fancy, she said. Mam had lived in the East long enough to appreciate the blinds, so she only said it a bit wistfully.

After all the furniture was put in place and Dat set the woodstove on the brick platform by the new chimney, it was just like a brand-new house. The twins squealed and shouted as they raced each other across the glowing hardwood floor, sliding in their stocking feet until they crashed into furniture and Mam made them stop.

Mam and Emma painted the porch railing, the kitchen, the brick part of the house, and every doorway and windowsill to match the living room. Dat shook his head, saying it was dangerous to be in the house because you'd be painted to the wall if you held still long enough. He was only joking, his eyes twinkling, and the girls knew he enjoyed getting ready for Emma's wedding as much as Mam did.

They froze tiny little bags of corn, lima beans, and peas for Emma, in bags only big enough for two people. Emma beamed and giggled as she put

one cup of vegetables in each bag, saying how cozy that would be, cooking supper for Joshua in their old farmhouse.

They filled little pint jars with pickles, red beets, grape jelly, and applesauce. They put peaches and pears in quart jars. Mam said two people could eat a whole quart of peaches before they spoiled. They canned beef, sausage, and little chunks of ham, all in pint jars that looked so cute, Lizzie found herself wanting to be married and making supper of her own.

Mam went shopping, buying sheet sets, towels, and washcloths. They made comforters from flannel patches—any color—orange, pink, blue, and hideous-looking patterns. Lizzie got all huffy about that, saying there was no way she would put anything like that on her bed.

"Oh, yes, Lizzie! This is exactly what I always dreamed of—patchwork comforters and quilts. Just wait until you see my old upstairs. It's so cold up there in the winter that these warm blankets will be exactly what I need."

"That's right!" Mam agreed, around the pins in her mouth. "Just wait, Lizzie. Your turn will come, and these comforters won't seem ugly then."

Lizzie snorted a bit, thinking how they wouldn't look any better at that point.

Mam had two quiltings that summer after the new living room was finished, inviting the women from church to quilt Emma's quilts. Mam had pieced one the summer before called a "Dahlia," blocks

of small, star-shaped flowers made with lavender fabric on a background of white. Emma's favorite color was lavender, so after the quilt was finished and bound, she was absolutely delighted.

Late that summer, Lizzie helped the Amish parents of the community paint and varnish the walls of the brand-new schoolhouse. The small, square building sat on the side of a gently rolling hill on the edge of Elam Stoltzfus' farm. A little meandering creek wrapped through the pasture on the opposite side of the road, and pretty oak and maple trees lined its banks. The schoolhouse was about six miles from the Glick farm, so, of course, Lizzie had to go with the school van again.

Lizzie always thought it would be so much nicer to be able to stay at school later in the evening and arrive earlier than the pupils, but it would have been too expensive for the school board to pay for all that extra transportation. Sometimes, when there was a special event, she would drive Bess and the buggy to school, but Mam didn't like that too much, saying it was too far. Mam took good care of horses, always pitying them if they had to run too fast or too long.

When school started the last week of August, Lizzie was as excited as ever, only without quite as many sickening butterflies in her stomach as she had her first year. She had successfully taught her first year, loving every minute of it, so she had less qualms about the unknown this time around.

She couldn't believe her good fortune, being the first teacher in a brand-new classroom. The walls

were so smooth, and the windows were all square with new trim. There was a brand-new blackboard, closets, and even new desks that were actually fastened to the floor. Her own desk was not new, but it was a good secondhand one, large and not as high as her old wooden one at the Mennonite school.

There were a few more pupils this year, all Amish children from homes and farms spread throughout a large portion of Cameron County. Some of them drove their ponies or horses and buggies to school, but most of them came with a driver.

The pupils were as excited as she was on the first day, exclaiming about and admiring the finished new school. There were Kings, Beilers, Zooks, Stoltzfuses, and lots of other common Amish names. The children were all loving, none of them causing her too much grief or worry those first few weeks. At home, with all of the wedding planning, there was no rest for anyone, so school was actually a welcome reprieve from the madcap pace in the Glick household.

By late September, the wedding was still six weeks away, but Mam was a nervous wreck, Emma said. Lizzie agreed.

Lizzie was secretly pleased to hear Mam and Emma argue and get upset with each other. All her life, it had been those two working together, and Lizzie was the different one. Even Mandy made Mam happier than Lizzie did most of the time.

Even when they were little and Dat taught the three girls to read the Scriptures in German, Lizzie had upset Mam. Each Sunday morning, Dat read from the Scripture, Emma read the verse after his, and so on.

Reading the German language was a bit more difficult for Emma, so it had taken her longer to read a verse. German had always been easy for Lizzie, so she zipped through her verse. Dat smiled at her each time she finished. But as Mandy faltered through hers, Lizzie noticed Mam's unhappy expression. Now what had she done wrong? Evidently something, because Mam's eyebrows were drawn and her mouth stern.

On they read, with the exact same results—Dat smiled at Lizzie, then sighed impatiently if Emma missed a word, until Mam opened her mouth.

"Melvin, I can hardly stand it. Emma and Mandy are trying to read just as well as Lizzie. You need to have more patience with them. If Lizzie can read so much better than the others, why does she have to read at all? She knows everything there is to know about German."

Dat had stared at Mam. Lizzie felt like running out of the room and never reading a word of German ever again. Her feelings were terribly hurt. She had always been proud of her German reading ability. Emma did lots and lots of other things so much better than she did, just not reading German.

That's how Mam is, Lizzie thought. She always likes Emma so much better than me. I'm not going

to talk to Mam for so long she'll know she hurt my feelings.

They finished their session of German reading, and Dat told them they were free to do whatever they wanted. It was an in-between Sunday, meaning a day their district did not have church services. Old Order Amish have church every other Sunday. This is an old custom that allows ministers to visit other districts.

Emma and Mandy wandered into the kitchen for a snack, but Lizzie went straight up the stairs to her bedroom. She flung herself on the bed, stuck her face in her pillow, and pitied herself. She planned on crying, but the tears wouldn't come, probably because she was more angry than hurt.

After a while she felt a bit silly so she got up, smoothed her dress, and wondered what she could do to worry Mam. She didn't care what Emma said. Mam always took her side. Emma never did one thing wrong. Mam should be glad she has a daughter who can read German so well. If Lizzie was a boy, she'd probably be a preacher or a deacon, and then Mam would be so happy to hear her read German in church. Mam ought to be ashamed of herself.

Now, years later, Mam told Lizzie she just couldn't understand what got into Emma, it was a fright how determined she was to have her own way. And Emma cried to Lizzie in sheer frustration

because Mam put her foot down, saying there would be absolutely no more than 250 guests, the house was not big enough for more. Emma begged and pleaded, but Mam's nostrils flared, her mouth was set, and that was that. Lizzie felt very important, being in the middle of Mam and Emma.

A wedding was a mess. Everyone was on pins and needles all the time. Lizzie told Mam this wasn't right. When it was her turn to get married, she was going to run away and go to the lawyer or governor or whoever it is that marries you. Mam laughed at her, saying she'd have a hard time getting either of them to marry her.

Finally, the day of preparation—*risht dag* in Pennsylvania Dutch—arrived. Everyone was up at five o'clock, except for Mam who had been up since three o'clock to bake enough pumpkin pies to feed all of the relatives. Emma said that was too early. Now Mam would be too tired to enjoy the day. But Lizzie guessed that if she wanted to get up at three to bake pies, she could.

Relatives began to arrive very early that morning. The *risht leid*, or the four couples who made the chicken and filling, arrived first. There was lots of work involved in that process, and they had to start early to get the roasting chickens in the oven.

The *risht dag* was a jolly day, almost more fun than the day of the wedding, Lizzie thought. Everyone hustled and bustled, smiled and teased each other as they worked together. The farm was truly a beehive of activity.

There were so many old traditions to follow. Joshua and Emma and their bridal party cleaned the celery. An Amish wedding had celery in everything, Lizzie claimed, but Emma corrected her, saying only in the *roasht* and the stewed celery. Oh, yes, and in the afternoon whole stalks of celery to snack on were placed in tall vases and set on the tables.

"Why celery?" Lizzie asked, as she scrubbed yet another piece.

"Because over a hundred years ago, our ancestors served whatever was in the garden at the end of the season at their weddings. That's why we have chicken filling, mashed potatoes, celery, and cole slaw. The cabbage, potatoes, and celery all come from the late harvest," Joshua informed her proudly.

"They grew the chickens in the garden too, huh?" Lizzie cracked.

The aunts were in the kitchen, baking pies and cooking vanilla cornstarch pudding and tapioca pudding while they also chopped celery, baked rolls, and just fussed up a storm. What a day to remember, Lizzie thought, with everyone full of energy and enthusiasm because Emma was getting married.

After the celery was all washed and sorted, the whole group took a coffee break and snacked on all kinds of cookies and doughnuts. Lizzie was cold and wet from washing celery, so it felt good to be in the warm kitchen with all of Dat's sisters—the aunts—and Doddy Glicks.

The men measured rooms and set up tables and benches. Since the wedding service would be held in

the same room as the one in which the meal would later be served, they had to know the length of each bench, exactly which bench went where, and how many tables filled each room.

Everyone had a job. Usually, the older women of the church made the gravy, cooked the celery, and brewed the coffee, while the aunts bustled about setting out plates of doughnuts, cookies, and dishes of tapioca pudding.

Lizzie loved the whole whirl of this special day before the wedding. The kitchen sounded just like a henhouse when the chickens are afraid of an intruder and cackling madly. Mam's face was so red Lizzie was afraid she'd have heart failure if she didn't calm down. But then, this was her first daughter's wedding, and she did have plenty of reason to be nervous and flushed, Lizzie decided.

Amid the hubbub, Emma flitted about, looking radiantly happy and excited. She was to finally have her big day, the one she so looked forward to her whole life. Lizzie couldn't fully understand why Emma didn't mind moving so far away, but then, she didn't have to. She most certainly was not planning any future moves of her own.

The sun shone beautifully on the day of Emma's wedding. Mam was so pleased to be blessed with a lovely day. Not too cold for November, she said, just a nice moderate day for a wedding. Dat smiled

and smiled, hurrying about doing last-minute things in his white shirt and new black suit.

Lizzie wore the same new white cape and apron as Emma, because Lizzie was a *nehva-sitsa*, or Emma's attendant. Joshua's brother Ben sat with Lizzie on one side of the couple, while the other *nehva-sitsa* couple, Joshua's sister Mary sat with Marvin on the other side. Lizzie had worried that Mandy would feel left out since she wasn't one of Emma's attendants.

"Don't worry," Mandy said. "I'll be a *nehva-sitsa* for you."

"I'm not getting married," Lizzie said as she pinned her cape.

Emma, Lizzie, and Mary all wore identical blue dresses with white organdy capes and aprons and black coverings. Joshua, Ben, and Marvin wore new black suits and white shirts with black bow ties clipped to their shirt collars.

"Don't say things you don't mean," Mandy said. "I see how you look for Stephen every Sunday at church, even though he's still living up north with his uncle."

"Be quiet, Mandy," Lizzie said. She sat down on the bed so she could tie her shoes and hide her red cheeks. Mandy was right. She did check each Sunday to see if Stephen was attending church with his family that week. So far he hadn't, but Lizzie was certain he would return sometime soon.

They all took a long time to get ready before the service. Lizzie's hair was plastered down so close

to her head it would take a severe windstorm to remove one hair from its place. Marvin told her she should always be so neat, but Lizzie felt like her hair was greased with lard, even though it was actually hair spray.

The wedding party entered the kitchen and were seated side by side where they would remain for the whole service like six stick men, Lizzie thought. Dat smiled and told them they looked very nice.

Then he looked at Mam, she looked at Dat, and all at once their smiles melted into little watery pools in their eyes. Dat blew his nose, tears running over. Mam turned away quickly, dabbing fiercely at her eyes. Lizzie felt her own emotion welling up, prickling her nose. But the relatives started to arrive and everyone started to smile again.

"Do your shoes fit?" Mommy Glick asked as she entered the kitchen. She bent down to take a peek at Emma's shoes.

"Oh, yes!" Emma said, smiling at Mommy as they shook hands warmly.

"You have a lovely wedding day," Mommy said, clasping Emma's hand with both of her own.

Emma wore Mommy's high-top shoes that laced over her ankles like figure skates. Ministers' wives wore these shoes to church, and a bride traditionally wore them to be married as a sign of obedience and a humble spirit, virtues that are highly respected among the Amish. Joshua wore new shoes in the same style, which was really very touching, old-fashioned, and serious, Lizzie thought. Lizzie had to

admit, she hoped someday she, too, could borrow Mommy Glick's shoes.

The guests began arriving in earnest. Aunt Vera's eyes swam with tears as she rushed in, wrapping her arms around Emma. Mam was so glad to see her sisters that she started openly crying, but that was all right because she didn't see her sisters very often.

Mam had asked a bishop from Ohio to perform the marriage ceremony. She always said it seemed so unfinished the way it was done in Pennsylvania, with the couple seated as soon as they were pronounced man and wife. In Ohio, the bishop asked the congregation to stand while he said a prayer for the couple, which Mam had asked for and Dat agreed to.

The bishop preached an inspiring sermon in his Ohio accent, which was all very interesting. Emma looked so dark-haired, petite, and pretty as she stood soberly beside Joshua, saying her vows in a soft voice. He answered in a deeper masculine voice.

When they stood to pray, Lizzie cried. She had planned to stay dry-eyed and serene. But this was Emma, her own bossy big sister who was taking this very serious step, and everything seemed so holy and good and right that Lizzie cried until she had to get out her handkerchief and silently wipe her nose. When they all sat down again, she was so embarrassed by her tears that she looked at Ben's shoes for a very long time.

After they sang the last swelling strain of the old wedding hymn, the festivities began. The new

husband and wife with their *nehva-sitsa* went upstairs to change from their traditional, borrowed shoes into new ones they had bought for their wedding day. Emma, Lizzie, and Mary each took off their black church coverings and put on new white ones. Then came the best part of the whole day—sitting down at the corner table in the living room downstairs.

While the couples were changing their clothes, their helpers had set the bridal table with Emma's fancy tablecloths, her fine white china embellished with tiny garlands of flowers, the pitcher and glasses Joshua had given her, and the pretty silverware she had received from him, as well. Lizzie was even more excited by the food in front of them—bowls of fruit, cut-glass cake stands holding decorated wedding cakes, parfait glasses filled with a creamy gelatin dessert, and all kinds of other classy-looking dishes and food. It was a beautiful table with Joshua on one side and Emma on the other, both happier than Lizzie had ever seen them.

Tables were set up along every available wall, with aunts and uncles hurrying and scurrying, carrying steaming plates of *roasht*, bowls heaped high with creamy mashed potatoes, cooked celery swimming in a velvety white sauce, pitchers of thick gravy, and dishes of cole slaw. The food was delicious, but Lizzie tried to eat daintily, feeling almost bashful sitting at this lovely table with Ben.

Emma oohed about the cakes, carefully reading the small tags on their tops, which identified

the name of each person who had baked a cake for Emma and Joshua.

"Oh, this beautiful white one is from Uncle James and Aunt Becca!" Emma said.

"They're both pretty, and this one is from your parents, Emma," Joshua said.

After the wedding dinner, it was time to open gifts. They unwrapped what seemed like hundreds of packages, carefully keeping a record of who had given each gift.

Then it was time to go back to the corner table again for the "afternoon table," the time of the day when the youth assembled at the tables to sing wedding hymns. Each young man asked a girl to accompany him and sit beside him during the singing. It was a thrilling, very jittery time for any young girl, because you never knew when you would be picked, or if any young man would pick you at all, Lizzie thought. You just had to stand there, trying to look calm and nonchalant, when all that time your face was devoid of color because your heart was beating so fast, it was all you could do not to drop away in a dead faint.

Lizzie had often heard of this practice from other girls, but she had never participated in it before. She could well imagine how absolutely unstrung she would become if Ben wasn't already her partner, her life so much like the Chutes and Ladders game with its constant ups and downs. With her luck, no one would find her attractive enough to choose her to accompany him.

The girls told Lizzie that the boys didn't really choose someone because she was pretty, but she never believed that. Of course, they did. All the pretty girls will be picked right off the bat, you watch, she thought. She wondered if Stephen would have chosen her if she hadn't already had Ben as a partner. She hoped so. She had looked everywhere for him, but she hadn't seen him yet. But with so many people in the house, she might just have overlooked him.

But she was pleasantly surprised to see when the couples filled in that the prettiest girls didn't automatically get picked first. Most of the boys chose their friends, and once everyone was seated, they seemed to be having a genuinely good time. In between songs, the youth snacked on the potato chips, candy, and fruit that was passed from table to table.

The relatives, parents, and other wedding guests were assembled in the center of the room in neat rows of folding chairs. The singing swelled to the ceiling, rolling around the room in great waves until Lizzie became quite bored. When would they ever stop? Just when she thought surely no one could think of one more song to pick, someone started another one, louder than the last one.

"Those Glicks can really sing," Ben said, leaning close to Lizzie so she could hear him.

"I guess so. I hope they soon run out of air. I'm getting tired of sitting here," Lizzie answered, smiling.

Ben laughed, telling her they'd sing for awhile yet.

Finally it was supper-time. The young people at the afternoon table were free to go. Lizzie was glad to get up and leave, going upstairs with Emma and Mary where they talked with friends and some of the Ohio aunts until it was time to go to Dat's shop where the youth had already gathered. There Emma and Joshua assigned each young man a supper partner. Some of the men were pleased, and others were impolite enough to refuse. But it was all in good fun and, for the most part, Emma and Joshua did not have a hard time with anyone.

Then for the last time, the wedding party sat at the elegant corner table, watching the couples file into the room as their names were called. Lizzie felt a slight twinge of pain when Amos led Ruthie in and together they found their seats. Amos is just as handsome as ever, she thought wryly. I wonder what Stephen is doing, she thought. But she shook her head and pushed away those thoughts.

Then John Zook led Mandy to the corner table. He was so much taller than Mandy, and she looked as if she had seen a ghost and never got over it. Her face was colorless, her eyes huge and dark with nervousness, but she gave Lizzie a tight little grin as she found her seat beside John.

Supper was delicious, but no one was really hungry. Lizzie pushed the ham and potatoes around on her plate, wishing the wedding would be over now. It was interesting watching John trying not to watch

Mandy. Lizzie talked and laughed with him since she saw him almost every weekend, and he was a good friend. Mandy was new to running around, so she was unaccustomed to any of the young men from the youth group, and she sat shy and quiet.

John was quite enamored with Mandy, Lizzie could easily tell. He must have found her pleasant company, too, since by the end of the evening as the singing was winding down, they sat deep in a serious conversation. As far as they were concerned, Lizzie thought, there was no one else at the wedding.

Lizzie was not happy at first, but she had to admit to herself, although grudgingly, that she hoped Mandy could be blessed with a sure feeling about finding a husband like Emma had been.

After the house was quiet and the last guests had gone home, Lizzie came down the stairs, shedding her white cape and apron as she entered the kitchen. Mam stood washing dishes at the sink.

"Mam, why don't you just go to bed? We'll do these dishes in the morning," Lizzie said.

"Oh, I need to wind down. I've been wound up as tightly as an alarm clock for so long that this helps me relax before I go to bed. Wasn't it a lovely wedding, Lizzie? What would we do at a time like this without relatives? All the managing and the work they did!"

"It was a nice wedding, Mam. It really was.

Emma looked so happy, and Joshua is so in love
with her."

"I know. I hope their love can continue to grow
and flourish. We never know what lies before us in
marriage. We just have to trust that God will provide
strength for whatever we have to face together."

"Did you see Mandy with John Zook?" Lizzie
asked.

"Someone said he asked for her. Imagine! I sup-
pose that'll be another case like Joshua and Emma,"
Mam said.

Lizzie bit her lower lip, hard, then turned to Mam.

"Why doesn't anything work out for me, Mam?
Am I just meant to be an old maid who teaches
school, or what? I don't know how to understand
God's voice or have the right feeling like Emma and
Mandy do."

Mam took her hands out of the dishwater, dried
them on a tea towel, laughed wryly, and said, "I
don't think there's a dry dish towel in this entire
house.

"No, Lizzie dear, now listen. I'll tell you a secret.
I had lots and lots and lots of dates with boys in
Ohio, and not one of them was my 'meant to be.'
Then I met Dat, and I knew as sure as the sun rises,
he was the one. And let me tell you something,
Lizzie. I always feel the same about you. I think
your 'meant to be' is right under your nose. You're
just not seeing him." She patted Lizzie's shoulder
affectionately. "You will someday. God just isn't fin-
ished with you or him yet."

"Who do you mean?"

"You know, Lizzie."

"I don't."

Mam looked deeply into Lizzie's eyes, and they fell before the certainty she saw in Mam's.

"Lizzie, I think you're trying to run away from God's will. We have to be very careful in blindly searching for our own will and not even trying to discern the difference. It's a very serious thing when God puts a true, undying love in a young man's heart for us, Lizzie, and we're too wrapped up in ourselves to see it."

Lizzie didn't say anything as Mam began taking off her cape and apron, laying the pins on the countertop.

"You mean Stephen, don't you?" she whispered.

"Yes, I do."

"I like him."

"But you don't love him."

"What is love?"

"You'll know when the time is right. Now go to bed, Lizzie. We're both tired. It's been a long day, and you have a whole lifetime to figure it out."

"Thanks, Mam."

"For what?"

"For being you."

Chapter 10

Joshua and Emma planned their moving day for the third of February. Although Lizzie was a bit worried about life without Emma, she told Mandy it would be a relief to have the upstairs back to normal with all of their wedding gifts finally out of there.

Even Mam had to admit that there was a time for everything. She didn't like this whole idea of newlyweds living at home with their parents. But it was an old Amish custom for a couple in Lamton County to visit the homes of most of the guests who attended their wedding before they moved into their own home. During each visit, Emma and Joshua received wedding gifts. Soon Emma's room and part of the second-floor hallway were filled with snow shovels, rakes, hoes, saws, hammers, flashlights, Tupperware, canister sets, brooms, and everything else you need to set up a new household.

Mam snorted and harrumphed quite a bit about these "Lamton rules," which really, if you thought about it, was no small wonder. She wasn't raised that way, and when all her brothers and sisters were married, they moved away from home within a few days, skipping, in her words, "all of this constant visiting and goings on."

That was just how Mam was, and no matter how often Dat sighed and shook his head, she didn't change. Oh, she visited homes along with Joshua and Emma, doing her level best to conform to Dat's ways, but she didn't genuinely endorse the whole traditional practice.

So in some ways, the day Emma moved away was a happy time. The family loaded all of Emma's and Joshua's belongings into a large truck early that Saturday morning. When the truck was full, Emma rode with Joshua and the driver in the truck, while the rest of the family followed in a van.

Lizzie hadn't been to Allen County in several months. She had many good memories of her weekends there, and she still wrote quite regularly to Mary and Barbara. The two girls had been dear friends of Lizzie's, and even if she didn't see them much at all, she wanted to stay in contact with them through letters.

On Joshua's farm were a large, red brick house with a huge bank barn and outbuildings. Joshua's parents had recently remodeled the kitchen. Emma had brand new kitchen cupboards and shiny new green linoleum on the floor. The living room had beautiful,

glossy, hardwood flooring with freshly painted white trim and newly painted walls. The walls were old, uneven plaster, but with the cracks repaired and painted over, it really was a lovely room, especially with the long low windows along two sides.

A big bedroom ran along the back of the house, along with a spare room that could have been made into another bedroom. But Emma and Joshua stored their extra belongings in there instead and also used part of it as a pantry.

The upstairs had four large bedrooms, all empty and so cold you could see your breath in them. Lizzie didn't know which was worse, living here in Allen County with an old, cold upstairs or milking cows with your husband. The whole marriage deal just gave her the blues as she stood all alone on the second floor.

As the men moved beds and dressers, cedar chests and brand-new chairs up the stairs, they propped the front door wide open. The mild winter air warmed a few of the rooms on the second floor enough that Lizzie and Mandy could unpack Emma's things.

Emma was radiant and her cheeks flushed as she worked. Lizzie thought she seemed almost happier than she had been on her wedding day. She instructed Lizzie on which new sheet set went on which bed, and which comforter and quilt, showing her the proper way to make up a bed for guests.

Mandy smelled the fresh new quilts from Joshua's cedar chest. "His mom must be quite proper," she commented.

"Why?"

"Look at all this stuff!"

Lizzie peered into the opened cedar chest, smiling to see all the neatly folded items stacked carefully inside.

"You should feel this comforter," Mandy said.

It was the heaviest, warmest comforter Lizzie had ever seen. Emma told them it was stuffed with wool. The flannel cover on the outside was buttoned so she could take it off and wash it when she spring-cleaned the house. Emma was so pleased with everything Joshua's parents had given them, saying Joshua and she had more than enough to furnish this big upstairs.

"Emma, I can hardly wait to come here and stay for a weekend, sleeping under these wonderful heavy comforters," Lizzie said, patting a pillow to make it fit nicely under the quilt.

"I hope you come often, Lizzie. I'm going to miss you," Emma said.

Lizzie looked at her sharply. Emma still looked happy, but there was a bit of apprehension in her voice.

"Aren't you glad you got married, Emma?" Lizzie asked, her voice rising sharply.

"Ach now, Lizzie, there you go again, jumping to conclusions. It's no wonder you don't have a boy-friend. I honestly think you're afraid of getting mar-ried yourself," Emma said, sitting on the side of the bed and patting the area beside her for Lizzie.

Lizzie sat down close to Emma, and an

overwhelming feeling of nostalgia gripped her. Time moved on, bringing changes, and it didn't seem very long ago at all that they were little girls. They had been so close.

"To tell you the truth, Lizzie, being married is all I ever dreamed it would be. And today ... moving into our own house, and putting my quilts on my own beds ... it's just, well, it's just the happiest time of my life. Joshua is so good to me, and I can hardly wait for our life to begin here on the farm. But that new beginning still brings wistful feelings of the past, of you and Mandy and Mam. Especially you. I'm going to miss you. Promise me, Lizzie, that you'll write me a long, funny letter every week. Promise?"

"Promise," Lizzie whispered around the lump in her throat.

"Don't you cry, or I'll start!" Emma said, her voice shaking.

"I'm not crying," Lizzie said fiercely. "I'm just going to miss you. I wish I had appreciated you more already. Who is going to sweep the kitchen 10 times a day?"

Emma laughed. "I didn't sweep 10 times."

"Almost."

"I feel almost guilty with all I have, Lizzie, and you ... you ... " she broke off, looking earnestly into Lizzie's eyes.

"And I'm a pathetic old maid," Lizzie finished for her, laughing. "Don't worry about me, Emma. I know now, since I'm here today, that I'm not ready

for this. You want to know something? This upstairs
gives me the blues."

"Why? Whatever for? It's my very best place.
The one I always imagined for my quilts. I love my
upstairs," Emma said.

"Well, good for you, Emma. You know how very
different we always were."

"We sure were and still are, I suppose. But yet, in
our own way, we always had a special bond, as long
as you weren't too lazy. Remember all the things
you did to slip away from the jobs you had to do?"

"Or how bossy you were! Emma, you were so
bossy, that's probably why I don't have a boyfriend.
I have nightmares of him acting as bossy as you
used to be."

Emma slapped Lizzie playfully. "Now, you know
better."

They laughed together as they finished making
the beds, and Emma went downstairs to help Mam
with the kitchen cupboards, leaving Lizzie to hang
up pictures and finish unpacking. She smiled as
she came to a box filled with old copies of *Family
Life*, *Young Companion*, and *Blackboard Bulletin*,
monthly magazines published by Pathway Publishers in Ontario, Canada.

Emma loved the magazines, poring over each
story and copying recipes as soon as they arrived in
the mail. She saved each issue for future use, and she
got upset if someone lost or tore one of her precious
magazines. Lizzie enjoyed reading the magazines,
too, but she also quickly became bored with them.

After stacking the magazines neatly in a dresser drawer, Lizzie opened another cardboard box, labeled "Spare Bedroom." Inside she found Emma's old diaries, letters, birthday cards, and even her get-well cards from when she had rheumatic fever as a child. Lizzie was fascinated. Sifting through all of Emma's old belongings, she felt a keen sadness, the same feeling she often felt growing up. It was sad that people had to grow up. Why did they have to? It brought so many more responsibilities, decisions, and serious weighty matters that just well... that just made you old. Old and fat and wrinkly.

But then, God made things that way. He invented the whole concept of time, and people had to go along with that because they were just people. And besides, that Peter Pan story about the children going to Never-Never-Land and remaining children couldn't be true. It was all a fairy tale, and would she even be happy staying a child? She doubted it.

She sat down on the floor, leaned back against the wall, then sat forward immediately as a chill crept up her spine. Cold air wafted in from cracks in the floor and baseboard, and she shivered. See, it's stuff like this that gives me the blues about marrying, she thought. They should fix up this old upstairs, but they could never afford it, so they'll just have to live with it. And who knows? Every year these cracks in the floor could get larger, letting in more cold air until their woodstove in the kitchen can't keep out the cold, and they'll just freeze. Oh, well, if she did get married, her husband would just have to make

sure the house wasn't too old or damaged, because that would make her nervous.

Lizzie wondered fleetingly how Stephen felt about houses and wondered if he was happy way up north. It was brave of him to leave his parents and family like that. She had thought over and over about their conversation that night at the sledding party. Surely it wasn't as serious as he made it sound. The thing that really tormented her most, though, was why she kept fighting against his love for her. It had to be love, or he wouldn't be so serious. Why did she resist him? It should be so easy just to let the wall of defense down and become his girlfriend, and, of course, marry him in the end.

Maybe she read too many novels that made her expect some knight in shining armor to come along, some extraordinary person who would sweep her off her feet with such a great love that it wasn't even funny. Or, like Mam always said, maybe she was fighting against God's will.

Mam had always felt that Stephen was the one for her. But how could your mother know? That was so dumb it never failed to irk her. Just as if God could talk to Mam but not to Lizzie because she was too ... well, too thick-headed. The whole thing just gave her a headache, so she didn't think about it too much.

But the thing was, how could Emma and Mandy be so 100 percent certain that this was the right one? They were taking an awful risk in Lizzie's opinion. Oh, that was another thing. Mam always said it was

different for every person, no two situations were alike. Hmmph. That was not very reassuring.

❧

"Lizzie! Where are you?" Mandy called.

"Up here."

"You're supposed to come down now. Mam said we're to rake the yard."

"I'm not finished with these things for the spare bedroom," Lizzie said.

"Come on, Lizzie. You have to help me," Mandy said.

So Lizzie put the lid back on the unpacked cardboard box and went downstairs where Mam and Emma were arranging things in the kitchen cupboards. They were talking and laughing with Joshua's parents and his sisters who were cleaning the pantry.

Lizzie was hungry, but it didn't look as if anyone was preparing any food. There wasn't even any coffee or tea on the stove or cookies for a midmorning snack. She couldn't remember anyone talking about lunch.

"Aren't we having coffee break?" Lizzie asked Mam.

"No, we got started a bit late, so we'll just have an early lunch," Mam answered.

"Are you finished upstairs?" Emma asked.

"Not quite."

"That's all right. I'll do that next week," Emma said brightly.

Lizzie looked closely at Emma. Yes, that happy answer was genuine, there was no doubt about it. But when Lizzie thought about being all alone in that upstairs the following week, it just made her heart drop so far she could almost feel it in her stomach.

Lizzie and Mandy headed outside. Patches of snow sat under the large maple trees, but the rest of the yard was bare. Sticks, leaves, and debris littered the brown grass. Mandy and Lizzie grabbed a rake and started cleaning up in earnest.

The brisk, cold air and exercise lifted Lizzie's spirits as she worked. Mandy's cheeks were flushed as she raked steadily, her scarf fluttering in the breeze.

"Mandy," Lizzie said. She stopped and leaned on her rake. "Do you think Emma will be all right?"

"What? Lizzie, of course. She was looking forward to this for a very long time."

"But... but I'm afraid she'll get homesick so much," Lizzie said, her brow creased in worry.

"Not Emma. You would probably, and maybe I would a little, but not her. You know how she is."

❧

That afternoon, as the Glick family packed their things for the return trip home, Mam was fighting tears. Lizzie couldn't look at her, certain that she would burst into big, choking baby-like sobs at the thought of leaving Emma.

Everyone piled into the van while Joshua and Emma stood close together, their faces wreathed in

happy smiles. Mam put a few boxes under the seat, and Dat rolled down the window.

"Now come visit us soon. Take good care of Emma, Joshua," he said.

Joshua smiled and said of course he would, while Dat blinked back tears of his own.

"Good-bye, Lizzie! Don't forget to write! Good-bye, Mandy and Jason!" Emma reached through the window for the twins, hugging them good-bye, and still she did not cry. Lizzie wished the driver would just go now, because her tears might start to roll any minute.

Mam wiped her eyes as the van pulled slowly out the country road. Lizzie bit her lip and blinked steadily to keep the tears away. Her heart felt sad, almost as if a part of her stayed at the farm in Allen County. She would come visit them as often as she could, that was one sure thing.

"Well, there goes Emma," Mandy said quietly.

"Yep, there she went," Lizzie answered.

They grinned at each other, a special loving grin, so glad to have each other. Sisters were just the very best thing ever, Lizzie decided. Even better than boyfriends or husbands.

Chapter 11

Dᴜʀɪɴɢ ᴛʜᴇ ʟᴀᴛᴇ ᴡɪɴᴛᴇʀ, ᴀғᴛᴇʀ Eᴍᴍᴀ moved to Allen County, Lizzie struggled to remain enthused about teaching school. For one thing, she thought drearily, it's constantly raining, and the dismal playground is nothing but one huge muddy pigpen.

She stood on the porch, gazing out over the gray-ish brown landscape as more rain fell from a leaden sky. The children had already left for the day, collecting their muddy boots and coats before wending their way down the drive to their various forms of transportation—pony carts, buggies, on foot, or to the waiting driver.

It's high time for school to be over, Lizzie thought darkly. She had more than the usual discipline trouble that week, and her usual methods of control—keeping kids in at recess or asking them to apologize, or to write their misdemeanors over and over on tablet paper—were not solving the behavior problems. An

undercurrent of bad attitudes was threading its way through the upper grades.

She sank wearily on a dry spot of the concrete porch, tucking her feet in away from the raindrops. There were patches of white strewn across the playground, evidence that the children were throwing their paper or little plastic bags of snacks on the grass again. She had been giving the children points on the blackboard for littering on the playground, but it looked as if that wasn't working very well either.

Huge tears welled in her eyes, spilling over her cheeks until they splashed on her black apron. She felt as if the ground beneath her feet was crumbling and she was going to fall headlong into a void of despair. She could not stop the tears, nor did she want to. There was no one to see her, no one to care. Her driver would not be arriving for another hour, so she let the tears flow until she was finished crying. Using the corner of her apron to dry her tears, she sighed deeply and shakily as she continued to watch the rain come steadily down. Rivulets of muddy water trickled over the gravel that surrounded the steps as she thought.

Suddenly her despair was swept aside by feelings of anger. I would love to see some of these housewives put up with all this dirt and mud around the entrances to their houses, she thought. They'd have a fit. I bet they would.

Getting to her feet, she swept into the classroom, yanking open the door with the force of her angry thoughts. I'm going to stop at Jonas Beiler's house

on the way home and ask...no, not ask, *tell* him I need a load of gravel on this driveway and the entrances to the privies.

Then, she thought, as she clenched her fists on top of her desk, I am going to make a speech on Monday morning. I am going to talk to all the pupils and tell them exactly how I feel. This rebellion is going to stop.

Adrenalin flowed through her veins, giving her energy to finish her work while she thought about her speech to the pupils. Climbing up and down the rickety wooden stepladder to hang the student's new art on the classroom walls, she muttered to herself, thinking of the words she would use to convey her feelings of failure as a teacher.

Where has all the joy gone this winter? she wondered to herself. I always loved my teaching job, but lately something is missing. Maybe it's me. She didn't think the problems were entirely her fault, but she knew she had lost some of her enthusiasm, too.

When the van pulled up to the front door, Lizzie was ready to go, her jaw set in a firm line of determination. But as the driver turned in at Jonas Beiler's farm, Lizzie's stomach did a flip-flop of nervousness. She soon controlled it, knowing this was the only way to improve the school and hopefully her mood. She hurried up to the door and knocked timidly.

"Come in!" called a voice.

Stepping inside, she clasped her hands as she greeted the family who was seated around the table, ready to eat their evening meal.

"So, what brings you here? This is a pleasant surprise. Hopefully, you're not having any discipline problems or anything of that nature," Jonas said from his place at the head of the table.

"Uh... oh no," Lizzie said. "I... I... Well, is it too expensive to have a load of gravel or stones of some kind put down at school? The... the playground is simply a mess, and the entrance to the privies is just... well, like a hollowed-out path of chocolate pudding," she finished.

Jonas Beiler burst out laughing, a sound of deep, rolling mirth that swirled around Lizzie's spirit, gently lifting and carrying her own thoughts upward. Her hesitant smile widened as she felt the black cloak of despair lifting like curtains on a summer breeze.

"Chocolate pudding! That must be some mud," Jonas chuckled, looking at his wife who smiled back pleasantly.

"Well, it is a mess. We all kind of peepy-step along the side of the enclosure to keep our feet dry," Lizzie said.

"Yes, I believe it. That new schoolhouse should have had more gravel put down at the beginning of the term. But you know it's not just me who makes the decisions, and we have to watch our pennies so the school tuition doesn't get too high. Let me bring this matter up at our meeting, all right?"

"The next meeting! You mean I have to wait for another month?" Lizzie said, trying vainly to hide her disappointment.

"It's tonight."

"Oh, I'm sorry. I don't mean to be imposing, but...well, the floor, the porch, everyone's shoes, it's just..." Lizzie said.

"It doesn't surprise me," Barbara Beiler said. "I told Jonas if we housewives had to put up with that kind of mud, we'd have a fit."

Lizzie smiled at her. So they did think about it, she thought.

"Well, thank you very much. I just hope the rest of the school board will agree to the cost of a load of gravel," Lizzie said.

"We'll see, but I would imagine we'll do something for you. It probably gets a bit despairing this time of the year."

"A bit."

"You sure everything else is all right?" Barbara asked.

"Well, not really, but I think it's nothing I can't handle by myself," Lizzie smiled.

Later at home, after supper was eaten, Mam lingered around the table with Mandy and Lizzie. She put another piece of peach pie on her plate, added a bit of ice cream and said, "Mmm!"

Lizzie grinned at Mam. "I know. That pie is still warm. Did you ever notice how it is with pie and ice cream? You don't always have quite enough ice cream to finish your pie, then you don't have quite enough pie to finish your ice cream, and it just goes on and on."

Mam laughed. "Oh, I know exactly what you mean. I could eat that whole pie!"

The door opened and Dat appeared, his hat pushed down on his head, his hair disheveled as if he'd been running. "Mandy, the phone was ringing. It's for you," he said, his voice breathless.

Mandy's eyes widened in surprise. She started getting up from her perch on the bench. "Who is it?"

"Don't know," Dat said, grinning.

"Is it a boy or a girl?" Mandy asked.

"She has an awfully gruff voice if it's a girl," Dat said.

Mandy shrieked, slapping Dat's arm as she rushed past him and out the door, running as fast as she could to the end of the drive where the Glick family's phone was housed in a small building. Amish families in their community kept their telephones outside because they didn't have electricity or many more modern conveniences in their homes.

Lizzie anxiously peered out the kitchen window after Mandy as she related her miseries to Mam, telling her about the thread of rebellion that was steadily growing among the upper grades and about the amount of gooey mud in the playground. Mam listened attentively, clucking her tongue in sympathy, nodding her head as she agreed with the Lizzie.

Finally, she said, "But Lizzie, you know we can't expect our children to be respectful if we aren't being the type of person who earns that respect."

"Whatever that means," Lizzie grumbled.

"What I'm saying is... Now, don't take this as an insult, all right? But you haven't been too happy

yourself lately. I mean, around the house. Especially with the twins. They were playing dolls, and one of them kept slapping her poor baby, saying she was Lizzie."

Lizzie glanced at Mam sharply. "So?"

"Well, I'm just saying this as nicely as possible. I'm afraid your lack of enthusiasm and happiness in school goes a lot deeper than just the mud or the children's behavior."

Lizzie wrung the dishcloth over the sudsy water, turning to wipe viciously at the countertop. Then she straightened, putting her hands on her hips.

"So you think I have this deep depression or something?" she asked.

"No, Lizzie. No, I don't. It's just that…"

The door was flung open as if a whirlwind had hit it full force, and Mandy fairly danced into the kitchen. "I have a date!" she shouted, grabbing Lizzie's hands and whirling her around the room.

"Let me guess!" Lizzie said sarcastically.

"John Zook!" Mam finished for her.

"Yep!"

"Not much of a surprise!" Lizzie said, smiling at Mandy.

"Whew! I need to catch my breath. I'll faint," Mandy said, gasping as she folded herself on the bench along the wall. She lifted both hands to flap them in front of her face, as she breathed slowly in and out.

"So, where are you going?" Lizzie asked, trying to sound all excited and not even the least bit envious.

"Guess what? Just guess what? He's taking me to a really nice sit-down restaurant. Not just to McDonald's," she said, batting her eyelashes.

That did it. Lizzie gave in to all her envy and feelings of frustration about her own life, which at the moment was only one insurmountable mountain after another. "What's wrong with McDonald's?" she burst out. "If I had my choice, a big hamburger dripping with sauce, ketchup, pickles, onions, and all that good stuff or some fancy restaurant, I'd pick McDonald's!"

"Now," Mam said.

"You're just jealous," Mandy said angrily.

"I'm not jealous! I am not one teeny bit jealous. You can have John Zook. You're going to end up with a farmer and get up every morning at four-thirty and milk his sloppy cows for the rest of your life. You can just have him and gladly," she flung in Mandy's direction before opening the stair door and clomping up the stairs. She wasn't sure, but she thought she saw Mam and Mandy give each other that look, the one that meant Lizzie's pathetic.

Lizzie spent the remainder of the evening in her room writing letters, correcting papers from school, and mulling her sordid life around and around in her head. So a person had the right to be grouchy occasionally, didn't they? Schoolteachers were cooped up with dozens of noisy children all day in all kinds of weather, day in and day out, and nobody, not one single solitary person, appreciated it.

That's what was wrong. She wasn't sad or depressed. The parents should come visit school much more often than they did. Maybe if she'd get more praise and appreciation from the parents, she'd be a better teacher.

Then she thought of the Valentine's Day surprise that Rachel Beiler and Mary Lapp had brought her. She remembered the bouquet of carnations and roses Jonathan King gave her, and she couldn't help thinking about Samuel Glick's warm handshake and sincere thanks for teaching his children. All the kindness the parents had shown throughout the year slammed into her self-pity, sending it flying like sparks into a dark night sky until not one trace was left.

She sat back in her chair and blinked, the feeling of warm gratitude bringing tears to her eyes. Yes, Mam was right, she decided. Maybe there was something deeper.

"May I come in?" Mandy whispered, opening the door a tiny bit.

Lizzie grinned. "Of course."

Mandy tried to walk quietly and sedately, but there was an extra bounce to her step, one she couldn't quiet down. She plopped on Lizzie's bed, patted the pillows, and sighed. She rolled over, stared at the ceiling, and sighed again.

Lizzie glanced over at Mandy and smiled in spite of herself. "As soon as you're done passing out, you can talk to me about your date," Lizzie said.

"Oh, goody! Okay, I'm done passing out."

Mandy jumped up, bounced back down, and then arranged herself on the bed so she could see Lizzie better. "At least for now."

Lizzie smiled, twirling her pencil. "So, what did he say?"

"Oh, as soon as I lifted the receiver and heard his voice, I knew it was John." She rolled her large green eyes dreamily. "And, oh, Lizzie, I have to tell you, he was so polite, so manly, so... well, he knew exactly how to ask me out on a real date. It was the most... the most..."

Mandy clasped her hands to her heart, looked at the ceiling, and sighed deeply. "It was the most memorable moment of my entire life," she finished.

"What did he say?"

"Oh, he just said he knows he should wait longer to ask me out, but it seems like he's already waited forever. Imagine, Lizzie! He probably liked me from the very first time he saw me, exactly the way I felt. Oh, it's just all meant to be. I can just see God's hand in all of it. It's the most wonderful feeling," she said, sighing in rapture.

"That's nice," was all Lizzie could manage as she pushed the lemon tinge of jealousy away.

Mandy paused, watching Lizzie's face closely. Finally she said very quietly, "Lizzie, I'm sorry to go on and on. You're not really, seriously jealous of me, are you?"

Lizzie straightened her shoulders, briskly turning to sort through her stack of papers.

"Oh, no, of course not," she said airily, waving

her left hand as if to dismiss the very thought. "Of course not."

"I'm so glad, Lizzie. You are such an absolute good sport about me having my first date. You know what? You should help me pick out fabric for a new dress and make it for me. Would you?"

"That would be fun!" Lizzie said. "What color are you planning to wear?"

"Oh, my! I don't know. What should I wear?"

They opened Mandy's closet door and paged through the sleeves of Mandy's colorful array of dresses.

"This one would be perfect, Mandy. You really don't need a new one just to go out for supper," Lizzie said, taking down a soft dress of sage green. "This matches your eyes perfectly."

"You think so?" Mandy gathered the dress in her arms and held it up in front of her, turning left and right as she examined herself in the mirror. Lizzie watched as Mandy's slim figure floated back and forth in the glass, her bright smile emphasizing the green color of her eyes. "But... it's so green!" she said doubtfully.

"It's perfect, Mandy. You look lovely. I've hardly ever seen you wear it," Lizzie assured her.

"You really, really, honestly think so?"

"Yes, Mandy. I do. If I were you, that's exactly what I would wear."

"All right. I'm going to."

Lizzie smiled as Mandy went twirling across the room, the green dress flapping wildly. Who could be

jealous of Mandy for any length of time? She was so young and happy. Her excitement kind of grabbed you and spun you along, like one of those little whirlwinds that went twirling across a dusty lane on a dry summer day just before a thunderstorm. Lizzie felt much like one of those pieces of dust. She was just swept along by Mandy's infectious joy.

"Mandy, let's ask Mam if we can go to Falling Springs on Saturday and go shoe-shopping!" Lizzie said, bouncing on her bed.

"Let's do! Do you have any money?"

"We'll ask Mam. She can give us some."

They sat side by side making plans, talking about boyfriends, school troubles, muddy playgrounds, self-pity, first dates, and anything else they thought of.

A comfortable silence fell over the room as each one became lost in her own thoughts. The kerosene lamp flickered as a lone ladybug buzzed into the lamp chimney, evidently banging its head as it fell to the dresser top.

"One more thing," Mandy said, clasping and unclasping her hands nervously.

"Hmm?" Lizzie asked, thinking more about the ladybug, her mind relaxing, slowly easing her hectic thoughts into a softer, dreamier state.

"Now don't laugh. Promise?"

"I promise."

"You know we don't eat at a restaurant very often?"

"Mmm-hmm."

"What if I don't know how to order? I mean…
now don't laugh!"

"I'm not laughing."

Lizzie was still thinking about the ladybug, won-
dering how it had ever gotten into the house in the
first place.

"You know how awkward I feel when I do order
at a restaurant. Like I can't talk fancy enough or
don't know how to pronounce the words, or… I
just feel so stupid," Mandy said miserably.

"Oh, you aren't that low class that you can't
order a dinner at a restaurant. You will do just fine.
I'm sure you'll be able to pronounce the words,
since Amish people don't go to places that are so
fancy you can't pronounce the name of the dishes
you're ordering."

"Are you sure? John comes from Lamton origi-
nally, and those people are classy."

"Not that classy."

"You don't know."

"Yes, I do know," Lizzie said quickly. "We are
only as pitiful as we allow ourselves to be. We are
someone, too. I mean, you can't always feel like a
nobody, being intimidated by the slightest thing.
You are a very attractive young girl who is being
escorted by a handsome young man, and you can
say fancy words just as well as anyone else."

Mandy looked at Lizzie with disbelief.

"You sound so English. Lizzie, stop it," she said,
frowning.

"I mean it. I don't want you to feel like a country

mouse, just because we're poor and live on this old farm. That evidently doesn't bother John Zook or he wouldn't have asked you out."

"True, true," Mandy said, her spirits visibly lifted. "That was dumb of me, wasn't it? Of course, I'll be all right. And you know what? I could always just tell the waitress I'm having whatever John orders."

"Of course. Good idea," Lizzie agreed.

"Thanks, Liz. I don't know what I'd do without you. You're my best friend, best sister, best advisor, best everything. G'night!" And with that Mandy was off in a twirl of green.

Lizzie sighed as she stared out the window to the tops of the old apple trees in the pasture. She decided she was truly, from the bottom of her heart, happy for Mandy. And then she admitted wryly to herself that what took away the worst of that awful sting of jealousy was John's plans to farm with his brother. John was handsome, and, of course, there had been a time when Lizzie would gladly have accepted his offer to go out, but those cows definitely put a damper on any romance.

Vaguely she wondered if Stephen's uncle in northern Pennsylvania was a serious farmer and if Stephen would want to farm after working with his uncle. She couldn't even remember what Stephen looked like anymore. She wondered idly if he had a girlfriend picked out by this time. Probably.

Suddenly, she picked up her pencil and started writing on a sheet of scrap paper. She scribbled her name, Elizabeth Glick, leaving an empty space

beneath it. Slowly, she wrote Joshua and Emma, then John Zook and Amanda Glick. Smiling pensively, she drew a question mark in the empty space beneath her name. Slowly she erased it and lightly wrote "Stephen" in that space. Leaning back, she nibbled on the end of her pencil, wondering how she would feel if he called her and asked her to go with him to a restaurant. It would be nice, but... slowly she erased the name.

Dear God in Heaven, she prayed, You know the space is still empty. I am no longer running away from you. I'm just walking, and I think I am listening for real this time. Guide me and show me the way like you showed Emma, and now I think Mandy, too, so... just show me the way. Amen.

Chapter 12

The clanging of Lizzie's alarm clock jolted her out of a deep, peaceful slumber. Turning over, she pressed the button to stop the annoying jangle before pulling the covers up over her shoulders and snuggling down for a last moment of comfort before facing her day. Just as she started to doze, the abrupt memory of what this day held jarred her consciousness, and her eyes flew open.

Today she had to make a speech to the pupils. She could no longer push things away or pretend that there was nothing wrong or hope that this rebellion would fade away. She had to face this problem head-on, not wavering in her ambition to correct it nor run away from it. Did God know how nervous she was? Was courage something he supplied at the last minute? Probably he would. Well, actually, he was going to have to help her, because just the thought of making a serious speech in front of those upper-grade boys turned her knees to jelly.

Dear God, please help me, she prayed, but then she couldn't think of any words to continue her prayer. She supposed that was enough anyway, rolled over, threw back the covers, and got out of bed.

Mandy was helping Dat and Jason in the barn, so the upstairs was quiet as Lizzie brushed her teeth, pinned her cape to her dress, and combed her hair. She took extra pains to make sure she looked nice, carefully rolling her hair sleekly along the side of her head before pinning her hair in a bob.

How would she start her speech? How about, I have to talk to everyone this morning? No, that sounded too... well, she didn't know. Before we start our work this morning, we need to have a discussion. No, that would never do. It wasn't really a discussion. The pupils were going to have to be told how it was.

Setting her mouth in a determined line, she leaned forward over her dresser to pin her covering, asking God again to help her, to go with her to school today.

Mam smiled at Lizzie, and they talked about the events of the day as she packed her lunch. The thought of food made Lizzie's stomach churn unexpectedly, so she didn't bother packing much.

"Are you on a diet, Lizzie?" Mam asked, as Lizzie clicked the lid of her lunchbox shut.

"No. Remember, Mam, this is the day I have to straighten out the problem in school," Lizzie said, nervously pleating her sleeve with her fingers.

"Oh, yes, that's right. Well, I'm certainly glad I'm not you. But you'll do fine, I'm sure. You always did have more pluck than Emma or Mandy when it came to something of this nature. God surely knows who the schoolteacher is in this family."

"Really, Mam? You really mean it? You think I'm an honest-to-goodness schoolteacher?" Lizzie asked, her mouth open in disbelief.

"Why, of course, Lizzie. You're doing a great job!"

And so Lizzie went off to school carrying Mam's encouragement like a banner of bravery, which really is what it was. It was amazing what a bit of praise from Mam could do, she thought. It bolstered her failing spirit and gave her a great big warm, woolly cloak of love that wrapped around her all day.

The children arrived in groups, chattering and laughing as usual. Their enthusiasm dampened Lizzie's, especially as they came in the door smiling their usual noisy, "Good morning, Teacher!" Oh, I'll just ignore it. They look so innocent and unassuming this morning, she thought for a moment.

But when the older pupils came in to put their lunches in the cloakrooms, some with averted eyes or mumbling an unintelligible version of "Good Morning," her resolve bounded back with more determination than before. Definitely something needs to be done, she thought.

Morning devotions went as usual, although some of the boys scuffled their feet on the way to singing class, punching each other, lifting smiling eyes to

Lizzie as if daring her to make them stop it, while the girls quietly giggled.

Lizzie's heart sank but she stared back steadily, saying nothing because she wanted to avoid a confrontation in singing class.

Singing was quite an accomplishment that morning, with her heart rapidly beating and her mouth feeling as dry as sandpaper. Tears threatened to spring to her eyes at the slightest thought of her speech, but she bravely withstood any sign of emotion, knowing there was no other way if she wanted to retain her dignity and authority.

After everyone was seated, the lower graders dipped their heads, reaching into their desks for their arithmetic books, knowing out of habit that their class came first.

Lizzie stood behind her desk, clutching the back of her chair until her knuckles turned as white as her face. She took a deep, shaking breath.

"This morning," she began, her voice quavering, "we're going to have to have an understanding."

The classroom became as quiet as the lull before a storm as the students sat up in their desks. They laid down their pencils and placed their books on their desktops. The students in the lower grades glanced uneasily over their shoulders at the older students.

Lizzie steadied herself before continuing. "I've noticed recently that there seems to be an atmosphere of rebellion among the upper grades, which is slowly filtering down to the little ones."

She paused to clear her throat, looking up to see some of the older pupils' faces turn pale. "I have no idea what started all of this or when it began. It's just suddenly very evident that some of you older boys seem to get a big kick out of irritating me, or rather, seeing how far you can push me until I lose my temper."

Lizzie found herself clinging desperately to her desktop for support, willing back the rising flood of tears. "Perhaps it's all my fault. Maybe I'm being grouchy every day without realizing that I am. At any rate, we need to understand each other, because I can't go on this way."

To her absolute horror, a huge, noisy, rasping sob caught in her throat, followed immediately by a torrent of genuine tears. There was nothing to do except stand in front of her class and let all the pent-up frustration and misery of the past month flow down her cheeks. Quickly, she reached for a tissue from the box beside her desk.

"What have I done to encourage you to, well ... in plain words, just turn against me like this?"

Fresh tears rose unbidden as her eyes searched the older pupils' faces, hoping for, and yet dreading, their answers. There was dead silence. Lizzie waited, alarmed to see tears rise in the eyes of the most timid of her little girls. She tried to summon a reassuring smile for her, feeling sorry that she had to put her through this lecture.

Slowly, an upper-grade girl lifted her arm.

"Yes?" Lizzie said.

"It started with the boys."

Lizzie looked at the boys, her eyes never wavering, until one by one, they dropped their eyes from her gaze. "I know, Rachel. I know that's where the problem started, but you girls were willing accomplices these past few weeks. But, to be perfectly honest, I can't put the blame 100 percent on the boys. I know I don't have a happy, carefree attitude myself. I haven't come to school and remained enthused about ordinary, everyday lessons. Maybe I was a worse teacher than I thought I was."

The oldest of the boys, Melvin, raised his hand.

"Yes?" Lizzie said, raising her eyebrows.

"You give us too much work. You're always pushing us too hard, and we never hear one word of praise. That's what started it."

Lizzie's eyes opened wide in disbelief, and she struggled to maintain her composure. Of all the nerve! Spoiled child! He was so lazy, it wasn't even funny. How dare he?

"But... but..." Lizzie sputtered. "You're supposed to do all the assigned work the teacher tells you to do. I can't cut back on lessons just because the pupils think it's too much. Don't you have any spare time at all? Ever?"

Rapidly, heads began to shake back and forth, and a few of the boys snickered.

That's when a hot, white anger coursed through Lizzie's veins, and she pulled herself up to her full height, surveying her classroom much as an eagle watched its prey. "All right. That's enough. I made

the mistake of being less than happy some days, grouchy really, and that is my fault. I'm sorry. But you boys are just not doing your job either. You are not trying to do your work nearly as well as you could. As for spare time, the library books are being used much more than necessary. How many of you have a book you're reading in your spare time?"

Every hand shot up.

"How many of you are finished with yesterday's vocabulary?"

Only a few of the girls raised their hands.

"And…how many have finished the art I assigned you on Friday?"

Not one hand was raised.

Lizzie sighed before she began again, "So you see, what we have going all wrong is a vicious circle of me being grouchy and you pupils being lazy. None of us has the enthusiasm we should have. But as far as me assigning too much work, I find that extremely hard to believe. How can I offer any praise for lessons that are rarely completed on time or with so little effort put into them?"

Mary, an older pupil, shook her head slowly. That gave Lizzie the courage to continue.

"So there are going to be a few changes. There will be no recess for pupils with unfinished work. I know for a fact that every one of you is perfectly capable of completing every assignment on time, and if any of you has a problem with that, you may raise your hand."

No one raised their hands. Lizzie sighed as she searched the boys' faces anxiously.

"Now, does anyone have an idea about how we can all stay enthused and energetic with our work?"

Two of the girls raised their hands.

"Yes, Sally?"

"You could give us points for 100 percent, then have a prize after we have so many points," she said.

"Not 100 percent! Anything over 92 percent. It's too hard to get every single problem right," Allen, one of the boys, shot back.

Suddenly Lizzie saw the opportunity to win over Allen.

"Good idea, Allen! Of course, it is hard to get 100 percent in every subject. But 92 percent is a bit lenient, so why don't we say 95 percent, or anything over that, is a point?" she asked, smiling at him.

His face reddened, and he looked flustered but said, "Sounds good."

"All right. That's what we're going to do. Now how are we going to keep track of each individual's points? And, how many points are a fair amount before we have the prize? What will the prize be?"

Over half of the classroom's hands shot up, some of the children raising their hands as high as they would go while they opened their eyes wide with anticipation, bursting to tell Lizzie what they thought.

One by one, the pupils told her their ideas, until they had come up with a feasible plan. Stars were the answer, they said. Those little foil stars you

licked on the back and stuck on a chart. After they each had over 500 stars, the whole school would go on a hike.

"That is just a great idea," Lizzie said. "Tell you what! The day of the hike, we'll ask permission to roast hot dogs and marshmallows!"

"Crackers and peanut butter!" shouted a fourth-grader, who instantly slunk down in his seat after receiving some lowered eyebrow looks from the upper-graders.

"I love a burned marshmallow between Ritz crackers with peanut butter on them," Lizzie said, smiling to reassure him.

❧

That evening, Lizzie found four notes attached to workbooks. Her heart swelled with love and gratitude to her pupils, especially the upper-grade girls who wrote endearing little notes of apology. The boys didn't write notes, but they may as well have, she thought.

One by one, they wandered up to her desk, starting friendly conversations with Lizzie until they were talking and laughing like old friends. Then they picked sides to start playing baseball on Monday morning, teasing Lizzie because she was no longer the first one to be picked.

❧

The change in Lizzie's enthusiasm was almost unbelievable. Every day she sensed the pupils brought equal eagerness to arriving at school, playing baseball at recess, raising averages during class, and bending their heads studiously as they all tried to receive good grades.

The weather was beautiful with soft breezes beckoning them all outside at recess. Often she allowed them 15 minutes extra playtime, mostly because the baseball games were extremely competitive, which Lizzie enjoyed more than anything. There were still minor discipline problems, but she no longer went home with a sinking feeling of failure, of not knowing which way to turn.

A few weeks later there was a knock on the schoolhouse door. Lizzie opened it to find the porch filled with the school board members and their wives. Her knees felt as if every bone and muscle had turned to gelatin. "Come in," she said, trying to smile calmly and naturally, although her mouth had instantly turned into the texture of a cotton ball.

She put out folding chairs and directed a few of the school board members to empty seats on a bench along the back wall while her heart hammered in her ears. Please, please let my pupils behave, she thought.

After everyone was seated comfortably, Lizzie resumed teaching her German classes. Good, she thought, I'm glad we're having German. Most of her upper-grade pupils were good readers in the German language, which Lizzie knew impressed

their parents, and especially school board members.

As usual, Melvin read clearly and properly, followed by Rachel who did just as well. She stole a cautious glance at the men and was gratified to see them raising their eyebrows at each other.

That is a good sign, she thought. Hopefully, things will be all right. Next she reviewed flashcards with the fourth-graders, who loudly pronounced each German letter.

After the lessons were completed, the children all filed to the front of the room to sing for their visitors. The pupils minded their manners, walking quietly without whispering or punching each other. Oh, bless them, Lizzie thought. She chose songs that normally went well, and as the music rose in volume, swirling around the classroom with its warm melody and touching words, she was very grateful to her pupils for putting their hearts and souls into the singing.

She couldn't praise them with the school board there, but she rolled her eyes and hissed, "Thanks!" to the older girls, which brought a smile to their faces.

After the children were dismissed for recess, she talked with the visitors, answering questions and thanking them for the fresh gravel that had been put down in the driveway.

"Well, it looks as if you needed it," one of the women answered.

"Oh, we did. I even had the nerve to ask for it," Lizzie said, laughing.

Before the school board members left, they all mentioned that they hoped she would consider teaching at least another term.

"Oh, I don't know," Lizzie said, flustered. "Does this mean you're asking me seriously or ...?"

"Oh, no, we'll come around to ask you," Jonas Beiler said. "This is just to warn you."

Lizzie was left with a warm feeling of accomplishment after the school board members left. There was something satisfying about winning their approval that made her want to become an even better teacher, to exercise all of her ideas and plans because she was doing some good for the community.

Teaching school was like that. It continually held Lizzie's interest and fascination. It was like being at the helm of a little boat filled with children on an unpredictable body of water. You never knew what would happen from one day to the next, and you couldn't always depend on smooth sailing. But in spite of it all, every day was filled with love from the children. They were, indeed, such unique little individuals, each having their own separate needs. Each one teaches me something, Lizzie thought wryly.

She sat down on the front porch steps, her chin in her hands as she reflected on the past year. It certainly had not been without its ups and downs, its trials and challenges, but through it all, she wanted to continue teaching more than ever.

What else would I do, she thought. Grade eggs until I'm gray-haired and bent over from old age?

School gives me the blues sometimes, but not always. Not nearly always. Actually, only a small fraction of the time.

Now that she was 18 years old, she felt every inch a young woman, capable of handling her job, looking forward to another year of teaching, achieving goals, and finding fulfillment doing something she loved.

Lizzie watched the creek that ran beside the school, babbling over the rocks, winding its way to the river, meandering through the green, sleepy pasture. Yes, she decided, she was happy. Genuinely happy being a teacher. But deep down, she knew she did not want to be a teacher forever, or rather, until she died. She wanted to have a home of her own, a husband and children, just like every ordinary Amish girl. Just like Emma.

She shook her head, thinking about Mandy and John. Boy, if they weren't off to a running start. She accepted the idea of Mandy dating, no longer struggling with jealousy, thanks to John's farm and his cows, but still... sometimes she longed to have a special friend of her own. Not always. Boys can be so... immature sometimes, acting so childish. 'Course, I better watch it. Mandy says I act the same way at times.

She was just ready to get up and go inside when she heard the distinct rattle of wheels, along with the steady clip-clop of a horse-drawn buggy approaching. She watched as the black horse slowed and turned in, coming to a stop in front of the porch.

The door of the buggy was pushed open from inside, and Rebecca stuck her head out the door.

"Hi!" she said, her blue eyes sparkling from beneath her heavy, black lashes.

"Hi, yourself!" Lizzie grinned, genuinely glad to see her friend. "What are you doing?"

"Oh, I had to help Sarah for the day and finished early, so I came to talk to you for awhile."

"Good! Tie your horse to the fence and come see my classroom," Lizzie said happily.

"I can't. I have to get going. We're planting the garden tonight."

"Really? Already?"

"It's late this year."

"I guess."

"What are you doing this weekend?" Rebecca asked.

"I don't know. Why? Come over."

"Elmer Riehls have the supper for us on Sunday," Rebecca said, swatting at a fly that tried to enter the buggy.

"Good!"

"Did you know Stephen's coming home?" she asked.

Lizzie's attention was suddenly riveted on the horse's ears. For some strange reason, she could not meet Rebecca's gaze at that moment. She straightened her black apron belt, running her hand quickly across it to eliminate some imaginary dust. Wiping a hand across her forehead, she finally turned to face Rebecca.

"Is he? When?" she asked.

"Saturday. He's going to stay home, he thinks. I hope he does. I miss him too much when he lives so far away."

"I bet," Lizzie said absentmindedly.

"Well, see you, Lizzie. I really do have to go."

Before Lizzie could answer, Rebecca was off down the hill, rounding the turn at a dangerous speed before racing down the road on her way to plant the garden.

Stephen is coming home to stay. Oh, my word. Now what? How am I supposed to feel? She sat back down on the concrete steps of the schoolhouse and held perfectly still, lifting her face upwards to trace the pattern of two swallows who were dipping and weaving their way across the blue sky.

Quite unexpectedly, she felt the soft strains of music in her heart. The tune grew louder and louder, like an iridescent bubble beginning to form. It grew in volume until she thought of the mound of bubbles running over the side of the sink when she washed dishes as a little girl.

She wondered if God spoke to a person in bubbles. Or feelings like bubbles. She breathed deeply, sighing happily as all the imaginary bubbles floated toward the sky, joining the soaring swallows with music on their wings.

Chapter 13

Lizzie stood in front of her open closet doors, flipping through the sleeves of her dresses, trying to decide what color she should choose. None of her dresses fit her mood. She should have made a new one for this evening.

She considered the light aqua blue dress. No. Too pale. Just wore it a week ago. Navy blue. Don't think so. Too dark for Saturday evening. Burgundy. Deep, dark red. Hate those sleeves. Too short. And on and on, until she was almost through her row of dresses.

"I have nothing to wear!" she wailed out loud, hoping Mandy would hear her and come to her rescue. She didn't like to admit it, but Mandy's choices were sometimes better than her own. That, or it boosted Lizzie's self-confidence to have Mandy say she looked nice in a certain color.

As nervous and edgy as she felt this evening, nothing, not one color, looked right to her.

Mandy's face appeared at the doorway, laughing. "Red. Deep, dark burgundy would look nice on you tonight with your tanned face."

She disappeared, swiping furiously at her wet hair with a fluffy blue towel.

Lizzie pulled at the sleeve of her burgundy dress, liking the feel of the soft satiny material, thinking that Mandy was probably right as usual.

She pulled on the dress, gazing at herself in the mirror, nervously biting down on her lower lip. She whistled under her breath as she combed her hair, wondering what the evening would bring. Her heart thudded, almost stopped, then went racing on every single time she thought of Stephen.

As soon as Lizzie and Mandy arrived at Jacob Beilers, Rebecca and Mary Ann raced out of the house, hopped into the buggy, and rode with them into the barn. Laughing and talking, the friends remained in the buggy, catching up on all the latest news, admiring each other's dresses, and laughing at Rebecca's antics as she imitated her failure at combing her hair into a bob earlier that evening.

Lizzie laughed along with the rest of them, although her laugh felt a bit forced and strained as she kept glancing furtively over her shoulder, wondering where Stephen was at that moment. Maybe he hadn't even come home this week, she thought. She didn't have the nerve to ask Rebecca, although

her curiosity almost overwhelmed her common sense. Better to be quiet, she knew.

"And then," Mary Ann concluded, "she told me I have to chop my onions even *more*! Can you imagine? The tears were already running down my face!"

"Oh, I envy you! I wish my mom would let me work in the kitchen of a restaurant!" Lizzie burst out.

"It's okay. I enjoy it. But it's harder work than you think, Lizzie."

Lizzie smiled back at Mary Ann, thinking how fortunate she was to work in a restaurant. Mam was so strict. She always told them a restaurant was no place for her girls—too many men, too many temptations, which Lizzie thought was just ridiculous. What was the difference? She had dealt with temptation in the egg-grading room when that English truck driver, Don Albert, had flirted with her. She enjoyed teaching school, but a part of her longed to work as a waitress in a real-life restaurant. But Mam would never agree.

There was just something so glamorous about lifting a tray of glasses or dishes of steaming food in one hand while walking swiftly to serve a table of waiting patrons, she thought. When she was a little girl she had often practiced that maneuver, playing restaurant for countless hours, holding a small tablet, asking her "customers" what they would like.

"The volleyball net is set up," John called to the girls. "Let's play."

They clambered down from the buggy and headed across the neatly mowed lawn to the playing field where the volleyball net was stretched between two heavy poles. A few of the boys tightened the pegs holding the poles.

The girls called hello to the young men as the game quickly began in earnest. Lizzie didn't see Stephen anywhere. He wasn't here. Well, all right, he probably never came home. After all, Rebecca hadn't mentioned a thing.

As the evening wore on, the volleyball game became more intense. Competition was fierce, and Lizzie forgot about Stephen as she was swept up in the heat of the game.

"Time out!" one of the boys yelled.

"Game over!" John shouted.

Lizzie laughed and shook her head. Her breath was coming in short gasps from the exertion, the constant movement of the game, and all of the shouting. Her side had lost in spite of her efforts. The group drifted away from the volleyball net. The girls laid out the food while the boys carried out a cooler filled to capacity with ice and sodas. Lizzie bent over to choose a drink when she felt a tap on her shoulder. Straightening, she looked directly into Stephen's face.

Quickly she took a step back, her mouth open in disbelief. "Stephen!" was all she could say.

"Hello, Lizzie. How are you?" Stephen said, his face thinner and somehow, much older.

"I'm, I'm doing okay. How about you? It's been months since I've seen you."

"Yeah."

That was all he said. Lizzie glanced up nervously, not knowing exactly what to say to that. Did he mean it seemed like a long year and he was glad to see her again, or did he mean it was almost a year, but so what? Lizzie couldn't tell. She looked at him again but he said nothing, just stood there with his hands in his pockets watching her face.

Lizzie looked down at the top of her soda can and toyed with the top. Say something. Say anything. Just make him stay here. She snapped at the small silver ring to open her can of soda.

Stephen laughed softly. "Here. Give me that. You never could open a can of soda the right way."

Before she could protest, he reached down and took her soda. He opened it expertly and handed it back.

Her eyes met his as their fingers touched. His blue, blue eyes pierced her very mind, and this time there were no walls of resistance around Lizzie's heart. She looked at him steadily, knowing that her eyes told him how much she had missed him, had thought about him, and that she was very, very glad he had returned.

Her gaze dropped, shyness overcoming her need to let him know that she was not the same Lizzie he had left. Laughing a bit shakily, she said, "How do you know I can't open a can of soda?"

"Oh, I just remember. I remember how much you like fish sandwiches at Joe's restaurant, and I remember the habit you have of chewing on a

plastic straw after your Pepsi is finished. I remember our ride to Dan Lantzes in the pouring rain, when I couldn't hold my horse and you were having a fit. I remember..."

They were startled by a resounding "Hey, Steve! Remember me?" A small dark-haired girl walked rapidly up to Stephen and shook his hand.

"Don't you remember me? Miriam! The girl from Lamont. Surely you remember. Was it a year? It wasn't that long, was it?" she asked.

She wedged herself firmly between them, and Lizzie backed away a few steps, watching closely as Stephen looked down and smiled, shaking his head and laughing when she said something much too quietly for Lizzie to hear.

Turning, Lizzie walked away blindly, furious to have been so rudely cut off from her conversation with Stephen. But he remembered all that! Sighing rapturously, she made her way over to Rebecca and Marvin who were sitting together at the wooden picnic table.

She sat down beside Marvin.

"Oh, my niecely! Here's my niecely!" Marvin crowed.

Lizzie ground out between clenched teeth, "Who is she?"

Marvin raised his head, looking over the crowd of young people.

"Who?" he asked loudly.

"That little dark-haired girl who is talking to Stephen."

Rebecca grinned and Marvin pointed at the new girl.

"You mean her? That one?" he said noisily, pointing with his forefinger.

"Shhh! Not so loud. She'll hear you!" Lizzie hissed. "And stop pointing."

"Oh, her. That's … mmm … What's her name? Miriam, I think. Stephen had a date with her one weekend when he was in Lamont with me."

Lizzie's eyes opened wide and she turned to face Marvin. "When was that?"

"Oh, I don't know. A year ago?"

"Why didn't I know about it?"

Marvin lowered his head, looking straight into Lizzie's eyes. "He can date whoever he wants to, Lizzie. You never wanted him."

"But … but … " Lizzie floundered.

"But, what?" Marvin said, clearly enjoying Lizzie's lack of composure.

Lizzie shook her head, cupping her chin in her hands as her gaze wandered over to Stephen who was bent down and talking to the dark-haired girl, clearly enjoying the way she animated her sentences with her hands. Her laughter reverberated through the lantern-lit darkness, and Lizzie snorted, getting up quite suddenly.

"Where are you going?" Rebecca asked.

"Nowhere."

"You want me to go along?"

"No."

Lizzie stalked off into the soft darkness, away

from the light of the gas lanterns and Stephen and the new girl.

Little flirt! She has the nerve. Biting down hard on her thumbnail, she kept walking across the newly mown hay field. So this was how it would end. Despair washed over her in long, drowning waves as she remembered Amos.

She was just unlucky in love, that was all there was to it. She was most likely cursed, like God cursed the different tribes of Israel in the Old Testament when they did wrong. She tried very hard to think of some major sin in her life, like stealing, hating someone, lying, but there was no huge thing she could think of that would cause the curse. Perhaps she shouldn't even try to think of such an unfortunate thing. Maybe all of this was to teach her patience, or maybe oh, horrible thought—maybe Stephen was not God's will for her life. How in the world were you supposed to know?

She had thought in the past months that maybe, just maybe, thinking about Stephen so much meant that she might be falling in love. She never told a single soul, not Mandy or Mam, not even Emma. No one. Then when she was so nervous about choosing the right dress, she was almost 100 percent certain that Stephen was the one. Then, finally, she had let her barrier of resistance down, trying to convey her feelings like some bold... Oh, my. She lifted cold hands to her flaming face, hating herself and her jittery nerves until she could barely breathe.

Stopping, she listened. Were there footsteps behind her? She froze, both hands covering her mouth, as solid footsteps followed her in the darkness. "Wait! Lizzie, wait up."

Stephen!

She remained frozen, her feet rooted to the ground as her strength left her body. Blood pounded in her ears, and she was seriously afraid her knees would no longer support her, that she might crumple to the ground.

Her breath left in one soft whoosh of sound as she felt Stephen's hands on her shoulders. She shrugged them off, wanting to run away faster than she had ever run, yet wanting to stay here close to him.

"Where are you going?"

She could not answer because of the huge lump in her throat. Tears pricked her eyelashes as she fought down the strong desire to tell him everything. She wanted to tell him how she felt, how different things were now, how grown up and mature and attractive he was. Suddenly he seemed so different now, but just as she finally came to this conclusion, here was Miriam, a small, pretty girl, appearing like a bad dream from the past.

Stephen turned her around to face him. His hands fell to his sides and his fists clenched as he stepped away from her. "Why did you run away?"

Lizzie lifted her chin. "I just needed to go for a walk. I have a headache," she said.

"Oh, well. I was afraid it had something to do with Miriam talking to me." He laughed a low

laugh of derision. "I...I mean, I probably couldn't be so lucky that it would even matter to you whether Miriam talked to me or not."

Lizzie didn't know what he was talking about. She was too unstrung to understand him. Suddenly, she could no longer remain standing and she sank to the ground, her knees quite seriously refusing to hold her.

Instantly Stephen was beside her, reaching out to help her up.

"No," Lizzie said in a tiny voice laced with tears. "Let's just sit here awhile."

Watching her closely, Stephen sat down slowly on the grass beside her, staying a polite distance away from her.

Sighing, Lizzie watched the night sky as she struggled to dissolve her feelings of despair and regain control of her swirling thoughts and emotions.

Stephen didn't say anything. Lizzie remained quiet, too, listening to the night sounds. A dog barked hysterically somewhere in the distance as the youth group shouted and laughed as they returned to their volleyball game.

"Do stars blink?" Lizzie asked suddenly.

"I guess. I don't know. It looks as if they do," Stephen answered.

There was an awkward silence as Lizzie battled with her pride and her new feelings for Stephen. Quite suddenly she blurted out, "Who is Miriam?"

"Miriam? That short girl? Someone I know from Lamont."

"Do you like her? Marvin said you had a date with her."

Stephen went completely still. He did not move a muscle, until Lizzie felt quite sick in the pit of her stomach. Here it came. Now he'd tell her what he followed her to tell her. He loves Miriam. And sorry about that look you just gave me over that can of soda, but you waited too long, Lizzie, he would say. My heart belongs to Miriam. You'll find someone else.

Then he turned his head, his hair lifting on the soft night breeze. He ran a hand through his bangs, shook his head as if to clear his sight, and said, "Look at me, Lizzie."

"Just tell me," Lizzie whispered, a sob catching in her throat.

"All right. I will. I'll tell you everything. Maybe I'm just stupid enough to tell you because I'm feeling bolder right now since you seem to care whether I like Miriam or not. But you know how it has always been since the first time I saw you. There was never anyone else in my heart. Never."

"Until Miriam," Lizzie finished miserably.

"No."

"What?"

"No. She means nothing to me."

And then Stephen started talking. The flow of his words rippled and swirled around Lizzie's heart like a myriad butterflies flitting from one heaven-sent spring flower to the next. She listened quietly as he told her things he had kept in his heart for

years, his memories of her which kept him at his uncle's farm in northern Pennsylvania because he knew she needed time and space to decide what she wanted. He loved the way she threw a baseball with her left hand, he loved the way she drove his horse and waded in the creek and ate stick pretzels two by two.

Lizzie threw back her head and let all the happiness escape in one long sigh that turned into smiles, and then into a mix of tears and laughter.

"Yes, Stephen, you were right. I needed time. I was blind for so long. I think I'm finally beginning to see how I am. I mean, that may sound like I'm a bit full of myself, but I truly think some young people are born with a nature that makes them want what they can't have, and *not* want what they can have. Or, in other words, I may as well admit it, maybe I've been resisting God's will. That's the way Mam puts it."

"Lizzie, does that mean that... Well, does this conversation really mean anything to you? I mean, do you even care about the things I said?"

Slowly, Lizzie nodded her head up and down. "Yes, Stephen. It means everything to me. I thought about you constantly these past couple of months, and now that you're here, you certainly seem older and more... more..."

"Does this mean that...?" Stephen stopped suddenly.

"What?"

"Nothing."

They sat awhile in silence, Lizzie feeling a bit self-conscious as she plucked aimlessly at the grass in the hay field. Quite unexpectedly, Lizzie jumped to her feet. "Let's go back, okay?"

Stephen sighed and then slowly stood up. They started walking back to the volleyball game, their steps becoming slower and slower. They said nothing until Lizzie laughed a low, happy sound.

"We're not exactly in a hurry to get back to the volleyball game," she said softly.

Stephen reached for her hand, holding it tightly in his own as he turned toward her and said, "Lizzie, I've thought of doing this so many times, that I'm not sure it's real. But... may I... can I pick you up Sunday afternoon?"

Lizzie smiled a small smile to herself. "You mean for a real date?"

"Yes."

"Oh, Stephen, of course. Yes, you may."

Feeling very shy, Lizzie continued walking with Stephen beside her, her hand securely held in his. It was a moment she would never forget, the feeling of having committed herself to a relationship, unsure of what the outcome would be. It was a shaky, scary, exhilarating feeling, and yet at exactly the same time she knew without a doubt, just like Mandy said, she just knew it was right. She would have to ask God over and over probably just to be positive, but so far, it seemed very, very good.

Chapter 14

THERE WAS NO USE TRYING TO HIDE ANYTHING from her family the following morning. She was the first one down the stairs, smiling widely the minute Mam turned from the stove to say, Good morning.

Lizzie thought she would suddenly burst apart if someone didn't mention her broad smile. She smiled with all her teeth showing, fairly dancing between the stove and the breakfast table. Mam was preoccupied and didn't say anything more. Lizzie cleared her throat, intending to tell Mam about her upcoming date with Stephen if she didn't notice soon.

The door burst open and Mandy hurried into the kitchen, quickly washing her hands at the small sink by the door.

"Hey, Lizzie, you and Stephen must have gone on quite a walk. What's going on? Come on, you have to tell me."

Turning, Mandy's eyes teasing, she dried her hands on the fluffy blue towel hanging on the side of the cupboard.

Lizzie took a deep breath, leaned against the counter, and adjusted her bib apron. Straightening her shoulders, she said clearly and slowly, savoring every minute of her important announcement, "I have a date with Stephen."

Mandy squealed and Mam stared, open-mouthed.

"I knew it!" Mandy shouted, throwing the towel up against the ceiling. "I just knew it! You know why? Stephen was talking to John for awhile after the game. He was probably making plans to do something with *us*!"

"Well, congratulations, Lizzie," Mam said quietly and almost reverently. "I've always felt right about you and Stephen."

Lizzie beamed at Mam, basking in her words of praise and acceptance. This all felt so very right and good, so she just continued smiling and laughing as she helped Mam with breakfast, chattering happily with Mandy about their upcoming weekend.

The door to the back porch opened as usual as Dat and Jason came in to hang their hats on the hooks against the wall.

Suddenly there was a loud banging sound, and Dat's frustrated voice saying, "Whoa! What is going on here?"

"Are you all right?" Jason asked.

Quickly, Mam moved toward the back porch. She met Dat halfway, her eyes full of concern.

"What? What happened, Melvin?"

Dat came through the door, shaking his head in disbelief.

"I stumbled across the doorstep," he said. "My legs both feel tingly, almost as if they are numb."

"Have you felt like that for very long?" Mam asked, hurrying toward him.

He sat heavily in a chair at the table, lifting one foot gingerly and flexing it.

"My feet felt that way for a few weeks, but I didn't think it was necessary to become anxious or concerned. I thought it would disappear after awhile as it had before."

❧

Lizzie stood against the counter, her arms crossed tightly in front of her. The joy of her morning was fading away, replaced by heartbreaking pity as she saw bewilderment on Dat's face as he shook his head. She was sure now that there was something seriously wrong with him. There just had to be.

He had gone to the optometrist several weeks ago to have his eyes thoroughly examined and then the prescription of his lenses changed. But still he complained about days of foggy vision and a complete blind spot in his left eye. Mam said he would just have to learn to live with his failing eyesight because the doctor had said he seemed healthy otherwise. But now this.

Lizzie turned toward the kitchen window, staring blindly out to the horse barn. Dat had to stay healthy. He had to. Everything depended on his health and well-being to keep the farm running

smoothly, the shiny, stainless steel tank filled with milk, the milk check coming in the mail to pay the mortgage payment and the accumulated bills. How in the world would they ever go on farming if he was unable to work?

She caught her lower lip and bit down hard, physically trying to keep back the panic she felt creeping up on her. We'll just be horribly poor with Dat not being able to work. There will be nothing in the house to eat. Mandy's paycheck and mine will have to go toward the mortgage payment. Mam will have to get a job. Did the church help people if their father couldn't work? What about her first date with Stephen? He probably wouldn't want to be married to someone as poor as she would be.

She could not let the wolves come any closer, tightening the panicky feeling in her chest. Turning, she shook her head as if to clear away the fear and faced Dat squarely.

"Dat, what... what do you really think is going on here?" she asked.

Mam and Mandy shared a knowing look, realizing how hard it was for Lizzie to calmly accept a situation like this.

Dat looked into Lizzie's eyes, and she read the fear in his. No, Dat, not you. You can't be afraid. You're Dat. You are the one who makes everything right for us so that we don't have to be afraid. She felt almost angry at Dat for being frightened.

"You have to do something, Dat!" she burst out.

"Lizzie," Mam said calmly.

They all looked at Mam.

"I think there really is something wrong other than a passing ailment," she said. "Chiropractic treatments have done nothing to correct the numbness in Dat's feet or help his feelings of exhaustion."

"Why didn't you tell us this before?" Lizzie asked.

"We kept a lot of his symptoms quiet because we didn't want to frighten everyone," Mam said. "We'll go see the family doctor as soon as I can make an appointment, and he'll very likely refer us to someone who can do further examinations. We really need to find out what is going on," she concluded.

Dat hung his head and sighed wearily. Mam put a hand on his shoulder as if to reassure him that everything was going to be fine. Mam seemed so solid, so courageous, so in control of this helpless, frustrating situation, that Lizzie took a deep breath, calming herself in the wake of Mam's bravery.

When Mam and Dat got home from their appointment in town, Lizzie was preparing name charts for the upcoming school year. Quickly, she got to her feet, nervously running to the window as she heard a vehicle's tires crunching on the gravel drive.

Dat was smiling as he paid the driver, and Mam carried a few bags of groceries into the kitchen, looking quite unperturbed. As Mam had predicted,

the family doctor referred them to a large hospital in Maryland, but their appointment wasn't till the following month.

Dat pulled out a box of chocolate marshmallow ice cream and went to the cupboard to get out a small stack of plastic dishes.

"Who wants a dish of my favorite ice cream?" he said.

Lizzie watched Mam and Dat suspiciously, sure they were just trying to put on a cheerful front. But they both looked and acted so genuinely like her normal parents that Lizzie finally smiled, relaxing. She was so glad to see Dat didn't have a horrible, fearsome, life-threatening disease.

What Lizzie did not know about was Mam and Dat's talk late into that night after all the children were asleep. They had been told by the kind, knowledgeable family doctor that there was a possibility that Dat had MS or multiple sclerosis. They had never heard of the disease and didn't know very much about it.

They discussed the farm. Jason was old enough to work side by side with Dat on the farm. But what about a dependable income? If Dat actually had some disease that would render him helpless in years to come, they needed to discuss the possibility of giving up farming.

Lizzie did not see the tears in Dat's eyes that night or hear Mam's fervent prayer to God to help them all, to have mercy on her poor husband and to realize the struggles in both their hearts as they wrestled

with fear of the unknown.

And so, with the impending knowledge weighing heavily on her shoulders, Lizzie felt a bit subdued when Stephen came to pick her up after church services on Sunday. The day was perfect, absolutely gorgeous, one of those days when the blue of the sky was so rich, the leaves on the trees so brilliant, it almost hurt Lizzie's eyes to absorb it all. Little white clouds floated lazily in the azure sky, for all the world like little cotton balls stuck on a brilliantly hued, first-grade art project.

Stephen had curried and brushed his horse to perfection, the horse's reddish brown coat rippling in the sunlight. He had combed his black mane and tail until they flowed together perfectly and cleaned and oiled the harness. Lizzie smiled to herself when she saw the light playing on the freshly washed spokes of the black buggy wheels. Stephen disliked washing his own buggy. Probably Rebecca had done it.

Stephen stopped his horse at the sidewalk and Lizzie hurried out, waving to her parents who stood smiling on the front porch. She knew Jason was peeping out somewhere, and she hoped fervently he would be quiet. Stephen and Jason had learned to know each other during a hunting trip they had taken a few years earlier. Jason was happy to hear that Stephen had asked Lizzie on a date. Now she just hoped Jason would be discreet, at least until she was safely on the buggy.

She sighed with relief when Stephen's horse responded to his "C'mon" and tug on the reins.

Soon they were well out the drive and away from the house, safely out of earshot. Just as Stephen turned to look at her, asking how her week was, an earsplitting whistle sliced through the air. Stephen pulled back on the reins, grinning as Jason charged through the milk-house door, his grin spreading widely across his face.

"Hey!"

"Hey, Jase."

"What are you doing with Lizzie in your buggy? Do you have enough room for her?" Jason asked.

Lizzie could feel her face heating up, but Stephen laughed easily, reaching out and knocking Jason's hat sideways.

"You can come along with us!" he said.

"There's no room!"

Lizzie tried to laugh, which ended in a small giggle, and she turned toward Jason, glaring at him, her eyes telling him in no uncertain terms to go away and behave himself.

As they turned onto the road, the horse picked up speed, and Stephen pushed open the door on his side of the buggy to let in a burst of warm air.

"You want your window open?" he asked.

"It is warm enough. I'll get it," Lizzie said, reaching out to pull in the window before hooking it to the clasp on the ceiling.

They rode in silence for awhile until Stephen looked over at her. He cleared his throat.

"You're so quiet today," he said.

"I guess I am, Stephen," Lizzie said. She added

quickly, "It's not you or anything. It's just my Dat."

Stephen lifted his eyebrows, looking at her with so much care and concern in his eyes she thought for one wild moment she would burst into tears, sobbing and hiccupping and snorting the way she used to when she was a small child.

She didn't. Calmly, her breath catching in her throat, she told him how Dat fell through the doorway, about his doctor's visit and the upcoming appointment at the huge hospital in Maryland.

Stephen listened without comment until she had finished, then he shook his head and said, "Wow." Lizzie watched him as he shook his head again, as if he was trying to comprehend what she had said. He turned his head and watched the scenery on the other side, saying nothing. He said nothing at all for a very long time, but for some reason, Lizzie wasn't uncomfortable. The silence wasn't awkward because she knew this was just how Stephen was. Lizzie smiled to herself, thinking about all the times he disappeared and reappeared without making any sound at all.

When they came to Elam Zook's home and Stephen turned in the drive, Lizzie's heart began pounding with excitement. She tried to appear calm and composed, but deep down she knew this was quite an event, her very first date.

She felt a bit important, knowing it always caused a commotion when a couple started dating. She arranged her black apron carefully, adjusting her cape and straightening her new navy dress. Of

course, she had to have a new dress. Mam always told her she looked best in dark colors like dark blue. Lizzie had chosen the rich, blue fabric because of the way the soft, thick material hung in graceful folds.

Her Uncle Marvin was unhitching his own horse as they approached, and he turned to greet them with a wide smile and raised eyebrows. Lizzie grinned back at him, casting a sidelong glance at Stephen who was trying to keep a straight face.

The whole day was special for Lizzie, and when Stephen came to ask her, a bit timidly, if she was ready to go with him to the hymn-singing, her heart swelled with pure happiness. What a feeling! It was just the greatest thing! She felt like Stephen was hers and she was his, an overwhelming feeling of belonging, of security and togetherness.

She took a deep breath, looking around at her group of friends to see who was watching, and answered a bit louder and slower than was absolutely necessary. "Yes, I am, Stephen. I'll be right out," she said, trying to bat her eyelashes and look a bit humble at the same time.

It didn't work. As soon as Stephen was out of earshot, Mandy threw back her head and laughed an unladylike guffaw of pure, unrestrained mirth.

"Oh, my! You laid that on thick enough!"

Mandy batted her eyelashes while the other girls laughed, a bit hesitantly at first, but seeing Lizzie laugh with Mandy and get up to slap her arm affectionately, they burst into laughter.

"Hey, Mandy, give her a break. It's her first date with him," Mary Ann said, coming to Lizzie's defense.

"See?" Lizzie said.

"That wasn't so bad!" Mary Ann said.

Lizzie smiled at her, a smile of knowing and acceptance. Friends were just the best thing in the world—other than Stephen, anyway.

On the way home that evening, Lizzie and Stephen talked easily about all kinds of different subjects, or rather, Lizzie did most of the talking while Stephen listened, occasionally adding his flat "Wow."

She became a bit nervous and ill at ease as they turned in the drive, wondering what would happen next. What if he didn't like the food she had prepared for a snack? She hadn't actually baked the chocolate whoopie pies herself or the cream cheese cupcakes either. Mam had taken care of all that since Lizzie hated to bake.

But there was nothing to worry about. John and Mandy had arrived home first and had already arranged an array of snacks on the kitchen table.

John and Stephen knew each other well, so they had a good time discussing numerous things until it was time for them to leave.

Lizzie walked with Stephen to the barn to help him with his horse, while John and Mandy remained on the porch swing.

She could sense Stephen's nervousness as he was hitching up his horse and buggy. He didn't say anything at all, but his movements were hurried.

Suddenly he went very still standing beside his horse, one arm crooked against the side of the harness. Lizzie stood quietly, waiting to see what he would say. Would he ask her for another date? Did he even want to continue seeing her? She lowered her head, kicking self-consciously at the graveled driveway.

"Lizzie."

Her head snapped up. "Hmmm?"

"I don't want you to continue dating if you're not sure. Okay?"

"Wh ... what do you mean?"

"I mean, this is very serious for me. You know how I've always felt since the first day we met. Don't go on dating me if you don't feel the same."

Lizzie was bewildered. "But Stephen! You haven't asked me yet!"

"I'm not going to."

Her heart sank way down, miserably, horribly. This is it, then.

"Well, then ... "

"Let's think about it this week. I'll probably see you Saturday evening then, all right? G'night, Lizzie."

She stepped back, bewildered, surprised, humiliated even. "G'night."

The gravel crunched under the buggy wheels as he drove out the lane at a good clip, leaving her standing on the darkened slope before she turned to make her way slowly into the house.

"Wow," she breathed.

Chapter 15

A FEW WEEKS BEFORE SCHOOL STARTED, ON a hot August day, Charlie Zimmerman drove his battered old pickup truck in the drive, parked at the end of the sidewalk, and honked the horn loudly.

Mam and Lizzie were husking corn under the walnut tree, and when Mam saw Charlie drive in, she gasped, her hand over her heart. "Oh, I wonder!" she breathed. Quickly, she laid down the brush and the ear of corn she was holding and hurried to the pickup truck.

Lizzie watched, holding her breath in anticipation as Charlie smiled as he talked. When Mam said, "Oh, my!" with both hands held to her mouth, Lizzie dumped her corn from her lap and raced over.

"What? What?" she asked excitedly.

"Joshua and Emma have a little boy!" was all Mam could manage to say. She laughed and cried, she smoothed her apron over her stomach, pulled her covering over her ears, threw back her covering

strings, and said, "Oh, my!" at least three times. Charlie beamed as she ran quickly to the barn, calling for Dat in a voice thick with tears.

Lizzie smiled at Charlie.

"Sorry, I guess she's a bit overwhelmed."

Charlie placed a hand on her shoulder, saying, "She has reason to be. She has reason to be."

Dat appeared at the barn door with Mam, a huge grin on his face. Charlie pumped Dat's hand up and down, congratulating him on his first grandson as Mam stood beside them and pulled her covering over her ears again. The three of them stood talking while Lizzie returned to the wheelbarrow load of corn, her thoughts spinning.

Emma had confided in Lizzie in a recent letter that she was "in the family way," as she put it. Amish families didn't talk very much about babies before they arrived. Lizzie hadn't even known about Mandy and Jason until after they were born.

She was very happy that Emma had a son, but this was some time to have a baby! August, right before school started, with all the canning and freezing. Someone would need to go and stay with Joshua and Emma, and although she desperately wanted to go, she knew she should stay at home and work on school projects.

That evening when Mandy came home from work, Lizzie and Mandy had a fierce argument about who would be allowed to go to stay with Emma. Lizzie wanted to go with all her heart, and so did Mandy. Mam settled it by saying she would

go the first few days, and after that Lizzie could stay till the end of the week, and Mandy could go for the whole week after that. Lizzie grumbled because Mandy got to stay longer, and Mandy grumbled that Lizzie could go first.

No one wanted to see Mam stay at Joshua's for a few days, but Dat said Emma needed Mam more than the rest of the family did, and they would all be just fine without her. First, though, they would all go to Allen County to see the baby and drop off Mam.

The corn was finished in record time that evening as they chattered about the baby. When they were finished, Mandy fairly hopped up and down with her eyes shining as she ran to the phone shanty to call John with the news.

Lizzie scrubbed the kitchen floor after the last of the corn had been taken to the cold storage in town. Mandy was so lucky to have a 100 percent steady boyfriend, whom she could trust completely and tell him everything she knew.

Lizzie knew she would love to be able to share this happy event with Stephen. But, oh, no, he hadn't asked her for a date for the coming weekend. It irked her. Kind of. Why didn't he ask her out again? Probably so she would wonder all week long if he really liked her or not. He *told* her he cared about her. Then why didn't he ask her?

❧

The next day the whole family went to see the new baby. When they arrived, Joshua's and Emma's house was quiet, the gas lamp in the living room hissing softly as the evening shadows lengthened across the house.

Mam reached the small white bassinet next to the sofa, oohing and aahing as she expertly picked up the small blue bundle inside. Emma got up from the rocking chair, beaming with happiness. Joshua's face reflected his joy as Dat exclaimed how the baby was every inch his father's son.

Lizzie took a good long look at Emma's little son, Mark, and decided he was actually really quite cute for a baby boy. He wasn't deep dark red or grotesquely swollen like some newborns. His eyes were little half moons, with a button nose, well, bigger than a cute button, but a nice nose, and his tiny little mouth puckered into a bow.

Lizzie looked at Baby Mark, then a bit dubiously at Jason. Now there was a case of one of life's greatest mysteries. She remembered very well the shock she felt when Mam came home from the hospital with Jason. He had been alarmingly homely looking, and most of his young life Lizzie had pitied him because of his wild-looking curls. But as he was growing into a young man, she thought he was the most handsome person she had ever seen, now that his curly hair was under control. He had blue-gray eyes with thick curly lashes and a kind smile that melted anyone's heart. So who knew? This cute baby might not be very good-looking at all when he got older.

Joshua and Emma both looked well and happy, so Lizzie decided it must not be too traumatic to have a baby. The biggest test was probably going to be in the coming weeks since a helpless infant could really scream. Babies yelled and cried horribly at times until you were reduced to a quivering mass of nerves and crying yourself. Like Mam had been with Jason.

Lizzie tried hard to put those thoughts to the back of her mind, focusing instead on how cute Mark was and how happy and relaxed Emma looked, her love for Joshua shining from her eyes every time she glanced at him.

❧

Lizzie returned later that week to stay with Emma and Baby Mark. She enjoyed her time with Emma immensely. Working for your sister was definitely more fun than working for someone else, Lizzie thought. It was so easy to relax at Emma's house, feeling right at home, getting something to eat when she was hungry, asking to take a nap when she was sleepy, and learning all the while to appreciate a newborn baby.

Mark very seldom cried, and when he did, Emma could always quiet him easily. She would feed him or throw a soft white diaper over one shoulder and hold him there, his soft little face snuggled against the flannel diaper. Emma rocked him in her pretty new rocker while Lizzie curled up on the sofa. They

had long, serious conversations while Emma cuddled her newborn.

"But, Lizzie," Emma said, smiling, "I am *so* happy for you, starting to really, truly find your life partner."

Lizzie eyed Emma skeptically. "What do you mean, 'life partner?' You don't know for certain, Emma."

"No, I don't. That's true. But…I don't know. Mam always had this feeling…"

"Mam's feelings aren't always right."

Emma stopped rocking as she watched Lizzie closely. "Why are you so testy about this subject?"

"You mean I should be all starry-eyed and gushing about how much I'm in love? Well, surprise! Maybe I'm not."

Lizzie picked at a loose thread in the blue and white afghan on the arm of the sofa. She smoothed a finger nervously across the arch of one eyebrow as her eyes fell before Emma's.

"Don't you like Stephen, Lizzie? Nobody said you *have* to date him. I mean it's your individual choice."

"He doesn't like *me*!" Lizzie spat out, annoyed at the huge lump beginning to form in her throat.

Emma began rocking again, patting Mark's back nervously with her hand. "Now *that*, Lizzie, I do not believe."

Lizzie lifted bewildered eyes to Emma. "You don't?"

"No, I don't."

"Well, then, why didn't he ask me for a second date? He said we should both think about it for awhile. Now that was a dumb thing for him to say. It just makes it seem as if he isn't sure if he likes me, or if he wants to date me seriously. I mean, what in the world is there to think about?"

"Lizzie, it seems bold of me to say this maybe, but for someone as smart as you are in book learning—a teacher even..."

She caught her breath as she let out a low laugh. "Remember how desperately I tried to keep up with you at school?"

"No. I forgot."

"Anyway, you can be so simple and dense and blind. Lizzie, think! Why wouldn't Stephen want you to think this over? He has always adored you, no, actually, adored the ground you walked on, and you never, not once, worried about his feelings. First, there was Joe and John, then Amos, and through all that..." Emma stopped.

"Neither Joe or John wanted me," Lizzie burst out. "Amos didn't either."

"Well, you know what I mean. Mam told you over and over to pray for God's will, and did you ever? Huh? Did you?"

"Sometimes. But, Emma, I know I'm older now, but sometimes God still seems way out of reach. Honest. Sometimes when I pray my prayers bounce against the ceiling and fall right back down. I feel silly on my knees."

Emma watched Lizzie seriously. "You should

have joined the church earlier."

"Why?"

"I don't know. Maybe you would be more comfortable with God if you gave your life over to him. You never really thought about that, did you?"

"Well, not really. I didn't want to join church too early. You have to be so plain and can't do one fun thing. Besides, this joining the church thing is all about the *ordnung* and obeying the rules, and I can do that anytime."

"No, Lizzie, joining church is so much more. It's learning how to live for Jesus Christ, your Savior, after you realize that you are a sinner and want to live a better life."

"Oh."

That was all Lizzie said. How could she confess to Emma the fear in her soul? How could she tell anyone that she was scared to death to actually come right out and admit to God that she was a sinner? She was afraid of God as it was, always trying to assure herself that she wasn't all that much of a sinner.

She still couldn't quite figure this whole thing out. If you confessed that you were a real sinner who was going to go to hell, you had to depend on something to help you out of that. Lizzie still was not convinced that she wasn't at least somewhat good enough to make her way to heaven. She helped Mam with the work at home, she wasn't outright terribly disobedient, and she even helped with the milking. Now that was a chore she absolutely hated with a passion, but she did it without complaining too much.

She threw the afghan off her lap, sat up, and smiled at Emma.

"Why don't you lay him down and we'll each make ourselves a cup of peppermint tea and a toasted cheese sandwich? I'm hungry."

Emma smiled back, relieved to see the dark look on Lizzie's face turn to a lighter one.

Their cups of tea steaming between them, they sat down together. The rich, buttery smell of the sandwiches made the kitchen seem warm and homey, Lizzie thought. Even as she felt the dark cloud of doubt return.

"What?" Emma asked, as only sisters can ask, that perfect opening when one perceives that something is troubling the other.

Lizzie swirled a spoon in her tea.

"This sinner thing, Emma. I know Jesus died on the cross for us, and I understand that. The new birth they preach about is all over my head. I don't get that, really, and Mam said I don't have to, that I will in time, that we can't of ourselves become born again.

"So that doesn't bother me so much. It's just that, how do we know for sure that if we do feel like a sinner, I mean, a bad one, then how can we be certain that Jesus' blood is for us, too? I mean me, just for me?"

Emma took a bite of her sandwich and chewed slowly. She wiped the crumbs from her mouth with a napkin.

"We never are. We just have to have faith and

believe it. It's kind of like a gift that seems too good to be free, so it's hard to humble ourselves to admit that we even need it in the first place. But you'll understand more as you grow older. We don't need to understand every little thing before we try to live for God."

"I guess."

Lizzie paused before telling Emma that Mandy and she would join church the following summer, and probably by then she would be ready to start that serious journey.

"In the meantime, you'll wait until Stephen asks for another date, right?" Emma teased.

Lizzie snorted. Emma laughed as she told Lizzie about how insecure she felt when Joshua asked her out the first time.

"But he asked you again that Sunday evening for the coming weekend, right?" Lizzie asked.

"Oh, yes! I would have had a fit if he hadn't."

That was no comfort at all, but Lizzie didn't say so. She needed to get out, get some exercise, clear her head of all these troubling thoughts wrapping themselves around her.

"Emma, do you mind if I start mowing the yard? I could do it all tomorrow, but I need the exercise."

"No, of course not. Why do you want to? Didn't I help much with whatever is troubling you?"

"Oh, of course," Lizzie said, meaning every word. There was still no one like Emma to explain things to her in a clear, uncluttered fashion that made everything more hopeful. Emma was like that.

Walking steadily behind the reel mower with the grass clippings dusting her feet and the hot August sun on her back, she did feel much better. Hearing the drone of a low airplane, she stopped to watch its course across the blue sky.

Airplanes were amazing things, an engine keeping that heavy craft in the sky and moving it along at that speed. Why weren't Amish people allowed to fly in airplanes? What would be wrong with one little ride? It would be the most wonderful feeling to be flying along above the earth and looking down on the little dots that were towns or houses and barns.

She sighed, returning to her grass mowing, and thought about how much it would cost to ride in an airplane. She'd ask Joshua; he knew such things.

"Lizzie!"

Joshua was hurrying toward her, a white piece of paper fluttering from his hand. Lizzie stopped, swiping at her loose hair with the back of her hand, watching him questioningly.

"I was in the phone shanty and the phone rang. Someone wants you to call him right away!" he said, a broad grin spreading across his face.

"Who?" Lizzie asked, her mouth becoming dry as her heart started banging too fast.

"Go find out!"

Lizzie grabbed blindly at the piece of paper, trying to read the numbers while running. She stumbled down over the bank beside the road, her thoughts scattered into a jumble that made no sense. Stephen? Would he? Did he even know where she was? He

would never call in the middle of the day. He was at work. It was probably Jason. Or ... or the school board. Or Dat. Joshua had said *he*.

She wiped her perspiring face, and then with shaking hands she spread out the piece of paper as she sank onto the stool in the shanty. She definitely did not recognize the number. Oh, this was so terribly unnerving. She was afraid to dial and afraid not to pick up the phone.

Taking a deep breath, she dialed the number quickly, just sure she would have heart failure if it was Stephen. Or if it wasn't.

It rang twice before a voice said, "Hello!"

Lizzie's heart sank. Marvin! What did he want? Trying desperately to keep her voice from showing the disappointment she felt, she said, "Marvin! Why are you calling me?"

"Stephen wants to talk to you."

Lizzie's mouth flew open as if to protest, but there was nothing she could do as she heard him yell for Stephen.

Then, "Hello."

"Hi ... hi!" Lizzie breathed.

"What are you doing?"

"I was ... was mowing grass, actually."

"Oh."

Typical Stephen. Just "oh."

"Why ... why are you calling me?"

There was silence for the space of a few heartbeats before Stephen told her that he was doing some concrete work with Marvin and that Marvin

had told him about the new baby. Stephen paused.

"How are you feeling about our date, Lizzie?" he asked finally.

He laughed before she could respond.

"Marvin didn't think I was very smart," he said. "He thought I should have asked you out again."

Lizzie bit her lip, squeezed her eyes shut, and then opened them wide as she tilted her head back to look at the ceiling. Good old Marvin, coming to her rescue like this.

"Well, I guess that's up to you whether you want to see me again," she replied.

"You know how I feel, Lizzie," was all Stephen said.

"Does that mean you're asking me out... or... or what?" Lizzie asked.

When she hung the phone on the hook, she definitely did have a date the following weekend. Dashing into the house, Lizzie let out a most unladylike yell of excitement, causing Emma to sit up from her nap on the couch, struggling to orient herself after all of Lizzie's hollering.

Baby Mark snuffled in his bassinet as Lizzie shouted, "Stephen called. I have a date!"

Laughing wearily, Emma sank back against the cushions.

"Lizzie, you're acting as if you're the only person ever asked for a date," she said, closing her eyes.

"I don't care!" Lizzie said, flopping into a chair and gazing happily at the opposite wall. "I have another date with Stephen!"

Chapter 16

Summer days turned sticky with August's humidity, and the heat hovered like a warm, wet blanket. Even getting up in the morning was a chore, and brushing her teeth brought a small sheen of perspiration to Lizzie's upper lip. The sun was already a hot, orange orb rising mercilessly across the east pasture when she headed outside with Mandy to do yard work after breakfast. It was going to be another uncomfortable day with the thermometer hovering between 90 and 100 degrees.

English people had air-conditioned homes, that was the thing. They could escape into their shaded, cool houses where that wonderful invention purred endearingly at the window, bringing waves of refrigerated air into a miserable house. They could lounge about in perfect comfort as long as they didn't go outside, Lizzie thought.

But not Amish people. No electricity meant no air-conditioning. So summer was miserable, and

you had to go about your day with a smile on your face and sweat dripping off your nose and down your back and into your eyes, especially when hoeing in the garden or mowing lawn.

The weekends weren't as much fun in the summertime, either, once the heat became this uncomfortable. For one thing, they had to wear Sunday dresses and capes and aprons, which were not designed for August heat at all. Long sleeves, a lined cape, and a black apron pinned around the waist amounted to layers and layers of heavy fabric.

Lizzie brought this fact to Mam's attention when she was getting ready one Sunday afternoon before Stephen picked her up. Her hands were moist with perspiration, and the pins would not go smoothly into the black belt of her apron. Her good humor had disappeared.

"Mam, help me pin on my apron," she said.

Mam glanced up from the *Family Life* magazine she was reading.

"It's too HOT to dress up!" Lizzie yelled as she accidentally pricked her finger with a pin.

"Now..." Mam began.

"I mean it, Mam. Think about it. We have facing on our dresses—that's two layers of dress material—and till the cape is pinned on, that's two more. Then, there are another two in the belt of our aprons. That's six layers. Six!"

Lizzie was almost screeching in exasperation, and Mam roared, helplessly caught in waves of laughter.

"Ach, now Lizzie. It's not that bad. I guess as long as the world has stood, it's been summer and winter, and we just take it as it comes."

Lizzie flounced off before Mam had a chance to help her pin her apron, deciding that if she was going to be in that kind of mood, she'd do it herself. As long as the world stood, thought Lizzie. What an ancient expression! The world didn't stand, it hurled itself around the sun at unimaginable speeds, whirling so fast it made no sense that you didn't feel one thing.

Stephen had continued to ask Lizzie for a date each weekend, and their relationship had quickly become more serious. They talked easily now, a more comfortable, effortless conversation, and it didn't really matter whether they kept small talk flowing or not. Silence between the two of them was content and easy, too.

Dat kept his appointment at the large hospital in Maryland. The doctors put him through a battery of tests to determine why his eyesight was failing and what caused the numbness in his legs and feet. He was often very tired and discouraged after his appointments, worried because his feet and eyes no longer wanted to do what his brain told them to do.

A few weeks after his examination, Mam went to the phone shanty to find out what the tests revealed. Lizzie watched her walk out the lane with a sinking feeling in her heart. Soon Mam came striding back in the driveway, her thumbs curled under her four fingers as she did when something upset her.

She took up the corner of her apron and wiped her eyes before reaching the porch. Lizzie steeled herself for the absolute worst, watching anxiously as Mam approached the steps.

Lizzie glanced nervously at Dat who sat at the kitchen table, drumming his fingers on the tabletop. As Mam came through the door he looked up anxiously, his eyes seeking reassurance.

Mam shook her head, making a soft, clucking noise. "Ach, the doctor wants to see you in his office in Maryland. I guess they don't realize how much it costs for us to go that far with a driver, but he didn't give us much choice."

"How soon does he want to see me?" Dat asked.

"Tomorrow forenoon."

Lizzie dreaded her return from school that day, knowing this was the actual day they would find out why Dat wasn't well. As always, she predicted the worst, her thoughts swirling around in her mind until she was in quite a state. She wanted the day to end swiftly, and yet she did not want to go home at all.

But there was no avoiding the cold, hard truth when Mam's words hit her with all the impact of a sledge hammer.

"He has MS," Mam said, not softly or loudly, just in plain ordinary words without tears or any display of emotion at all. She just said the words, simply and matter-of-factly, like carefully laying Scrabble tiles in the proper blocks to complete a word.

Lizzie threw down her book bag, folding into a kitchen chair with a sigh.

"What does that mean, Mam?" she asked, her fingers plucking nervously at the rip in the plastic tablecloth.

Mam turned from the sink where she was peeling potatoes for the evening meal. Taking up the corner of her apron, she dried her hands on it before sitting down at the table.

Her eyes looked tired. The red veins running through the whites of her eyes were more noticeable when she took off her glasses and wiped them with the dry corner of her apron. Putting her glasses back on her face, she smiled at Lizzie, only to have one corner of her mouth drop immediately as her nostrils flared and tears came of their own accord, despite her best effort to hold them back.

"I don't know, Lizzie, really, I don't," Mam said softly. "We have plenty of literature the doctor gave us to read, so I'm sure till the evening is over we'll know more. The way I understand, it starts with a virus which somehow gets into the spinal fluid, and, in time, that messes up the brain signals, which is why Dat doesn't have the full ability to walk like he used to. Same thing with his eyes."

"But there has to be something doctors can do," Lizzie said. "Isn't there some type of medication they can give him to make it go away?"

"No. Not the way the doctor described the disease. There are many types, some much worse than others, or with some the muscles deteriorate faster, I suppose. Ach, Lizzie, I really don't know too much about it yet. I just know that we have this to live

with now and we have to make the best of it."

Mam went back to peeling potatoes with a tired sigh, and Lizzie watched her, a feeling of overwhelming pity making it hard for her to speak normally. "Where is the literature the doctor gave you?" she asked.

"On Dat's desk."

So Lizzie curled up on the sofa, devouring every word she could about the disease that evidently was living in Dat's spine. Multiple sclerosis. Whoever came up with those words? she thought. Her whole being rebelled against this horrible intruder that had so rudely interrupted their lives.

She opened one pamphlet and looked at a few drawings of spinal fluid and odd-looking bacteria.

"This slowly progressive disease involves various parts of the central nervous system and presents numerous symptoms which tend to come and go, only to return again in greater severity," Lizzie read.

She found out that although a tremendous amount of research was being carried forward in the hope of discovering the basic cause, as yet there was no known cure.

Another pamphlet described in more detail exactly what was occurring in Dat's body. The lesions of multiple sclerosis which interrupt the nerve pathways are characterized by a loss of the usual insulating material called myelin, which covers the nerve fibers. In other words, Lizzie thought, little tiny scabs are messing up the nerve fibers, making everything more difficult for him to do.

She flung the glossy little folders on the arm of the sofa and marched back out to the kitchen.

"Does this mean that we have to stay home on weekends and everyone is going to be all serious and sad and I can't go camping this weekend?" she burst out, leaning against the countertop as she searched Mam's face.

Mam smiled a very small smile. "No, of course not. Dat is still alive and well and will continue to be all right for quite some time. Actually, he shouldn't be showing too many signs of the disease for up to a few years, other than his stumbling and blurry vision. So, no, Lizzie, you can go camping, of course. Our family life will just go on much the same as it always has."

"What about the farm?"

"We'll keep going as long as Dat is able. We'll see. Now go change, and you can start getting the wash off the line."

Chapter 17

THAT SATURDAY AFTERNOON STEPHEN DROVE up the lane and past the barn in a spring wagon. Two horses pulled the wagon which was covered with a tarp, forming a makeshift roof and sides so it looked almost like a modern-day covered wagon. Rebecca sat beside Stephen, smiling and waving her long, thin arms the minute she spied Lizzie.

Stephen's eyes were shining with excitement as he jumped down to hold the horses while Lizzie loaded her sleeping bag, pillow, ice chest, box of food, and folding chairs into the back.

Dat came out of the barn and shook his head at Stephen.

"Looks like a lovely pair to me!" he said, pointing to the horses.

"They'll be all right," Stephen replied, laughing.

"You better not let them see the contraption they're pulling," Dat laughed.

"That's just in case it rains."

"Hopefully it won't."

Smiling and waving, they were off, after Dat told them to be careful and behave themselves.

"That's what he always says," Lizzie said to Stephen.

"Well, at least he's friendly about us going camping," Stephen answered.

"I'll say," Rebecca added.

Lizzie's parents hadn't liked the idea of a group of youth traveling together for so many miles and camping overnight, especially in an unknown place. Stephen knew a very nice English couple, good friends of his parents, who had made arrangements for them to pitch their tents on their campground. This, however, made little difference to Lizzie's parents.

Finally, Dat spoke to Stephen's parents at church one Sunday. After a long discussion, the parents finally decided it was all right to let the youth go camping this once, but if they heard of any unruliness, they could never go again.

They were instructed in rather serious terms how to behave, Lizzie thought. They were to be very careful of traffic and take good care of the horses, especially as they pulled the wagon up the mountain. They couldn't yell or be just plain down noisy or put themselves or the horses in danger.

It was, Lizzie thought, a bit uncommon for the small group of youth in Cameron County to even have the audacity to ask their parents to go camping overnight, but those are the kind of things that made

life exciting. They all sat together and talked about their upcoming adventure after the hymn-singings on Sunday evenings. Mam and Dat should realize how fortunate they were that she asked permission to just go camping. What if they all decided to go white-water rafting? Or go for an airplane ride? Camping was mild compared to that.

The air was chilly so Lizzie wrapped a blanket around her shoulders as the horses trotted faster. They were on their way to pick up Marvin and Stephen's friend, Reuben, before heading to the campground across the West Mountain. Lizzie had never seen Stephen in such high spirits nor heard him talk as much as he did on their way to pick up Marvin.

The horses traveled together all right, although Stephen had to hold back Bob, the small chestnut brown one. Bob tossed his head up, then threw it down, worrying with the bit in his mouth until Lizzie began to be a little afraid.

"Why is that small horse so agitated?" she asked Stephen.

"He'll settle down once he gets good and tired," he answered, quite unperturbed.

So Lizzie tried not to let the little horse bother her as they picked up the two other boys and headed west. It was, after all, a perfect fall day, a bit chilly, maybe, but otherwise just a great day to be off on an adventure like this.

But Lizzie could feel Bob's agitation, and she was afraid he would wear himself out, raising and lowering his head, chomping down on the bit, prancing, stepping sideways, until the sweat turned to foam and flecks of foam coated his harness. If he would only calm down, he would use maybe only half of his energy.

She didn't blame him. It would be awful to be hitched to that long wooden tongue with a horse he had never met before, with those leather blinders on each side of his face. He wanted to run the way he was used to, run free and swift, without that weight hanging on his collar.

What if one of the horses began balking and they began drifting backward? They were going up, up, always on a slight incline, very different from the rolling up and down terrain of Cameron County.

Lizzie could no longer remain quiet, so she brought up the subject to Stephen again.

"Don't worry about it," Stephen said shortly.

Lizzie glanced at him sideways and shrugged her shoulders. All right, be like that then, she thought. She was hurt. That wasn't very nice of him to tell her off like that. She watched him again, but he was talking and laughing with Reuben without noticing that Lizzie was quiet. Actually, a bit miffed.

She wished Stephen would reassure her more verbally and help her overcome her distress about Bob. He probably wouldn't be very comforting about anything, Lizzie thought as she realized the night would be very dark so far away from any towns or

houses and the campground so far away from Mam and Dat and Mandy.

Golden leaves floated to the ground, and little wrinkled brown ones scudded across the road as the breeze pushed against the covered wagon. Stephen and Marvin discussed the best places to pull off on the side of the road to let the horses rest and drink water.

Just as Stephen had predicted, the horses slowed to a walk once the road turned gradually uphill, because they needed to conserve their energy for the long haul to the top of the mountain.

The five young people settled in and relaxed, laughing and talking about all kinds of ordinary subjects. Lizzie told them about Dat's disease and how hard it was to think of him being unable to walk in the coming years, which brought quick sympathetic tears from Rebecca. She's such a dear, Lizzie thought, and not only because she's Stephen's sister, just because she's herself.

As the afternoon continued, Rebecca and Marvin got out of the wagon and were now walking behind it to make the load lighter for the horses. Up front, Reuben and Stephen were having so much fun while Lizzie sat in the back seat, her arms crossed tightly in front of her, and pouted. She tried not to pout seriously, just enough to make Stephen notice that he had hurt her feelings. But if he noticed, he gave no sign.

Bored all alone on the back seat, she cleared her throat and coughed. Nothing happened. Stephen

kept having fun with Reuben, so she dug in her purse until she found her pack of chewing gum. "Anyone want a piece of gum?" she sang out.

"No, thanks!"

"Nope!"

Lizzie stuffed two big pieces into her mouth and chewed vehemently. She peered through the plastic side flap to see where Rebecca and Marvin were, but they weren't even in sight. She sighed and flopped back against the seat.

"I'm bored," she said loudly.

Stephen turned to look at her and laughed.

"You'll soon be a lot more bored than you are now, if you get bored this quickly," he said.

After he said that, Stephen laughed, bringing bright color to Lizzie's cheeks. Now she wasn't just hurt and bored. She was angry. How dare he? Her very own boyfriend.

"Let me off," she said curtly.

"Why?"

"Just let me off."

Stephen shrugged his shoulders, stopped the team, and watched as Lizzie climbed down over the back step.

"What are you going to do?" he asked, really noticing her this time.

"Walk."

"By yourself?"

"Of course."

"Do you want me to come with you?"

"No."

She soon found Rebecca and Marvin and had a good time walking with them along the leaf-strewn country road that wound its way to the top of the mountain.

They stopped almost at the very peak of the mountain and had a long, delicious lunch, while the boys watered the horses at the spring which bubbled out of the rocks. It was a beautiful spot, one Lizzie would never forget, sitting surrounded by thick foliage that provided a brilliant background to the sweating horses.

After lunch they climbed back onto the wagon and started down the opposite side of the mountain. Lizzie fought down her panic as the brakes, which were blocks of rubber, scraped and screeched against the back wheels, helping the horses hold the wagon to a safe speed.

She sat back against the seat with Rebecca, put her fist to her mouth, and whispered, "Aren't you afraid?"

"No. The horses are taking it easy. Stephen's a good driver."

But Lizzie was immensely relieved when they finally rolled into the campground. It was so good to be on level ground—on good, soft, green grass— that she chattered happily on about anything and everything. She felt so much better. She would never tell Stephen how absolutely petrified she had been.

After talking to the owner of the campground, the boys fed and watered the horses and then set up the girls' tent and one for themselves. As the sun

slipped behind the mountain, Marvin and Reuben started a roaring campfire while Stephen got out folding chairs. They all started roasting hot dogs and burning marshmallows to a black crisp.

Stephen brought his chair over close to hers and sat down beside her. Lizzie smiled.

"Are you having fun?" he asked quietly and only for her ears to hear.

"Oh, yes. Except for a while back there when you were mean to me," she said, trying to pout prettily.

"Mean to you? When was I mean to you?"

"You and Reuben were laughing at me."

Stephen sat back and looked at the stars twinkling down between the leaves of the treetops. "We didn't want to make you feel bad, Lizzie, but I don't like when someone nags at me when I'm driving a horse. Especially not two horses."

"I'm sorry," Lizzie whispered.

"That's okay," Stephen said gruffly. Stephen and Lizzie sat quietly side by side until it was time for bed.

Rebecca and Lizzie had a great time in their tent, settling in for the night. They arranged and rearranged their sleeping bags and adjusted their pillows. Finally, sometime after midnight they dozed off fitfully, each trying to reach a comfortable position on the hard ground.

In the middle of the night, Lizzie awakened to a shrill scream, which sounded so much like a genuinely terrified woman that she sat straight up and grabbed Rebecca, her eyes wide open in terror. The

horses were going crazy, whinnying and snorting and stamping their feet as they strained on the ropes that held them to the trees.

"Rebecca! What is it?" Lizzie hissed.

"How would I know? I didn't hear it. You woke me, grabbing my head!" Rebecca shouted.

Then at that moment another terrifying, high-pitched wail sliced through the thick darkness. The horses snorted again and whinnied restlessly.

Rebecca and Lizzie cowered in their tent, half whimpering with fright. This was awful. Was it a woman who was hurt and afraid, or worse yet, a huge mountain lion out there on the mountain somewhere, just waiting to rake its claws through the thin material of their small tent?

Just when Lizzie thought she would scream loud and long without any restraint whatsoever, she heard the boys' tent zipper, and bright spots of light moved across the campground to the horses. The boys gently steadied the horses, calming them in soothing tones.

Another ear-splitting scream rent the night air as the girls sank lower in their sleeping bags. Lizzie was close to tears as she wriggled out of her sleeping bag and quickly pushed up the tent zipper. Just as she was ready to call out to Stephen, she heard him tell Marvin that he was almost positive that sound was a bobcat.

A bobcat!

They aren't even very big, Lizzie thought. About twice the size of a house cat.

Quickly she stuck her head out and called, "Are you sure, Stephen?"

"I think so, but just to make sure, we'll walk around with flashlights after we get the horses calmed down."

Lizzie crawled back into the tent, smiling to herself about how calm and grown up and handsome Stephen looked out there, taking charge of this terrifying situation. He would protect her, making her feel so much less afraid and alone. She guessed she could forgive him for being uncaring on the way across the mountain. She definitely was not going to bring it up ever again, that was one thing sure.

Stephen was her boyfriend now, and if she wanted to continue their friendship, she would have to learn to be quiet, keeping her thoughts to herself at certain times. Emma said that was important when you got married, and she believed almost everything Emma said.

Chapter 18

MANDY THREW A PILLOW IN LIZZIE'S direction and let out a fierce yell. Lizzie reached down and picked up the pillow, firing it back at Mandy as hard as she possibly could. Tiny pellets of cold, hard snow whacked against the upstairs windows of the old farmhouse as another winter storm began to pick up speed, dropping icy snowflakes on the brown frozen landscape. Inside, Lizzie's bedroom was suffused in the soft yellow glow of the kerosene lamp, the wick turned up as far as it would go without sending black smoke billowing out of the glass chimney.

It was the week before Christmas, a busy time in the Glick household. Mam loved Christmas shopping and Dat gladly let her go ahead with it. He was no shopper, he always said, which was just fine with Mam, as she certainly was. Mam always saved money somehow, somewhere, even if it meant doing with less grocery money through November.

Lizzie just knew that on Christmas morning there would always be three or four good-sized packages piled around the drop-leaf table in the living room for each family member, while Mam hovered about, her cheeks pink with excitement. Every year Lizzie had a long list of things she wanted. This year's list included ice skates and new dresses and a warm robe, as well as things for her room, like a new picture for the wall and a nice new candle with an artificial flower ring around the base.

Oh, my! Nothing surpassed the spread of food at Christmastime. Mam was always a very good cook and a wonderful baker, but over Christmas she completely outdid herself.

Each year she would start by looking through all of her cookbooks, particularly her red hardcover Betty Crocker one. Then out would come her gray metal recipe box with the tattered yellow recipe cards that held all the wonders of Christmas. Among them was date pudding, which was so rich you couldn't eat too much, although Lizzie always managed to eat so much her stomach hurt a bit.

There was hardly an end to the rich desserts and drinks Mam would cook and bake for weeks before Christmas. She made butterscotch pie, chocolate pie, sand tarts, Grandpa cookies, Christmas layer salad, banana pudding, and Christmas cake. Mam mixed ginger ale with grape juice, or she bought soda— Mountain Dew, Pepsi, or root beer—and vanilla ice cream to make root beer floats. Which, Lizzie discovered as a child, you should never eat with olives.

Sometime Mam roasted a turkey for Christmas, and other years she baked a ham. She would always arrange pineapple rings on the ham and baste it with a bit of the juice while it baked.

The best part of Christmas dinner was the Ohio filling. It came out of the oven moist and steaming with a golden brown crust on top. The crust was the best. It tasted like toast with too much butter, Lizzie thought. Mam's version was from her native Holmes County, Ohio, and included potatoes, carrots, and celery chopped into tiny pieces, cubed bread, chicken, and chicken broth. It was so good. There was no other way to describe it except to say it was almost the best thing about Christmas food.

Mam made all kinds of cookies and candy, too. Rice Krispie treats and chocolate-coated peanut butter crackers were Lizzie's favorites.

Lizzie and Mandy always worked very hard to clean the entire house for Christmas, while Mam baked and cooked in the kitchen. They didn't decorate the house because that would be too worldly. Sometimes Mam allowed a few red candles on the windowsill or a candle set in the middle of the table.

Amish people did not believe in Christmas trees. Lizzie always wanted one though. Her favorite argument was that Laura Ingalls had one, decorated with popcorn and cranberries. Mam said Laura was English, but Lizzie said she wore longer dresses than her own. Mam said they were still English, and her

nostrils flared a bit, and Lizzie knew it was time to stop pressing Mam on the Christmas tree issue. Christmas trees were fancy and not in the Amish *ordnung*.

At Christmas the festivities also extended to the youth gatherings, especially the large Christmas hymn-singing that all of the parents were also urged to attend. It was just a special time, where all the voices blended together as the group sang old German favorites.

They often sang the verses in German and the chorus in English of songs such as "Joy to the World" and "Hark the Herald Angels Sing." Lizzie's favorite was *"Stille Nacht"* or "Silent Night" in German.

Dat loved singing, and especially at Christmastime he was in his element, sitting in the middle of the room at the singing, leading many of the songs with his beautiful voice. He knew all the words to all of the songs. Lizzie was secretly proud of Dat because she knew that when he started a song, the singing would become especially rousing. Dat was probably the community's best voice.

Two days before Christmas, Lizzie and Mandy were wrapping their Christmas presents for John and Stephen. Picking out a gift for a boy was a new experience for Lizzie, and one she was decidedly not comfortable with. Mandy teased her mercilessly, which was quite funny for awhile, but now Lizzie didn't think it was so humorous anymore.

She dreaded exchanging gifts with Stephen because she was worried about how to act properly

and politely. She just didn't know how and when to say the right thing.

What if she didn't like what Stephen gave her? Of course, she would fuss over it and tell him it was beautiful even if it wasn't. But Mandy laughed when Lizzie told her how she would react, being calm and polite no matter what she received.

"Your face is a dead giveaway," Mandy said. "You can't hide your true feelings."

"That's not true!"

"You'll say, 'Oh, how lovely!' and promptly burst into so many tears that you'll need a whole box of Kleenexes to keep blowing your nose," Mandy continued, clinging to the pillow that landed in her face.

Lizzie flipped back her long, brown hair, which was still wet from the shower, and scowled at Mandy.

"So. You weren't exactly thrilled with that cheap picture John gave you for your birthday," she said.

"I was! Where did you get that idea? Huh? He gave me my water set, too, not just the picture."

Mandy got up from her perch on the bed and ran a towel across her wet hair.

"You're just jealous," she said.

Lizzie shook her head vehemently. "Oh, no. Huh-uh. I wouldn't want a water set. I'm not getting married anytime soon."

"Then why are you dating Stephen?"

"'Cause I like him. He's fun to be with."

"Is that all?"

"Well, for now."

Mandy sat back down on the bed and straightened the gold bow she had tied around John's gift. The enormous box was wrapped in a dull red paper and done up with a gold bow, which looked very masculine. It was the perfect paper for a young man's present, Lizzie thought. She and Mandy had bought the same thing for their boyfriends, a small shaving cabinet with sliding glass doors and a wooden towel rack. They were very popular among the girls' friends and considered the perfect expensive Christmas gift to give to their boyfriends.

Lizzie's package for Stephen was wrapped in forest green paper. She was very happy with it, except she secretly thought the red looked more Christmasy. She would never admit this to Mandy, who was already too smug and self-assured about that package of hers.

"So, Mandy, you give John his gift Saturday evening, and I will give Stephen his Sunday evening, okay? Because you most definitely are not going to watch us exchange gifts or hear us or anything."

Mandy laughed easily. "Oh, relax. We're going to be down at the farm with his brother."

"Over the entire holiday?"

"No, of course not. John says he has something special to tell me or show me. I'm not sure what he meant."

"He's going to ask you to marry him!" Lizzie said loudly.

"Hush, Lizzie! You'll wake the twins! No, he's not. I'm not even near old enough and haven't

joined the church yet."

"Oh, that's right. I forgot."

They sat and talked awhile longer as the snow pinged against the windows and the soft hiss of the kerosene lamp made everything seem homey and cozy. They talked about Dat and how they hardly ever noticed there was anything different about him since his diagnosis. It always made them sad to think of Dat's disease, but since Mam was so upbeat, encouraging Dat to keep doing all the things he was used to doing, it helped the girls to see that it really wasn't so terrible to have multiple sclerosis.

"Not yet, Lizzie," Mandy said wisely, shaking her head slowly. "But sometime it will be."

"I know," Lizzie said soberly.

They sat in comfortable silence, Mandy with her chin on her knees, her arms wrapped around her legs. Lizzie plumped the pillows and flopped back, crossing her hands behind her head.

"So, what do you say when you give your boyfriend his present? Just, 'Here,' or 'Do you want this?' or 'Open this,' or what?" Lizzie asked.

Mandy rolled over and collapsed in a fit of laughter. She laughed until she could hardly get her breath, gasping and wheezing as she slapped at Lizzie.

Lizzie laughed with her, but only because she always had to laugh when Mandy did—that's just how it was.

Wiping her eyes, Mandy said, "Yes, Lizzie, just hold out the box and say, 'Here!'"

"You're a big help!" Lizzie said, pushing Mandy

off the bed where she collapsed into another fit of giggles on the rug.

"Are you really so nervous about giving Stephen that gift?" she asked, sitting up and watching Lizzie incredulously.

"Of course I am! I never had a boyfriend before," Lizzie said.

"Don't worry about it. You know how Mam says, 'Everything will work out.' You and Stephen are so relaxed and comfortable together, I can't see why you're making such a big deal out of this."

Quite honestly, Lizzie was uncomfortable with formalities, even ordinary everyday little ways of being nice and polite and knowing exactly what to say at the exact right moment. Oh, she could talk to English people, go shopping, pay drivers, and get along all right in the world, but receiving a gift from someone or acknowledging a compliment always made her feel completely at a loss about how to act.

So when Stephen and Lizzie drove home that Sunday evening after the hymn-singing, she was in a state of panic. Stephen talked easily while she chewed desperately on one fingernail after another, nodding her head or saying, "Mmm-hmm."

Suddenly Stephen reached over and took her hand away from her mouth. "Quit that. Either you're really hungry, or you haven't clipped your fingernails in a long time."

Lizzie laughed but didn't say anything.

When they reached her home, Stephen unhitched his horse and went around to the back of the buggy. Lifting the back door, he extracted a box which was so beautifully wrapped that, even in the dim light of the forebay, it looked so expensive it took her breath away. Oh, she wondered, what was inside?

She looked at Stephen questioningly, but he didn't notice or pretended not to. Without saying a word, he started toward the house. There was nothing for Lizzie to do but follow him, and since he wasn't saying anything, she guessed she may as well remain silent as well.

Stephen said he wasn't hungry, so Lizzie asked if he wanted to exchange gifts first.

"Let's do," he said.

Sitting in the living room in the quiet house lit with the soft yellow lamplight, she took the package he handed to her as naturally as breathing, and about as uncomplicated. After putting aside the huge foil bow, she tore off the paper and found a golden glass object wrapped in white tissue paper.

She was puzzled, unable to think of anything shaped like that. The glass, a translucent golden color, had a bumpy design in it, almost like little bumps with lines between them.

Unwrapping it carefully, she held it up to the light.

"A shade! A glass shade!" she exclaimed. Quickly she dug into the tissue paper again and came up with a huge, intricately designed kerosene lamp with a

clear glass chimney and a bracket to hold the big, beautiful shade.

Lizzie was so pleased she couldn't find words to express herself. John had given Mandy a blue one exactly like this, but Lizzie just figured she would never have one of her own because John came from Lamont, where everyone knew the latest style in gifts and things like that. She had tried hard to admire Mandy's beautiful lamp, even though she was thinking how perfect a gold one would be in her own room. And now she owned one!

She didn't struggle with what to say. She was too delighted about owning that perfect lamp.

"Thank you, Stephen," she said sincerely, her whole heart meaning the words. "I just love it."

"I'm glad," he said.

"Oh, I almost forgot yours!"

She handed him the large package, watching eagerly as he ripped off the bow without bothering to save it, just like boys always did when they opened gifts, Lizzie thought. He tore open the box and smiled quietly when he saw the golden oak wood of the shaving cabinet.

"Just what I need," he said.

"Really?" Lizzie asked breathlessly.

"Yes. I do need this to keep small things in my room. It's beautiful oak wood, too."

"You really like it?"

"Of course I do."

Lizzie sighed happily, and Stephen handed her a large white envelope.

"Your card."

"Oh, oh, yes, of course. I put my card for you inside the shaving cabinet."

Separately they opened the cards and read the words. Lizzie had agonized for a great length of time at the card shop in town, trying to find a Christmas card with the perfect words.

Should her card say "To the One I Love," or should it say "To a Dear Friend"? If she got the first card, it would tell him she loved him, and that would be dumb because she had never told him that. Not yet. If she gave him the one that said "To a Dear Friend," it sounded like a card she would give to Mary Ann or Rebecca or just any ordinary girlfriend.

And Stephen was definitely more than that. But to say "I Love You" on a Christmas card was a little too bold, she thought. She had finally settled on a card that said "For a Special Friend," which really was a nice safe card that didn't seem as if it was meant for the mailman or the milk-truck driver or Charlie Zimmerman.

She opened the large white envelope Stephen handed her and stifled a gasp when she saw the words, "To the One I Love at Christmas," in large beautifully written words across the entire face of the card. The inside had soft paper, almost like tissue paper, folded along both sides, and Stephen had written beautiful words about how his life had changed since they had started dating and how much she meant to him, especially at Christmastime.

Below it he had written, "I Love You, Stephen."

Lizzie remained seated, reading the card a lot longer than was absolutely necessary, simply because she didn't know what else to do. She was afraid to look at Stephen, and horribly embarrassed at having chosen that simple friendship card. Color crept into her cheeks as she watched him close the card and return it to the envelope with a soft sigh.

"Stephen, I ... I ..." she stammered.

He turned to look at her, and she met his gaze for only a moment before dropping her eyes in bewilderment.

"It's okay, Lizzie. It really is. I'm just glad you consider me your special friend."

She laughed softly. "Well, if you must know, I spent some agonizing moments at the card shop, trying to figure out which card was appropriate. And now your card says so much more than mine. It's just that, well, sometimes I think I must be the only person in the whole world who doesn't really understand ... understand ... well, what I mean, I mean ... what I ... what love is."

There was a long, uncomfortable silence as Lizzie sat miserably twisting the hem of her apron in both hands. Just say something, Stephen, anything, she thought.

But he didn't. He sighed again and stood up abruptly, gathering the wrapping paper that was strewn across the sofa.

"I'm hungry," he announced. "Let's go have our snack."

In the kitchen, the mood was dispelled, the atmosphere lighter, and Stephen bantered lightheartedly, as usual, while they ate the Christmas cookies and drank hot peppermint tea. After he left, Lizzie put the mugs in the sink, absentmindedly letting the flow of warm water splash on the back of her hand, her thoughts ebbing and flowing.

Why could she never find solid ground where Stephen was concerned? It was like walking through a maze or a puzzle where she could never find her way with absolute clarity. Did anyone ever love beyond a doubt, totally and absolutely committed to one other person, their only desire to spend the rest of their days growing old together?

She shook her head wearily, knowing she was tired from the long holiday so that now was not a real good time to be contemplating anything. As she made her way up the steps to her room, carrying the lamp, she felt old and weary from constantly battling her doubts and fears.

She wished Emma still lived at home so she could ask her if she ever felt unsure of herself where Joshua was concerned. Well, she was going to get some sleep and not worry about anything till morning. She ran her hand across the beautiful gold lamp, still in awe of actually owning one like Mandy's, only prettier. It had been a good Christmas, with all the presents from Mam and Dat, the love they had for each other, and, most of all, the fact that the old farm and Cameron County was their home, really and truly.

Chapter 19

Lizzie marched down the middle aisle of her classroom, her face contorted with disgust. She reached out and grabbed Eli's arm, yanking him back into his seat. He looked up at her, his face a mixture of mockery and fear.

"If you don't stay in your seat, I'm going to have to get out my paddle," she ground out between clenched teeth. "Sit down and stay there!"

The classroom became very quiet, the only sounds coming from a few nervous pupils clearing their throats. Lizzie turned on her heel and stomped angrily back to her desk, her hands shaking as she picked up her pen.

Why were the pupils being so disruptive today? Was it the long, boring winter months that made the children restless, or were they all just trying to drive her as far as she would go? Swallowing her threatening tears, Lizzie tried to calm herself before a feeling of panic completely took control of her senses.

Normally her teaching duties were a happy time, a time of feeling fulfilled, busy, and as if she was doing a service to the children and their parents, an important part of the community. But lately, everyone and every little incident worked on her nerves, making her feel as if she was inadequate, especially with the children misbehaving, getting low grades, and ignoring their schoolwork.

She gazed out at the dark scudding clouds which hung low above the small schoolhouse. The bare branches of the trees along the creek whipped back and forth in the stiff winter wind. Shivering, she got up, grabbed the coal stoker, poked at the red-hot coals inside the black stove, and then adjusted the draft. Stifling a yawn as she called on the fourth-grade English class, she crossed her arms in front of her, keeping her back to the stove.

Hannah raised her hand impetuously, shaking it over and over trying to get Lizzie's attention.

"Hannah?" Lizzie asked, raising her eyebrows.

"I'm not finished."

Elam raised his hand, a defiant look in his black eyes.

"Elam?"

"I'm not done either."

Lizzie sighed. She longed to go home to her room, bury herself in the warmth of her comforters, and sleep. Everything was overwhelming her until there was nothing left but a great weariness. But she had to go on and make an effort to complete this long, dark, and dreary day.

Mentally shaking herself, she took a deep breath.

"Why were you unable to finish?" she asked evenly. In response, two pairs of shoulders lifted and dropped as two pairs of eyes dared her to do something about it. She knew that today was not a good time to undertake an important discipline measure because of how tired and discouraged she was, so she steadied herself and smiled.

"Well, please try harder to complete today's lesson," she said.

The afternoon finally came to a close, and when Lizzie locked the schoolhouse door and turned to climb into the waiting van, she knew this had been one of the longest days she had ever lived, especially since she had begun teaching school.

At home she told Mam she didn't want any supper and went straight to her room. Pulling pins from her cape and apron while kicking off her shoes, she dropped into bed, yanking the heavy down comforter completely over her head, and fell into a deep, blissful sleep. She didn't hear the door opening, or see Mandy stick her head through the doorway, or hear the door close carefully behind her as she went back down the stairs.

When she woke up, the light was fading in the west, leaving her room in gray twilight. Blinking, she sat up, bewildered. She knew instinctively that it wasn't morning, and yet it didn't feel like it was evening, either. She grabbed her alarm clock and saw it was only five-thirty. Then she remembered how tired she had been when she climbed into bed.

Slowly she threw back the covers, put her feet on the floor, and sat, her back rounded and her head hanging in dejection. Immediately worries and fears surrounded her, banging incessantly like a child playing with the lids of its Mam's pots and pans.

What if... what if... what if I'm dating Stephen and I don't even like him one bit? What if I mess everything up my whole life and just continue to go on this way, not knowing if I'm truly in love and if he is the right one for me?

All winter she had harbored these doubts. Christmas had heightened her uncertainty again when they exchanged cards and he had been so sure on his card, professing his true love, and she stumbled and hedged, unable to really commit herself, or at least unsure about what to say. Why was it so complicated? It wasn't that she didn't like Stephen, and she certainly did not like, or long for, any other young man. Something—she didn't know what—was not right.

She had tried opening the subject with Mandy, but her sister had been very little help. Oh, yes, she had said she went through a time of being tempted to date others, but those feelings weren't from God. It was only the devil trying to make you miserable, she said, and you had to deal with it. Mandy was wise, but she could be a bit lofty at times, making Lizzie feel as if she was seven years old.

Raising her head, Lizzie rubbed the small of her back. There was no one to talk to. Mam wouldn't give her any choice at all, because her verdict about doubts was exactly the same as Mandy's. They were

all from the devil. Well, how much power did that guy have, she wondered to herself. Surely it was not only he who was swirling her thoughts like some endless electric blender whirring everything together until nothing made any sense. Besides, she couldn't think of the devil too much, knowing how badly he scared her.

Oh, God, she groaned as her head sank into her hands. Guide me. Tell me what to do.

That weekend Lizzie was in such a state of despair that she would not have minded if Stephen hadn't picked her up at all for their date.

Everything he said and did irked her, setting her teeth on edge. No, she really did not believe that this relationship could go on, and the more she dwelled on this, the more evident it became. Why, of course it couldn't. She definitely felt better, almost light-hearted and less dejected, when she thought of ending her relationship with Stephen.

So as they drove in her drive that Sunday evening, she was calm and sure. As he pulled into the forebay, she laid a hand on his arm to stop him from unhitching his horse.

He turned to look at her.

"Stephen," she said quietly, calmly.

"Hmmm?"

"There's no need for you to come in tonight, because … because … well, I would like to end our friendship this evening."

"You what?" Stephen was incredulous, disbelieving.

"I don't think we should continue seeing each other. Really, I'm not happy during the week. I'm depressed and grouchy at school, and I think it's because I'm not happy with you."

There was a long silence before Stephen sighed, his shoulders slumping in defeat. "Well, there's not much for me to say then, is there?" he said quietly.

"No."

"It won't help for me to beg, huh?"

"No."

"You feel sure this is what you want?"

"Yes."

They sat together in silence, their shoulders touching, the lights of the buggy shining on the forebay wall. The horse nodded his head, wanting Stephen to unhook the rein that held his head up.

The chains in the workhorses' stalls rattled as they lifted their heads, and a calf bawled in the distance.

"Well, Lizzie, it's hard for me to let you go, but I know it'll only make it worse if I don't give up. So..." he swallowed hard, "there's nothing I can do. You know my feelings will never change, but if yours ever do, don't hesitate to let me know."

Calmly, Lizzie threw back the buggy blanket, slid back the door, and climbed out. She could barely stand and look at him, and he averted his gaze completely.

"Good-bye," she whispered.

There was no answer, so she turned away and walked slowly across the gravel drive. She had done

it. She had ended this troubling thing, and no one, not even Mam, had advised her or told her what to do. She felt independent, a bit proud of herself for having conquered her worst enemy, her doubts about Stephen.

She still felt peaceful and unperturbed as she climbed into bed, thanked God for having led her to this victory, and fell asleep a few minutes after her head touched the pillow.

Her alarm clock jangled without mercy that morning, jarring her senses into wakefulness. She jabbed viciously at the shut-off button and groaned, rolled over, and then stuck her head under the comforter. Her room was freezing cold, as usual, and she just couldn't quite face the chilly air.

Then it hit her. Like the force of a sledgehammer, the thought slammed into her. Stephen was no longer her special friend. She had ended it. Dry, sour-tasting panic rose in her throat, causing her to sit up abruptly, her eyes wide open. What have I done, her mind screamed. How does he feel this morning? Will he even go to work? Does his family know? What will Rebecca say?

She had the distinct feeling that Stephen was whirling around in outer space, and she was one little black dot a million miles below on a round blue earth, and there was absolutely no way possible to ever see him again. Her whole being recoiled at the

thought of Stephen disappearing forever. I won't be his girlfriend. Or his wife. Not ever.

A deep, horrible, rasping sound tore from her throat as she flung herself back on her pillow. No. No. This was all wrong. Horribly, terribly, 100 percent all wrong. If she thought she had felt despair before, she had never experienced remorse so real that it cut like the sharpest knife.

She had to do something, go tell someone. Somehow, she had to let Stephen know right this minute, no, this day. Surely she could pull herself together long enough to go to school. Grabbing her bathrobe and a handful of Kleenex, she hurried down the stairs, honking her nose noisily before entering the kitchen.

"Mam!" she burst out, wild-eyed.

Mam whirled from her usual morning place at the stove, her eyes wide with alarm.

"L... Lizzie!"

"Mam, you have to listen to me," Lizzie sobbed. "I told Stephen our friendship is over, and now..."

Mam's shoulders slumped with relief when she heard the words.

"Oh, I thought something really awful had happened. This had been awhile coming, Lizzie."

"And now..." Lizzie continued. "I can't stand it. I feel as if I'll never see him again, and it's just... just horrible!"

Mam turned off the gas burner, laid down the spoon she was holding, and came to sit in front of Lizzie. Putting a hand on her shoulder, she rubbed

it gently to comfort her, letting her sob into her Kleenex.

"There, Lizzie, now that's enough. This almost had to happen, knowing how undecided you were for so long. It's amazing how God answers prayers," she said, shaking her head.

"But Mam, I felt so calm, so peaceful when I ended it."

"Yes, I believe it. God was leading you to do that. He knew you had to know how it felt to no longer have him in order to understand the depth of your real feelings."

Lizzie looked up, her eyes swollen and her nose red as she swabbed at yet another river of tears.

"Now get yourself pulled together, Lizzie. You can make it through today."

"But... Stephen! Mam, he'll go English, or do something awful, and it will be all my fault. I have to let him know this morning that I do... Oh, Mam, I do love him."

She launched into another fit of weeping, while Mam sat quietly, rubbing her back.

"Why do you always choose the rockiest path, Lizzie? You hurt yourself so much more than Emma and Mandy. I guess each child's nature is different."

"Well, Mam, how can I let him know how I feel? I have to right now, right away, this minute."

"No, no, Lizzie. God will provide a way if you'll only calm down now. If nothing else, you can always write him a letter. Hopefully, he did say you could do that. I mean, he's willing to try again."

Lizzie's face lit up with fervent hope. "Oh, yes, Mam!"

"All right, then, get ready now, and off to school. You'll survive."

❧

And Lizzie did survive three whole days before she and Mandy received an invitation for a surprise birthday party for Mary Ann, their friend from church. Lizzie dressed carefully, choosing Stephen's favorite color, but she was no longer in a state of panic about his well-being. She actually felt calm and quiet. Way down in the deepest center of her heart, she sensed a sure and steady bud of love unfolding, and the feeling was the most restful, abiding thing she had ever experienced. The doubts had been driven away, she guessed by God, because no other thing or person could heal and calm in such a wonderful fashion.

But her heart still thumped in agitation when she saw him standing in Mary Ann's kitchen. His usual dark tan seemed a bit lighter, and his eyes were sad as he spent the evening standing at the edge of the room, saying very little. He never said a whole lot, but tonight he barely smiled at all.

After the evening's festivities were over, she knew it was now or never, so she walked over to the group of young men.

"Stephen," she said. He turned.

"Can I talk to you?"

He didn't answer, just followed her quietly until she stopped a good distance away from the group.

"It's cold," she said, turning toward him.

"Yeah, well," was Stephen's answer.

"Stephen, I... I do want to... I mean, I'm sorry I ended our friendship. When I woke up the following morning, I knew without any trace of doubt that what I did was so horribly wrong."

She heard Stephen inhale sharply. "Are you sure, Lizzie?"

"Yes!"

Her heart seemed to stop when she felt Stephen grasp both her hands, keeping her from twisting her apron hem. He held her hands gently, and she slowly quieted under his strength.

"Lizzie, I'm not good with words. You know I don't talk about feelings easily. But... I... just hope...

Slowly Lizzie raised her eyes to his, and the steady, glowing light in his eyes showed the true love he felt in his heart.

Then, there was nothing to say. No words were sufficient. Lizzie felt a soft pressure on her hands, and then in one flowing movement she was enveloped in his strong arms. Her cheek rested on his chest, and an indescribable feeling of warmth, of being wanted and needed, of being understood, all washed over her, much like a gentle spring rain. It was sort of like she imagined Heaven to be. But Mam's words admonishing her to keep their courtship pure kept her feet firmly on the ground.

Stephen really did love her. He really, really did, and that knowledge kept her there in his arms, safe, secure, and slowly realizing that her own love for him was developing, like a rose, slowly opening to the sun's warmth. It seemed so right at this moment, close to his heart, but would she always feel this way?

Stephen said very quietly, "I can only hope you can someday return my love."

As they clung together, Lizzie began to cry as Stephen struggled to blink back his own tears. Releasing her, he stepped back, but only for a moment as they both began talking at once. He told her of the struggles of the past few days, the terrible rebellion that raged in his heart to abandon the Amish way if he had no chance with her. Lizzie could only nod her head in understanding, feeling closer to him than she had ever felt before in her life. She wanted to stay in the circle of his arms forever.

Maybe this was why the Amish people tried to teach their youth about the respectability of a clean and honorable courtship, she mused. If this is what real love feels like, oh, my! she thought happily.

Looking up at Stephen, she loved the way his straight, brown hair fell over his eyebrows and how he brushed it away every 10 minutes. His eyes shone with a new light of joy and hope redeemed, and Lizzie giggled to herself, thinking they probably were only a reflection of her own.

Suddenly her future was spread out before her as clearly as a picture. Stephen and Lizzie. No, Stephen

and Elizabeth. She was all grown up now. They would probably join the church and be married in the fall and live happily ever after, just like Cinderella and her prince.

Oh, glorious thought. No more doubts. No more what-ifs. What Lizzie did not quite comprehend was the fact that they were still both human beings who lived in a real world of trials and sorrows, which would balance the joy.

Chapter 20

It seemed as if suddenly every one of Lizzie's friends started dating at once. Uncle Marvin asked Mary Ann to a singing, and they began dating soon afterwards. Just when Lizzie thought it couldn't become more exciting, Stephen's sister Rebecca began dating Reuben.

The couples often drove to the mountain on a Sunday afternoon, or had skating parties by the pond, or just spent time together as winter turned into spring. Lizzie looked forward to the weekends when she and Stephen joined the other couples in different activities throughout the community.

Lizzie soon discovered that living happily ever after, or rather, dating happily ever after, was only a fairy tale, a myth, just like lots of things in life that are far too good to be true.

She didn't feel like ending their relationship again, but this thing of dating was not always 100 percent perfect. Actually, last weekend had barely made the 75 percent mark.

That Monday morning Lizzie was in a vile mood. She didn't want to go to school, but neither did she feel like staying at home under Mam's scrutiny. Mam had a way about her that never failed to irk Lizzie if she was having problems. Mam would start by looking at her a few extra moments, then purse her lips before asking what she had done that weekend. By then, Mam already had a very good idea that she didn't have a great time, not even a very good time, so why did she ask? So Lizzie would mumble something vaguely unintelligible and wish Mam would go away and let her alone.

Lizzie held her shoulders as high and stiff as she could manage and posed her eyebrows in a perfectly worried arc as she dashed between the table and countertop, slamming her lunch box a bit harder than was absolutely necessary. No wonder, she thought angrily. It just made no sense whatsoever. Who had ever heard of walking the Appalachian Trail when you were dating? That was one of the stupidest things she had ever heard of. Imagine, leaving your girlfriend for a month while you went striding along a string of mountains just to see how far you could go. For all the world, it reminded Lizzie of that song about the bear going to the other side of the mountain to see what he could see, and only that. To see what he could see—that was the only reason.

Oh, it wasn't that she hadn't tried to persuade Stephen to give up the whole silly idea. At first she had listened patiently as he tried to explain where

they would go—they, meaning Reuben, Marvin, and him. He told her in detail how many miles they would hike each day, and that it would probably be close to a month till they reached their destination.

She gasped audibly when he said that, then launched into a full-blown tirade of protests. What made him think he could do this? Why, if a young man had a girlfriend, it was his moral responsibility, no, his duty, to stay at home and spend his weekends with her. She saw Stephen's jaw set as he turned away from her to watch the scenery out the buggy window. He also let his horse run faster than was absolutely necessary, which only increased her foul mood.

When she realized she wasn't getting anywhere with him by threatening and protesting, she tried to get him to change his mind by being sweet, batting her eyelashes demurely as she told him how terribly she would miss him. Was he really sure he wanted to do this? After all, he had to think about the dangers out on those unfamiliar trails, the mountain lions, black bears, bobcats, and other dangerous creatures.

What really upset her was how he laughed at her for saying that. He laughed long and loud, with kind of a snort at the end that made her feel as if she was in first grade and didn't know anything at all. So she set her mouth in a firm line and refused to talk. If he was going to be determined to do this senseless thing, then he was going to have to suffer for it.

The rest of the way home she sat back against the corner of the seat, her arms folded in front of her,

and pouted. Stephen kept asking her questions and she would answer with a small, "Okay," or "Fine," until he gave up talking to her.

Needless to say, their Sunday evening had ended on a sour note, with Stephen taking Lizzie's peevishness in stride, but never coming close to considering how she felt. He just went right ahead talking about his plans to walk the Appalachian Trail. That was the trouble with boys. They did what they wanted to do, and it was up to their girlfriends to be agreeable, and supportive even, no matter what their personal feelings were.

Look at Mam and Dat, she thought bitterly, as she slapped a piece of cheese on top of a slice of bologna. He just went and moved if he felt like it, and it was up to Mam to pack up and go along, even if she didn't want to one bit. Lizzie stifled a yawn and clicked her lunch box shut. Oh, Monday morning and the school year almost at a close, with most of the pupils being very tired of their lessons and, no doubt, their teacher as well.

She sat down hard on a kitchen chair and stared morosely out the window. Mandy had gone to work an hour earlier, so that left only Mam to finish the breakfast dishes and do all the morning chores, sweeping the house, shaking a few rugs, straightening the toy shelf, and other little duties necessary to keeping everything organized.

"Lizzie, why don't you help with the dishes until your driver comes?" Mam said kindly.

"He'll be here any minute," was her curt reply.

৵

Nothing, not one thing, or hardly anything, went right that day. To start with, the fire in the coal stove was out completely. There wasn't even a spark, not a hope of finding a few red coals to rekindle the blaze. The schoolroom was uncomfortably chilly, so chilly in fact that you could see your breath.

Where was Elam King? Why hadn't he come to the schoolhouse as usual and stirred the coals and turned up the draught so that she was greeted with a warm rush of air when she opened the door?

Muttering to herself, she started scraping down the cold ashes, coughing as the dry coal dust irritated her throat. She bet anything there was no kindling in the coal shed, and she was not about to hike to Elam King's farm to find some.

The door opened behind her, and Elam King's breathless children hurried up to Lizzie.

"Dad forgot to fix the fire, Teacher! We have a sick cow," they announced, all in one sentence.

Lizzie told them it was all right, she'd get the fire going, when really, it was not all right. But what else could she say? It wasn't the children's fault, or Elam King's. So she would blame the cow, which was quite easy, knowing how cows tended to become sick or have a calf at the unhandiest moments.

Midmorning little Jonas cried because he wasn't finished with Friday's arithmetic lesson. Lizzie gritted her teeth, resisting the urge to grab a handful of his tangled curls and give them a good, hard yank.

He was never finished. He was just a natural-born little procrastinator who always pushed away his lessons until the very last moment of the day, and then panicked when the rest of the children put their books away to go home.

Lizzie had tried making him stay in at recess, but he was so amicable about it that it was no punishment at all. He would sit in his desk while the other pupils hurried out the door, his sunny expression never wavering as he launched into a vivid account of his weekend.

She had tried standing behind his desk, urging him almost continuously to work, but that was not the answer either. It left her feeling frustrated, and Jonas so nervous that he kept chewing on the corner of his shirt collar and repeatedly blinking his eyes, until Lizzie was afraid he'd ruin his eyesight.

Besides the problems with Jonas and the lack of a good warm fire, she felt the constant irritation of thinking about Stephen nonchalantly telling her that he planned to traipse all over creation for a whole month. She was writing on the blackboard when she heard a snicker, followed promptly by a rubber band hitting the blackboard beside her. Slowly she returned the chalk to the tray, turned calmly, and addressed the crowd of tittering boys.

"All right, who was it? Who snapped the rubber band?"

No one answered and no one lifted a hand. A complete silence fell over the classroom.

"You may as well tell me because I'll find out,"

Lizzie said, her cheeks flaming with anger. Blatant disrespect, that's what it was.

"It was me," one of the seventh-grade boys said, raising his hand, staring at her as if to challenge her to do something about it.

All the frustrations she had endured over the weekend, and especially this morning, hit her with the force of a cannon, leaving behind only blind, white anger. She marched back to his desk, grabbed his shoulder, and smacked his face as hard as she could. His head snapped back, and his expression changed to one of disbelief, then shame, as he lifted both hands to his face as if to ward off more blows.

"There! That is something I will not tolerate. You boys have been trying me to the limit these past couple weeks, and you don't even have enough respect to be ashamed of your misbehavior. I will not take it!" she said loudly, punctuating each word angrily.

The classroom instantly quieted down. In fact, it was so quiet you could almost hear the creek rippling across the rocks in the schoolyard. Little Rachel, who was in first grade, started sobbing quietly into her handkerchief as she rolled her large eyes in Lizzie's direction. The upper-graders all bent their heads, resuming their work with averted eyes.

"So everyone can just straighten up, and I mean it," she finished. She walked back to her desk, sitting in her chair with shaking knees as she absently toyed with her red pen.

An aura of alarm hung over the classroom like an impending storm, and Lizzie swallowed down

her own fear, after the realization of what she had just done settled into her conscience. Suddenly, she felt like a huge, green ogre, complete with horns, who had swung her club and terrorized innocent children.

What had she done? What would the boy's parents say? She was almost positive she was in trouble now. Oh, mercy. Well, it was all Stephen's fault, really, if you thought about it. She had lost her temper because of trying to deal with him walking the Appalachian Trail. It was frustrating if your boyfriend just did what he wanted with no regard for your feelings whatsoever. It was all his fault. It was.

The remainder of the day, everyone was quiet and well-behaved. They kept their distance, knowing that this was not a good day to go to their teacher's desk to talk because she was in some vicious mood.

Before she dismissed the pupils at the end of the day, she agonized between apologizing to Alvin or standing firm. He would go home and tell his parents, no doubt about that, but, oh, well, the damage was done now. The only way was to stand firm, she knew, as he had no business snapping that rubber band.

When she got home that evening, she poured out her whole miserable day to Mam and Mandy. They listened attentively, and Mandy gasped when she told her about smacking Alvin across his face.

"Mercy!" Mam said. "Lizzie!"

"Do you think his parents will be upset with me, Mam?" Lizzie asked, fear wrapping its tentacles around her chest and squeezing.

"It's hard telling. I just don't know how they'll react to this. Why did you do it?" Mam asked.

"Because! He made me so mad!"

"You know it probably wasn't for the best," Mam said gently.

Lizzie glared at Mam rebelliously, still determined in her heart that Stephen was to blame for her outburst. So she told Mam about his plans, and to her consternation, Mam burst out laughing.

"It's not funny!" Lizzie shouted, flouncing over to the kitchen counter and lifting the lid on a stainless steel pot. Sniffing, she said, "Mmmm, chicken and dumplings!"

"Ach, Lizzie, now listen here," Mam said.

Lizzie returned the lid and watched Mam warily. If Mam said, "Now listen here," she knew there was a stern lecture coming, whether she liked it or not. Mam's serious lectures were like a dust storm in dry areas or a storm at sea. You just battened down the hatches, gritted your teeth, and hoped it wouldn't get too fierce.

"If you think for one minute that you're going to marry Stephen and never learn to give up to him, you have another guess coming."

Well, the storm was a heavy one if she said "you have another guess coming." That was her age-old tool used to drive a point home with all the force

of a sledgehammer, wielded by a strong, muscular man.

"Men are like that. They are allowed to do things, and it's up to us weaker vessels to be submissive. That's why we wear a covering—to show that God comes first, and we obey him, and then our husband comes next, and we obey him as well."

Lizzie snorted and stammered, her face turning red as she tried to express herself.

"You mean...you mean, husbands can do exactly what they please, and we follow as meekly as half-dead sheep and adore the ground they walk on? No, I don't believe that, Mam, not for one minute. If that's the order of things, then I'm not getting married. Never. I'll be an old maid and teach school till I'm so fat I can't fit between the desks!"

Mandy laughed gleefully, and Mam's shoulders shook as she got up to check on the chicken and dumplings, bending to adjust the flame of the burner.

"What does your Bible say, Lizzie? Read it," she said.

"No."

"All right. If you're going to become rebellious, there's no point in discussing it. Nine chances out of 10 you'll have to learn the hard way anyhow," Mam said forcefully, the color in her cheeks heightened.

Lizzie watched Mam, knowing she had irked her. Good. If she wanted to become so high-minded about how a marriage should be, then she was not going to listen anyway. Her husband was not going

to sit on his throne and touch her lowered head with his kingly scepter, while she bowed her head in total submission like some trembling servant who was grateful to breathe the same air as her beloved husband. The whole concept inflamed every fiber of her being.

"All right, Mam, I'll discuss it with you and try to listen to what you have to say, but you can't tell me that the husband is to be a lordly person who rules over his lowly wife with absolute authority."

Mam remained quiet, thinking, while Lizzie and Mandy waited. "Ach well, Lizzie, you think too much. I don't really know how to answer that. No, not really, in a sense, and yes, really, in another sense, I guess."

"You guess! You don't even know?"

Lizzie was appalled to think Mam had been married for 20 years, and she still didn't know how it was supposed to be.

"What I mean is—there is no black and white in marriage. Not really. The Bible has plenty of verses to ask us, no, *tell* us, to be submissive, a helpmeet to our husbands. Even in the Old Testament, Sarah called Abraham lord."

"That was in the Old Testament. They stoned people then. We don't do that now, do we?" Lizzie broke in.

"No. No, we don't. But the Old Testament is filled with lessons and good examples for us to follow. All right, now, I want you and Mandy to read your Bible this evening and see what you can find

about marriage. Then come show me, okay?" Mam said, smiling.

She got up, asking Mandy to set the table. That officially brought the whole conversation to a close, leaving Lizzie seated high and dry in the middle of a frightening desert of constantly shifting question marks.

Well, if she was lucky, Stephen would be bitten by a rattlesnake the first few miles of the Appalachian Trail. Not fatally, of course, but just enough to make him return back to where he belonged.

She was also going to have to read her Bible tonight to prove to Mam, somehow, that total submission was absolutely not necessary, because that would be a sad way to live. Really, if that was the case, why did any girl in her right mind ever get married?

They just didn't think far enough ahead, that was all there was to it.

Chapter 21

"WIVES, SUBMIT YOURSELVES UNTO YOUR own husbands, as unto the Lord."

There it was in black and white. Lizzie's heart sank, and she swiped a finger nervously across her nose. Her hopes sank even further, like an anchor plunging to the sea floor as the rope unraveled, when she read the next verses.

"For the husband is the head of the wife, even as Christ is the head of the church: and he is the saviour of the body. Therefore, as the church is subject unto Christ, so let the wives be to their own husbands in everything."

Lizzie put her finger on the verse where she had stopped reading and gazed unseeingly out her upstairs bedroom window. There was no getting around it, hardly. Mam was right. The whole idea of marriage and submission settled around her shoulders like a suffocating wool blanket. There was no possible way that Scripture could be true.

In *everything*, it said. Not just some things, or most things. *Everything*. Every single thing. Well, what if the husband did something really dumb, like walk the Appalachian Trail, for instance, or if he turned nasty and hit his wife and yelled at her or beat the children, if there were any. Then what?

She opened her mouth to yell for Mandy, but closed it again, deciding to read further.

"Husbands, love your wives, even as Christ also loved the church, and gave himself for it."

Yes! See? Lizzie pulled up her knees, laying the Bible aside as she wrapped her arms around her legs, happily smiling at herself in the mirror.

There, that was the bottom line. If the husband loved his wife the way he was supposed to, he would give his life for her, or rather, to Lizzie's way of thinking, give up his own will sometimes. Actually, come to think of it, if he loved her very much, he would do anything she asked of him, because he was giving up his own life for his wife.

Lizzie continued reading the chapter and her spirits lifted considerably. When she reached the end of the chapter, her eyebrows were drawn down in confusion again.

"Nevertheless, let every one of you in particular so love his wife even as himself, and the wife see that she reverence her husband."

Well, that reverence word was a bit strong because it conjured up for Lizzie that kingly husband who sat on his throne, his scepter hovering over his trembling wife. But then, if he loved his wife as much as he

loved himself, he would be very kind to her. He'd make her life easier if he could, like helping her with the hard work—gardening or mowing grass—and not go off hiking for three weeks. It would make it so much easier to submit to him if he acted half normal.

Ah, well, Lizzie mused. I just don't quite get it. Mam never said the husband was supposed to give his life for his wife. I bet she doesn't even know that's in the Bible. Maybe she just doesn't really want to bother with that verse, knowing her husband didn't always. If you were going to be honest about this, Dat didn't give his life for Mam when they moved to Cameron County. He knew it was not what she wanted to do. But then Mam didn't always reverence Dat either, and maybe that was because he didn't deserve it.

So this marriage thing wasn't quite as hopeless or mysterious or depressing as Mam made it sound with her submission speech. The husband had to stay in his place, too. Lizzie closed her Bible and went downstairs to find Mam working on her cross-stitch quilt patch by the light of the softly hissing gas lamp. She sat in the chair across from her and said, "Mam, you were wrong."

Mam looked up, adjusted her glasses, and smiled at Lizzie.

"About what?" she asked.

"It's not *just* the wife who has to be submissive. Didn't you ever read that part about the husband giving his life for his wife, like Christ died for the church?"

Mam put down her cross-stitch patch and sighed. She gazed absentmindedly at Lizzie as if she wasn't really seeing her at all and sighed again. "Yes, Lizzie, I know it's in there," she said softly.

"Well, then, if he stays in his place, what is there to submit to? Huh? Nothing, Mam."

Lizzie was elated, quite jubilant actually. She was immensely relieved to know that her husband couldn't just go off and do exactly as he pleased whenever he felt like it. He had a responsibility to give his life to his beloved wife, who would obey him with sweet reverence like the Bible said.

"I'm afraid it's not that easy," Mam said.

"What do you mean?"

"Well, for one thing, we're very human, and on the day we marry each other, we still have our own wills intact. Each of us has a pretty good idea of what we expect of our husband, and he has a pretty good idea of what he expects of his wife. Unfortunately, his wife is not always as he wants her to be, and vice versa. He is not all that she expects either. So we have troubles, trials, rainy days, whatever you want to call it, and it isn't all roses. That's why we have those verses in the Bible, something we can live towards, something we can hope to become, that perfect merging of two souls, two wills, two individuals who become one through marriage."

Lizzie frowned. "You sound exactly like a preacher. An English one."

Mam laughed. "Maybe I do, Lizzie, but I don't want you filling your head with sweet visions

of a perfect husband who gives his life for you. Because..." Mam leaned forward, a touch of, what was it—hardness? Bitterness? Honesty born of experience? "Very few men do give their lives for their wives," she finished.

Lizzie said nothing, and the pendulum on the living room wall clock rocked steadily back and forth, back and forth, as the gas light kept up its soft, hissing sound.

"I think I'll go to bed," she said finally.

"Good night," Mam said, a touch of wistfulness in her voice.

"Good night, Mam," Lizzie said.

❦

Lizzie lay awake, an open book beside her, the kerosene lamp on her nightstand flickering in the night air. Her thoughts were rapidly spoiling her peace of mind, like Jason shooting his dart gun into her brain. Those annoying little plastic, yellow darts with orange, rubber suction cups at the end, that if they landed squarely, hung there, quivering, until you pulled them loose.

So then, the truth of the matter was, men often did what they wanted, probably because they knew their wives were supposed to submit themselves and revere them. Boy, that just wasn't right. The thought made her so angry she felt like throwing her pillow against the wall. She rolled onto her side. She didn't know why that thought brought out so much

rebellion and so many hateful thoughts.

She wondered vaguely where love came in. Love was supposed to be the reason for getting married in the first place. Wasn't that simply liking someone so much that you would do absolutely anything for them?

So now if Stephen were her husband, and he would tell her that he was walking the Appalachian Trail for three weeks, then, if she loved him whole-heartedly, she would say, "Oh, of course, my darling husband! You deserve to enjoy yourself on a vacation away from me, and I hope you have a lovely time."

And he would be so grateful for her sweet nature, her love and support, that he would go hiking for three weeks, have a great time, and tell all his friends what a wonderful, kind, loving wife he had at home. Somewhere along the line she had to get rid of her anger against men being the stronger vessel, the head of the house, the boss, in plain words, the king, which only brought on a fresh case of rebellion within her.

Oh, the whole mess was hopeless. Throwing off the covers, she stalked over to Mandy's bedroom door, yanked it open, and stuck her head inside.

"Are you still awake?"

"Mm-hmm, what do you want?"

Lizzie walked in and sat down on Mandy's bed, as she scooted over to make room.

"Oh, I can't sleep. I'm thinking too much. Did you read your Bible about marriage like Mam told us to?"

"Yes."

"Well, what did you think?"

"That's just how it is, Lizzie. It's really quite simple. We both live for each other and not for ourselves, and it'll go okay."

"It's not *that* simple!" Lizzie exclaimed, appalled at the thought of entering marriage with that tiny amount of concern. "What if your husband would want to go on vacation for three weeks, and you thought it was a dumb idea? Huh? Then what?"

Anger crossed Mandy's features, and she said impatiently, "Well, if you're in one of those moods, just go to bed. Go on. You're just mad because Stephen is going hiking, and you are acting like one huge, overgrown baby, pitying yourself, determined to justify your own selfishness with those Bible verses. Now go to bed. I'm tired."

Mandy rolled over and pulled up the covers, or tried to, but she couldn't with Lizzie sitting on them. She lifted her head and glared at her. "*Go!*" she shouted.

So Lizzie went.

Back in bed she tossed and turned, thinking and rethinking what Mandy had said. She was clearly on Stephen's side, so what was the use of talking to her? Selfish. So Mandy thought she was being selfish. Well, Mandy had better watch it. She just better watch who she called selfish. Lizzie could feel the heat rising in her cheeks as she thought about what Mandy had said about her justifying herself, and her rebellion. She was quite sure she meant that anyway.

Oh, that Mandy. She may as well be a little bearded man living high in the Himalayan mountains, a small wrinkled philosopher around whom people gathered for words of wisdom. She knew Mandy could see right through her, and she was as exposed as if she were made of air with little banners blowing that said she was selfish, childish, and rebellious.

She flipped onto her left side, reached out, and peered at the face of her alarm clock. Eleven-twenty-five. She groaned. It would soon be time to get up and she still hadn't slept a wink. She'd have to resort to counting sheep, she supposed. It was an awful thing when you thought too much, planned too much, and worried far too much about the future.

Oh, that's right, she thought. I forgot to pray. I wrestle around with all my problems and forget to hand them to God. She wished it would be as easy as two hands reaching down through the ceiling to retrieve Lizzie's bundle labeled "Troubles." The minute the bundle was in God's hands, it would be lifted up through the ceiling and gone out of sight, out of her mind, never to be seen again.

Life, however, was not that easy. Real life, real problems. Dear God, you're going to have to help me with this husband and wife thing. I will give up now and not be selfish. Help me, Lord, to be truly unselfish. Keep Stephen safe on the Appalachian Trail, and keep me safe from rebellion. Amen.

She breathed deeply, relaxing, and even giggled to herself as she dared to hope—although she stopped

short of asking God to let it happen—she just hoped a mountain lion would scare them so hysterically they'd come back home two weeks earlier than they had planned. Or a bobcat. The way they screamed, it would probably work even better.

When Stephen brought her home after the hymn-singing on Sunday evening, Lizzie was a bit better prepared to hear him say that their plans were finished now, and they would be leaving Tuesday morning. She managed a small smile as he talked, listening attentively to his plans without once resorting to rebellious feelings.

"I want to be sure and thank you, Lizzie," he finished, watching her face attentively.

"For what?" she asked, in a genuinely small, quiet voice.

"For being nice about me being gone so long. I know you don't want me to go, but you're being an awfully good sport about it, and I do appreciate it."

"You wouldn't stay home for me, would you? I mean, give up the whole adventure if I didn't want you to go?"

Stephen was quiet for a very long time, before he said with a soft laugh, "Probably not."

So there. She had a notion to give him the whole lecture and bring the Bible to show him that he was supposed to lay down his own life for her. She knew that wouldn't be a good idea, mostly because they were not married yet. He had never asked her to be his wife, so really being so pointed would be a very wrong thing to do.

Lizzie wanted to assure him that it was all right for him to go, to let him know that she wanted him to have a good time. She really did, but she also wanted him to worry a bit that she wasn't happy because he was going and leaving her. So she didn't answer.

And in that silence, her own battle of right and wrong raged in her spirit. She knew the right thing to do, but she couldn't let go of her own desires to make him feel bad, at least a little. She wanted to punish him somehow for going against her will, so she remained silent while right fought wrong with a clashing of swords.

Finally, Stephen cleared his throat, watching her carefully as she sat in her self-induced little war of wills.

"Maybe I better go. It's getting late. Good-bye, Lizzie. I'll send you postcards, if I can."

Lizzie got up to go along to the barn as she always did, feeling perfectly miserable. "Wives, submit yourselves unto your own husbands," was constantly in her thoughts, but she reasoned that little bother away by telling herself she wasn't his wife. She didn't have to submit yet.

When Stephen was ready to step into the buggy, all of Lizzie's battles and miseries came crashing down around her, and she reached out to touch his arm.

"I...I'm sorry, Stephen. I *do* hope you enjoy your vacation, and I'll be patiently waiting till you come home. I'll miss you so much, but you know that, don't you?"

She was rewarded by the most loving look she had ever received from him as he told her again how he appreciated her attitude and how much he would miss her.

After he left, and the battle of her own will won, she felt as light as a feather floating on a soft white cloud. So that was the answer, she thought happily as she fairly danced up the stairs to her bedroom. If you could give up a teeny-tiny bit, God would supply all the feelings of love you needed. He filled your cup way full until it ran over the sides and made a big puddle beside it.

Chapter 22

THE GIRLS SAT SIDE BY SIDE ON THE PORCH swing, pushing their feet lightly against the concrete floor to keep it in rocking motion. It was one of those quiet twilight times, not yet dark, although the sun had slid behind the mountain for awhile already. The birds were twittering and fussing, scooping up the last mosquitoes for their babies' bedtime snacks. The barn door slammed, sending a few noisy robins into startled flight as Jason came walking across the drive and up the sidewalk to the porch.

He would turn 16 years old soon and was looking every inch the young man that he was. His shoulders and arms were heavier, the muscles showing beneath his shirtsleeves, and he had grown at least three more inches that summer, or so it seemed. Lizzie and Mandy adored him, their handsome young brother with the kind blue eyes that twinkled back at them as they teased each other or had long,

serious conversations. His eyes always twinkled. He was naturally kind, Mam said.

But then, that Mam, Lizzie thought. She just loved Jason because he did anything she asked of him. If she needed manure for her flower beds, or a bit of mulch brought, or even if she came home with a load of groceries, Jason ran to help. Sometimes Lizzie felt a bit jealous about how much Mam loved Jason, but not very often, knowing he deserved her devotion, as kind as he was to her.

"Hey," he said quietly as he threw himself down on the porch steps, sighing as he ran his hands through his shock of curly brown hair.

"Hey, yourself," Lizzie answered.

"You're awfully dirty," Mandy observed.

"You would be, too. It was a long day and I'm about beat."

"You work too hard, Jase," Lizzie said.

"Shh!" Jason put his finger to his lips and rolled his eyes in Dat's direction as he came across the yard. He didn't really hobble or limp; he just had a dragging gait, almost as if he couldn't lift his feet properly.

Dat stopped at the porch, grabbing the railing before looking at Jason. "Tired?" he asked.

"A little."

"You work too hard, Jason."

Dat shook his head, a frustrated look in his eyes, his hands gripping the railing firmly. He knew he wasn't able to do some of the fieldwork anymore, and that ever so gradually more and more of the

heavy jobs, as well as the responsibility of the farm, fell on Jason's young shoulders.

Mam came out to join them. The twins were in bed already. Mam was wearing her blue summer housecoat that still smelled like talcum powder, the same as it always had. It didn't matter which scent of powder she used, they all smelled like Mam. Even when Lizzie was a little, worried girl, Mam's housecoat had smelled the same, a soft, flowery Mam aroma that wrapped around you, comforting and instilling a sense of peace, of belonging, of love as warm and sure as the sun that rose and set each day.

"Do we have any ice cream in the freezer?" Jason asked, lifting his eyes to look at Mam.

"Oh, yes! Your favorite. I just got two half-gallons in town today," Mam said, as she hurried into the kitchen to fill a dish with his favorite treat.

"Anyone else?" she called out the kitchen window.

Everyone had a dish of ice cream as they had a serious conversation about farming. Dat broached the subject, saying matter-of-factly that he couldn't see any sense in continuing, seeing how hard Jason had to work just to keep everything afloat. He admitted that the cows weren't doing as well as most of the other farmers' cows in the area, and that it was a constant struggle to keep the bills paid with enough left over to live on decently.

Mam had known for a long time what Dat was now admitting. She had often fussed to the girls, her face red as she toyed nervously with the straight

pins in her dress, saying how she wished Dat would give up farming.

"He's just not cut out to be a farmer," she would say wearily, before giving in time after time, hoping that Dat would see it for himself.

Now it seemed as if Dat had finally arrived at this conclusion. Mam could not hide the excitement in her eyes as she listened to what Dat was saying, and Lizzie could tell she felt like shouting her delight at his words.

"So some changes are going to have to come," Dat said.

"Like what?" Jason asked, his spoonful of ice cream stopping halfway as he turned to face Dat.

"Well, we're going to have to make a living somehow. I have MS, which isn't that big of an issue, really, because I can still do a good day's work. But…" Dat said, his voice softening, "it won't always be this way."

Lifting his head, he looked out across the fields to the creek. "I always liked to build things, carpenter work. What do you think, Jason? Could we run a carpenter crew?"

Jason shrugged his shoulders. "You could, maybe. I don't know much about building anything, although I suppose I could learn."

"Sure you can learn. Building is just a matter of common sense and hard work. In a few months you'll probably be working circles around me," Dat smiled.

Praise from Dat was scarce, so when he did

congratulate someone on a job well done, or whatever, it meant the world to them. Jason ducked his head, flustered, not quite knowing how to handle this compliment, but Lizzie could see a small smile of embarrassment on his face. Dat had given him a real compliment, like one man to another, telling him he was a hard worker.

So the day came a few weeks later, when a tractor and trailer rolled down the country road, and were barely able to make the turn at the end of the drive. The driver had to back up and keep trying at a few different angles, barely inching his way past the wooden corner post of the fence lining the driveway. One wheel went down so far into the ditch Lizzie felt sure the whole truck would twist sideways until it snapped in two.

Dat got quite fussed up, almost running out the drive, waving his arms, trying to be helpful, which, probably wasn't of much assistance to the driver, who was used to handling his truck quite well by himself. But that's how Dat was. When he hitched up a horse, he said, "Whoa, Whoa," almost continuously. Even if the horse stood rock still, he kept saying "Whoa."

Dat was small and became agitated easily, putting in lots of effort to accomplish a task. He was also very meticulous about things, making sure everything was done to his specifications, so that was probably the reason he became so excited, knowing how he would dislike having the corner of his fence run over by a tractor and trailer.

After the truck was properly parked, the driver lowered the large steel gates, and Dat and Jason started loading cows. Lizzie felt no emotion at all as each homely-looking cow lumbered precariously up the ramp with a minimum of prodding by the shocking stick.

One good thing about cows being so dumb, Lizzie thought, was the small amount of effort it took to load them onto a truck. The only thing a cow thought about too much was chewing its cud, so they probably wanted to hurry onto the truck so they could get on with their cud-chewing.

The rest of the afternoon, different trucks and drivers rolled down the lane until every single cow, heifer, and calf had been sold. The whitewashed cow stable seemed strangely silent and eerie, with only a few ambitious barn swallows left to make it their home. The drop seemed deep and dry with no fresh cow manure or water in it, the milk house vacant and lonely.

Silence hung over the whole barn until it gave Lizzie the shivers, reminding her of a tomb. Maybe they shouldn't have sold the cows, she reasoned. What if there was no blessing in Dat's carpenter crew because he had sold the cows? What if Dat only thought he could build things like pole barns and houses, and he really couldn't? The empty cow stable gave her the creeps so she hurried out into the bright sunshine, back to the normalcy of the farm.

Dat had reminded the girls that the farm equipment and horses would also have to be sold

eventually, which made Lizzie feel sad, loving the sound of those magnificent horses dragging their chains across the worn wooden boards of their feed box. There was just something about watching a workhorse eating mouthfuls of oats, with some of the grain spilling out the sides of their mouths, that was delightful to watch. The way they used their huge mouths to nibble up every little bit of grain was so amusing. They ate corn that was still on the cob so cleanly, it was almost as if they were humans eating corn off the cob. Lizzie often wondered why the horses didn't chomp down the entire cob, but Dat said they tasted bitter to the horses.

But there was hardly any use in keeping the workhorses if they had no work in the fields. If there were no cows to feed, there was no sense in making the horses plod their way around and around a field, their heads nodding, harnesses creaking, as they pulled on the thick leather tugs attached to their enormous collars, heaving with their powerful neck and shoulder muscles.

Lizzie never tired of watching a team of horses working in a field. Sometimes there were only two hitched together to pull a wagonload of hay or a cultivator. Sometimes, for heavier equipment, there were four in the harness, side by side, pulling together. In the spring, Dat hitched six horses to the large plow so that each horse could pull his fair share of the plow without tiring too much.

Well, she reasoned, they still had Bess, the driving horse, Rocky, the better driving horse, Billy, the

beloved oatmeal-colored Shetland pony, and Jason's riding horse. Dat loved riding horses, so as soon as Jason was old enough, he bought a fine Morgan stallion for him. Mam wasn't too happy about that horse, but she didn't say much, just pressed her mouth into a firm line and shook her head ever so slightly.

Jason's riding horse was named Charmer, and he certainly was that. His coat glistened in the sun, a deep reddish brown, with a rippling black mane and tail. He had three white "stockings," or white hair above his black hooves, which only made him look fancier. Dat said he was almost too nice-looking for Amish people to own him, but he said it in a twinkling, humorous way, so that Lizzie knew he was very proud of Jason's horse.

Jason was an extremely good rider, sitting back, relaxed in his saddle, moving with his horse as if they were one. Lizzie and Mandy were thrilled to watch Jason and Charmer, exclaiming to each other that surely no other girls in Cameron County were lucky enough to have a kind, handsome brother like theirs, especially now, with his riding skills developing every week.

Shortly after selling all of the cattle, Dat hired a driver with a heavy pickup truck and bought ladders, scaffolding, saws, and all kinds of tools and equipment to begin building things for customers. He placed an ad in the local paper, made phone calls, and had business cards made. It wasn't long before he had a few months' work waiting for his crew.

Dat was the kind of person who thrived on changes, any kind of new and different changes that occurred in his life. So this carpentry business was just as challenging and exciting for him as farming had been when the family first moved to Cameron County. He didn't seem to be sentimental about the cows once they were gone, never saying too much about missing them and instead taking this new endeavor in stride.

Lizzie teased him about the cows, saying he didn't like them as well as he wanted the rest of the family to think he did.

"I miss milking cows, Lizzie," he said.

"I bet you don't."

"I do!"

"Not too much!"

Then Dat had to laugh, and, as he always did, he blinked his eyes in that certain way, which meant, Behave yourself. But what he said was, "Now, Lizzie!"

So she felt better about the empty cow stable, glad that Dat and Jason enjoyed their work building things. Dat loved going away every day, traveling away from home and seeing the sights along the way, talking to different people, just getting out and about. He often brought home a watermelon or cantaloupes from a farm stand along the way, or candy for KatieAnn and Susan. The supper table was always filled with lively conversation about the progress of a building, an eccentric customer, or a wreck on the highway.

These were happy days on the farm. Dat built a small room off the dining room that was mostly windows, with a skylight in the ceiling, which made it a greenhouse of sorts. Mam was overjoyed with her new room. She spent many happy hours in it, growing all her own plants for her ever-expanding flower beds around the yard.

Her favorite were her "cheraniums," as she called geraniums. Because of Mam's origins in Ohio, she always pronounced her "g's" and "j's" with the "ch" sound. Jacob was "Chakob," and jelly was "chelly," and so on. She never changed the sound or pronunciation of her words, tossing her head impatiently when the girls teased her about it, and she never fully accepted the eastern Pennsylvania Dutch. She always rolled her "r's," and said, "Fact!" to exclaim about something and "Ei, nay" when she wanted to be emphatic, driving a point home.

Mam was a bit different from proper eastern Lamton Amish, but that was who she was, and she never changed. She still clung to some of the old traditions from Ohio, in spite of the ever-changing world around her. Joshua genuinely liked Mam, as did Stephen and John, although they remained shy, staying away from Mam and Dat, as is the Amish tradition when youth are dating. But the times they were there for Sunday supper, Lizzie would often catch Stephen chuckling to himself as Mam fussed away in her Ohio accent.

Lizzie was glad that Mam and Dat were resilient and brave. They took life and made the best out of

what God handed them. Mam had a deep-rooted faith and believed that whatever happened in their lives held a special purpose, a deeper meaning, a lesson from God that they didn't always comprehend.

So when the cows were sold and Dat quit farming, Mam felt it was a reward for being submissive to something she had fiercely resisted. She was blessed now with a happy husband who worked well with his son and with a farm she had grown to like. Not love. Mam never loved the old farm, but she accepted it resignedly, appreciating every new thing Dat built for her.

After the cows left, life on the farm changed drastically for Mam. She had no men to cook for, no milk house to keep clean, and her days turned quiet and peaceful as she went about her work while Lizzie and Mandy were off at their jobs.

And, of course, not getting up in the morning to help milk was one of the best things that had ever happened to Lizzie in her entire life. Never again would she have to stumble out to a smelly cow stable, in frigid temperatures, as well as on sweltering summer evenings when she detested every cow permanently.

Mam said it was a blessing to be given a life without cows, which was probably true, but anything in life is like that, Lizzie thought. If some source of irritation is no longer around, of course it's a blessing, but to Lizzie it was more than that. If was a gift. An undeserved gift.

Chapter 23

ONE WARM SPRING DAY, SHORTLY BEFORE Stephen left to hike the Appalachian Trail, he drove in the lane to pick up Lizzie for their weekly date. He had slid both buggy doors back and fastened both windows to the ceiling, held there with leather straps. Bob was already wet with sweat from traveling the three miles to Lizzie's house. The buggy shone a brilliant black, the gray canvas washed spotlessly clean. The blue interior made Stephen's eyes bluer than ever, and Lizzie's heart skipped a few beats when he smiled at her.

"Hello, Stephen," she said, smiling back at him.

"How are you, Lizzie?"

"Too warm," she said emphatically, plopping down beside him on the seat, lifting her apron to cool herself. She still wasn't happy that he was leaving her for a month to go hiking, but she was excited about their date today and decided not to let his upcoming trip spoil her mood.

"It's not too warm. I love this weather."

"Do you really?"

"Sure. Makes you feel good to sweat. I tie a red handkerchief around my head at work. Soaks up the perspiration."

Lizzie imagined this and laughed.

"So, what are we doing this afternoon?" Lizzie asked.

"I thought we'd ask Reuben and Rebecca to go to the dam for a boat ride. It would feel nice and cool on the water."

"It would be cooler IN the water," Lizzie laughed.

"I could push you off the boat if you want."

Lizzie punched his arm while Stephen clucked to his horse, and they started slowly out the drive. That was the nicest part about having a boyfriend, Lizzie thought. This slow, easy pace and never having to hurry became the best part of Sunday afternoons. She looked forward to this time each week — riding around in the breezy buggy, just the two of them, enjoying each other's company, talking easily, laughing, getting to know each other better.

"Whose boat?" Lizzie asked.

"We're building an addition for Mr. Wright who lives on the other side of the dam. He has a big aluminum boat he takes out on the water quite often, and he said I'm welcome to use it anytime I want."

"Really? Are we going to use it today?"

"Mm-hmm."

"Wow!"

Lizzie loved the whole idea. Water didn't scare Lizzie. She was a good swimmer, having learned in the river in Jefferson County, so the boat ride didn't worry her at all. Actually, on a day like this, it would feel wonderful to fall into the lake. Of course, boys and girls weren't allowed to go swimming together, and falling into the lake would be considered exactly that, even with her dress on. And her cape and apron and covering.

"Reuben and Rebecca will meet us at Maybury," Stephen said.

"Do they have their own team? What will we do with the horses? Isn't too hot to make them pull us up the mountain? What about the flies that are so pesky to horses in hot weather? Do you have fly spray?"

"Whoa!" Stephen laughed.

"What?"

"Yes, Reuben and Rebecca have their own team. The horses can be put in Mr. Wright's barn. And, yes, it is too hot to go the whole way up the mountain, but we'll only go a short way till we turn down the road that goes to the dam." He paused.

"Oh, and, no, I don't have fly spray, but this guy has a barn so they'll be fine."

Lizzie relaxed then, enjoying the ride to the little town of Maybury, a small grouping of houses, two churches, a post office, a tractor business, a general store, and gas station, all tucked cozily near the bottom of the mountain.

Reuben's team was already parked by the general store, and the purple skirt of Rebecca's dress hung

out the buggy door. Stephen stomped on the brakes, and they lurched to a stop beside them.

Reuben and Rebecca leaned forward in unison, equally big smiles on their faces.

"Hi!"

"Hello youself!"

"It's too hot for the horses!"

"We're not going up the mountain very far."

"Ready?"

"Do you have any food?"

"I packed a whole pile."

"Let's go!"

They wasted no time pulling out of the parking lot, and the horses trotted steadily through the town of Maybury and out toward the dam. The dam sat on a huge reservoir with the concrete embankment holding the water in a large valley between a high ridge and the mountain. It was a beautiful clear lake, continually fed by springs and creeks from the mountain to the north.

The horses sensed the adventure, their ears pricked forward, their necks arched, as they trotted close to the mountain. On the left, they passed a happy little creek that gurgled and tumbled along over smooth, slippery sandstone, quieting to a soft sigh in deep, dark pools beneath overhanging hemlock branches. Cattails swayed in the hot breeze, and bumblebees and butterflies hovered along the banks. Wild strawberries grew in profusion, the sun gently coaxing them up and out of the wet fertile soil.

Stephen made a sort of groaning sound, which

startled Lizzie.

"What?" she asked.

"Those deep pools are probably loaded with big heavy trout. Wish it wasn't Sunday and I had my fishing pole."

"That's all you think about," Lizzie said, in what she hoped was a pretty, pouting little voice.

"Oh, no, it's not."

"What else do you think about?"

She hoped with all her heart he would say something like "sitting by that deep pool with you" or that "you are as pretty as the wildflowers" or that "you are much more important than the fish." Which she definitely was, she thought.

Stephen adjusted the reins, thought a bit, then said dryly, "Where I would get good bait."

He roared and laughed when Lizzie made an exasperated sound, then slid his arm across the back of the seat and pulled her close.

"No, Lizzie, I think of you much more often than I think of fishing. Especially on Sundays, because I can't fish then."

Lizzie sat up straight and grabbed a handful of his long, sun-streaked, brown hair and pulled with all her might. Stephen easily pulled her hands away, yelling how much it hurt, but they were both laughing until the buggy wheel dipped down into a culvert. Stephen tugged at the reins to straighten out the buggy.

"Hey!" Reuben called from behind them. "You better watch where you're driving!"

And then the road wound steadily uphill and the horses slowed to a walk. They kept a steady pace, their heads moving up and down, up and down, the harnesses creaking against the shafts as the horses drew the buggies steadily up the mountain.

They came to a dirt road that turned down the side of a ridge, and before long, Lizzie could see the sparkling blue waters of the lake shimmering between the trees. Water was like that. It wasn't really blue, it just reflected the blue of the sky. It wasn't gray or black either. Sort of silver, but really no color. And yet it was so beautiful.

They arrived at a small brown house set in a little wooded cove by the lake. It was the cutest thing Lizzie had ever seen. Sort of ramshackle, not really kept up very well, but still very homey and cozy and friendly. Even the two large cats straddling the arm of the wooden porch rockers were smiling.

Blue morning glories wound their way up the side of the porch, and a bed of yellow snapdragons were nestled between large, pink hollyhocks. Dandelions and orchard grass grew among them, but it was all very colorful and gave the whole place an air of serenity and relaxation.

The door opened gently and a bent, grizzled old gentleman came to the porch.

"Hello there! Get down. Get down! Come on in."

Mr. Wright helped them put the horses in his little barn filled with banty roosters and pigeons. Then he showed them his boat which was rather large, much to Lizzie's relief. Not that she was afraid of

the water. It just seemed safer, especially if they were going to have their lunch in the middle of the lake.

Reuben and Stephen carried the boat down the bank to the lake, and they all climbed aboard a bit gingerly. Rebecca held one side of the cooler containing the food and Lizzie the other.

There were three seats in the boat, but the four of them could easily fit two to a seat, each couple facing the other. After a few tries, they got the oars in the oarlocks, and with a swift, smooth push of the oars, Stephen steered the boat toward the middle of that deep, cool water.

Rebecca told Stephen he had better not go too close to the lip of the dam. Just suppose if they went down over that great steep expanse of concrete, they'd all be killed.

Stephen pooh-poohed that idea, but Lizzie felt the same apprehension, although she bit down hard on her lower lip to keep from nagging him along with Rebecca.

Reuben trailed his hand in the cool water, flicking it at the girls, which was just fine with Lizzie. It was so hot Lizzie guaranteed you could fry an egg on the seat of the boat. Her cape felt like it was made of wool, her dress was itchy and she could have screamed, she was so uncomfortable.

Why in the world would they sit in the middle of the lake with no breeze on this startlingly hot spring day? She was hungry, the sun was hot, and she was thirsty. She wished she was a fish. Stephen would care more about her then.

"Hey, it's too hot!" Rebecca yelled in a very unlady-like voice. Lizzie burst out laughing.

The boys agreed and rowed to the north side of the lake where the merciful shade welcomed them with open arms, the boughs of the huge oak and maple trees forming a sort of canopy for their picnic.

Rebecca poured ice-cold meadow tea into plastic cups, which Lizzie drank gratefully. As soon as her cup was empty, she asked for more. In all the world, there is nothing more refreshing than meadow tea on a hot day, Lizzie thought.

They ate thick roast beef sandwiches with slabs of Swiss cheese and lettuce from Rebecca's garden. Rebecca had thought to pack small Tupperware containers of mayonnaise and mustard which made the sandwiches taste so good.

Lizzie had packed a bag with potato chips, homemade dill pickles, peanut butter chocolate chip cookies, and large red apples, polished until they looked like a picture in a storybook.

The whole picnic lunch was so delicious, the cookies melting in Lizzie's mouth and then washed down with that wonderful ice-cold meadow tea.

Stephen's eyes held hers as they ate, and she felt such a closeness to him. For the very first time in her life, she thought she might know what it felt like to be in love. Not just kind of, or sort of, but for real.

When everyone was finished eating, they packed the remains of the lunch carefully into the cooler, and Stephen announced that they would row around the lake again to see if they could find any fish. Oh,

great, Lizzie thought resignedly, remembering the sun's rays beating down on her six layer of fabric. Oh, great.

"You guys better row as fast as you can," Rebecca said loudly. "It's hotter than ever out on the lake."

"We will," Reuben assured her.

And they did. They cruised around the lake, the boat creating an actual wake like a speedboat, only a lot smaller and gentler. A nice, wet breeze cooled the girls. Stephen yelled at regular intervals whenever he spied the flash of a trout or the yellow speckles of a sunfish, bemoaning the fact that he had no fishing rod.

Rebecca and Lizzie sat back and let their hands trail in the deep, cool water as they chatted and watched the boys handle the oars, propelling them along. It was a wonderful day. It was so good, in fact, that it made Lizzie's heart hurt with the fullness of it. Rebecca was her best friend, Stephen might just be the love of her life, and Reuben was such a dear, very good match for Rebecca.

For the very first time in her life, she wondered when or if Stephen would ask her to marry him someday. They could live in the little brown house by the lake, if Mr. Wright would just sell it to them. She would weed the flower beds and paint the porch rockers. She laughed. But then, living here by the lake would have one big disadvantage. She would have to compete with the fish for Stephen's love and attention.

LINDA BYLER

BIG
Decisions

LIZZIE SEARCHES *for* LOVE
• *Book 3* •

Chapter 1

THE LEAVES TURNED SHADES OF BRIGHT orange, red, and yellow, and the squirrels scurried in short swift trips up the rough bark of the trees. Their cheeks were stuffed full of acorns and nuts which they stashed away in a deep, dark, cozy chamber for their winter nourishment.

Lizzie and Stephen walked together on a Sunday afternoon along a creek, kicking the brown leaves and bending their heads to the stiff autumn breeze. Lizzie wrapped her sweater tightly around her chilled body, crossing her arms in front of herself to keep warm.

"I should have worn a scarf!" she said her teeth chattering.

"Hey, Lizzie, I just had a great thought. Thursday evening I'm going archery hunting again. Would you like to come along?" Stephen asked.

"Archery? Bow and arrow? I can't shoot a bow and arrow," Lizzie said.

"No, you don't have to shoot. Just go along and be with me. There's nothing quite like it. Honestly. It is the most exciting, the most intense sport there is. To sit in a tree somewhere, waiting quietly until you hear leaves rustling, or maybe spot a reddish-brown color gliding along through the trees, is an incredible experience. Your heart starts thumping so hard you feel like your head will burst. There's just an unbelievable amount of excitement in all hunting, but archery is my favorite."

That was quite a speech for Stephen, so hunting must be more than a hobby—closer to an obsession, Lizzie thought.

"How can it be so thrilling? Actually, all you do is sit in the woods," Lizzie said, still less than enthused.

"No, that's not true, Lizzie. Come along, and I'll show you."

So that was how Lizzie found herself careening across the mountain at breakneck speed in an old, white work van, driven by a friend of Stephen's. His name was Ryan Gustin, and he was quite a character, speaking the Pennsylvania Dutch dialect as fast as he drove his rattling old van.

Lizzie enjoyed his company, sometimes laughing uncontrollably at his version of a Dutch expression which served to take her mind off the alarming rate of speed he maintained down the winding road.

Stephen seemed quite comfortable in the front seat beside him, so Lizzie decided Ryan must be a competent driver if Stephen was so relaxed.

Turning north, they came to a valley between two mountains. Old buildings and beautiful, prosperous farms dotted the scenery, while simple family dwellings sat along the road. The mountains were colored with every brilliant hue imaginable, and Lizzie was content to ride along and enjoy the beauty. She was just starting to become a bit bored and uncomfortable when Stephen yelled for Ryan to stop. This was the place. Ryan stomped on the brakes.

As the van shuddered to a stop, Lizzie peered out of the splattered window at a dilapidated, old, three-story house. Broken shutters hung from single hinges, the porch railing looked as if it had been ripped from its base, and pieces of gray siding lay strewn across the yard. The porch roof gapped where the wind had torn shingles loose.

Lizzie shivered, wondering if the house was haunted at night. She knew there was no such thing, but old, unoccupied houses always gave her the blues. The real, sad blues. Not that she felt depressed. Not the crying blues. Just the kind of blues where the sun was hidden behind a dark cloud in her feelings.

She didn't really want to get out of the van as she looked a bit timidly at the steep, brush-strewn hillside directly behind the creepy old house. The sloping fields led to dense forest, real mountain woods that suddenly looked quite dark and spooky.

Stephen and the driver were already out, unload-
ing their archery gear, still talking and laughing
and having the time of their lives as Lizzie pulled
her white cotton scarf tighter under her chin. She
sniffed nervously, running a hand hastily across her
hair to straighten it.

She wished she had worn some heavy material
around her legs, because her thin woolen knee socks
were not going to be heavy enough to wade through
the unkempt woods. She remembered the hillside
along the ridge in Jefferson County and the horrible
scratches she and her sisters got every day from the
long, spiny raspberry bushes that lined the trail.

She sniffed, squinting nervously to see if she could
locate any brambles, but then sighed, gave up, and
sat back against the old plastic seat. Stephen would
take care of her, she decided, so she would relax.

"Ready?" Stephen stuck his head around the
door, extending his hand to help her down. Lizzie
took it gratefully, searching his eyes for reassurance.
Stephen smiled, and her heart melted as she stood
beside him. If your boyfriend was so nice to you, it
didn't take much to believe you could do anything
at all.

Ryan strode off in the opposite direction, and
Stephen swung his bow under his arm as he headed
out. Lizzie followed, determined to be a good sport.
She would certainly not be a hindrance to him or
hold him back by telling him she was uncomfortable.

Stephen parted the tall weeds as they started
the gradual uphill slope. Lizzie grimaced as heavy

seedpods slapped her cheeks, raining prickly, granular seeds down the neckline of her coat. She slapped at the heavy pods, shaking the front of her dress to get rid of the itchy feeling, her mouth pressed in a line of determination. She would not grumble or complain, knowing Stephen would not appreciate a whiny girlfriend tagging along.

Stephen stopped after a short distance and said, "Whoa."

"What?" Lizzie asked, trying to peer around him.

"These brambles are pretty thick here. Think you can make it without getting scratched too badly?"

"I think so," Lizzie answered, with all the false bravado she could muster.

"I'll try and hold them for you," he reassured her.

He must have forgotten about her the minute that statement was out of his mouth. Lizzie found herself in one of the worst situations of her life, trying to hold back a long bramble with one hand, only to rake a thorn across the palm of her hand, while two more long whips with briars intact tore across her thin woolen socks.

Grimly, she untangled herself, putting the injured palm to her mouth as she tried to free her legs by tramping on the briars. As she bent to hold back the brambles, a long vine yanked her hair, pulling horribly as her white scarf slid around her neck. She grabbed quickly to retrieve the scarf and was promptly scratched by another sharp branch.

"Ouch!" she yelled, completely undone by this thorny predicament.

Stephen's instant response was, "Ssshhh!"

"Why? Why can't I holler? These brambles are unbearable!" Lizzie wailed, close to tears.

Suddenly retrieving his manners, Stephen mumbled an apology and came to her rescue, holding aside the long spiny branches until they came to the forest's edge. Lizzie shook her head grimly, smoothing her hair with scratched fingers and adjusting her white head scarf.

"Okay," Stephen whispered, "step as quietly as you can, and when I come to a suitable tree, I'll motion for you to follow."

"F ... f ... follow?" Lizzie whispered back, aghast.

"Yeah. Up the tree. We have to sit in a tree so the deer don't see us."

"I can't climb trees!" Lizzie hissed, her eyes narrowing.

"Pine trees are easy. Now be as quiet as you possibly can."

That was how Lizzie found herself halfway up a scaly pine tree, positioned so that she had the same view Stephen did. The bark was rough and very uncomfortable. She sat on the side of her leg, holding onto a branch beside her. The first five minutes weren't too bad. She rested from the strenuous climb, breathing in the pine tar and admiring Stephen's profile as he stood alert and absolutely motionless in the tree, waiting breathlessly for the sight of a deer.

The wind swayed the branches as Lizzie strained to see through the thick growth. It would definitely

be exciting to see a deer with huge antlers come walking across the pine needles, but who knew when that might happen? Deer roamed acre after acre of woods, but having one walk in front of you seemed about as possible as finding a needle in a haystack, so what was the sense of sitting in this tree? The deer were probably all on top of the mountain or in some farmer's cornfield having a bedtime snack.

Her leg ached and her arm became very stiff, so she shifted her weight to her other leg. Instantly, a small branch broke loose, rattling down through the pine boughs with the noise of a shotgun, or so it seemed.

"Sorry!" Lizzie hissed.

Stephen drew his eyebrows down. "Shhh!" he warned, putting a finger to his lips.

Boy, he was serious. All right, she would be more careful. So she sat quietly. And sat. And sat. Her nose itched, her feet hurt, her whole leg was numb, and still she sat. The sun slid behind the opposite mountain, casting long shadows through the thick forest, and still she sat.

This is a lot worse than council meeting or communion or sitting at Emma's wedding, she thought grimly. A hard bench would seem like a recliner if you compared it to this pine tree. Sitting like this for hours in a darkening woods would be a good form of torture if you wanted to force someone to talk. She would gladly say anything to get out of this tree.

She tried shifting her weight to the opposite side as slowly and quietly as she possibly could, loosening

some bark in the process. She looked at Stephen beseechingly, but he only frowned seriously. She groaned inwardly. She wished she had never agreed to go hunting with him. It was the most uncomfortable, boring thing she had ever done in her entire life. She hated hunting and was never, ever going to get herself in this predicament again.

Suddenly there was a decided rustling in the underbrush. Stephen's head turned slowly, and he brought his bow up to a more ready position. The rustling continued. Lizzie listened with bated breath, watching carefully in the direction the sounds were coming from. Would they actually see an honest-to-goodness deer? She didn't know if she could stand to see Stephen put an arrow into the poor, innocent animal.

She didn't know if she wanted to be disappointed or relieved when a busy gray squirrel emerged and raced across the thick pine needles.

"There's your deer!" Lizzie mouthed.

"Shh!" Stephen warned.

What was the use of holding so perfectly still? It was getting dark, and there was no possible way he could shoot a deer now. She was getting very tired and impatient, wishing with all her heart that the night would be over. If Stephen didn't soon come down out of this tree, if he kept up this stupidity of sitting in a tree when it was almost dark, she was going to say no if he asked her to marry him.

What about returning to the van? How would they get through those dreaded brambles again?

"Stephen!" she whispered.

"Shh!"

This time he was serious. Turning his head slowly, he peered intently into the semi-darkness as, much to Lizzie's disbelief, two deer stepped out of the thicket. How could they be so quiet? Lizzie's heart rate increased, but mostly out of fear for the deer's safety. She so definitely did not want them to be killed with arrows stuck into their hearts. They were such beautiful creatures, completely at ease roaming their mountain, so why did anyone have to kill them?

Then as Stephen started to raise his bow to the proper position, they walked just as silently back into the forest. When Stephen finally turned to Lizzie and spoke to her in a normal tone, she knew the whole hunting ordeal was over. Carefully, with aching limbs, she made her way out of the pine tree. Rubbing her back, stretching, and sighing, she regained a sense of normalcy, grateful to be standing on solid ground and able to move at free will.

Lizzie stared at Stephen in disbelief when he turned to her and said cheerily, "That was fun, wasn't it? I bet you really enjoyed it."

"It...it, yes, well, it was all right. Mmm-hmm." That was the closest thing she could say that was honest and still not hurt his feelings. She couldn't say just how tedious her evening was, but he must have known because he laughed out loud quite suddenly.

"Not exactly a hunter, are you?" he said, smiling mischievously.

"Just get me off this mountain safely, and I'll be fine," Lizzie said.

They took a detour under a barbed wire fence, which Stephen held so Lizzie could easily slip through, before walking across a nicely cropped pasture until they came to the old house. Lizzie stared up at the attic windows in spite of herself, wondering who had built this huge three-story house and why it had been left to rot away, the wind and rain and snow all taking its toll on the sturdy structure. Probably the squirrels and the rats had a grand time gnawing at the lumber that held it together.

Ryan appeared shortly and shared his story with Stephen about having spotted a few deer but too far in the distance to have a decent shot. They stowed their hunting gear in the back of the van before climbing in. Finally, Lizzie was on her way home, away from the pine tree, the dark forest, and the creepy, sad, old house.

They turned into a little restaurant, Ryan saying he was starved because he hadn't eaten anything since lunchtime.

Lizzie was only too happy to sit in the tiny booth, eating French fries with plenty of salt and slathered with ketchup. They were the most fattening, most unhealthy thing, Mam said, but one of the most delicious foods in the world. Lizzie enjoyed every one, and then ate her way down the entire length of a tall chocolate sundae topped with whipped cream and nuts.

"Mmm!" she said, smiling genuinely at Stephen.

"Better than hunting?" Stephen asked.

"Much better," she grinned back at him.

That evening, she decided marriage was probably a lot like hunting. You had to take the good with the bad, because God himself knew circumstances would not always be as pleasant as French fries and sundaes. There would be times of sitting in pine trees, but that was only normal. If the good was balanced with the bad, life could be leveled off into happiness. Maybe a mature, quiet kind of happiness, if you learned to care about each other's feelings enough not to always say exactly what you thought.

If she had told Stephen how horrible her evening really was, he would have been hurt. And if Stephen had been as impatient with her as he seemed to be when she struggled through the briars, she would have been terribly insulted.

So it definitely paid to keep your mouth closed when you would love to air your grievances loud and long. After all, Stephen knew hunting was not her favorite thing to do, but she bet anything he admired her for sitting in that tree so long. She had proven to him that she could keep quiet for a good long time. And that was amazing.

Chapter 2

Lizzie missed her older sister, Emma, a great deal, mostly because she thought about marriage so much herself. She wished Emma was in her bedroom down the hall, ready to talk whenever Lizzie had important questions that needed answers. But Emma had married Joshua last year and moved to Allen County.

Mam and Dat were all right to talk to about such matters. But they were so old, it seemed that when they talked about being newly wed, it was like they had gotten married in the 1800s. You couldn't really compare things, like homes and furniture or anything like that, because things were so different after their wedding than now.

What really alarmed Lizzie is how Mam would throw her hands in the air and laugh about the fact that they had to borrow 50 dollars to buy a kitchen table for their first house. Dat would join in and relate how old and freezing cold their first rented

home was, and they would laugh together, as if it was all one big hilarious joke to be so poor and not care one teeny bit about it.

Lizzie wondered everyday when Stephen would ask her to marry him. She needed to talk to someone who got married in this day and age, like Emma. She had nice furniture that Dat and Mam had provided, things like a new hutch cupboard which held the set of china Joshua had given her before their wedding day. She had a brand-new table you could pull apart and put leaves in until you had a table spread clear across the kitchen, and as many as 18 or 20 people could sit around it at one time. Emma even had a new sofa and rocking chairs and a really pretty bookcase with sliding glass doors.

Lizzie didn't know if Stephen had any money or not, so she worried a great deal. For one thing, she hated being poor or having to make do with cheap or broken things, like a torn, wrinkled plastic tablecloth. She wanted a nice new house with new linoleum on the floor and varnished, wooden cabinets with a pretty canister set perched on the Formica counter top. She daydreamed for hours about her new house, and the closer a marriage proposal seemed to be, the more she wondered about Stephen's finances.

Mandy told her airily, in quite a lofty manner actually, that she cared more about her classy new home than she cared about Stephen. "You need to remember, Lizzie, that a nice new house doesn't make a happy home," she repeated.

Sometimes Mandy could be so infuriating with her wisdom and knowledge and always being right, that Lizzie found it easier to talk to Emma about these things.

So when Lizzie came home from school, and there was a long letter from Emma in the mail holder, she was ecstatic. Her excitement increased as she read how they wanted Mandy and John and Stephen and Lizzie to come on Saturday evening.

"Oh, good, good, *goody*!" Lizzie yelled exultantly, waving the letter in the air as she marched around the kitchen.

Mam smiled, and Dat drew his eyebrows down in displeasure. He shook his head and mumbled something about acting your age, before his head disappeared behind his paper again. Lizzie stopped to look at Dat, or rather at the paper he was holding. Dat just was not the same since he had been diagnosed with multiple sclerosis. He was often tired and, of late, irritable and short with his children. He would have laughed in the past, his blue eyes twinkling at them, but now he often frowned or showed his displeasure with a sharp word. Most of the time the girls shrugged it off, but sometimes it hurt, even though they realized he struggled to accept this disease more than they would ever know.

❧

So they hired a driver and traveled to Allen County. Lizzie could hardly wait to see Emma

and Joshua, the old farm, and especially their new baby, Mark. Stephen wore a light, cream-colored shirt that made his skin look very tan. His hair was always bleached to a lighter color by the fall after a long summer of working in the sun. Lizzie thought he looked very handsome and wondered if Emma would think so, too.

After you dated awhile, it was much easier to relax and fully accept the fact that your boyfriend really did like you the way you were. It was no longer quite as big an issue for Lizzie to be a bit overweight, because Stephen certainly didn't seem to mind.

Lizzie didn't worry so much about her appearance like she had in the beginning of their relationship. It seemed as if dating for a year or so took care of the flutter of nervousness, the agony of indecision about which dress to wear, or, when you really thought about it, a lot of silly insecurities.

They no longer had strained silences. Instead, it was normal for them to have a good, healthy discussion about something they didn't agree about. But the one thing they didn't discuss was marriage. Of course, Lizzie wanted to get married now. She wasn't really tired of being with the youth, but she wanted to go forward with her life.

For one thing, she was tired of teaching school, of helping Mam at home, and especially of the endless yard and garden work around the old farm. Lizzie wanted her own house, a nice new one, to be exact, with only Stephen to worry about.

The van turned into the farm lane. Emma greeted them from the porch of her brick farmhouse with a huge smile. As soon as they climbed down from the van, Joshua made John and Stephen feel at home with his warm manner as he showed them around the farm, pointing out where the pigs and steers were housed, and walking them to the pastures and the fields.

The sisters sat together in the living room and talked as fast as they could until they all stopped and admitted that no one was listening because all three of them were talking at once. There was just simply no one else on earth like a sister, they all agreed, and before they were aware of it, they were all talking at once again.

They fussed over Baby Mark, admiring the cute shirt and pants Emma had made for him. He was a big boy, toddling around on the glistening hardwood floor, pulling himself up with a mighty effort as he hung onto a sofa cushion. Emma said the best thing that ever happened to her was having a baby.

"I want lots and lots of children," she said.

Lizzie eyed her a bit skeptically.

"Emma, now you know they won't all be as good as Mark is right now. Suppose you'd have a baby that screams and cries like Jason used to? Or Aunt Becca's baby girl?"

Emma leaned back on her glider rocker, gently massaging Baby Mark's back as she tried to get him to sleep. She laughed easily as she looked at Lizzie in disbelief.

"Boy, you sure haven't changed, have you? Worrying about a colicky baby before you're even married!"

"Not *my* baby. Your next one!" Lizzie shot back.

Mandy laughed. "Oh, boy! Here we go. Sounds like home!"

"Don't you ever long to be a single girl at home again, Emma?" Lizzie asked.

"No! Absolutely not. Never. I'd much, much rather be married to Joshua and have a baby boy. Right, Mark?" And Emma proceeded to hug and kiss her precious boy until he struggled to be put down on the floor.

"Come. I have to show you what I made for our snack tonight," Emma said, as she led Lizzie and Mandy to the kitchen. Handing Mark to Mandy, she triumphantly produced two Tupperware containers and whisked the lids off, watching eagerly as Lizzie bent down to see what was inside.

"Emma! You didn't make these. You bought them at a bakery!" Lizzie gasped.

"I made them! I absolutely did. I would never buy something like this at a bakery," Emma laughed, beaming proudly.

Mandy oohed and aahed about the lemon jelly roll Emma held, while Lizzie said the chocolate one looked like a picture in a magazine. It did. Emma had made two perfect cake rolls. The lemon one was piped full of a light lemon filling that smelled so delicious Lizzie's mouth watered. The other cake was a rich chocolate filled with creamy vanilla frosting.

Emma had dusted both with confectioners' sugar. The cakes were perfectly round without a crack or a burnt edge in sight.

"I just can't believe you did that," Lizzie said, absolutely impressed.

"Oh, Lizzie, you know how I always was. There's nothing I'd rather do than spend hours in my kitchen, meticulously producing something like these jelly rolls."

Emma's eyes lit up, and she hurried back to the pantry. "Look at this," she said, holding a perfect loaf of homemade bread. It looked exactly like the loaf of bread in the children's book about the Little Red Hen who baked a beautiful loaf of bread with the wheat she raised.

"Emma, you are genuinely talented at baking," Lizzie said sincerely.

"And having baby boys!" Mandy added, scooping up Baby Mark and squeezing him affectionately.

When Joshua came into the kitchen followed by John and Stephen, there were no awkward moments, no times of feeling ill at ease. That was just how it was when you went to Emma and Joshua's place, Lizzie thought happily. They both loved to have company and made you feel so welcome and relaxed. Maybe it was because Emma was her sister, but whatever the reason, Lizzie loved to go visit them.

They all sat around the kitchen table as Joshua put on the teakettle for hot water. He drank black instant coffee almost continuously throughout the evening—that boiling hot, dark brown, bitter brew

that Lizzie could positively not enjoy. She had often tried to drink coffee like Mam did. She tried it with milk, with sugar, with cream and sugar, but no matter how many attempts she made, it just wasn't good. Stephen drank coffee, too. He seemed to enjoy it as much as Joshua did, telling Lizzie he filled a quart thermos with it every morning.

That's why Lizzie found it so fascinating to watch Joshua enjoy his coffee. It was steaming hot, so he would sit back in his chair and stir it for awhile, talking and laughing easily until the coffee cooled enough for him to take the first sip. That black awful stuff.

Emma carefully arranged the cake rolls on a cut-glass oblong tray, putting a sharp stainless steel knife beside it. Her cheeks flushed, she scurried back and forth between the refrigerator and the pantry, slicing cheese and arranging Ritz crackers around it. She poured tall glasses of ice-cold peppermint tea and opened a bag of pretzels, placing them in a dish that matched the oblong tray.

"We don't go to town often," she said breathlessly, "so we can't serve a lot of fancy things like Pepsi and other snacks."

"Emma, that wouldn't seem like being at your house," Lizzie said. "It seems homier and 'farmier' with the food you have."

Emma gave Lizzie an appreciative look, glancing a bit nervously at Stephen and John.

"Don't worry about me. We live very simply at my house," Stephen said.

Lizzie was so proud of Stephen she could have hugged him, but of course she didn't. That was a very nice thing to say, making Emma feel comfortable with the fact that her food was just right exactly the way it was. Emma continued to dash between the table and the counter top, making everyone comfortable, seeing that they had everything they needed, until Joshua told her to sit down and relax or the cake rolls would be all gone before she could enjoy a slice of them.

"Maybe I had better before Lizzie eats all of them!" Emma said, teasing her.

"I could eat the whole thing," Lizzie said seriously.

Joshua's eyes sparkled as he turned to Stephen. "You sure you want to marry her? She may turn out to be expensive!"

"Joshua!" Lizzie cried, horrified.

Stephen thought it was very funny, although his face definitely deepened in color. Lizzie knew her face was bright red, but everyone laughed so genuinely, and Stephen gave her such a reassuring look, that Lizzie could laugh with them. The exchange broke all the reserve they had left, and as the evening wore on they had a genuinely good time playing their favorite card game, Rook.

Lizzie decided during the evening that being married to someone you loved was a very worthwhile goal. It was an exciting idea, one that made her feel happy through and through. She wanted her very own home so she could have her friends over and

serve them all her good food, although she knew without a moment's hesitation that it wouldn't be homemade cake rolls like Emma made. She could barely bake a decent chocolate chip cookie.

She sat back in her chair, watching Stephen shuffle the Rook cards. She wondered a bit apprehensively if he could be a good husband and father, and if he had enough common sense to make good solid decisions and protect her. He could be very grown up, especially when he talked about his work, so that Lizzie was sometimes in awe of him. But he could also be hopelessly funny at times, acting as if he didn't have a care in the world.

He turned to smile at her, that secret little gesture of belonging, and Lizzie's heart melted in gratitude that he was her boyfriend. Probably there was no such thing as an absolute, 100 percent, perfect boyfriend, and so far, Stephen was everything she had hoped for.

"No, I'm planning on buying the herd in a few months," she heard John say.

Lizzie snapped to attention, her eyes riveted intently on John's face. She watched Mandy as she blinked her huge green eyes, listening carefully.

The herd! He meant cows! Oh, poor Mandy.

"How many are you planning to milk?" Joshua asked, bending for yet another sip of coffee.

"Around 40, hopefully," John answered.

Forty cows!

"Who in the world is going to help you milk 40 cows?" Lizzie blurted out.

"My brother will help me get started. Then we'll see," he said, turning to scoop up the Rook cards.

Lizzie's eyes narrowed as she watched Joshua's slow grin spread across his face.

"You need a wife," he said, smiling broadly.

Emma and Lizzie exchanged knowing glances and hid their smiles. Mandy cleared her throat nervously and quickly grabbed a pretzel, chewing rapidly.

"Looks as if his wife got hungry for a pretzel very suddenly," Stephen said slowly.

Mandy drew back her arm and threw a pretzel, hard, hitting Stephen's face. He ducked, grimacing, and laughed with Joshua at John and Mandy's discomfort.

Everyone laughed then and settled down to a serious discussion about courtship and marriage. It was no wonder you wanted to get married when you were at Emma and Joshua's house, Lizzie decided. They portrayed marriage as one of the greatest ideas God ever invented. Joshua could go on and on about the merits of living with Emma. He didn't try to hide the fact that she was one of the best things that had ever happened to him, and the time he spent on the farm with his wife were the best days of his life. Emma beamed and smiled, naturally basking in the warm words of praise from her husband.

"Surely, though, there are some things that you would change. Surely you're not always blissfully happy every day," Lizzie broke in, always the pessimist.

Joshua shrugged. "I wouldn't know what!"

"Me neither," Emma said softly.

"Come on. Not one thing?" Lizzie asked.

"Oh, maybe little things like not frying the corn-meal mush exactly as crispy as I like it," Joshua laughed.

"Or watching you eat chocolate cake in your oatmeal," Emma said, smiling.

"What?"

"Oh, he fixes a dish of oatmeal like ordinary people with sugar and milk, then he plops a piece of chocolate cake in the middle, stirs it up, and eats the whole mess," Emma said.

"Now that is definitely different," John said.

"You want to taste it? I've been eating it for years. It's so good it's habit-forming, like coffee. Tell you what, I'll make you some."

With that, Joshua got up and opened a drawer, selected a small saucepan, filled it with water, and settled it on the stove.

By the time the evening was over, they had all had a taste of warm oatmeal with chocolate cake stirred into it. The group gave Joshua's concoction mixed reviews. Stephen liked it, and John grudgingly pronounced it edible. Mandy turned up her nose, but then that was Mandy, skinny thing, about most food, Lizzie decided. Lizzie loved it but didn't really elaborate on the fact, mostly because it was embarrassing the way all food tasted delicious to her.

When it was time to leave, Lizzie wished the evening wasn't over yet. She loved spending time with

Joshua and Emma and told them so.

"You need to invite us again," she said, as Emma hugged her tight.

On the way home, Lizzie sincerely hoped the longing to be married had settled squarely into Stephen's heart and would not let him rest.

Chapter 3

"WHAT REALLY GETS TO ME THE MOST," Lizzie said, waving her arms for emphasis, "is why does a covering have to be a certain size, or an apron belt a certain width? What does that have to do with your soul?"

Her sister, Mandy, didn't say anything, just rearranged the driving reins in her hands as she guided Bess, their horse, toward the small grocery store. Lizzie slumped in her seat as the buggy climbed the hill. That was typical of Mandy, not saying much when she wasn't really sure of herself.

Lizzie and Mandy were about to become members of the Amish church. It was a time of learning for Lizzie, of truly seeing for herself what it meant to be *gehorsam*, or obedient. It wasn't all roses. Not even close.

When they reached the small village of Knobstown, Mandy pulled Bess to a stop. The sisters jumped out of the wagon and tied Bess to the

hitching rack before going into the small grocery store.

"How are the girls?" Mr. Tibbs called out, his blue eyes twinkling behind his heavy eyeglasses. His plaid flannel shirt was stretched tightly across his round little stomach, his short fingers ringing up an order as swiftly as any cashier in town.

Mr. and Mrs. Tibbs, who ran the little friendly and efficient store, were always happy to see the "Amish kids," as they called them.

"We're fine," Lizzie said, smiling back at him.

"Speaking for your sister, too?" he called, winking jovially at Mandy.

"Same here," Mandy grinned.

"Good! Good!"

He leaned forward, his palms down on the counter, and asked what he could get for them.

"Mam has quite a list here, so it'll take a while," Lizzie told him.

After the two grocery bags were filled and the items paid for, Lizzie and Mandy each chose an ice cream bar to eat on the way home, even though the weather was bitterly cold. They took big bites of their ice cream as the buggy wound down the hill toward home, Lizzie holding Mandy's bar between bites so she could drive Bess.

Mandy giggled, telling Lizzie that she was getting some strange looks from passing motorists. Lizzie sat on the spring wagon seat with an ice cream bar in each hand, while Mandy, the skinny one, was driving and had none.

"You mean, I look like I eat all the food away from you? Mandy!"

They drove on in companionable silence until Lizzie brought up the subject that was troubling her.

"Mandy, why do the ministers make such a big deal about the smallest things?" she asked.

"Lizzie, just be quiet. I don't understand everything fully. We probably won't until we live to be a ripe old age. You make the biggest fuss about all this. What is your problem with changing some things? You don't want to comb your hair fancy after you're married anyway. Nobody does."

Lizzie thought Mandy was being awfully short with her. She had to talk when something troubled her. Mandy knew that was a vital part of Lizzie's well-being, bringing things out in the open and discussing what lay so heavily on her heart.

"Oh, all right, Miss High and Mighty. I apologize for disturbing Her Majesty's peace," Lizzie said, turning to look squarely at Mandy.

There was no response, only a faraway expression as Mandy looked at Bess's ears.

"Grouch!" Lizzie finished, before turning away to watch the scenery in the opposite direction.

When they brought the groceries into the kitchen, Mam smiled and examined every item before putting it in the pantry or refrigerator. Lizzie made herself a cup of peppermint tea, sat down at the kitchen table, and stared into space. Mandy went straight to her room, with only a few short words to Mam.

Mam lifted her eyebrows.

"What's wrong with Mandy?" she asked.

"I don't know. She was not very nice about my questions on the way home."

"What questions?" Mam asked, sighing as she straightened her covering.

"Oh, just this *ordnung* thing. Joining church."

Mam's eyes narrowed as she watched Lizzie's face closely. "What now?" she asked.

"What does being plain have to do with your soul?" Lizzie burst out miserably.

"Well, Lizzie, obedience to the rules of the church is an outward sign of a change on the inside," Mam said.

Lizzie snorted.

Mam sighed.

"You know a humble spirit is the surest sign of a change in your heart," Mam said. "You want to do what's right, Lizzie. That's why you're joining the church and no longer rebelling against God. After you're baptized, you'll no longer live for yourself and your selfish will, but you'll have started on a journey where God is your Master. Now it's up to you to lead a new and obedient life."

Lizzie sighed. Mam made it sound so easy.

"So, Lizzie, if you can't be *gehorsam* in small things, how can you expect to be willing to obey God in bigger things?" she concluded.

"You mean that's what it's all about?" Lizzie asked.

"Yes. In a way it seems that church rules are all man-made things that God doesn't care about, but

if you look at it in a spiritual sense, they aren't."

"What about English people, Mam? How come they can get to heaven so easily and never have to worry about one stitch of their clothes. They polish their fingernails, wear all kinds of beautiful clothes, use make-up, and do their hair, and they never have to worry about obedience and solemnly joining a church with a bunch of rules."

"They were born into that lifestyle. It isn't wrong for them. They wouldn't even think of dressing like we do."

"It still doesn't make much sense," Lizzie said, finishing her tea.

Mandy clattered down the stairs, slumped against the wall on the bench behind the table, and began chewing her fingernails.

"You must be in some terrible mood, chomping down on your fingernails like that," Lizzie said.

Mandy glared at her before she smiled a bit wryly and confessed about being upset, actually a bit more than that.

"John would have liked to get married next fall, but he thinks I'm too young," she said.

"Yes, you *are* too young!" Mam said.

"I'm not too young!" Mandy burst out, her frustration making her eyes look wide and dark.

"I'll say, Mandy! You're way, way too young. I would never want to get married this year, and I'm older than you," Lizzie said, her voice rising.

"Remember, Lizzie, we're not all alike," Mandy sang out in a squeaking voice.

❧

So throughout that winter the girls went to church every two weeks and listened closely as Grandpa Glick and the row of solemn ministers explained the way of the cross, of Christ's suffering, and how to follow his footsteps. The ministers explained to them in minute detail the way they were expected to dress, to behave with decorum, and to learn to be obedient to the rules of the church.

Mostly, Lizzie understood the German phrases and could benefit from the ministers' words. She clearly grasped the concept of learning to fear God, to come before him with due solemnity, and to respect the admonishments of her elderly grandfather.

There was, however, one thing that bothered her during that summer. In the *Light from Heaven* book, the one she had read to her pupils, Joseph Armstrong, the main character, went through great personal anxiety. He searched his own soul deeply and felt a certain transformation after he gave his life to God, as did many young people in other books she had read.

She didn't understand all of this too well. Either the Amish people didn't believe in having an experience like a new birth, or else they were taught to view their spirituality much the same as they viewed everything else—calmly and stoically accepting—kind of like putting a lid on too much joy, too much sorrow, or too much rejoicing.

Sometimes Lizzie wanted to be like the Baptist churches in the South that she had read about where people shouted and sang and clapped their hands, swaying to the "Glory, Hallelujah!" in their soul. They were rejoicing in the Lord, and Lizzie often felt like crying when she read about their religious experiences. It touched a spot in her heart so that it felt right to rejoice with them.

She felt elated, joyous actually, that Jesus had died for her. Mam always smiled and shook her head in that certain way that meant she knew exactly what Lizzie meant. But Mam also told Lizzie she had to be careful. She told her she could rejoice in other ways than clapping and shouting, like when she was all alone and stepped out of the house on a beautiful spring morning and heard the birds singing and saw the sunrise and the green leaves on the trees.

Lizzie promptly informed Mam that it wasn't the same if you didn't have someone thumping on the organ or piano while the people around you sang as loud as they could, just all caught up together in that moment of rejoicing.

Mam's quiet, "Tsk, tsk," was her only response, before telling Lizzie she read too much.

"Contentment and continuing the quiet way of life are the virtues I most admire in Amish people," Lizzie always said. Of course, she wanted to be Amish. She never even thought of not being a part of the Amish way of life. She just wanted to really let loose sometimes.

Being Amish was the only thing she had ever

known. She had no real longing to leave her parents, go into the big, wide world, and try to become an English person. That would seem all wrong. Some Amish people did that, so she guessed they were comfortable with that, but she wouldn't be.

That winter, Lizzie learned in lots of different ways what was expected of her when she became a member of the church. The ministers explained lots of the lessons in the Old Testament, as well as what happened to people when they rebelled openly against God. The ministers also spoke a great deal about the difference Lizzie and her friends would experience when they lived within God's will, serving God and not idols. That was not hard for Lizzie to believe, and she learned to appreciate the stories in the Old Testament, as well as the words Jesus spoke in the New Testament.

But sometimes Lizzie despaired, overwhelmed by the fear that she would never be good enough to be baptized in the fall.

"I'm not *that* different than before, Mam," she repeated sourly as she sat in the kitchen with Mam and Mandy.

"Oh, but you're making an honest effort, Lizzie. That's all you can do. Grace supplies everything, really, in the end," Mam said.

Lizzie eyed her suspiciously. She was just about sure that Mam didn't always know what she was talking about. For one thing, she claimed "all your own righteousness was like filthy rags in the sight of God," and yet, all winter they were instructed to

live righteously. What sense did that make?

So now if you tried as hard as you could to do good, to live in the way you were instructed, then it was nothing to God, and it all amounted only to grace? So why didn't people just go out and do what they wanted to? They may as well, if grace took care of everything.

Mam scooped out some cookie batter and dropped it onto the baking sheet, using the back of her hand to brush away a strand of hair from her cheek. Beads of sweat clung to her forehead and the color in her cheeks had heightened as the heat in the kitchen had escalated during the afternoon.

"Mandy, be careful there. You're trying to put too many cookies on that sheet, all right?" she instructed.

Mandy nodded, pushing up her sleeve with one hand and sending the glass mixing bowl full of batter onto the floor where it smashed into a hundred pieces.

Mam gasped, then sighed impatiently.

"Who's going to clean it up?" she asked.

Lizzie thought that was an excellent example right there. "Okay, Mam, so why didn't you get angry and yell at Mandy? You used to when we were little girls. So is that all your own righteousness now, and it doesn't amount to a hill of beans in God's eyes? That's what you claim."

Mam looked sharply at Lizzie, but then she smiled.

"Now there, Lizzie, is the beauty of becoming a Christian. If we are all good and holy, acting

righteous and prim and proper so that other people think we are such awfully good Christians, *that* is filthy rags. But if we live to become more like Jesus, if we just have a desire to be good, he quietly, without our knowing, molds and shapes us into a vessel of his own making, and we aren't even aware of it. I would never have noticed any difference at all, girls. None."

"Really? You're a lot different than you used to be," Lizzie said.

"And, hopefully, 20 years from now I'll be so much different than I am now. More patient, more compassionate, not so easy to criticize, oh my, the list could go on and on," Mam answered.

Lizzie fiddled with a cookie, saying nothing. Now that made a lot of sense. She was beginning to grasp only a bit of what it meant to walk with Jesus. It was as if you were only a lump of raw, gross-looking clay, and through life's sorrows, disappointments, and trials—just look at Mam, having to move here to this old farm—you were shaped into a vase or a bowl that pleased him. You never knew what he might make out of the rough beginning, she supposed.

Several weeks later, Lizzie and Mandy were baptized on a cold Sunday morning. There was no doubt or fear, no despair or confusion anywhere for Lizzie. She realized one thing as surely as the sun rose and

set. She had set her face toward heaven, promising to live and obey within the Amish church, and she believed very sincerely that Jesus Christ was the Son of God.

She also learned, to her surprise, that Amish people were not as unemotional as she thought. She had been to baptisms before, of course, but now that it was her turn, she saw how the adults cried openly, using huge white handkerchiefs to staunch their tears of joy. They were sincerely grateful that more of the young people had come to the knowledge of the truth, Lizzie knew. It was a moment in her life she hoped to remember as long as she lived, tucked away, kept like a precious jewel.

Her tears ran with the water the ministers used to baptize her and became wet spots on her white organdy cape. She heard small, subdued sobs from the women's side, which was very touching to Lizzie. She guessed Mam and all the aunts and all of the other women in the church must really love the youth who knelt before them. It was a great feeling to know you were accepted into this group of people who had gone before you, setting an example of right and wrong. These people, most of them her family and friends, genuinely cared about her and wanted her to be a part of the growing community of Amish people.

After the service, she ate her bread and cheese, snitz pie, and red beets with the rest of the church just as she did each Sunday. But she knew there was a difference this Sunday. She was now a sister in

the church, her sins were forgiven, she was washed clean, and she would learn to apply her faith to the temptations and trials she encountered along life's way. Maybe she was only a shaky new Christian, but she would certainly try as hard as she could. Everyone was just going to have to have patience with her, because, after all, Mam was pretty old when she quit yelling at them.

Chapter 4

T HAT WINTER BROUGHT THE USUAL SNOW, frigid temperatures, and ice, which meant skating, tobogganing, and even sleigh rides across the snowy fields. It was one of Lizzie's favorite seasons, and she looked forward to spending time with Stephen and her friends who were now all dating. That winter was a time of relaxing in her lasting friendship with Stephen, a time of contentment and happiness which seemed to radiate through to the children at school. She loved teaching and being outdoors playing sports, almost as much during the week with her pupils as she did on the weekends.

Lizzie decided that the children needed to go skating one more time before the thaw set in and the ice melted. Lizzie announced one morning that the school would take an afternoon at the pond, if the students earned 100 perfect scores on their work.

Every 100% grade, no matter which age group or subject, was carefully recorded with a stroke of the

chalk on the farthest left-hand corner of the large blackboard. When they recorded the hundredth 100%, the entire school would go skating.

Lizzie smiled to herself as little heads bent to their goal of 100%. The classroom became so quiet and well-ordered that Lizzie heard the wall clock's homey ticking. Little eyebrows were lowered in their focusing and tongues were bitten as erasers appeared. Students diligently erased work that was not good enough to achieve the prize. Hands held heads and twirled straying hair in concentration. Dictionaries were pulled from the back shelf and put to earnest use by students who normally would have chosen the faster, easier route of guessing when they were unsure of an answer.

She loved her teaching job so much at times like this. Dear hearts, so innocent, responding to such a small prize. It almost didn't seem fair. Lizzie loved ice-skating, and yet she didn't need to work for it the way her pupils did. After about 10 days, Lizzie drew the hundredth stroke with a flourish, turning to her pupils.

"Very good! I do think the first grade contributed almost half of them! It's just wonderful, first grade! Good job," she said.

Anticipation ran high the following morning, as the pupils brought extra food in their lunchboxes. Thermoses of hot chocolate and a large container for water were set on the sleds, cushioned with old quilts. A toboggan, for the little ones, was carefully lined with buggy robes.

Two older boys, Amos and Ben, went ahead of the group, pulling a sled loaded with a box of firewood and newspapers for the fire they would build next to the pond. The upper-grade students would stay warm all day, eventually shedding mittens, coats, and scarves as they heated up from the exertion of skating. But the little ones grew tired and cold, even crying that their poor little feet felt as if they were frozen.

Lizzie bundled up, placing a whistle in her coat pocket. She blew the whistle only when absolutely necessary, but it never failed that some errant person drove her to blowing the whistle as hard as she could. The disobedient person had to sit on a bale of straw for 15 minutes.

The day was sunny, the warmth of it promising spring. The air, however, was still wintry, swirling bits of loose snow across their faces as they bent to walk up the hill, then down the other side toward the pond. The day was so bright, Lizzie squinted against the glare of the snow. She wished she could wear her black sunglasses, but that would seem a bit *gros-feelich*, or conceited, she feared.

Mandy said those big black sunglasses didn't look quite right with an Amish covering, which was something to consider. But the truth was, they made Lizzie feel sort of cool, almost like former President John Kennedy's wife, Jacqueline. She admired that woman so much, and secretly, when she wore those sunglasses, she felt the way Jackie Kennedy looked. Oh, well, no sunglasses today. She was a teacher

who commanded respect, and she needed to remain in control.

The pond loomed ahead, a bit grayer than the snow. The top of the ice was not perfectly smooth. There were skaters' marks all over it, and bits of snow, straw, and wood ashes left from other skaters on earlier evenings.

The boys soon had the fire started. They put their skates on and slid across the ice, pushing the scrapers. Scrapers were homemade bits of aluminum fastened to broom handles that smoothed the ice on the frozen pond.

As the boys worked, Lizzie helped the little ones tie their skates, arranged quilts on straw bales, and stoked the fire. Then she sat on a bale of straw and squinted into the sun as the pond became alive with black-garbed figures flying across it, looping and swerving, in a sort of intricate dance.

She decided to drink a cup of hot chocolate before lacing up her skates. There was just something about a steaming cup of hot chocolate on a cold winter day, Lizzie thought, that made your heart so cozy you could hardly stand it. It felt like the softest cashmere scarf around your stomach, soothing it and warming your whole body until you felt fluffy all over.

Hot chocolate tasted even better with a chocolate chip cookie to dip into it. Chocolate chip cookies were funny things, though. They were almost a staple in an Amish child's lunchbox. All the mothers made chocolate chip cookies. They made molasses

cookies and whoopie pies and snickerdoodles and raisin cookies, too, but the most popular was always chocolate chip.

But chocolate chip cookies were as unpredictable as the weather. Each mother had a different recipe. Some cookies were hard as a rock, but they were the best to dip in hot chocolate.

Others were high and dry and, the minute they hit that creamy liquid, dissolved into a warm mushy mess. You couldn't get them to your open mouth fast enough before they disintegrated and landed in the bottom of the cup. If you were lucky, a few chocolate chips floated to the top, and you could at least rescue them.

Aunt Becca's chocolate chip cookies were the best, hands down, Lizzie thought. They were firm and chewy and a tiny bit overbaked. If you broke one in half, you could hold it in the hot chocolate for a long time, and then lift it to your mouth with style and grace.

Lizzie never did, though. She just wolfed them down, dripping hot chocolate on the front of her coat. She was dismayed to find that she had already eaten four cookies and probably could have eaten four more.

Sally and Dorothy giggled, sitting beside her on the bale of straw.

"Are you hungry?" Sally ventured.

"Mmm-hmm!" Lizzie said emphatically.

"You ate a bunch of cookies!" Dorothy said, giggling.

"I'll go skating now and work them off," Lizzie said, smiling down at Dorothy.

Energized, she quickly laced up her white figure skates, hit the ice running, and with swift strokes soon caught up with the upper-graders who were already organizing a game of "freeze tag."

That was a game they never tired of playing. When the students who were "It" caught someone, that person had to stand at the very spot where he or she was caught. That student was guarded by those who were "It," while the others tried to dart in and free him or her.

As the sun climbed toward noon, hats and scarves, stocking caps and mittens were flung off near the fire. The owners skated off as fast as they could before being caught. The students dodged, twirled, and sprang away from each other until they were all gasping for breath, their cheeks red from the cold and exertion.

After lunch, the boys were allowed to play hockey, but they had to leave an area of the pond for the girls and smaller children. All afternoon, Lizzie taught the girls how to gracefully skate backward and in a circle, lifting one foot over the other, distributing weight onto the inside skate so that the skater naturally turned in a circle. The girls practiced, fell down, laughed hard, sat on the ice and talked, drank more hot chocolate, and kept trying.

It was all delicious fun. There was no other word to describe it. On the ice, Lizzie forgot the task of being a teacher and was genuinely happy, almost

like a child with her pupils, if only during those pre-
cious hours of ice-skating.

<center>❧</center>

The following Monday morning, Mandy flew
down the stairs and literally burst into the kitchen.
Her eyes were wide and very green in the soft lamp-
light as she told Mam and Lizzie the reason for her
excitement.

"I'm getting married!" she said breathlessly.

Lizzie stopped halfway to the table with a hand-
ful of knives and forks, her mouth dropping open
in disbelief.

"Surely you mean this fall? This coming Novem-
ber?" she croaked.

"No. This spring!"

Mam turned quickly from the sink, her eyebrows
drawn down in a serious display of disapproval.

"Not this spring, Mandy. Amish people have
their weddings in the fall. In November. You can't
get married in the spring."

She turned to stir the scrambled eggs, the subject
closed, swept away by her refusal. She calmly con-
tinued her work of getting breakfast on the table
for her family as Mandy glanced at Lizzie, raised
her eyebrows, and shrugged her shoulders help-
lessly. Going over to the stove, Mandy leaned for-
ward, peering closely at Mam to get her undivided
attention.

"You don't understand, Mam. You really don't.

John wants to get married in March because his—our—herd of cows is arriving the first week in April, so … Well, Mam, we can, can't we?" she implored.

"But … but …," Mam spluttered. Then she did what she sometimes did when she was at a loss for words. She scolded. Clicking the gas burner lower, a bit more forcefully than was absolutely necessary, she said angrily, "Now see, Mandy, you made me burn these eggs. Lizzie, don't just stand there doing nothing. Get the juice poured. There's no jelly on the table."

The subject was closed until Dat had finished his breakfast. Then Mam brought it into the open, abruptly and unexpectedly.

"Mandy says John wants to marry her in March."

Dat's eyes flew open as he stared at Mam.

"This coming March?" he asked.

Mandy nodded eagerly, fairly bouncing on her chair. "Yes! This March, Dat. He's—we're—getting a herd of cows in April, and he thinks it's wiser, smarter, or whatever to be married in the spring so I can help on the farm."

"Will the preachers agree to it, even?" Mam asked.

"Well, I don't know why not. It's done sometimes, although rarely. It's not really forbidden; it's just different." Dat sat back in his chair, adjusted his suspenders, and smiled a watery smile at Mandy. "So I guess if we have to get rid of you, we may as well do it in March as wait until November. It's all right with me."

Mam turned a very light shade of green, Lizzie thought, as reality sank into her head. This was the middle of January, and that meant eight weeks at the most to prepare for the wedding.

Mam threw up her hands. "Oh, dear!" she said, resignedly.

Lizzie gazed unseeingly at her dish of cereal, her appetite gone. Oh, this was just great. Little Mandy would be getting married before her, making her feel like a spinster, an old maid who just couldn't manage to get married in turn. Why couldn't they wait until fall; then she would get married first, the way it should be. John and his cows! That was nothing but a stupid excuse.

She slapped her spoon down on the tablecloth.

"It's senseless that Mandy gets to get married first, all because of a herd of cows," she snapped. "How unromantic is that? So now our whole peaceful winter is over. Mam's nerves will be on edge, and she'll boss everyone around for the remainder of the season."

"You're just jealous, Lizzie," Mam said. "There's absolutely no reason for you to be so childish. If John and Mandy want to get married in March, they can get married then. There is no shame in that. Actually, it is a very grown-up, sensible thing to do."

Lizzie snorted, but she didn't say anything more.

So over the next eight, very short weeks, Mandy glowed with happiness and anticipation as she unpacked and repacked her ridiculously expensive set of china, caressed her linen tablecloths lovingly, hummed, sang, and whistled. It all amounted to an enormous housefly in Lizzie's soup of life. She tried to be generous, happy for Mandy, rejoicing with her, but it wasn't always possible. That's just how Lizzie was. She wanted to marry Stephen, but so far, he hadn't even mentioned getting married. All he talked about was hunting or ice fishing or the boat he would like to buy, and it made her nervous, wondering if he was not going to ask her to get married until they were old.

Lizzie threw herself into her teaching duties as a way of dealing with the maddening pace at home. The school was full of excitement as they planned a Valentine's Day party. The pupils' eyes shone with anticipation, little beacons of happiness on a dull winter day. They would have cookies and candy and punch, the children decided. The students would each bring a covered dish instead of their usual boring lunchboxes.

Macaroni and cheese would stay hot on the back of the stove. Ham sandwiches, applesauce, carrots and dip, and chocolate pudding rounded out the Valentine's Day menu. Lizzie would supply the paper plates and cups and choose all the games.

Lizzie sat at her desk while the children planned, writing notes to the mothers explaining what their children should bring for the party. The pupils each

folded Lizzie's notes and stored them carefully in their lunchboxes.

Valentine's Day was such a big event in the one-room schoolhouse, even if the upper-grade boys pretended to hate it. Many mothers bought Valentines at the K-Mart in town, although some of the more conservative mothers sent homemade cards with their children, deeming the store-bought ones too worldly.

So in the middle of gray February, the school was filled with a festive air as the students took a break from studying to decorate the classroom for the party. The children attached red paper hearts to the windows with double-sided Scotch tape. They stretched chains of pink and red construction paper from each corner to the middle of the room. Red balloons dangled in great clumps above Lizzie's desk.

Little first-graders squealed and clapped their hands, jumping up and down. They spilled their chocolate milk out of their lunchboxes, and chased each other until Lizzie had to tap the bell to quiet everyone. Planning a Valentine's Day party was as much chaos as the party itself, but Lizzie loved every minute of it.

The week before Valentine's Day, Lizzie sat at her desk and frowned at the upper-grade boys near the back of the room. All day four boys had huddled together at Levi Lapp's desk, whispering. Lizzie got up to help the first-graders write their math problems on the blackboard. As she was correcting one

of Anna Miller's sums, she heard an almost inaudible giggle, but a giggle nevertheless.

She slowed her writing, every muscle tensed. Yes, there it was again. She whirled, just as Levi quickly opened his desktop and shoved something inside. The remaining three boys bent studiously over their desks, the picture of demure, engaged scholars working on their English.

"All right," Lizzie said loudly.

Four pairs of innocent eyes stared back at her. The classroom became very, very quiet.

"Levi, what did you just place in your desk?" she asked quite firmly.

In the silence that followed, little Rachel Esh picked nervously at her apron, dropping her English book.

"First grade, you may return to your seats."

They sat down quickly, turning to watch the big boys.

"What is it?" she asked, in a voice she hoped was authoritative, even scary.

"Nothing," Levi announced, impudently.

Marching back to his desk, she yanked the lid open and bent to peer inside. Levi leaned back nonchalantly. He didn't seem to have a care in the world, which only fueled her anger. The desk was empty inside except for a matchbox.

"What is in the matchbox?"

"Nothing."

The classroom was as quiet as a lull in a storm, and about as threatening. The lower-graders were

terrified, their eyes open wide, their faces mirroring the tension.

"Why did you throw it into your desk in a hurry, then? Give it to me."

Levi grinned as he handed it over.

Lizzie grasped the matchbox firmly and slid the cover off without at any hesitation. Nestled inside was the cutest mouse she had ever seen. His beady, little brown eyes stared up at her, unblinking and quite unafraid. It's fur was brown and so neat and shiny. Perfect little ears protruded from its cute, rounded head.

There were chocolate cookie crumbs in a corner of the large matchbox, and unbelievably, a plastic soda bottle lid filled with water, which had spilled a bit when she pulled it out of the desk. Lizzie's eyebrows lowered, but her mouth began to twitch. It was just so charming! What a darling little mouse!

Lizzie wasn't afraid of mice. She could never bring herself to kill one, and she hated mousetraps. It was the cruelest thing anyone had ever invented. How would people like it if a huge steel bar snapped them to their death in such a horrible manner? She always pitied the mice, hoping they could somehow escape the house, avoiding Mam's broom and Dat's trap.

Lizzie knew she should be stern and strict and punish Levi, while warning the other boys about doing something that distracted the whole classroom. But she couldn't bring herself to do it. Didn't the way Levi had fed this little mouse show real

responsibility and kindness? He even gave it water to drink.

"Well," she began, and then her mouth just opened into a smile. She gave up.

"Isn't he cute?" she asked.

Instantly there was bedlam in the classroom as children started giggling, holding their hands over their mouths as they laughed. The students in the lower grades rose in their seats for a better view as Lizzie walked down the aisle to show them, amid oh's and ah's of approval. After everyone had properly seen the mouse, she returned it to Levi.

"Now, why don't we keep him as a pet for a little while? He's a fat little country mouse, and I think he would be very happy with plenty of food and some shavings. Does anyone have a small cage?" Immediately a number of hands shot up, and the children bounced in their seats with enthusiasm.

The rest of the day the entire school was upbeat, except for Levi. Lizzie kept him after school for a serious talk about respect.

"You lied to me when you said there was nothing in the box," she said.

"Well, nothing besides the mouse. Plus, I guess, cookie crumbs and water."

"Still, Levi, no matter how you say it, it still really wasn't the truth. Telling lies, even littler white ones, will land us in a heap of trouble if we're not careful."

He looked at his desktop, avoiding her eyes. Lizzie sighed. Levi had a good heart. He was simply

drawn to mischief just as a duck or goose is naturally attracted to water. He thrived on paddling around in his own little pond of schemes and pranks like this one. Harmless, perhaps, but disruptive nevertheless.

A certain quality in Levi spoke to Lizzie's own heart. She had been very similar to Levi when she was in school. When she had gotten bored, she could always think of ways to make life more exciting. Then, when she was reprimanded, she was so embarrassed, until she thought of another prank.

The Valentine's Day party went off without a hitch, although Lizzie ate so many cookies that her stomach hurt. Stephen gave her a beautiful Valentine and a huge box of chocolates. Lizzie couldn't help eating just a few, even after all the cookies she had consumed earlier in the day.

Holiday or not, there was no rest at home. As soon as she sat on the sofa to catch her breath and read the comics in the daily paper, either Mam or Mandy asked her to do something like paint the basement.

For one thing, painting the basement was ridiculous. She had just painted it a nice coat of glossy white paint the summer before. But, oh, no! It had to be done again in the middle of the winter. It was the same all over the house and barn. No rest for mind or body.

No one cared what she thought or paid any attention to her. That was why she ended up at the family doctor's office with a huge infected area on the back of her lower leg.

A week earlier, the winter temperatures had risen enough so that rain fell instead of snow. The rain froze immediately that night when the temperatures dipped, covering the drifts of snow with a slick coat of ice. It was the perfect mixture for wonderful sledding on the steep hill behind Lizzie's schoolhouse.

The children careened wildly down the long, steep hill on sheets of plastic, cardboard, and sleds—anything they could cling to as they raced downward. Lizzie allowed the children an entire hour of extra recess, knowing this sledding was a rare opportunity for some exciting thrills.

Lizzie joined in the fun, flying down the hill with her students until one of Lizzie's knee socks slid down, and the back of her leg scraped on the ice during a wild ride across the snow. She didn't notice that she was injured until the children pointed, shrieking, to a large brush burn that ran down the entire back of Lizzie's leg. She looked and gasped, stunned by the deep scrape. The cold had already numbed her leg, and she wasn't in any pain. She limped back to the warmth of the schoolroom, bandaged her leg, rang the bell, and resumed classes.

That evening, Mam fussed and clucked over the size of the scrape, saying it looked more like a burn.

"Soak it in Epsom salt and put Union Salve on it," she said, her usual, never-fail cure for every ache and injury.

"Now just how am I supposed to soak the back of my leg in Epsom salt?" Lizzie asked, a bit upset because Mam wouldn't help her more.

Mandy glared at her, as if to tell her without words what an absolute baby she was.

"Just fill a dishpan almost full and hang your lower leg over it," she said sternly.

So with a great deal of snorting and displays of her foul mood, Lizzie managed to wet the injured area, spread the dark brown salve painfully across it, and slap a paper towel on top, because, as usual, there was no gauze bandage in the bathroom cupboard.

But now it was only a week before the wedding, and her leg still had not healed. At night, she tossed fitfully, the throbbing pain keeping her awake as she resolved not to make a fuss to anyone. She had actually reached the point where she was truly happy for John and Mandy. Her jealousy had finally dispersed like storm clouds on a sunny day. She had wanted desperately to stop feeling so jealous of Mandy and even prayed earnestly about it. Once she really, really wanted to overcome this, she actually had.

Mandy was so sweet, so easy to like, and so in love with her tall, handsome John that she made everyone else happy, too. Little bursts of happiness shone from her green eyes, and Lizzie told her she reminded her of a fairy scattering stardust.

"Oh, Lizzie," Mandy said sincerely. "I want the same thing for you. I hope with all my heart your turn will be in November."

"I'm about 100 percent sure he'll ask me. I mean, why wouldn't he? Look how long we've been dating."

"Sure he will, Lizzie."

"Look at this, Mandy." Lizzie turned the back of her leg to show her the now-infected wound, and Mandy gasped as she peeled off the bandage. It was clearly a bad infection, and at Mandy's yelp, Mam came to see what all the commotion was about. She took one look at Lizzie's leg and immediately bundled her off to see the doctor.

Armed with antibiotics, salve, gauze, cloth tape, hot and cold compresses, and orders to keep her leg elevated, Lizzie returned to the hubbub of preparing for Mandy's wedding.

By the time the relatives came the next week on the *risht-dawg*, the day of preparation for Mandy's wedding, Lizzie's leg felt much better, and she was able to help get the house ready for the big day. There was the usual happy banter as the food was prepared. Lizzie's aunts baked pies, cooked tapioca pudding, washed the celery, and baked bread until the whole house was a regular beehive of activity. In the living room, the men set up rows of benches and tables.

"When Amish people have a wedding, they even wash their barn windows," Lizzie commented.

"Oh, yes, of course. The cow stable is white-washed, and everything that isn't painted gets a fresh coat," her aunt laughed.

"Our cow stable isn't in use anymore, so it didn't get whitewashed, just cleaned," Lizzie laughed.

Joshua and Emma arrived, all smiles and happy to be waiting on the *eck*. The married sisters and

brothers of the bride had the special job of waiting on John and Mandy and the other members of the bridal party, or in the Pennsylvania Dutch language, the *nava-sitza*. It was a very important assignment, and Emma's cheeks glowed with anticipation as she laid out the table linens, china, silverware, and all the pretty cut-glass dishes they would use. Mandy was not allowed to see what Emma and the cousins were doing, because it was all a surprise for her when she sat at the corner table the day she was married.

The women cut butter into fancy wedding-bell shapes, covering it carefully with plastic wrap and refrigerating it for the big day. They made special Jell-O dishes, fruit dip, and all kinds of delicious food for the bride and groom.

"What beautiful china!" Emma gasped.

Lizzie was hurrying past with a basket of clothes and turned to smile at her.

"Isn't it? I was so jealous of Mandy's china for so long that it actually cured me. Kind of like getting a severe dose of the measles. Once it's that bad, you're immune to it."

Emma laughed. "Ach, Lizzie, you couldn't be too envious of Mandy. She's too sweet. Your turn will come."

Lizzie smiled as she hurried up the stairs with her basket of clothes. Dear, dear Emma. She had so much plain-down goodness and common sense, such a well-grounded attitude about everything. She never got too much in a tizzy about anything, just

took it all in stride matter-of-factly, never questioning God or fretting needlessly.

She probably didn't even think there was anything to feel bad about if Mandy was married first. That was how God intended it, and Lizzie would just have to be patient and wait until Stephen decided to ask her. Mandy and Lizzie had laughed plenty, sitting in their rooms, trying to decide what you could say to your boyfriend to get him to ask you to marry him. But still, there was no getting around it, the ultimate timing, the big question was all up to Stephen, no matter how many broad hints Lizzie threw at him.

She never said too many shameless things, just coyly suggesting the colors she liked for a kitchen or the style of cabinets. Typically, Stephen never answered or mentioned the fact that he liked a certain type of house or anything at all.

The wedding day dawned bright and clear, a perfect late March day. Buses and passenger vans packed the driveway, mixed with teams of horses and buggies, people hurrying and scurrying everywhere.

John's family and friends were all from the Lamton area, so it seemed as if over half of the crowd arrived in vehicles. Lizzie liked John's parents immediately, a nice-looking, friendly couple who were from an old Lamton family, obviously hard-working

and very proper with impeccable manners.

Lizzie told Mam they reminded her of the old Southern families she had read about in books. Mam said, yes, they were probably much the same. They were all well-to-do Amish farmers, though, and not plantation owners, although their ancestors, like the Southern families, probably came from a certain circle of people in England or Germany.

Hmm, Lizzie thought. So now Mandy is marrying into the "gentry" from Lamton. Oh, dear. Next thing, I'll just be her common servant, and she'll snap her fingers to have my absolute obedience.

When John and Mandy stood before the minister from Ohio, they looked so sincere and serious, pronouncing their vows with such quiet solemnity, that Lizzie was quite overcome by emotion. Unexpectedly, a huge lump formed in her throat, and quick tears sprang to her eyes at the thought of Mandy's serious step, this embarking together on life's river with John by her side.

John was as handsome as he had been the first day Lizzie saw him. It had taken her a while to accept that John wasn't interested in her, but instead in skinny, big-eyed Mandy. Lizzie glanced over at Stephen who sat straight and still on his bench. Well, things had worked out for the best, just as Mam had said they would.

Still, Lizzie didn't want Mandy to be married. First Emma, now Mandy. The thought of life without sisters, except for her twin sisters, KatieAnn and Susan, who were still too young to be much fun,

was depressing indeed. But this was a day of happiness, of joy and celebration, so Lizzie put aside all thoughts of losing Mandy to John and his dairy farm. There was no sense in becoming absolutely morose on Mandy's special day, so she did her level best to smile brightly, talking and laughing happily with all the guests after the service was over.

But once the buses and vans motored out the drive, and the tired aunts and uncles finished washing dishes and putting benches and chairs away, and she could finally collapse into bed, she cried great tears of genuine self-pity. She wallowed in her sad feelings like a pig in its mudhole, actually enjoying the fact that she could release her pent-up emotions after spending all day with that artificial smile pasted on.

She wished with all her heart that Mandy wouldn't have married so young. Now she'd never be the same. She'd turn into this proper walking stick who didn't laugh hilariously and kick Lizzie out of bed or do other unladylike things that were so... so sisterly and had long ago secured a bond between them that no proper Lamton family could even touch.

Oh, she could just see it. Now, when she'd go visiting Mandy on the dairy farm, she'd open the door, her hair combed sleek and smooth, not even a trace of any stray hairs, her covering ironed to perfection, and she'd inquire with genuine warmth about her trip. And Lizzie would stand on her doorstep and feel like a genuine hillbilly, fat, with her hair going

in every direction and her covering crooked, and say, "Fine, thank you. Isn't it a beautiful day?"

They would never again, not once, throw back their heads and laugh uproariously or go swimming in the creek or drive Billy. Mandy was *married*. A great wave of regret and nostalgia carried Lizzie along until she thought she would just stop breathing with the awful pain in her chest.

And another thing. Stephen hadn't even been very romantic at the supper table. He was having too much fun with Marvin and Aaron, who sat across the table. He was having a great time, laughing and teasing poor Sara Ruth until Lizzie was embarrassed. He could at least act as if he planned to grow up someday and seriously ask her to be his wife.

Well, I'm not going to live here alone without Mandy, she decided. If he doesn't ask me to marry him, I'll have to ask him myself. It had been hard when Emma left home to live in Allen County, but Mandy getting married was even worse.

Why hadn't Stephen tried to give her some special attention and hint about it being her turn to be the next bride? Not a word, not a serious look, nothing.

She punched her pillow, flipped on her side, and groped for the box of Kleenex in her nightstand drawer. Blowing her nose loudly, she wiped her eyes, rolled over, and resumed pitying herself. The next morning, when Mam asked her what was wrong with her eyes, Lizzie glared at her and told her she had eaten too much wedding cake.

Chapter 5

John and Mandy moved 10 miles away to their dairy farm soon after they were married. Lizzie went back to school where she was quickly swept up in her teacher's duties again. The easy routine of teaching made it easier for her to accept the fact that Mandy was married and that she had gone to live with John.

It wasn't that she didn't miss her; there was just nothing else to do about it. Life went on as usual, the sun rose and set in the same sky, and Mandy lived under the same sky with the same sun and moon, except now she was 10 miles away. Emma was even farther away, and Lizzie had soon become accustomed to that, so she would survive.

Dat's health seemed fairly stable in the spring. He loved the challenge of building. Mam said that his giving up farming was one of the best things that could have happened. He was always eager to go to work, he was happy while he was there, and he had

only minor frustrations, like stumbling occasionally or bouts of blurry vision.

One warm Sunday evening, Stephen and Lizzie decided to sit under the old apple tree in the pasture instead of sitting as they normally did in the living room. The grass was soft and cushiony, so after their walk, they sat side by side in the soft, warm darkness.

Stephen was acting a bit strange, Lizzie thought, having less to say than usual, which really, on ordinary days, was never very much at all. Lizzie tried gamely to keep up a lively conversation, but she didn't get a very positive response from Stephen.

Finally, she could stand it no longer, so she blurted out, "Why don't you have anything to say this weekend? You're much quieter than usual."

Stephen didn't answer until Lizzie became quite uncomfortable.

Then, all he said was, "I'd like to build a house someday."

"A house!" Lizzie squeaked, her heart plummeting to her stomach.

"Yes."

"You mean to sell? Or for yourself, or … I mean, where would you build it? Do you know how to build a house by yourself?"

"Of course. That's what I do."

"Oh, yes. I guess."

There was a soft silence as dogs barked in the distance. Headlights created an arc of light as a car rounded the bend, the kitchen door slammed as someone went out to the front porch, and still

Stephen said nothing.

Lizzie gnawed at the corner of her thumbnail, cleared her throat, sighed, glanced nervously in Stephen's direction, and wondered what was going on. Surely he wasn't contemplating marriage this weekend, as he had been having the time of his life with all of his friends, playing baseball, going on day trips, talking about walking that dreaded—in Lizzie's opinion—Appalachian Trail again. Stephen's first trip had just about ended their relationship, and Lizzie wasn't sure she could handle it if Stephen went hiking for a month again.

And then, oh sickening thought, she wondered if he wanted to end the relationship, to have absolute freedom to go on long trips or just do as he wanted. He had acted like it lately, now that she thought about it.

She held her breath as he reached down and took away her hand.

"Don't do that. You'll chew a hole in your thumb."

There was a space of a few heartbeats as his hand tightened on hers, and he leaned closer.

Then, very softly, he said, "Lizzie, do you think we could build a small house on an acre of your dad's land?"

"W ... We?"

"Yes, we."

"I ... I don't know. I guess we could ask him sometime."

"No, not sometime. Next week. We have to

know if we want to live in our house this winter."

Lizzie drew a deep breath. "You … you mean … ?"

"Would you live in a new little house with me, Lizzie?"

"We'd … I … we'd have to get married first?" she breathed.

"Of course. If I asked you tonight, would you marry me?"

"Well, are you asking?"

"Yes."

Lizzie sighed happily, turned to him, and said, "Yes, I will. I will marry you and live in a little house with you."

Stephen laughed happily. "All my hopes and dreams have come true, Lizzie!"

Lizzie, as usual, felt awkward and wasn't sure how to answer. For one thing, she was so happy she had to fight back her tears, and for another thing, the lump in her throat threatened to choke her, so she just sat there and swallowed. She couldn't speak at the moment, although a thousand questions rained in from every direction, wherever thoughts came from. For once in her life, she was absolutely speechless. She wanted to tell him it was a dream come true for her, too, which it was, but to be perfectly honest, she was a bit afraid. How did they know the dream come true would remain a good dream?

So she said, "We'll be very happy, I'm sure."

There was nothing wrong with that, was there? Of course not. Of course they would be very happy

together. Maybe not 100 percent of the time. Like all the Amish preachers said, they would have their rainy days and their sunshiny days.

Stephen got to his feet quite suddenly, pulling her up with him. His hands closed firmly around hers, and she felt the difference in him as he placed her hands around his waist. Her own heart beat with his, and it was the most natural feeling she had ever experienced. This beating of two hearts together was as light as a moth and as powerful as a large magnet.

Lizzie raised questioning eyes to him. The lights from the back porch reflected the love in his blue, blue eyes. As naturally as their hearts beating, he slowly bent his head, and their lips met in an honest-to-goodness kiss of love.

It wasn't that the world stood still, the way the books said. But the dark sky, the apple tree, the soft summer night's breeze, disappeared for a very short time. In that moment, there was only Stephen and this all-consuming love she felt for him.

"Lizzie, I love you so much," Stephen said, his voice shaking. "Thank you for promising to be my wife."

"I do love you, too, Stephen," she said.

And she did.

The spoken words, that mutual kiss empowered Lizzie, drowning any doubts or fears she had ever felt. They would stand together, in love, with God at the helm, and even if they stumbled and fell sometimes, he would pick them up.

After a moment, Stephen pulled back.

"You know, Lizzie, I don't have a lot of money. I have very little saved up, but I think if we had a bit of land, we could borrow the money from the bank to build our house."

"Do you really think we can borrow the money?" Lizzie asked. "I mean, how do you know we could even qualify?"

"We probably won't unless we own an acre of land," Stephen answered.

Then he laughed softly. "Here we are, planning our house as if our life depended on it and acting as if our relationship—actually getting married—is of no consequence. Do you think we can get along?"

"Oh, of course," Lizzie said airily. "We don't always agree on everything now, so I'm sure there will be times when we don't agree in the future. And you know me. I can't keep my thoughts and opinions to myself, and I might get a bit loud and judgmental, don't you think?"

Stephen laughed. "Yes, definitely."

"And," Lizzie continued, "you'll just stay quiet and never say what you think but do exactly as you please, no matter if I fuss and carry on like a wild person."

"Not always. Not if I love you as I should," he said soberly.

Lizzie was amazed at that statement. He must have read his Bible about that subject as well, which was very good. Stephen was not the type of person to be verbal about God or what certain passages

in the Bible meant. He was taught to keep his faith to himself, as most Amish youth were. They were instructed to live their beliefs and let their lights shine, which was good.

Stephen did not think highly of himself or his opinions, especially when it came to spiritual matters. Lizzie had realized early in their relationship that he was not comfortable with speaking about God. Lizzie had mentioned this to Mam, and Mam said that it was nothing to worry about. That would come in time, as he matured spiritually, which was comforting to Lizzie.

Lizzie clasped her hands, sighing joyously. "Oh, I can hardly believe this! Really, Stephen, are we actually going to live in a new house? How did you know I always wanted a new one? You know I'm not like Emma. She always wanted an old house with old quilts and stuff. I'll even have new kitchen cupboards, won't I? And I'll get to pick out the color of my linoleum, no, not *my* linoleum, *our* linoleum," she said, laughing happily.

So they sat and planned, talking about many different subjects, until Stephen said it was past his usual time to leave.

"You ask your dad about the land, all right?" he concluded.

"No, you come over Wednesday evening, and we'll ask him together," she corrected him.

"You know, it's funny about your dad. I don't know how often I've heard him say he would gladly have all his married children live on the farm, and

so far, they've all moved away to farms of their own. I always thought he'd probably be glad to offer us some land. Do you think I'm right?" Stephen asked.

Lizzie laughed. "Oh, you know how Dat is, Stephen. He talks almost as much as I do!"

She helped him hitch up his horse, and as he drove out through the darkness, his lights blinking as they always did, Lizzie thought they blinked a bit faster and brighter than before. She and Stephen were so happy that even the buggy lights felt it, she thought, then told herself to stop being so downright silly.

Wednesday evening Stephen was a bit late, which had Lizzie in an absolute dither. For one thing, she had tried so hard not to talk about the marriage proposal and the acre of land to anyone, but unable to help herself she had confided in Mam the very first thing on Monday morning.

Lizzie thought Mam seemed quite pleased, especially about their plans to build a house somewhere on the farm. So that made Lizzie feel good inside, thinking how happy Mam was to welcome Stephen warmly into the family as a new son-in-law. Of course, she reasoned, Mam and Dat had always approved of Stephen, she was sure of that.

When Stephen finally did turn into the drive, she breathed a sigh of relief. Dat had just finished the barn chores and was sitting on the porch for a minute's rest. He looked questioningly at Lizzie as

Stephen pulled up to the barn door.

"This isn't Saturday evening," he said bluntly.

Lizzie ran lightly down the steps, calling over her shoulder, "I know. He has something he wants to ask you."

"Hello, Stephen," Lizzie said, smiling up at him warmly as he walked toward her.

"Hello, yourself. Did you tell him?"

"No."

She hadn't told him, that was the truth, but she was almost certain Mam had said something to him about it.

"Hi, Stephen," Dat called. "We didn't expect to see you this evening."

Stephen grinned at him.

"How are you feeling?" he asked Dat.

"Oh, I'm fine. I would hardly know I have MS, except my legs don't always want to do what my brain tells them to do. My eyesight is largely improved by the new prescription from the specialist in Warm Springs. He knows what he's doing. It took him two whole hours to thoroughly examine my eyes, and he found some things an ordinary doctor would never have found. I got a new pair of glasses. Almost fell over backward when he told me the price. Three hundred dollars! I almost told him to keep the glasses. That's ridiculous."

He stopped for breath, but before Stephen could get a word in edgewise, he started rambling on again.

That was Dat, Lizzie thought, smiling to herself

as she walked to the porch with Stephen. As long as he had someone who listened without saying much, which Stephen was very good at, Dat would talk.

"You ought to start working with me and Jase. We need a good block layer right now. Are you familiar with masonry?"

Dat barely paused long enough to hear Stephen's "Mm-hmm," before launching into a lively description of a concrete job they were doing.

Stephen sat down next to Dat and listened, nodding his head, or shaking it in disbelief, and laughing at appropriate times. His eyes were crinkled at the sides, and he looked as if he was enjoying the whole conversation, although Dat was doing all the talking.

Jason came up on the porch, greeting Stephen with a quick smile.

"Are you mixed up, Stephen? It isn't Saturday evening," he asked, interrupting Dat.

"I know. I came to ask your dad a question," Stephen said quietly.

"What? What?" Dat was fairly hopping up and down on his lawn chair, if it was possible to hop up and down while still sitting.

Stephen took a deep breath, and Lizzie could tell he was nervous. He wasn't good with words, long speeches, or talking when he felt embarrassed, so she felt a bit sorry for him.

"I guess ... Did Lizzie tell you we want to be married in the fall?" he started.

"No! Really? She didn't tell me!" Dat leaned

forward, slapping his knee. "But do you think a secret like that would survive 10 minutes in this house? Of course, I know. Annie told me."

"Well, anyway," Stephen said, grinning shyly, "we wondered whether you would be able to give us some land if we want to build a house."

"Land? Would I give you land? How much?"

"Oh, just a small plot, enough for a house and barn. Maybe an acre."

"An acre? Oh, of course. We could do that. I don't know how much money you have, but you know if you have an acre of ground, that's enough collateral to be able to acquire a loan to build your house. Did you know that? And if you don't build a very big house, you know not a real big one—you don't really need it the first five years that you're married—you can always add on later, you know."

Stephen nodded.

"And another thing. If you build your house close enough to ours, you won't have to build your barn right away. You can always use our barn to keep your horse in. But then, maybe you wouldn't want that either. Where do you want to build? Surely not down in the flats. If we get another flood like Hurricane Agnes, your whole house would be under water. No, that's not going to work, building your house in the flats."

Stephen nodded.

"You could build your house along the road, there where those three ranch houses were built recently. That would work. The only thing is, it's on

top of a hill. Do you mind building your house on a hill? Now me, I always liked a view. To be able to look around and see for miles. That's a good feeling, a real good feeling. If you don't mind living on a hill, I'll give you an acre. Do you want to walk up there and see it?"

Stephen looked at Lizzie, and she nodded her head eagerly.

"All right," he said.

"Let me get my hat," Dat said on his way to the kitchen.

"You sure you're not too tired?" Stephen asked when Dat returned.

"Nah."

Lizzie smiled to herself, thinking how self-assured and confident Dat sounded. He probably felt proud to be able to be Stephen's benefactor, the person who made it possible for them to build a house. He was all excited, waving his arm for emphasis as he talked almost continuously while they walked behind the barn and up over the alfalfa field adjoining the pasture behind it.

"Yes, it spites me not to be able to farm this land anymore, but I guess it's like Annie says. If you're not cut out to be a farmer, you never will be one. I guess that's me. I still can't figure out what happened, but the cows died, we had dry weather, and in no time flat, we were struggling to keep our heads above water. Then I got this MS, and I knew it was time to give it up."

Stephen nodded.

"Another thing. Not farming makes me grateful for my job, too. A farmer never gets done. He just quits in the evening, and the way my legs are now, I can relax in the evening when I come home. Now, here. Right about here."

Dat stopped, waved his arm, and asked, "What do you think?"

They stood in the middle of an alfalfa field on top of a rounded slope that led gently down to the small country road below. There were three new ranch-style houses out farther along this road, but a good distance from where they stood. There was a field across the road, a low one that led to the creek and was filled with small locust trees.

Stephen looked around without saying anything. Lizzie was so thrilled, she was afraid if she said anything at all, it would break this wonderful, too-good-to-be-true feeling of standing on this hill, thinking this would be the exact spot where her new house would be. So she didn't say anything.

"It looks all right," he said finally. That was all. Just that.

So Dat started talking again, waving his arms while Stephen smiled. Lizzie wrapped her arms tightly around herself and took a deep breath, straightening her shoulders as she did so. The sun was setting behind the distant mountain, casting the green hillside in a soft orange glow. Birds twittered in the brush, and a car passed slowly on the road below, the driver honking his horn softly as he waved to someone in the lawn.

How perfect! How absolutely unbelievable! Mam and Dat lived just down over the hill and would always be there for them if they needed them. There were English neighbors to the right of their acre, and their house would be on a hill overlooking a sweeping little woods and fields.

What kind of house would Stephen build? Would they agree on the size, the color, the layout? Well, of course, they would. She was so happy to have a brand-new house of her own, she would let Stephen do exactly as he pleased. Yes, she would. Surely good intentions, coupled with a sense of pure happiness, would be sufficient for her to be a quiet, submissive wife. Lizzie's thoughts swirled around in her head, and she vowed to be everything she should be for Stephen, very much the same as counting a flock of chickens before they are hatched.

Chapter 6

Lizzie pulled on the reins, pressing her lips together to make a buzzing sound.

"Come on, Bess, hurry up," she said aloud as she sat alone in the buggy on her way to John and Mandy's farm.

She didn't want to push good, old, faithful Bess too hard, as the morning was already warm, and she still had about half the distance to cover.

She could hardly wait to see dear Mandy again, so the drive down to their farm seemed twice as long as usual.

Route 842 wound across the rolling countryside and past large dairy farms and chicken houses. Some of them were homes where Amish people lived, and when she saw someone at the wash lines hanging out laundry, she smiled and waved.

The cornfields looked richly green with young tender stalks standing about as high as a person. She wondered if there would be sufficient rainfall,

since Cameron County land with its deep shale deposits tended to lose its moisture faster than some areas. She hoped sincerely, for John and Mandy's sake especially, that God let lots of rain fall on the cornfields, and the alfalfa fields as well, so their dairy farm could prosper and give them a good start financially.

She was grateful all over again that Stephen was not a farmer. She was afraid she couldn't stand the suspense of not knowing if it would rain enough to grow a decent crop to feed the cows so they could make their farm payment. Wouldn't it just be sickening to stand outside hanging up clothes week after week, while the corn curled its leaves and changed in color from a brilliant, healthy green to an olive-colored dryness, and you knew that was your profit?

She was afraid her nerves would not be able to hold up under such a strain, so it was very good she was marrying Stephen and that Mandy was married to John. Probably she'd snap, almost like losing her mind but not quite, and do a rain dance in the front yard, which would look awfully suspicious. She grinned to herself. She wondered what Mandy would say when she told her about Stephen asking her to marry him and about the new house.

"Come *on*, Bess," she hollered, slapping both reins down hard on the poor, unsuspecting horse's rump. Startled, Bess took a few fast steps, then settled down to her usual slow, steady trot. Lizzie sighed.

She didn't know why Dat didn't let her drive Red, his fiery sorrel gelding. They had a horse named Red when she was a small child, and now Dat owned a horse almost like him and had named him Red. Lizzie begged Dat to let her drive him to Mandy and John's house, but the answer was always the same. Her arms weren't strong enough. No. So here she sat, watching the cornfields and thinking of rain to while away the time, as Bess hung her head straight out like a cow and took her good old time getting there.

Finally, at the bottom of a sloping hill, "Bigler Road" appeared on a flat green road sign, and Lizzie tugged slightly on the left rein. Only a mile anymore, and she would top the familiar little rise before the road sloped down to Mandy and John's farm.

A small, red-brick house was situated under towering maple trees with two barns behind it. John had built the new round-roofed dairy barn next to the old structure, but both were painted red, so the new one looked as if it had always been there, really. There was an implement shed on the left, opposite the house, and various corncribs and other outbuildings here and there.

Lizzie looked appreciatively at Mandy's neatly mown grass and the growth of new petunias arranged neatly around the flower beds. Mandy was a good little worker, she surely was, Lizzie noted happily. That was all the time she had to think anything, because the door of the brick house was flung

open and skinny little Mandy appeared, her smile stretched across her face as far as it could go.

"Lizzie!" she yelled in a tone of voice that conveyed gladness and disbelief at the same time.

Lizzie leaned forward as far as she could, as if that would get her there sooner.

"Surprised you, didn't I?" she called, savoring this moment she had been waiting for.

Bess stopped, and Lizzie hopped out of the buggy as Mandy ran to meet her.

"Oh, Lizzie, I'm so-o-o glad to see you. I didn't have real homesickness—not really. I just wished so much one of you would come see me today or tomorrow, because I'm not really busy this week."

Mandy helped her unhitch Bess, chattering happily as they led her to the water trough for a long drink. Barn swallows swooped and chirped about the forebay, as Lizzie looked around at the almost, but not quite, finished barn.

"John still busy?" she inquired.

Mandy was tying Bess in a new box stall, but Lizzie could hear her sigh as she said, "I mean it, Lizzie, he works all the time, constantly, steadily, except to eat his meals."

Together they walked back to the house, and Lizzie admired her neat lawn.

"Of course, you know it was you and me that kept our yard looking nice, so what would you expect?" Mandy said, batting her long, thick eyelashes.

Lizzie slapped her arm playfully.

"*Gros-feelich*, are we?" she laughed.

"Just a little."

After touring Mandy's house, which was small, but filled with new furniture and pretty accessories, Lizzie pronounced it the cutest, homiest farmhouse she had ever seen.

"Do you like it?" Mandy asked, clasping her hands together eagerly.

"Oh, I love it, Mandy. It's so cute, it's almost like a little doll house."

"We're going to need an addition built on if we have children, though."

They settled on Mandy's new sofa facing each other, Mandy with her blue dress smoothed over her pulled-up knees, as she always sat. Her thick, heavy brown hair was smoothed back tightly, like married women wore their hair, which only accentuated her large, heavy-lashed green eyes. Lizzie thought she looked better than ever, with a rosy glow on her cheeks, a picture of health and contentment.

"You look so nice, Mandy. Almost beautiful. Marriage becomes you, I suppose. Are you as happy as you look? Like Emma?"

Mandy smiled genuinely. "Of course, Lizzie. There you go again, asking me a million questions in that worried, eyebrow-tilted expression of yours."

"Well, see, I guarantee you that things can't be absolutely perfect after you get married. How can you move away from Mam and Dat and Jase and never get homesick, never wish you weren't married? Mam told us over and over, there's more to

marriage than a happily-ever-after story. And here are you and Emma, acting as if it's the greatest thing that ever happened to you, living on your farms!"

Mandy laughed long and heartily. "What a pessimist!"

"I'm not!"

"Yes, you *are*!"

Lizzie shrugged and then sat straight up, remembering her big news.

"Hey, Mandy, guess what? Just guess!" Lizzie leaned forward, her gray eyes alight as she searched Mandy's face.

"You're getting married!" Mandy said positively, without a doubt.

"How do you know?"

"You told me to guess."

"Well, guess what else."

"You're going to live close to us."

"No!"

"He's building a new house for you!"

"Yes! Oh, Mandy, I mean it. Can you just imagine how excited I'll be? Mam will live just down over the hill from me."

Mandy clasped and unclasped her knees, trying to remain genuinely happy, but like headlights on a car, she had hit the dimmer switch. Lizzie instantly caught on.

"What? What's wrong with that? Huh? Your smile kind of melted to a smaller one."

"No, no, Lizzie. That's just *great* that you'll live

close to Mam in a new house. I'm really, really, genuinely happy for you."

Lizzie watched her with narrowed eyes. "That's not all of it. What is it?"

Mandy picked up a cushion and pulled at a button that was sewn in the middle of its top as if her life depended on it, her head lowered, averting her eyes. Finally, she sighed and looked up, straight into Lizzie's eyes, honestly. "All right, here goes. It's just that, well … nothing."

"Mandy, stop it. If you don't stop that and tell me what's on your mind, I'm going to go home."

"No, don't. Don't. All right. Okay. When we were little girls, and Mam bought us something, like a new scarf—actually, it *was* new scarves that I'm thinking of. You *always* and, Lizzie, I mean *always,* got to pick the best color, then me, then, of course, Emma. These three scarves were bright pink, yellow, and a dull green. Guess who got the pink one?"

"Me. I remember," Lizzie said flatly.

"Okay. See what I mean. You're used to getting what you want, right?"

"No!" Lizzie protested vehemently.

"I'm just saying you've always wanted a new house, and now Stephen is building you one. You never wanted to live far away from Mam, and now you don't have to. Which is good, but just so you aren't … aren't … "

Mandy floundered for the right word, and Lizzie sighed, rolling her eyes.

"Selfish."

"Yes."

Mandy said it evenly and meaningfully, not unkindly, just dropping the word like the colored little pill you drop into warm vinegar water to dye Easter eggs. It was only one little word, but it immediately changed the ordinary water into one brilliant with meaning.

"So you think I'm selfish?" Lizzie asked, her eyebrows drawn low, suspiciously.

"Not always, Lizzie. Just sometimes. I'm afraid you'll be selfish with Stephen. Like expecting him to do everything perfectly and on time, and just ... well, Lizzie, marriage is just not for you to sit on a pretty cushion and expect your husband to keep you happy."

"I know that," Lizzie spat out, thoroughly riled now.

"I'm sure you do."

"Well, I do. I don't care what you say."

"Let's not argue," Mandy said agreeably, gazing unseeingly out the window.

"I'm not arguing, Mandy. I'm not selfish, either. Well, I know what you mean, though. It seems as if I get my own way in lots of things, and that I don't appreciate it enough but just expect more. I'm sure that's the way you see me from your perch on top of the Himalayan Mountains with the rest of the little grizzled men who dish out wisdom to us failures!"

Mandy laughed genuinely, then jumped up and tugged on Lizzie's sleeve.

"Come on, let's eat an early lunch. I'm starving. John isn't home today. He's helping his brother with hay and will eat there. So let's make those huge sandwiches like we used to make on Saturday evenings before church."

They went to the kitchen, finding Swiss cheese, leftover chicken, tomatoes, and mayonnaise, which they slathered thickly on two slices of soft, chewy, homemade bread. Heating the griddle, they slowly toasted them while Mandy poured peppermint tea into two tall glasses, adding ice cubes from the refrigerator.

Mandy told Lizzie that she was indeed very happy, and John was a sweet, kind, and loving husband. But like Mam told Emma before Baby Mark was born, having a baby is more than a woolly pink blanket, so it is with marriage. There were days, of course, when things went wrong, and your husband was not always the way you thought he should be. But when you averaged everything out, she would much rather be married, living right here on the farm, than anything else in all the world. Lizzie took a bite of her sandwich and chewed thoughtfully while she listened. Of course, Mandy was right, just as she almost always was about important matters.

When John came home that afternoon, Mandy begged Lizzie to stay and watch them milk. John agreed laughingly, knowing her dislike of cows and anything that went with them.

So Lizzie tagged along with Mandy while she tied her *dichly*, the little triangular bandana most Amish

women wear to do chores or help with farm work. She watched as Mandy went to the milk house and started assembling milkers, looking around at the brand-new interior of the large building.

"Wow!" she breathed. "Classy farmers!"

"You think so?" Mandy asked, pleased at Lizzie's compliment.

"Of course. Our old milk house wasn't even half as nice as this one. Maybe I wouldn't have minded milking so much if our facilities had been better."

She watched as John let the cows in who walked as ungracefully as any other cows, new cow stable or not. Cows didn't change, that was for sure. John worked with deliberate swiftness, if there was such a thing. He didn't seem to move fast; in fact, he hardly moved, and yet, he did everything at once. Mandy went from cow to cow, washing udders, exclaiming over the amount of milk in the milker from one of their best cows. They worked together in complete unison, and Lizzie could tell that Mandy had a genuine interest in the cows' well-being, which in turn made John feel proud to have such a good helper.

Well, Lizzie thought wryly, God sure doesn't make mistakes, does he? As much as I wanted to marry John, I could never be Mandy and love to milk cows the way she does. She doesn't have to pretend one tiny bit. She truly enjoys her work on the farm.

They talked and laughed while they worked, the milkers clicking away in their usual ka-chink,

ka-chinking rhythm. It reminded Lizzie of her mornings with Dat, which she never once had felt even a twinge of nostalgia about now that the cows were all gone. Milking cows was just not something she enjoyed, and she probably never would.

John was awfully good-looking, though, in his straw hat and everyday work clothes, and his small dark beard. She told Mandy about her observation after chores were done, and Mandy laughed agreeably.

"Of course, Lizzie, he's the most handsome man in Cameron County, you know."

As Lizzie drove out the driveway to start her long trek home, she looked forward to the time alone, driving Bess. She needed to think. No use looking back, that was one thing sure. Life went rolling along like a gigantic wheel, and all human mortals had to go along, whether they wanted to or not. But did she really want to go back to when Mandy and Emma were still at home, before Joshua and John were part of the family? Probably not really.

She did so look forward to the time when she would live in her own house with Stephen, even if she was worried about marriage sometimes. If there were trials and troubles, everybody got through them. Well, Amish people did anyway. Some English people were divorced, but they were allowed to be, and Amish people weren't. Although when Mam heard of some far-off people who were having marital problems, she would shake her head and say, "They should live apart for awhile." Stephen was

quiet, that was one thing, so Lizzie would probably do most of the talking, but that was all right. She did that now, and Stephen listened. He liked to hear her talk.

Oh, there were countless things to look forward to when she got married. Stephen would buy her a set of china, a water pitcher and tumbler set, and silverware in a nice wooden chest. Mam would go furniture-shopping with her. It was all just too good to be really true. Already, Mam was piecing two quilts for her, and one was a yellow and white Dahlia pattern that she would put on her guest bed. If she had one. She didn't know how many bedrooms Stephen was planning on having in the house.

She missed her pupils, thinking back to the last day of school a month earlier. She wasn't sure if she wanted to try and keep on teaching in spite of getting married or not. They had asked her to return in the fall, but she really hadn't decided. The money she made would be nice, but maybe it would all prove to be too stressful with the new house underway and planning her wedding.

Mam was really the one who carried most of the stress when it came to having a wedding. Lizzie often wondered what kept her from popping like a balloon when you blow it up too far; that's how nervous she became about the day before the *risht-dawg*. Oh, well, a lot of Emma and Mandy's wedding-day tensions could have been avoided if they hadn't cared so very much about things like the amount of guests they invited, the menu, or who did what.

It didn't matter a whole lot to Lizzie, because a wedding was just a wedding, and then it was over. Who knew or remembered who was invited and who was not, or what they ate, for that matter. She slapped Bess and told her to hurry up. It was time to get home.

Chapter 7

STEPHEN SPREAD OUT THE SHEET OF PAPER with blue markings all over it. After he turned it the proper way, it resembled a rectangular pattern of sorts, the lines running every which way, outlining walls, doors, and windows.

"There. Hold that corner," he said.

Lizzie held down the one side of the drawing to keep it from rolling up and peered eagerly at the sketch of their house.

"Here's where the front steps go up to a small porch," Stephen explained. "This door goes into the kitchen. You said you wanted the floor plan open— kitchen, dining room, and living room in one, or almost. What do you think?"

Lizzie drew down her eyebrows, concentrating intently on the small squares that were rooms.

"Do that porch and door face the road?"

"Mm-hmm."

"Oh."

Two bedrooms made up the back of the house; the bathroom sat on one side with the basement stairs across from it. An open stairway in the living room divided it from the back bedroom. The dining room and kitchen seemed like one room except for a small wall on each side that separated them, and the living room was off to the left, creating an L-shaped living area.

Lizzie loved the sensible house plan. For a small house, it was very open, the space flowing together in a way that allowed for the maximum amount of light and air on summer days.

"We don't need two bedrooms, though," Lizzie said doubtfully.

"I thought we'd use the one to put my desk and gun cabinet and all my hunting and fishing things in until we need it," Stephen said.

"How many bedrooms are upstairs?"

"Three small ones. It's only a story and a half, you know. The dormers out the front allow for extra space for windows."

"What color is our house going to be?" Lizzie asked eagerly.

"What color do you like?"

"Brown."

"We'll have brick halfway up to the windows, so we'll need to decide what color we like. I like white bricks with brown mortar. I think that will look nice with that brown siding that resembles wood."

Lizzie looked at Stephen. She was incredulous.

White bricks! White! He couldn't be serious. He liked white bricks. She knew in one swift moment that she shouldn't say anything, but she so desperately disliked the idea of ruining her dreamed-about little brown house with white bricks, that she blurted out, "White? I hate white bricks."

Stephen turned to look at her, his eyes narrowing. "You do?"

He was surprised at her outburst, Lizzie could tell. Well, he's just going to have to be surprised, because I won't have my dream house ruined by that strange idea.

Her own will overrode her common sense, even the things Mam had tried to teach her about being submissive. Like a gray storm cloud across the sun, the atmosphere between them became a bit chilled as Stephen cleared his throat.

"Yes, I do. They look like a prison or a doctor's office," she said emphatically, completely sure of herself now that Stephen was wavering.

Her heart sank as she saw Stephen turn to the drawing, his jaw setting as he worked the muscles along his face.

"Well, that's too bad, Lizzie. I happen to like them. The light-colored bricks set against the dark brown mortar look neat."

Lizzie's mouth literally dropped open in disbelief. He was openly disagreeing, without considering her point of view at all! How could he do that? Wasn't he supposed to love her enough so that her every whim would be his command?

She panicked. She didn't want to have white bricks on the house, so she burst out, "Well, then I guess you'll have to live in it alone, because I won't live there if you use white bricks."

"Lizzie!" Stephen said sharply.

She crossed her arms in front of her, leaning back against the chair. Stephen stared at her, and she glared back defiantly. Silence stretched between them like a taut rubber band, ready to snap in either direction.

Stephen sighed.

Lizzie breathed quietly, her heart hammering in her chest. She knew she was hurting his feelings, but she so hated the idea of white bricks that she didn't care how he felt.

He rolled up the drawing, stood up, and said, "Well, I may as well go home then, if we're going to disagree."

"No! No! I don't want you to go," Lizzie said, gazing up at him with eyes that she hoped would melt his heart. Maybe if she whined and begged, even shed a few tears which were very close to the surface anyway, he would give in to her.

"I'd better go. It's getting late. Your parents will think I shouldn't be here anyway, the middle of the week like this."

"Are… Aren't you going to talk anymore about the… the bricks?" Lizzie implored him.

"There's no use. Lizzie, I'm a builder, and I know what looks nice. You aren't used to building houses, so how could you understand what I'm talking about?"

That was like throwing kerosene on an already smoldering fire. Lizzie completely lost all sense of right and wrong, of caring whether she hurt his feelings, of anything at all. She was so angry she leaped to her feet, her eyes flashing as she faced him squarely.

"Oh, you! You make me so angry. You don't have to be a builder to know what looks nice and what doesn't. Women have more taste than men, and they always know what looks pretty. Men don't, and you don't either."

All he said was, "I think white bricks would look best," and then walked out to the kitchen, through the door, and out to the barn, while Lizzie fumed and sputtered all by herself.

All right. Let him go. She was not going to go help him with his horse or say good-bye. Good for him if he had to go home like this. She watched, barely breathing, as he backed the horse and buggy out of the forebay and gathered up the reins. Switching on the headlights, he climbed in, and gravel spit against the wheels as he turned to drive out the lane at a fast pace.

He meant what he said! Surely he'd turn around and come back to her. He'd pity her and tell her brown bricks were the best choice just because she thought so, and that he loved her much more than the house, and that she was the light of his life and he would do anything in his power to make her happy. Then she would feel so adored and be so happy in her little brown house that would look exactly as she had always pictured it.

She stayed by the window, watching and peering anxiously into the darkness for a glimpse of the bluish white lights of his headlights as he returned to apologize to her. Crickets chirped steadily, and the night sounds remained exactly the same with no horse's hooves clopping on the road. Sighing, she smoothed back her hair in agitation, chewing on her lower lip as a lump began forming in her throat. Her nostrils burned and quivered, and tears stung her eyes.

Turning, she marched up the steps to her room, determined not to give in to her absolute misery with a display of emotional tears. He was completely out of his rightful place. She had every right to choose the bricks for her house. She was the wife, or soon would be, and who would live in the house the most? She would. He would be away at work over half of the time anyway.

See, that's how Dat was, she thought angrily. If he wanted to move somewhere, he just said he was moving, and it was up to Mam to go along. Men were all alike. *Gros-feelich*. Conceited. How could he think that just because he was a builder, he knew what looked good?

Lizzie fairly snorted as she buttoned her nightgown and turned down the covers of her bed. Climbing in, she pulled them up to her chin and stared wide-eyed at the ceiling.

Dear God, she tried to pray. Please make Stephen see his big mistake.

That didn't work.

Her prayer seemed to bounce against the ceiling and come back down, landing like a great crushing weight on her chest, making her feel worse. She was so miserable that she didn't feel like getting married at all, especially if he was going to be so stubborn about bricks.

She rolled over, punched her pillows, and squeezed her eyes shut. Then, like cold, hard little hailstones, she was accosted by doubts and fears. Her thoughts ran completely rampant, as she lay all alone in the dark with only her own will and anger to keep her company. It was not a peaceful or restful kind of company.

How much were you expected to give up after you were married? Bow before your husband, the king, and say in a quiet, hushed, humble tone, "Oh, of course, Your Majesty, white bricks are beautiful." Stuff all your own wants and desires in a deep recess of your brain, like a garbage bag full of forbidden fruit, stuck away into the darkest corners of the attic?

And so her rebellion raged, fighting off any hope of ever falling asleep. What was best? Living in a house that didn't even come close to what she had imagined and submitting to the will of her husband. Or, like a fiercely determined warrior, sword and shield drawn, hack her way through until he finally relented? Oh, she so wanted to have her little brown house encased in brown bricks with pretty shrubs growing around it, exactly as she had always pictured it.

Maybe her whole life would be easier if she never married but remained single and taught school until she was 70 years old. She could hold Emma's and Mandy's babies and eat all she wanted, because she would not have to worry one tiny bit about her figure if she had no boyfriend or husband. For one thing, she could do exactly as she pleased. If she ever saved enough money from teaching school, which was highly unlikely considering teachers' wages, she would build her own house and use brown bricks. Just like the last little pig in the "Three Little Pigs" nursery rhyme, she thought grimly. The wolf could not get in.

Maybe I'll just break up with Stephen, she thought. Immediately his dark face and long brown hair with blond streaks in it, his blue, blue eyes, and just him, the image of Stephen, appeared in her mind. She knew without a doubt she could never be happy without him. A quiet sob tore at her throat as she buried her face in her pillow and cried great tears, soaking the pillowcase in the process.

Suddenly there was a soft knock on her bedroom door. No, it couldn't be. Nobody knocked on bedroom doors in the Glick household, especially in the middle of the night.

Knock, knock.

Her heart leaped to her throat and cold shivers chased each other up and down her spine. Grabbing her woolly housecoat, she wrapped it tightly around her body, her arms crossed over the front protectively.

"Who is it?" she called weakly, her mouth as dry as if it were full of cotton.

There was no answer, then in the space of a few seconds, a quiet, "Me."

Stephen!

Lizzie drew a sharp breath, and in one rush, she was at the door.

"Stephen!" she gasped, "you're not supposed to be up here."

"I know. Can we talk?"

Placing her hand firmly in his, she crept down the stairs, carrying the kerosene lamp from the bathroom. She set it carefully on the kitchen table and turned to face him with red, swollen, questioning eyes.

"What is it?"

In a gesture of helplessness, Stephen raised his hands beseechingly, then let them fall to his sides.

"I... I'm not real good at expressing my feelings," he said in a quiet tone of voice, "but... well, I got home and just couldn't unhitch my horse. I had no right to be so bullheaded. You know how much I love you, and I want to be able to do anything for you. But I'm self-willed, too, and if I want something, I think that's how it has to be. I'm sorry. That wasn't right."

Lizzie tried to laugh softly, to float lightly over the top of his unaccustomed deep emotion. But her tears were still too close to the surface, and her laugh, when it did emerge, was more like a sob, followed by more dreaded tears.

"It's all right," was all she could manage before she walked across the kitchen to the box of tissues.

Stephen sank into a kitchen chair, then looked at her across the lamplight. "No, it isn't all right. I was being mean to you."

Lizzie wiped her eyes, and this time her low laugh was genuine. "No, Stephen, I was the one being mean. I should have tried to picture the house the way you did. It really is not so significant, either, whether we live in a house made of white or brown bricks."

"Why did we have that senseless disagreement?" Stephen asked.

"Because we're us. You and I are so much alike." Lizzie shook her head, feeling very wise at that moment.

Stephen leaned forward.

"Lizzie, you pick the color for the bricks," he said. "I don't mind either way. Honestly, I don't. I don't know why I acted so sure of myself in the first place."

Lizzie watched his face, his eyes soft with emotion, and thought that if he ever did seem like a king, it was at this moment. She loved him with her whole heart and knew without a trace of doubt that white bricks were going to look absolutely fantastic. Oh, she wanted to be a sweet, submissive wife when he was so unbelievably kind and good.

"So," he finished, "it's up to you."

Clasping her hands in her lap, taking a deep breath of pure happiness, she said, "I think white

bricks would look very nice."

Stephen laughed. "You don't."

"Yes, I do. Stephen, when you are so kind, it's easy to want what you want. Don't you think that's very important after we get married? We just have to remember to consider each other's feelings instead of saying outright anything we want."

After a while, Lizzie asked him how he even got up the stairs without waking Mam and Dat.

"You have the creakiest stairs in Cameron County," he grinned. "It took me a long time to get to the top step, believe me."

She laughed. "I'm sure Mam and Dat never heard you."

How different she felt as she hung up her house-coat and climbed into bed. Her prayers were now of thanksgiving and praise. It felt as if God beamed down on the old farmhouse, straight through the ceiling to her heart and soul. How light her heart felt!

Finally, she understood this submission thing, this giving and taking, and it seemed very possible that she would be able to be happy and submissive at the same time. Oh, they would have their flare-ups, their disagreements and sad times, same as all couples who were married, but wasn't it just something? Wasn't it just unbelievable?

She bounced onto her back, patting the covers into place. Imagine! He said he couldn't unhitch his horse until he drove all the way back, he felt so bad because he was mean. He wasn't really being mean,

just... well... And here she was, thoroughly miserable, unable to sleep because they had parted coldly, without wishing each other well. She felt as if she had been rescued out of a pit of quicksand full of despair, her feet planted now on firm ground while birds and butterflies twittered and darted around her.

A house made of white bricks, filled with love and understanding, with peace and submission, was so much better than one with brown bricks, filled only with her own determination and her lack of love. Maybe she would be as old as the hills before she understood everything or learned to be submissive in all things, but this much she understood. It was easy as pie to submit to a kind, loving husband.

The following morning she hid her smile when Mam said she declared there were some strange creaks in the night. Dat told her when the nights became cool, the aluminum siding on the new part of the house expanded and contracted, causing creaking sounds.

"No," Mam said wisely. "It was the stairs."

When Dat left to go to work, Mam's eyes bored into Lizzie's, and she said, "All right. Out with it. What was going on?"

Lizzie burst into happy laughter, telling Mam everything. Mam's eyes became soft and watery, and her nose turned red as it always did when she became emotional. "Ach my, Lizzie, I would say you're off on the right foot." It was like a large pat on the back, hearing Mam say that.

Chapter 8

LIZZIE UNHOOKED THE BUGGY WINDOW FROM the ceiling and lowered it into place with a decided click. Rubbing her hands across her sweater sleeves, she shivered and said, "Brrr."

Stephen smiled at her.

"I wondered how long you'd keep that window open. This is real hunting-season weather."

Lizzie slapped his arm playfully. "That's all you ever think about."

"Oh, no. Not this fall. I'm thinking about you, then the house, then hunting. See? Hunting is way down on the bottom of the list."

"Don't you ever think about getting married? About the wedding?" Lizzie asked, smiling happily.

Stephen's face became quite sober, and he watched the horse's ears intently. "Yeah, I do."

"You don't sound very thrilled about it."

"Oh, I am, Lizzie. You know I am. It's just that I'll be glad when the actual wedding day is over. I don't

like crowds of people all packed together in one house, even if it's our wedding. I mean, I don't want to make it sound as if I don't want to marry you. I just wish there wouldn't have to be quite so many people there."

Lizzie patted his arm reassuringly. "I know, Stephen. I know very well how you dislike crowds of people. I'm just the opposite, aren't I?"

Stephen nodded quietly.

"I'll just love all the attention, the relatives, the gifts, the food! Actually, I can hardly wait for our wedding day."

The horse picked up speed without being urged when it spotted another buggy on the road ahead of them. Horses did that, Lizzie thought. They could be clopping along, a bit bored, and suddenly, their ears would prick up when they spied another team ahead of them. Instantly, their ears turned forward, and they surged ahead, no longer content to amble along by themselves. Stephen pulled back slightly as his horse lunged into his collar, racing toward the other team.

They were on their way to Ben King's house to a supper for the youth. It was one of the farthest places they had to travel in their district. Stephen had let his horse walk up a few of the steepest hills to save his strength for the miles ahead. At the rate the horse was traveling now, it certainly looked as if he had conserved more than enough energy.

The gap between the two teams narrowed until Lizzie could see someone waving and a face in the mirror peering back at her. "Rebecca," Lizzie laughed. "The only person who waves like that!"

Stephen grinned.

Rebecca was Stephen's sister, as well as Lizzie's closest friend now that Mandy and Emma were both married. She had a great sense of humor with an endearing manner that made her easy to talk to and so much fun to be with, Lizzie thought.

Rebecca had been dating Reuben after they had gone on a camping trip together with Lizzie, Stephen, and other friends. Now they were making their own plans for their wedding. Lizzie's Uncle Marvin and Sara Ruth, as well as her friends, Amos and Sally, were also planning their weddings in November or December. This would be one of the last youth gatherings that Stephen and Lizzie would attend since most of the group was getting married.

They reached a steep hill that wound through a wooded ridge, so both horses slowed to a walk. Lizzie gasped as Rebecca hopped lightly out of Reuben's buggy while it was still moving and stood in the middle of the road, grinning at Lizzie.

Lizzie slid back the door of Stephen's buggy.

"What are you doing, jumping out of the buggy like that?" she asked.

"I'm tired of sitting. Jump down. Let's walk the rest of the way."

Glancing questioningly at Stephen, who was busy keeping his horse from balking on the hill, she hopped out of the buggy, almost stumbling before she stood beside Rebecca.

"Hi!"

"Hi!"

They both burst out laughing for no reason at all.

"Rebecca, you know what? We shouldn't be quite so silly anymore. We're both getting married soon. Can you imagine? We'll be old married ladies, sitting at our quilts, sighing about our arthritis way too soon!" Lizzie laughed.

"Just because we're getting married doesn't mean we can't laugh," Rebecca cried.

Lizzie caught her breath, grabbing her side. "Don't walk so fast. I have side stitches."

"What are they?"

"Not so fast!"

Quite suddenly, Rebecca headed straight for the leafy bank and sat down so fast that little puffs of dust rolled from under her skirt and leaves whirled away with the dust. "Okay then, we'll sit."

Lizzie plopped down beside Rebecca, gasping. "I don't know how you can walk up a hill that fast and keep talking at the same time," Lizzie said wryly.

"That's because I'm skinny," Rebecca announced.

"Do you think I'm fat, Rebecca? Seriously, tell me honestly, am I too fat to be getting married? Would you go on a diet if you were me? Huh? Tell me."

"Well... let me see. Hmmm." Rebecca leaned back, eyeing Lizzie carefully. "Yes, you're fat."

Lizzie pinched her hard on her upper arm. "Stop it."

"Well, you are."

"What?"

"Fat."

"I'm not! Do you think so, for real?"

"Yes, you're fat."

They both doubled over with laughter before Rebecca wiped her eyes and said, "You're not skinny. You're a bit heavy, but Stephen likes you like that, so I would never, not even once, worry about it."

"Did he ever tell you he likes me a … a … bit heavy?"

"No, but I know he does. He likes you."

"I would hope so. We're getting *married*, Rebecca."

"We are, too."

"Do you want to?"

"What?"

"Get married?"

"Why do you ask such a silly question? Of course."

Lizzie smiled, but the smile kind of slid downward into a soft sigh, like an ice cream cone that was melting in the hot sun.

"Don't you ever wonder if you're doing the right thing? I mean, what if … after a couple gets married they suddenly decide they really don't like each other all that well, and they're Amish and can't get a divorce and are miserably unhappy all the rest of their lives."

"O … o-oh, Lizzie. You think of the dumbest things."

"Do you know of one couple, just one Amish couple that that happened to?" Lizzie asked, peering anxiously into Rebecca's face.

Their conversation was brought to an abrupt end by the appearance of two teams coming up over the

hill. The first one was Marvin and Sara Ruth, followed by Amos and Sally.

"Jump out!" Rebecca shouted, gesturing to the approaching women to join them. Both women leaped nimbly out of their buggies as Marvin and Amos waved and said hello before moving on up the hill to follow Stephen and Reuben.

Sara Ruth and Sally were both small and blond. They were each only a bit over five feet tall, weighing slightly more than a hundred pounds. Lizzie always envied their slim figures, looking so little and girlish, so light-haired and dainty. But she guessed not everyone could be so perfect.

After saying hello, Sara Ruth felt the sleeve of Rebecca's dress. "Is it new?" she asked.

"Yes, I made a few new dresses for the weddings this fall. We'll all be going in with the 'young married ones,' so we have to look nice and neat and a bit plainer, you know. Comb our hair flat."

They all laughed at Rebecca, but each one knew what she meant. The "young marrieds" were the couples who were engaged. They got special treatment at each wedding. They were seated first among the youth, which was always an honor. Even if you weren't married yet, only engaged, you were still seated first. These girls combed their hair more demurely, like the married women, and looked very mature and ladylike, Lizzie always thought.

She tried to savor every moment here on the leaf-strewn, wooded hillside, chattering as only young women can. This was almost their last time together

at the youth's supper, and it all took on a surreal quality as Lizzie listened to Sally and Rebecca, smiling to herself as she tore a brittle leaf into many pieces.

It was a bit sad to think that there would be no more weekends of running around with her friends. Not really sad, just nostalgic maybe, kind of wishing you could go back and be 16 all over again. Would there ever be another time in her life quite as exciting as going to Allen County with Emma that very first weekend just after Lizzie turned 16? Probably from here on until she died, nothing would even come close to it. She would just grow old and fat—fatter, according to Rebecca—and have a whole houseful of children with runny noses and bottles dripping milk all over the floor. In a brown house with white bricks, instead of a brown house with brown bricks.

Suddenly she wanted to never, ever get married. Like a dark cloud hiding the sunlight, all of her happy anticipation disappeared. She pulled up her knees, stretching the blue fabric of her dress tightly around them, resting her chin on her folded legs.

Rebecca stopped talking and looked at Lizzie. "You're being very quiet."

"Don't worry about it."

"Grouch!"

Lizzie smiled.

The other girls chattered on, Sara Ruth giving them a vivid account of sewing her own wedding dress. They talked about how nervous they were about their actual weddings when they would stand

facing the minister in front of hundreds of pairs of eyes.

"Mary Ann is lucky!" Lizzie said finally.

"Why?" Sally asked.

"Because she's been married for almost a year, living in her cozy new home in Lamton, and all this nerve-racking stuff is behind her."

"You think getting married is nerve-racking?"

"Well, kind of. In a way."

The truth was that while Lizzie looked forward to all of the food and attention on her wedding day, she also got very nervous whenever she thought about it. Would Stephen know how to do everything right? She remembered Joshua and Emma, and also John and Mandy, practicing the day before their wedding, each turning the proper way so that the groom never turned his back to his bride. Things like that. She knew Stephen was completely ill at ease in a crowd, so the whole wedding day was something that gave her a severe case of butterflies in her stomach.

"Oh, it won't be so bad when the time comes," Rebecca comforted her.

"Come on, let's go. It's almost time to eat," Sara Ruth said.

So they walked the remainder of the way up the wooded hillside, the four of them in their bright dresses making a colorful scene against the backdrop of green leaves. As they neared Ben and Lydia King's home, they all remarked over Lydia's perfect flower beds and garden.

"She even has cabbage and lettuce that looks

absolutely healthy!" Rebecca said excitedly.

"What's so thrilling about that?" Lizzie wanted to know.

"Oh, a lot. We're moving onto a produce farm, you know, so I'll be busy helping Reuben with all kinds of vegetables and things. Imagine! We'll have about a hundred times the amount of this garden."

Lizzie looked at Rebecca closely. Sure enough, the enthusiasm shining from her pretty blue eyes was genuine. Unbelievably, she did look forward to all that work.

Lizzie shook her head incredulously. "Rebecca, I can't believe you. How can you look forward to toiling in a huge garden every day?"

Rebecca stopped and stared at Lizzie. Then she spread her hands wide and laughed. "See, Lizzie, you just don't get it. Not everyone is alike. Look at Mandy, way down the 842 on her dairy farm. Is she happy? Huh? Is she?"

Lizzie burst out laughing. "Stop it, smarty."

"Well, just because you don't like cows and get depressed thinking about growing produce doesn't mean Mandy and I do, too. We're just not all alike."

All the girls burst out laughing. It was just Rebecca's way, turning an ordinary sentence into a statement.

Lizzie slipped her arm through Rebecca's and squeezed her hand. "All right, I understand. Stop acting like Mandy."

Rebecca grinned at her, and Lizzie's heart swelled with love for her true friend, because that's what she was. Stephen's sister or not, she would always

be a special friend, one whom she hoped to remain friends with all the days of their lives.

That evening on the way home from the hymn-singing, Lizzie felt so much love and gratitude for having Stephen in her life. He was not a dairyman or a produce farmer, and he was building a new house for her, albeit with the white bricks he had chosen. She sighed happily, thinking how perfect he was for her.

"Tired?" Stephen asked.

"No, just happy. Stephen, I'm so glad you're not a dairy farmer or a produce farmer, I mean, a person who grows vegetables on one huge acre after another. I don't think I would marry you if you were. Can you imagine Reuben and Rebecca?" she asked.

"Sure, I can imagine Rebecca. She loves to garden."

Lizzie slipped her arm into his and said softly, "But, oh, Stephen, I'm so glad you're a carpenter."

They rode together in silence for a short time before he asked her if that was the only reason she had agreed to marry him.

"Of course not, Stephen. There are many other reasons. But you know as well as I do that I could never look forward to slaving in a produce field or milking cows. I would give up to it if I had to, but I probably wouldn't be very happy, at least sometimes."

Stephen laughed wryly. "Likely not. Giving in is not one of your strong points."

"Ouch!" Lizzie said, smiling.

"That's all right. I will probably like a wife with a little spunk."

Lizzie smiled to herself. Stephen was so right for her. She wondered what had taken her so long to see it. Life was amazing, or rather, God was amazing, the way he worked things out. Even if you resisted his will at first, he just did what was best for you until you were ready.

Like knowing Stephen was the one for her. How could she have known if he hadn't gone away for a while? And how did he know she had to have that time without him? Probably God, same as always. He put in people's heads things that were right until his perfect will was made manifest, like the Bible said.

"Stephen, you know what, though? Sometimes we so barely manage to find the Lord's will. You know? Kind of like a needle in a haystack? If you keep searching and want to find it with all your heart, you will. Right?"

"Sometimes you know where it is, you feel deep down that you found it, and then, you can't have it," Stephen said very quietly.

A slow smile spread across Lizzie's face. "You mean me, don't you?"

"Yes, I mean you. Although you're a lot bigger than a needle in a haystack."

Lizzie laughed.

Chapter 9

A FEW WEEKS LATER, ALL THE BUILDING permits had passed through the network of township ordinances, the bank had obligingly loaned Stephen and Lizzie the amount they needed for Stephen to get started on the house, and the bulldozer was scheduled to arrive.

Dat was fairly dancing with excitement. Mam said she declared he was getting better, MS or not. His mind was fully occupied with Stephen and Lizzie building a new house on the acre of ground Dat and Mam had given them. It was still a one-way street when Dat and Stephen were together, Dat doing all the talking, or rather, the greater portion by far, and Stephen quietly deciding things his way without much ado.

Mam said she was afraid Dat was a bit pushy, shoving all his own ideas on Stephen, but Lizzie assured her that Stephen could take care of himself. He just didn't say much, then went ahead and did exactly what he wanted to do in the first place.

When Lizzie stood on the hillside and watched the huge bulldozer backing down off the trailer that had transported it, she put both hands to her mouth to hide her excitement. KatieAnn and Susan were with her, their eyes big with awe around this noisy, rattling monster.

Stephen and Dat walked over to them and grinned.

"Think he can dig your basement?" Dat asked.

"He's certainly big and noisy enough!" Lizzie yelled above the clanking and chugging of the big machine.

The driver waved down at them, pulling levers and working pedals as he turned the bulldozer toward the four wooden stakes with plastic orange streamers tied to them, outlining where the house would be built. And then, just like a gigantic spoon over a dish of hard, frozen ice cream, he scooped up a layer of sod and set it aside.

Lizzie felt a bit sad for the poor warped little alfalfa plants which were taken from all the rest of the alfalfa plants on the hillside and cast aside by the bulldozer to die. It didn't seem right. The little plants had to sacrifice their lives so she could live in her house on the hill. Sorry, little alfalfa, but you'd have to withstand the winter winds anyway, and then only to be cut and dried and eaten by a cow, she thought.

The huge yellow machine kept chewing and scraping at the alfalfa-covered hillside until a decided hole appeared, which swallowed up parts of the bulldozer as the driver dug away, or so it seemed.

Stephen stood and watched, his blue eyes alight, as Dat kept walking here and there, swinging his shovel and talking fast and loud whenever he passed by Stephen. Stephen smiled at Lizzie over Dat's head, and she burst into laughter of pure joy. That was Dat! That was just how he was.

"I'm cold!" KatieAnn said, grasping Lizzie's hand tightly as she burrowed her head into her sweater.

"Are you?" Lizzie asked, glancing at the twins, surprised to find their noses red with the brisk wind.

"Okay, come on. We'll go down to Mam. This is long enough now. We know what he'll be doing the rest of the day, right?"

Susan nodded, and turning, Lizzie walked briskly down the hill, the twins hopping and skipping along on either side, clinging to her hands.

They burst through the kitchen door. Mam stood at the stove, stirring something that smelled wonderful, the steam enveloping her face. She stepped back, lifting the spoon and knocking it against the rim of the kettle before smiling at them.

"Cold, isn't it?" she said.

"Mam, you should see the big hole he's digging…" Susan shouted.

"With his big yellow digging machine!" KatieAnn finished.

Mam gasped in mock excitement, her eyes opening wide. "Really?" she asked.

"Mm-hmm."

"Stephen and Lizzie's house!" KatieAnn exclaimed.

Lizzie sat down at the kitchen table, eyeing Mam eagerly. "Mam, how long—usually how long, anyway—does it take to finish a house? I mean from the time the bulldozer starts digging until we can move in?"

"Ach my, Lizzie, I forget. We only built one house, and I can't remember the actual time it took. But, my goodness, you're not married yet, you know. You still need to have a wedding and buy your furniture and lots of other things."

"But I want time to go faster. Mam, do we have to live at home here with all of you in this house all winter? Why is that an Amish custom? Stephen doesn't say anything, but I guarantee he doesn't want to do that. Why do we have to?"

Lizzie got up and lifted the lid from the kettle, taking a deep sniff of the bubbling contents. "Mmmm!"

"Chicken and dumplings," Mam said. Then she sighed and said, "Ach, I don't know why either. It's not done that way where I come from. In Ohio, the custom is to move right after the wedding, and you don't have to run all over the creation 'young married visiting' either. Whoever thought up that scheme must have wanted an extension to the wedding. Same as Easter Monday."

"Now, Mam!" Lizzie chided.

"I know. You can't change an old chicken, can you?"

"'You can't teach an old dog new tricks' is the actual saying."

"I'm not old. It's just hard for me to conform sometimes. Guess I'm too thick-headed, as Melvin would say."

She got up and headed for the stove, taking up the wooden spoon. She peered closely through the steam and held it lightly over the dumplings. Lizzie knew exactly what she was doing. She would insert the spoon into a dumpling to test the middle of it, and when it was light and fluffy the whole way through, it was done. Mam made the best chicken and dumplings in the world. Not that Lizzie had ever traveled very far to taste many other varieties, but she knew Mam's were just delicious.

A week later, the footer for the house was poured and the first concrete blocks laid. Dat and Jason, as well as Stephen's father and brothers, helped Stephen with the construction. Stephen's dad was a thin man, about Dat's age, who owned a farm and raised lots of pigs. He enjoyed farming, working hard from sunup to sundown as most dedicated farmers do.

Stephen's two brothers, Daniel and Henry, were a merry twosome, especially Henry who was always laughing about something. Dat said when Stephen's brothers were both there, it was almost less help than if there were only a few people working, because they were always distracting everyone with their stories.

Lizzie discovered she had one huge problem, which quickly ballooned quite out of proportion. Her eyebrows were drawn up in the middle, which is what happens if frustration is allowed to rule your face, she thought. She wished it wouldn't take so long to lay the block basement walls. Every time she walked up to the top of the hill, the brothers were either sitting somewhere talking, or Henry was throwing mortar at Stephen, which caused Lizzie's eyebrows to shoot straight up.

At the rate they were going, they wouldn't move into that longed-for house until next summer. With all the stress of the upcoming wedding and no furniture, or hardly any yet, this was ridiculous. How could Stephen be up here on the hill acting like a 12-year-old with his brothers?

So she became increasingly irritable, trying to keep her lack of patience from showing, especially when she was around Stephen. She tried to keep her eyebrows straight, which was an awful job, giving her a constant headache. She had to think continually or remember to flatten them, pasting a make-believe smile on her face when Stephen was near. Lizzie's impatience turned the much-anticipated time of building their house into a long, weary ordeal.

Lizzie's undoing came that Friday evening when they were sitting on the hillside, Stephen covered with dirt and mortar, his eyes tired. He took off his hat and ran his dirt-covered fingers through his hair, sighing wearily.

"Guess I'll take tomorrow off and go squirrel-hunting with Daniel," he said, replacing his hat and turning to look at her.

Lizzie was caught totally off guard. Her eyebrows shot straight up as an alarming note crept into her voice. "Why?" she squeaked, determined not to become hysterical.

"Why? Because I'm tired, Lizzie. I work during the day, go to the livestock auction on Tuesday evenings, and then work some more, besides spending every spare moment over here building the house. So don't ask why," he said flatly, a bit irritably even.

Lizzie knew instinctively what to say. Of course, he worked too hard and was tired. He deserved at least one Saturday off to go squirrel-hunting. But her impatience had taken over her life, and like a bird flying out of its cage, and Lizzie making only a half-hearted attempt at catching it, she turned to look at him

"Aren't you worried one bit about getting this house finished? At the rate you and your brothers are going, we won't live in it until next summer," she said.

The look in Stephen's eyes drove home the fact that she had said something awful. It was a lot worse than letting Mam's parakeet out of a cage; it was more like throwing some precious item into a deep, swiftly-moving river where it could never be retrieved. She knew her words had done a lot of damage, and she could not bring them back. They were out. Said. Done.

"You think I'm not working fast enough?" he asked, disbelief in his eyes. "Well, if you're going to act like a regular taskmaster, then I'm going hunting for sure."

Lizzie sat up straight, fuming. She didn't care if she had said something to hurt him now. He was being ignorant. Throwing all caution to the wind, she burst out, "Oh, go ahead. If you think I'm so difficult, maybe you'd better not marry me at all."

Stephen snorted. He actually snorted, and it was not a nice snort.

"As tired as I am, maybe I won't."

"Fine."

Stephen turned and headed down the hill in the gathering darkness with short, swift strides, so that Lizzie knew he was very angry. Quickly she got up and followed him, hurrying, knowing she had to make this right. He had only told her innocently that he was going squirrel-hunting. He had not intended to get into an argument. It was all her fault, all her own stupid fault, because she had no patience.

Catching up, she caught his arm, but he shook her off.

"Stephen!" she cried.

He walked straight ahead, down to the drive and into the forebay of the barn. There was nothing for Lizzie to do but stand there like some senseless person and watch him go.

"Oh, dear. Oh, dear," she said out loud to no one in particular except herself. "He is really mad."

That thought spurred her into action, and she ran

after him, stumbling on some rocks at the bottom of the hill. Before she reached the barn, she slowed to a steady walk so that he wouldn't think she was really racing after him. She had her pride, after all, and he was not going to see how worried she was.

He was placing the bit in his horse's mouth when she sauntered into the barn. She put her hands behind her back and cleared her throat for attention. Stephen said nothing, just fastened the chin strap on the bridle as if his life depended on it. Turning to walk past her, he never slowed or looked at her, so she had no choice but to step out of his way.

Turning, she held the shafts for him while he backed his horse between them. She helped him hitch up, fastening the proper straps to the proper hookups. She watched in disbelief as Stephen climbed into the buggy and without as much as a "Good-night" or his usual "See-ya," he was gone.

They had just argued like this before about the white bricks! A giant wave of despair washed over her until she felt tumbled about, soaked, drowned in the maelstrom of feelings that encircled her heart. She wasn't fit to become his wife. Well, he wasn't acting very mature either. Big baby!

Turning on her heel, she marched across the gravel driveway and up the steps, yanking open the kitchen door before throwing herself into a chair. Jason looked up from the magazine he was reading.

"What gives?" he asked.

"O…o…h, that *Stephen*!" Lizzie said, two red spots in her cheeks showing her anger.

"Why?"

"He plumb went home without saying good-bye
or good night because he's all upset about me saying
something or other about him going squirrel-hunt-
ing. Can you imagine? He's going squirrel-hunting,
and those concrete blocks will never, ever be fin-
ished. Does he care? Oh, no. Not as long as his silly
brothers are around."

Lizzie looked up to see Mam in the doorway, her
thin white scarf tied around her head, wearing her
old light blue housecoat, smelling as she always did
of soft, flowery talcum powder. Mam smiled a very
small smile and shook her head ruefully. Turning to
sit in the chair opposite Lizzie, she looked straight
into her eyes until Lizzie flinched, dropping hers.

"What did you say to make him mad?" she asked
softly.

"Nothing!"

"Yes, you did."

"Just that ... well, how can he go squirrel-hunt-
ing when the house isn't coming along as fast as it
should? He doesn't even *care*!" she burst out.

"Boy, Lizzie!" Jason said loudly. "Big baby. I
wouldn't marry you if I were him. Can't you see
how hard he works? I mean, he looks almost hag-
gard. He sleeps so little from working two jobs
besides trying to get this house built."

"Jason's right," Mam said, softly and not un-
kindly.

"So you're both on his side?" Lizzie burst out.

"Now you listen to me, Lizzie. I saw your eyebrows

go steadily higher all week, and I figured it would come to this. You're going to have to learn to give up if things don't go exactly as you plan. I know I can talk about it until I'm blue in the face, but you're going to have to learn the hard way if you don't listen to me. Stephen is doing more than enough, and to have you nagging at him about hurrying with this house is simply not going to work. You're going to find out after you're married, mark my words."

"It takes a long time to build a house, Lizzie," Jason said.

"I know that. I do. I guess I'm just panicking."

"Now, if Stephen said he wanted to take you shopping for your china and silverware on Saturday, would you have said 'no, the house is being built too slowly'?" Mam asked wisely.

"Of course not."

"See, it's called being selfish, Lizzie. How can we enter marriage and figure it's going to work as long as we hang on to our own selfishness? Never wanting Stephen to go out and do something fun, because you think he should stay home and please his little princess."

"Stop it, Mam. You're being mean."

"No, I'm not being mean. I'm being truthful."

Jason got up and stretched, running his fingers through his mop of curly hair, yawning. "I'm not going to get married for a long, long time. Girls are a big bother."

Lizzie said nothing as he slapped her arm playfully, peering closely into her face, saying in a high,

singsong voice, "Good night, sweetheart!"

Lizzie punched his arm and laughed in spite of herself. "You better fix that hair of yours before you ask anyone for a date," she teased.

Mam sat quietly after Jason went upstairs. The clock ticked steadily as a warm, companionable silence settled over the two of them. Lizzie caught a soft whiff of Mam's talcum powder and was instantly transported back in time when she was a very worried little girl, checking on her kitten, Snowball, in the middle of the night, certain that she was hungry or scared. Then Mam had smelled the same, a warm, comforting, clean Mam smell that never ceased to make Lizzie feel loved and comforted, secure and safe in the middle of a very uncertain world.

"Mam, am I going to make a decent wife for Stephen, if I have all this impatience and—what do you call it—'Wanting what I want and wanting it right now'?"

"Why, of course, Lizzie. I don't doubt for one moment that you and he are meant for each other. I always felt that way. He's the perfect one for you. You're not going to walk all over him. You might not have the easiest road, which, for some reason, we mothers want for our girls. I mean, we've had some tough times, your dad and I. Yet I think that each daughter, as she gets married, will have this perfect little love story and live happily ever after, when I know real life just isn't that way. We struggle; all of us do."

"Well, if it's so tough, why bother getting married

in the first place?" Lizzie asked, a bit wearily.

"It isn't tough. It's what we make of it. Getting along with a brand-new husband is the first serious step in putting all that love and romance to the test. We *think* it's all roses, and we're so in love. But just wait until he does something, like now, squirrel-hunting, that you think is absolutely unnecessary. So what do you do? You tell him, and probably not in a very peaceful or kind tone of voice."

"Whatever is a 'peaceful voice'?" Lizzie snorted.

"Not exactly 'peaceful.' More like a 'peace-making,' understanding tone of voice. I do it too, Lizzie. You're not alone in this. I hurt Dat's feelings at times by being critical or unsubmissive. But once we learn, and often, actually, by trial and error, we see that our unkindness is often what starts an argument in the first place."

"That's quite a speech, Mam, and it comes dangerously close to that dreaded king and his humble servant theory."

Mam laughed deeply and genuinely. "Yes, I guess it does, Lizzie, but at least it brings a lasting kind of happiness. The kind of happiness where you start singing in the middle of doing something you don't even want to do, not knowing or understanding why. You're just happy. That comes from doing God's will, which is more often than any of us care to admit, from submitting to our husbands."

"Who are out traipsing around in the woods shooting squirrels while the house is on hold?" Lizzie asked.

"Exactly."

"Hmmph."

"Well, if you don't believe me, try fighting against Stephen and everything he does, and see how often you feel like singing."

Lizzie looked at Mam, clearly understanding what she meant. The difference between the white bricks and the coveted brown ones.

"All right, I get it. So if you hear me singing tomorrow, you'll know I'm in my rightful place."

"In order to do that, your rightful place is on your knees this evening. Only God can give you the power to overcome your own selfishness."

Dat appeared in the doorway, buttoning a clean shirt, his hair wet from the shower.

"Very good speech, Annie." He laid a hand affectionately on her shoulder. "When I hear you talk like that, I think of all the times I required too much submission from you. You've been a good and faithful wife to me."

Quick tears welled up in Mam's eyes, and she blinked with embarrassment. "Oh, not always, Melvin. Not nearly always."

"Take care of Stephen's feelings, Lizzie. It's worth it," Dat said, clearing his throat gruffly at the unaccustomed emotion he felt.

When Lizzie dropped to her knees beside her bed, she could only thank God for two parents who were often imperfect, but who had gone the way before her and wanted only what was best. That was a huge thing, really.

Chapter 10

Wᴇɴ Sᴛᴇᴘʜᴇɴ ᴄᴀᴍᴇ ᴡɪᴛʜ ᴀ ᴅʀɪᴠᴇʀ ᴛᴏ ɢᴏ to Falling Springs the following week, Lizzie was waiting eagerly on the porch swing, her sweater wrapped closely around her body with her arms folded. It was getting close to their wedding date, and they had to choose the remaining furniture they needed to furnish their small house.

She was quite beside herself with anticipation. She had very seldom gone shopping with Stephen, as he certainly did not enjoy doing that, he had informed her firmly. But today he had no choice, she told him. He had to buy her china and her water set, which was really a water pitcher and six glasses she'd use on the day of their wedding. She also needed a set of silverware and a nice wooden chest to put it in.

Mam had given her all the money left in her savings account to buy kitchen chairs and a rocking chair for her living room. She had frowned about Lizzie's determination to have captain's chairs for

her kitchen table, telling her those "furniture store chairs" don't last. They're not built as well as the Amish-crafted ones. But Lizzie was adamant. She loved the look of the low, round back and the arms you could rest your elbows on when you sat back in the chair.

Their first stop was the furniture store. Lizzie hopped out of the vehicle almost as soon as the wheels had stopped. Stephen laughed and shook his head at her.

"Why don't you just calm down a bit? At the rate you're going, you'll be completely worn out long before we're finished selecting our things."

"Oh, okay," Lizzie answered, trying to walk slower and act more demure, which really, if she thought about it, was how a girl who would soon be married should act.

She stopped at the big glass door, and Stephen reached around her to open it for her, allowing her to walk in first. It impressed her so much that he knew how to behave politely in the presence of English people. Besides, it made her feel special, cherished, even a bit queenly, when he allowed her to go first. She glanced up at him with a look she hoped conveyed her appreciation of his good manners. She was rewarded with a warm smile that melted her heart.

How could they forget their argument about squirrel-hunting so soon and love each other so much again? That was one of life's greatest mysteries, she supposed, how angry you could become and how soon you could forget that emotion when

love came flooding back, like the sun warming you after it had been hidden by dark clouds. She wondered how long it would keep working like that, or if eventually, if you got too angry too many times, that the love wouldn't work anymore? That was scary to think about.

The salesman came over to them, danced over, actually, Lizzie thought, and asked them quite eagerly what he could help them with. He introduced himself and shook hands with Stephen, which was a bit too friendly when he was only a salesman in a furniture store. He looked like the cat in the Pinocchio book, so Lizzie took an instant dislike to him. She bet anything his chairs were expensive and very low quality.

He showed them different dining room sets, hovering over them like a bothersome mosquito, reciting the best merits of every set. He works on my nerves, Lizzie thought. I wish he'd go away.

As if reading her thoughts, Stephen asked him politely if they could have a bit of time by themselves to decide which chairs they wanted.

"Oh, of course! Certainly! Certainly!" and he was off as if his shirt was on fire.

Lizzie stifled a giggle, and Stephen grinned.

"All right. Now with him gone, do you like any of them?"

They looked at each one, compared prices, and finally decided to buy four oak captain's chairs, but no table. Mam had ordered their table from an Amish furniture shop in Lamton, one that you could

stretch out far enough to add 12 leaves and seat as many as 20 people at one time. That's the kind of table all Amish women owned, a very necessary and practical piece of furniture with all the company they would serve over the years. Some women had their tables for 50 years, that's how well they were built, Mam said.

They also bought a Boston rocker which was a wooden rocking chair with a high back and two pretty beige and brown cushions. When the over-enthused salesman totaled the bill, the amount was still 100 dollars less than the amount Lizzie had in her purse. She was so happy because she could buy something more now, maybe a coffee table or some extra dishes. After Stephen made arrangements to have the furniture delivered in a month, they were on their way to the little shop on Main Street to buy a wooden silverware chest.

Lizzie was a bit apprehensive, not knowing how to let Stephen know that he didn't have to spend an exorbitant amount of money on her without making him feel as if he didn't have enough money to buy her pretty things. He opened the door for her, and a little bell tinkled above their heads. A small, heavy-set man on a wheelchair turned to greet them, an easy smile spreading across his round face.

"Hello, there!" he greeted them.

They both answered with hellos of their own before looking around the tiny shop. The walls were covered with cut-glass or crystal dishes, displays of silverware, and wooden chests to store them in.

There were also clear glass cases of jewelry and glistening gold and silver trophies, awards for having won a certain sport or event.

"If there's anything I can help you with, please let me know," the man told them in his soft, polite manner.

Lizzie's eyes lit up, and she pointed to a clear glass water pitcher set. The pitcher was round and a bit low with the most wonderful-looking handle coming up from the bottom, shaped into a graceful arc with the rounded end resting against the top of the pitcher. There were eight tall glasses, each with a clear glass bottom and one delicately stemmed flower etched on it. The set was beautiful, absolutely perfect, but she hesitated before she could summon the courage to look at the price.

"One hundred thirty-nine dollars!" she gasped.

Turning to look at Stephen, she said, "You can't buy that for me. The price is outrageous!"

"Do you like it?" he asked.

"Oh, I love it. It's so beautiful! I never saw anything like it. I wonder how they can make a handle like that out of glass." She bent over the set, lifting a glass and turning it against the light.

"Well, you said you don't mind getting inexpensive china, didn't you? I could buy this set for you if you don't mind less costly dishes then," Stephen said, as she watched the sunlight playing on the clear glass.

Lizzie returned it to the shelf, clasped her hands together in excitement, and said, "Of course! That's

what we'll do! You can buy this ridiculously expen-
sive water pitcher set, and we'll go to K-Mart for
my china. That's exactly what we'll do!"

When they emerged from the quaint little shop,
Stephen carried a box containing the beautiful water
set, and Lizzie carried one which held a oak silver-
ware chest. It was lined with beige-colored felt and
had different compartments to hold knives, spoons,
and forks, with a small drawer beneath.

"Oh, Stephen!" Lizzie breathed. She couldn't
think of one thing to say other than that simple state-
ment. She meant to say, "Thank you," but it seemed
so inadequate. She was, quite easily, thrilled beyond
words.

However, they had not bought the silverware to
put into the chest because it was simply too expen-
sive. Lizzie didn't mind at all. She knew that at
K-Mart there was a set she had often admired for
about one-fourth the price, which really was smart,
because how often did you use your good silverware?

Before they went to the big K-Mart store, they
stopped for their favorite treat—pizza. That was
one thing they never disagreed on. Pizza was their
favorite restaurant food. Lizzie knew that pizza and
all the big sandwiches, French fries, fried mush-
rooms, and whatever, were terribly high in calories
and everything else that was not good for you, but
she never cared, figuring a few such meals weren't
going to hurt her.

Lizzie liked going to restaurants with Stephen.
He always told Lizzie the same thing—that he didn't

know how to pronounce the words, so she should order for him. Then he would show her the item he wanted and pronounce it in some outrageous fashion, so that she always laughed when the time came to order.

Over piping hot slices of thick pizza, loaded with mushrooms, sausage, and pepperoni, just as Stephen loved it, they talked of their house and how much they looked forward to arranging their new furniture in it.

"I just wish I could buy china like John gave Mandy," Stephen remarked.

"Please don't, Stephen. I wouldn't even feel right, knowing you're putting every penny you have into our new house. To tell you the truth, I'm not interested in dishes much anyway. If a set of china is arranged in a hutch cupboard, who can tell if it's expensive or not?"

That was how she felt, too. K-Mart china was just fine for her and perfect for Stephen's budget. She knew that sometimes she would run her hands over the unbelievably smooth surface of Mandy's plates and cups, marveling at the luster of those dishes, but she never once wished she could have some just like them.

They were pushing a cart up the long aisles at K-Mart when Stephen began showing signs of impatience. He said something about where they kept their hunting stuff, then leaned against a shelf and tapped his foot while Lizzie browsed, or he whistled a slow tune under his breath. He sighed,

asked Lizzie where the clock was, and asked if she couldn't choose silverware without him.

"No, Stephen, I want to get my things with you!" Lizzie said, sharper than she had intended.

"Oh." That was all he said, and afterward he started looking at the ceiling, humming and tapping his shoe against the tile floor.

"Stephen, look. Which design do you like best?" Lizzie held up three different knives to show him the handles.

"That one!" he said, so quickly that she knew he hadn't even considered.

"You didn't even *look*!"

"They're all nice. I like them all. Just buy all three."

Lizzie laughed. "You don't even care!"

"Why would I? You don't see the handle of your fork while you're eating. You look at your food. Just get whatever you like best."

He resumed his humming and foot-tapping routine, which was soon accompanied by drumming his fingers against the shelf he was leaning against. Lizzie tried hard not to let it bother her, but she was starting to feel a distinct twitch in one eye. Her back began to ache with tension, and she chewed her thumbnail.

She liked the design that looked as if little blocks were hammered into the handle, but then, what about the rose design? Of course, there were no roses on her water pitcher set, so maybe that wouldn't look right either. She simply could not decide, and

Stephen was acting like some huge dolt by this time.

"Let's go look at the china," she said evenly, although she had to clench her teeth so she wouldn't lose her temper.

He followed her meekly, saying nothing, leaned against another shelf, and looked at the ceiling. Then the foot-tapping began again.

"Stephen, do you like this design?" she asked quickly. Anything to stop that incessant foot-tapping.

He walked over and peered down at the plate she held in her hands. "That's pretty. Actually, if your mashed potatoes covered that one row of flowers, and the gravy ran over to the opposite side, it would look exactly like every other set of china."

"If you don't act normal, I'm going to break this plate over your head," Lizzie said, trying to joke but falling a bit short.

"You would, wouldn't you?" Stephen said.

"If you don't stop tapping your foot and staring at the ceiling, I will."

"Lizzie, I hate to go shopping. Why do I have to stand here so long? Just buy something, anything, so we can go home. I want to work on the house," he said beseechingly, spreading his hands for emphasis.

"I'll tell you what. You go to the sporting goods section and look at fishing rods or guns or whatever it is that holds your interest, and I'll choose my china all by myself."

"You sure?"

"I'm sure."

She had never been more certain of anything in her life, letting out a huge sigh of relief the minute his tall form disappeared around a corner. Men just weren't made to go shopping. Mam said the very same thing about Dat. After he left, she calmed herself considerably and chose the hammered design for her silverware and a beige and gold flower pattern for her china. A salesperson helped her with the two boxes of china, and she wheeled it toward the sporting goods section, hoping both boxes would stay intact until she found him.

Sure enough, there he was, bent intently over the gun case, muttering to himself. She stood and waited to see how long this would go on. He didn't look up or notice her for a few minutes, then caught sight of her from the corner of his eye.

"Oh! There you are! Sorry!"

He looked at her closely to see if she felt any resentment or anger toward him. But, oh no, Lizzie was smiling serenely, determined not to ruin the rest of this outing.

"I'm not a very good shopper," he admitted wryly.

"You're doing just fine, Stephen. It did take me too long to decide," she said, smiling sweetly up at him.

She felt no resentment because it made her very happy to think of future shopping trips when he would be at work, safely away from any store where she needed to go. She knew the reason Stephen tried his best to be apologetic and very helpful, loading

the boxes of china onto the checkout counter, was because he was thanking his lucky stars that you only got married once, and from now on, it was up to her to go get the things they needed. Large stores gave him a severe case of claustrophobia, and he couldn't breathe very well if he didn't look at the ceiling.

∽❦

What a clamor when they arrived home! The twins squealed and jumped up and down, and Jason asked Stephen dozens of questions about turkey-hunting before they had even finished unloading all of their purchases from the buggy. Mam exclaimed over and over about the beautiful water set, and Dat sat at the kitchen table and shook his head, smiling at Stephen.

"Aren't you glad you'll only be getting married once?" he asked.

"Funny you say that," he said. "That very thought is the only thing that kept me going through all this!"

Dat threw back his head and laughed. "Oh, how well I remember that very same feeling! Although back when we got married, we didn't buy all these fancy things like they do nowadays. I would never have been able to afford it. I wasn't even 21 years old yet."

Lizzie sat down beside Stephen and smiled. "Was it really that bad going shopping with me?" she asked.

"Not the first part of the trip, no. I enjoyed buying the kitchen chairs and the rocking chair. It was the china and silverware that fixed me!"

Jason laughed uproariously, which didn't impress Lizzie at all. She glared at him and told him to wait and see how much he would like to go shopping with Sharon a few years from now.

"Sharon!"

"Don't act so shocked," Lizzie said in a singsong tone of voice.

Jason very seldom blushed, but Stephen laughed when his face turn a decided shade of red.

"Now, Jason!" he said.

Lizzie unpacked her plates and showed Mam the pattern and texture of her silverware. Mam told her she had done very well and that she was proud of her for being careful of Stephen's money since he was building the new house and all, until Lizzie's heart swelled with love and gratitude.

Why, even when you had a boyfriend and were getting married, did your parents' approval still mean so much? Was it something you sought your whole life long? She supposed it must be so, because even with loving Stephen and having him in her life and looking forward to getting married, she cherished her parents more than ever.

Maybe love was just like that. The more you loved, the more you were given to love, until your cup was full and ran over and even splashed on the floor. It was a wonderful thought, and Lizzie hoped it would never end.

Chapter 11

LIZZIE WAS UPSTAIRS ON HER KNEES, BENDING over to paint the wide, heavy piece of baseboard in Jason's room. The wedding was only a week away, and they were putting the finishing touches on the freshly painted and cleaned upstairs.

She dipped her brush into the gallon of thick white paint, than ran the brush carefully along the bottom of the board, very slowly so she wouldn't ruin the linoleum. Sighing, she sat back on her heels. Time and a bit of paint had certainly made a huge difference in this old house, especially in the rooms that had new flooring.

She heard the kitchen door banging and wondered if it was already lunchtime. She sure was getting hungry, but it seemed too early to be noon. Then she heard the stairs squeak in protest as Mam came up at a fast pace. She appeared at the doorway, her scarf coming loose, her hair windblown, and a hand over her chest as she struggled to regain her breath.

"What is it, Mam?" Lizzie scrambled to her feet, her face ashen.

"It's Mandy! She had a doctor's appointment today, and they have a pair of twin girls!"

"No!" Lizzie screeched.

"Yes, they do!"

Then she was laughing and crying, and Lizzie was laughing and crying and dropping her brush and picking it up again. Mam was gasping and fixing her scarf, trying to speak, but all that came out were little gasps and hiccups. Finally, she dug in the pocket of her dress, found her handkerchief, and blew her nose. Then she handed it to Lizzie, and she wiped her eyes and blew her nose.

"S ... s ... six weeks early! Oh my goodness. *Siss ken fa-shtant!*" her favorite Pennsylvania Dutch phrase which means there's no sense. Mam used the only way she knew to fully express her feelings at a time like this. It didn't make much sense, but Lizzie knew exactly how she felt.

Then the thought hit Lizzie like a slap in the face. "The ... the ... my wedding!" she screeched again.

"Yes, the wedding! No, we can't have a wedding without John and Mandy. We'll just have to move the date to December sometime."

"Ma-a-m!" Lizzie wailed. "What will Stephen say?"

"It can't be helped, Lizzie. You're going to have to give in. Mandy will need help and lots of it, so there's no way we can have this wedding in a week."

Lizzie struggled to give in to this unexpected turn

of events. The doctors had assured them that Mandy would be fine to attend the wedding. Why did she have to go have those twins now? Lizzie stopped that ugly thought, knowing it was completely selfish and uncaring. Dear, sweet, big-eyed Mandy. So young, with such an awesome responsibility placed on her shoulders. She took a deep breath and steadied herself as Mam watched the display of emotion move across her face.

"Stephen will be all right with this, Lizzie. He's not the kind of guy who gets all upset about having his wedding a few weeks later. He's not that childish," she said firmly.

❧

So that evening Lizzie's family all took early baths, changed into clean Sunday clothes, and got on their way in a van to the hospital in Falling Springs. Their first stop was at Stephen's parents' place.

Lizzie was met at the door by his mother, a small, round person with big blue eyes like Stephen's. She wore glasses and was dusting her apron with her hands, removing the flour that clung to it.

"Lizzie! This is a surprise!" she said.

"Yes, it is, isn't it? Is Stephen at home?" she asked.

"I think he's upstairs. Let me call him."

She turned to get Stephen, and Lizzie smiled at Daniel who was seated on the wood box.

"Hi!" she said.

"Hi, yourself," he answered and grinned at her. He is almost better looking than Stephen, Lizzie decided. That dark hair and those blue, blue eyes.

Stephen appeared with his mother.

"John and Mandy have twin girls, Stephen! That means we have to postpone our wedding for at least two more weeks."

Stephen's mom held both hands to her mouth and said, "Ach my! *Siss ken fa-shtant*!" exactly like Mam.

In typical Stephen fashion, he didn't say anything at first, then he smiled and shrugged his shoulders. "So I guess we'll be getting married later then."

"I guess. We're going to have to write a bunch of postcards and make a pile of phone calls."

Stephen's mom bustled out to the van to congratulate Dat and Mam, and Lizzie stepped closer to Stephen, putting a hand on his arm. "Stephen, I feel so bad about all this. I'm sorry."

"It's all right, Lizzie. Really. She couldn't help it. At least we're still getting married, and you're not here to tell me you decided against it."

He looked down at her with so much love shining from his blue eyes that quick tears sprang to Lizzie's own.

"I would never decide against it. You know that."

She hurried out to the van as Stephen's mother stepped back, and Lizzie and her family were on their way to the large hospital in Falling Springs.

✧

KatieAnn and Susan's eyes grew very large at the sensation the climbing elevator gave them. When it clunked to a stop on the fifth floor, they both suppressed their giggles. Mam was in a fine tizzy. Two bright red spots appeared on her cheeks, and her nostrils flared the way they always did when her excitement ran high. She hustled the twins off the elevator and into the waiting room, giving Jason quiet orders to stay with them until the rest of them found Mandy's room.

"We could stay here by ourselves," KatieAnn snapped, shrugging off Jason's hand from her shoulder. Jason laughed and steered the twins toward a set of chairs.

Lizzie smiled to herself as she walked down the hallway to find Mandy's room. She was surprisingly nervous. Would Mandy look the same? Would she be awake? Was she in pain? How would she react to being the mother of twins at such a young age?

"There it is," Mam said much too loudly. Mam always spoke loudly when she was nervous or agitated, but nobody told her to quiet down. Dat winked at Lizzie. Hospitals put them all a little on edge ever since Mam's long stay several years earlier when she had pneumonia. Lizzie smiled at Dat, glad that they had a happy reason for visiting the hospital this time.

Lizzie followed Dat and Mam into the room. There was Mandy, lying sound asleep in an elevated hospital

bed, her head sagging a wee bit to one side. The curtains were drawn, casting a quiet evening shadow across the room. There were no babies in sight.

Mam walked up to Mandy's bedside, and Mandy's eyes flew open in an instant. "Mam!" she exclaimed and then burst into tears as Mam hugged and hugged her, fussing like Lizzie had never heard her.

"Honestly, Mandy. Ach, my. *Dess iss net chide*," she kept saying, laughing and gasping while tears rolled down her cheeks. Dat kept wiping his eyes, and Lizzie hugged Mandy, becoming quite undone as she tried to congratulate her.

"Where's John?" she finally asked.

"He went home to milk the cows and change clothes. He should be in soon," Mandy said in a soft voice.

When everyone calmed down, Mandy grinned mischievously at Lizzie and announced, "So, my twins and I thoroughly messed up your wedding plans!"

"You *would* do that to me, wouldn't you?" Lizzie grinned back. Knowing how well Stephen had accepted this made things much easier for Lizzie. What were a few weeks to wait if they could spend the rest of their lives together?

They all walked to the nursery and peered through the glass at the tiny cribs containing the smallest babies Lizzie had ever seen. There were white cards put in a holder that only said "Zook," so they didn't know what their names were. They hadn't even thought to ask Mandy.

The twins weighed almost five pounds each, although Lizzie had a hard time believing this. They were so skinny! Their little hands looked too fragile to be real, and their faces were actually almost gaunt. Mam said that was because they were born prematurely and weren't filled out yet.

Lizzie could not imagine being the mother of those tiny, fragile, little human beings. It would be too much responsibility for her. She could never do it. She knew she couldn't. She became very quiet and sober, pitying Mandy so intensely she could barely make herself go back to her room.

When they got back, John had arrived, greeting them all with so much genuine warmth and enthusiasm. There were tears in his brown eyes.

"Congratulations!" Dat said, beaming warmly.

"Thanks. Thanks. Isn't it something though?" John answered.

"Their names, Mandy! We forgot to ask their names," Mam gushed.

"Sarah and Sylvia!" Mandy announced happily.

Everyone talked and exclaimed about the birth of these tiny twins, but Lizzie sat on the wide window ledge and became steadily depressed, thinking about being a mother to two tiny babies all at once. What in the world would Mandy do if they both cried at the same time during the night and there was no one to help her, especially if John was out milking cows? What if they were both hungry? How could she feed two at once?

Like a soft, stifling vapor, the thoughts of inadequacy enveloped her until all the bright, happy moments from just a few minutes earlier were obliterated. She stared at the floor, chewing her lip and scuffing the toe of her shoe against the nightstand. She wasn't completely sure she was normal where babies were concerned. They quite simply gave her a sense of helplessness, of weary, endless responsibility.

Did you ever want babies? Was it normal to get the blues about having babies? She shrugged her shoulders, shaking off the feelings of despair, and decided she was just tired and struggling to accept this sudden change in plans. Of course, she wanted babies, and, of course, she would be a good mother. Anyone that could teach a roomful of children and thoroughly enjoy it could surely take care of one harmless little baby.

Mandy and John brought the twins home the following Friday, and Lizzie was there to greet them on their arrival. She had hustled and bustled, cleaning every corner of Mandy's small house, doing the laundry and raking some of the lawn that was strewn with maple leaves. Mam brought another small crib, and they set them up side by side in the living room. They fussed with and arranged the tiny baby clothes, sleepers, tiny socks, and T-shirts. Lizzie loved the smell of the baby lotions and powders, spreading some on her arm to keep the scent close by.

"See, Mam, it wouldn't be so bad if you had one baby at a time. I do love babies, honestly, I do, and, of course, I want children after I'm married. It's just that I can't see how in the world Mandy is going to manage," she said worriedly.

Mam shook her head wisely. "Well, let me tell you, Lizzie, having a baby is more than a woolly pink blanket. Indeed it is. But I so love babies, and I thoroughly enjoyed the twins. I'm hoping Mandy will feel the same way. No doubt, two babies are a big responsibility, but I enjoyed every minute."

Lizzie watched Mam in amazement, thinking how capable and courageous she really was. Everything that happened in her life, she took in stride. She made the best out of each situation. Moving, old farms, sicknesses, twins, whatever, Mam always stayed the same. She just marched up each hill as it was presented, in her high-strung, take-charge kind of way. That is just how Mam was. Lizzie wished with all her heart she could be more like her.

As if Mam read her mind, she stopped folding the snowy white diapers and said, "See, Lizzie, you think too much. You're always supposing this or supposing that about the future, making yourself extremely anxious when it is absolutely unnecessary. You should learn to place your trust in God and not in your own power. If God thinks you're capable of managing a pair of twins, he'll give you a pair."

Lizzie dropped a tiny T-shirt. "Mam!"

Mam looked up, surprised. Seeing the expression

on Lizzie's face, she burst out laughing, a real deep laugh that shook her stomach.

"It's not funny!" Lizzie burst out, which only increased Mam's mirth.

"Oh, my! Yes, it is funny."

"Mam, seriously, what are the chances of me ever having twins? How many daughters, I mean, genetically, have a pair of twins if their mothers have some. I don't ever, ever want two babies at one time. Surely God knows that. Should I pray not to have twins?" Lizzie asked anxiously.

"I don't know," Mam chuckled. "As long as I can remember, from the time I was a little girl, I prayed for twin girls."

"Whatever for?" Lizzie asked incredulously.

"Oh, I wanted them. Here they come!" she said all in the same breath. Lizzie ran to the window just in time to see the van pull up to the sidewalk. John bent his head to pay the driver, and Mam and Lizzie hurried out to Mandy and the babies.

Mandy looked pale and tired, but she smiled happily when she saw Mam. Lizzie climbed up to receive one of the babies. It felt as if almost nothing was in the blanket, the baby was so tiny. For a moment, Lizzie panicked, worrying which end of the blanket held the head and which the feet. She lifted a corner of the blanket, and sure enough, she had the wrong end up! Glancing hastily at Mandy, hoping she wouldn't see, she switched ends, hurrying into the kitchen, red-faced. See? That just proved how hopelessly inadequate she was with babies.

There wasn't much time to think about that, with getting Mandy settled on the sofa and finding a cool, clean white sheet and pillow for her. John was hungry, and it was getting close to milking time, so Mam hurried around the kitchen, fixing toasted ham and cheese sandwiches and tomato soup while Lizzie unpacked the accumulation of things from the hospital.

The twins just slept. That's all they ever did, Mandy said, because they were born so early, and that's what premature babies did.

Lizzie sat in the rocking chair opposite Mandy's sofa and marveled at her good spirits and her calm demeanor. She didn't seem nervous that her twins just slept and that sometimes she could hardly waken them when it was time for a feeding.

"The nurses in the hospital were a great help. Sometimes they had to take their sleepers off so they'd cool off and wake up. They showed me lots of ways to rouse them out of their deep sleep when their feeding time comes."

Her voice became quieter and quieter and, to Lizzie's astonishment, Mandy drifted off to sleep. Imagine, she thought. How could a person be so relaxed after bringing home two babies to care for? What Lizzie didn't know was how utterly exhausted Mandy really was. There was not much time for sleep in a hospital with all the IV lines, the checkups, and tests. They had no mercy on a sleepy young mother.

So Lizzie rocked all by herself as Mam and John

had supper. She was hungry, but her wedding was only a few weeks away, so it was high time to lose some weight. She watched Mandy's pretty face, her eyes perfect half-moons in sleep, and hoped with all her heart she would remain strong and optimistic as she accepted this major responsibility.

Suddenly, a high-pitched squeak pierced the air, and Lizzie jumped straight out of her rocking chair. "What was that?" she cried.

Mam turned to look at Lizzie, saw one little bundle in the crib moving, and burst out laughing. There was another high-pitched squeal, and Mam laughed until she had to get out her handkerchief and wipe her eyes. John's laugh rang out, and Mandy's eyes fluttered open, followed by a smile when she heard everyone laugh.

"One of the babies is awake," Mam said, coming over to the crib and lifting her out. Bending her head, she cooed and fussed, saying all kinds of things to this tiny infant who, Lizzie was sure, could not understand a word she said.

"What? What's wrong with my little girlie? Huh? Do you need a clean diaper? I bet you do! Little squirrel. You know, Mandy, they look like little squirrels with their thin faces," she said, misty-eyed with love for these tiny babies.

Lizzie still felt weak from her scare. Watching Mam with narrowed eyes, she wondered how a mother and daughter could be so completely opposite. She guessed she would just have to charge into marriage like Mam did and trust God about babies.

Chapter 12

THE FOURTEENTH OF DECEMBER DAWNED bright, clear, and cold. Of course, the entire Glick household had been awake long before dawn, because this was Stephen and Lizzie's wedding day.

Lizzie was upstairs, her hands clammy with nervous perspiration as she tried to pin her white organdy cape perfectly. Her royal blue dress had been made to perfection, but her difficulty with putting on an organdy cape sure never changed, wedding day or not.

Stephen knocked on the door of her room, then came in to have his bow tie adjusted, just as she finally put the last pin into her cape. She forgot all about her frustration, catching sight of Stephen, her handsome husband-to-be. Doesn't he look so good? she sighed to herself. His tanned face was cleanshaven, his streaky brown-blond hair cut and combed neatly, and he was wearing his new black suit with a crisp white shirt which set off his dark skin.

Lizzie reached up to secure the bow, straightening his collar a bit, as he watched her face intently.

"Nervous?" he asked.

"Oh, yes. Actually, more nervous than I thought I would be. Are you?"

He laughed a bit ruefully. "Afraid so."

"Just be glad you don't need to pin on a white cape and apron."

Stephen came over to stand beside her, telling her she had nothing to worry about—that she looked lovely just the way she was. "You are just perfect, Lizzie," he said soberly. "I feel like a very lucky—no, blessed—young man today."

Lizzie didn't say anything; she just let her eyes tell him what was in her heart. If she ever had any doubts at all, they were completely banished on this morning of their wedding day. She understood deep insidethe exact meaning of "meant-to-be," the rock-solid assurance that this day, this time in her life, was where God wanted her to be.

Emma dashed up the stairs, her cheeks pink with excitement. "Hey, you two. Mam says you're supposed to be down in the kitchen sitting on that bench in 15 minutes."

"Oh, dear!" Lizzie whirled around to grab her white apron from the bed.

"Emma!" she hollered. "You have to help me with my apron."

Rolling her eyes at Stephen, Emma came in and began adjusting the apron for Lizzie. Joshua and Emma had come from Allen County the previous

day to help on the *risht-dawg*, the day of prepara-
tion before an Amish wedding, just as they had done
for Mandy.

Baby Mark toddled around and squealed with
excitement most of the day until he wore himself out
completely, falling asleep on a corner of the couch
in the dining room. The whole house had been in
a frightful uproar, same as the previous weddings,
but Mam seemed a bit more unruffled, not quite as
upset about things, as this was, after all, her third
wedding.

Dat was always the same at wedding time. He
loved it, thriving on the action and the attention
from relatives on both sides, but most of all, he
loved the singing. He would always lead quite a few
songs on the day his daughters were married, just
for the pure joy of "getting the singing going real
well."

Mam and Lizzie hardly argued or disagreed on
anything. Mam was much calmer, and Lizzie wasn't
particular about little details, like who was invited,
or how many of the youth were included, or what
kind of pies they served.

Aunt Vera made mountains of date pudding at
home in Ohio, bringing it all the way to Pennsylva-
nia with buckets of whipped topping for the big day.
Date pudding was Lizzie's favorite dessert, ever since
she had first tasted it as a little girl in Ohio. It was a
soft, moist cake baked with dates and nuts, then cut
into tiny squares and layered with a caramel sauce
and whipped topping. It was rich and creamy with a

nutty texture that was simply delicious. They served it on every table throughout the house, with small squares of red and green Jell-O on top, because their wedding was so close to Christmas.

Lizzie's room soon filled up as the remainder of the bridal party moved over from the adjoining room. During the wedding, Jason would sit with Rebecca, and Daniel would sit with Lizzie's cousin Esther, who, along with Lizzie's sisters and their husbands, made up the six individuals who would be the honored guests.

"Hold still, Lizzie; I mean it," Emma hissed around a straight pin in her mouth.

"Get that pin out of your mouth, Emma!" Lizzie hissed back.

Emma straightened up, giving the smooth white belt an extra pat and said, "There!"

Lizzie stepped up to the mirror, surveying the finished attire, her eyes wide with apprehension.

"Do … I … I … Does it look all right? Emma, you made a nice covering for my wedding day. Thank you. You are a dear. Honest."

"You look lovely, Lizzie, and I'm glad you like the covering, because I sure went to enough pains with it. I must have opened and redone that one side three times."

"Ready?" Stephen asked.

Lizzie looked around her room wildly. "Where are the decorative throw pillows for my bed?" she asked.

Jason produced them from behind his back,

grinning, and Lizzie pounced on them, arranging them carefully, making certain everything looked just right.

"Do we remember who goes first?" she asked.

"Of course," Jason said airily, and they all filed solemnly down the stairs and sat side by side with their backs against the stairway wall, as straight as stickmen on a hard wooden bench in the kitchen.

Suddenly Lizzie thought she would be sick to her stomach from sheer nervousness. The house was already full of people, and every minute another horse and buggy or van load of people arrived. Where would they all sit? Suppose there was not enough room for everyone? Maybe this would actually be the first wedding the Amish people could remember that didn't have enough seating space. People would talk about it for 50 years. Like the story of the bride who changed her mind at the last minute and would not join her groom to stand in front of the minister to be married. The minister asked if there was anyone else in the room who would marry this man, and the bride's sister got up and married him, and they lived happily ever after. Was that really true? No one seemed to know who these people were, so Lizzie always doubted the story.

Why did she sit here on her wedding day, thinking all these ridiculous thoughts? She was so nervous this minute that she felt like crying. She wished she could hold Stephen's hand for comfort, but then she was so clammy with sweat he probably wouldn't want to hold her hand. This was awful.

Oh, dear, a whole load of people Lizzie had never seen before walked up to them, and she didn't have the slightest clue who they were! She swallowed hard, glancing wildly at Stephen, but he was smiling genuinely at a tall, plump lady and greeting each strange person who shook his hand.

Lizzie wondered what would happen if she panicked and burst through the door and ran down across the flat pasture to the fencerow by the creek and hid. Would they come looking for her? Why did she think these thoughts? She had to calm down, really seriously calm herself, and remember what day this was. Her wedding day. After today she would no longer be Lizzie Glick. It was high time people started calling her Elizabeth, now that she was a respectable married woman who combed her hair sleek and flat.

After shaking more hands than she had ever shaken before, at least in one sitting, she took a few deep breaths to calm herself so she could smile at bustling aunts and greet her friends as they filed into the room. She began to feel comfortable enough to enjoy her wedding day.

The singing started, which was the official signal that the ceremony was now in progress. The ministers all filed upstairs to hold conference, with Stephen and Lizzie following them. The ministers each took turns speaking to them about marriage and what was expected of them in their life together.

As Lizzie listened, she knew that beginning with this day, she had entered into a permanent union,

one rooted as deeply as the largest oak in the forest. Seasons would come and go, the heat of summer, the winds of autumn when every branch moved in the gale, the ice and snow in winter, which bent every branch to its limit, sometimes even breaking sturdy limbs, and yet she and Stephen would endure.

When spring came, new growth would replace the broken limbs, strengthening the tree, just like their argument about the color of the bricks on their brown house had deepened their relationship.

There was no turning back now.

She peeped at Stephen beneath lowered lashes, overwhelmed by happiness and her faith in him. He was so serious, his tanned face so solemn, his hair shining, and cut in the proper *ordnung* for this day.

All she needed to do was place her hand in his and follow him back downstairs as the singing congregation waited. He would lead her to the minister who would unite them in holy matrimony. With the singing wafting up from the house below, Lizzie felt like crying again because of the interest of these kind ministers, and well, just everything.

When they were finished, Lizzie and Stephen filed slowly and solemnly into the living room with the rest of the bridal party, sitting across from each other on the new wooden chairs that Stephen's grandfather had made for them in his little woodworking shop. They had been a gift from Stephen's parents and pleased Lizzie immensely.

Lizzie kept her head bowed demurely, her hands folded in her lap. She couldn't look up—she didn't

dare look at Stephen—so she just looked at her lap. It felt as if hundreds of eyes were staring intently at her from every direction, so the safest thing to do was keep her head lowered.

The singing stopped and someone chose another song—that familiar tune that had been sung at hundreds of other weddings. It was a very cozy feeling, Lizzie thought, to know that this ritual, this form of *ordnung* or set of rules the wedding was based on, had been the same for Mam and Dat, for Stephen's parents, and their parents before them, and on and on for generations. That was a good and calming thing, the realization that everyone in this house knew what to expect and how to go about running this wedding.

It certainly had not seemed very orderly yesterday. The whole house had resembled a chicken house after a fox makes an appearance. Well, that was a stretch, perhaps, but how could 10 or 15 women get anything accomplished and all talk at the same time? Because talk they did. Laughed and planned and stood in small bunches with pieces of paper, writing down who did what, and who was seated where, and how many platters of chicken and filling went on which table, and on and on.

Sometimes Mam got a little snorty if the rules were a bit stringent, and she would shake her head and say, *Ach, voss machts aus?* What does it matter? She was from Ohio, so she was no stickler for tradition, although she had a few practices of her own from her growing-up church that Lizzie didn't

particularly like. But when all the dust settled from the *risht-dawg* and the sun rose on a perfectly prepared wedding day, who knew what an unbelievable fuss had occurred there the day before? That's just how it was.

Now the preachers all walked into the room, quiet and solemn, and took their seats in the same row as the bridal party. After the singing was finished, the first minister stood up, cleared his throat, surveyed the crowd of people, and began to speak. After his sermon was over, there was a short prayer, the scriptures were read, and then the bishop from Mam's home church in Ohio stood up to preach the long sermon. He was in his 60s, Lizzie guessed, according to his white hair and beard. He proved to be a good speaker. He touched on many interesting aspects of marriage, including living together in harmony with your neighbors, as well as with each other.

However, Lizzie became fidgety, her palms began to perspire again, and her back started aching. She knew the minister would talk about the Tobias story, the tale from the old German storybook where a young man of God set out on a journey for his father and discovered love and then marriage. It was a good, rather touching story, but after the bishop mentioned Tobias's name, Lizzie's heart never really slowed down. She knew that soon the bishop would call Stephen and her to stand before him.

Her heart jumped in one frantic flutter when he started the Tobias story and went racing on until

he stopped to announce that today there were two who were prepared for matrimony. He announced their names, and Lizzie ignored her swiftly beating heart and her nervousness. She solemnly did what was required of her, getting up from her chair, holding Stephen's proffered hand, and following him to stand in front of the bishop.

The minister cleared his throat and asked the congregation if there was anyone who wished to put a stop to this wedding. Of course, there wasn't. Then he asked Stephen if he wished to take Lizzie as his wife. Would he promise to love her and take care of her, through sickness and other trials of her life? Stephen quietly answered, "Ya."

Then the minister asked Lizzie the exact same questions. Lizzie's voice shook only the tiniest bit as she said, "Ya." The minister asked them more questions of faith, to which they both responded in turn with another "Ya."

The minister covered their joined hands as he pronounced them man and wife, then spoke a blessing in the name of Jesus Christ. Lizzie and Stephen turned and sat down across from each other. Only then did Lizzie take a deep breath, and her heartbeat slowly returned to normal. Only after the ministers had given testimony, another long prayer was read, and the last exultant song was started, she dared to sneak a look at Stephen's face. His eyes were very blue, and he gave her a small, special smile, which she returned before lowering her eyes properly to her hands in her lap.

The singing rose and swelled around them. Of all the slow, old German tunes that were sung, this was the most lovely of them all with its words about God and a bride and groom. Lizzie pressed her lips firmly together to hold in her emotion. The song was sung so beautifully.

Joy flooded her heart, and a sure feeling enveloped her soul. She had sought God's will in her own fumbling, unsure way after many errors. But now she had come home, securely bound to her husband by her love and, most importantly, by God.

The last soaring note of the song died away. It was almost time for the celebration to begin. Finally Lizzie could look at Stephen and see only him, hold his hand, and go back upstairs to change her covering from a black organdy to a white organdy one. She and Stephen also changed from their borrowed, old-fashioned, high-topped shoes to their afternoon slippers.

Then the festivities of an Amish wedding day officially started. Men quickly rearranged the living room, carrying in long tables and setting them up around the room. Lizzie and Stephen were told their dinner was ready in less than half an hour after the service was over. The wooden benches where people were seated during the ceremony were placed around the tables, tablecloths were put on, and dozens of hands passed out plates, water pitchers, rolls, butter, jelly, applesauce, coleslaw, filled doughnuts, trays of cookies, fruit, and hot platters of food before the guests were again seated.

Lizzie tried hard to keep a mature, serene expression on her face, but her smile just kept sliding out of control. She was deep-down, really happy, genuinely pleased to have become Stephen's wife, to spend this wonderful day of celebration as the honored guest who sat in the most important seat, the *eck*, or corner.

Her nicest tablecloth covered the table, and it was set with her china, silverware, and, best of all, the expensive water pitcher and glasses Stephen had given her. A cut-glass bowl held fruit, two cakes sat on glass cake stands, and a variety of fancy dishes were filled with good things to eat. Even the butter was molded into wedding bells with little sprigs of parsley adorning it. The whole corner table looked so grand. Joshua and Emma, John and Mandy, and Aunt Vera's two children, Leroy and his wife and Mary Ann and her husband, served as their waiters.

After finishing their delicious meal, Lizzie and Stephen went upstairs to Lizzie's bedroom to open the gifts that were piled on Lizzie's bed. Many of the aunts and cousins came up to watch them open the beautifully wrapped presents.

After the gifts were unwrapped, Lizzie couldn't imagine what she would do with all the stuff! She would need a large pantry and plenty of cupboards in her new house, no doubt about that. She smiled.

"Where will we keep all of this?" she asked Stephen.

"We'll have plenty of kitchen cupboards, Lizzie," he told her, which made Lizzie glad and happy all over again.

After that, the afternoon singing began, and Lizzie and Stephen and the rest of the wedding party all filed back to the *eck*, their table, again. Each of the single young men chose a young girl to sit with him at the table, and they shared a songbook between them during the hymn-singing. All the older folks stopped their dishwashing and other various duties to watch "the *youngie* go in." There were quite a few giggles and rib-punching and some whispering among them, as they watched to see who had picked which girl.

Stephen told Lizzie he was so glad he never had to do that again, and Lizzie could very easily agree with him. The singing started again, slow hymns and also faster ones which the youth led, while candy dishes, fruit, drinks, and other delicacies were passed from person to person.

There was lots of talking and visiting going on, and one part of the table became a bit rowdy, with some of the young boys tossing small pieces of candy or celery at each other. Their companions either giggled or looked horrified, depending on the type of girl. It was all familiar and very dear to Lizzie and Stephen.

The last event of the day was pairing the boys and girls for the evening meal. This was Lizzie's duty. Each boy took a girl to the table. They would eat supper together and join the hymn-singing later in the evening. This was a big event in the life of a teenager. Sometimes, after being taken to the table, a couple would begin dating, so it was considered a

good way to meet a companion. It was the hardest part of the day for the bride, because after thinking that she had everything down pat, finished up, and that everything was fine, a few of the boys would refuse to accompany the girls she had paired them with for the evening.

The air had turned sharply colder after a snow shower that afternoon. Lizzie was getting tired and a bit irritable with some of the couples' slow response to her pairing. It was getting late, she was almost in tears, and she couldn't find Stephen.

Finally he appeared, and she made a dash to be at his side. "Stephen, where were you? I need help badly. David and Lee won't take Susie and Fannie. Now what do I do? Everyone else seems to be okay with the partners I assigned."

Stephen put his arm around her waist and held her firmly, soothingly, while Lizzie struggled to keep her emotions in check.

"Let me take care of it," he said and marched her along with him, confronting the two boys who were acting reluctant to join their dates.

"If you don't want the girls she gave you, I guess you won't be getting any supper then, will you?" he said in a firm voice.

"Aw. Come on!" Lee wailed.

"Sorry. It's either Fannie or no one," and he steered Lizzie away.

"You mean... Can you do that?" she asked.

"Sure. I can act as stubborn as they are."

Lizzie giggled.

"They'll get over it," he finished. And that was that.

Lizzie decided on the way to the *eck* for supper that she had better appreciate Stephen all her days. What would she have done without him?

The buttered potatoes, corn, and meat loaf tasted good to Lizzie after a day of traipsing around in the cold, trying to keep everyone happy. She soon forgot her frustration after all the youth filed in and they sat eating the good food and listening to the singing. Lizzie looked for David and Lee but couldn't find them, so she figured they must be all right.

Stephen sat back, his blue eyes drooping with sleepiness after the tension of the day. Lizzie watched him, then asked if he was glad the whole day was over, or almost.

"Oh, am I ever! Even if it's my wedding day, all these people really make me tired in a hurry!"

Lizzie laughed. "You look beat."

"I am."

After the guests said good-bye, and Lizzie and Stephen were wished congratulations one last time, the aunts and uncles started washing dishes, filling garbage bags with candy wrappers, leftover apple cores, and celery tops, all the while still smiling and joking. Some of the relatives continued singing heartily, although Lizzie wondered how in the world they could keep going without their voices wearing out.

For the last time the bridal party left the table, glad to have had a wonderful time together, but

at the same time, grateful it was all over, and that they could get on with their normal lives. Of course, life for Lizzie would be a new "normal." She was no longer a single girl at home, helping Mam and being one of the family. She was Stephen's wife now, whatever that entailed, though all she felt was joy and anticipation.

Even if marriage was a bit like jumping off a cliff, never completely certain where you would land, there was no other place she would rather be than here in this torn-up, messy house that had just held such a joyous celebration.

She loved Stephen. Wasn't that amazing? Each disagreement, each time one of them hurt the other's feelings, actually brought them closer as they forgave each other, which in turn, brought them a deeper affection. So what was there to be afraid of? Nothing really, unless, of course, the disagreements became too serious.

Chapter 13

STEPHEN CLIMBED INTO THE BUGGY. HE wrapped the blue and green plaid buggy blanket around Lizzie's legs before settling it around his own. He lifted the reins and chirped to George, the horse. The buggy rolled forward.

Outside, the air was frigid with gray clouds scudding across a backdrop of dull blue and white sky, as if the sunshine had frozen along with the rest of the world. The buggy wheels screamed that thin high squeal of metal on frozen snow, which always set Lizzie's teeth on edge. She shivered and snuggled closer to Stephen, glad for the warmth of another person and the heavy blanket wrapped securely around them.

They were on their way to visit yet another family in the community and to receive the wedding gift that awaited them. It was the custom among the Amish of Lizzie's community for newlyweds to visit the home of each guest who had attend their wedding

and receive a gift, becoming better acquainted with each other in the process. Sometimes the new couple stayed for a meal; other times only for a short visit or a "call." Lizzie couldn't understand why some families went to a lot of work preparing a meal, while with others, you sat for a short time, collected your wedding gift, and kept going. Kind of like a drive-through gift collection. She thought the short variety was pretty dumb.

But, being Amish, Lizzie knew that it wasn't up to her to say how things were done or not done, no matter what she thought. She was a member of this Amish church, and she never even thought of being anything else. She was perfectly content to follow its customs and dedicate her life to living happily within the church's rules. Well, not always. She still wanted nice things. Sometimes she wished she didn't have to comb her hair like all the other married women, so completely flat and smooth and up off her forehead with only thin, flat rolls along the side of her head.

No wonder everyone waited until they were married to comb their hair like that. Suddenly the unsuspecting husband found his wife looking quite different, and there wasn't a thing he could do about it. He was married to her. Of course, Lizzie reasoned, she had combed her hair almost the same way on their wedding day and Stephen still went ahead and married her. Mam said looks had nothing to do with love, but deep down, Lizzie knew that wasn't completely true.

Her mind wandered to the table set up in her bedroom with gifts stacked on top, beneath, and on both sides. Gifts everywhere. In her opinion, it was time to move into the little house on top of the hill that Stephen was building. She didn't like living with Dat and Mam and the rest of the family for the first months after she was married. But that was how things were, so there was no use fretting.

Mam wasn't too enthused about it either, but she never let on, except when Stephen and Dat were at work. Then she would tell Lizzie how it was done in Ohio where she was born and raised, the newly-weds moving the day after the wedding, the way it should be, she said, her eyes snapping behind the wire rims of her glasses. But she never said much to anyone else. She packed Stephen's lunch along with Dat's and Jason's, cooked delicious meals, and in general, seemed quite thrilled to have them in the house, in spite of the newlywed tradition in Ohio which she preferred.

Mam was a good sport about most things in life, a trait that Lizzie had come to appreciate as she became older. Actually, when she really thought about it, Mam was more dear to her with each pass-ing day. It seemed especially so since Lizzie knew she would soon leave their farmhouse, the place she had spent the past seven years of her life.

Lizzie slid a sideways glance at Stephen, wonder-ing what he was thinking, and wondering, too, if he truly was the exact right person for her to spend the remainder of her life with, now that she had

promised to love, honor, cherish, and obey him. She sincerely hoped so.

The thing about Stephen, though, was his inability to talk very much at a time, which kept her chattering on, kind of like a fish out of water, flopping around on the bank until it flopped its way back in. Sometimes when he became too quiet it worked on Lizzie's nerves, and she said senseless things that annoyed him, she could tell.

His head was turned as he stared intently out the window of the side door, watching for deer again, the way he always did on the Water Mill Road. He should know that there would be no deer in broad daylight, especially in the frigid weather, and most of all, with the squeal of the buggy wheels that could be heard a mile away.

"You're not going to see any deer," Lizzie said, flatly.

"I might."

"Not in this weather."

He didn't bother answering, so Lizzie toyed with the fringe of her black woolen shawl under the heavy blanket and felt nervous. He didn't look very happy, and she was almost 100 percent sure she knew why. He simply didn't enjoy this going from one place to another the way he should, and that made Lizzie feel very anxious, afraid that he might no longer want to go. What would people think?

After the last meal they had had almost a week ago at Aaron King's house, Stephen had definitely been subdued, shrugging his shoulders noncommittally

when she asked him why he was unhappy.

"I'm not, really. It's just that ... well, nothing."

"What?"

"Nothing."

"Come on. You didn't enjoy tonight, did you?"

"Well, your Uncle Marvin says everything, so there's nothing left for me to say."

Marvin and Sara Ruth and Amos and Sally were the other two couples who went visiting with them through the winter months, and Lizzie enjoyed them immensely. It was a bit of a shock to hear Stephen talk about her beloved Marvin that way. He was a very sociable person, easily conversing with anyone about almost any subject, which Lizzie thought was an extremely admirable quality. It was the way most of the Glicks were.

She thought Stephen was acting like a baby, but knew she shouldn't say so because it simply wasn't nice. She wanted to though.

"Marvin was always fussy and outgoing."

"I know."

So that conversation came to an end in a hurry, and Lizzie glanced at Stephen again. She still wondered if she should tell him he was being childish and that she couldn't understand why he couldn't enjoy listening to Marvin talk. Suddenly she remembered when she was 15 years old at a pajama party at her friend Sharon's house, and how terribly left out she had felt, all because the girls loved Mandy. She had even cried all alone in the bathroom and had never told one single soul, certainly not Mandy.

Maybe that was how Stephen felt now, like going
to the bathroom to cry all by himself because no one
had noticed him. Sometimes you couldn't help it
when you felt like that, even if it was terribly child-
ish and dumb. It wasn't Marvin's fault, not one bit.
He was just being Marvin, oblivious to the fact that
Stephen wished he'd be quiet and let him say some-
thing occasionally.

They pulled into the driveway, and John Mill-
er's wife, Suvilla, stepped out onto the porch and
waved. While Stephen tied up the horse in the barn,
Lizzie picked her way across the frozen ground to
the house. Suvilla welcomed Lizzie warmly, holding
the door open and shaking her hand over and over
before directing her to the bedroom. A kerosene
lamp offered its cozy glow in the quiet room. Lizzie
took off her black shawl and bonnet, unbuttoned
her coat, and slid her arms out of the sleeves. She
laid her coat on the bed and took her covering out
of the covering box, pinned it securely on her sleek
hair, and tied the strings, gazing disapprovingly in
the mirror.

The thing was, her forehead was twice as high as
it used to be with her hair pulled back so severely
now. She looked like that picture of a turtle in the
Tommy Turtle children's book. No matter how she
tried, she just couldn't get used to seeing herself with
that high forehead.

She heard Suvilla chattering on as she returned
to the hallway just as Sara Ruth and Sally arrived.
Lizzie smiled with the familiar pleasure she always

felt when she was with her two dear friends who had also just gotten married. Visiting was twice as much fun when you had good friends to share the evenings with. They giggled and laughed together, shivered and commented on the weather, all agreeing how glad they would be to have homes of their own and to be able to stay at home on evenings such as this.

Their husbands came into the house, and they all sat down around the dining room table. The supper was delicious. Lizzie enjoyed everything thoroughly, running her hand worriedly across her stomach under the table. Oh dear, this will never do, she thought unhappily, as she finished a whole piece of chocolate cake with peanut butter frosting. I have to stop eating so much this late in the evening.

She glanced at Stephen, who seemed to be enjoying himself, talking to Marvin and Amos. John was getting into the conversation as well. Good, Lizzie thought. Maybe it was just that one evening that was a problem and everything will go well from here on.

After the dishes were done, the Millers gave the couples their wedding gifts—stainless steel bowls for the young women and pitchforks for the men. These were good, useful items they were grateful for, and Lizzie thanked her hostess genuinely, telling her she didn't have that size bowls at all. Aaron would not let them leave before they had played a few tricks, including "Where's Jack?" a game where a blindfolded player stumbled across the kitchen, trying to

reach his opponent. It was as hilarious as always.

Lizzie left the house with Stephen, filled with a warm happy feeling, thankful for the gifts, and appreciative of the good meal and secure relationship with older members of this close-knit group of Amish people. As they left this home, Lizzie felt keenly the strong ties of love she had for each family, never wanting to say anything bad about these evenings.

So she was relieved when Stephen seemed happy on the way home, talking more than usual. He told her that Marvin and Sara Ruth were planning to move into temporary living quarters in their new shop, and then take their time building a new house, instead of rushing as he had to for his and Lizzie's house.

Rushing along? Lizzie lowered her eyebrows and tried not to say what she thought, she was so incredulous. Rushing? In her opinion, the house was coming along at an unbelievably slow pace, so she couldn't understand what Stephen meant.

"Rushing? Do you think we're hurrying on our house?" she asked.

"Why, of course!" he said, loudly.

"But...?"

"Oh, I know. It's not fast enough for you. But to think we're only working in the evenings and on Saturdays, I think we're pushing it."

"But... but... at the rate the house is going, we won't be moved in till spring!" Lizzie said in a voice that tried very hard not to be a wail.

"We can move before that. I was thinking of moving into the basement anyway, now that we have running water. If I do a bit of plumbing, and if we bought a heating stove and some carpet, we could move."

"Really?"

"If you want to. I'm ready to live by ourselves, even if it means living in an unfinished basement."

"Oh, goody!" Lizzie clutched Stephen's arm excitedly. "That will be so cozy!"

"You won't think all the sawdust seeping through the ceiling is cozy, Lizzie," he laughed.

"I don't care. You can wipe sawdust away. Oh, let's do! Let's move in a week!"

"We could."

❧

And so they did. The following week, Mam helped Lizzie clean and scrub. Dat and Jason put up temporary shelving for Lizzie's dishes, they laid pieces of carpeting on the fresh concrete, connected the plumbing, and generally made the basement quite livable.

On the day they moved the new furniture to the basement, the weather turned surprisingly warm and balmy for February. Lizzie thought happily that this was very likely a good omen. Perhaps they were being a bit impatient—unwise, actually—but, oh, it would be so good to have a home of their own.

The gas stove sat beside the makeshift sink with enough counter-top space to prepare a meal and wash dishes. The refrigerator stood beside the sink. The hutch, or "combine," as the Amish called it, stood against the opposite wall, with the new table and chairs in the middle.

It was all very cozy, and Lizzie chattered happily all the while she unpacked her brown ironstone dishes, setting them in the combine. They strung sturdy wire from the chimney to the back wall and then over to the north wall, hanging old sheets to partition off a bedroom. The men brought in Lizzie's bedroom suit from the farmhouse to fill the temporary room.

Joshua and Emma had not been able to come because their children were sick. Their absence almost ruined the day for Lizzie. She felt sorry for Emma, who, she was sure, would have loved to help arrange furniture the way Lizzie had helped her. But there was nothing to do about that now, so she tried not to pity Emma, knowing she probably didn't mind as much as Lizzie did.

John and Mandy arrived late because of doing the morning chores, having two babies to bundle up, and then driving 10 miles with their horse and buggy. Lizzie squealed with excitement when they arrived, running over to Mandy and grabbing her arm, while Mandy's grin spread the whole way across her face as she looked about the new basement.

"Lizzie, I can't believe you're going to live in this

groundhog hole," she said.

Lizzie stopped in her tracks, truly insulted.

"It's not a groundhog hole!" she protested.

"I know," Mandy smiled. "It's just..."

"Not finished!" Lizzie completed the sentence rapidly.

Mandy laughed.

Mam didn't think Mandy's twins should be in the new house. Susan and KatieAnn kept them in the farmhouse so Mandy could be with Lizzie. The sisters worked side by side down to the last detail, hanging curtains over the small windows and putting a new tablecloth and place mats on the table, before they all trooped down the hill for Mam's late dinner of chicken stew and dumplings.

Halfway through dessert, Lizzie could hardly swallow because of the lump in her throat. This was it. This was truly it. She would never live at home again with Mam and Dat in the old farmhouse with the new addition and Mam's porch filled with "cheraniums" in the wintertime, all kinds of seedlings and transplants in the spring, and bountiful houseplants in the summer.

Now who would mow the grass and trim along the flower beds? That had been her job as long as she could remember, although Susan and KatieAnn had begun to do a lot of the mowing the previous summer. It certainly wasn't Mam's job. She never mowed lawn. She cooked and baked, cleaned the kitchen counter, tended her flowers and quilted, and the girls did the remainder of the work.

It wasn't that the family couldn't survive without Lizzie's help, she knew. It was just sad to think that it was all over now. Her new life with Stephen would begin this evening when they were all alone in the funny little unfinished basement on the hill behind the farm. Lizzie looked up to see Mandy gazing intently in her direction. She lowered her eyes, willing herself to finish this last piece of butterscotch pie.

In Mam's wise way, she opened the subject when the men returned to the new house and Lizzie stayed to help with the dishes. Dumping leftover applesauce into a Tupperware container, she turned to face Lizzie.

"So, this is it for you, huh?"

Blinking rapidly, Lizzie answered. "I suppose so."

"Well, it's the way God intended, Lizzie," Mam said, sighing a bit as she wiped the container where she had spilled some of the applesauce. "He didn't mean for us to be tied to our mother's apron strings after we reach a certain age. Nature, the animals, everything God created, has its times and seasons. Birds leave the nest, baby calves are weaned, and on and on."

"I know, Mam, but I just hate to think of this part of my life being over. All the closeness we shared as sisters..."

"I know exactly what you mean, Lizzie," Mandy broke in. "And let me give you a bit of sisterly advice. Prepare yourself, because marriage isn't all

roses, no matter how much you love your husband. I'll never forget the almost overwhelming nauseas before the twins were born, and..."

She giggled, holding a hand to shield her eyes for a minute. "I mean it, when I think back to those first months! What a baby I was—upstairs crying, wanting desperately to be home again, just wanting to be one of Melvin Glick's girls again, and poor John was downstairs eating cold sandwiches for supper. All alone! Oh, how horrible."

Mam threw her head back and laughed long and genuinely. Taking off her glasses, she wiped her eyes, still shaking with silent laughter, and said, "Ach my, Mandy. I remember that very same feeling. It's all a part of life, of growing up and learning to become a more mature person."

Lizzie leaned back in her chair and glared at both of them. "You think it's funny, Mam. Well, I don't. And I'm not going to have one moment like that. Stop talking such things. It gives me the blues."

"All right, Lizzie. But really, it isn't all roses and sunshine, just like Mandy said. You'll have days when you wonder why you ever got married in the first place."

"I don't believe that," Lizzie said staunchly. "I refuse to think that could be possible. You just weren't... well, maybe you didn't love John the way you should have."

Mam's eyebrows went straight up, followed by Mandy's, and they had a genuine, "She'll learn" look between them. Lizzie was so angry that she got

up and said it was time for her to go back up to the house. So much for a tearful farewell, she thought, as she stalked up the hill into her little basement that promised to be a haven of pure marital bliss.

Chapter 14

A COLD FREEZING RAIN POURED FROM LEADEN skies, driving in from the east in long, wet slashes against the small basement window as Lizzie pinned her cape once again for another visit. This evening they would be going to visit Elmer and Malinda Esh, a young couple who rented a farmhouse about six miles away. Lizzie looked forward to the evening since the Eshes were not much older than they were.

She was grateful for a good woolen shawl and the bonnet that afforded some protection from the freezing rain as she climbed into the buggy.

"Whew!" she gasped. "This weather!"

Stephen nodded.

"I'm worried about leakage in the basement, no spouting on the house, and the cement blocks offset the way they are, for bricks. I just hope the ground will contain the seepage."

"Oh, it'll be all right," Lizzie said airily.

"I'm not so sure," Stephen replied.

"Well, what's the worst that could happen? Some water on the floor that will surely go down the drain?" Lizzie asked.

Stephen didn't reply, only grunted, so she remained silent, although the thought of rain water coming into the basement made her bite down hard on her lower lip. Her eyes darted nervously to the rain streaming against the buggy windows.

She forgot the pelting rain, the basement home, or anything worrisome after she entered the cozy farmhouse kitchen and found the table set with Malinda's prettiest dishes. The only light in the dining room came from real candles burning in their delicate holders.

Oh, but that was just about the classiest thing Lizzie had ever seen! She clasped her hands in front of herself excitedly. How romantic for newlyweds to eat by candlelight, which was always flattering to anyone's looks. The imperfections of your face were well hidden by the small amount of light candles afforded.

The food was delicious, although it was different, without the usual meat and potato fare. Lizzie enjoyed the evening tremendously, eating too much as usual, promising herself that she would do much better at the next meal.

Their wedding gift was a Tupperware pitcher, something new, with a lid that sealed so you could shake the liquid inside without it leaking out. Lizzie thought it was a wonderful new invention to be able

to mix a drink without having to stir it with a spoon. Iced tea mix would no longer settle on the bottom of a container because you could keep shaking it at intervals, and the sugar would always be mixed through. Before this, you ended up with watered-down iced tea at first, and then tea that was much too sweet when the pitcher was almost empty.

When the evening was over, Lizzie dashed through the rain and scrambled quickly into the buggy, slamming the side door shut with all her strength before wrapping the blue and green blanket securely across her lap. She watched Stephen's face as he frowned at the streams of icy water cascading down the window of the buggy.

"Still no let up," he murmured, more to himself than to her.

"No. It's been raining like this for..."

"All day," Stephen broke in.

He urged George forward, and they went flying along, homeward bound. Lizzie was glad to go home to their own little house, even if it was unfinished. As usual, they took the team down to her parents' farm, because there was no barn on their property yet. Stephen asked if she wanted to be dropped off at their house, but she shook her heard no, assuring him she could run up the hill through the rain as well as he could. They ran through the downpour together and arrived at the basement door, gasping for breath, completely soaked. Stephen turned the knob and unlocked the door, stepped inside, and stopped.

"What?" Lizzie squeaked.

Then she heard it. A decided splashing sound where Stephen stepped. Oh, no! Her heart escalated to her throat before banging way down to the pit of her stomach, spreading fear and anxiety through her. Water! Water everywhere! Her new furniture, the sofa, the recliner. Everything would be ruined, of this she was positive.

"Oh, Stephen!" she wailed, absolutely heartsick. "Where is all this water coming from?"

"Just be quiet!" Stephen almost shouted at her.

Lizzie was horrified. Water, cold rain water, spread across the entire floor, swirling beneath her new sofa and recliner, swishing along the table and new chairs, and now Stephen was yelling at her, clearly angry just because she squeaked one frightened little question.

It was pitch dark in the basement, but Lizzie knew she needed to find a pack of matches to light the gas lamp. Flashlights! That was the answer, but by the time she had sloshed over to the cupboard, Stephen had already found one, which by the sound of his muttering, wasn't cooperating.

"Doesn't that one work?" she managed, in a tiny voice.

There was no answer; only the sound of a flashlight being hurled against the unpainted cement block wall, accompanied by Stephen's frustrated accusation that she had lost all the flashlights.

That did it. Lizzie felt the anger course through her body, followed by a rush of adrenaline. She

stopped in the middle of the wet basement, curled her hands into fists, and took a deep breath.

"I didn't touch your precious flashlight!" she yelled, "So don't go blaming me for everything that goes wrong!"

"There were two flashlights against the left cupboard wall. Now there's only one, and it doesn't work."

"I didn't use it!" Lizzie screeched.

There was only a resounding "Humph" from Stephen, and Lizzie became so angry she wished she had a flashlight to throw at him. All right, if that's how he was going to be, she'd just stand there with the water sloshing around her, slowly seeping between the leather layers of the soles of her Sunday shoes and soaking her feet with a miserable, cold wetness. She knew where the matches were, but she wasn't going to tell him. Let him figure it out.

Which, of course, he did. He rummaged around in a few drawers before sloshing over to the table and lowering the gas lamp that hung above it. Striking two matches, he heated the mantles until they ignited. Brilliant yellow light illuminated the entire basement as he carefully hung the lamp on the hook suspended from the ceiling joist.

Lizzie looked around very slowly, hardly daring to look at Stephen, knowing he was angry. A significant amount of water covered almost the entire floor. Water seemed to still be entering the basement through the east wall, where rain continued

to pelt against the house. Lizzie felt panic rising in her throat. They couldn't even begin to sop up the water with towels and buckets. They'd be working the entire night.

"Stephen, what are we going to do?" Lizzie asked, wringing her hands in despair.

"Open the drain, for one thing," he said shortly, grabbing the broom and flipping it upside down as he searched for the drain opening.

Oh, that was it! They had a drain! Of course! All the water would run down the drain pipe, out into the yard and down the hill. Why hadn't she thought of that before? Why, of course. They would have a clean, dry basement in no time.

She almost cried when Stephen bent down and pulled at the top of the drain, and she heard a distinct gurgling sound as water began to flow down the new pipe. She watched in awe as a little whirlpool of water formed above it, the water continuing its spiral down this wonderful little outlet. Never had there been a sweeter sight in her entire life. Her new furniture wouldn't be ruined after all.

"Oh, Stephen, it's going down!" she breathed happily.

"Yeah, but more is coming in along that back wall, so don't get too excited.

"You mean... you mean, it's still coming in?"

"Of course. As long as it continues to rain like this, it'll come down through those offset blocks. There's no spouting on the house, remember?"

Lizzie nodded miserably.

"You can start sweeping some of the water toward the drain awhile. I'll set up the things we can lift out of the water."

He started picking up the new kitchen chairs and placing them upside down on the table top, while Lizzie reached for the broom and began sweeping water towards the drain from the farthest corner. The water kept up its swirl down the lovely little drain. They didn't speak, just worked silently, each one doing what had to be done at the moment. Lizzie swept as if her very life depended on how much water went down that drain. When she reached the bedroom, she couldn't stop the wail that threatened to turn into a torrent of genuine little girl tears.

"My bedroom suit! My new bedspread!" she wailed. "Stephen, I mean it, everything will be ruined!" she cried.

"Not if we get it dried out as fast as we possibly can," Stephen answered, "The only problem is the water is still coming in."

"How … long do you think it will keep raining?" Lizzie asked, her mouth dry with anxiety.

"How would I know?" Stephen answered brusquely.

That did it. Lizzie began crying in earnest. She stopped trying to be brave and grown up, resorting to the heartsick despair she felt so keenly. She wanted to run to her old bedroom upstairs in her parents' farmhouse, crawl safely into her own bed way off the ground, and listen to the rain drumming on the attic roof. She would be dry and secure, and

Dat would take care of everything. She shouldn't have married so soon, she thought sadly. Then she felt so horrible for having that thought and she started crying harder than ever.

Perhaps this was what the preacher meant at their wedding when he said they would experience the joys of sunshiny days as well as the trials of rainy days. She supposed you put this experience smack dab in the category of trials and rainy days, for sure. The same preacher had also spoken at length about the trials in their lives producing fruit; in other words, making better people out of all of us. Lizzie couldn't see how this was possible. How was she ever supposed to like Stephen again? He was mean to her.

That was the thing about being married to someone. What if you could hardly stand them when they didn't act right? It was all so scary. How in the world did that preacher figure any good could come out of a mess like this? She doubted if even God could find the good in this situation.

Tears running down her face, and sniffling and coughing like a little girl, she kept sweeping water toward the drain. She made absolutely sure Stephen heard her crying, so he would feel sorry for her and feel bad that he had made her cry so soon into their marriage. She blew her nose loudly, sighed, looked in his direction, and sighed louder.

He kept on moving furniture out of the water, never stopping to glance in her direction. Bringing pieces of lumber down from upstairs, he set the sofa

and recliner up and out of the water, which, Lizzie admitted to herself, was a wonderful idea.

"You'll have to help me with the dresser, Lizzie," he said, stopping to look at her.

"I'm still crying. Wait," she answered, finding the perfect opportunity to let him understand that she was, after all, completely heartbroken. Stephen's shoulders sagged, and he made a sound between a snort and a sigh. Mostly a snort. Lizzie blew her nose loudly again, then stepped over to receive her instructions.

"Now when I lift this end of the dresser, you slide that piece of two-by-four under it. Be careful."

Oh, it was a great idea, it really was, setting her precious furniture on two-by-fours. The things that were on casters—the hutch cupboard, the table, and the light stand—could all sit in the water without serious damage, so Lizzie began to feel better. Much better, in fact.

The rugs were soaked, so there was nothing to do except roll them up and place them close to the drain. Stephen put more wood in the stove, building a roaring fire, and soon Lizzie noticed dry spots on the new concrete floor.

Glancing at the kitchen clock, she saw it was almost midnight, and suddenly she felt very, very tired, actually on the verge of collapse. Her arms hurt from all the sweeping, which was why she was tired, she decided. She wondered vaguely if Stephen was tired, too, and fervently hoped so.

The following morning they were awakened by brilliant sunshine slanting through the east window of their basement home. Lizzie sat bolt upright and said quite loudly, "The sun is shining!"

"It usually does," Stephen said dryly from the depth of his pillow.

"Not when there's a rainstorm!" she said happily.

Oh, she could not believe their good fortune as she tiptoed around the basement in her bare feet, evaluating their situation. A small amount of water was still seeping through the block wall, but only in a few places, and not very much at that. The soaked rugs continued to leak water, but most of it ran down the lovely little drain.

They were saved! No furniture was ruined. All would be well, and Lizzie's joy knew no bounds.

"Oh, Stephen, I'm so glad it quit raining. Everything is drying out!" she trilled.

She made eggs and toast, heating the canned sausage Mam had given them with the remainder of their canned goods. She would have liked to make pancakes, but she didn't know how, and besides, she had no pancake syrup. She would have to remember to buy some when she went to town with Mam.

They ate and talked, Stephen saying they'd need to plan a few frolics on Saturdays to work on the house, since this basement was not the ideal place

for new furniture. They needed to finish construction as soon as possible. Lizzie clasped her hands together with sheer happiness, hearing Stephen talk like that. Finally, he was going to hurry! Soon she would be living in a new house!

It was amazing how easily and completely she could forgive Stephen for being so short with her last evening. She guessed that must be because she loved him, believing that if you didn't love someone you didn't get over things that easily.

A new thought struck her then, and she looked at Stephen when he wasn't looking at her. Maybe he had thought she was being a frightful, big baby last night, sweeping water and crying, but he wasn't mad at her this morning, at least not that she could see.

"Were you mad at me last night?" she blurted out in her forthright manner.

"Not really. You burned this toast."

"What do you mean, 'not really'? Were you sort of?"

"Hmm-mm."

"Yes, you were."

There was no answer.

See, that was the thing about Stephen that irritated her. You couldn't get to first base about how he felt. She had always shared all her feelings with Emma and Mandy. Everything. But with Stephen....

Well, the sun was shining, the basement was partially dry, and life was definitely better than last evening. They had gotten through a very big trial

in life, in Lizzie's opinion. They had come through quite well, considering Stephen only threw one flashlight, not both of them, and she had cried only once. Well, the crying had gone on for quite some time, but it wouldn't have if Stephen had been kinder and put his arms around her and pitied her the way she thought he should have.

She guessed that was how most men were. She was sure Stephen thought she had been terribly childish; that's why he chose to ignore her. So really, he had something to get over, too. Perhaps he could hardly stand her this morning.

That was a new thought, so she vowed to do better and never cry again. She bet most men didn't like it when their wives cried, especially when the tears were produced by a situation they had no control over. It wasn't Stephen's fault they had a rainstorm. Yes, she would figure this out and learn by her mistakes, becoming a better wife as time went on.

When Stephen got a clean, new tea towel and asked if she wanted him to dry dishes for her, she smiled at him genuinely and was very grateful. He was a good husband in so many ways, so what did it matter if he didn't tell her all his feelings? Putting up with her crying and drying dishes for her was a lot.

And when he said he wasn't going visiting anymore, that he was thoroughly tired of it, that they had plenty of wedding gifts, and that he would rather stay at home with her, she agreed heartily. That was fine. Perhaps the rainstorm had come so they would

agree on this one thing and learn to accept each other in the process. Maybe that preacher knew what he was talking about after all.

Chapter 15

THAT SPRING, THE GLAD DAY ARRIVED WHEN the house was finished. Mandy and Mam helped Lizzie clean the new rooms so they were ready for the moving day they had set for Saturday. Stephen's whole family would come to help, as well as Joshua and Emma.

For a small house, their floor plan was very wise, Lizzie thought. The kitchen was in a part by itself, although the dining room and living room were all open, laid out in a kind of L shape. That meant Lizzie could set up her table with all the leaves in it if she chose to have lots of company for a meal.

She loved her new kitchen cupboards, stained to a medium walnut shade. She had plenty of cupboard space, plus a small pantry with deep shelves that held an amazing amount of things. The refrigerator sat along the opposite wall by the window, and the table and chairs were placed in the middle of the dining area near the back door that faced the east.

The linoleum was a shade of brown with a small brick design. The laundry room had hardwood flooring, with an open stairway going to the upstairs. The living room was small, but it flowed into the dining area, with only the line where the hardwood flooring stopped, and the brick brown linoleum started, marking where one room began and the other ended.

There was a small hallway off the dining area, where, on the left, the basement door opened to the stairs going down, and on the right, another door led to the bathroom.

Lizzie was very proud of her bathroom with its long vanity attached to a tall cupboard built into the corner. She had so much space for towels, washcloths, sheets, pillowcases, and anything else she chose to store there. It was really wonderful cupboard space, a part of the house that she loved the most, she thought, smoothing the towels properly as she placed them one by one into the tall shelves. She put the sheets there on the top shelves, all folded evenly. In her opinion, it looked exactly like a picture in the Sears' catalog.

At the end of this small hallway, a door led to their bedroom, a nice-sized one with less expensive linoleum in a shade of white with a small stone design. The bedspread was blue, but she hadn't made curtains for the windows yet, so it wouldn't seem finished until that was done. There was a second bedroom adjoining their room. Stephen had lots of things to put in this room, like guns, a gun

cabinet, a bow and arrow, strange looking boots, gun cleaning kits, and a spare desk.

One thing bothered Lizzie, although she decided not to make a fuss to Stephen about it. It was the fact that no door joined these two rooms, which meant that any nice summer breeze wouldn't flow from one room to the next. A door between the rooms would take care of that.

But today was moving day, and there was so much to be happy about. She couldn't imagine making a big issue about the lack of one door.

Stephen's parents arrived early, eager to help carry the new furniture up from the basement. His mother brought more sheet sets, towels, and a brand new comforter made with purple and blue flannel and knotted with blue yarn. It was very pretty and of a medium weight that would be perfect for their bed. The wood stove in the living room was not very far away, so their bedroom probably wouldn't become too cold.

She didn't need to worry about that now, however, because spring was here and promised to bring beautiful sunshine and warm breezes nearly every day.

Joshua and Emma arrived. It was always a happy event when they traveled the 45 miles from their own farm in Allen County.

John and Mandy came up the hill with their black horse, the twins sound asleep in their little car seats in the back seat of the buggy. Mandy had made cookies for their coffee break, and Mam soon

had the coffee ready, bringing it up the hill from the farmhouse below.

Lizzie would never forget this whole day. Everything was taken care of, down to the last detail. The curtains were all hung, the bathroom fixtures were in place, and even the canister set Mandy had given her was lined up on the counter top and filled with flour, sugar, oatmeal, and tea.

The canisters were made of glass, not ceramic, with the words "sugar," "flour," "coffee," and "tea" labeled across their fronts in brown, fat letters. It was an unusual canister set, Lizzie knew. No one else had one exactly like it, so she felt very classy and modern.

After everyone had gone home, wishing them the best, Lizzie's heart was filled to overflowing. How blessed she and Stephen were! They had so many caring relatives, so much love to absorb and be thankful for. She felt as if her whole life had built up to this moment. She was settled in a new house with everything the way she wanted, and Stephen was her husband. She was living a dream come true.

Before long, however, Lizzie was finished making curtains, cleaning the basement, baking Stephen's favorite chocolate cake, and sewing a few items of clothing, and she became very, very bored.

She wanted a lawn. That was the thing. She

wanted a bulldozer to come level the mounds of topsoil that were lined up on the south side of the house so they could rake them evenly and then sow grass, plant shrubs, and make flower beds and a garden. Lizzie had nothing to do.

Stephen told her they could not have a lawn that summer, because he was laying all the white bricks himself. There was no use putting a lawn in when he would just ruin it by trampling the grass while laying brick. Lizzie nodded, understandingly. She really did. But inside she saw no sense in it. Couldn't he lay brick by staying close to the house where the flower beds would be?

One evening, after she had literally been sitting in the recliner twiddling her thumbs, she opened the subject of having a lawn once again.

Stephen sighed, his eyes narrowing, and he laid down his fork.

"Lizzie, you just don't get it. How can I push a wheelbarrow across the newly seeded lawn? Or drag a water hose across it? Or set up the scaffolding? It simply won't work. Besides, it's too late in the season. The sun will be too hot, and we'd have to water constantly if we seeded now." Picking up his fork, he resumed eating his mashed potatoes and hamburger gravy.

Lizzie didn't say anything and only watched him eat, thinking he had an awfully big mouthful of food and that she didn't like him very much.

That was the trouble with having a husband. He was the one who made the decisions; not you.

What if you knew better? What if that lawn could be seeded right now?

Stephen took a sip of water, then tipped back his chair and looked at her.

"Besides, we can't afford to pay someone to spread the topsoil, and the best time to seed a lawn is late August or September. Not the beginning of summer.

"How do you know?"

"I asked."

"Who did you ask?"

"A guy that was planting shrubs at the house we're building."

"Oh."

Well, there wasn't much Lizzie could say to that since he had asked the landscaping fellow. He probably knew what he was talking about.

She sighed.

"But, Stephen, I'm terribly bored. I have nothing to do. Not one thing. If I had a lawn and flower beds and a garden, I'd be busy all summer long."

"Lizzie, you have to give up on having a lawn this summer. You'd make it a lot easier on yourself if you would."

"I should get a job," she said glumly.

"Why don't you?"

"I hate to think of grading eggs again."

"It would give you something to do, and we could save money and buy all kinds of nice shrubs this fall."

That did it. If there was anything Lizzie loved

more than a nice house it was a beautiful lawn. She would get a job, even if it meant going back to grading eggs.

❧

The following morning she marched resolutely down the hill to the phone shanty they shared with Mam and Dat. She dialed Darwin Myers' number and waited anxiously till his wife answered the phone. Yes, they would be glad to have her work part-time, they really would. Yes, they could come pick her up, although Mrs. Myers was almost sure Lizzie could make arrangements with Fred Martin's wife, Dorothea, who had just started working there the week before.

Lizzie hurried in to the farmhouse to tell Mam, who was busily planting a few late purple and white striped petunias in her flower bed by the sidewalk.

"Good for you, Lizzie!" she commented when Lizzie told her she was going back to work. "That's a good idea. You know in Proverbs there's a chapter that speaks of a woman who is an honor to her husband by making things and selling them in the marketplace. Stephen will be glad if you help with the income."

Lizzie nodded happily.

"Yes, he will. He's the one who suggested it to me."

"Well, I'm glad. Idle time is the devil's time, Lizzie."

Lizzie's eyes narrowed, not sure how she should take that comment from Mam.

"You mean, if I have nothing to do, it's the devil's fault?" she asked suspiciously.

Mam laughed.

"No, no, no. I mean, to sit around doing nothing is not good for our minds. It's a time when, being human, we tend to think of ourselves, have dissatisfied thoughts, or whatever."

"Hmm, maybe that's why I become miserable because Stephen isn't finished with his brick-laying and we can't have a yard. Mam, you know how happy I'd be if I could mow lawn."

"Knowing you, Lizzie, you'll mow lawn three times a week with the mower set much too short."

Lizzie laughed. "Probably."

Mam bent to her task, and Lizzie decided to go home.

Dat and Jason were at work and the twins in school, so there was no one to talk to other than Mam, and she was, by all appearances, terribly busy planting her petunias.

"Do you need help?" she volunteered.

"Now Lizzie, you know I like to plant my own petunias. Did you see these 'cheraniums'? These new pink ones? Aren't they the prettiest color? I found them at the new greenhouse in town. They were a bit too expensive, but I love my 'cheraniums.'"

Lizzie nodded, knowing Mam's flower beds well. A complete mixture of colors, every petunia and geranium she could find for miles around, planted in

a profusion of brilliant hues. Mam spent hours with a wheelbarrow, a bag of peat moss, and a bucket of water, planting flowers until her face became almost as red as her geraniums.

So Lizzie began a routine of working for the Myers three days a week, standing at the egg-grading machine sorting eggs. Since she had worked there before, the Myers had built a new chicken house, installed an updated grader, and hired more people.

The second week, Lizzie thought she saw a new and different car parked in the parking lot. It was a small black car with blue stripes along the side.

"I wonder if someone new started," she said to Dorothea, who picked her up in the morning.

"Looks like it."

Sure enough, when Lizzie walked into the egg-grading room, a new girl stood by the egg-grader, looking a bit uncertain. Lizzie felt suddenly a bit shy, mostly because this new woman was very pretty. Her dark hair was cut neatly and swung in glossy smoothness down her back. Her eyes were brown, and her mouth looked different than any Lizzie had ever seen, maybe because her teeth were perfectly straight and white. She wore a beautiful blue sweater with a navy blue skirt, and looked quite English. She seemed to be a woman of the world and very sure of herself, except on this first day at a new job, when everyone felt a bit ill at ease.

That bit of uncertainty helped Lizzie to move toward her.

"Hi, I'm Lizzie," she said.

"Hi! I'm Julie Morton. It's nice to meet you. I guess we may as well learn to know each other, as close as we'll be working together."

Lizzie laughed, Julie smiled, and a friendship sparked that instant.

At lunchtime, Lizzie was amazed to discover that Julie had just gotten married in a long white gown and veil with all of the English wedding traditions at her parents' home, even though her parents were members of the German Baptist group, or River Brethren, as they were commonly called in this immediate area.

Her parents were plain! How fascinating. Her mother wore a large white covering, and her father cut his hair and beard almost like Dat. As Julie talked about their way of life, Lizzie was reminded that there are lots of different denominations, different groups of plain people who were, really, much the same, with only a few differences. Although Julie's parents dressed plainly, they drove black cars and trucks and had electricity and other modern conveniences that Lizzie was not allowed to have. Yet they had basically the same views and values as the Amish.

The lunch hour flew by, and they both gasped to realize they had already talked five minutes past the allotted time. They hurried back to work, still smiling as they reclaimed their positions at the

egg-grading machine.

Throughout the summer, their friendship deepened. Lizzie looked forward to her days with Julie. One day while they sat side by side eating lunch, Julie told Lizzie that she and her husband, Gary, had decided to give their lives to God and join the River Brethren. They would dress plain, as their parents did.

Lizzie blinked, surprised. She could see Julie was very serious.

"You mean you'll dress with a covering and a long dress? Completely different than now?"

Julie nodded soberly.

"But then ... You'll be different? You won't laugh and talk the way you do now?"

Julie laughed. "Of course I will!"

Lizzie was hugely relieved. She had been afraid Julie would no longer be the same talkative, fun-loving person she was now when she started to dress plain.

At work that afternoon, Lizzie kept glancing sideways at Julie, at her beautiful dark hair and her pretty sweater, and wondered if she wouldn't turn out to be one huge disappointment, becoming so pious and holy that she would think that Lizzie no longer qualified to be her friend. It made Lizzie nervous, thinking about someone becoming a much, much better person, going from a carefree young English woman to being a good plain one. That evening she fretted about this to Stephen, telling him everything about Julie and her church.

"Why are they called River Brethren?" she concluded.

Stephen shrugged his shoulders, turning back to his *Outdoor Life* magazine.

"Stephen, you're not listening to me again."

"I'm listening."

"But what if I come to work and she's almost like, well, like an angel? She'll be all freshly baptized and good and pure, and her clothes will be so different, and I'll be... well, the same sinner I always am."

"Lizzie!" Stephen scolded.

"I mean it. I did so many wrong things since I was baptized and gave my life to God, that sometimes I'm not sure if I did."

"What?" Stephen said absent-mindedly.

"Gave my life to God when I got baptized."

"Well, if it's as hard as you make it sound, we'd never make it." he said dryly.

Lizzie didn't know what he meant by that remark, and he soon laid his magazine aside, tilted back the recliner, and closed his eyes, after which Lizzie knew the discussion had ended then and there. That's how Stephen was. He didn't keep rambling on about nothing in particular, so she got up and sighed, knowing the conversation was over.

When Julie came back to work the following week, Lizzie was very nervous about her again. She tried to be polite and not stare at her or ask rude

questions, but she studied Julie a lot when Julie wasn't looking at her.

She was still pretty, only in a subdued way. Her white covering covered most of her hair and all of her ears and tied snugly beneath her chin. Her dress had a cape over the shoulders and a belt around her waist and hung in folds almost to her shoes. She seemed sweet and old-fashioned, almost like she imagined the characters in the Laura Ingalls Wilder series of books looked. Thankfully, she was the same Julie, her smile coming quickly and easily. She seemed, like her clothes, a bit subdued and serious, but friendly and welcoming.

Lizzie had tried to comb her hair flatter than ever that morning, jerking her covering as far over her ears as it would go, feeling as if she would be more equal to Julie if she was well within her church's *ordnung*. It was just something she wanted to do to make herself feel better, since she definitely wanted to appear more pious herself. She didn't know whether Julie noticed her flat hair—she just hoped she did—and believed that Lizzie was with her on the road she had chosen to get to heaven someday. But the thing that really bothered Lizzie most was when Julie mentioned the fact that they would be farming her father-in-law's farm soon. Lizzie's eyes became big and round, and she swiveled her head instantly to stare at Julie.

"You mean milk cows?" she squeaked.

"Oh, yes. Gary is a real dairy farmer. He loves cows."

"Then ... then ... does that mean you will, too?"

"Oh, yes!" Julie said happily. "I'm looking forward to milking cows."

"Oh."

"Why, don't you like cows?"

Terribly afraid that she would fall way on behind, as far as being a good person, Lizzie assured Julie that yes, she liked cows, just not milking them. She thought Julie gave her an awfully funny look but had the good manners to let it go at that. Lizzie wondered how much sinning was involved in hating cows. She had never enjoyed milking cows at home with Dat, but maybe if Stephen became a dairy farmer she would learn to appreciate them. Although, if she was very honest with herself, she doubted that she would like Stephen very much if he wanted her to milk cows with him.

Chapter 16

ALL SUMMER LONG, STEPHEN CAME HOME from working with Dat and Jason, ate his supper, and then went outside and laid the white brick with brown mortar around the base of their house. He enjoyed his work very much. In fact, he told Lizzie they should have planned to brick the whole house. Lizzie didn't say anything, but she was extremely glad he hadn't thought of that, thinking how frightfully ugly that would look. Like a prison, or something. But, since Stephen hadn't planned for that, there was no use saying exactly what she thought.

All summer long the weeds grew around the house and on the piles of topsoil heaped beside it. There wasn't a thing Lizzie could do about it, as long as Stephen meticulously laid his bricks, one by one, in perfect succession. Fortunately, since starting her work at the egg-grading room, she was no longer bored, so the days flew by.

One evening after Stephen had laid the very last brick, Lizzie helped him sort the few remaining ones, rinse the wheelbarrow well with the green rubber hose, and stack the few leftover bags of brown mortar. Then she went to the house to make a pitcher of lemonade. The sun was beginning its descent, dipping below the mountain, and a small flock of blackbirds fussed and twittered their way across the evening sky, the way blackbirds did when they started to sense the end of summer.

Stephen watched their flight, drank his lemonade, and said nothing. Lizzie clasped her hands around her knees, pulling her skirt down till only her bare toes were visible, and sighed happily.

"Oh, Stephen, I'm so glad those bricks are finally finished," she said.

"I'm not."

"Why not?"

"I enjoy laying brick."

"I know, but… weren't you even, not even once, a bit impatient to have the job done?"

Lizzie was incredulous, watching Stephen with narrowed eyes as he shook his head back and forth.

"Really? You were never in a hurry?" she asked.

"No use hurrying if the best time to seed a lawn is in September. That's another whole month."

"You mean you're not going to get started on the lawn next week?" Lizzie asked, trying to keep the desperation from her voice.

"No."

"Well… well… well… what ARE you going to

do in the evening?" she asked, her heart sinking.

"I don't know. Just relax."

"But... why would you relax, when... ?"

"Lizzie, there's more to life than hurrying to finish everything as fast as you can. What would you suggest that I do?"

"Well, nothing. I mean, if you don't want to."

"We only have enough money to have this topsoil spread by an excavating company; then our loan is completely used up. I'd love to have a new bow. A compound bow. Archery season comes in October, so I thought maybe I could do a few jobs in the evening, save the money, and buy a new bow."

Lizzie stared off across the hills of topsoil, trying so hard to say the right thing, but she imagined Stephen working in the evening and not having her precious yard put in until spring.

"You mean...? Stephen! Surely not!" she wailed, losing all her premeditated composure.

She wanted a new lawn, shrubs, and flower beds so badly, especially now that they seemed so close, and he'd go prancing off, working for someone else to buy a bow! Just for himself!

"What?" Stephen asked, his head swirling in her direction, staring at her in disbelief.

"You wouldn't put in the lawn?" Lizzie said quite forcefully, her eyebrows lowered as she stared back at him.

"Yes, I would. How long does it take to put in a lawn? One day? A few evenings? We have a whole month before September."

"Oh."

Lizzie's relief knew no bounds and was followed by a rush of love for Stephen, and the fact that he would not go archery-hunting until the lawn was seeded. Now that was so nice of him, she thought, slipping her arm through his and laying her head on his shoulder.

Suddenly she remembered the Mennonite produce farmer, Robert Weaver, who had asked if there was anyone available to help pick tomatoes. Mam had told him her girls were no longer at home, and she wasn't sure who would be available to help. Tomato-picking was a good thing. Lizzie and her sisters had picked tomatoes for a farmer when she was only 15 years old, and they had made a substantial amount of money for Mam. Why couldn't they do that now? She and Stephen?

"Stephen, I know! We can pick tomatoes!" she said, beaming.

"Pick tomatoes? I guess not," Stephen snorted.

"I'm serious, I really am. You can make 20 dollars in a hurry picking tomatoes, and it's enjoyable work. I mean, as long as your back doesn't begin to hurt."

"A bow costs a lot more than 20 dollars, Lizzie."

"How much more?"

"More like 200."

"Really? Well, we could work about 10 evenings, and that would do it," Lizzie chirped, undaunted.

The thing about this whole bow business was the fact that if she wasn't nice about Stephen spending

money for that bow, then perhaps he would become all strict and proper, deciding not to spend money for shrubs and mulch and other unnecessary but nice things she dreamed about.

All her life, Lizzie had admired neat lawns, closely trimmed shrubs, and meticulously cared for flower beds, always determining how she could achieve that look of perfection in her own yard. Even when she was at home on the farm, she mowed grass constantly. She cut away at the edges of the flower beds to make precisely straight borders until Mam had yelled at her from the porch, telling her to go store that hatchet before she hacked the entire yard away.

It made her nervous to think of wanting something so badly, to have it so nearly within reach, and yet to know that Stephen may not want to plant expensive shrubs. The new house was there now, and finished on the outside, anyway. All she needed to achieve her dream of a beautiful little home was a seeded lawn and shrubs.

"We could try it," Stephen said slowly.

So the following week when Stephen got home from work, Lizzie had supper ready and waiting so they could quickly eat. Then Stephen hitched up George, the horse, while Lizzie hurriedly washed dishes, and they were off. George was feeling frisky, and the two miles passed in a blur before they pulled up to the hitching rack on the Robert Weaver farm. Stephen hopped down and went to find Robert while Lizzie waited, watching the tomato-pickers

bent over as they worked in the flat field.

It was a pretty sight, the sun beginning to take on its evening glow, the colorful prints of the Mennonite girls' brightly colored dresses brilliantly lighted against the backdrop of green tomato plants dotted with black plastic hampers filled with bright red tomatoes. She wished she could take a picture, but Amish people don't believe in having cameras, so she knew she couldn't and that was all right.

Stephen returned with Mr. Weaver, tied George to the hitching rack, and then they were off across the drive and down the lane leading to the tomato plants. Lizzie had to walk fast to keep up with Stephen. Robert had shown him where they could start picking, which proved to be farther away than it had appeared at first.

There was a stack of black plastic hampers turned upside down at the rows where they would begin. Eager to show Stephen what an accomplished tomato-picker she was, she stepped right up to the hampers and easily pulled several from the tall stack. She walked along, scattering a few ahead of them. She turned to find Stephen with his hat pushed back, scratching his head in bewilderment.

"Lizzie, it's going to take all evening to fill 10 baskets, and that's two dollars and fifty cents. This is not the smartest thing we've ever done."

Bending to the task, Lizzie lifted the dying tomato vines to find an absolute trove of large ripe tomatoes all piled in one heap.

"Look, Stephen. This is no problem. Watch. How long does it take to fill a hamper when there are so many of these huge red tomatoes on top of each other?"

She began pulling at the tomatoes, remembering how easily they were removed from the stalk, and slamming them into the bin as fast as she could. She pulled tomatoes, showing off for Stephen and going much faster than what was absolutely necessary.

Stephen watched, then grabbed a hamper.

"I'd rather be building pole barns," he grumbled, but he soon began throwing tomatoes into the hamper, keeping up with Lizzie.

She said nothing, grimly determined to pick as many tomatoes as she possibly could. The sun slid down, the air began to cool a bit, and still they kept picking tomatoes. Lizzie's back hurt horribly, but she was determined Stephen wouldn't know, as he showed no signs of slowing.

They were both on their tenth basket now, so Lizzie figured at 25 cents a basket, they would have five dollars for 20 baskets. That was far from 20 dollars, though, and her back could not stand one more basket before she would collapse into a heap in the tomato stalks. Straightening up, she rubbed her back with both hands, grimacing as she did so.

"Doesn't your back hurt?" she asked, watching intently as Stephen kept on picking, whistling under his breath.

"Hmm-mm."

"Not one bit?"

"Hmm-mm."

No use showing her weakness now, she thought grimly. I can't stand bending over picking things too long at a time, but he's not going to find out. This was my idea. Groaning inwardly, she bent over and began her eleventh basket, glancing over her shoulder to see how far away the sun was from dropping behind the mountain. Pretty far.

"Stephen, what time is it?" she asked.

He straightened, pulled his watch from his pocket and said, "Six-thirty."

"Is that all?"

"What do you mean, is that all? If we're going to make 20 dollars, we still have a long way to go."

Lizzie nodded, bent her back, and picked tomatoes as if a mad bull would attack her if she didn't keep up with Stephen. Now the backs of her legs hurt miserably, a dull ache that went clear down to her ankles. But on she toiled, her only source of energy derived from her stubborn will and determination to prove to Stephen that she could pick tomatoes as fast or faster than he could.

Lizzie kept going, trying to think of any subject to take her mind off the pain in her back, but nothing worked for very long. She thought of shrubs, lawns, flowers, the porch Stephen wanted to build, but nothing made her feel better. She thought of the way they tortured prisoners during wars to get them to talk about secrets they needed to know in order to win a battle. Tomato-picking could work

as torture. She wondered if anyone had ever thought of that before. It would be a very good idea. Lizzie decided she would tell anyone just about anything to get out of this torturous backache. She would even tell Stephen her back hurt, she finally admitted.

"Stephen!" she blurted out.

"What?"

"My back hurts. Let's quit."

Stephen straightened and looked quizzically at her face. It bore the pain of the past hour, with her eyebrows poking straight up in the middle, her eyes resembling a coon hound's, sad and begging for pity. He tried desperately to keep a straight face, certainly not wanting to laugh at his wife if she was suffering. But the suffering was only half as bad as she portrayed it, of this he was positive.

In the short time they had been married, he had learned to know her quite well. She preyed on his pity, which really was all right, actually a bit endearing, except for now. Whose idea had this been, anyway?

"How many baskets did we pick?" he asked.

"Don't worry about that, Stephen. Don't you care one tiny bit about my back? I'm going to ruin it for the rest of my life, I mean it."

"Lizzie, this was your idea."

Suddenly her face turned beet red and she leaned forward, clenching her fists. "Stop saying that, Stephen!" she yelled. "You didn't have to come with me. It's your fault, too!"

He hurriedly bent his back, picking tomatoes so she couldn't see him laughing. His shoulders shook, and he sputtered to keep from laughing out loud, knowing her anger would only increase if she saw that he thought it was funny.

"Why don't you say something?" she asked, still angry.

"Oh, go pick tomatoes, Lizzie. You'll be all right," he managed, behind the huge grin on his face, which by now he had turned away.

By the time the sun actually, finally, slid behind the mountain, casting a spell of shadows across the abundant field of tomatoes, Lizzie was seriously afraid she would not be able to find enough strength to return home. She would probably need to spend the remainder of the night in the tomato patch.

Stephen rubbed his grimy hands together.

"That was fun! We made 25 dollars! A good start. If we return tomorrow evening, that will be 50. A fourth of what I'll need. Probably not even that much."

Lizzie hobbled between the rows, rubbing her lower back and glaring at her husband.

"I'm not coming back," she said shortly.

"Really?"

"No."

"Ach, come on, Lizzie. Be a sport. Till tomorrow evening you'll be used to it."

Lizzie was going to answer, she really was, but nothing would come out of her mouth. For one

thing, she was almost crying, and for another, if she didn't answer, then maybe he'd worry about why she didn't and start to say things husbands should say. Things like she did so well, and he appreciated her help, and he loved her very much, and he never saw anyone pick tomatoes as fast as she did. Things that would make her want to help him save money to buy his archery supplies.

They finished up in the field. After they were paid, Stephen untied the horse and they headed home. It felt very good to sit beside him in the buggy and pity herself, but it bothered her that he was whistling low under his breath, intently looking out the side door for deer. They wound their way up the hill beside the creek and through the woods until they came to a halt on the main road. George chomped impatiently on his bit as they waited for a few cars to pass.

It was a lovely evening, the last glow of light making everything look prettier than it actually was. Farmhouses and barns that weren't perfect because of a rusted roof, faded siding, or sagging shutters suddenly appeared almost brand new and beautiful in the fading half light of a summer evening. Cows grazing in the pasture after milking seemed much cleaner, and the pasture itself appeared even and dark green with no thistles or cow dung in it. It was amazing. Without thinking, she told Stephen this, and he turned to look at her, slid an arm around her, and held her tightly against his side. Lizzie was startled, then grinned smugly to herself.

Ah-hah! He DID appreciate her. He just wouldn't tell her in so many words the way her family did at home. Snuggling against him, she already looked forward to another evening of picking tomatoes, backache or not.

So during the course of a few weeks, Stephen and Lizzie made 184 dollars. Lizzie's back actually became used to the work, and she learned how happy you could become by doing something unselfish for your husband. Stephen even asked her to go along to the archery shop, but she declined, knowing he would enjoy it more without her waiting impatiently by his side.

Then, one glorious week in August, the excavator spread the topsoil. They let it settle for a few weeks, then bought grass seed and fertilizer. Stephen brought bales of straw from his father's farm. Their friends, Dan and Leah Miller, offered to help them with their lawn since they had seeded their own yard the year before.

The evening Stephen and Lizzie decided to seed the lawn turned into a fun-filled, festive evening. First, everyone raked the soil until it was fine and smooth, removing small rocks and leveling uneven hills of dirt. Dat and Jason arrived with their own rakes, Mam brought homemade cinnamon rolls, and they all worked on the new lawn, moving along the front of the house, down the opposite side of the driveway, and all along the sides and back of the house.

Then, while everyone else rested, Dan and Stephen spread the fertilizer and seeds, raked lightly

again, and spread straw to absorb the moisture and protect the tiny little seeds. Lizzie washed her hands well, made coffee, mixed iced tea, and then served a good snack. They all sat around the table, enjoying each other's company and Mam's delicious cinnamon rolls.

No one knew, though, quite how happy Lizzie actually was. All those weeks of anticipation and waiting until Stephen was ready to seed the lawn had been very hard for her. She wanted things done right away without waiting four weeks. But now here they were on a warm, balmy evening with their very own lawn properly seeded. Lizzie was quite confident she would have a beautiful lawn by the next spring.

She chewed happily, smiling at Leah, who was a petite, tiny woman, about eight years older than Lizzie. She was indeed a good friend, giving Lizzie advice about different things, including how to get along with your husband, which Lizzie really appreciated. Lizzie was a bit dubious about being the willing servant that Leah talked about, but it was something to think upon, especially the part about never grumbling or nagging, which was very hard for her.

What other way was there if you wanted something done? Especially if you wanted it done now and not two months later? Oh, well, tonight nothing mattered except the friendship of these two kind and helpful people, Dat and Mam and Jason, and the fact that, finally, at long last, they had a lawn. Now for the shrubs.

Chapter 17

Lizzie was enjoying a dish of strawberry ice cream while sitting at a picnic table in the park with her friend, Julie, who she worked with while grading eggs. Suddenly, the ice cream tasted like Pepto-Bismol and the succulent strawberries took on a shiny, grainy quality that turned her stomach. Waves of nausea rippled up her throat, and she looked over at Julie, a bit wild-eyed.

"I don't feel one bit well," Lizzie said shakily.

Julie raised an eyebrow.

"We're not expecting a baby, are we?"

"No," Lizzie said firmly. "It has to be a bug."

"Oh, but Lizzie, some bugs turn into a serious malady called pregnancy."

"I know, Mam told me that."

Lizzie was a bit miffed, sitting there feeling so terribly sick and miserable, the ice cream melting in it's Styrofoam dish and sliding farther and farther down her lap as she held it in her nerveless fingers.

Julie didn't have to talk to her in those condescending tones, as if she was only 12 years old.

The ride home was pure torture. Lizzie was humiliated beyond words when the movement of the car made her so dizzy that the strawberry ice cream churned in her stomach. She had no choice but to ask Julie to please pull over and stop as soon as she could. When the car came to a stop, Lizzie opened the door, lurched into the deep weeds at the side of the road, and threw up the strawberry ice cream.

"Oh, dear, I am so embarrassed," she said, as she climbed back into the car.

"It's all right, Lizzie. There's a bug going around."

Lizzie glared at her friend, and they both burst out laughing.

Julie was right. Lizzie and Stephen were ecstatic to find out they would be parents. Stephen smiled everywhere he went—to work, to church, to visit his parents—which only increased Lizzie's own anticipation.

Mam smiled and nodded when Lizzie told her the news. They discussed babies, mother, hospitals, doctors, buying baby clothes, just everything. Mam told her in a serious sort of way that having a baby wasn't easy.

Lizzie took this to heart, although she told Stephen she could handle her pregnancy just fine. She was tough. She could work as hard as he did, well, almost, and she was healthy, robust, and certainly not weak or skinny.

The weight gain began then, which was a constant source of frustration for Lizzie. The doctor told her 25 to 30 pounds was ideal, and she was determined to stay within those boundaries. At first, it was easy. Foods that were ordinarily delicious turned into vile, unappetizing concoctions that propelled her in the direction of the bathroom, and she threw up almost anything she ate.

Saltines and ginger ale. Pepsi. Ginger tea. Dry toast. Pretzels. It all came back up. Just when she thought she must surely die, unfairly, at a young age, she noticed that the smell of vegetable soup was no longer quite as nauseating. She could eat cheese sandwiches with mustard, which perked her up considerably.

After her nausea passed, her appetite came roaring back. She wanted to eat everything she saw, from the time she got up until she went to bed. She baked whoopie pies, wrapped them individually in plastic wrap, and kept eating them just about all day.

The thing about whoopie pies is that they stick to the plastic wrap in chocolaty layers, and when you pull the wrap away, the part underneath is so soft and good and so close to the creamy white frosting that you take one big bite after another, and before you know it, it's all gone and you want another one.

Lizzie faithfully swallowed her prenatal vitamins, ate healthy foods—orange juice, peas, tomatoes, peaches, and corn—as well as whoopie pies. She went to visit her doctor regularly and immensely

enjoyed all the attention she received. Emma and Mandy were overjoyed that Lizzie and Stephen would soon be parents. So much joy, Lizzie thought, as she headed to the hospital with Stephen the night her labor started. I just can't wait for this baby.

Hours later, Lizzie was startled by a strange sound in the hallway, waking instantly when she realized where she was and why she was not at home in the little house on top of the hill. She and Stephen were parents now. She had given birth to a little girl the morning before at the hospital in Cedar Falls.

The baby, her baby, weighed seven pounds and one ounce, a perfect miracle, with a deeply tanned complexion, almost as if she had been lying in the sun before she was born. Her eyes were blue, her nose was only a little bump—not really a nose yet— and her mouth was small and perfect. Lizzie was thrilled and very, very scared of this little human being that she was suddenly responsible for forever.

They hadn't decided on a name. Lizzie had informed Stephen quite early that if the baby was a girl, she would name her Laura for Laura Ingalls Wilder, the heroine of Lizzie's life. Stephen didn't say no or yes. He just smiled and didn't make a comment at all, but Lizzie figured his smile must have meant something like an approval, so she went right on thinking about a baby girl named Laura.

She felt a tiny bit guilty about that fancy name. Amish people were encouraged to give their babies plain names like Sarah, Barbara, Anna, and Rebecca, old Bible names that the Amish had used for generations. The thing was, if you really wanted to know which Sarah or Barbara someone was speaking of, you had to add her grandfather's name and her father's name to identify her. You couldn't just say Barbara Zook or Anna Stoltzfus. You had to say, "She is one of Dan's Sammie's girls." It was quite frustrating.

Take her own name, for instance. Lizzie Glick. Her dad's name was Melvin. But which Melvin Glick? There were lots of Melvin Glicks in the large Amish community surrounding them. So you had to say Doddy Glick's name, and then Dat's, before people knew who she was.

Besides, she liked something different, something pretty. Like Laura. It was old-fashioned, for English people, anyway, and it had a nice sound, especially when she added the middle name, Anne.

So here she was, waking up in this strange place, her heart sinking when she thought of the previous night. She had been so very tired, wanting to sleep so desperately, but they kept bringing Laura in, saying it was time for her to eat. But no matter how much the kind nurses tried to help, or in what position she held Laura, she refused to nurse for longer that a few tense seconds. The whole night had been a complete disaster. Lizzie fought tears of despair, she was so upset about the ordeal of trying to breast-feed her baby, who, apparently, was absolutely clueless

as to what was required of her.

Lizzie sighed and smoothed the blanket a bit self-consciously as a very large nurse opened the door with her foot and bustled efficiently about the room. She checked Lizzie's blood pressure, took her temperature, poked and prodded her, and asked questions fast and furious like a game of ping-pong. Lizzie was having trouble keeping up with the ball.

"Time for your shower!" the nurse chirped. "Breakfast at eight!" Lizzie groaned, thinking about getting out of bed, but soon realizing that she had absolutely no choice whatsoever, without even a minute of reluctance. Her sheets were pulled back, a pair of very large solid arms were extended toward her, and she was propelled out of bed, her head spinning, the room seeming to tilt permanently to the left. She shuffled to the shower, depending on this solid pillar of strength beside her.

Lizzie had to admit that the soothing hot water and soap, and having her hair washed squeaky clean, were great spirit-boosters, for sure. Her breakfast tray did not stir her appetite at all. In fact, the smells assaulting her from beneath the brown plastic covers made her feel nauseous. She sat in her bed, her back propped against pillows, and wished with all her heart she could figure out why she felt so alone and insecure. She tried to swallow the lump in her throat.

Surely something was wrong with her. Wasn't this supposed to be a time of great love and joy?

She had often looked longingly at pictures in maga-
zines of a wife holding a sweet, perfect, newborn
baby. The father always had his arm around both of
them, looking so happy because he simply adored
his beautiful wife and baby. That was what she had
always imagined, the perfect moment from which
they would live happily ever after.

Mam had told her once, in her wise way, that
having a baby was more than just a soft woolly
blanket and cute baby clothes. Lizzie had blinked
her eyes a few times and watched Mam suspiciously
for awhile after she said that, trying to gauge her
level of seriousness. As far as she could tell, Mam
was pretty serious. Oh, well, she had thought then.
Having a baby was something she was quite cer-
tain she could handle. Weren't there thousands and
thousands of babies born in the United States every
day? It couldn't be that bad.

But, now, sitting alone in the green, sterile envi-
ronment of her hospital room, her head back
against the white pillows, she closed her eyes and
tried desperately to fight back the feeling of dread
as she thought of the nurse bringing baby Laura to
be breast-fed. The whole thing was so devastating.
Laura simply would not nurse right. Lizzie sighed,
casting a sideways glance at her roommate, Dorie,
who was serenely eating great forkfuls of scrambled
eggs. Lizzie watched her and wished she could pull
the curtain between them.

Chewing happily, Dori swallowed, and then
trilled joyfully. "Good morning!" Lizzie quickly

gathered her trembling mouth into a quivering smile and answered, "Good morning!"

"Did you sleep well?" Dori asked, spearing a piece of bacon with gusto.

"Not really. Well, only when they didn't bring my baby in."

"Yes, she was a bit fussy, wasn't she? Oh, well, the first few days won't really determine how she'll be once you get her home."

Lizzie nodded gratefully, her eyebrows held high, the lump in her throat swelling to gigantic proportions when Dorie spoke so kindly.

Why in the world did she always feel like crying? This was awful. Perhaps she would become mentally ill now. Biting her lip and struggling to regain her composure, she squeaked, "Is that what they say?"

"Oh, yes!"

Lizzie nodded, a ray of hope beginning to dissolve the lump in her throat. Yes, she would be fine, she really would. She could handle this.

"Aren't you eating?" Dorie asked, concern in her voice.

"I'm not hungry."

"But you should eat. It'll give you strength."

Lizzie nodded, biting her lip. She felt like crying all over again but was saved from another battle with her emotions by two nurses bringing in the babies.

"Time for the little ones' breakfast!" they announced happily.

Lizzie's heart took a complete nosedive, down, down, until her stomach actually hurt from the dread and fear of another despairing episode of trying to feed her baby. But the sight of little Laura made her temporarily forget her fear, as she pushed the white flannel blanket aside and gazed at the small brown face beneath it.

She was so cute, except her forehead was too high, creating the impression that her eyes, nose, and mouth were all one little package, farther down on her face than it should be. Holding the blanket away, Lizzie closely examined the amount of hair Laura had. She had enough not to look bald and ugly like some babies, but not so much that she would need it to be brushed immediately. Yes, she was indeed a cute baby girl, exactly what Lizzie had always dreamed of.

Then, to her amazement, the nurses both left. Just like that, with no warning, they both walked out the door, leaving Lizzie to fend for herself. She felt very much like she was afloat in the middle of nowhere, on a boat with no oars or engine or much sense of direction. She sat bolt upright, clutching Laura as she watched the girl beside her expertly position her little red-haired boy, lean back, and smile. The baby began nursing, as if he knew exactly what he was supposed to do, and went about his business.

Oh, dear, Laura thought wildly, as she cradled little Laura, who promptly threw her head back and began screaming and crying in earnest. No matter

which way she held Laura, her response was the same—screaming until beads of perspiration formed along Lizzie's forehead. She was quite seriously afraid she might faint away, letting her baby fall in the process.

Desperately, she kept trying, with Laura consistently refusing, until they were both in no shape to resume breast-feeding. Lizzie glanced around wildly, afraid her baby's constant crying would upset Dorie and her little boy.

"I'm sorry," she offered contritely.

"It's O.K. We're fine."

Maybe she should sit on a chair. Gingerly, she laid Laura crosswise in the middle of the high, narrow hospital bed, and then slid out. Better go to the bathroom first, she thought nervously, as she headed in that direction, quickly glancing at Laura who was still crying at the top of her lungs.

When she emerged from the bathroom, a nurse was bending over the baby, crooning, but as Lizzie approached, she gave her a disapproving glare.

"Never, ever, leave your baby lying alone across a bed. Do you want her to fall and break her head? Fracture her skull?"

Lizzie was shocked, her eyes opening wide as she tried to fathom why the nurse was speaking to her in this way.

"But...I...I..." she stammered, trying to maintain a bit of composure.

"No. There are no excuses. You cannot leave a crying baby in the middle of a bed."

Lizzie bent her head to hide the onslaught of tears, bit down hard on her lip, and shuffled weakly to the chair.

"Have you fed her?" she asked.

"No," Lizzie answered in total and absolute defeat. "I can't get her to nurse."

"I'll take her to the nursery and give her some formula," the nurse announced, whisking the crying baby out the door.

Lizzie sagged weakly in her chair. She never, ever wanted another baby. Why had she ever wanted one in the first place? That nurse should be fired immediately before she hurt more young mothers' feelings. There was absolutely no way her baby could have fallen off that bed when she was in the bathroom for only two minutes.

She lifted her head when Dorie turned and clucked her tongue.

"That wasn't nice," she said softly.

Lizzie shrugged her shoulders, unable to speak, then sat back and thought more sad thoughts. Stephen should have stayed here, and Mam should come for a visit right now.

"What time are visiting hours?" she asked.

Dorie held her little boy over one shoulder, softly patting his little back, and was rewarded with a perfect little burp.

"There you go, my little man. Visiting hours? I think from four to eight."

Lizzie became sad, then, really sad. So sad, in fact, that she stared out the window at the gray

November sky and truly wished she didn't have a baby. Why didn't anyone send her flowers? All the bright, colorful bouquets on the wide green windowsill were her roommate's, not hers. No one thought of her down here in Cedar Falls at the hospital, and likely no one would send her flowers anyway. English people were nicer than Amish people. A beautiful flower arrangement was very, very necessary right now.

So what would happen if they gave Laura formula? She would drink it nicely from a bottle, then go right off to sleep, but what about the next time Lizzie tried to feed her? There had to be a next time. Lizzie heaved herself out of the chair, climbed back into her high, narrow bed, pulled the snowy white sheets over her shoulders, turned her back to Dorie, the perfectly successful mother with all that calm serenity shining from her face, and closed her eyes and cried. Great big, gulping, quiet sobs, with a steady river of tears that ran out of the corners of her eyes, across the bridge of her nose, and onto a puddle on her clean white pillows.

The truth was, she had never felt quite so frightened or quite so alone in all her life. This baby was such an enormous responsibility, something so scary and so defeating. She wasn't a fit mother. That was it. That was the whole thing. She remembered the times when other girls always wanted to hold babies in church, and she had never really wanted to. Not at all. She tried to like babies, often, but they grabbed your covering strings and threw up a

thick white substance that smelled like sour milk, scratched your face with their tiny white fingernails, and were just not pleasant to hold.

Now here she was with a baby of her own, and what was she supposed to do with it? She hardly wanted it very much right now, if she was honest. She wished Mam was here. She had to find out right now if she was normal or not. She couldn't believe for one moment that any young mother had ever felt this way before.

You were supposed to be absolutely enamored, so much in love with your baby so that all you wanted to do was hold and cuddle her constantly. Yet here she was, relieved to find the nurses taking her back to the nursery to give her a bottle of formula.

Just when she thought she was stuck in this deep dark moment of panic, the door swung open again. A nurse, dressed in the usual white uniform, stepped in, shaking a bottle of liquid and smiling as she turned to look behind her.

"Someone's getting flowers!" she announced.

Lizzie rolled over and dragged the sleeve of her hospital gown across her eyes, trying desperately to conceal the fact that she had been crying.

"Stephen and Lizzie!" The florist's delivery person read from the card that was attached to a beautiful flower arrangement, looking at Dorie and Lizzie expectantly.

"That's me." Lizzie managed to say a bit shakily.

"You! Good for you! They're gorgeous!"

The nurse rolled over a tray on wheels, set the

flowers carefully on top, and the delivery person left with no more fuss.

Lizzie was amazed! She had never received flowers from a real florist before. Mam said they were terribly expensive. Slowly, almost in awe, she took the envelope from the plastic holder that was stuck into the potting soil and extracted a pink card that said, "Congratulations! Dad and Mom Glick."

How lovely! That was so thoughtful of Mam. It was the most beautiful bouquet Lizzie had ever hoped to see. Real greenery—little ferns, a palm tree, and other real plants which she could pot into larger separate containers when she got home—filled the base of the pretty ceramic pot. Pink and white carnations topped the colorful, perfectly aligned bouquet. A huge pink bow was attached to one side, making Lizzie very happy that she had a little girl.

Then, because Mam had been so kind to think of her and Laura, she began to cry again. There was not a single thing she could do to stop, so she kept crying. She just sat in the middle of the hospital bed and squeezed her eyes shut while tears ran from behind both lids, like a pot of potatoes boiling over when there was no one around to turn down the burner.

"What?" Lizzie's eyes flew open as the nurse stopped at her bed and clucked her tongue.

"Tsk! Tsk! Crying, are we? Baby blues?"

Lizzie nodded miserably as the nurse brought a box of Kleenex, perched on the side of the bed, and

tilted in, putting both arms around her in a soft, motherly hug. Lizzie leaned against the softness of her clean, white uniform and inhaled the smell of soap and something that smelled like Mam's ironing. That made her cry some more, the memory of Mam ironing, standing in the old kitchen running the gas iron back and forth, back and forth, singing softly.

"There, there, honey. It happens. It happens all the time. Is this your first one?"

Lizzie nodded, sniffing, dabbing her eyes.

"You'll be fine. Is she doing all right for you?"

Lizzie shook her head back and forth. "She won't nurse. They took her back to the nursery and gave her formula."

"Let me go get her for you."

With that, the nurse was off through the doorway, and Lizzie cried fresh tears because the bouquet of flowers was so pretty, and the nurse had given her a hug, and she was so kind, and just maybe she wasn't abnormal after all, crying like this.

When the nurse returned, Lizzie's tears stopped momentarily, as the kindhearted woman made quite a fuss over Laura's complexion, her perfectly shaped face, and how fortunate she and Stephen were to have a darling little girl. Lizzie felt deeply ashamed then, chiding herself seriously for being such a big baby as she set about the task of trying to feed a very upset newborn girl. In the end, the nurse was perplexed, the baby screamed, and Lizzie was soaked with perspiration from all the effort of trying to get

Laura to nurse.

That evening Mam and Dat came to visit, bringing Stephen. Lizzie's world seemed to turn right side up again with him by her side, gazing at her as if she truly was a wonder. Dat said he picked out Laura in the nursery. He didn't even look at the name tag on the little crib to know which she was.

"She's as dark as Stephen," he crowed, so proud of his granddaughter. Mam just kept holding the baby and laughing and laughing. Mam was like that when she saw newborns for the first time. She laughed. A lot, actually. Then she would talk to them, cooing and fussing and giving them funny names, pursing her lips in the most serious manner. While Mam was there, Lizzie did not feel afraid, depending on her to guide her through this bewildering maze of being a mother to a newborn.

"Oh, she doesn't like your milk," she said matter-of-factly when Lizzie explained this huge obstacle called breast-feeding. "Nothing wrong with the bottle. I'll get you some formula on the way home and don't worry about it."

But Lizzie did. She wanted the best for her baby, and mother's milk was the best. Mam didn't think it was a big deal, but Lizzie did. She felt like a failure and wished some miracle would occur so her baby would quit screaming when she tried to nurse. She looked forward to going home tomorrow, learning if she could handle one tiny, dark, complicated, screaming baby named Laura.

After they were settled in at home, Lizzie felt

much, much better. This whole thing of having a baby to care for seemed so possible now, with Stephen helping her and Mam just down the hill from the little house.

Chapter 18

"BUT LIZZIE, JOSHUA, AND EMMA ARE LOOKING for us," Mam protested, looking troubled as she gazed at her daughter.

"But, Mam. I feel so alone with my baby. I wish you wouldn't go."

"Stephen is here. You'll do fine. There's nothing to it. Just make sure the formula is not too hot when you put it in her bottle."

It was Saturday afternoon, and Mam had come up the hill to say they were going to Allen County to church services at Joshua and Emma's house. Mam knew Lizzie would be all right, although she wished she could put a stop to her fits of crying. When Mam said that, Lizzie said nothing, only nodded her head in acceptance, and Mam hurried down the hill to prepare for their weekend in Allen County.

The truth was, Lizzie thought Mam was not doing her duty. She should stay right here with her and Stephen. Joshua and Emma could have church

without them. But, no, off they went, just like that. It made Lizzie mad. Then she felt guilty for becoming angry. Then she started crying again. This was the third day of mostly crying, and Lizzie felt absolutely at the end of her rope. She had given up even trying to be happy. There was no use. She shuffled around and heated formula, sterilized bottles and pacifiers, cried, and listened to Laura scream.

Stephen came home and tried to help, hanging his clothes on their proper hooks, making small talk, trying to hold Laura on the rare occasions when she didn't cry, and, in general, struggling to keep his small family afloat. Lizzie sat on the sofa and cried as Stephen came in and leaned against the wood stove, his arms crossed in front of him as he watched Lizzie, softly sniffling on the couch with Laura beside her.

"Now what's wrong?" he said, kindly.

"Mam was here. They're going to Allen County to Joshua and Emma's for church services."

"But … what's wrong with that?"

"They don't have to go, Stephen. They could stay here with us," Lizzie's voice caught on a fresh sob.

"Lizzie, we can be alone. You're going to have to get ahold of yourself and stop being so terrified."

"I'm…I'm not. It's just that she…she cries so much."

"But Mam said some babies do."

"I know, but when she cries all the time, I feel like I'm a horrible failure. What am I doing wrong? Why does she cry?"

Stephen laughed, running his hands through his hair.

"She's quiet now."

Crossing the room, he sat beside Lizzie and pulled her against him, holding her gently.

"You're not a failure. You're doing the best that you can. Maybe she's just a grouchy baby and that's simply how she's going to be."

Lizzie sat up and looked at Stephen.

"You mean, you think I'm doing the best I can?"

"Of course. You're doing a great job. She takes the bottle well, she's clean and dry and warm, and sometimes she sleeps and sometimes she cries, just like babies do."

Lizzie looked at Stephen, then dubiously down at Laura who was wide awake, looking around with her small bright eyes.

Lizzie laughed, then sagged against the back of the couch.

"I wish I could take a pill to quit this awful crying and sense of helplessness. I feel like a boat that weathered one storm, and before it's really recovered, another storm starts battering it."

"You're probably overtired, and once you sleep more regularly, you'll feel happier."

Lizzie sighed, then resolved to try harder. Stephen always had a lot of common sense when he spoke about matters like this. She would try and get her rest and see if that stopped the crying.

But now, when she did lie down at night, or during the day, she was so tense and nervous about having

a new baby that she couldn't sleep anyway, or not for a long time. She had never known that a person could get so tired and still go on living. She doubted very much that she would ever fully recover. In fact, she believed she would always shuffle around like an old lady and never truly feel strong and laugh for real.

But she and Stephen did survive the weekend without Mam, although Lizzie struggled every hour, trying mightily not to resort to endless unexplained tears. It was like a summer rainstorm that showed up at the most unexpected moments. Dark clouds threatened to overtake her sense of stability, the well-being and genuine happiness she was accustomed to feeling most of her life.

The worst part came after Laura finally settled down for the night, tucked into the small wooden crib in the corner of their bedroom, covered cozily with soft pink and white blankets. Lizzie lined up her bottles in the kitchen on the counter top and placed a small saucepan on the stove, ready to heat the formula during the night. Then Lizzie would climb into bed, feeling as if she would melt into the mattress and never be able to get up again. She was so tired, but there she would lie, her eyes open wide, staring at the ceiling. Meanwhile, every snuffle, breath, and whimper from the crib seemed to be amplified 10 times.

She was completely overwhelmed with the responsibility of caring for this tiny, pink human being, who depended on her for her every need. Lizzie was

worn out with diapering, bathing, feeding, burping, and deciphering what Laura wanted every time she opened her sturdy little mouth and yelled, which, in Lizzie's opinion was far, far too often. Lizzie was sure she was doing something wrong.

So, much like she had done when she was four years old and had gotten Snowball, the kitten, Lizzie lay and worried about her baby. Sometimes babies spit up and choked, or simply died in their cribs. What if that happened to Laura? Or what if Laura cried and cried and cried, and nothing, not one thing Lizzie tried, would stop her?

Lizzie tried to pray, to ask God to help her, she really did, but that only brought more tears. She only felt more pitiful. Probably God was very kind to young, scared, first-time mothers, so she cried because God was so loving. Stephen's breathing, slow and steady, was a source of comfort for a reason she couldn't explain. Probably because he was a rock-solid human being that could help if everything spun out of control, even if she still had to go down the hill for Mam's advice.

❦

On Monday morning, Stephen's sister, Mary, arrived with his mother while Lizzie was sweeping the kitchen floor. They tied their small black horse to the hitching rack and breezed into the house, bringing a whole new world of optimism with them.

First of all, Stephen's mother, Annie, grabbed the

broom from Lizzie and, in her forthright manner, told her to go sit down. Young mothers should not be sweeping their kitchen when the baby was only a few days old, she said, clucking her tongue while Lizzie sat down, bewildered. No one had told her that, so she smiled to herself and figured it wouldn't hurt to listen to her mother-in-law.

"Where is she?" Annie asked, looking around for a crib in the living room.

"She's sleeping in her crib," Lizzie answered.

"In the bedroom?"

"Yes."

"Oh, you don't want her in there. You should have a small crib out here, so she's with you during the day."

Bustling into the bedroom, she came out with Laura, clucking and exclaiming about her complexion.

"Lizzie, she's really cute!" she said, beaming happily.

Mary smiled, talking to the baby. Lizzie sat back against the cushions, a real bubble of happiness beginning to well up inside. She was thrilled that they made such a fuss about her baby. Knowing that Mary would stay with them the whole week made everything seem more secure and possible. Actually, there was hardly a reason for her to cry at all. Stephen's mother continued to fuss and ask questions, and Lizzie completely forgot about herself, or how she felt, as Mary gathered the laundry and tidied the house.

"You know, you need to keep babies very warm," Annie chided, as she wrapped the soft, white, thermal, knit blanket securely around Laura again. "They don't stay warm on their own, the way we do. Maybe that's part of the reason she's fussy. Maybe she's not warm enough. Mary, check the fire. See if there's more wood."

While Mary did the laundry in the basement, Annie made coffee and put away the things she had brought, including shoofly pie and some of the fresh sausage from the hogs they had just butchered. Lizzie felt very cozy, knowing that having a baby was a special event, especially since Laura was Annie's oldest son Stephen's baby.

That day, Lizzie had her first, deeply restful nap since Laura was born. Mary kept Laura in the living room with her while Lizzie slept. Lizzie awoke feeling so refreshed and happy, she couldn't believe it.

Mary was holding Laura, who was sucking peacefully on her pacifier, her eyes wide open, when Lizzie walked into the living room. Lizzie was surprised to feel a genuine rush of affection for her little bundle in Mary's arms. Reaching for her, she bent to kiss the soft little forehead, and held her tightly against herself. Suddenly she realized that she was perfectly normal, and she genuinely liked her baby. What was so bad if she cried? All babies cried.

Mary proved to be a good *maud*, cheerfully going about her duties, laughing about everything, which was like a good spring breeze to Lizzie's battered emotions. Mary did laundry, cleaned, baked

cookies, ran errands, folded clothes and put them away, anything Lizzie asked of her. Lizzie felt quite queenly, sitting on the recliner asking her maid to do things for her.

When Stephen returned from work in the evening, Mary had supper ready for them. Lizzie's appetite returned with full force. It seemed as if Laura knew exactly the time they sat down for supper, and she would begin crying from her little crib.

But now, that was all right. Lizzie knew it was something she could handle quite well, in fact. Laura was either hungry or had to be burped or just wanted to be held for a while, which made Lizzie feel very capable and very motherly. Mary thought she cried an awful lot and was most certainly a grouchy baby. One day she peered in over the sides of the small porta-crib in the living room, lifted the blankets, and said, "She even looks grouchy when she sleeps!"

Lizzie looked over Mary's shoulder to see why she said that. Indeed, Laura's eyebrows were drawn down in an expression of displeasure, her little mouth puckered into a pout. Mary giggled and Lizzie laughed softly.

The glad day arrived when Emma came from Allen County, and Mandy came all the way to the farm in her horse and buggy. Lizzie wore her best everyday dress and bib apron, taking special care in the way she combed her hair and put on her Sunday covering. She felt very thin and pretty that morning, weighing less than she weighed on the day she

became Stephen's wife. She was so excited to see her sisters. Her cheeks were flushed and her eyes finally looked the way they were supposed to, now that all the crying had stopped.

Mary had baked chocolate chip bars, and the coffee was hot, waiting on the back of the gas stove. She bustled about the kitchen, tidying the counter top, while Lizzie watched from her position on the recliner. It was almost uncanny the way Mary resembled Stephen, with the same dark, nut-brown complexion, sun-streaked, dark brown hair, and large heavily-lashed eyes. Today, Mary wore a pale-colored dress which made her appear even tanner. She was thin as a reed and ate more than Lizzie did, which only assured Lizzie that there was a difference in people's metabolisms. Some people just burned calories faster and more fully than others.

"Here they come!" Mary said, from her vantage point at the kitchen window.

"Do they?" Lizzie asked, jumping up, rushing to the window. Sure enough, Mam, Emma, Mandy, Susan, and KatieAnn all came walking up the hill, along the little pathway worn down through the grassy field.

Mam was carrying one of the twins and Mandy the other. Emma carried her baby while KatieAnn held on to Mark's hand. Lizzie watched and fairly skipped to the back door to open it for them, exclaiming in delight that they had all come together for a long anticipated visit.

Emma cried as she hugged and hugged Lizzie,

but that was all right. Emma always cried when a baby was born to someone else. She thought, as did Joshua, that babies were the greatest blessing there ever was, and they had always wanted a large family. Mandy laughed and looked at Lizzie and told her she looked very skinny—for her—and her face looked nice, and did she have on a new covering?

Lizzie cried with Emma—only a little bit—then laughed with Mandy while Mam stood by and wiped her tears. Her nose became red the way it always did when she cried. KatieAnn and Susan took off the children's coats and laid them on the bed in Lizzie's bedroom, knowing their mother and older sisters would be incapable of thinking about normal things for the next five minutes, at least.

Then Lizzie walked over to the small, wooden porta-crib and held Laura out for her sisters to see. She had put her in the prettiest sleeper she owned, a pink and white one with two small appliquéd hearts on the shoulder, and wrapped her well in a pink blanket.

"Oh, oh, oh, my goodness!" Emma exclaimed, fluttering her hands, clearly beside herself. "Lizzie!"

Mandy, in her self-contained, quiet way, said quite firmly, "Lizzie, she's the cutest baby I've ever seen!"

Then Mam's nose became even redder, and she laughed and cried at the exact same time. Lizzie had never felt quite so important to her Mam and sisters as she did at that moment. Not even on the day she got married.

They all took turns holding Laura, while Katie-Ann and Susan entertained the other children with Mary's help. Everyone chattered and exclaimed and talked all at once, and no one truly listened much to what other persons were saying. After the initial frenzy of seeing the baby and saying the most important things had died down, they had coffee around the kitchen table, savoring the chocolate chip bars, and talking at a much more normal volume and speed.

Mandy's twins were walking now and beginning to say whole sentences. They looked just like two little girls exactly the same age, except they were different in every way. One was dark-haired and dark-eyed while the other had blond hair and blue eyes. John and Mandy had been blessed with another little girl, named Sadie, who was nine-months-old and as blond and blue-eyed as the one twin. Mandy was a very busy young mother, very capable and sure of herself, now with three little girls. Joshua and Emma had a third baby, too, a little boy named, Isaac.

They listened sympathetically as Lizzie recounted the horrors of her hospital stay, her baby's crying, her own helplessness, the mean nurse, and her roommate who successfully nursed her red-haired baby boy.

"But, Lizzie, I don't even know what you mean. I have never once in my life felt that way," Mandy said.

"Not even with the twins?" Lizzie asked, incredulous.

"Never."

"Me either," Emma chimed in.

"Well, why? Why would I be the one to have those awful blues?" Lizzie asked, becoming anxious all over again, her eyebrows raised in bewilderment.

"You were always like that, Lizzie. Always." Mam chimed in.

"I didn't cry about stuff, Mam."

"No, but you think ahead too much. You worry about things, not taking it a day at a time. Remember how you acted about Snowball, the kitten?"

"I did think about that, really I did, Mam."

"Well, if you'd relax and quit thinking about situations that could happen, but very likely never will, you'd be much better off," Mam said wisely.

"But you can't help the way you are," Lizzie answered, a bit miffed.

"You can learn from this, though, Lizzie," Mam assured her.

"Well, I won't have to worry, because I don't plan to have another baby. Not ever."

Lizzie said this quite forcefully, much to Emma's consternation. Mandy was aghast. Mam's nostrils got bigger, and her eyes snapped behind her glasses. No one said anything for awhile.

"Lizzie, you wouldn't do that," Mandy said finally.

"Not just one," Emma said kindly.

"Do you have to have a whole pile of babies?" Lizzie asked. "Does it say anything in the Bible about how many babies you should have?"

Mam shook her head back and forth slowly, swallowing a mouth full of coffee. She raised her hands in the air and brought them back down on her lap, the way she did when she laughed.

"I don't know, Lizzie. I just know that babies are a blessing, and 'blessed is the man who has his quiver full,'—meaning children are the arrows—which is a verse in Proverbs. There's no real law about how many babies each individual family should have, but among the Amish, especially, we're expected to have children."

"Why?"

Emma and Mandy looked at each other in their superior, "that poor thing," kind of way, which made Lizzy cross her arms and stare at them rebelliously.

"Tell me why one baby isn't enough."

"Lizzie, just wait. You'll want more children as Laura becomes older."

"No, I won't."

"What about Stephen?" Emma asked gently.

"He didn't say anything about having more children," Lizzie snapped.

"Lizzie, there's another verse in the Bible about women reaching salvation through childbearing," Mam said flatly.

"I thought our salvation is through Jesus on the cross. You know, grace, and that we can't earn it," Lizzie countered.

Then Mandy, in that wise, prophetic way she always had, said Lizzie probably didn't need to

think about more babies now. And then Mandy went on, "Did you know that the other day we had a cow with a twisted stomach, and the vet could do nothing, not one thing, and the cow died?" They all returned to the living room, the subject changed to much safer ground. Lizzie's happiness was restored as she thought about a dead cow instead of having more babies.

"Wasn't that quite a loss?" Lizzie asked.

"Not really. She was not a good milker, and we're butchering her, so we'll have ground beef you can buy from us for a good price," Mandy answered.

"Oh, goody! Then I can make meat loaf and barbecue sandwiches and vegetable soup and lots of good things for Stephen's supper," Lizzie said, smiling.

The rest of the day passed in a happy glow, with good advice from Mam about being careful not to give Baby Laura more than two ounces of formula before burping her. She also told Lizzie to hold Laura's head up when she gave her a bottle, although Lizzie still felt inferior watching Emma and Mandy peacefully nursing their babies, relaxed and at ease with the whole deal. Oh, well, sometimes life just was that way, and you had to do the best you could, even if it meant giving your baby formula from a bottle.

Chapter 19

In spite of all of Lizzie's insecurities and her lack of expertise when it came to babies, Laura thrived and grew, although crying lustily much of the time. Lizzie switched to a different formula, but with no success. One evening Stephen's mother, Annie, persuaded Laura to try goat's milk, which was natural and she thought as close to mother's milk as nature could provide. Laura drank well, cried just the same, and smelled exactly like a baby goat. Lizzie switched to a soy-based formula, and Laura smelled exactly like a little soybean.

But they continued on with the soybean formula, simply because her crying bouts were fewer, her nights were better, and she seemed more relaxed. That, in turn, made Lizzie feel better and calmer about babies in general.

The winter was a harsh one, with many snowstorms and temperatures hovering around zero degrees many days. The township plows, with their

bleary-eyed drivers, did their best, but still some of the less traveled roads remained closed for days with snowdrifts making the roads impassable. Still the snow fell and the wind blew great walls of it to distant places, blowing anything shut that bore even the semblance of a dip. Lizzie loved the snow and the excitement of seeing cars slip and slide, revving their engines as they tried repeatedly to make their way to the top of the small, steep incline below their house.

On one of those days after yet another snowfall, when the weather turned bitterly cold and a strong, steady, forceful wind began to blow during the night, Lizzie was awakened by the tingling of her nose. She lay shivering beneath the heavy comforter, listening intently to the steady whine of the wind, ever increasing outside the window.

That morning, Stephen got up a bit earlier to make sure there was plenty of wood in the box beside the stove in the living room. He had a good strong fire going by the time Lizzie got up to make breakfast and pack his lunch.

"I'm glad I have work inside today," he said.

"Won't you have a problem getting to your job?" Lizzie asked worriedly, knowing their weekly paycheck had been decreasing during most of the winter months because of the weather, but their mortgage payment was due on the same date every month.

"I don't think so, not with Jerry," he replied, grinning. "He's not afraid of anything with that four-wheel drive."

"Just be careful," Lizzie said.

"I want you to be careful, too," Stephen said seriously. "Don't let the woodstove get too hot in this wind. Sometimes I don't really trust the chimney. I don't think it's built well enough with just the flue liner and chimney block."

"Doesn't everybody build their chimney that way?" Lizzie asked.

"Pretty much. But I'd still feel more comfortable if we had built a better one."

Lizzie tried to heed Stephen's advice, but the house would not warm up sufficiently. Laura's little hands were cold, and shivers went up and down Lizzie's spine as she sat at the sewing machine. She stopped treadling just to listen to the wind as it wailed and howled around the little house, rattling anything that wasn't securely nailed down. She felt thankful for their good sturdy home, covered with bricks, white or not. They kept out the cold, increased the strength of the little structure, and helped her feel safer.

She added a few pieces of wood to the stove and opened the draft in the back, telling herself there was no sense in being chilly all day, especially with Laura shivering. She returned to the sewing machine, quickly becoming engrossed in putting in a difficult sleeve, and forgot about the draft in the back of the woodstove.

Suddenly she felt quite warm, so she stopped sewing and went to check the fire. She was alarmed to find the stove radiating much more heat than

usual. She quickly turned the knob to shut down the draft and was rewarded with an instant crackling sound as the wood lost the draft that had caused it to overheat. Anxiously Lizzie put her hand close to the stovepipe. It didn't feel red hot. Everything would be all right, she thought, hurriedly returning to her sewing while Laura slept.

The wind increased its fury, whining and making the snow swirl in great expanses across the countryside. Lizzie could hardly understand how Stephen could get to work on a day like this. But she shrugged off her concern, knowing he would be safe as long as his crew worked on the interior part of the new building.

She resumed sewing, then stopped to listen. What was that noise? A bumping sound seemed to be coming from upstairs. Bump! There it was again. It sounded like someone dropping a stone or a brick on the floor.

Hurriedly she left the sewing machine and stood, barely daring to breathe, at the open stairway listening. Bump! Another one! What if someone was up there, trying to lure her upstairs so he could grab her as she opened the door?

Now she heard another sound, only a bit lighter, like popping. Pop! Pop! Oh, dear! Lizzie looked left and right frantically before realizing there was only one thing to do. She had to charge up the stairs and see for herself what was making that unusual noise.

Quickly, she raced up the stairs, flung open the door, and peered inside. Nothing. The bed with

its multicolored Sunshine and Shadow quilt stood against the opposite wall. The rugs lay straight beside the bed and in front of the dresser.

She dashed across the hallway, opened the door on the opposite side, and instantly knew there was something wrong when a wall of warm air hit her. It was much too hot in the room. Reaching out tentatively, she touched the wall surrounding the chimney and yanked back her hand when the drywall burned her fingers.

Pop!

Now she heard the sound quite clearly, coming from the chimney. The chimney was on fire, popping and crackling in its ferocity. Laura! Her baby! She was all alone and had to call the fire department with no telephone in the house. Dat's phone shanty at the bottom of the hill was farther away than their next-door neighbors, a young English couple named Lance and Alice Wingert, with three children. She wondered wildly if Alice was home and which direction she should go. She could not waste one moment. The chimney was burning, and perhaps their little house would be next.

Dashing down the stairs, she grabbed the heaviest homemade comforter in the bedroom, threw on her coat and scarf, rolled Laura in the comforter, hearing her cries of protest, and dashed outside, running a short distance from the house.

The cold and the wind hit her with unbelievable force as she turned to look at the top of the chimney. She began crying as the evil-looking flames leaped

out and danced around the top of the chimney while black smoke pour out in thick plumes.

Oh, dear God, don't let our little house and all our stuff burn, she prayed, as she ran as best she could, carrying Laura in the heavy comforter. Never had the short distance between her house and the Wingerts' home seemed so far. She finally slipped between the shrubs by their back door. She tried not to pound madly, but knocked louder and more quickly than usual until Alice opened the door, peering out at Lizzie.

"The … the house! The chimney is burning! I need to call 911!" Lizzie burst out.

"Oh, my! Where? Your house! Come in! Hurry!" She stood aside as Lizzie hurried past, then reached for the phone and dialed 911, those blessed three little numbers that meant help would be on the way soon. Alice spoke in a clear articulate voice, giving the operator the correct address and describing the house.

"You go back now, stand in your driveway, and direct the fire trucks," Alice ordered, taking control of the situation quickly. "I'll watch Laura."

"But … she doesn't have a bottle!" Lizzie said hopelessly.

"She has her pacifier. She'll be fine. Go!"

So Laura ran, sobs catching in her throat as she saw the bright orange flames still leaping from the chimney. She had never felt quite so helpless or so inadequate in all her life. What would Stephen say? That was the most terrible thought.

She stood, then, in the gently curving driveway in the bitter cold with the strong winds blowing her skirt around her legs. She watched the chimney burning, until she finally, blessedly, heard the wail of the fire siren. Even then, it seemed like a very long time before the huge red trucks, with all the white and gold lettering, the fancy silver grillwork, and the yellow whirling lights on top of their cabs, actually came into view.

Lizzie waved her arms, pointing, but it was a useless gesture, as they had likely spotted the burning chimney half a mile away, since the house sat on top of a hill.

"We can't get up the drive!"

The firefighter rushing past her explained this to her, as he held a large fire extinguisher with both arms. He was followed by another, and then another fireman. There was nothing left for her to do except follow as they dashed up the front porch steps and into the living room, already on their way upstairs before Lizzie entered the house.

She stood at the bottom of the stairs, breathing hard, hearing the sound of chopping, followed by the hiss of the fire extinguishers. More men came charging in through the front door and up the stairway, their heavy firefighting gear clanking as they went. Then there was nothing to do but wait. She listened anxiously to the firemen stomping about upstairs, talking in low tones, until she smelled a smoky sulfurous odor wafting down the stairway, swirling around the living room.

Lizzie coughed, barely able to contain her curiosity, wondering if her house would burn down after all the firemen did to stop the burning chimney. She bit down hard on a fingernail and watched anxiously up the stairway as a fireman came back down, looking as if he wanted to talk to her.

"Do you live here?" he asked kindly.

"Y...Yes," Lizzie answered uncertainly, not sure if he would scold her for letting the stove become overheated.

"Let me tell you, you are a very fortunate young lady. The chimney block was so hot the rafters were beginning to burn behind the drywall. Five more minutes and your roof would have been aflame."

Lizzie watched him speak, her eyes wide, barely able to comprehend what he was saying.

Five more minutes!

What if she hadn't heard that sound? Or had not gone immediately for help? Or what if Alice had not been home? Oh, surely God had heard her prayers and had not let the house burn to the ground. Their very own house!

"You have a bit of a mess upstairs, but everything is replaceable. I suppose your husband isn't home?"

"No, he isn't. He'll be home around six."

"The fire in the stove will be out, so you'll have to find another source of heat until he returns. In this cold...Is there any way you can get ahold of him at work?"

Lizzie nodded, remembering the phone number stuck to the refrigerator door. After thanking the

firemen, she ran over to the Wingerts, made the phone call to Stephen, and then ran back to the house with Laura still wrapped in the comforter. Already, the house was cool, so she turned the oven on and propped the door open, figuring that would help a small amount until Stephen arrived. Laura was screaming at the top of her lungs, protesting the great weight of the comforter wrapped around her, trying with all her mighty little strength to worm her way out of it.

Lizzie laughed, calm now and so relieved that the fire was extinguished. She wrapped Laura tightly, telling her she should be grateful for the warmth of the big comforter instead of complaining like that. Finally Stephen arrived. His face was pale; his eyes wide with alarm. Lizzie felt like crying when she caught sight of him climbing out of the truck, but she didn't.

"What in the world, Lizzie!" he burst out, as he came through the back door.

"It … it just … "

"Are you all right? What about Laura?" he asked, coming over to peer into the heavy comforter.

"Yes, we are both all right, Stephen. It was…was my fault, letting the stove get so hot."

"No, Lizzie, not entirely. I never did feel safe building that chimney cheaply like that. Now we'll do something different. I'll go to the lumber company in town today and ask them what to do."

Lizzie followed him upstairs to see the damage the firemen had made in order to extinguish the

flames. There were huge, ragged holes chopped in the drywall, and when they peered into the wall, they could see the shiny blackness of the charred rafters. The entire room had a smoky, sulfurous smell, and the chimney still radiated some heat behind the battered drywall.

Stephen gave a low whistle as he laid his hand on the chimney block.

"That's scary, Lizzie. We came so close to losing everything."

Lizzie nodded soberly.

"But...you and Laura are all right, and that's what matters most."

Lizzie blinked back tears of gratitude as she hugged Stephen, thankful that he was not angry and that it had not been her fault. Well, at least not completely.

❧

That evening Dat and Jason helped Stephen install a new stainless steel chimney. Stephen explained everything to Lizzie. He showed her the instructions, and how black soot, the buildup from burning green wood, couldn't accumulate on the sides of the chimney.

When the whole setup was complete, Lizzie could not believe how thankful she felt as the fire crackled and popped, and the heat spread throughout the cold house. Everything felt safe and secure, cozy and homey again. She was so grateful that they were

here in their own little house with their possessions intact, and with the danger that had threatened to take everything extinguished.

That spring, after the harsh winter winds had slowed to a warm, gentle breeze and the melting snow ran in little rivulets into the spouting, splashing onto the ground and turning it into soft, spring mud, Stephen built a barn. The nice little building with brown siding matched the house and had a roof that wasn't straight, but was bent in the middle—a hip roof Stephen called it.

Lizzie loved the little barn. It completed the property, making it look much more like an Amish homestead and not just a house on top of a hill. Stephen built stables, one for George and one for an extra horse when company came, or in case they ever decided to buy a new horse, which Lizzie doubted would ever happen. Stephen thought one horse was enough. She would have loved to fill the barn with miniature ponies like Teeny and Tiny, the ponies Dat bought when Lizzie was little. But Stephen did not like ponies at all, saying they were stubborn little creatures, and why would she want a pony? If she wanted a pony, she could just walk down over the hill and drive her parents' ponies.

He would get a dog, he said. Lizzie said, no, she didn't like dogs. If she couldn't have ponies, then he couldn't have a dog. She didn't feel very virtuous

after she stated that a bit too forcefully, but she figured it didn't hurt Stephen to hear it. Otherwise, he'd become too selfish and just walk all over her, and didn't the marriage books say the wife shouldn't be a doormat? Lizzie figured she was coming pretty close to being a doormat, not being allowed to have ponies. Stephen wanted to go and buy a dog that ran all over the neighborhood and dug in her flower beds and barked up an insane storm every time someone came for a visit. She didn't like dogs, and that was that.

She thought Stephen was being very quiet after she said that, so she kept watching him out of the corners of her eyes when he wasn't looking. Was he angry, or just thinking about buying a pony for her?

Probably that's what it was. He was planning a surprise for her, putting a cute pony in that extra stall when she least expected it. But when she asked him a question at bedtime and he didn't answer, she figured it didn't take that much thinking to decide to buy a pony. He was mad.

Oh, well, he'll get over it, she thought unhappily. We're not having a dog. In fact, she so desperately didn't want a dog that she didn't care if she was being virtuous or not. Dogs were annoying.

Chapter 20

LIZZIE LOVED TAKING HER BABY TO CHURCH. There was just something about it that made her feel quite capable, so much like a real mother who knew what she was doing, even if she didn't. Every two weeks, on Saturday evening, she would get out the little straw basket with a lid on it, called a *kaevly* in Pennsylvania Dutch. Stephen's mother had ordered it for her and had given it to her as a baby gift.

In this little basket, Lizzie put a neat stack of snowy white cloth diapers, smelling so fresh and clean, she loved to bury her nose into them and take a deep breath of the scented softness. On top of this stack of diapers, she folded a pair of rubber panties, the stretchable little outer garment that held the wetness against the diaper, a clean pair of white tights, and a clean T-shirt, just in case she might need them.

Beside that pile of baby necessities, she placed one little jar of baby food, usually fruit-flavored. Lizzie's favorite flavor was Tutti-Frutti. It tasted so

good she probably ate half of it, licking the spoon while she fed Laura. She aĺso had a small container of rice cereal with a tiny bit of sugar sprinkled on top, a small baby-sized spoon, and a bottle containing a wee bit of apple juice mixed with water. She also added bottles of soy formula, two extra bibs, and the best part, baby toys.

It was fun to pick out the cutest toys to put in her *kaevly*, because she felt classy when other mothers watched what she gave her baby to play with during church. A string of pink and white glass beads with small key chains attached and little plastic rings kept Laura entertained for awhile.

She picked out a dress for Laura the evening before, sometimes pink or navy blue, just whatever she felt like. Often she would match the color with her own, especially if she was wearing a pretty color, like burgundy or forest green.

She completed Laura's outfit with one of the little homemade bibs Lizzie had bought at the dry-goods store in Lampeter. The bibs were usually crocheted or surrounded by lace of the same color as the baby's dress. Oh, it was all so much fun and exciting to take your baby to church, that she wished they would have services every Sunday instead of only on alternating ones.

In the wintertime, she dressed Laura in a little pink sweater set with a pretty blanket to match. On top of that Lizzie pinned a little black, woolen shawl securely around her that was just like her own, except it was baby-sized, of course. On Laura's

head, she placed a stiff little royal blue bonnet, just like her own, except baby-sized as well, and tied it securely under her chin.

She thought the shawl and bonnet were the cutest things she had ever seen, with Laura's little brown face peering out from the dark shades of fabric. So cute, in fact, that she squeezed and squeezed her before putting her own shawl and bonnet on. She carefully held Laura beneath the folds of her shawl when they went outside to protect her from the cold. She carried the *kaevly* with the other hand and went down the steps to where Stephen was waiting with George and the buggy.

When they arrived at church, Mom or KatieAnn or Susan would come with their arms extended to take Laura. Lizzie felt so loved and important and so Amish and motherly. Stephen's mother would fuss over her, making Lizzie feel happy and cuddly and warm inside, secure in the fact that she belonged to a group of family and friends. A complete circle of contentment.

Sometimes Laura would have a genuine crying spell, when nothing seemed to pacify her. Lizzie would take her away from where the service was being held, often upstairs, and rock her or feed her or do whatever it took to get her to stop crying. Often a friend and her fussy baby joined her, and they talked about babies, their sleep patterns, how much they weighed, or whatever.

Church wasn't nearly as boring when you had a baby to take care of, especially when a minister droned

on and on and wasn't very interesting. Then Lizzie just up and took Laura upstairs, whether she was crying or not. People didn't know what was wrong with her baby, and really, they didn't need to know.

Sometimes she would put a package of cheese crackers in her *kaevly* and eat them while she fed Laura, because it got late and she became very hungry. The thing was, when they served lunch, she was never able to sit at the first women's table because they were seated according to their ages. So she had to wait with the younger women and girls till the older ones had eaten. It seemed as if that table of older women always took their time, drinking coffee and talking way too much.

<center>❧</center>

On this fine spring morning, Stephen brushed and brushed George with careful attention, put the glossy black harness on his back, and then attached all the buckles and straps before putting the horse back in his stall. He went to the house to dress in his traditional white shirt, black broadfall pants, and black vest with hooks and eyes that closed down the front.

Humming under his breath, he opened the back door. He was amazed to find Lizzie hunched over the table with a small dish of water. She held a fine-toothed black comb, called a *shtrale*, in Dutch, and two tiny pieces of metal he remembered his mother using at home.

Lizzie did not look up when he entered, so he walked over to the table, peering down to see how she was faring.

"Bobbies?" he asked.

His wife nodded grimly, intent on parting Laura's silky baby hair in the middle and creating a wet strand on each side of Laura's forehead. Lizzie intended to roll the tip of each strand upward and around a sliver of soft bendable metal. With that action, she would form a small roll of hair on each side of Laura's forehead, called bobbies. It was an old traditional way of keeping a baby's thin hair from hanging in her face without cutting it.

Stephen soon sensed that Lizzie was pretty close to panicking, so he walked quietly away, down the hallway and into the bedroom. Lizzie wet the *shtrale* once more in the tiny dish of water and pulled it through Laura's hair on the left side of her part. Carefully holding the small bendable piece of metal, Lizzie began rolling upward, just as Laura turned her head, leaving Lizzie holding the metal, but no hair. She glanced with apprehension at the clock. Only 15 more minutes and they would have to leave, no doubt about it.

"Hold still," she hissed, putting her fingers on each side of Laura's cheeks and pulling her face to the desired position.

Once more, Lizzie tried, rolling upward until the bobbie was at the right spot on the side of Laura's forehead. Sighing with relief, she patted Laura's cheek and said, "Good girl."

"Now hold still," she murmured, and began the other one. That was when Laura decided she had had enough. She clearly saw no sense in putting up with these atrocities. She pulled her little body into a cramped position and howled shrilly.

Instantly, Lizzie bent over her, whispering, "Shh-shh-shh."

But Laura was indignant now, and she was not about to be lulled into submission by anyone. She kept screaming, one bobbie firmly in place and the other pieces of hair becoming drier by the second. Scooping her up, Lizzie held her distraught baby. They would never make it to church on time. She felt like crying but knew that would only make matters worse. She had to get that other bobbie in place.

"Sh-sh, you'll be all right. I know, it's not nice. Sh-sh-sh," Lizzie kept saying, bouncing Laura up and down.

Finally, with only five minutes to go, Laura quieted enough for Lizzie to lay her back down on the table top. She gave her a bright little toy to play with, anything to get her mind off whatever Lizzie was doing to her hair. Swiftly, she wet the comb, raked it through her hair, adjusted the soft piece of metal, and began rolling, just as Laura twisted her little body to roll over.

"No, Laura! No!" Lizzie wailed. Laura promptly began crying again.

"Stephen!"

In the bedroom, Stephen jumped, then rushed to the door, adjusting his suspenders, alarmed at the

panic in Lizzie's voice.

"Stephen, I can't make bobbies! She just turns her head! We'll be late for church!"

"It's not that bad, Lizzie. We still have a quarter of an hour."

"We don't! Remember last time? We left at eight-thirty and were last."

"We weren't last. Some of the youth were."

Lizzie turned her back without bothering to answer. They were the last ones to arrive, she knew that.

"Hold her still," she barked.

"How?"

Stephen looked helplessly at his screaming daughter, then at his upset wife, and wondered if this was the way things were going to be from now on.

"I have to make the other bobbie. Just hold her head on each side so she can't turn it. Sh-sh, Laura. It's not that bad!"

So Stephen bent down, his elbows on the table, his hands gently cradling Laura's head, while Lizzie concentrated on the bobbie. He wasn't prepared when Laura suddenly turned her head hard to the right, twisting her entire body.

"Stephen!" Lizzie shrieked.

It really irked him when Lizzie yelled at him like that. He was doing the best he could. But he said nothing.

"You have to hold her head firmly," she ordered, wetting the comb for what would be the twentieth time.

"Why don't you just stick her head in a vice?" Stephen asked sarcastically, as he bent to his task.

Lizzie shot him a withering glance but said nothing, returning to her task with desperation now.

Laura screamed, but Stephen held her head more firmly, murmuring to his daughter. Lizzie deftly rolled the hair and clipped it into place, standing back to view the two bobbies.

"They're crooked!"

Straightening up, Stephen picked up his wailing daughter and patted her back, soothing her over and over while glaring at Lizzie.

"You're not going to redo that bobbie," he said firmly.

"But they're not straight, Stephen. I have to."

"Give it up Lizzie. She looks fine to me. It's time to go!"

"I'm not ready."

Grimly, Lizzie scooped up the dish and comb, swiped the tabletop with a wet cloth, then reached for Laura as Stephen hurried to the bedroom to finish dressing. Lizzie's heart sank seriously when she looked at Laura's forehead. One bobbie was up higher and closer to the middle of her face while the other one hung to the side. Oh, it was so pathetic-looking. She couldn't take her baby to church with those bobbies.

Weighing her options, she decided that arriving at church late would create more of a stir than two bobbies that were not quite straight, so she put the bottles of formula in her *kaevly* and said nothing.

Stephen emerged from the bedroom looking as handsome as he always did in his Sunday suit, and Lizzie forgave him readily for not allowing her to fix Laura's bobbies.

❧

"Is it chilly this morning?" she asked, hoping he had forgiven her for acting so hysterical.

"A little."

So Lizzie put the little black woolen shawl around Laura's shoulders, secured it with a pink safety pin, put the blue bonnet on her head, and tied it beneath her chin. She stood back to look at her, chuckling softly.

"Oh, Laura, you look so cute and so Amish with your bobbies!" she exclaimed, then swept her up into a tight hug.

Grabbing her *kaevly*, she went outside where Stephen had gone, put her *kaevly* into the *doch-veggley* or buggy, and climbed in, holding Laura firmly. Stephen gathered the leather reins, then reached up to George's neck and attached the neck rein, that part of the harness which held George's head up.

Lizzie always disliked neck reins. Always. They were the cruelest invention anyone had ever thought of. How would a person like to pull a load up a hill without being allowed to hunch over to pull? She always felt a small sense of rebellion every time Dat, and now Stephen, attached that thing. It was cruel, that's what.

As Stephen climbed quickly into the buggy beside her, George tossed his head, made a running leap, and was off down the curving driveway. Lizzie clutched Laura tightly, nervously hoping Stephen could handle George. She was not in a good mood after all the tension of the morning, and it only elevated her bad humor to start off like that.

"I guarantee one thing," she said dryly.

"What?"

"If you wouldn't attach that neck rein quite as tightly as you do, George would behave himself better as he starts off."

"That rein isn't tight. What do you mean?" Stephen asked, turning to look at her quite sharply.

Too sharply, in Lizzie's opinion, so she didn't answer.

Stephen tried again. "What do you mean 'that rein is tight'? He's running with the rein loose now."

Lizzie still didn't answer, only because it felt too good to see him trying to get her to talk. So he shrugged his shoulders, thinking he'd never understand women as long as he lived, at least not Lizzie, anyway. She could be a strange duck.

They drove on in silence, Laura relaxing against Lizzie after the traumatic morning she had just endured. Her eyelids fell heavily as she fought sleepiness, the way she always did when they went away in a buggy. Lizzie shifted her arm more comfortably, then sat back against the blue upholstered buggy seat, sighing as her shoulders slumped in relaxation.

What a morning it had been, she thought wryly.

She sincerely hoped this was not a harbinger of things to come. It wasn't right. Here it was Sunday, the Sabbath, the Lord's day, and she had already panicked, lost her temper twice, and was still coddling ill feelings toward her husband. She thought the devil sure didn't take Sundays off, the way he had made her carry on.

She glanced at Stephen, who appeared a bit worn and weary for so early in the morning. She wondered what he was thinking, but she was still a bit too miffed about that neck rein deal to ask him. That was the trouble with being married. If that harness were Lizzie's, she would have seriously lengthened the neck rein, but since it wasn't hers, she had no business speaking her mind. She should sit back and leave it entirely up to her husband's judgment, with absolutely no will of her own.

It was all so weird, strange, and stupid. Whoever heard of such a thing? She thought she had this all figured out when she was dating Stephen. Yet here she was, upset about that short neck rein, while he drove along, contently secure in the fact that he could drive with that rein exactly the way he wanted. He was the husband and she was the wife, and that meant he was the boss. She would have to figure out how to live with that.

She was just angry all over again. No one ever talked about the husband giving his life for his wife, as Christ gave himself for the church. To Lizzie's way of thinking, if Stephen loved her so that he gave himself for her, he would lengthen that rein because

it bothered her. Then when he came to church and the men asked him why his horse's neck rein was so long, he should smile nicely and say his wife liked it that way, and that since it bothered her, it bothered him as well.

Then all the men would think what a good husband Stephen was and how fortunate Lizzie was to have him. Wasn't that the way the Bible said it should be? But no, here they went, racing down the road, Stephen secure in his kingly position and she wrestling with this huge mountain called submission.

Suddenly the whole thing was unbearable and, forgetting to pout, she said loudly, "Doesn't it bother you that George's head is held up so high?"

"Lizzie, would you get off it? The rein is loose. He's comfortable. It's the way he naturally holds his head."

"Oh, no, it isn't, Stephen."

"Lizzie, now stop. You're still upset about making those bobbies, and you can't give up that they're crooked, so you're taking it out on me. Now stop it."

That really made Lizzie see red, so much so, in fact, that she felt like crying. The nerve of him! How did he know?

"You... you..."

"You can sputter around all you want to. It's true."

"You're mean."

"I don't try to be."

"I'm just telling you the truth."

So Lizzie thought about the truth for the next mile or so, finally coming to the conclusion that he was probably right. That rein bothered her a lot more than usual because of her own frustration. Well, she wasn't going to let him know she thought he was right. That would for sure only make him feel more superior than ever.

But when the visiting minister spoke eloquently about the blessing a family receives by a quiet, well-spoken, godly mother staying in her rightful position, Lizzie bent her head and cried a few tears in her rose-colored handkerchief. It touched a part of her soul that wanted to be good, but which her own willful nature made extremely difficult.

Glancing around furtively, she looked to see if other women felt the same desire to be such a person. Rather a large amount had tears in their eyes, and a few were blowing their noses. Lizzie felt very righteous and good inside, feeling as if she actually was like that. Well, not really, but by the time they had a larger family, she would be a virtuous woman. After all, these things take time.

Chapter 21

LAURA WAS OUTGROWING HER LITTLE BROWN porta-crib. Lizzie's mind began churning, trying to figure out a way she could fit a big, normal-sized crib into their small bedroom. Any way she arranged the furniture in her mind, the room was still too crowded. So she decided she would approach Stephen about transforming the room where he kept his gun cabinet and desk into a really cute little nursery.

As she hung her Monday's washing on the line, she thought about it. When she ironed coverings she thought about it, and when she cleaned the basement she thought about it. In fact, that was all she could think about most of the day, becoming more and more excited as the day went on. She would make little gingham pink and white curtains and cover the bumper pad around the crib to match. Perhaps she could make a tiny comforter with pink and white flannel, knotting it with pink yarn. Or

would white be better? Maybe white.

By the time Stephen came home from work, she had thought herself into quite a stew, her cheeks flushed, her eyes bright with anticipation, eagerly waiting to see if he was in the proper mood for her to ask such a huge favor.

Her heart fell as he climbed out of his co-worker's truck, his trousers covered with mud, his face dark and very, very tired. Even his hands and thermos were muddy. It didn't look too promising, she decided, so maybe the best thing was not to ask him at all this evening if he was tired and grouchy.

She waited nervously as he entered the basement, took off his shoes, and washed up at the sink, puttering around down there for far too long, she thought. When he finally did come upstairs, he did not have his usual smile of welcome.

"Long day?" Lizzie asked, too quickly and much too brightly.

"Yeah," he said brusquely.

So Lizzie kept quiet as she served the good supper she had prepared—mashed potatoes and beef gravy, peas and carrots, and macaroni and cheese, one of his favorite meals. Lizzie tried to keep the conversation light and happy until Stephen pushed back his chair and sighed, finally smiling at her. Instantly Lizzie dove straight into the subject, plying him with all kinds of questions about many different subjects pertaining to that particular room.

"But you know, Stephen, the biggest problem is that there isn't a doorway between your gun-cabinet

room and our bedroom," she stated quite firmly. Stephen lowered his eyebrows.

"Why would you need a doorway between our bedroom and the other room?" he asked.

"Well, I'd have to walk all the way through the living room, and besides, I couldn't hear Laura very well when she cries," Lizzie said.

Stephen didn't say more after that. He just got up and walked into the living room, sitting heavily on the brown recliner and picking up a fishing magazine. Lizzie crossed her arms and glared at him. Of all the nerve! There he goes, tuning me out and refusing to talk. Well, she wasn't finished yet, so she'd talk anyway. Sitting opposite him on the sofa, she leaned forward and began speaking in a sweet voice. Or so she hoped.

"But listen, Stephen, we can't get a full-sized crib in our bedroom. It's too small. You know that. I know you don't want to give up your hunting room, but you're going to have to anyway. You can't just have that room for your stuff if we need it for the baby. And besides, you can keep all that junk upstairs."

Stephen sat straight up.

"Junk! My hunting stuff isn't junk!"

"Well, kind of."

"That does it, Lizzie. I'm not moving out of there. We can arrange a big crib in our bedroom somehow."

Lizzie sat straight up, gripping a small square pillow with both hands, her eyebrows reaching for her

hairline, her eyes wide with disbelief and sorrow.

"You have to, Stephen!" she wailed.

"I don't have to do anything," he said, very quietly, but very determinedly.

He may as well have been a judge in a courtroom, raising his gavel, banging it down, and passing a sentence that would send her to prison, Lizzie thought wearily. All her dreams of pink gingham curtains and a little changing table flew out the window, disappearing somewhere above the sun.

She was afraid of the firmness in his voice, so she sighed as loud as she could, hoping her eyes would convey how hard it was when he refused to do her bidding. When he didn't respond, she slowly returned to the kitchen. Cleaning all the dishes off the table in slow, sad, little movements, she watched him out of the corner of her eye to see if he felt badly. She fervently hoped so.

There was nothing to do but give it up. Well, there was half of a small saucepan of macaroni and cheese left. She got a clean fork from the drawer and ate great comforting mouthfuls of the gooey, cheesy dish. She didn't care if she gained five pounds. Actually, if he was going to be so mean, maybe she'd just keep eating macaroni and cheese until she gained 20.

Turning on the hot water, she grabbed the bottle of dish soap and squeezed it angrily, creating way too many suds. She had to rinse the dishes twice as long, and there were suds over everything. She had always loved that feeling as a little girl, but now, the

bubbles only irked her more.

After she wiped the counter clean, she felt very thirsty. She drank a large glassful of cold water from the refrigerator, then felt fat and uncomfortable and worse than ever. She didn't want to join Stephen in the living room, because she wasn't planning on talking at all. All evening—not one word.

She supposed she could go sit in the bedroom, but Laura was asleep, and she certainly did not want to wake her. She had two options: continue to stand right where she was, against the kitchen counter where he couldn't see her, or sit in the bathroom, which would seem a bit suspicious.

Maybe she could pretend to be sick and make terrible retching noises, and he would become extremely alarmed and so sorry. Then he would put his arms around her and tell her he loved her and would do anything she wanted. He couldn't bear the thought of living without her.

Well, knowing Stephen, he'd go right on reading his fishing magazine without worrying about retching noises in the bathroom. She sighed and then blew her nose, which sounded a lot dryer than she had hoped. She wanted desperately for him to think she was crying, standing all alone in the kitchen, sobbing so pitifully. Taking a few soft steps, she peeped around the partition, wondering if he looked her way at all.

He was lying back against the extended recliner, his eyes closed, looking very, very tired. A wave of love and pity washed over her then. She knew she

was acting very spoiled and immature. But the thing was, her dream of a nursery far outweighed her guilt from being childish. If you put the nursery on one side of the scales, and her guilt on the other, the nursery won by a long shot. So what was she supposed to do?

Persuading a husband to do something he didn't want to do was an acquired skill, she thought. Certainly with Stephen. He could act exactly like a donkey when he wanted to.

Suddenly she brightened. She would wait a few days, and then when he was in a better state of mind, she would buy him a new shirt or tell him he could get a dog, or something like that, and he would give in. She told herself, Never, ever call your husband's hunting gear junk again.

So she walked into the living room, picked up her unfinished dress, folded it neatly on the sewing machine, and cleared her throat. She picked up the corner of the rug, pulled it into place, and cleared her throat again. Stephen stirred, then opened his eyes, raising his eyebrows as he straightened his chair.

"You know why I'm grouchy?" he asked, in his straightforward manner.

Glory Hallelujah! He wasn't angry!

"Why?" Lizzie responded, eagerly.

"Because I'm tired of working with your Dat and Jason."

"But … but …" Lizzie floundered, her heart sinking. Dat was their paycheck, their security, their house

payment and groceries and...and...everything.

"I want to start my own business with my brothers."

This was too much. Lizzie's thoughts filled with a hundred unnamed fears, which whirled around inside her head like a whole flock of frightened blackbirds. She was unable to comprehend much of what he was saying.

"What do you mean?" she finally managed, a bit weakly.

"Just that. I don't have anything against Dat and Jason. I just feel as if we'll always live here and never get ahead as long as I'm only being paid by the hour."

"But...I mean..." Lizzie simply didn't know what to say, so she stopped and sank into a rocking chair.

"But, Stephen," she finally said, in a very small voice. "It's so scary."

"Not really."

"But...what about Dat? What does he say?"

"I haven't said anything. And don't you say a word to anyone, either. I'm not sure exactly what I'll do. I like to make furniture, too, so maybe I could build a small shop, attach it to the barn, and work there in the evening."

Oh, that sounded like the perfect solution to Lizzie and she told him so instantly, adding that it seemed so very much safer to stay with Dat and build furniture in the evening.

They sat for quite a while, discussing both ideas.

Stephen became more enthused about building a small furniture shop as additional income. After Lizzie realized he was now in a much better state of mind, she asked a bit timidly if he really meant what he had just said about putting a doorway between the two rooms.

"Are you still chewing on that?" he asked, amazed that she had not forgotten one bit.

"Well, yes, Stephen. I want a nursery for Laura. The only thing in that room is your desk and gun cabinet, and the desk will fit nicely in the dining room. How often do you use your guns? Huh?"

"A lot," Stephen said, scowling.

Determined to have her own way, Lizzie pushed on, fueled by her single-minded desire to have that nursery.

"You don't. Only in the fall. Deer season, and that's it."

"Turkey, squirrel, pheasant, dove, rabbit," Stephen said, loudly.

"So? That's in November and December."

"October!"

"Well, whatever. But that gun cabinet could go upstairs. I'll fix up a room for it and everything. The only difference is you'll need to climb the stairs."

Stephen said nothing, only picked up his fishing magazine again.

"Stephen, if you're going to sit there and read that thing without answering me, I'm going to go get a saw and cut a hole in that wall! Put it away!"

Stephen put the magazine away and looked

straight at her, giving her his undivided attention.

"Okay, and how do you plan on sawing through that wall?" he asked.

"With a saw," she said archly.

"Once you set your mind to something, you just don't give up, do you?"

"Sometimes I do."

"When?"

"I don't know."

"I don't either. I'll tell you what. If you help me in my new shop in the evening, I'll put my gun cabinet upstairs. I'll cut that much-needed hole in the wall if that's what it's going to take to keep my very determined wife happy."

Lizzie could not believe her ears! She was so happy, she shrieked like a little girl, hugging Stephen and waking the baby. She talked nonstop as she ran into the bedroom to pick up a bewildered little Laura. She told her she would soon be sleeping in a big crib in her very own room, and wouldn't that be the most delightful thing ever?

The days that followed were busy, happy ones for Lizzie. Stephen helped her move the furniture, and then, true to his word, he brought his tools in one Saturday morning and cut a door in the bedroom wall. There was a lot of noise and dust everywhere, but she did not complain about anything, not ever. She was far too happy to have the nursery she had dreamed about.

She even stood beside Stephen, telling him he was very handsome in that gray shirt. It made his eyes

look almost silver. He grinned, then told her she was just saying that because she was getting her own way. Would she stand beside him right now and tell him he looked handsome if he lay on the recliner and refused to cut this door?

Lizzie said of course not. Husbands who refused to do anything nice for their wives never looked handsome. Stephen said they looked exactly the same, just not in their wife's eyes. "You always look the same, no matter what you did," he said. Lizzie laughed and laughed, and then Stephen grinned, and they sat on the floor and talked a while about other things.

Those were the times Lizzie was glad she was married and lived with Stephen in the little brown house on top of the hill. If your husband was kind and did a nice favor for you like cutting this door, life was so happy and rosy, and your husband looked very nice when he worked.

But if you sat in a buggy beside him and the rein was too tight on the horse, and he didn't think so and refused to loosen it, your husband didn't look nearly as handsome. Actually, on Sunday on the way to church, Lizzie thought Stephen's nose was really growing and that his hair was cut too square in front of his ears. It was amazing how his looks changed when he was kind.

The nursery turned out just as pretty as Lizzie had imagined a few weeks later. She painted the walls a pale pink color. Stephen read directions from a small white manual and assembled the crib without once losing his temper. Lizzie sewed the pink gingham curtains and covered a bumper pad she had bought at a garage sale with the same fabric.

They went to town and bought a nice dry sink at the used-furniture place, which they probably should not have bought, since it was over a hundred dollars. But Stephen said it wasn't too bad, so Lizzie thought he was surely the best husband anyone had ever had.

The closet in the nursery was one of the things she was most thrilled about. She arranged all the little dresses on little pink plastic hangers, then hung them on a silver rod in a colorful row. On the shelf above it, she placed Laura's little black shawl with her navy blue bonnet on top, and then the diaper bag which she used to go everywhere, except to church when she used the little woven basket *kaevly*.

On the floor of the closet, Lizzie put the blue stroller that folded up neatly.

Now all she needed were some rugs. She still wanted soft, fuzzy, pink rugs, one to put in front of the crib and another to put in front of the dry sink, mostly because the floor was a stone-patterned linoleum. When they built the house, they planned this room for Stephen's things, not a baby's, which, if you really thought about it, wasn't too smart. They should have thought of having babies, but, then,

some people never had any. You just never knew about that kind of thing, which, Lizzie supposed, was completely up to God.

Sometimes she wondered why God was the way he was. Why he let some people have a whole pile of babies. Others, who desperately wanted children, he left childless, and they had to adopt someone else's babies if they wanted any. It was hard to figure God out sometimes, never knowing what he would do next. But then, Mam helped Lizzie to understand that nothing was stressful as long as it was the way God wanted it to be. Most likely everything was the way he chose anyway. Good or bad, it was God working in people's lives, which was a calming, very restful thing for Mam, but just as scary as could be for Lizzie.

The real issue here was the idea of having more babies. As Lizzie finished placing all the cute baby things where she wanted them, she wondered if Laura would be their only child for a long, long time. She certainly did not want another one, not now, not ever. But she could not tell Mam that. Or Stephen. Or anyone, really. For one thing, Mam would start in about God's will. He meant for women to complete a family with children, she would say. But Mam loved all babies—homely ones, fat ones, even noisy, slobbering babies that weren't a bit cute. She loved them all.

Of course, Lizzie loved Laura, but she wanted only her for now. Maybe when Laura went to school, she could think about having another one. Lizzie

really wondered what the Bible said about having babies. How many was a good number, how many was an excellent number, and how would only one look to God?

English people didn't have 10 children. They had only two or three, and sometimes, only one. But Amish people had a whole pile. Some families had 14 children, or 12 or 10 or whatever. So did that mean the Amish woman would have it nicer in heaven? Or find more grace in God's eyes?

She would have to get her Bible and figure this out. So she did. Stephen eyed her warily as she searched her Bible each evening before she went to bed. He thought that if she wanted to talk about whatever was on her mind, she would. And sure enough, one evening she started in with dozens of complicated questions and reasonings about having a large family versus a small one, and did it make a difference to God in the end?

Stephen shrugged his shoulders and said he didn't know, but the truth was, her endless questions about life made him tired. Why did she need to make a relatively simple existence so complicated by having to understand every tiny little thing? But that was Lizzie, and she was his wife, so he guessed he'd better learn to live with it.

Chapter 22

Lizzie could not let the matter of having more babies rest. She thought about it constantly, always resisting the idea. She searched her Bible until she became quite frustrated with the lack of direction it gave about the proper number of children God wanted in each family.

Stephen never said much about the subject. He rolled his eyes and sighed loudly whenever she approached him yet again with her endless wondering about having a large family, especially if you didn't want one.

Lizzie finally decided he was no help at all and marched down the hill with Laura in her arms to visit Mam. Mam was puttering around in her flower beds, carefully clipping the brown leaves off her picturesque "cheraniums."

KatieAnn and Susan came running for Laura, who started waving her arms and wriggling all over the minute she saw them approaching. KatieAnn

held her while Susan looked over her sister's shoulder, both talking to her at once while Laura squealed with excitement. Lizzie watched and decided that it was amazing how much the twins loved Laura. She wasn't even their own baby. Maybe KatieAnn and Susan were like Mam, truly loving all babies, constantly wanting to hold them when they were around her. Mam straightened her back and wiped the sweat from her brow, her face red with exertion.

"Come on in, Lizzie, and I'll fix us a cold drink," she said.

"You go on working in your flower beds, Mam. You don't need to stop because I'm here."

"Oh, no, I'm not that busy. I always have time for you girls," she said, smiling.

Lizzie thought things really changed after you got married and moved away. Mam treated you more like company, becoming more smiley and polite when you came home. That was because you were no longer a real daughter, but now partly Stephen's wife, so Mam was much kinder and didn't boss you around anymore. That was nice.

Mam opened the door for Lizzie and got out two glasses from the cupboard, filling them with ice cubes and grape Kool-Aid, which tasted like Lizzie remembered home to taste. Suddenly she had a sharp pang of homesickness, and she wanted to sit around the kitchen table with Emma and Mandy and drink grape Kool-Aid while Mam bossed them around.

"What's on your mind, Lizzie?" Mam asked,

noticing the worried arch of her brows, accompanied by a most troubled expression.

"Oh, not much. Well, yes, a little."

Mam waited.

"Why do Amish people have so many children?" Lizzie finally asked.

Mam raised her eyebrows, then took a long drink.

"That's a good question, Lizzie," she said.

"Is it?"

"Yes. And you know, I don't really know how to answer it. I wanted all my babies, every one of them, even if they were born almost every year."

"But you're not normal, Mam. Not where babies are concerned," Lizzie said.

Mam laughed and laughed, her round stomach shaking as she did so, until she looked quizzically at Lizzie and shook her head. She took off her glasses to wipe them with the corner of her apron, the same way she always did.

"Oh, now, Lizzie, I think I'm quite normal."

"Then I'm not. Mam, I don't want another baby. Not ever, and it's so hard to find anything in the Bible about that subject. It doesn't say anything about the number of babies you're supposed to have," Lizzie said.

"Lizzie, now listen. The Bible doesn't say one thing specifically about the way we dress. It doesn't say we're supposed to wear capes or make our dresses a certain way or any of that. Someone hundreds of years ago decided this is the way we should dress so we remain modest, and the tradition has

been maintained all these years. Having babies is very likely much the same. Did you find the passage in the Bible where it says about women reaching their salvation through childbearing? I forget exactly where it is, but it's there."

"Mam, the preachers say grace is free. A gift. Isn't grace our salvation? Then how come we have to have a whole pile of babies to get to heaven? That's trying to earn our way in—you know that."

Mam was quiet, turning her empty glass around and around.

"Lizzie, you think too much," she said. "Why don't you just stop trying to figure everything out and learn to accept whatever God sends? No matter what, and it's hard to explain this, but having babies is a very good method of learning to give up our own will."

"So, when you say that, you're saying you had to give up every time a baby was born? Right? Huh?"

"Well, not really. I looked forward to each one, wondering if it would be a boy or girl, what it would look like, how much it would weigh. I was always happy with my babies."

"Not Jason."

"Yes, I was, Lizzie," Mam said, becoming slightly perturbed, Lizzie could tell.

"He was homely-looking, you know that. And you cried in the bedroom, all by yourself, because he cried so much. I saw you."

"Lizzie, with each baby you have, your motherly instincts become better. You become more relaxed,

more focused on the baby's needs and less and less on your own. That's why it's a good thing to just let God direct in your life, bearing children, learning through that to become more and more unselfish as time goes on. It is good for a woman to have children."

Lizzie thought of the hospital and the grouchy nurses, her inability to nurse Laura, her overwhelming feelings of inadequacy. She had cried constantly, feeling as if she was washed overboard in stormy seas and would surely perish, all because of having had a baby. It was definitely not something she wanted to do ever again if she could help it.

"But then, what if I don't have more children? What if I would be one of the first Amish women in the world to have only one? Does that mean God would be mad at me?"

"Ach, Lizzie, you make me tired. Sometimes I don't know how to answer your questions."

"So, you don't know, right?"

"No, not really."

"Look at Aunt Vera, in Ohio. She had two children, Leroy and Mary Ann. And I'm pretty sure she'll go to heaven, Mam, as kindhearted as she is."

Mam laughed. "Ach, yes, Lizzie. Vera is one person who had only two children. She had Leroy and Mary Ann and decided that's enough of that. Bless her dear heart, I miss her. It's time we go for a visit again. Did you know Homer bought a coal business now?"

"He did?" Lizzie said absent-mindedly, still worrying with the baby subject.

"Well, if I do have more babies, I'm not going to the hospital. I didn't like it there. That one nurse was so mean, and I still think that's what got me started crying," she said.

"Lizzie, I've been to the hospital many, many times, and I've never had a nasty or mean nurse. Are you sure it was as bad as you say it was? Maybe you were overly sensitive."

Lizzie shook her head.

"Huh-uh, Mam. She scolded me terribly for laying Laura crossways on the bed. I'll never forget how that only added to my feeling of being overwhelmed with the responsibility of a new baby. She made me feel as if I wasn't fit to have a baby, which, I suppose, I wasn't, because she wouldn't nurse right."

"Your next one might be so different, Lizzie. You know and have learned a lot with Laura. Stephen wants a little boy, and after that, you'll want more. You'll see."

On her way back up the hill, Lizzie was glad Mam didn't have better answers She couldn't prove that having a large family instead of a smaller one was a rule enforced by God. Big families were just an Amish tradition, the same as her clothes.

But, if she was quite honest with herself, the traditions of the Amish—of the forefathers, as the ministers said—was not something she took lightly. She supposed a church was the same as a school. You had to have rules or else everybody would just go out and do their own thing. What sense of structure and order would there be otherwise?

Yes, she would continue to wear a black shawl and bonnet to church, to wear black shoes and stockings, to comb her hair sleek and flat, to light her propane gas lamp and trim the wicks. She would wash with a wringer washer propelled by a gas motor, keeping up the old traditions and way of life because she wanted to. She never really wanted to change. Never. She loved her way of life, and she wanted to do these Amish things. She loved belonging to a group of people who believed in the same order.

Not that she perfectly followed every tiny aspect of the rules and regulations. She was supposed to wear a shawl and bonnet wherever she went in the wintertime. Even to town, when she went shopping. But a large woolen shawl was quite cumbersome in a store, the trailing fringes sometimes knocking things down.

Once, a little English girl had been terrified by Mam's shawl and bonnet, running to her mother and hiding. Lizzie had been embarrassed, knowing the little girl was not used to seeing someone dressed in all black, especially with a long flowing shawl. Lizzie just wore a sweater, or a coat and a bonnet only when it rained or was very cold. Most of the young women did the same.

Well, she would wait and see. She would pray about this matter of children and, like Mam, leave it to God. Perhaps she would come to want one more baby, in time, and never any more after that. She bet no one except God knew how she dreaded the thought of having another baby.

Maybe God keeps record of families in the Book of Life. Kind of a report card for mothers. If you have 14 children you get an A+, if you have 12 an A, and on down to an F for having only one. But still, with report cards you can get away with an F if it's only in one subject, as long as you have A's or B's or even C's in other areas. Perhaps if she was as kind as she could be to Stephen and would not say one nasty thing if he got a dog, or call his hunting gear junk, she would earn an A in that category. Then if she only had two children, she'd still pass.

All these thoughts were silly and unnecessary, Lizzie decided, especially if salvation was a gift and was handed down free of charge. This was about the most confusing thing ever. If salvation was so free, why did you have to bother to live right and plain and simple? Why couldn't you go out and do exactly anything you wanted and never have to worry if anything was right or wrong?

How nice were you to your husband if you gave him all he wanted, but refused to have more children? What if he was much too kindhearted to tell you he wanted a baby boy more than anything? A childish, selfish girl who didn't want any more babies would probably earn a grade lower than an F on her report card, maybe a G, if there was such a thing. Someday, when she had the courage to approach Stephen about this subject, she would.

❧

Not too much time elapsed until Lizzie had a good opportunity to ask Stephen that very question. He was sitting on the front porch, relaxing after his shower, tired from the day's work, and glad to have the company of his wife and baby daughter. Lizzie settled beside him, and he reached for Laura, who gurgled happily and nestled against his shoulder. He patted her little bottom and smiled at Lizzie.

"She's growing so fast. Can you believe she's nine months old?"

"I know," Lizzie said tightly.

"Is she crawling all over the place?"

"Not really all over the place. She doesn't like the hardwood floor in the living room. It's too slippery, and she flops down on her stomach and yells as loud as she can."

"She's some Maidsy," Stephen said, grinning.

Maidsy was the pet name they used for Laura, and she recognized the word, lifting her head and looking at them when they said it.

Without warning, Stephen said, "About time for another one." It wasn't a question. It was a statement.

Lizzie's heart jumped, flipped, then resumed beating normally, only a bit faster.

"You think so?" she breathed.

"Oh, yes! I'd love to have a little boy. An Andy!"

Lizzie swallowed, then looked away from Stephen, out over the hilltop, down to the tree line by the creek. For once in her life, she had absolutely nothing to say.

There it was. Stephen, Mam, God, and the Bible were all on one side, and she was on the other. She was pretty sure Emma and Mandy would stick with that first group of people and tell her the same thing Mam did. Men wrote the Bible, not women.

She knew what Mam would say about that, too. It wasn't humans that wrote the Bible, it was the Holy Spirit. It was inspired by God, so really, those men, Malachi, David, Peter, John, all of them, were only vessels God used to write things he wanted everyone to know.

She may as well forget arguing about any of that.

"You're not saying anything, Lizzie," Stephen said gently.

"No. I'm not."

Her words were sharp, a bit too loud, and very certain.

"Why not?"

"I...I...Stephen, we don't want another baby!" she burst out.

"Not ever?"

"No!"

She got up, flounced into the house, and sat heavily on the sofa, feeling more miserable than she could ever remember. Why did everyone have to be so mean? Now Stephen, yet! At least Mam could be on her side if Stephen wasn't. She was surprised to hear the front door opening. Stephen came in and sat beside her, handing Laura to her.

"Lizzie, don't be upset. I didn't mean anything by it."

Those were tender words, coming from Stephen, and they melted her heart into tiny little droplets that formed into real tears as she turned to him gratefully.

"I'm not upset, really. I just…well, I need a bit of time to think this thing through. I wish I would like babies better, and I wish I was a better mother, and I wish the Bible would say more about babies," she said, tearfully.

"The Bible doesn't spell things out in black and white, Lizzie. We have to figure out what makes us feel right with God and what doesn't. We have choices."

That statement from Stephen held a wealth of peace for Lizzie. Why, of course! He was so right. It was so simple and uncomplicated and worry-free! You could soon tell whether you had made a wrong or a right choice, simply by the way your conscience bothered you. She had often experienced that in her life.

So Lizzie calmed down and forgot about her anxiety at the prospect of having another baby. She figured she'd let the whole thing up to God. Like a heavy backpack strapped to her back, she loosened it and left it by the wayside for God to pick up and take care of.

The next morning, Lizzie was walking down the hill with Laura when she met Dat coming from the barn, his face lighting up at the sight of them.

"Hello, there! How's our Maidsy?" he asked, grinning happily, and then stumbled on an uneven patch on the driveway. He fell heavily on his side as his legs gave way beneath him.

Lizzie rushed to his side.

"Dat! Oh, my word, Dat! Are you all right?" she asked, as she retrieved his straw hat from where it had rolled.

Grunting, Dat turned over and sat up, shaking his head in dismay.

"I'll be all right. Just give me a hand."

Setting Laura on the grass, Lizzie hurried over to grasp his hands, alarmed at the amount of strength it took to pull him up. For a terrifying moment she thought she wasn't able to, and they would both fall heavily back down on the gravel.

Standing straight again, Dat gave a low laugh.

"Ach my, this M.S. is about as hard on my will as anything I've ever seen. I don't have a choice. Suddenly, without warning, my brain doesn't tell my legs to do what I want them to, and bang! Down I go!"

He shrugged his shoulders.

"Nope, don't have a choice. God decided to give me multiple sclerosis, and here I am. I gotta deal with it."

He sighed, looking off into the distance.

"I don't know what the future holds, but I know God will help me handle it. Me and Annie."

He said this with so much pride in his beloved wife, and with so much courage and assurance that

God would be there, that Lizzie felt inspired to the core of her being. Surely, if Dat could handle this dreaded disease, this loss of muscle control that would steadily worsen, she could give up enough of her own will about having a family.

Dat's eyes were very blue and kind as he looked at Laura.

"She still looks like she's been in the sun too long. She's the cutest little thing. Bring her in and we'll have a piece of shoofly pie, Lizzie."

Lizzie loved Dat with all her heart. If Dat could look at his grim future with that much confidence, couldn't she? She was, after all, his daughter. Slowly Lizzie was softening her grip on her own determination to have only one baby.

Chapter 23

AND SO, ONE GLAD DAY IN AUGUST, LITTLE Andrew Lee was born at a midwife's home-birthing center in Jefferson County. The midwife and her unmarried sister were Amish. Mam was a bit unenthusiastic about the prospect of having Lizzie go there, but Lizzie maintained her aversion to a hospital, telling Mam there was no use arguing, she simply was not going back to the hospital.

Stephen had his wish, a baby boy named Andy, and his smile was wide and genuine for a long time after Andy entered the world. Lizzie was a bit disappointed, surprised at the sight of her little boy. Laura had been so adorable, with dark skin and a nice amount of hair, but Andy was very white with only a bit of hair on top of his head. She didn't say anything about it, of course, especially not to Stephen, but Andy just wasn't very cute.

It was a great consolation to think of Jason, her brother. He was about the homeliest baby she had

ever seen. Now, as a teenager, he was so handsome with his curly brown hair and crinkling blue eyes.

Mary and Barbara Swarey, the midwives, were the exact opposite of that grouchy nurse at the hospital. They were quiet, encouraging, and often smiling. They held little Andy for no reason at all, except because they wanted to hold him. That was so inspiring to Lizzie, because he wasn't really a cute baby. Mary would come to Lizzie's room, wrap Andy warmly and securely in a fuzzy blue blanket, then sit down in the little wooden, armless rocking chair and rock him, all the while talking to Lizzie about babies and children and life in general.

Oh, it was truly the greatest blessing to be there, and Lizzie valued every hour she spent with the midwives. At night, when Andy would become restless and cry, one of them would appear like some magical person in a light-colored housecoat with a white scarf tied around her head and quietly murmur to the baby. She expertly scooped him up and took him away, cuddling and consoling him as she went. Lizzie drifted off into another few hours of blissful slumber.

Sometimes they brought him to be fed and then stayed to help her. They arranged the pillows, quietly encouraging her, telling her over and over to relax and hold her baby gently, until she had truly mastered this hopelessly difficult art of breast-feeding.

It was the most wonderful, rewarding feeling to know she was quite adept at feeding her baby. He would burp soundly and go right off to sleep, warm and contented, trusting her for all his needs. It was so different from Laura's birth, this feeling of accomplishment. She had a newfound confidence that taking care of this baby was something she would be perfectly able to do.

When one of Mary's girls brought her supper tray, Lizzie opened her eyes wide as a smile of appreciation spread across her face. On the tray were two large yellow ears of corn, perfectly cooked, with a small dish of salad full of sliced tomatoes, carrots, and other fresh vegetables from Mary's garden. Alongside was a thick slice of homemade oatmeal bread and a small dish with a pat of bright yellow butter made from the cream of their own cow. There was also a small glass dish of golden honey from the midwives' own beehives down by their orchard, which Lizzie thought was simply the most extraordinary thing she had ever heard of.

When Lizzie began to eat, she wished there were two slices of bread on her tray and two more ears of corn. Salad wasn't very filling, but then Mary and Barbara ate healthily and weren't overweight. They knew that good nutrition without a lot of unnecessary calories was the best for a nursing mother, especially when she tended to be on the heavy side the way Lizzie was.

After Lizzie had eaten everything, Barbara brought a pretty glass dish piled high with ice-cold

chunks of watermelon. The fruit was delicious. So good, in fact, that Lizzie resolved to turn her own dry, little hilltop garden into a garden just like Mary's. She would plant plots of herbs and teas and have different flowers and vegetables all growing in neat squares, one complimenting the other like pictures of gardens in seed catalogs.

She even wanted a cow to make her own butter. She would ask Stephen to get a few hives of bees, and she would get the recipe to make this light, spongy, oatmeal bread. She had, quite simply, never been as inspired to eat healthy things and grow them in her own backyard as she was now with this supper tray.

That evening Stephen brought Laura to meet baby Andy. She was not quite two years old, and her eyes were very large and scared as Stephen carried her into Lizzie's room. She had gotten carsick on their trip across the mountain. Stephen had cleaned her up as best he could, which tugged at Lizzie's heart. Laura was so brown and smelled bad and was so afraid, seeing her mother in such a strange place. Mam walked behind Stephen, barely able to conceal the urgency she felt to see the new baby boy.

Lizzie reached for Laura, but she turned her face away and clung to Stephen.

"Maidsy!" Lizzie said pleadingly. Laura turned her head a tiny bit so that she could peep out with one eye from her position on Stephen's shoulder.

Mam picked up Andy, whom she had finally found in the little wooden crib, and was delightedly

pulling on the blankets, trying to have a better view of his face.

"Oh, my goodness!" she chuckled, laughing the way she always did when she saw a new baby for the first time.

"Ach, my! Isn't he cute, Lizzie? Why, he's about the prettiest baby I've ever seen!" she exclaimed, clearly enamored of this pale little grandson.

Lizzie's heart was filled with gratitude.

"Do you think he's cute, Mam? Really?"

"Why, of course!"

She said this as if there was absolutely no question that anyone would ever think he was a homely baby. Why, of course he was cute with those adorable big blue eyes and that wispy hair which would grow in thick and blond. Mam laughed and laughed, her stomach shaking the way it always did, as she unwrapped Andy, checking him fully from head to toe, while Stephen held Laura and peered over her shoulder and laughed with her.

Stephen liked Mam. He always had. Lizzie thought it was very nice to have her husband like her mother. Weren't there a whole pile of mother-in-law jokes around? They didn't apply to Mam and Stephen, which always made Lizzie feel secure and happy.

When Laura finally did leave the safety of Stephen's shoulder, she sat a bit stiffly on Lizzie's lap. Mam brought the new baby for her to meet. Lizzie couldn't help but notice the haughty indifference with which she met her new brother, her back held

stiff and straight. She glanced at him with no emotion before burying her head in Lizzie's shoulder and crying her little heart out.

Lizzie quickly bent her head to console her. Stephen reached for her, and Mam laughed some more, telling them that Laura's behavior was perfectly normal for a child. She would likely be a bit difficult for a few weeks until she became accustomed to the idea of sharing her parents with someone else.

After her family left to go back home, Lizzie had a few moments of unsteadiness, knowing those feelings of inadequacy would return unless she was strong. Right now it was very much like keeping a boat afloat on choppy seas, bravely keeping her eyes on the lighthouse. God was there, she supposed, and would keep her from sinking whenever a wave of despair hit. She would not allow herself to sink or to be intimidated by feelings of inadequacy.

Mary and Barbara were a great help. To them, there was almost nothing that rivaled the blessings of motherhood and babies. It was all a gift from God and not something to allow to bury you. They didn't think the way Lizzie did. They had a whole bright attitude about having children, which amazed her.

They actually thought of babies as a very special gift, a blessing straight from heaven. Why wouldn't someone want lots of precious babies? They were so cute and special and sweet, binding a family forever with bonds of love.

So was it any wonder then, that Lizzie felt very much like a queen in her own little world when she

slipped on her navy blue dress, pinned her black apron around her waist, adjusted her white covering, and bade Mary and Barbara good-bye? They had helped her view motherhood in such a different light so that the resistance that had made her first year with Laura quite miserable completely vanished.

She was a mother now, a real mother with two children and a house. She had a husband beside her, and, if things got really scary and crazy, a mother who laughed at babies and said they were a lot tougher than they looked. New babies never frightened Mam, even when they choked or got sick or wouldn't nurse or had diarrhea. There was always something that worked, and if nothing else, you whisked them off to the doctor in town and he'd know what to do.

In the weeks that followed, Lizzie found it so much easier to cope with having this second baby. On one afternoon, however, Laura simply refused to cooperate with anyone, even Mam, throwing fits until Lizzie spanked her. Afterwards, Laura cried brokenheartedly, and Lizzie pitied her so much she started crying herself, telling Mam she was going to take a nap. But in truth, she lay on her bed with little, stubborn, angry Maidsy beside her and cried and cried and cried.

But that was it. Never again did she come close

to feeling so overwhelmed. She found that when she got up in the morning, her first thoughts were with the children and not of herself and how she felt.

She also found that you could survive quite well on five or six hours of sleep. And Laura learned to love Andy more with each passing day, which made Lizzie's life quite a bit easier. Stephen was so kind and attentive. He was a very good father to Laura, even if he felt clumsy and ill at ease with newborn Andy. He could do almost anything with Laura, and she would listen amazingly well.

Stephen built his furniture shop as an addition to the barn. He made different articles of furniture in the evenings. He loved the work, learning as he went along, making hutch cupboards and desks, among other pieces. He would start a fire in the woodstove, then bundle Laura up in her coat, the little navy blue one with a round collar that his sister, Sharon, had made for her. He tied her little white scarf securely around her head, straightened up, and took her small brown hand in his bigger one. Together they would go to the shop while Lizzie cleared away the supper dishes.

Laura would play quite contentedly beneath his worktable for hours. She played with blocks of wood or shavings, along with any tool he would allow her to have. When they returned, smelling of wood shavings and wood smoke, Laura would smile

happily and have her bath willingly, telling Lizzie in her halting language about her evening with Dat.

Andy, however, was a bit of a problem when it was time for his feeding. He would not always nurse well, so Lizzie became a bit flustered about it again. She tried different ways of holding him, but she became increasingly frustrated at his lack of skill. He refused to take a pacifier.

One day when Lizzie was feeling particularly stressed, she heard footsteps on the front porch and then a small knock. The door opened a bit and someone called, "Are you home, Lizzie?"

Edna! Lizzie recognized her voice immediately. Her cousin Edna from Jefferson County!

Instantly she was at the door, warmly greeting her favorite cousin, Edna, who had walked up the hill from the farm where Uncle Elis had gone to pay a visit to Dat and Mam. Edna was also married and had two children, and because she lived in Jefferson County, Lizzie did not get to see her or her family very often. So it was a special treat for Edna to come to see her new little boy.

They settled themselves in the living room, talking as fast as they could until they both laughed, suddenly unsure if they were actually listening to what the other was saying. Edna exclaimed over Andy, then sat back on the sofa as Laura began to nurse him.

She clucked in her usual frustration, then looked at Edna. "Why can't I nurse a baby right?" she asked.

Edna's eyes narrowed as she watched Lizzie's hurried attempts.

"Well, for one thing, sit back. Relax. Put up you feet and sing as loud as you can!"

They both burst out laughing, although Lizzie felt like crying.

"I'm serious, Lizzie. You're way too nervous. No wonder he doesn't nurse. You're holding him as tightly as you possibly can!"

"I'm just not good at this," Lizzie wailed.

"Yes, you are. Learn to relax and then try it."

With Edna's guidance, Lizzie did begin to see what she meant. Frustrated, she was holding her baby much too tightly. He kept squirming and crying, trying to free himself from her hold.

After Edna's visit, the situation vastly improved. By the time Andy was a few months old, Lizzie could finally understand why mothers nursed their babies and didn't use formula. Lizzie guessed she was just not quite a natural mother the way some women were, like Emma and Mandy. Or Mam. Or almost anyone else.

She had to learn by trial and error and lots of self-inflicted hardships. She wasn't naturally inclined to be a calm, serene person when it came to having babies, no matter how Mary and Barbara made her feel. But she was learning. She no longer thought that having a baby was an affliction, something terrible that you tried to avoid as determinedly as possible.

It was just all in one's head. She had to stop

worrying and relax, as Edna had shown her, and each new problem would eventually take care of itself. That thought was extremely comforting.

Chapter 24

THE YEARS PASSED, MUCH AS TIME PASSES FOR
any family. The day came when Lizzie had her for-
tieth birthday, which made her feel very old. In fact,
the thought of being halfway through her years here
on earth was quite alarming. Didn't most people die
between 70 and 90 years of age? She had better do
some very serious thinking, that was all there was to it.

Was she prepared to die anytime soon? Didn't
people say it was all downhill after 40? Her side
often hurt a lot; in fact, quite often and severely,
now that she thought about it. She was at the age
where people got cancer or pneumonia or arthritis
and became quite sick and died.

She didn't know exactly how one went about
preparing to die. Just walk into the living room, sit
down on a chair, look up at the ceiling, and ponder
all your sins, she supposed. But when she did that,
she felt so hopeless, the amount of sins that piled up.

Her worst sins, she felt quite sure, were her lack

of patience, her love of beautiful things, and want-
ing everything perfect all the time. She yelled at the
children, six in total now. She also talked about
people behind their backs. Honestly, Lizzie thought,
she was hopeless, she really was.

She had often decided to stop saying anything
negative about a person, ever, but it had only lasted
for a day, maybe less, before she started gossiping
again. The same thing happened when it came to
yelling at her children, although, she reasoned, that
was getting better as she became older, so she didn't
really know how serious that was in God's eyes.

So, as hopeless as it all seemed, this trying to be
good enough to get to heaven on your own, fortu-
nately there was grace. She did believe Jesus died on
the cross, shedding his blood for everybody. That
was the only hope of salvation, the only boost to
Lizzie's confidence when she thought about dying.
It was tremendously reassuring.

So turning 40 years old increased her faith in
Jesus' power of salvation. She grasped more fully
the futility of trying to be perfect so God would like
you, as she had so often tried in her younger years.
She guessed God knew her nature. After all, hadn't
he given it to her? He would mold her and shape her
the way he saw that was best.

That was comforting but often hard to grasp,
although Mam insisted that was how it was. Mam
knew a lot about the Bible because, for as long as
Lizzie could remember, she read it every morning.
Lizzie could never get into the habit of reading her

Bible every day. Sometimes reading your Bible was boring, and you just read it to ease your conscience because you knew it was a good thing. Sometimes when you sat down to read it, instantly pressing thoughts or worries crowded in, and you were reading but not even comprehending one tiny little thing. Lizzie supposed that was the devil trying to keep you from doing something that was right and good.

That spring, on the third day of April when Andy was not quite 16 years old, Christopher James was born. He was a big boy, weighing almost 10 pounds, with large wide-set eyes like Stephen's.

Lizzie was still, at the age of 40, as happy and appreciative of Mary Swarey, the midwife, as she ever had been. Mary's sister, Barbara, the other midwife, had married a widower from another community and went to live with him and his family. Mary's daughters had come to help her, which was much the same as having Barbara there.

Stephen wanted to name his little son Neil. Lizzie thought she had never heard of such a dull name as Neil, but she didn't make too many arguments against it, not wanting to hurt his feelings. Stephen was so proud of his new son. As it was, they soon agreed on Christopher as his name, but then, when they returned home, Laura was a bit miffed because she wanted that name for her own son someday. She was 17 years old now, and, of course, was thinking

about these things, although Lizzie thought that was a bit dense. What if she chose not to get marry until she was 24 or more?

And so Christopher, a strapping little boy, joined the family. Andy was thrilled to have a brother, although it hardly seemed as if he was a real honest-to-goodness brother with the age difference. When Andy held Christopher he seemed a bit unsure of himself, uncomfortable even, and was glad to hand him over to one of his eager sisters who were much happier holding a baby.

"Babies just aren't my thing," he admitted rue-fully and went on his way.

Lizzie felt as if seven children was the right amount. Her quiver was full, as the Bible said. Ste-phen was more than thrilled to have another son, a small boy to tag around with him when he was actually old enough to have a grandson.

And wasn't life like that? Lizzie mused. As you aged, you naturally became mellower, more patient, not as quick to lose your temper when things went wrong. If you thought about it, the youngest person in the family profited by having parents who were more willing to accept the ways of a child. Before, when she was younger, she hadn't quite realized that a young child is exactly that, a little person who is not perfect. She had expected perfection from her older children, even when it seemed to be a losing proposition.

So she had teenagers, school-aged children, and a baby. Her daughter, Emily, was six years old and would be attending school in the fall, and here was

Lizzie, 40 years old with an infant to care for and no little ones to run for a diaper or a pacifier.

Laura was a schoolteacher now at the new school the community had built on Stephen's parents' land along the winding country road that passed in front of the big house. Stephen had been dead set against Laura teaching school, saying she would never make a teacher with her lack of self-confidence. He reminded Lizzie about the fact that Laura couldn't say a poem at the Christmas program in school without crying. How in the world did Lizzie expect her to teach school?

Lizzie insisted that Laura was quite capable. Didn't she have the same Mennonite teacher for all eight years of school? She was taught well, consistently having been given work that challenged her. Of course, she could teach school.

And Laura did. She taught school for eight years after that and enjoyed her time in school immensely. Andy went to work on Stephen's construction crew. Lizzie and Stephen's daughter, Becky, taught school for two years, then worked for a landscaper after that. Trials and troubles, laughter and tears came and went in the big house. Life was much the same for Stephen, Lizzie, and the children as it was for everyone else.

The wooden rockers on the front porch were filled with friends, neighbors, Lizzie and the girls, and sometimes Otis, the big black Labrador Retriever. Crocks and other planters filled with impatiens and geraniums lined the porch, the sun rose and set,

each day bringing new challenges and inspiration.

As Lizzie grew older, she often sat on the porch to unwind. Every morning in good weather she drank her coffee on the rocker that faced west, thinking about things and musing about life in general. That porch corner was her mainstay, her sanctuary before starting the day.

Sometimes Stephen joined her, which reminded Lizzie that they were getting older. Hopefully, they would be able to live the remainder of their years growing old together, sitting on these very same porch rockers, finding greater portions of peace as they aged. Wasn't that what life was all about, learning to love more fully, becoming a person who quite naturally became more loving and closer to God?

Things like open stairways and neck reins on horses' harnesses and porch railings and everything Lizzie had cared so intensely about no longer held quite the significance they had in the moment. That was just how life was.

She was even making peace with her weight, that ever-present source of consternation and serious frustration. How could a person weigh so much and feel so skinny and hungry? It was one of the biggest mysteries of life. It wasn't that she sat down and ate a whole package of Oreo cookies or anything like that. She tried to eat healthfully and responsibly. But she couldn't really help it if she wasn't quite full after having eaten a sandwich and ended up making part of another one and eating that, too.

Food was such a comfort, such a cozy thing to

have when worries assailed you. All you had to do was make a toasted cheese sandwich with plenty of butter, the Velveeta cheese dripping off your fingers as you ate it, and the world instantly became a better place. But if you weighed a lot, then eventually you'd just have to accept that you were fat. Lizzie was not an accomplished dieter. She could cut way back on her food intake, lose five pounds with the best of them, eat a piece of cake, and regain the entire five pounds in no time flat.

She faced a losing proposition from the start, that's all there was to it. Mam and Dat Glick had both been heavy in their early years, and large uncles and aunts abounded everywhere on Lizzie's family tree. Right there you had it, and she didn't care what anyone said. If your ancestors had a weight problem, nine times out of 10, so would you. That was the way it was. So to try and be thin when you knew it meant that you'd never enjoy the foods you loved was far too depressing, and anyway, what did it matter?

Stephen loved her the way she was, which was a huge blessing right there. She would absolutely hate to be married to someone who watched every bite she put in her mouth, raising his eyebrows and sniffing, the way men do when they don't approve of someone.

Stephen never made her feel unattractive, although she knew full well she often was. Especially when she wore a *dichly*, that small triangular piece of handkerchief, to do work around the outside. When Lizzie wore that, her whole ears were exposed, and not just part of them as they were when she wore a covering.

Ears continued to grow as long as you live. So did your nose. But especially ears, and Lizzie's were not small. In fact, her earlobes were rather long and fat, which that made her feel very homely. But that was all right. Stephen didn't think she was homely, but Lizzie knew her girls thought so, the way they tried to help her pin her *dichly* on just so, sniffing a bit and trying not to laugh.

That was the thing about having teenage girls. They certainly kept Lizzie humble, or tried to. But she didn't go down easily. She was like a balloon that is squeezed, but just keeps popping up some other place because it still has air!

Lizzie supposed that's just how it was for everyone with daughters. They just kept on correcting you all the time. Even the way you pronounced words. She had always been proud of the fact that she could pronounce words correctly. She had been very good at vocabulary in school, read books all her life, and, actually, always thought of herself as fairly intelligent. Until Laura grew up. Then it was one correction after another, and Lizzie lived for the day when she could correct Laura about how she pronounced a word. It was all in good humor, and they didn't actually fight about it. They just let each other know when the other said a word and it didn't sound quite right.

And so, Lizzie had large ears, was overweight, and seldom pronounced all her words correctly, according to Laura, who really didn't know everything. Lizzie sincerely hoped she would always remember to laugh at herself, because life is so much easier if

you didn't get too dead serious about trivial things.

That's what caused big bad feelings, she decided, and so she hoped to enjoy the rest of her journey of life with a good sense of humor about most things and a smile on her face. Anything else was of the devil, Mam would say. And, whether Lizzie admitted it or not, even at age 40, she knew that what Mam said still counted.

Dat was nearly a complete victim of multiple sclerosis now, spending his days in a hospital bed by the low window where they wheeled him each morning. He was able to watch the birds at the bird feeder, the traffic on the road, or whatever caught his attention. His patience was a constant reminder of the resilience of the human spirit and gave Lizzie courage to face the future. You just did what you had to do, she had learned. Some people said that was God-given strength once life got really serious, and she supposed they were right.

Dat was amazing, the way he spent his days in bed, often miserable but seldom complaining, waiting for the hour when angels would come to take him home.

And so, with the love of family, especially from Stephen and her children, Lizzie would enjoy the remainder of her life with a smile on her face, large ears and all.

The End

The Recipes

Lizzie's Favorite Recipes

Whoopie Pies

Makes about 4 dozen whoopie pies

2 cups sugar
1 cup oil
2 eggs
4½ cups flour
1 cup dry cocoa powder
½ tsp. salt
1 cup sour milk
2 tsp. vanilla
1 cup hot water
2 tsp. baking soda

FILLING:
4 cups confectioners sugar, *divided*
2 egg whites, beaten
1 tsp. vanilla
1½ cups vegetable shortening

1. To make pies, cream sugar, oil and eggs together thoroughly in a large mixing bowl.

2. In a separate bowl, sift together flour, cocoa powder, and salt.

3. Add these dry ingredients to creamed mixture alternately with sour milk.

4. Stir in vanilla.

5. In a small bowl, dissolve baking soda in hot water.

6. Stir into batter until smooth.

7. Drop batter by rounded teaspoons onto cookie sheets.

8. Bake 8-10 minutes at 400°.

9. Remove from oven and allow to cool.

10. While pie tops/bottoms are cooling, make Filling.

11. In a medium bowl fold 2 cups confectioners sugar into beaten egg whites.

12. Stir in 1 tsp. vanilla.

13. Beat in shortening until smooth.

14. Beat in remaining 2 cups confectioners sugar until smooth.

15. Assemble pies by spreading a dab of filling over a cooled bottom and topping it with a second cookie.

928

Creamsticks

Makes about 2½ dozen doughnuts

PASTRY:
 1 cup milk
 1 cup warm water
 2 pkgs. yeast
 ½ cup vegetable shortening
 ⅔ cup sugar
 2 eggs, beaten
 1 tsp. salt
 6 cups flour
 vegetable oil for deep-frying

FILLING:
 3 tsp. flour
 1 cup milk
 1 cup vegetable shortening
 1 cup sugar
 1 Tbsp. vanilla
 2½ cups confectioners sugar

TOPPING:
 1 cup brown sugar
 half a stick (4 Tbsp.) butter
 ⅓ cup milk
 ½ cup vegetable shortening
 2 cups confectioners sugar

1. To make pastry, begin by scalding 1 cup milk. Allow to cool to room temperature.

2. In a separate bowl, dissolve two packages yeast in one cup warm water.

3. In a large mixing bowl, cream ½ cup shortening with ⅔ cup sugar, 2 beaten eggs, and 1 tsp. salt.

4. Combine cooled milk and dissolved yeast with creamed mixture.

5. Add flour 2-3 cups at a time (for a total of about 6 cups), and mix until you get a soft dough.

6. Cover and let rise in a warm place until double in size.

7. Roll out on a floured surface.

8. Cut dough into rectangular strips, approximately 4 inches by 1 inch. Place on baking sheets about 1 inch apart.

9. Cover and allow to rise again in a warm place until almost double in size.

10. Deep fry in vegetable oil.

11. Cool and cut slits in top.

12. While pastry is cooling, make filling.

13. Make a paste by combining 3 tsp. flour and 1 cup milk in a medium saucepan over medium heat.

recipe continues on next page

14. Stir continuously until mixture boils and becomes smooth.

15. Remove from heat and allow to cool completely.

16. Combine 1 cup shortening, 1 cup sugar, and 1 Tbsp. vanilla in a large mixing bowl.

17. When smooth, mix with flour and milk mixture until well blended.

18. Stir in 2½ cups confectioners sugar.

19. Force filling into creamsticks with a cake decorator or cookie press.

20. Make topping by combining 1 cup brown sugar, 4 Tbsp. butter, and ⅓ cup milk in a medium saucepan.

21. Bring mixture to a boil, stirring frequently to prevent sticking.

22. Cool.

23. Blend in ½ cup shortening and 2 cups confectioners sugar.

24. Spread topping over filled creamsticks.

Molasses Cookies

Makes 7-8 dozen cookies

3 sticks (1½ cups) butter, softened
2½ cups brown sugar
3 eggs
1 cup Bre'r Rabbit molasses
7 cups flour
2 tsp. cinnamon
2 tsp. ginger
1 Tbsp. baking soda
granulated sugar

1. In a large bowl cream butter and brown sugar together.

2. Add eggs and molasses.

3. Stir in flour, cinnamon, ginger, and baking soda to form a firm dough.

4. Pinch off about 1 rounded tsp. dough and roll into a ball.

5. Roll each ball in granulated sugar.

6. Place on cookie sheet and flatten a little to make a cookie shape.

7. Continue until all batter is used.

8. Bake 10 to 12 minutes at 350°.

Apple Pie with Crumb Topping

Makes 1 pie

FILLING:

1½ cups water
1 cup brown sugar
2 Tbsp. cornstarch
1 tsp. cinnamon
1 Tbsp. butter
2 to 3 cups grated apples

9" unbaked pie shell

CRUMB TOPPING:

1 cup brown sugar
1 cup dry old-fashioned, or quick, oatmeal
½ cup flour
3 Tbsp. butter, softened

1. Combine water, 1 cup brown sugar, cornstarch, and cinnamon in a large saucepan.

2. Heat over low heat to dissolve sugar and cornstarch. Stir frequently to prevent sticking.

3. Add 1 Tbsp. butter and grated apples.

4. Remove from heat.

5. Spoon filling mixture into pie shell.

6. Combine brown sugar, dry oatmeal, and flour in a good-sized bowl.

7. Cut butter into dry ingredients to create crumbs, none larger than pea-sized.

8. Sprinkle crumb topping uniformly over apple filling.

9. Bake at 350° for 45 to 60 minutes, or until well browned.

Sand Tarts

Makes 12 dozen cookies

DOUGH:
2 cups granulated sugar
2 sticks (½ lb.) butter, softened
1 tsp. baking soda
3 eggs, beaten
2 tsp. milk
3½ cups flour

DECORATIVE GLAZE:
1 egg, beaten
½ cup milk
colored sugar

1. Mix all dough ingredients together in a large bowl until smooth.

2. Chill dough overnight.

3. Roll thin on floured surface.

4. Cut into shapes with cookie cutters.

5. Mix egg and milk together to make Glaze. Brush tops of cookies with glaze mixture.

6. Sprinkle with colored sugar.

7. Bake at 375° for 8 to 10 minutes.

Banana Pudding

Makes 15-20 servings

3 3½-oz. pkgs. instant vanilla pudding
5 cups milk
8 oz. sour cream
1 large container frozen whipped topping,
 thawed
2 8-oz. boxes vanilla wafers
12 to 15 ripe bananas, sliced

1. Make pudding according to box instructions

2. Assemble in large serving dish in layers, starting with vanilla wafers, sliced bananas, and pudding. Continue to alternate layers, making as many layers as you wish.

3. Cover. Refrigerate until ready to serve.

Christmas Salad

Makes 15-20 servings

⅔ cup dry lime gelatin
3½ cups cold water
20-oz. can crushed pineapple, drained, with
 juice reserved
2 Tbsp. dry clear gelatin
⅔ cup cold water
8-oz. pkg. cream cheese, softened
1 cup heavy cream, whipped until stiff and
 sweetened to taste
3½ cups cold water
⅔ cup dry strawberry gelatin

1. Mix lime gelatin, 3½ cups water, and crushed pineapple, drained (juice reserved), in bowl.

2. Pour into 9 x 13 baking pan.

3. Chill until firm.

4. Heat pineapple juice to boiling point.

5. Dissolve clear gelatin in ⅔ cup cold water. Stir in pineapple juice. Cool.

6. Stir softened cream cheese into clear gelatin until smooth.

7. Fold in whipped cream.

8. Spoon on top of lime-pineapple layer.

9. Mix strawberry gelatin and 3½ cups cold water together. Chill until firm.

10. Spoon over top of creamy layer.

11. Refrigerate until completely firm.

12. Cut into squares and serve.

Christmas Nut Cake

Makes 12-15 servings

CAKE:
2 cups granulated sugar
1½ sticks (12 Tbsp.) butter, softened
4 eggs, separated
1 cup milk
3 cups flour
4 tsp. baking powder
¾ cup walnuts, chopped
vegetable oil

CARAMEL FROSTING:
1½ cups brown sugar, packed
1½ sticks (12 Tbsp.) butter
⅓ cup milk
1 tsp. vanilla
confectioners sugar
¼ cup walnuts, crushed

1. To make Cake, thoroughly cream sugar and butter.

2. Separate egg yolks and whites.

3. Add 4 egg yolks to sugar and butter and beat well.

4. Add milk, flour, and baking powder. Beat well.

5. Beat egg whites in a bowl.

6. Fold egg whites into batter.

7. Mix in chopped nuts.

8. Divide batter by pouring into 3 round cake pans that are oiled and dusted with flour.

9. Bake at 350° until toothpick inserted in center of each pan comes out clean, about 30 to 35 minutes.

10. Meanwhile, prepare Frosting by cooking brown sugar and butter over medium heat.

11. Boil for one minute.

12. Add milk.

13. Continue cooking until it boils again, then remove from heat.

14. Let cool completely.

15. Add vanilla.

16. Add confectioners sugar to thicken frosting to desired consistency, about 3-4 cups.

17. Frost cooled Cake.

18. Dust with crushed walnuts.

Grandpa Cookies

Makes 10 dozen cookies

2 sticks (½ lb.) butter, softened
3 cups brown sugar
1 cup sour cream
5 eggs, beaten
4¾ cups flour
1 Tbsp. baking soda

1. Cream butter and brown sugar together well.

2. Add remaining ingredients, finishing with baking soda. Mix well.

3. Drop by big teaspoonfuls onto cookie sheets. Big round cookies are best.

4. Bake at 375° for about 12 minutes.

5. Frost with caramel frosting or plain vanilla icing.

Chocolate-Covered Ritz Crackers

Makes 20 servings

1 box Ritz crackers
1 medium jar creamy peanut butter
1 lb. milk chocolate wafers

1. Make cracker sandwiches with peanut butter spread between two crackers.

2. Melt chocolate.

3. Dip cracker sandwiches into melted chocolate to coat completely.

4. Lay dipped crackers on waxed paper. Allow to cool completely.

TIP

Successfully melting chocolate means never allowing it to get too hot. Melt in a double boiler over boiling water, stirring repeatedly. If the temperature is too high, the chocolate will turn into hard clumps.

Date Pudding

Makes 20 servings

PUDDING:
 1 cup chopped dates
 1 tsp. baking soda
 1 Tbsp. butter
 1 cup boiling water
 2 eggs, beaten
 1 cup flour
 1 cup sugar
 1 tsp. vanilla
 ¾ cup chopped nuts

SAUCE:
 2 cups water
 1 stick (¼ lb.) butter
 1 cup brown sugar
 ½ cup flour
 2-3 Tbsp. water

 whipped topping

1. In a large mixing bowl, pour boiling water over dates, soda, and butter. Mix together well.

2. Let cool.

3. Add eggs, flour, sugar, vanilla, and chopped nuts.

4. Place in greased baking pan.

5. Bake at 325° for 30 to 35 minutes. When a toothpick inserted in center of Pudding comes out clean, the Pudding is done. Allow to cool.

6. Cut Pudding into 1" squares.

SAUCE:

1. Combine water, butter, and brown sugar in saucepan. Bring to boil.

2. In a small bowl, blend ½ cup flour with 2-3 Tbsp. water until smooth.

3. Stir into hot syrup mixture and bring to a boil again. Stir frequently to keep it smooth and to prevent sticking.

4. Cool completely.

5. Layer ⅓ of the squares of cut-up Pudding into a trifle bowl. Top with ⅓ of the Sauce. Top that with big spoonfuls of whipped topping.

6. Repeat those layers twice, ending with whipped topping. Chill and serve.

Chocolate Cake

Makes 15 servings

CAKE:
2 cups sugar
¾ cup vegetable oil
3 large eggs
2 cups flour, sifted
¾ cup cocoa powder
2 tsp. baking soda
2 tsp. baking powder
1 cup sour milk
1 cup hot coffee

1. In a large bowl, beat sugar, oil and eggs together until well mixed.

2. In a separate bowl mix together dry ingredients.

3. Alternately add sour milk and dry ingredients to creamed mixture.

4. Last, add 1 cup coffee. Beat all together until thoroughly mixed.

5. Pour into a greased 9 x 13 baking pan.

6. Bake 45 minutes at 350°, or until tester inserted in center comes out clean.

CARAMEL FROSTING:
 1½ cups brown sugar
 1½ sticks (1¼ cups) butter
 2-3 cups confectioners sugar
 1 tsp. vanilla
 ⅓ cup milk

1. Cook over low heat until bubbly, stirring continually. Then boil 1 minute, stirring constantly.

2. Add ⅓ cup milk carefully, and bring to boil again.

3. Immediately remove from heat.

4. Cool to room temperature.

5. Stir in vanilla and confectioners sugar until frosting is of spreading consistency.

Cinnamon Rolls

Makes about 2 dozen rolls

ROLLS:
½ cup milk
½ cup sugar
1½ tsp. salt
¼ cup shortening
½ cup lukewarm water
2 tsp. sugar
2 Tbsp. dry yeast
2 beaten eggs
4 cups flour
half a stick (4 Tbsp.) melted butter
1 cup brown sugar
2 Tbsp. cinnamon
⅔ cup raisins, *optional*

FROSTING:
1 cup confectioners sugar
¼ tsp. vanilla
enough milk to make a spreading or
 drizzling consistency

1. Scald milk in 1- or 2-qt. saucepan.

2. Add ½ cup sugar, salt, and shortening to scalded milk. Pour into large mixing bowl.

3. Cool to lukewarm.

4. In a separate small bowl, sprinkle yeast over ½ cup lukewarm water in which 2 tsp. sugar has been added. Let stand 10-15 minutes.

5. Stir and add to milk mixture.

6. Add the beaten eggs.

7. Work in about 4 cups flour by stirring, and then kneading until dough can be easily handled.

8. Cover and let rise in a warm place until double in bulk.

9. Divide the dough and roll each half into a 9 x 12 rectangle.

10. Brush each rectangle with melted butter.

11. Sprinkle each half with half the brown sugar, cinnamon, and raisins if you wish.

12. Roll up each rectangle like a jelly roll.

13. Cut in 1"-thick slices. Lay slices about 1 inch apart in greased baking pans.

14. Cover and let rise until double in bulk.

15. Bake at 350° for 35 minutes.

16. Frost while warm.

Chocolate Pie

Makes 16-18 servings

8 oz. pkg. cream cheese, softened
1¼ cups sugar
2 tsp. vanilla
½ cup cocoa powder
¾ cup milk
16 oz. container frozen whipped topping,
 thawed
2 large, or 3 small, pre-made graham cracker
 pie shells

1. Beat together cream cheese, sugar, and vanilla.

2. Add cocoa powder alternately with milk.

3. Fold in whipped topping.

4. Spoon into two large or three small pie shells.

5. Cover. Refrigerate for at least 3 hours before serving.

Broccoli Cauliflower Soup

Makes 6-8 servings

4 cups chicken broth
2 tsp. chicken bouillon granules
1 large bunch broccoli, diced
2 cups cauliflower florets, diced
2 cups milk, *divided*
1 tsp. salt
2 cups cooked chicken, cut up
6 Tbsp. cornstarch
6 slices white American cheese, or other
 cheese that you prefer

1. In 4-quart saucepan cook broccoli and cauliflower in chicken broth and bouillon until soft.

2. Add 1½ cups milk and salt.

3. In a small bowl, stir cornstarch into ½ cup milk. When smooth, stir into saucepan.

4. Cover and heat over low heat, stirring frequently.

5. When soup is hot through and thickened, stir in cheese until blended into mixture.

Potato Chowder

Makes 8 servings

2 Tbsp. butter
¼ cup onion, diced
½ cup celery, diced
3 cups potatoes, diced
1 carrot, shredded
6 cups milk
10¾-oz. can cream of celery soup
14-oz. can chicken broth
6 slices white American cheese
salt and pepper to taste

1. In a large saucepan, sauté onion and celery in butter.

2. Add enough water, a cup or more, to cook potatoes and carrots until soft.

3. Add milk, cream of celery soup, and chicken broth. Cook over low heat until very hot.

4. Add cheese, stirring until melted.

5. Salt and pepper to taste.

Chicken Stew

Makes 6-8 servings

3 cups cooked chicken, deboned and
 cut in chunks
1 qt. chicken broth
2 tsp. granular chicken bouillon
2 cups potatoes, cubed
2 cups peas
2 Tbsp. onion, chopped
2 cups sliced carrots
1 Tbsp. parsley
1 tsp. salt
pepper to taste
flour
water
1 box buttermilk baking mix

1. Put first 10 ingredients into an 8-qt. kettle.

2. Cover and bring to a boil.

3. Reduce heat. Simmer until vegetables are soft.

4. Thicken or thin with water and/or flour as desired.

5. Make dumplings according to buttermilk baking mix box.

6. Drop dumplings on top of cooked stew.

7. Simmer until dumplings are cooked through.

Dressing (Mam's Ohio Filling)

Makes 15 servings

2 loaves bread, cut in cubes
1 stick (¼ lb.) butter, melted
6 eggs, beaten
5-6 cups milk
1 cup chicken broth
2 cups chicken, cut up
1 cup celery, cut up fine and cooked until
 tender
½ to 1 cup carrots, cut up fine or grated,
 and cooked until tender
1 Tbsp. chicken bouillon
½ tsp. pepper
1 tsp. seasoned salt
2 Tbsp. parsley

1. In a very large bowl, toss bread cubes with melted butter.

2. Spread bread cubes on 2 baking sheets.

3. Turn oven to 350°. Toast bread for about 20 minutes, or just until nicely browned.

4. Combine eggs, milk and broth in large bowl.

5. Gently stir in rest of ingredients.

6. Bake in a large roaster or baking pans at 350°, uncovered, for 1½ to 2 hours, stirring occasionally, until hot and crusty on top.

Chicken Filling, or Lancaster County "Roasht"

Makes 15 servings

1 stick (¼ lb.) butter
2 cups celery, chopped
2 loaves bread, cut in cubes
3 cups chicken, cooked and shredded
1 tsp. salt
1 tsp. pepper, or less, to taste
6 eggs, beaten

1. Melt butter in large skillet.

2. Sauté celery in melted butter.

3. Combine all ingredients in a large greased baking dish.

4. Bake, uncovered, at 350° for 1 to 2 hours.

5. Stir occasionally until nice and brown.

Barbecued Meatballs

Makes 10-12 servings

MEATBALLS:
3 lbs. ground beef
12-oz. can evaporated milk
2 cups dry oatmeal, old-fashioned or quick
2 eggs
1 cup chopped onion
½ tsp. garlic powder
½ tsp. pepper
2 tsp. salt

1. Mix together well.

2. Form into 1" balls.

3. Place in lightly greased baking dish.

4. Cover Meatballs with Sauce. Bake uncovered for one hour at 350°.

SAUCE:
3 cups ketchup
1¼ cups brown sugar
½ tsp. garlic powder
½ cup chopped onion
1 Tbsp. liquid smoke

Mix together in a bowl.

Spaghetti Sauce

Makes about 44-46 cups

½ bushel fresh tomatoes
3 garlic cloves, diced
3 lbs. onion, chopped
4 green bell peppers, chopped
1 pint vegetable oil
4 12-oz. cans tomato paste
1 Tbsp. dried oregano
1½ cups sugar
1 Tbsp. sweet basil, dried
⅓ cup salt

1. Cut stem ends out of tomatoes.

2. Cut tomatoes in half.

3. Cook tomatoes and garlic in large stockpot over medium heat, covered. Stir frequently to prevent sticking.

4. When tomatoes are very tender, put through tomato press.

5. Cook chopped onions and peppers over low heat for ½ hour. Stir frequently to prevent burning.

6. Combine all ingredients in stockpot over low heat. Bring to a boil, stirring frequently.

7. Put in jars and seal, following instructions for using your canner.

Farmer's Market Tomato Casserole

Makes 3-4 servings

2 cups stewed tomatoes
½ tsp. salt
¼ tsp. pepper
a bit of onion powder, garlic, and
 oregano to taste
1 Tbsp. sugar
1 cup croutons
4 oz. sharp cheddar cheese, grated
Parmesan cheese

1. Mix all ingredients except Parmesan cheese in a greased baking dish.

2. Sprinkle with Parmesan cheese.

3. Bake uncovered at 350° for 30-45 minutes, or until heated through.

Baked
Macaroni and Cheese

Makes 4-6 servings

2 cups cooked macaroni
half a stick (4 Tbsp.) butter
3 Tbsp. flour
2 cups milk
2 cups cheddar cheese, shredded
½ cup white American cheese, shredded
½ tsp. salt
dash of pepper
3 Tbsp. butter
¾ cup bread crumbs

1. In a large saucepan melt half a stick butter.

2. Over low heat, stir in flour until sauce is smooth.

3. Gradually add milk. Continuing over low heat, cook and stir constantly for 2 to 3 minutes, or until sauce bubbles and thickens.

4. Stir in cheese. Continue heating until cheese melts and sauce is smooth.

5. Stir in salt and pepper.

6. Place cooked macaroni in a greased 9 × 13 baking dish.

7. Pour cheese sauce over macaroni.

8. In a small saucepan, melt 3 Tbsp. butter. Stir in bread crumbs.

9. Cover macaroni and cheese with buttered bread crumbs.

10. Bake uncovered 1 hour at 350°.

Homemade Baked Beans

Makes 20-25 servings

1 gallon Great Northern beans, drained
1 lb. bacon, cooked until crisp and drained
1 medium onion, diced
1 Tbsp. salt
¾ cup brown sugar
½ cup molasses
1 cup ketchup
1 pt. tomato juice
2 tsp. cinnamon

1. Pour beans into a six-quart roast pan.

2. Crumble cooked bacon over beans.

3. Add remaining ingredients and stir together.

4. Bake covered 2-3 hours at 350°. Stir at the end of each hour. Beans are done when they're heated through and are the consistency that you want.

Red Beet Eggs

Makes 24 servings

1 dozen hard-boiled eggs
1 qt. pickled red beets with juice

1. Cool eggs and peel.

2. Place in a good-sized jar or bowl.

3. Pour pickled red beets, including juice, over eggs.

4. Stir so each egg is surrounded completely by juice. Make sure eggs are fully submerged in juice.

5. Cover. Chill in refrigerator overnight.

6. Cut each egg in half lengthwise and serve.

Bread and Butter Pickles

Makes 4-5 pint jars

1 gallon thinly sliced cucumbers
2 large onions, thinly sliced
½ cup salt

1. Mix together well in large pot or crock.

2. Cover with ice water.

3. Cover with a heavy plate for three hours.

4. Drain thoroughly and pack in pint jars.

5. Mix in large bowl:
 4 cups vinegar
 4 cups sugar
 4 tsp. mustard seed
 1 tsp. celery seed
 1 tsp. turmeric

6. Fill jars with this mixture.

7. Process in boiling water bath, following instructions for using your canner.

White Bread

Makes 2 large or 3 medium loaves

½ cup lukewarm water
1 package yeast
1 tsp. sugar
2 cups lukewarm water
1¼ tsp. salt
⅓ cup sugar
1¾ Tbsp. shortening
7-8 cups flour

1. Dissolve the yeast and 1 tsp. sugar in the ½ cup lukewarm water.

2. Mix the 2 cups water, salt, ⅓ cup sugar, and shortening in a very large mixing bowl.

3. Add the yeast mixture and, gradually, the flour.

4. Knead until smooth and elastic.

5. Place in greased bowl, cover, and set in a warm place to rise until double.

6. Punch down. Let rise again.

7. Put in two large loaf pans or three medium ones. Let rise until double again.

8. Bake at 350° for ½ hour.

The Glossary

Ach, voss machts aus? — A Pennsylvania Dutch dialect phrase which means, What does it matter?

Bobbies — A common hairstyle for little Amish girls. Bobbies are two small, tightly rolled knobs of hair, designed to keep their uncut hair off their faces.

Broadfall Pants — Pants worn by Amish men and fastened with buttons, rather than a zipper.

Cape — An extra piece of cloth which Amish women wear over the bodices of their dresses in order to be more modest.

Combine — A hutch or piece of furniture where dishes are stored.

Covering — A fine mesh headpiece worn by Amish females in an effort to follow the Amish interpretation of a New Testament teaching in I Corinthians 11.

Dat — A Pennsylvania Dutch dialect word used to address or to refer to one's father.

Der Saya—To wish someone God's blessing.

Dichly—A Pennsylvania Dutch dialect word meaning head scarf or bandanna.

Dochveggley—A Pennsylvania Dutch dialect word meaning buggy.

Doddy—A Pennsylvania Dutch dialect word used to address or to refer to one's grandfather.

Driver—When the Amish need to go somewhere, and it's too distant to travel by horse and buggy, they may hire someone to drive them in a car or van.

Eck—One corner of the room reserved for the wedding party during the wedding reception.

English—The Amish term for anyone who is not Amish.

Fadutsed—A Pennsylvania Dutch dialect word meaning plain.

Gehorsam—A Pennsylvania Dutch dialect word for obedient.

Gros-feelich—A Pennsylvania Dutch dialect word meaning vain or conceited.

Hold Conference—A time during the wedding ceremony when the bride and groom meet with the ministers (away from the congregation). Traditionally the ministers offer the couple words of encouragement and advice.

In-between Sundays—Old Order Amish have church every other Sunday. This is an old custom that allows ministers to visit other church districts. An in-between Sunday is the day that a district does not hold church services.

Kaevly—A Pennsylvania Dutch dialect word for a little straw basket with a lid on it. Lizzie fills her kaevly with Laura's toys.

Lebbley—A Pennsylvania Dutch dialect word referring to a small piece of cloth, attached to the center back of the waist of a dress.

Mam—A Pennsylvania Dutch dialect word used to address or to refer to one's mother.

Maud—A Pennsylvania Dutch dialect word meaning a live-in female helper, usually hired by a family for a week or two at a time. *Mauds* often help to do house-, lawn-, and garden-work after the birth of a baby.

Mennonite—Another Anabaptist group which shares common beliefs with the Amish. The differences between the two groups lie in their practices. Mennonites tend to be more open to higher education and to mission activity and less distinctly different from the rest of the world in their dress, transportation, and use of technology.

Mommy—A Pennsylvania Dutch dialect word used to address or to refer to one's grandmother.

Mutsa—an Amish man's suit coat.

Nava-sitza—A Pennsylvania Dutch dialect word that refers to a bridal party.

Nehva-sitsa—a wedding attendant.

Ordnung—The Amish community's agreed-upon rules for living, based upon their understanding of the Bible, particularly the New Testament. The *Ordnung* varies some from community to community, often reflecting the leaders' preferences and the local traditions and historical practices.

Patties down—Putting one's hands on one's lap before praying, as a sign of respect. Usually includes bowing one's head and closing one's eyes. A phrase spoken to children who are learning the practice.

Risht dag—The day of preparation for an Amish wedding. Since Amish weddings typically take place at home, this is the day when the family prepares much of the food for the wedding and sets up the benches and tables used during the ceremony and the meal that follows.

Risht leid—the four Amish couples who prepare the Roasht for an Amish wedding.

Roasht—Chicken filling. Mam prepares both a Lancaster County and an Ohio roasht.

Running around—The time in an Amish young person's life between the age of 16 and marriage. Includes structured social activities for groups, as well as dating. Usually takes place on the weekend.

Shtrale—A Pennsylvania Dutch dialect word for a fine-toothed black comb.

Siss ken fa-shtant!—A Pennsylvania Dutch expression which means, It makes no sense.

Snitz Pie—Made from dried apple slices, Snitz Pie is often served at the lunch which follows the Amish Sunday church service.

Vocational school—Attended by 14-year-old Amish children who have completed eight grades of school. These students go to school three hours a week and keep a journal — which their teacher reviews—about their time at home learning farming and homemaking skills from their parents.

Whoopie Pies—Two round, soft cookies filled with a sweet, creamy icing. Whoopie pies were originally chocolate, but pumpkin and oatmeal varieties are also common.

Young Married Ones—The couples who are recently engaged. They receive special treatment during their engagement, especially at weddings. In some areas, after these couples are married, they visit members of the community together, sharing meals and receiving gifts.

The Author

Linda Byler was raised in an Amish family and is an active member of the Amish church today.

Growing up, Linda loved to read and write. In fact, she still does. In addition to the *Lizzie Searches for Love* series, contained in this *Trilogy*, Linda is also the author of the *Sadie's Montana* series, which includes three novels: *Wild Horses*, *Keeping Secrets*, and *The Disappearances*.

Linda collaborated with her daughter and mother to write *Lizzie's Amish Cookbook*, featuring authentic recipes for the food that Lizzie loves so much.

Linda is well-known within the Amish community as a columnist for a weekly Amish newspaper.

Other Books by Linda Byler

Sadie's Montana Series

BOOK ONE BOOK TWO BOOK THREE

Available wherever books are sold. Or to order directly from the publisher, call 800/762-7171, extension 221, or e-mail orders@GoodBooks.com